Death's Lady

Book 1: Prelude: The Year's Midnight

Interlude: Chase

Book 2: Of Absence, Darkness

Book 3: As Shadow, a Light

Death's Lady

by

Rachel Neumeier

Copyright © 2021 Rachel Neumeier
Cover art and design © Kristy Avery Midnight Coffee
All rights reserved.
ISBN: 9798503199413

This is a work of fiction. Names, characters, businesses, situations, or events are the products of the author's imagination. Any resemblance to actual persons, businesses, situations, or events, living or dead, past or present, is purely coincidental.

DEATH'S LADY

Prelude: The Year's Midnight	1
Interlude: Chase	110
Of Absence, Darkness	157
As Shadow, a Light	403
Endnotes	785

Many thanks to Kristi Thompson, Elaine Thompson, and especially Kim Aippersbach for their invaluable critiques; and to Linda Schiffer and Dolores Neumeier for proofreading the manuscript.

1

Tenai told Dr. Dodson, long after the event, that her first vision of her new world was of light. Light laid over darkness: she stepped out of a cold midwinter night, and found the star-lit darkness she left behind was nothing like the shattering confusion of headlights and streetlamps and glaring reflections she entered. Half-blinded, surrounded by bewildering violence—the squeal of brakes, the shattering crash of one vehicle into another, shouts of alarm and anger—Tenai left her dangerous sword Gomantang buried in the hood of a gray Ford truck, there in the middle of the intersection into which she had stepped.

In time, Daniel Dodson got the sword back for her. The police found reasons to return it when the request made its way to them—after all, no major crime had been committed with it, and besides, somehow no one really wanted to keep this particular sword near at hand. Daniel did not give the sword back to Tenai right away. When he showed it to her, she smiled her narrow, secretive smile and agreed that it might be as well if he kept it for a time.

"Gomantang was forged in the dark country," she told him. "He is not a kindly weapon, but his song can be sweet. I would not suggest you put him where your daughter can touch him, Doctor."

"I'll leave it in my office here. But you keep your hands off it too," said Daniel, who by that time was comfortable with her, and Tenai smiled again and said, "I will not touch him until you give him to me, doctor; but you do not touch him, either. Yes?" And of course Daniel agreed.

That was how Tenai spoke, once she decided to speak; with a turn of phrase that struck the American ear as odd and foreign. She might actually have been foreign; no one could tell. She was a dark woman: dark of hair and eyes, skin of an ambiguous shade that made it hard to mark her race on the hospital forms. She was dark of mood as well, and capable of violence when she wished; tall enough to be intimidating—an inch or so taller than Daniel himself. She was not beautiful, but she compelled attention.

Tenai had come into Dr. Dodson's care raging with a fury so tightly contained that a casual glance might have judged her calm. She was not calm. Daniel did not need to be told this. He knew it from the first moment he saw her.

He inherited her three months after her arrival at Lindenwood, from Dr. Margaret Wilson, who was moving to a research hospital with the intention of concentrating on theory for a while. Daniel could understand that. Clinical work with real patients carried real consequences. Even a place like Lindenwood was harder on the heart than research. So many patients here would never really be well. A doctor could burn out on this work.

He had never intended to return to clinical work himself. He had expected to remain in an administration position—or possibly accept that teaching position at Yale. Something that would give him time to write. But here he was.

"Jane can be violent," Maggie warned him. At that time, they did not know her name. She was on the hospital records as Jane Doe IV. "Be careful of her, Daniel."

"But you have her out on the low-security ward." Daniel let a questioning note enter his voice.

"She's easier to handle down here." Maggie grinned, a warm, good-humored grin that showed in her eyes. "You'll find out, Daniel. We tried her on Anafranil. Bad call: it kicked her into a more violent mode instead of settling her down. We damn near lost her right then, but fortunately we all got ourselves calmed down just in time."

"Sounds exciting."

"Yeah, you have no idea. These days, the staff knows how to manage her. Watch them with her. You'll do all right with her too, I expect. In fact, that's one reason I suggested Russell give you a call when I heard you were, um, at loose ends."

Russell Martin was the director of the hospital. Daniel hadn't yet met him; he was out this morning and wouldn't be back until early in the afternoon. Maggie gave Daniel a thoughtful look at odds with her casual tone. She added, "Russell's a good guy. He really is. You already know this place is one of a kind. Wallace might've had the money and the strings to pull, but Russell's the guy who set Lindenwood up and keeps it going. Wallace knew what she was doing when she got him for the job. I'm telling you, you'll get along fine."

A very wealthy woman named Suzanne Wallace had founded Lindenwood, endowed it, lined up a board of trustees in line with her vision, persuaded Martin to take the directorship, and set the whole thing up with the director running the board, not the other way around. Daniel knew all that. He was skeptical that any institution, even a small, privately funded, one-of-a-kind institution, could live up to Maggie's sales pitch. But ... he'd needed a place to go. A place to start, if not *over,* at least *forward.* Whatever else it might be, Maggie had promised—and Daniel believed—that Lindenwood was nothing like Belfountaine.

"All right," he said.

Maggie was going on. "This particular Jane won't tolerate doctors who go off on power trips. She doesn't like anybody trying to control her."

Daniel snorted, and Maggie rolled her eyes. "I know. Don't say it. Not the best traits for an institutionalized patient, even here. She'll do better with you than she has with me, I hope."

Daniel clicked his tongue reprovingly. "Maggie, have you been bullying the patients again?"

She laughed and shook her head. "You've been working with mutism, I mean. If you can get her talking, she might be all right. If you can't, she'll likely be out at the end of June. Six months for a charity patient, that's the rule, which is a damn sight more generous than most, you don't have to tell me that. But put this one out on the street and she'll probably assault somebody, kill somebody, who knows. If she goes to prison, she'll kill somebody for *sure,* there is no way this woman could take the pressure in a place like that. She'd sink like a stone." She made an eloquent gesture, *Down she'll go.*

Obviously she thought this Jane Doe was worth saving, if they could do it. "Elective, you think?"

Maggie shrugged. "Yeah, my guess is, there's nothing organic wrong with her. I think it's all history. And a good dose of pure cussedness. She talked for the first couple days, just not English. Not Spanish, either. Nobody could figure out what lingo she was slinging. Then she shut up like a clam. Not one word since. She's a real mystery. You're good with the weird ones. Wait till you read her admissions history. Serious nuttiness. You'll love it."

"Sounds exciting." Daniel honestly was getting intrigued by this description.

"Oh, yeah. Her whole record makes exciting reading. The police tried to trace her, figure out who she is, but no dice. No fingerprints on file or hits from missing persons or DNA matches or whatever they do these days. If anybody anywhere is missing this woman, they haven't said so loud enough for it to make waves."

"How'd she wind up here?"

"Oh, you know how it goes, the state hospital was full up, and everyone knows we take half a dozen charity cases a year, whatever Russell can manage. But he does like to patch 'em up and move 'em out if he can. The board gets antsy if he tries to hang onto one longer than six months, and he likes to keep the board happy when that's reasonable. Keeps everything purring along smoothly, he says, and he's not wrong. Plus, this time we haven't even come up with a good diagnosis. I've been juggling a handful of lame-ass guesses that don't really fit. You can read all about it in her file, but I'd suggest you meet her first, get a feel for her, maybe you'll figure her out better if you don't get yourself tangled up by a bunch of bullshit theories."

"Maggie, you're a fine diagnostician."

"Yeah, you can say that now. I hope you do reach her. Three months doesn't give you much time, but if anybody can do it, I'm betting you can. I leave it all to you," Maggie finished, with a dramatic wave of her hand that encompassed the small office she was bequeathing to Daniel, and all that went with it: names and histories and all the various miseries several dozen human beings could suffer, crammed into a pair of black filing cabinets. "Enjoy."

"Right," said Daniel.

"You'll do great." She hesitated, just enough of a pause and just awkward enough for Daniel to guess what was coming. "And ... how are *you*?"

"Fine, Maggie."

"I was sorry to hear about Kathy. More sorry than I can say."

"Yes," Daniel said distantly. "Thank you. I appreciated your card." He had tensed despite himself, waiting for the pain ... but that, too, seemed at the moment distant. Lindenwood, at least, held no memories. And it was the nights that were worst, anyway.

"And Jenna? How's she holding up?"

"She's stopped asking when Mommy's coming home. This new start ... I needed it, but I think Jen needed it more." He didn't mention the nightmares, the tantrums, the tears ... all the volatile flotsam and jetsam thrown up by this particular storm. All that had been tapering off anyway over the past few months. This move had helped. He thought it had. He said instead, "She's bouncing back faster than I am, I think."

"Kids are resilient. They have to be."

"Ain't that the truth." Both doctors were silent for a moment, thinking about that. Both of them saw proof every day that all resilience had limits.

After a moment, Maggie added, "And the ... aftermath must have been rough on you, too. Though Russell's lucky to have you here. It's an ill wind, they say, but yours was ... kind of a hurricane."

"That doesn't matter, Maggie."

"All right." There was another slight pause, not quite so awkward this time because they were over the hard part. "Move in okay? Got yourself settled?"

"Yes, pretty well." Daniel was more than happy to switch to small talk. "We're renting right now, but I'll buy a place as soon as I have a chance to look around a little. Someplace near a good school, I guess. I've got Jenna at St. Paul's right now."

"That's good. All the Catholic schools around here are good—speaking as a mom myself. You Catholic?"

"Episcopalian. But ... Kathy was Catholic." He got his wife's name out with only a little difficulty. "Jenna's always been in Catholic schools. I didn't want to change that, on top of everything else."

"St. Paul's is a fine school. Its high school is good, too. My oldest is graduating from high school this year. How time flies, hey? Have me over for coffee sometime and we'll catch up for real, okay? No shop talk—we'll talk kids and schools and stuff, how about it?"

"That sounds wonderful. I'll take you up on that."

"Sure. And in the meantime, give me a call if anything comes up. Don't hesitate." Maggie Wilson gave him a brisk nod and was gone.

She left him with a ... not a warm feeling, precisely, but a feeling that the emotional landscape might not be altogether bleak. She'd done it on purpose, Daniel thought: Maggie had always been quick and accurate with off-the-cuff therapies. Maybe he *would* take her up on that offer of coffee and informal family chat.

At the present moment, the patient files offered distraction and interest. As Maggie had intimated, the file for Jane Doe IV was short, but exciting. Also as she'd suggested, he left aside all of Maggie's own comments, just glancing over the admissions notes. No English or Spanish, okay, lots of other languages in the world. Odd clothing too—that was a little more unexpected. Plus the sword. Quite a few peculiar details. This woman *was* interesting.

But no admissions notes could substitute for going to see the woman for himself, out in the ward, where he could get a look at her without the stiffness of an official appointment.

Daniel toured nearly the whole ward before he turned through a wide doorway, looked across the breadth of the TV room, and laid eyes on the woman herself. He did not need anyone to point her out to him, not only because her personal stats were laid out in her file.

Lindenwood's current Jane Doe was not watching the television. She was leaning against the wall, looking out the corner window. The window was wide open, taking advantage of a cool but pleasant spring day. The bars outside the screen did nothing to block the crisp breeze. The woman had her arms folded over her chest and one knee drawn up, her foot resting on the wall behind her. Her head was bent a little, her expression abstracted. To Daniel, despite her quiet attitude, she looked in that first moment like a burning flame; like a stroke of lighting captured and frozen in human form. He had to fight an impulse to shield his eyes with his hand, as though she had literally been alight.

Daniel just watched the woman for a little while. The hospital routine made extra room for her, that was clear. When the other patients were rounded up for lunch, Jane Doe IV stayed exactly where she was. Daniel, watching her, mentally agreed that he would not have wanted to try to force her to do anything she didn't want to do.

One of the orderlies went over to her finally and told her, "Jane, if you're hungry, lunch is on the table. Soup and sandwiches. Applesauce. Anything sound good?"

The woman spared him some fraction of her attention. She

shook her head, so at least she wasn't non-responsive.

"All right," the orderly said. "Don't skip supper, all right? You're thin enough already."

This received a grave inclination of the head, and the man nodded to her and left the room.

Then the room was empty but for Daniel and Jane Doe IV, which seemed too good an opportunity to waste. Daniel went over to her. He didn't get too close, suspecting that this woman valued her personal space and needed a lot of it.

She looked at him, a swift summing look so penetrating that Daniel was taken a little aback: he had thought she might ignore him. This intense examination was not what he'd expected.

Tall, built long and lean. Unusual, angular features. Somehow, despite having been institutionalized for several months, she looked fit. Like an athlete. Just looking at her made Daniel feel thoroughly out of shape. He felt himself flush, physically self-conscious in a way that he seldom was—and never just because a patient looked at him.

The expression in her dark eyes was not quite neutral. More ... assessing. Judging.

Daniel took a breath, refocused, and said, "My name's Daniel Dodson. I'll be your doctor for a while, if that's all right with you. You're on the hospital books as a Jane Doe. That's such a bland name, I thought I'd ask, what *is* your right name?"

The woman did not, of course, answer. Daniel waited, letting the silence stretch out. And out. Finally he said, not speaking any more loudly, but with a little more intensity, "I'd appreciate it if you'd tell me your name, please."

And a little later, more intensely still, "What's your right name, please?" And then, "What *is* your name? Perhaps you would tell me your name?"—each time with greater intensity and a longer pause, waiting for a response.

The woman's expression did not change. Her face, her eyes, had become as blank and closed as though she had been carved out of wood. On the other hand, she didn't hit him, either. She didn't even walk away. There was a tension in the set of her body that suggested either might be a possibility. Her self-control seemed ... formidable. Both a strength and, Daniel feared, a serious weakness.

He gave up. "Well," he said, "you'd be surprised how often that works, but I suppose you're no child, to be bullied or surprised into speaking against your will. I hope I haven't offended you. The problem with mutism is, the habit of silence can get to be so strong it's almost impossible to break. A brand-new doctor has the best chance of helping a person out of that habit, and I'll never be brand-new for you again. I'm sorry—sorry if I've offended you, and sorry it didn't work. I hope you're willing to have me as your doctor."

For a long moment, the woman continued to regard him, face blank and still, and his heart sank. It seemed all too possible that he would be looking to reassign Jane Doe IV to a different doctor pretty soon, and that would not be a great way to impress Lindenwood's director.

Then ... expression, seeping visibly into the woman's face. One narrow eyebrow lifted, giving her a sardonic look. "Yes," she said. "Doctor." Her voice was surprisingly deep for a woman's voice, but not rough with disuse as might have been expected. No. Her voice was rich, smooth, even velvety, as though she'd spent her spare time for the past year singing opera rather than silent. Even with only two words, it was plain she spoke with a strong accent, nothing Daniel could identify.

Daniel refused even to blink in surprise. "Well, good. I don't suppose you'd tell me your name? It does make conversation easier."

The woman tilted her head to one side, studying him. "Tenai," she said.

He did blink at that. "Tenai? Is that your name?"

The woman seemed to consider this. "Yes," she said finally. "Tenai. That is my name."

"Do you have a last name?"

Both eyebrows went up this time: sardonic, yes, and amused. "A *last* name. At the last ... at the last I was being called Nolas-Kuomon. That was my *last* name."

Daniel could make little sense of this. "Tenai Nolas-Kuomon?" he suggested. Did this sound like any language he knew? It rang no bells.

"No. *You* do not call me Nolas-Kuomon." The woman said it emphatically, with a direct stare. Even in that smooth voice, it was an order, unmistakably. Daniel filed that tone away with everything else he knew or guessed about this woman: little enough, so far.

"So Nolas-Kuomon ... that isn't your family name, then?"

"Ah. The name of my *family*." Her dark eyes measured him. "My family was Ponanon. Or later ... Chaisa. Chaisa was ... my land-name. But Tenai is all my name, now."

Her stare was a little uncomfortable in its intensity. A normal person never looks so closely at a stranger, reserving that kind of gaze for a lover, or a child. Daniel made no judgments, not yet. He only answered mildly, "All right. Tenai, then. Will you tell me where you're from, Tenai?"

It took time for the woman to answer. At last she said, "Somewhere else."

"Ah." Daniel sat down in one of the many chairs and lifted a hand toward another chair. "May I ask you a question, Tenai?"

She did not move. She stayed exactly where she was, studying him. "Yes," she said. "Ask."

"Are you crazy?" Daniel asked this question seriously. Patients in a mental hospital had little tolerance for euphemisms, and quite often a pretty fair grasp of their own conditions. And this one, he guessed, might particularly dislike any attempt to weasel around the truth.

Tenai did not seem offended by the question. She hesitated, and he had the sense that she was choosing her words carefully. "Sometimes, I think, yes," she said at last.

"You mean, sometimes you think you might be crazy? Or you think you might be crazy some of the time?"

Tenai turned away from him, and for a moment Daniel held his breath, but she only paced away a little and then spun, neat as a cat, and came back, and he understood that she only moved because moving helped her think. Or helped her deal with her thoughts. She came back and sank down on the floor by his chair, sitting back on her heels, arms resting on her knees. She was as bonelessly graceful as a dancer.

"I think, some of the time I am being crazy," she said, that strange accent stronger than ever.

"What makes you think so?"

She looked up at him, a swift, unveiled stare, intense as before. Fury flickered in her suddenly opaque eyes, a rage so dangerous and so out of proportion to any offense Daniel might have given that he froze where he sat, breath catching, waiting for the explosion.

It did not come. Static suddenly buzzed from the television, startling, and they both glanced that way. Tenai blinked, and blinked again, masking the rage behind a wall of self-control so strong ... so strong it was frightening. Daniel let his breath out. His palms prickled with sweat. He slid them into his pockets.

Tenai, watching him, said harshly, "I will not ... let go, Doctor."

"Where—why—" Daniel collected himself, and asked more steadily, "Why are you so angry, Tenai?"

The orderly came back in; his eyebrows lifted when he saw the silent Jane Doe speaking to Lindenwood's newest doctor. Daniel flicked a glance at him, and the man vanished at once. Daniel hoped he would have the sense to keep everyone else clear.

Tenai had turned her head at the orderly's brief intrusion. She glanced back at Daniel, and this time her eyes were veiled. It was possible she'd closed herself off again, refusing the intrusion, refusing her doctor, repudiating them all ... but she did not get up, or walk away.

Daniel asked again, "Tenai, why are you so angry?"

For a long, long moment—it probably seemed longer than it was—he thought she would not answer. But she said at last, her deep voice concealing a wealth of expression beneath a veil of dispassion, "It is not to you I am angry." A slight pause, and she corrected herself. "Not *with* you."

Daniel leaned back in his chair, giving her as much room as he could. He said nothing, simply waiting, to see whether she would continue if given a chance. And she did, standing up and moving away and then back, as before, although she did not drop down to the floor again. This time, she rested her hip on the arm of a heavy chair and stared at him from that distance; a safer distance, perhaps. She said, her accent seeming if anything a little stronger, "I do not want to be in this place. I do not like the people here. I want to go somewhere else."

"You want to leave the hospital," Daniel murmured, reflecting this statement to see where it might go.

"Yes. But it would be a bad idea. So I stay. I am going to be stay," she said, and then frowned. "I will stay. I will stay, to learn."

"You want to leave, but you will stay. I think that would be best, Tenai. You seem to learn very fast. English isn't your first language, is it?"

Her dismissive gesture expressed such intense rage Daniel

could hardly believe it didn't crash into open violence. The television buzzed again, sudden and loud, and Daniel told himself that was why he flinched. But he knew it was actually the impact of that harshly contained fury.

"I see you're angry," he murmured, trying to show that he respected her anger, her right to be angry, trying to recognize and legitimize her emotion. "But I don't know why. I'd like to help you, but I don't know how. Why are you so angry, Tenai?"

This time, the pause stretched. And stretched. But he had opened up lines of communication. Maybe that was enough for this first unofficial session ... maybe he should let her go, let her relax ... Daniel thought of that heart-deep rage he'd seen in her and wanted to suggest a halt, a little pause; they could pick up this conversation later, when she was in the mood ... he sat still. It took an effort.

And, damn, the woman saw that effort. He could tell from the way she looked at him, that half-derisive tilt of her eyebrow. That savage rage was still very much in evidence, if you looked for it behind the derision. She crossed her arms over her chest and looked at him, not with that devastating vivid intensity, but decently reserved, like a normal person. She said, drawing out the word as if exploring the concept behind it, "What are you, man, that you are sitting there asking me ... questions like that?"

"I want to help you," he said, and knew it sounded banal.

"Why?"

Why? Daniel paused, taken aback. He asked at last, "Don't you need help, Tenai?"

It was her turn to pause.

Daniel did not press her. He waited. He wasn't holding his breath, but it felt like that, in a way. People went by, in the hallway. Voices were audible, muffled and indistinct. No one came into the room, thank God and orderlies with good sense.

Tenai was no longer looking at him. She stared at the floor, seeing ... Daniel had no notion what she might be seeing. Linoleum wasn't high on the list of possibilities, if he were any judge. He continued to wait.

At last, she looked up again. Rage, yes: in the set of her shoulders and the tension of her neck, and in that opaque dangerous stare ... yes. Daniel put down a surge of fear; he let his breath out and sat still, hands open on his knees, leaning back in his chair, open and relaxed. She had done nothing threatening, nothing at all, and he found himself more afraid of physical violence from this woman than from any violent male patient with whom he had ever worked.

But Tenai did not move, except to look into his face. She said, in that smooth, accented voice, "Perhaps. Yes. Perhaps that is so."

Thank God.

It took Daniel an hour of puttering around in his new office, getting everything squared away, before it occurred to him that he had, for that length of time, managed to get absorbed in other peoples' problems. Forgetting his own for that whole time. Guilt and relief mingled as he continued with the automatic tasks of getting himself sorted out in this office and this hospital. Guilt because he had briefly forgotten Kathy ... relief because he understood the psychological pattern of recovery he was going through, and understood that the pain would lessen in time; that it was already less than it had been. More guilt, that he should hope for an end of pain, when pain and memory were so entwined.

On top of that, apprehension about starting over in a new place. Anxiety about whether he'd made the right choice, about whether he still had the ability, the necessary emotional steadiness, to handle clinical work. Worry that he might be using Lindenwood's patients to escape from his own grief, when every one of them deserved his full professional attention for her own sake

Every bit of that was perfectly normal. None of it was more enjoyable for that understanding.

Nine people dropped by in that hour, to offer greetings and congratulations to the new doctor who had got Jane Doe IV talking in fifteen minutes after three months of silence. Daniel nodded and smiled and chatted about trivial things, and did not say, *That was the easy part. Everything else is the hard part, and I don't have the foggiest idea if I can find a way forward for either Tenai or myself.*

At five minutes before three o'clock, he made his way over to the administrative wing. Dr. Martin's secretary glanced up with a smile when he pushed the door of the outer office open and said in a cheerful tone, "You must be Dr. Dodson. Dr. Martin's expecting you. Go right in, and welcome to Lindenwood."

"Thank you," Daniel said automatically, and followed the

wave of the woman's hand to the first door on the left. *Russell Martin, Director*, it said on the door, in small unostentatious letters.

Dr. Martin, in a perfect contrast to the lettering, was a big man, built like a football player. He reminded Daniel of a slow and sleepy bull. Although Daniel did not know him well, he had read some of his papers. In another life that now seemed very long ago, he had even run into him from time to time at conferences. Appearances aside, he knew the man had a first-rate brain.

Dr. Martin obviously recalled that glancing acquaintance as well. Standing, he offered Daniel a friendly nod and a hand across the cluttered expanse of his broad desk. "Doctor Dodson. Good to see you again."

Daniel returned the handclasp, meeting the other man's eyes and trying to look relaxed. "Sir."

Dr. Martin released his hand and gestured toward the chairs set up for visitors. "Have a seat." He sat back down himself, his chair creaking as it took his weight, and studied his newest doctor. "Maggie recommended you highly."

Daniel nodded. "I'm glad to hear it. She's a fine doctor."

"She is that. You went to school together, I understand."

"Yes. That was a while ago."

"Right. Right." The other man paused, his look at Daniel both assessing and sympathetic. "I was sorry to hear about your wife. Tragic. I'm very sorry for your loss."

"Thank you," Daniel said, aware he sounded stiff.

"You all right?"

"It's been almost a year."

"Sometimes it takes more than a year, Doctor. I would completely understand if you needed to talk about it with someone. Let me just mention that we're well supplied with shrinks here. Doctors who treat themselves, you know."

"I'm fine," Daniel said, aware his tone was too sharp.

The director only nodded, unoffended. "You also fine with what happened at Belfountaine?"

"What about it?" *Far* too sharp, and Daniel made himself breathe deeply, trying to relax.

Dr. Martin leaned back in his chair. He looked calm enough for both of them. "I figure it's best to get the air cleared as quick as possible, Dr. Dodson. A whistleblower's never popular. Especially if the guy he blew the whistle on was right at the top. Even more especially if the whole business winds up putting *Belfountaine*, of all places, on the wrong end of half a dozen lawsuits. I have to say, that's one *hell* of a way to make waves in the field, Doctor."

The director was evidently a fan of the *extremely* direct approach. Daniel had no idea what to say—no idea what he even *could* say. It wasn't as though Dr. Martin were wrong. Every single word of that was the gospel truth.

After a moment, Dr. Martin went on. "I would not want some damned hothead with an axe to grind and a liking for the limelight anywhere near Lindenwood. Maggie swears that's not you. She says you're conscientious as hell, you discovered bad stuff going on, and you didn't give a crap about bureaucratic bullshit or institutional reputation. But what *I* figure is, right at that moment, you were probably *spoiling* for a fight. Just wound up tight as hell. Probably a real sizeable dollop of self-destructiveness to top it all off. That's why you didn't have one shred of hesitation about blowing the whole thing wide, wide, *wide* open. How about it? That in the right ballpark?"

Daniel had to take a moment to recover. That had gone way beyond *direct* and straight to *brutal*. But the director was not wrong. That assessment was actually extremely perceptive. Daniel drew a slow breath, let it out, and admitted, "Probably that's not far off. It wasn't just Hinkley's abuse of his patients. It was admin's response. Any bureaucracy's first, last, and only instinct is to cover up problems. *Solving* the problem is never a priority. That's even more true when there's real reputation at stake." He met the director's steady gaze. "I knew that. But, yes, it made me angry to see it happen You're probably right that I was ready to get angry. But if I was reckless, it was with my own career, not with my patients' well-being. If I was careless, it was with Belfountaine's reputation, not with the truth." Daniel managed, barely, not to add that any institution, no matter how prestigious, that covered for a man like Hinkley richly deserved to have its reputation stomped into the mud.

"Uh huh." Dr. Martin studied Daniel without the slightest break in his massive calm. "Okay, so, you over that now? Got it out of your system? I'm asking because I think I run a pretty good hospital here, Dr. Dodson. I try to make our patients my first priority. But I don't fool myself Lindenwood's perfect. That crap at Belfountaine turned my stomach and if you dropped a mountain of hurt on 'em, as far as I'm concerned they had it coming in spades. But it'd bother me a hell of a lot if any member of Lindenwood's staff spotted a problem here and ran to the press or the hospital commission or the board right off. I'd want that doctor to *come to me first*. That seem reasonable to you?"

Daniel nodded. "Absolutely, sir." He hesitated. He didn't want to sound like he was making excuses. But it seemed important to be clear. Dr. Martin obviously put a serious premium on clarity. He said, "I did go to Belfountaine's director first. It didn't ... she didn't ... I ran into a wall."

Martin nodded. "You ran into a wall and decided to blow a great big hole right through it." He leaned forward, resting his powerful arms on his desk. Met Daniel's gaze with steady, deliberate sincerity. "Dr. Dodson, if you bring a problem to me, I will not drop it in the deep freeze. That's a promise. If you run into any kind of trouble with this hospital, or our staff, or with *me,* come to me about it, and I *will* take your concern seriously. *You* will give me a real good chance to deal with any problem before you even *think* of going someplace else. That seem fair?"

Daniel nodded. "Yes, sir. More than fair."

"All right." The director leaned back again. "And if I have a problem with you, I will let you know before anyone else figures that out. That work for you?"

"Yes, sir," Daniel said again.

"Then I bet we'll get along fine." The director deliberately took a brisker tone. "I'm looking forward to having you here, Doctor. You have a sterling *clinical* reputation. We're lucky to get you, and I know that. So. Your case load okay? Your office okay?"

Daniel exhaled, deeply relieved the director was willing to move on to easier topics. "Fine." Busier than he'd been accustomed to, and smaller than he'd been accustomed to. But Lindenwood was a small place. Prestigious, but small. And a clinical psychiatrist was not an administrator. Regardless of Dr. Martin's polite comments to the contrary Daniel knew the truth: he had been lucky to get a place at Lindenwood. Lucky that Dr. Martin liked to do things his own way and had the authority to run the hospital exactly as he liked. *Very* lucky that Maggie had put in a good word for him. Oh, he could have tried to go into private practice ... but he was terrible with the bookkeeping and other paperwork starting a private practice would have entailed.

And then, the months after Kathy's death would have been the worst possible time to try to strike out so boldly. He'd been holding himself together with ... he didn't know quite what. But he knew he'd been ... breakable. Fragile. Was still fragile. Lindenwood was the sort of place that could help him get back on his own feet.

Not since he was six had he depended on someone else to help him get up after a fall. It was not a comfortable feeling.

"Then welcome aboard," said Dr. Martin, his tone warm now. "And good job with our Jane Doe. I hear you got her talking right off. I am impressed."

"I was lucky."

"Lucky. Sure you were. That's the kind of luck a doctor makes for himself. Keep me in the loop, okay? Let me know how it goes with her. She's three months in. You know it's usually six months for an indigent patient, right? We try to keep to that if we can. I'd like to hear she's ready to move out on schedule. Following the rules keeps the board happy, and when I don't have to spend half my time soothing ruffled feathers, *I'm* happy. But the patients are the priority, so if that's not gonna happen, let me know asap. If you lay out a persuasive argument she needs more time and can *profit* from more time, I'll bend a rule or two to make that happen. Okay?"

"Yes, sir," Daniel agreed, relaxing a little more. "Thank you." He didn't specify for what. He certainly didn't say, *For getting everything out in the open, and thank God we don't have that whole mess sitting there with everyone thinking about it and no one talking about it.*

He didn't say it. But he bet Russell Martin knew it. He bet the man was a damn good psychiatrist when he tossed his director hat on his desk and had a chat with a patient instead. Or with staff. Or, yes, no doubt with the board of trustees. He didn't doubt, now, that Martin had set a solid personal stamp on Lindenwood.

It had all gone a good deal better than Daniel had had any right to expect. It was just one more piece of evidence, as he realized later, that the things we worry about are not the things that are most likely to trip us up. No. That would be something else. Something unanticipated.

There was the usual round of department meetings to get through after that: meetings in which Daniel was brought up to speed regarding hospital procedures and policies; meetings in which he could begin getting acquainted with the doctors and the staff; and far more interesting meetings in which truly baffling cases were discussed—another round of congratulations for getting Jane Doe IV talking—and through the praise, Daniel flashed repeatedly on that furious blank stare. Yes, all right, the silence was just the tip of the iceburg, that was obvious. What might be lying in the depths out of sight ... that was far less clear. He scheduled Tenai into an hour block for the next day, and knew that whatever detailed and sensible plans he might make tonight, this was one patient he was going to have to play by ear.

He left the hospital at four thirty on the dot and drove through the city in such a state of preoccupation that afterwards he recalled nothing at all of that drive. He arrived a little late at his daughter's school and parked in the first space he found, then ran up the stairs and walked, puffing, down the hall to the after-school area, glancing distractedly at the bright artwork decorating the walls. His daughter met him at the door of the room with her usual run-and-jump, and he whirled her around and said, a little more heartily than he should have, "How's Daddy's best girl?"

"Look at my hair!"

"I couldn't possibly avoid it," Daniel assured her. "Very, um, unusual."

"Yeah!" said Jenna, and dashed off to get her things.

Daniel nodded to the after-school coordinator as she came up to meet him, and was relieved when she nodded back.

"She was fine," the woman murmured as Jenna dashed off. She was young, one of the nuns who chose to wear blue and white street clothes rather than the blue habit many of the older nuns preferred. Her name was Sister Mary Catherine. Aware of Jenna's recent loss, aware of the trouble the child had had all through first grade, aware of the move across the country and all the dislocation, she said now, "Her teacher tells me she handled your leaving better this morning. She's making friends—nice girls who ought to be able to help her come the rest of the way out of her shell. She and Nicole braided each other's hair."

"I noticed," Daniel said drily. Lots of slender, uneven braids of all different lengths, the ends done off with bright blue and red and yellow rubber bands. Though it was a very good effort ... for a second grader.

"They both agreed she looks cute that way. Which she does,

of course! You say she used to be a happy, extroverted child?"

"Yes. She was."

"Then she will be again, and I think I'm seeing signs of it now." Sister Mary Catherine nodded reassuringly.

He had hoped this would prove to be the case, and ignored Jenna's storms of protest about the move. Or pretended to ignore them, while they tore his heart. He had been sure that his daughter could not actually miss the first-grade classmates she had never shown any signs of accepting. He had been positive that it was the very idea of change that frightened Jenna—more change, after everything that had already happened. But he had not been completely confident of his own judgment—in that matter or in any other—not then. But it looked like he had been right. "Thank you," he said warmly.

"I'll keep you informed," Sister Mary Catherine assured him, patted his arm, and turned back into the room with a brisk wave.

So that was one part of his life that seemed to be falling back into order. And Lindenwood looked like it would be all right. Daniel still felt as though he had to brace for disaster ... but for the first time in over a year, it was becoming possible for him to believe that maybe disaster might not actually come crashing down.

2

The next morning, Tenai came into Daniel's office, escorted by one of the nurses, with the wariness one might expect from a person picking her way through a minefield. Or from a patient in an institution. She pulled attention toward herself, as a tiger might have pulled attention: no one with sense—or sensitivity—could possibly concentrate on anything else when Tenai came into a room. This was such a perfect relief to Daniel that he would have concentrated on this one patient alone, if he could have done so and still somehow met his other professional responsibilities.

The nurse told him, "Tenai says—" there was a world of suppressed but honest delight in that word— "Tenai says she would like a corner room instead of the one in the middle of the hall, and that's okay with the staff if it's okay with you, Doctor."

"Certainly. Thank you." Daniel was looking at Tenai, and was hardly aware of it when the nurse departed. Sixty minutes. It wasn't much. It was probably as much as he could handle.

Tenai looked very much as she had on the previous day: vividly present, with a burning conflagration barely hidden behind those dark, contained eyes. She stood just inside the door of Daniel's office, poised to retreat—no. Not *retreat*. Withdraw, perhaps, but there was no *retreat* in the woman.

"Will you have a seat?" Daniel gestured to the couch, a dusky-rose color that was meant to be soothing and at least did not clash with the dove-gray walls and black metal desk and filing cabinets.

A moment passed. Another. Then Tenai walked across the room and settled, with all her wariness, on that couch. It was a comfortable piece of furniture. She made it look stiff.

Daniel came out from behind the desk, met her mistrustful stare, and went immediately back behind its sheltering width. Sheltering for whom ... he was not quite sure. He sat in the desk chair, leaned his elbows on the neat surface, and looked at Tenai.

Most people would start to speak quite soon if the doctor stayed quiet. Tenai, of course, was comfortable with silence. Daniel became ruefully aware how stupid an expectation it had been.

So Daniel broke the silence himself. Starting with something important, why not? Small talk seemed ... far too artificial, somehow. So he simply asked directly: "Tenai, why are you so angry?"

"What *are* you?"

Daniel blinked, and chose the simplest answer. "A psychiatrist. Do you know what that is, Tenai?" And, at her mute stare, he explained, "A doctor who specializes in problems of the mind and emotions. We're medical doctors first, but then we specialize in those kinds of problems. We help people who are depressed, people who have trouble perceiving what's real and what's not, people who suffer from violent mood swings ... do you know what I'm talking about, here, Tenai?"

"Yes." And she offered after a second, "I watch the people here, so I know what is a doctor. I do not know ... I wonder how a doctor, a psychiatrist, is made. I wonder what you are, that you made yourself into a psychiatrist."

"Well, everyone has to do something, I guess, Tenai. I'm good at this." Sometimes, anyway. "I like helping people, I suppose." Corny as it sounds, Daniel thought. But it was true. And he had the impression that truth was important to this woman. "What have you done, in your life, Tenai? What are you good at?"

He had expected a withdrawal. Or silence, another kind of withdrawal. He had not expected what he got: a sharp bitter laugh, and Tenai on her feet, stalking toward the desk. Catching his breath, Daniel made himself hold still. Tenai did not hit him. She picked up the pen on his desk, and broke it with one quick snap.

"I destroy things."

"Ah." She was still standing there, rather too close for comfort, with that burning rage right under the surface ... sometimes one must proceed blindly, but that is seldom a comfortable way to go on. Daniel asked, keeping his tone gentle, "And people?"

Tenai gave him a burning look. Then she spun in place, went back to the couch, and leaned her hip against its arm, watching him. "No," she said, and added, not so reassuringly, "Not here, or now."

"Can you ... give me an example of how you destroy things?" No answer. Nothing. Resistance? Mistrust? Or something else, some less obvious possibility? Daniel tried again, "Where are you from?"

Again, no answer. Daniel observed, "You know, no one gets very far with this kind of thing unless she's willing to trust her doctor."

That registered. Tenai's head went back a little, in surprise, maybe. Her narrow eyebrows lifted. After a second, she said, "Would I do ... good, wise, wisely ... would I be *correct* to trust you, Doctor?"

Daniel leaned back in his chair, studying her. "Well, trust is a relationship that one builds up over time, I know. But, Tenai, how much time are you willing to spend deciding? You've already been here three months."

"*I know,*" said Tenai. Anger, again. Not hidden. No. Right out on the surface.

Daniel observed in his calmest tone, "I can see anger eating you up from the inside, Tenai, so much it frightens me. I can see that you're trying to carry every kind of weight through life all by yourself and it frightens me when anyone tries to do that, because no one can, in the end." He added gently, "And you don't have to, now, you know. That's what we're for, the doctors here. What I'm for. That's what psychiatrists do. No man is an island. Nor are you."

Surprisingly, Tenai laughed. The anger was still there. But humor was there, too, and it seemed real. It occurred to Daniel that this was the first evidence he had seen that this woman had any sense of humor at all. "Is that what you think?" she asked.

"Am I wrong?"

"Doctor, you are wrong. In the end, everyone must carry every kind of weight alone. No one can carry another person's burden so much as a single step. You must twist your soul out of the hands of fate if you can, and no one can help you do it. An island? We are no one of us so solid. We are leaves, carried each by the breath of a separate wind. If we are coming down one moment on the same place of earth, the next breath of wind will carry us apart once more."

The violence of it was a revelation all on its own. "That's a very harsh view of life," Daniel commented.

"It is true."

"Why do you think so?"

There was another grim pause, filled with tension. Daniel broke it. "Tenai, I can't help you if you hide in silence. Start with something easy. Tell me where you were born."

"Nothing is easy."

"In that case, start with something hard."

Arms crossed, she stared at him. Or maybe not at *him*, after all. Her eyes, dark and watchful, had turned inward. Seeing ... what?" Daniel did not break the silence, this time. He tried not even to breath audibly.

And eventually Tenai rewarded his patience, his instincts. She said, "I was born in Talasayan, in Goshui-sa-e." She stopped. Daniel made a small encouraging noise, trying to remember if he had ever heard of those places, if those words sounded like any language with which he was familiar.

After a moment, Tenai continued, in a level, flat voice, "That tells you little enough, I think, doctor, because you do not know the white walls and beautiful carved doors of Goshui-sa-e. The people there used to rub the dark wood of their doors with scented oil for every festival, but you have never seen that place, never smelled the fragrance of the oil. You do not hear the calls of the birds from the places built for them under the edges of the roofs, or the voices of the people quoting poetry to each other as they bargain for bread in the streets. They were very fond of poetry in Goshui-sa-e.

"What picture does my speech paint for you, doctor? It will not show you the land of my childhood. You will not know that land. There is still a city where Goshui-sa-e stood, but it is not the city of my childhood. The people there no longer care for carving or birds or poetry. The city I knew is gone. And the girl who knew it and loved it as her own, that girl is gone also. What will you do to recapture the things that are past, doctor?"

Daniel drew a slow breath, trying to think if he'd ever heard of any place similar to the town she described. He said, "None of us can go back, Tenai. Perhaps I can help you find a way to go forward instead."

The woman said with some violence, "We will all go forward, whatever we do. Whether we wish to or not."

Since this was hard to deny, it took Daniel several seconds to find an answer. At last he said, "But we all choose *how* we do it."

"We do what we must," Tenai said. She had not moved from her half-seat on the arm of the couch, but her pose had become taut and dangerous.

"And what have *you* done, Tenai?"

There was a frozen, tense silence. Then the tall woman snapped to her feet and walked away. To the door, open its customary inch. She slammed it back against the wall with a hard blow and stalked through it, out and gone. Behind her, Daniel let his breath out slowly.

The following week, Tenai did not keep her appointments. Time running through their hands, seconds ticking away, but it would do no good to say *We've only got through June, Tenai, so let's get a move on.* He was positive pushing from that kind of practical perspective would do a lot more harm than good. So Daniel patiently scheduled that block of time free for her, and let her go her own way when she did not show up. He did administrative jobs during that slot, rather than scheduling in another patient. And he inquired after her among the nurses and orderlies. She was still talking. Just not to him.

She was hiding. Not in rigid silence this time. Not from the whole world. But she did not want to be seen, not for who she was, not by him.

But what was she hiding *from*? Life? That didn't feel quite right, and Daniel thought about it again. Things she had done in her life, or experienced in her life, maybe. Things she was afraid she might do, if she started living again.

Daniel let Tenai alone. He could do that for a little while longer. Another week, maybe.

His other patients were interesting. Dr. Martin, possibly following Maggie's advice, had found him quite a collection of complicated cases that fell rather outside the normal categories.

There was Kitty Stevens, for example, a bright girl with Tourette's and severe depression on top of that. Maggie had thought the depression was caused by the Tourette's, and had been trying to help the girl deal with her feelings about the Tourette's in an effort to help the depression. Daniel wasn't so sure. He suspected the depression, even if originally precipitated by the Tourette's, might have become an autonomous remnant of the original condition, more effectively treated separately. And he also suspected, for no reason he could quite put a finger on, that the overt depression might in fact mask a more primary anxiety that was not overt at all.

Maia Patel, a woman just approaching middle age, might be schizophrenic. Or maybe not. She was one of those patients who defied easy classification; theoretically fascinating but personally tragic. To Daniel, schizophrenia did not quite feel like the right diagnosis. He found other vague, hardly defined disorders drifting through his mind—minimal brain dysfunction, maybe a strange *forme fruste* of epilepsy. She had not yet been tried on Dilatin. Daniel wrote the order after his fourth session with her.

Bess Poole was an elective mute, and severely depressed, Daniel suspected. He had no idea how to get her talking. She wasn't like Tenai. Rather than using silence as a wall against anger or other emotion, Bess was absorbed by an apathy so complete that the nurses almost had to physically manipulate her through daily exercises as though she was a coma patient. Her emotional spectrum was so narrow it barely existed. Daniel wondered whether his chief job with Bess might not be to help her reconnect to her emotions; he suspected the apathy would take care of itself if he could manage this trick. At the moment, however, he had no idea how to proceed.

There were others: each a real person with real problems, each to be helped to the full extent that Daniel and Lindenwood could help them. It was impossible to ignore their needs. It was even easy to focus tightly on those needs. The Lindenwood patients, indeed, were all of them *exactly* the distraction Daniel had hoped for and needed. He immersed himself in their lives, letting himself forget, for the present, about his own lingering grief and anger. Refusing to expect failure; deliberately sharpening his own sense of efficacy. He could reach these women. He *would*.

It helped that Dr. Martin had more sense, or more delicacy, than to assign any bipolar patients to Daniel. Even so, working with any woman even prospectively suicidal sometimes brought back thoughts of Kathy so strongly that Daniel was forced to stop whatever he was doing and leave Lindenwood for an afternoon. He spent four hours outside Jenna's school once, sitting in his car and listening to the high quick voices of the children drifting through the open windows. Only later did it occur to him that he'd been lucky no one had called the police to investigate the man sitting outside the school.

Tenai did not come back to him. In the end, Daniel put himself deliberately in her way. He left instructions that when Tenai left the ward to walk in the hospital grounds, he was to be informed. That was how he happened to be strolling down the paved walk that ran around the perimeter of the wall when Tenai came that way.

When he saw her, Daniel went to the nearest bench and sat down. It was chilly, though well into April. He ran a hand absently over his scalp, wishing he'd thought to wear a hat. The concrete bench seemed to suck away what warmth there was. It wasn't comfortable. Daniel sat on it anyway.

For a minute or so, it looked like Tenai would turn around and leave him sitting there. But then she seemed to change her mind, and came forward instead.

"Good morning," Daniel greeted her when she stopped a few feet away.

Tenai inclined her head. "Good morning, Doctor."

"You've been missing our appointments."

"And so I see the limit of your patience."

"I already knew you were more stubborn than I could be, so why pretend otherwise?"

She almost smiled, the barest crook of her mouth. "Walk with me, if you wish."

Daniel rose with alacrity. The walkway ran beneath the new green of the willows and the red-tinged leaves of the oaks. Daffodils bloomed along the wall, and grape hyacinths. Flycatchers darted through the air, and robins hopped here and there on the lawn, and it was all very peaceful. Tenai looked peaceful, too. But now that he was within arm's reach, he could feel her tight-held rage, held hard, just out of sight.

As though she were not angry at all, Tenai turned her head to watch with detached interest as a pair of squirrels ran through the branches of an oak and into the trees of a neighboring yard, out of the hospital grounds. Considering a similar path herself, possibly.

"Are they different from the trees of your ... country?" Daniel asked her, with deliberately mild curiosity.

Tenai lifted an eyebrow. "Should they be different?"

"There is no place called Talasayan," Daniel said, still in that mild tone. "Or Goshui-sa-e. I checked every spelling I could think of."

"The land lies across the veil. It is not this land. The trees are the same, but the names are different. What is that one called, with such leaves?"

Daniel told her.

"Oak," Tenai repeated in a thoughtful tone. "A hard word, a strong word. A good name for such a tree. In the west of Talasayan there are deep forests of such trees, which the people there call *badan*. In the great plains of the south, in Imbaneh-se, these trees grow alone, vast and strong, and there they are called *tananar*, for though the people of Talasayan and the people of Imbaneh-se share a language, some of the words are different. On the islands of Tesmeket these trees grow throughout the mountains. There they are small and twisted, and when they speak their own language, the people there call them *tolt*."

"I wonder why the trees are the same here and there, in such different lands?"

Tenai shrugged, not very interested in the question. "What else would trees be like?"

"It explains a lot about you, if you're from another world."

"You do not believe me," Tenai said, not at all surprised. "I know this. It is not heard of that this should happen. I have listened for a long time. No one steps from world to world across the veil ... or no one speaks of it. At least that. But if you do not believe me, what do you think is true?"

Daniel, who tried hard not to lie to his patients, hesitated for a second. "I think you encountered something in this world that you couldn't live with, and so you invented another world to be from. A different life to have lived, that you liked better."

"You believe strange things," Tenai commented. The corner of her mouth had twisted in wry amusement. "Do you think I like that world better than this?"

"I think you see your problems in that world as more directly solvable than the ones you really faced. When their lives become unbearable, people must still find a way to bear them. Sometimes the ways they find are strange."

"*My* life is never what I have found unbearable." But she considered what he had suggested. "There is a woman named Kim in the ward where I am. She believes her son will come here and take her away, to a house in the country, where they will live in great happiness. She waits for this every day that visitors come. Her son never comes on those days. But the next morning she is waiting for him again. She speaks of nothing else. She describes each room of the house in such detail one can almost see it. Anna told me that her son hates her and will never come."

Anna was one of the other patients. "Yes. Kim isn't my patient, but I think that's true."

"That is sad. But, Doctor, I am not Kim."

"No. You are yourself."

Pursuing her thought, Tenai added, "I think I had forgotten until I came here that other people also have memory following at their heels like hounds behind the deer."

If she had become less absorbed in herself, that was excellent.

"There is a girl who sits in the hall all day and looks at nothing. She makes no noise. She does not speak or move. Everyone steps around her and forgets she is there."

"Michaela."

"Yes. She wants to forget that she is there, but she cannot forget. Doctor—"

Daniel gave her an encouraging nod. But she only turned on her heel and walked away, following the gradual curve of the high stone wall that separated the hospital from the world.

Daniel followed her. "Tenai," he called. "Tenai, wait!"

She stopped, although she did not turn to face him.

"Where are you?" he asked her. "Will you show me?"

"Where have I gone?"

"Into memory. Haven't you?"

Tenai did turn, then. Daniel, who was not in the habit of retreating from his patients, did not take a step back, although for a moment he had to fight the urge.

"Why do you want to know about me? What gives you the right to ask me such questions, to walk into my memory? Perhaps you can help Kim, perhaps you can help Michaela, but you are wrong about me, Doctor."

"Do I have to be right about you to help you, Tenai? "

She hit the wall with the heel of her hand. Daniel half-expected the stone to crack, but the wall stood there stolidly, absorbing her anger. That might have been why she had chosen it to strike. He took a step forward, and stopped, instinctively. Tenai stared at him, an aggressive, dangerous stare.

"Tell me about your life," Daniel encouraged her. "Why are you angry, Tenai? What have you done? What has been done to you? Who are you?"

"Go away," she ordered harshly.

"Well, Tenai, I can't, you know. You're my patient."

She took an aggressive step toward him, one hand half-raised. He stood still, pure instinct, and probably stupid stubbornness. But Tenai put her hand down. She said, almost pleadingly, "I do not want to hurt you, doctor."

"I'm glad to hear that."

"I should go. Over the wall, and gone." But she didn't move.

"Stay," Daniel said. "If you don't trust me, Tenai, whom will you trust? And if not now, then when?"

The April breeze was chilly on his hands, his face, stirring the limber willow twigs. He did not move. Neither did the tall woman he faced: head-on, like an enemy. If there was a battle, it was one he had already won, in the television room when Tenai had decided to answer him. Or Tenai had won it, by deciding to speak. But it was a battle that must be won again and again, by the doctor or the patient, and it would be nice if they both kept in mind that they should fight on the *same* side ...

Tenai said at last, harshly, intensely, *"I killed Encormio. I killed so many people."*

Daniel let his breath out, chilly wind forgotten. "Tell me about it, Tenai."

The woman made a sharp gesture, turned on her heel, and walked away. Over her shoulder she said abruptly, "Walk with me."

They walked down the path, the two of them. Tenai did not seem cold. She walked with a fast stride, hands jammed in her pockets, head down. Daniel matched her pace, which meant he was soon out of breath. Eventually, to his relief, her pace slowed. She let her breath out in a long sigh, angular features relaxing a little, dark eyes losing some of that opaque dangerousness.

"Encormio was the king," Tenai said. That odd liquid accent of hers gave her words the flavor of a story out of *The Thousand Nights and One Night*, some tale of magic and mystery, betrayal and loss and heroism.

Encormio was the king, and he was old. He had been king of the land for a thousand years. He was older than that; much older. He remembered the dark, wild era before the Martyr had been born or died, and he never ceased to long for those harsh ages of iron and blood—so it was said. Encormio ruled with blood and fire and fear: not only Talasayan, but Imbaneh-se and Keneseh as well, and sometimes, intermittently, Tesmeket. The tales of his cruelty were as numerous as his years and as broad as the span of his rule. But his throne of ivory and bone rested in Nerinesir, hundreds of miles from Goshui-sa-e. Goshui-sa-e was a peaceful town. Encormio might love blood, but he was not a fool, to destroy the land that supported his rule: folk so far away from Nerinesir might never feel the shadow of his hand pass over them. The stories remained only stories, in Goshui-sa-e.

"That's where you grew up?" Daniel asked. "What was it like, there?"

Tenai shrugged. "What is any place *like,* doctor? That was long ago. It was a beautiful country, and pleasing to the spirit. I was happy there, I think. But I was only a girl. I think I saw the sunlight and not the shadows."

"You talk like you're a thousand years old yourself, Tenai."

She gave him a swift look. "I am not quite so old as that, doctor. But I am older than I look. Although my bargain was not the same one Encormio made, nor did I pay the same price."

Daniel wanted to ask about that, but he felt those other questions would take them away from the heart of the thing she needed to talk about. He only nodded in acknowledgement. "So you grew up in a country ruled by a thousand-year-old king. What went wrong?"

A slow, inscrutable look. "I grew to be a woman, and in time I married Nolas-ai Salai Chaisa-na, the heir of Chaisa."

Chaisa lay to the north of Goshui-sa-e. It was a broad land, lying near the coast, between the rugged Namanah Mountains to the north, with the easy plains of the Kintavar peninsula sweeping away south. It owned access to a wide shallow bay, not usable in winter, but excellent in the summer. A fine land: a land good for grain and apples and cattle and people. The lord of Chaisa in those days was a man named Maririvar, a fine man with a gift for creating prosperity and two bold sons. The older of the sons was Salai, a beautiful and energetic young man who was all an heir should be, but restless, until one day he met a certain young woman in Goshui-sa-e.

"That was you, of course," said Daniel. They had paused in the shade of a barely-leafed oak; or rather, Tenai had paused there, and Daniel stopped with her. She stood with her hand on the coarse bark, looking up into the heavy branches as though their strength absorbed her attention. She brought her gaze down from the heights to look at him with faint surprise.

"That was the girl that I was. I do not remember that girl well, but I remember her first sight of Salai Chaisa-ai. He was a beautiful young man. His hair was black and soft, but his eyes were that light color one sometimes finds. Not blue, not gray. The color called silver. It is said that those with silver eyes can see into a man's heart and know whether he is true. Salai had eyes like that."

"You married him."

"Yes," agreed Tenai, as though the memory gave her no pleasure. "I married Salai."

"Most fairy stories would end with your living happily ever after," Daniel commented, knowing very well that not all stories came out that way in real life ... or in whatever sort of imaginary life Tenai was remembering.

The tall woman did not seem to hear this comment. She was walking on, hands in her pockets again, eyes unfocused, looking at nothing.

Salai Chaisa-ai was a fine man, and his brother lighthearted and good tempered, and his father wise and practical. A young woman might prosper in that country, married into that family. Travelers came from time to time, from Kandun and Antiatan and nearby Goshui-sa-e. Some few came from Nerinesir. The stories they told might be disturbing, but it was nothing to which a young woman concerned with her family need attend. She bore her first child, this young woman, a son, fine and strong, very like his father. The same dark coloring. The same silver eyes.

When the boy was five, the lord of Chaisa was summoned to Nerinesir, to attend on the king. To attend on Encormio. Maririvar did not wish to go, but one did not resist the king. He went. He did not return.

Chaisa mourned. The sons of Chaisa mourned most of all.

But the old lord was gone. Approaching the king to investigate or protest would not bring him back, and might call the king's attention north, which no one wished. No. It was wisest to attend to Chaisa, and let mourning ease with the passing of time. Everyone agreed. Everyone said so, the new lord of Chaisa, and his wife, and his brother, and all their people.

But the younger brother went south after all, without leave from Salai—well, he did not wish to worry him. He meant only to bring back the story of his father's last days, and the old lord's bones if he could get them, to burn properly with wood gathered in Chaisa. So the letter he left gave his family to understand.

Salai might have gone after him. But his wife was again with child. So he stayed. His brother did not return. No word came of him, although Salai inquired, sending letters and messengers and, at last, hired spies, to the capital.

The new child was a daughter, with silver eyes and a pretty disposition, swift to laugh and slow to cry, even as an infant. Her father cherished her, though he was slower to laugh himself than he had been in previous years.

Chaisa prospered still. If it seemed not so peaceful a place to the young mother as it had once, still it was a fine land. Seasons turned. Years died. No fire was lit for the lost brother. The house accounts listed the younger brother only as temporarily departed from Chaisa. And every month, Salai Chaisa-ai sent a letter to Nerinesir, inquiring after his brother.

These letters frightened his wife. She asked him not to send them. Then she asked him in stronger terms. Finally, she begged him to cease. And one spring, when little Marai was three years old and the boy Lonovai almost nine, he agreed. No letter was sent that month.

The next month, a letter arrived from Nerinesir, bearing the king's own mark. The letter contained a summons, a formal summons, the kind any lord might receive: I understand your son is of age to be made a page, come to Nerinesir and bring the boy, make him known to me, perhaps if his father agrees he would like to serve a royal household. A letter like that is an expected thing, of course. Some considered such service worth the risk, even under such a king as Encormio. However, in this letter was something else. Penned below the formal scribe's mark was a line in flowing script.

"I can see it still, when I think of that time," Tenai said, in her calm, abstracted tone. "It said, *Come to Nerinesir and I will show you what became of your brother.*"

"Grim," said Daniel. He had forgotten the chill of the breeze.

Tenai had never seemed to feel it. Her eyes were distant. There was no recognizable expression on her face. "I begged him not to go," she said.

"But he went anyway."

"Yes. He had no choice."

"Taking your son."

"He had no choice," Tenai repeated, still expressionless. The sun touched the horizon. Shadows, long and uncertain, stretched out along the ground.

"… What happened?"

"They did not return," Tenai said, her tone remote. "I received a letter from Encormio himself. It said, *To set your mind at rest, be informed that they are dead. Let it lie, Chaisa, and teach your daughter a prettier compliance than your house has shown in the past. She is the last of that line, which I would not wish to see end.* The day after that, my daughter caught the croup. Four days after that, she was dead."

There was no more expression in Tenai's voice. Daniel stuffed his hands in his pockets. They seemed colder than the chill in the air could explain.

"Do you have children, Doctor? A wife?"

Daniel managed, somehow, to keep his voice steady; to keep his mind on his patient's needs and not his own. "A young daughter. My wife ... died last year."

Tenai glanced at him. There was no trace of compassion in her eyes. For a moment, Daniel almost hated her, until he got control of himself. Few psychiatric patients had energy to spare for anyone else's problems. Tenai was at this moment wholly focused on her own. He knew that. It was one reason she was here. She said, "Then you will understand the taste of my despair."

Daniel said, making sure he meant it, "I'm sorry, Tenai."

"You believe this story?"

"I believe you lost people that meant the world to you."

"The pain passes," she said distantly. "The years run on like rain down a stone, until the stone at last is worn away. Grief passes. One forgets."

Daniel put down, again, a sharp feeling of resentment.

"Everyone is different," he said, his tone a little harsh despite every effort.

Tenai glanced at him. "You have not found this yet. Your loss is still with you. Live as long as I, and you will find that all things pass."

She looked about thirty, maybe thirty-five. "How old are you?"

"Ah. Old. Old." Tenai stared into the western sky, where the clouds had been painted with rich rose and amber by the setting sun. She said matter-of-factly, "I had lost everything. Encormio took them from me. I swore I would not rest until I had destroyed him, as he had destroyed me. I swore it before God. Under a dark sky, I killed a black bull and poured out its blood on the frozen earth. I lit a black candle and a white one, and I made a bargain with a new lord."

"A new lord?" Daniel asked cautiously.

"With Lord Death. I did not fear him, you see. So I called him into a night with no light but those candles. And we made a bargain. That if he would teach me all the arts by which a woman might destroy a king, I would give him—" She broke off.

"What?"

"Anything," Tenai said, her tone flat. "Anything I had; anything I would ever have. I was prepared to offer anything at all. And I found Lord Death did have one desire. The dark Gatekeeper took my bargain, and taught me ... everything. Everything I had asked. And in return I promised him—"

"What, for God's sake?"

Tenai met his eyes. Her own were dark, and secret, and ageless. "Never to die," she said, and walked away, leaving him there in the spring light among the trees, to think about that.

3

Daniel noted down the story Tenai had told him. It stayed in the back of his mind all that evening, even as he picked Jenna up from her school program and encouraged her to tell him all about her day and made supper for them both. When he read his daughter her bedtime story—and then her second story, and then her third—it struck him that Tenai's story had sounded just like that.

Well, not *exactly* like a second-grader's bedtime story, obviously. But exactly like the plot of a book. From time to time that would happen: a patient would tell a story she had read somewhere, and the doctor would take it too seriously. It could be embarrassing.

Yet Daniel had a feeling that this was not what had happened here. Or if it had, it was a story Tenai had absorbed into herself far too well. That night he stayed up for a long time, searching for any historical or literary references to a king named Encormio, or a country called Talasayan, or any woman at all who had made a bargain with the Lord of Death so that she would never die.

The next day, Tenai did not come to his office to keep their appointment. This time Daniel didn't wait. Both he and Tenai already knew he was less patient than she, so what was there to prove? He caught one of the nurses in the hallway and asked her to remind Tenai that she had an appointment at one o'clock and he hoped she was on her way.

The nurse raised her eyebrows. "Certainly, Doctor. And if she doesn't care?"

Daniel said, "Ask her if she likes walking out on the grounds. Point out that's a privilege patients normally have to earn. Then remind her about the appointment."

"Ooo-kay," said the nurse even more dubiously.

"Well, we'll see, won't we?" Daniel went back to his office.

And seven minutes later, there she was. Tenai pushed the door open and came in, stood in the middle of the room folded her arms over her chest and stared at him. Her expression was hard, contained, dangerous. "Am I in your service?" she asked him. "Do you call me to come and go?" Anger was in her voice, but also other things, less identifiable.

Daniel leaned back in his chair. "I didn't know whether you'd come, Tenai. You might have decided to tuck yourself into a corner of this hospital and close out the world. But here you are."

To his complete astonishment, Tenai turned, neatly, and put one fist through the gray-painted wall. She stood there afterwards, staring at the damage while Daniel worked to breathe evenly and not show surprise or alarm. She'd scraped her knuckles. Blood ran down her fingers ... not much blood, and if she'd really hurt her hand, she was hiding it well.

Daniel waited.

At last, Tenai said, still not looking at him, "I apologize, Doctor."

Daniel made a noncommittal sound.

Tenai watched the blood drip off her fingers. The drops made little round dots on the floor ... linoleum, fortunately, and washable. She watched them fall, and said distantly, "I remember too much. Too far back. I remember the girl I was, but she is gone. I remember the woman I became, and even that is too long ago. I do not know what to do with the person I became ... the person I am now."

"You began to tell me your story, and now you remember more than you want to?" Daniel asked gently.

A long pause. At last, in a low voice, "Perhaps. I do not know."

Daniel nodded. "You recalled that distant girl. She was you. Now you're here. You feel disconnected from your past. Perhaps it might help you to tell me how you got from that past to this present. Will you tell me the rest of the story?"

"You don't believe it is true."

"If *you* believe it's true—if you only half-believe it—if it's important to you in any way, then I would like to hear it."

Another slight hesitation. "Yes, Doctor."

"You'll tell me the rest?"

"It is a long story. But I will tell it to you."

Daniel leaned back in his chair again, letting out a deep breath. "All right. Please sit down, if you don't mind. We've got half an hour left today: perhaps you can't get through the whole tale, but let's see. You made a bargain with the Lord of Death so that you would never die. What happened after that?"

In the dark of the moon, in a frost-touched pasture, by the light of one black and one white candle, Tenai had poured out the blood of a bull and called down from the heights the dark wind that carries souls from life into death. She had tools to her hand besides the knife and bowl and candles: she had a lock of her husband's hair, and a dried flower her son had brought her when he was two, and the cleaned finger-bone of her dead daughter. She had her fury, and her despair, and her hatred. And she had nothing to lose.

When she quenched the small candleflames between her fingers, the darkness became absolute: no gleam of stars or moon to lighten the dark. It was a darkness that belonged to the deep places of the earth, not to the wide lands under the sky. It smelled of blood and fire. And it shaped itself into the form of a man, there in that pasture, and looked at her with hollow eyes that had seen everything. Even without light, it could be seen: an absence of form, like a hole in the night.

Everyone has something to lose, said Lord Death. His voice was passionless and still as the voice of the dark that had drawn it forth. It was not a human voice. It made no pretense to be human, or mortal, or familiar in any way.

"Nothing I care for," Tenai had answered, sharply. "Nothing I am not willing to give away three times over."

Youth, suggested that unhuman voice. **Health. The long span of years that lie ahead, perhaps, with all the possibilities they contain. The beauty of the world. The brilliance of passion. Friendship. Sorrow. The memory of joy. Life.**

"Nothing," repeated Tenai, "that I am not willing to give away."

The passionless gaze turned to look at the things Tenai had brought to the field: a lock of hair, a dead flower, a finger-bone. She could see them when Lord Death looked at them, despite the utter absence of light: they seemed picked out of the dark by his attention.

Then the hollow eyes turned back to her. It was not like meeting the eyes of a man. She would not look away. **Death comes to everything,** the voice said, out of the dark. **For everything, there is an ending. Death is not evil. The working out of providence is better left to God.**

Tenai had laughed. *"Where is God's hand, in any of this? Shall I wait for God to act, when the king has ruled a thousand years already? Where was your hand, Lord, when he should have died, a thousand years ago and more? I do not want to live. I want Encormio destroyed."*

Encormio is beyond my reach for this brief moment, said that dark voice, distantly. **But that will not last. In time he will come to me.**

"Not soon enough," said Tenai. "Lord—I beg you, who rules the turning of the seasons and the dying of the fire and the endings of all things, if you cannot destroy Encormio, tell me how I can."

I rule nothing, the voice answered.

"You rule all my hope," Tenai said into the dark. "You rule all my desire. Lord Death, can you help me achieve my desire? Can you give me what I ask?"

Yes, said the voice, though with seeming reluctance.

"Then what can I offer that you will take? Youth? Health? The brilliance of passion? The memory of joy?"

There was a long, lingering silence. The air was cold. The frost broke underfoot like glass. Dark within dark, Lord Death stood there, shaped into human form by blood and fire and pain. He said in that voice that was the merest breath out of the darkness, **Offer me your life.**

Tenai opened her hands in relinquishment, and grief, and a terrible joy. "It is yours, Lord."

Offer me your death.

"For the price I have named, Lord, that too is yours."

You will regret this bargain, stated Lord Death, in that still, quiet voice; so like and so utterly unlike the voice of a man.

"Then I will," answered Tenai. "That, too, I accept."

The dark shape of Lord Death held out a hand to her. In his hand he held an unadorned black goblet. **Drink,** he said.

Without hesitation, Tenai took the goblet from his hand. It was heavy: she held it in both her hands and still felt the weight. It was cold, as though it had been set in the snow to chill. The liquid within it was clear and pure as water. It might have been water. She did not ask, but drank. The liquid had neither taste nor body; it was like drinking mist, but it was ice-cold. As Tenai drained the cup, the cold seemed to rush through her body, spreading through her veins to the tips of her fingers and toes. The cold spilled into her mind and her heart, and for a moment that seemed to last a long time, it absorbed her awareness and stopped her breath. It was not unpleasant. But it produced a strange chill that ebbed only slowly.

At last, when she could breathe again, Tenai looked up at Lord Death. He was still dark. Still wrapped in darkness. But he looked altogether more real, more solid, more present, than he had. The stars had come out into the night. Their light was a distant and frail thing, but it was light. It slid across the dark plains of Lord Death's face, which was so nearly the face of a man and so entirely something else.

I will teach you all the skills of destruction, said Lord Death, and his voice, too, although still quiet, had gained depth and substance and might almost have been, to Tenai's ears, the voice of a man. **But in the end, Tenai Ponanon Chaisa-e, those will not be the skills you will need.**

"How not?" Tenai demanded. "Will these skills not suffice to achieve my aim? Will they not be enough to destroy Encormio?"

You will destroy Encormio. But that will not be the end.

And Tenai had looked into those hollow, empty eyes and declared, "Lord, if I destroy Encormio, that will be enough, and I will thank you for it, whatever comes after that."

"I did not," Tenai added, "know what bargain I was making. Although Lord Death had put it clearly enough. If I had known then what I now understand ... I would have done the same."

"Bargained away both your life and your death in return for the destruction of one man?"

"I wanted nothing in either life or death but that destruction," Tenai said flatly. "No one else could do it, or dared to try for it. And I achieved it. In the end, I hunted Encormio through the dark as the hounds drive the stag, and forced him through that last Gate. He *ran* to Lord Death, for fear of me." Bitter fury burned in her eyes. She was not seeing the office, or Daniel. She was seeing the past.

It was real to her. No matter how clearly confabulated it was, her story was almost real to him, as well. Tenai had, it seemed, something of a gift for story-telling. Daniel could almost see the dark Lord she had called up and to whom she had offered everything.

He said, trying to recall her attention to the real world and the real moment, "So how did you end up here?"

After a moment, those dangerous eyes focused on his face. The fury ebbed. She took a breath. Another, and she managed to smile: the narrow, bitter smile she offered from time to time, with a little humor tangled up with darker things. But it was a smile. "Doctor, that is far ahead in this story."

Daniel held up his hands. "All right, Tenai, I'll wait for it. Our time's up for the day, anyway. But I'll ask you another question. Not to answer, but to think about. Tenai, what is it you want out of life?"

She stared and then laughed, a harsh sound with no trace of humor. "Doctor, how should I know?"

"I told you, no need to answer. Just think about it. But I'll tell you what *I* want for you: that you understand your own necessities. That you let go of the past, whatever it held, and find a way to move on. That you let go of some of this rage you're carrying and regain a healthier emotional balance. Maybe you could think about whether you might also want those things."

She gazed at him without answering. But the expression in her dark eyes was wistful.

Daniel let his breath out. "I have a suggestion. Michaela. You mentioned her to me."

"The girl who is silent."

"You said she's silent because she's trying to forget she exists. Do you remember that?"

Tenai inclined her head. "I remember."

"I think that was a very perceptive comment, Tenai. She's had a tough time. I can't tell you the details, of course, but the heart of the problem is grief. You understand grief. I wonder if you might be able to help Michaela stop trying to turn herself invisible."

"How?"

Daniel shrugged. "If I knew, I'd do it myself. We've all failed to help her. But you understand stubbornness as well as grief, and you're right there on the ward with her. Everyone walks past her. No one notices her. Maybe you might try noticing."

After a moment, Tenai bent her head again. "Yes, Doctor."

"Second—can you read and write?"

Tenai tipped her head a little to the side, regarding him with interest. "Only a very little."

Daniel nodded, unsurprised. He would not have been surprised either way. Illiteracy was consistent with her delusional state—no English if you're from a different world, with kings and magic and bargains to be made with the Lord of Death. It was also consistent with her mutism—no English, not for a long time, so of course she had become mute. Her occasionally peculiar ways of speaking suggested she spoke English as a second language. Delusional backgrounds were not always so consistent and complete, but sometimes they could be. Especially if the patient had an obsessional component to her problems. He said, "You'll need to learn if you're ever to leave this institution. I'd like to ask you to work with Alice Pough. She's one of our volunteers. She used to teach GED classes at a prison. Now she teaches a few of our girls and women. I want you to start working with her. She's frightened of students who behave violently, which is why she left the prison. Don't scare her, Tenai. I mean this. We can't afford to lose her." He glanced at the wall, where the hole stood in mute testimony of Tenai's own barely-controlled violence.

The woman's dark eyes followed his own glance. She looked like she might even feel ashamed of that. Daniel didn't want that. Not that he wanted her to feel great about bashing holes in walls, but shame wasn't the feeling he wanted her to take out of this session. He said briskly, "Next time you need to let go, get outside and run it out. Or go to your room and scream. Or come to me and break up my walls, but preferably not too frequently. Okay?"

"Yes," she agreed, now smiling a little.

That was better. Daniel smiled back, picked up a pencil and leaned back in his chair to suggest the session was over. He watched her walk out with her dancer-graceful stride.

Then he called maintenance to repair the hole in his wall.

There were reports to write, notes to transcribe, other patients' cases to consider, administrative duties to pursue. His next scheduled appointment with Tenai was not for three days. But Alice Pough, forewarned about the new student she was getting, brought Daniel a report after their first session.

"I thought she might be a very difficult student," Alice said, taking her place on the rose-pink couch. "I mean, illiterate adult students usually either have severe learning disabilities, putrid educational backgrounds, or both."

Daniel made an interrogative sound.

"No, neither. Tenai's more like an ESL student from a good background. She's obviously got the educational background. Just not in English. She speaks well—I mean, she expresses herself well. And my, what a beautiful voice, I must say."

"Yes," agreed Daniel, half-amused.

Alice smiled back. "She's got a good memory, and she knows how to apply herself. She's an excellent student."

"I'm glad to hear it," said Daniel. "Emotional problems?"

Alice made a show of exaggerated surprise. "Does she have any?"

"Well—"

"Oh, I know she must be having some kind of trouble, or why would she be here? But she seems fine to me. A little reserved, maybe," the teacher allowed. "She's quite self-contained, isn't she?"

"You don't see ... anger, in her?"

Regarding him with interest, Alice shook her head. "Should I?"

Daniel shrugged. "As you say, she has a lot of self-control, and I told her to be nice to you. Tell me if she ever frightens you."

"Now, Daniel, you know I'm not that easy to frighten."

The doctor answered her smile with one of his own. "I know."

One of the nurses brought a report of her own to the doctor shortly after that. She stopped Dodson in the hall. "Your patient," she said, meaning Tenai, "is up to something, Doctor."

"Up to something?" Daniel inquired.

The nurse, an older woman whose equanimity made her invaluable to Lindenwood, did not sound alarmed or annoyed. She sounded quite cheerful. "Yes, indeedy. She's started a rescue project, I think."

"Has she?"

"She's been sitting with little Michaela all morning, Doctor. Just sitting by her. Sometimes she sings/ Tenai, I mean. Not in English. Sometimes she just sits quietly. But she's been there all morning."

"Has she really? Well, well." Daniel was immensely pleased.

"I don't think there's any harm in it," the nurse said, a little tentatively. "But I thought I should mention it."

"Harm? I don't think so, either. Quite the reverse, for both of them, I hope. And I'm glad you let me know. Please keep me informed," Daniel told her, and went on about his duties. When Tenai said she would do something, evidently she meant it. Pay attention to Michaela. Work with Alice.

Give away everything she had, to destroy an enemy ... she would have meant that as well.

Five days from Tenai's first paying her attention, Michaela finally showed signs of listening to her. She leaned heavily on the older woman, her head resting on Tenai's shoulder or knee. And the day after that, Daniel got word from one of the nurses that Michaela had been talking to Tenai. Softly. Almost whispering. But, for the first time in eighteen months, responding to and talking with another person.

"I've heard very good things about you," he told her at their next appointment. "I've heard, for example, that you got Michaela to start talking. How did you do that? What exactly was it you did?"

Tenai shrugged, a minimal movement. They were walking up the hospital's main drive, a long curving drive bordered on both sides by the willows, now thoroughly greened up with spring, and by flowing beds of daffodils. The big early yellow ones had mostly finished blooming, replaced by little white ones. Their light fragrance carried to the walkway. It had been Daniel's suggestion, that they might spend their hour out-of-doors. From Tenai's relieved agreement, it had been a good one.

"Michaela is very young," she said now, with the tolerant air of an ancient grandmother. "She is a child. She has no subtlety. But she is not one of the mad, the insane, you know. She is only unhappy."

"She hasn't said a word in the eighteen months she's been here, Tenai. Not to her doctor, or the nurses, or the other patients. Not even to me."

"Dr. Christie is a fool." Tenai's voice held a glitter of anger, but also a more dispassionate judgment. She stooped to pluck one of the little daffodils, held up the stem, turned the little spray of flowers in her fingers, but without truly seeming to see it. The narrow flowers were red, a bright, vivid crimson. Daniel glanced down curiously to see if any of the other daffodils were that color. He hadn't realized they came in such a vivid, strong shade. But all the ones he saw were yellow or white. Tenai seemed to have picked the only stem of red flowers.

She said, "He let her fall so deeply into silence that she could not climb out. You would not have done that."

Daniel, who couldn't agree with her assessment out loud, shrugged. "Some cases are harder than others."

"Michaela is not a hard case," Tenai said, with clearly no pun intended. "But it is true that a woman, another patient, may work with her more easily."

"So what are you doing with her?"

"I tell—am telling, no, I *told*, her stories of my childhood. Out of my childhood. The stories that all mothers tell their children," Tenai added, a little grimly. "It has been a very long time since I thought of these stories. The story of the wolf and the oak; the story of the dog who stole the apples; the story of the girl who caught the moon in her hair."

"Perhaps someday you will tell me those stories, Tenai."

She made an impatient gesture, tossing aside the remains of the stem she had picked. The flowers fell to the ground, looking like a spatter of blood against the early green of the lawn. "Yes, if you want me to tell you, Doctor. I asked Michaela to tell me stories. That is all."

"You asked her to tell you stories."

"Yes. So she did. Red Riding Hood, and the one about the beanstalk and the giants. They are good stories."

"Are they?"

"Yes. The monsters are always defeated. What kind of story could be better? They are the right stories for Michaela to tell me. She had forgotten that at the end of the story, the monsters die."

Daniel nodded. He didn't say *But you aren't a monster*. He said instead, "And the heroes live happily ever after. Happy endings are important." What he meant was, *You, too, are meant to live happily ever after*. He didn't say that either.

She shook her head. "*Just* endings are important, Doctor."

Not quite the direction he had wanted her to take. "Fairy tales can be cruel. Sometimes kindness is better than justice." But that was a little heavy-handed, possibly, so he added at once, "Do you think Michaela might start talking to other people now?"

"Not to her doctor. She might talk to you, I think. I did."

"She's not my patient—" Daniel, meeting her eyes, hesitated. Glad she cared enough about the girl to want this. Not quite certain whether he should point out to her that she did care or leave her to realize that one her own. "I'll see what I can do," he promised. "How about your English writing?"

Anger easing, Tenai smiled. "I think you did not tell me everything true about that teacher."

"Oh?"

"That woman would not be so very easy to frighten, Doctor." She held up a hand before he could speak. "I am careful. I am still careful. I do promise you. She teaches well."

"That sounds good."

"Do you not have reports of these things?"

"Certainly. But I like to hear it from you, too, Tenai."

She bent her head a little. "Yes." She was silent for a moment. Finally she said, "I understand what you are doing, I think."

"Yes?"

"You want me to think of other people, and not so much of myself. That is what you are doing, Doctor."

He didn't try to deny it. He merely agreed, "That's part of it, yes. Am I wrong?"

For a little while they walked on in silence. Daniel waited, knowing that Tenai would answer eventually. And eventually she did. "No. You are right."

"Good. Tell me, if you think I'm making a mistake."

Tenai gave him a look, sideways, out of the corners of her eyes. "I do not think that you make mistakes, Doctor."

That surprised him into laughing, though with more than a touch of bitterness. "My God, don't I wish that were true! You haven't been watching long enough, that's all. Everyone makes mistakes. Certainly I do."

Terrible ones, sometimes, and sometimes when it mattered most. Daniel shut his eyes for a moment, then dragged himself back to the moment and said, "Although at least I've never promised away my life and death in a moment of despair."

Tenai gave him another slanted look. There was no sign she had picked up his reaction, and he was grateful: it was nothing to load a patient down with. But she was involved with her own pain. There was tension, in the set of her mouth and in her neck and shoulders. "You wish to hear more of the story? It is ... hard. Dark."

Daniel paused, and turned to face her. "Would you rather go inside?"

The tension didn't ease, but Tenai shook her head. "It is better out here. Under the clean sky, where there is room to move."

Daniel found he agreed with her. "All right. We have lots of time today. So why don't you tell me what happened after you made your bargain?"

For a long time, or for a time that seemed long, Tenai dwelt outside of the world ... among the blowing veils, between the worlds, on the lintel of the Gate. In the sunless kingdom of Death.

"What was it like?" Daniel asked her, keeping his voice low, not to disturb the flow of the story.

Tenai shrugged. "My memory of that time is uncertain. You understand, it was not like any mortal place. I was sustained by the water that Lord Death gave me to drink, and I think that changed my way of seeing, of understanding."

"Like a ... drug?"

"I do not know, doctor. I would say, in its own way. Sometimes it would seem that I had been there only a short time, and sometimes for a very long time."

"Was anyone there, besides you?"

Tenai touched the smooth bole of a great beech, looking into nothing. "Sometimes it seemed like there might be others there. Sometimes it seemed like there might be vast crowds. There were teachers there ... soldiers, generals, armsmasters, held before the final Gate that they might teach me their skill. They would teach me and then go, released to pass through the Gate. But I think no one seemed real there. Except for Lord Death."

"Of course. Right. The Lord of Death."

He was not like a man. Sometimes he seemed almost like a man, but sometimes his form would shred into the dark wind or fade imperceptibly into the darkness beyond dark, the darkness that crashes down when one puts out the one lit candle.

"But you weren't frightened of the Lord of Death," murmured Daniel.

Tenai did not glance at him. "I had nothing to fear. I had lost everything already. But you should say Lord Death," she added. "Not the Lord *of* Death, as I am ... was ... the lady *of* Chaisa. Death is not a place to possess. Lord Death is like sorrow, which is Lord Sorrow, whose kingdom contains all worn, forgotten things, the grief of grinding years. Or like Lord Silence, who rules unspeakable truth. Lord Death is the Gatekeeper. His kingdom lies between the mortal realm and the realm of God. Any general or armsmaster who dies must pass through that dark kingdom. They taught me. What Lord Death taught me himself is less easy to explain. To wait. To be patient. To pay attention. To endure. The time of my childhood, the time of my motherhood, those things came then to seem the life of another woman." She sighed, slowly, as though looking back through a long age to the bright, nearly forgotten days of her childhood.

"It sounds very difficult," Daniel offered.

Recalled to the present moment, Tenai gave him a half amused, half sardonic look. "Difficult? It was the easiest thing I have ever done." Her eyes had gone blank and still and dangerous. "I will leave you here, doctor, if I may. I would like to be by myself for a little time." But, though obviously edgy, she waited for Daniel's startled nod of permission before she walked away, moving with long strides.

The afternoon seemed less bright and warm to Daniel after Tenai left him alone. Perhaps the temperature really had fallen, but he suspected it was the strange horror of her story. Lord Death, Lord Sorrow, Lord Silence! It seemed strangely suitable that there should be a lord of unspeakable truths. What truths were they, he wondered, that Tenai found so unspeakable she had been forced to invent such metaphors?

It seemed even more appropriate that there should be a Lord Sorrow. Sorrow ought to be personified. A dark, powerful entity with empty eyes and a hollow heart: that would suit sorrow. How had Tenai put it? The grief of grinding years? How apt. How *exact*.

Daniel stopped beside Lindenwood's driveway and leaned against one of the beeches. The smooth gray bark was warm under his hand; the early leaves trembled overhead. Lindenwood loomed to his left, clean formal lines and neatly kept entryway, warm in the sunlight, but with bars on all the windows.

Suddenly he could not face it: could not face the pain of its patients or the too-close camaraderie of its staff.

He had no sessions scheduled for the remainder of this afternoon, into which he might have poured his attention and so lose himself. He had merely intended to use this time to catch up on his paperwork and prepare for the end-of-week staff meeting. Instead, not even pausing to speak to Lindenwood's receptionist, he walked around to the parking lot on the east side of the building, got into his car, and drove down the long driveway and out the gate.

It was far too early to pick up Jenna at St. Paul's, even if he picked her up before the after-school program began. Daniel drove aimlessly around the city for some time. The neighborhoods around Lindenwood were filled with tall, narrow houses of brick and stone, with impersonal front yards and back yards hidden behind high wooden fences. Some had their curtains drawn, but even where the curtains were open, light slid over opaque glass that closed out any passing glance from the outside. Daniel passed a park and turned into its winding driveway, letting his car coast at last to a halt near a small lake as calm and blue as the sky.

Willows here too, trailing their green leaves in the water. A young family was picnicking by the lake, parents sitting close together on a blanket, three kids running and shouting at the edge of the water. A feeling of isolation and deep loneliness seemed to settle slowly out of the bright sunlight, like darkness hidden behind the day.

And yet, where Daniel would have been willing to treat a patient for persistent, possibly damaging grief, he found himself reluctant to define his own, even after a year, as anything other than a normal, healthy response to loss. That, of course, was reassuring in itself: major depression was not usually perceived as healthy or normal by its sufferers, but as a deficit of mood utterly devastating and alien to normal mood. But he perceived the dark grief that still lingered in his world as ... Kathy's due, he supposed.

I do not think you make mistakes, Tenai had said to him. Daniel didn't know whether to laugh at that comment, or weep.

He started his car and left the park. He tried to leave his grief there, turned his thoughts purposefully toward happier images. Jenna deserved better from him than this bleak mood. He thought about her, deliberately. For his daughter, at least, this move had been an unambiguous good. A new school, new friends, a new life:

positive stressors that, as he had hoped, had served to push Jenna toward healthy recovery.

The school parking lot was crowded and busy; Daniel had arrived with the first wave of parents, those who picked their kids up right after school let out. Jenna would be upstairs, of course. Daniel threaded his way through a mob of children and adults around the main door and made his way down the hall and up the broad stairway.

Sister Mary Catherine took in his appearance with a raised eyebrow and a smile. She had her group of after-school children engaged in a variety of activities: a couple of boys were messing around with paints at the easels; two girls and three boys were playing, and arguing over, some kind of homemade board game; and several children had taken books and tucked themselves into a corner filled with beanbag chairs.

Jenna, along with two other little girls, was playing with a collection of little plastic horses and talking a mile a minute.

"I can't thank you, and St. Paul's, enough," Daniel said quietly. "This is an incredible turnaround for the short time you've had her."

The sister smiled. "I think she was ready to recover, Dr. Dodson. I'm sure it's her close relationship with you that gave her the security she needed to meet us halfway." A slight pause and then Sister Mary Catherine added, "She wouldn't talk to Nicole's mother yesterday, though. She won't watch any of the children leave with a mother. She turns her back. And she likes the men teachers better than the women teachers—better than me."

Daniel winced slightly. "I see."

"But she's much improved in just this short time," the sister added firmly. "Come meet her friends—that's Terri on her left and Nicole on her right."

Jenna, intent on a rearing white horse, didn't see him until he was right by the table. Then she followed Terri's glance up, squealed, "Daddy!" and jumped to her feet.

Daniel caught her as she jumped, pretended to stagger with her weight, and collapsed into a tiny chair beside the table, making exaggerated faces at how small it was. All three of the girls giggled and bounced around.

"The white horse is the good guy!" Jenna told him.

Daniel inspected the plastic herd. "Is there a bad guy?"

"Not there," Nicole told him, and showed him a Tyrannosaurus hiding on a chair on the other side of the table. "You're lucky you didn't sit on him. He would bite you!"

"Look at those teeth," Daniel said admiringly. "The horses better watch out." He wondered if he should call, say, Nicole's mother and see if Jenna might be able to go over to Nicole's house to play. Would that help, or might it be too pushy? Maybe it would be better to let Jenna have a little more time before suggesting she tolerate some other little girl's mother.

"You're really early," Jenna told her father. She looked pleased about this, and a little surprised.

"I got away early." Daniel hesitated. Then he added, "I found a nice park—a lake with geese. Want to get ice cream someplace and go check it out?"

"Yeah!" And Jenna tore off to get her jacket, no sign of lingering grief there.

Daniel realized that the reason his own lingering grief did not feel wrong to him was that his daughter could so effortlessly take it away for minutes or hours, and put the sunlight back into the sky. Terrifying and reassuring both, to think that he was probably doing the same for her.

All right. A little more time, then, and he'd see about arranging one or two play dates and see how that went.

4

Tenai danced on the sun-lit lawn, in the empty circle of the hospital driveway: a dance of death that mimed the movements of battle. There was no opponent. It might have been harmless exercise, or equally harmless practice. It did not look harmless: there was a blaze of anger and violence behind every movement. Daniel had turned his chair to watch from his office window. Her dance made him uneasy.

Dr. Martin appeared in Daniel's doorway and for a moment just watched Daniel watch Tenai. "Got a diagnosis yet?" he asked.

"No," said Daniel, a little warily. "I haven't done the battery."

Dr. Martin nodded. "Trust your own instincts more than the tests, do you? That can be a good idea. Especially with the ones that don't fit any classic diagnosis real well. But you can give me an off-the-cuff opinion, I expect."

"Obsessive. But not typically. I don't see evidence of compulsiveness. Nothing with demanding rituals, nothing overt."

"But—" Dr. Martin invited Daniel to continue.

"But recurrent ideas, yes. Persistent impulses ... I think so. Destructive impulses, destructive ideas. Her memories didn't come out of nothing; they have to reflect a real past. It definitely must have taken some sort of obsession to build such coherent false memories and hold them together. And she has such somber affect. You know how that kind of serious attitude can be ... I don't know ... a penumbra of compulsiveness."

"Yeah. But you're not looking at any psychotic diagnosis at all, are you?" the director observed with a shrewd little nod. "Nothing organic. I've read your case reports, Doctor. You don't think she's out of touch with reality. Why not?" The director cocked his head to one side, interested.

Daniel ran a hand across his smooth scalp, hunting for words. "Because she may have invented a false past, but I don't see any sign that she's out of touch with her present."

"You don't think the screwball past is a problem?"

"Its symbolism tells us about her real past. The family she lost ... probably that one's simple enough. The king she fought and killed ... somebody she hated? Or—"

"Or killed?"

"I don't think so." Daniel didn't want that to be true, and knew it. He picked up a pen and turned it over in his fingers—a distancing technique, he recognized, signal of his own unease with the possibility. But in fact he also thought it was unlikely. "Nothing so literally true. I was going to say, it might be a part of herself that she blames for the very real loss she suffered."

"So she was at war with herself," Dr. Martin said thoughtfully. "A little pat, maybe, but sure. That's possible." He rested his hip on the arm of the couch. "I wonder who won?"

It was a good question, but ... "I'm not so sure that anybody *won,*" Daniel said, and looked pointedly out the window.

"Yeah. Or she wouldn't have wound up acting out a wild-ass delusion in the middle of the city. But you think she's got that under control now, huh, Doctor?"

Daniel gave the director a sharp look. "Under control? Maybe, for now. Under control enough to leave Lindenwood? That would not be my first choice for her."

"She'll have been here four and a half months this Friday."

"She won't be ready to leave in one and a half. Can we give her another six months?"

"I did ask you to talk to me about that as soon as possible. Six weeks is kind of last minute."

It was. Time had gotten away from him, Daniel realized. "Yes," he admitted. "I'm sorry. I would appreciate another six months, if that's at all possible."

Dr. Martin shrugged. "Write me up a progress report and a proposal for continuing treatment and I'll consider it. But we have patients clamoring for space—paying patients—and another charity patient came in last week. I do like to be able to show the board a hospital that doesn't lose too much money too fast. I can tell you right now, I am not super likely to approve that big an outlay for your Tenai Doe." He gave Daniel a straight look. "That hasn't changed in the past six weeks. It wouldn't have been any different if you'd come to me the day after you met her. You write me up a good, forward-looking treatment plan with an *honestly* optimistic prognosis and I'll think about what we can do to meet that plan halfway."

Hard to resent bad news when it came wrapped up with a big *Don't blame yourself* bow and an offer to help. Daniel nodded.

"You can tell me now how you see yourself moving forward."

A moment to gather his thoughts, put down his dismay at the thought of losing Tenai before she could make it on her own. Dr. Martin eyed him with slightly pointed patience, and Daniel said, "I need to hear more about this king, the battle she had with him, how he died. I want to see how she worked out the plot of this story; I think that could be important in symbolic terms. It might tell us more about what might have really happened to her. But I think she's working on building herself a bridge to reality. When she started talking, I think she made the decision to leave that delusional past in the past. When she accepted treatment, she started to work toward a future in the real world. I don't see any signs that she's trying to bring her confabulation forward into her present or her future. And I've been looking."

"Mmm. So?"

"Well, besides the obsessiveness, I suspect she's working through a subtle kind of depression. Which makes perfect sense. Whatever her symbolic past actually represents, to her she seems to have achieved a goal. Now she's experiencing some kind of profound emotional letdown. I think. But you're right. I don't see any indications of psychosis. I just don't think there's anything organic behind what we're seeing in this case." He put the pen down with a decisive little click.

"A purely emotional disorder."

Daniel hesitated, glancing out the window to where Tenai danced with Death. *"Purely* anything may be simplistic. But, yes. I think that's the crux of it."

"I know," said Dr. Martin. "Some patients refuse to fit into the categories we invent. So. Where do you think she got those 'memories' of hers from?"

Daniel shrugged bafflement. "A story she read once? A movie she saw as a child? A story her father told her when she was six? Though it's pretty dark for a bedtime story."

"A story she wrote herself when she was twelve?" Martin waved a hand. "Could be any of those, sure. Okay. Obsessive, but not classically. Mm-hm. Maybe subsidiary depression. You want to try her on Prozac? Or Anafranil?" The director's tone was neutral, interested, not challenging.

"I'm thinking about it. The core of the problem isn't depression or delusion. It's rage. If she's not ready to give that up, she may experience any lessening of her anger as an attack. Or ... perhaps as unjust. Justice is very important to her. She feels ... I think she feels that she has a *right* to her anger. Whatever truly happened to her, she probably does. Force that to level out and I think we may see much stronger resistance."

Martin nodded thoughtfully. "You think that's where the violence came from when Maggie tried Anafranil the first time. Sure. You could well be right. Still. Don't hesitate too long, if you can get her to the point where she *is* ready. Don't want to run out of time for a fair trial of Prozac or whatever, if she's on her way out." Dr. Martin paused for a moment, then toed the office door closed. Daniel stiffened, trying not to show it.

The director walked across the office and stood in front of the window, arms folded over his broad chest. Outside, Tenai slaughtered imaginary opponents with an invisible sword, her movements slow and graceful. The director said, his eyes on the woman, "And as for how she's doing ... I hear she's become more outgoing on the ward."

"I hear that, too," Daniel agreed cautiously.

"I hear, for instance, that she's drawn the little Alston girl, Michaela, out of her shell." The director turned, arms still folded over his chest, and gave Daniel a narrow look. "That your doing, Dr. Dodson?"

Ah. Right. Well, yes, it had been a risk, to ask Tenai to get involved with another patient ... especially a patient who belonged to one of the other doctors, and most especially to Dr. Christie, who did not like other doctors stepping on his toes. Daniel hadn't expected to be called on it, though. He met Dr. Martin's eyes. "I suggested Tenai might try being friendly with Michaela, yes."

The director's expression was calmly neutral. "Tell me about that."

Daniel shrugged. "That hyper-focus on herself is one of her biggest problems, the clearest sign of obsessiveness. I think she's been blind to the other patients. I wanted her to get involved with other human beings. Michaela also needs to get pulled out of herself. I thought it might help to point Tenai in that direction. Like giving her a puppy. Responsibility, protectiveness, a push to pay attention to another person's needs ..."

"And you didn't see how it could hurt. Even though, if the girl happens to push some button neither you nor I know about, she could certainly get flattened," Dr. Martin said. "As you know perfectly well, Doctor. And that leaves aside the possible psychiatric harm a *patient* might do, encouraged to muck about with *another patient's* treatment."

Daniel didn't drop his gaze. "As long as Tenai's on the ward, it's possible somebody might put a foot wrong with her. It was your decision to keep her out with the general population, sir, and I think that's been important in drawing her out of herself and her confabulated past, but it's also been a risk. Any human interaction naturally has the potential to help or to harm. Any friendly interaction is likely to help. Michaela had set herself up in solitary confinement. It's hard to imagine any way Tenai could have made her condition worse."

"So you unilaterally decided to set your *patient* onto another doctor's case. Without running this strategy past him, much less me."

Put that way, it did sound a little ... pushy. Daniel let his breath out slowly, not looking away. "I guess so. I thought it might work. I think it *has*."

"You are one free-wheeling son of a gun, aren't you? I think Maggie left that out of her description."

Daniel leaned back in his chair, folded his hands on his desk, and met the director's eyes. "I can focus too narrowly. I know that. I apologize. I did not intend to offend Dr. Christie. I definitely didn't intend to offend you. But from what I hear, Michaela's made substantial progress since Tenai got involved. Even Dr. Christie thinks so. He won't change his mind about that as long as he thinks theirs is a spontaneous friendship."

Dr. Martin snorted. "And the end justifies the means?"

"Success," said Daniel carefully, "is its own justification. I admit I put the patient's needs first. Is that the wrong priority?"

"It's not, by God, the *only* priority, Doctor. Dr. Christie would've howled at the idea, I can see why you didn't tell him what you had in mind, but the reason you didn't run your bright idea by me was because ... ?"

Daniel turned his hands palm up. "I didn't think of it."

The director shook his head. "You didn't think of it. For God's sake."

"What are you going to do?" Daniel asked him. He could imagine the director reassigning Tenai to some other doctor, and was surprised at the depth of apprehension he felt at the thought. "Don't take Tenai away from me."

"You think I ought to be thinking about that?" Dr. Martin studied him. "No," he said after a moment. "Or I should say, hell, no. I'm pissed at you, but not that pissed. You got Tenai talking and cooperating. You've got a solid connection with her, and I'd be an idiot to screw that up. Now you've got her to connect to Michaela, and I'm glad to see it, no matter how many corners you cut along the way. But, dammit, Dr. Dodson, you are not in private practice here. You are part of my staff and I want you to act like it. Is that clear? Are we communicating?"

Daniel took a long breath. "Yes, sir." Another breath. "I would like to continue encouraging contact between Tenai and Michaela."

"Damn right. Too late to turn that clock back now."

Daniel rubbed his mouth, carefully tamping out a smile in case it looked self-satisfied. Though Martin was probably perceptive enough to get it was relief, and appreciation for the director's rapid, practical decisions.

"I'll reassign Michaela to you. You give Christie that new patient of yours, Samantha Bowen. Don't take this as a reward. I don't mean it that way. Keep me informed, you got that, Doctor? Keep me in the loop," he said, in a not-unfriendly tone, and opened the door again. "Or if you need anything else." That last with a warning look. He gave Daniel another short nod and went out.

Outside, Tenai danced in the chilly spring air.

Daniel put aside the tension of the last few moments, scooped up his jacket and went to find her.

Tenai had chosen a rather ostentatious area in which to dance, or exercise, or practice, or whatever she was doing. The center of the circle drive held only a few trees, big white oaks and a single muscular beech. Many office windows overlooked the area. Daniel saw faces at a few of them, watching Tenai from above as he had done himself. Something he hadn't been able to see from his office: Michaela was watching too. She sat tucked up against the trunk of a big oak, surrounded by a scattering of daffodils, turning a fallen twig over and over in her fingers, watching Tenai. He could not remember ever seeing Michaela leave the building before, though she had the privilege. She had never cared to. Now here she was. He pretended not to pay any attention. Make a big deal about it, and she was likely to close herself off again, back inside her own head, tighter this time. So he just watched Tenai himself, pretending not to notice Michaela at all.

This close to Tenai, he could see more than the outline of her dance; he could see the blankness of her expression and hear the *whuff!* of expelled breath as she moved suddenly with her arm extended, completed an upward sweep, lunged, and recovered. It was impossible to tell whether she knew that he was there.

Eventually—Daniel thought it might have been as long as twenty or twenty-five minutes, but he had forgotten his watch and was not certain—the powerful movements stopped. The moment of cessation was unclear. The dance had been slow enough at times to appear at an end. The boundary between *slow* and *over* blurred, but when Tenai looked at Daniel and met his eyes, he knew it was over.

There was anger in her face, in the set of her shoulders, in the line of her neck. But there was something else there too, difficult to identify: Daniel thought that it might have been a strange kind of peace that somehow did not contradict the anger. He said, "Are you all right?"

Tenai gave him a summing look. She was breathing in long deep breaths that seemed to take away the anger when she let them out. "Are you?" Tenai turned the question back to him. "You have been angry, Doctor? With me?"

Daniel found himself unsurprised by her perception. "No," he said. "With myself, I guess, and with life, I suppose."

Tenai said merely, "Ah."

"Do you want to walk a little?"

She answered seriously, "I want to run and run and not stop. I dance instead."

"So you do. It was beautiful to watch."

Tenai shrugged, that minute gesture he had learned to recognize.

"It's almost time for our hour. Shall we go in? I'd like to hear a little more of your story."

Another shrug. "If you like, doctor." Tenai glanced toward the hospital's main entrance, framed with budding roses and generous swooping beds of irises. But before she moved in that direction, she went over to Michaela and crouched to say a few words to the girl. Michaela smiled and then looked shyly down. Tenai picked one of the last daffodils blooming beneath the high-branched oak and gave it to her. It was not yellow like most of the others, but a startlingly strong crimson. Daniel had not realized Tenai deliberately selected the red ones to pick, and it seemed a little odd that again, the one she had picked appeared to be the only red one in the whole bed, but he was more interested in Tenai's smile than the flower.

Then she straightened and came to join Daniel. "That was nice of you," he said, making sure he sounded casually approving but not surprised.

"Now that she is not trying to forget herself, she wants other people to know she is there. Especially she wants me to remember she is there." Tenai slanted a glance at him. "I had not realized that I ..." Her voice trailed off. But after a pause, she said, "I had not realized I had anything left to give anyone, except death. I thought I was nothing. Not in the same way as that child tries to be nothing. In a much more dangerous way: I thought I belonged entirely to Lord Death's kingdom. When you told me to make Michaela stop trying to disappear, you meant to ... make me think I should give her a flower. So that I would remember I am not dead, even when I reach into that dark kingdom."

Some of that was puzzling, but basically this was exactly true and Daniel thought that was enough. He said, "Well, yes. Do you mind?"

"No. I think I had forgotten that flowers existed." Her attention had turned inward.

"You forgot you were still living," Daniel suggested cautiously.

Tenai gave him a burning look. "My life was not important to me. I had set everything aside but vengeance."

Tenai rode out of Lord Death's sunless land and into the cold of a midwinter night, high in the mountains above Nerinesir.

Midwinter, those three days when the year dies and is reborn, is the time when it is easiest to pass through the veil that separates the land of the living from the realm of Death. For those three days, Lord Death walks abroad every night and anyone, it is said, can see him. Folk pen up their stock and shelter indoors. They light extra lamps and set candles at every window and before every door. Babies born during the dark midwinter nights are unlucky. Midwives will try to bring babies early or hold them off, whatever they can, to keep them from entering life during those long nights. If a baby is born during the midwinter dark, it may be given to the priests to raise for God, but there are also those who will sacrifice it, offering its blood to Lord Death to turn the luck. Death and fear and ill-luck: that is midwinter.

Tenai rode a horse that had recently foundered somewhere in Talasayan; Lord Death had taken it into his hand in that moment between dying and living. It was a good horse; Lord Death might have chosen any dying animal, after all, and had chosen this one. The horse picked its way down out of the mountains, until at last she rode around the shoulder of a mountain and looked down at the glittering city of Nerinesir, nestled into its high valley.

Nerinesir was a fine city. It had been built of the bones of the mountains: white and black and gray stone, strong and enduring. Its outer walls were stone as well, thirty feet high or more, with towers spaced around them for soldiers to keep watch ... although the watch in those days was kept only casually. Encormio held all the land in his fist. Only Tesmeket, where the folk always remembered their long-past history of free barbarity, broke free of the great king's grip from time to time. Then the fast little ships of Tesmeket might raid the lowlands along the coast, until Encormio drove them back again to their islands.

The River Gate led into Nerinesir from the north-east, the Sunrise Gate from the east, the Gate of Pearl from the south-west, and Death's Gate from the teeth of the great mountains that lay to the south of the city. Tenai sat on her horse on the high mountain road and smiled in the bitter cold, looking down at that gate. It was open. No one feared attack in those days.

On that first attempt, Tenai intended a swift and direct attack against Encormio himself. Why strive for subtlety when no one would look for her? She rode down from the heights through the gathering dusk on the horse Lord Death had brought her. She had no sword ... the dark sword Gomantang came later. She had the silver knife with which, so long ago, she had killed the bull in that frozen pasture. She had a black cloak stiff with frost, and a thousand memories, and a terrible purposefulness.

Encormio's palace lay on the west side of the city, near the Gate of Pearl. Tenai entered the city through Death's Gate. Buildings crowded close on both sides of the narrow cobbled streets, two and three stories high, but all the shutters were closed and barred. Although the moonlight did not often reach street level, abundant lamps hanging from tall poles cast a pale milky light across the cobbles and the faces of the buildings. The light was cold in this season, made of the distant winter sunlight.

The shod hooves of Tenai's horse rang on the cobbles and echoed through the streets, slow loud beats, like the ringing of a hammer on stone. Some of the people huddled indoors must have heard her pass in the silence of the night. No one put back shutters to look out, perhaps for fear they might see what made that sound.

Nerinesir was a city of concentric circles: outer city and inner, court and palace, with a wall dividing each from the next.

But before Lord Death, lord of all gates and all gatekeepers, no lock would hold. When Tenai came to the Serpentine Wall that enclosed the inner city, she laid her hands on the gate and it fell open before her, and she passed through into the inner city and rode past the great homes of the nobility. When she came to the Martyr's Wall, she flung the gate open in the same way and rode into the gardens and parks of the court that surrounded the palace itself; and when she came to the Wall of Glass, the same.

Lord Death was there before her, waiting in the dark. He did not speak to her, but when she rode past him, he turned his head and gazed after her.

Although it was the dead of night, Encormio was awake, and all his courtiers and musicians and sorcerers and soldiers, all his wives and children and their servants. He had known she was coming, or that someone was. He waited in his great reception hall, surrounded by his people, and his musicians played for him on harps and bone flutes, which are the instruments appropriate to winter.

Encormio was a broad man, heavy and tall, with powerful hands and thick arms. His eyes were silver: eyes that could see into the hearts of men. His hair was not black, but that dark brown that in certain lights looks almost red; unusual in Talasayan. He wore it long, bound with an iron ring. The king was dressed plainly, in a short outer robe of plain brown with an inner robe of blue showing at throat and hem. He wore a wide black ring on his thumb, and an ironic smile that hid his thoughts more effectively than a mask.

It was plain, even to Tenai who was not looking and did not care, that Encormio's courtiers and musicians and sorcerers and wives and children and servants were all terrified of him. Tenai herself, riding upon the magic of the midwinter night, was too intent on her goal to be afraid.

"Welcome!" said Encormio, in a voice as heavy and powerful as his body. He meant to say more, probably, but Tenai did not wait. She threw the little silver knife she carried at the king.

Encormio did not dodge, nor attempt in any way to guard himself. His soldiers made no move to protect him. His sorcerers invoked no spells or magic. There was no need. A darkly-glittering protective spell surrounded the king, visible in that odd sideways manner of magic when the knife touched it.

But Tenai twitched the veil of the world into the knife's path, and the knife flew into the veil and out of it and pierced Encormio's chest, four inches too far to the right to touch his heart. That far the protective spell succeeded, because Tenai did not often miss her mark with a thrown knife.

After that, everything seemed to happen both very slowly and all at once: the knife struck Encormio, and the king, silver eyes wide with amazement, staggered and put out his hand, catching himself on the shoulder of the nearest courtier. The glittering spell of protection blazed up and went out, like a candle in a sudden wind. A woman screamed. Men shouted. Two soldiers of the palace guard, quicker than the rest, drew their swords and attacked Tenai.

Tenai killed the first and took his sword, killed the second and walked forward, toward Encormio. She barely perceived anyone other than the king, even the soldiers, when more of them shook off their shock and tried to prevent her. But there were suddenly a great many soldiers and a fair number of sorcerers. Encormio fled, a swift flight through an inner door and away. Out of reach.

Tenai might have pursued him. **Too late,** commented Lord Death, standing unruffled amidst all the clamor, and Tenai was forced eventually to admit that this was true. She had drawn his blood. She had bled the king and driven him back; dealt out death within his walls and come close to driving him into the embrace of Lord Death. But she had missed, and Encormio was now on his guard, and, for this moment, out of reach.

"If that first flung knife had killed Encormio," Tenai said, pacing from one wall to the other in Daniel's study, "who knows what might have happened in the world? Certainly everything would have come to pass very differently. It would have been over, just so quickly. Over." She paused, gazing at the office wall without seeing it. "I would never have gone to Imbaneh-se to raise my first army, which led to such terrible things later between Imbaneh-se and Talasayan. Encormio would have been dead, and that son of his that was the eldest, I forget his name, that son would have become king. Even if the son was a fool, or vicious, he would never have been so powerful as Encormio."

"But you missed," Daniel prompted her in his most neutral tone, wondering what that failure might symbolize to Tenai.

"I missed, and that was bitter to me. I went out into the mountains and lived as the outlaws live for that winter, watching Nerinesir, learning the shape of it and the ways of its people. Sometimes I came into the city and lived there for a time, going by different names, watching the court and searching for Encormio's weaknesses. He guarded himself well after our first encounter. It would be many, many years before I came so close a second time. And many years more than that before at last I succeeded in my long desire."

"But you did succeed."

"Yes, in time," agreed Tenai distantly. "In time. Pardon me, Doctor. I believe I will go out again for a little while." And she did, five minutes early, leaving Daniel tapping his pencil on a blank pad and wondering what about this session and this story to put down. What the shape of reality could possibly be, behind the fantastic story Tenai had woven to hide it.

5

Anger management was not a term that often floated through Daniel's mind. It was a term associated in his mind with marriage counselors and stressed senior executives and child abuse; a term that carried with it a strong, dispiriting whiff of futility. So many angry men dropped out of programs that might have helped them: angry, yes, and impatient, and unwilling to admit publicly—or, more importantly, to themselves—that there was a problem at all.

There were ways to deal with anger. As many as there were to deal with grief, perhaps. But shoving it in some mental closet and pretending it didn't exist was not usually effective. It seemed to Daniel, as too many days ran past, that this might be exactly what Tenai was doing. It was a self-control issue. What had occurred to him when he'd first encountered this woman? Hadn't he thought then that that self-control of hers might be a weakness as well as a strength?

Out on the floor, the staff were delighted with every evidence of normalcy she showed. Like the staff, Dr. Martin was impressed. Daniel's own pleasure in this evidence of Tenai's re-connection to the rest of the world was more restrained, especially after the director told him he probably wasn't going to grant an extension for Tenai's stay at Lindenwood.

"She's doing too well," Martin told him. "You wanted her to develop relationships. She has. You wanted her to start interacting more freely with the staff and patients. She is. We all wanted her to show a peaceful attitude. One has developed. All this is good. Right?"

"Yes," said Daniel. "But ..."

This was a private discussion. Daniel felt he had to challenge Martin's decision, but he was having trouble putting his own lack of enthusiasm into words.

"But ...?" Dr. Martin inquired. "We've got engagement with

other patients and with staff, no more broken stuff, a lot higher comfort level all the way around. I look at Tenai and I think of our half-way house. Give her a couple months there, and I think of her moving on with a normal life. But I guess that's not what you see."

Daniel threw up his hands and stood up to pace, the short five steps down and back that the director's office afforded. After a minute, he stuffed his hands in his pockets, as though he might find words there that could express his hesitation. Dr. Martin said nothing more; made no effort to hurry him. The director had settled behind his desk, leaning back in his chair. He looked perfectly comfortable. Perfectly willing to sit there and wait for however long it took Daniel to get his thoughts together. That calm patience must be pretty effective with patients. It was certainly effective with Daniel.

"Say you force a river underground and cap it off," said Daniel, turning to face Martin. "You can say, There! Dry land! But the river's still underneath, and when it blows off the cap, there'll be one hell of a flood."

"You think she's repressing rather than recovering."

"She says she feels less anger. I don't think she's *trying* to fool me. But is a fish aware of being wet? She's been so angry so long, can she even tell the anger's there anymore? I remember—" Daniel said, and stopped.

Dr. Martin waited, his expression neutral and interested.

Choosing his words with some difficulty, Daniel said, "About ten months after my wife ... died, it occurred to me one day that ... that the grief I'd felt ... was changing to memory. That the grief, the initial weight of grief, had started to lift, somewhere in there. It was like ... I don't know. Like suffocating for months and then waking up to find I could breathe. And for most of the time during those months, I'd never felt the lack of air. If you'd asked me how I was doing, I'd have said fine, and I'd have believed it. I forgot air even *existed*."

"I understand," Dr. Martin said gently.

"I think ... I look at Tenai, and she's doing so much better. But I wonder if that's a real improvement, or just an apparent improvement. I don't ... I don't get the impression that she's gained any real self-knowledge, any improvement in understanding her own feelings. And I don't think that's something so easy to dispense with."

"That's why you still haven't put her on Prozac," Dr. Martin observed. "I thought you'd simply decided she didn't need it. I was inclined to agree."

Daniel shook his head. "No. No. Look, I guess we both agree that the psychotropic drugs are more apt to work properly to take care of the functionally autonomous remnants of past psychological trauma, right?"

"Right."

"And I can't tell what's functionally autonomous and what's ongoing psychological trauma, yet. None of us can tell, yet. Not me, and, with all due respect, not you, and not Tenai herself. That's the problem. She's becoming *more* resistant, not less. She won't tell me how her story ends, and I think she needs to do that. I think I need to hear it, and I think she needs to cope with it. I'm almost certain that if we put Tenai out the door at the end of the month, we're going to hear on the news how she lost it and slaughtered some guy who cut her off in traffic."

"I've been tempted myself." But Dr. Martin held up a broad hand to forestall Dodson's response. "No. I understand you. You could be right. So. I guess you still want another six months, right, Doctor?"

"Yes. Please."

"Um. I don't know. She just does not look like she's that big a risk. Not anymore." The director tapped his thick fingers on his desk, considering. "Tell you what, Doctor, you might try giving her a little push and seeing if something gives."

Daniel looked at him. "If something gives, it could be something big."

"If she's gonna snap, she better do it here instead of a week after we put her out the door. If we kick her out and she kills some guy who cuts her off in traffic, that's kinda on us. Especially on me, and I don't need that kind of karma." He tapped his fingers a little longer. "Let's say you give her a little push. Not too hard, mind you, but enough to show whether she ought to be able to hande the halfway house. If nothing breaks, maybe you're wrong and she's ready to take a baby step or two out of the nest. If something does, you get your extension. That sound okay to you?"

Daniel had to admit this made sense. He nodded.

"I thought half an hour ago that you were doing a damned good job with Tenai. Now I think so, more. So whatever you do, I expect I'll support you, even if it breaks bigger than I'd like. That fair?"

"Yes, sir. Thank you."

Dr. Martin waved a casual hand. "Yeah, we'll see how it goes. Keep me informed. Now. How're you coming with Bess? She's still talking just to you, I hear."

And so. So. All that remained was to decide on exactly the right kind of push. The kind that would move Tenai, if she actually was stuck, in the right direction. Or *a* right direction. The rest of the story might show him what direction that was—or show it to Tenai; so often the patient knew her own necessities best, if her doctor could get her to *look*. But Tenai refused. Days passed by, and grew uncomfortably into a week. Time ticked down, the passing seconds wearing away.

"Do you *want* to leave the hospital?" he asked her at last. "Do *you* think you're ready to leave us? Are you less angry than you used to be?"

They were walking on the grounds. Daniel thought he had memorized every rock and blade of grass and bush contained within the hospital grounds. If Tenai was bored with them, it didn't show.

The season was turning in its good time. The irises and peonies had passed their peak, but the roses were just entering full bloom. It was still spring, though summer was obviously just around the corner. A wonderful, fresh time of year. A fine time for a personal springtime. Daniel's own spirits had lifted, an involuntarily response to the sunlight and the season, but he would have admired the flowers more if not for the fear of losing Tenai, with disaster rapidly following.

There was no immediate answer. Tenai walked along the concrete walkway, hands in her pockets, head bent. Finally she said, meeting Daniel's eyes with her own dark ones, "Yes. Am I not?"

"I'm not sure," said Daniel. "I'd like to hear the rest of your story." Not the first time he'd asked. He expected the same answer this time. And got it. Tenai paused beneath one of the big trees, resting her hand on its rough bark, not looking at him.

"I do not want to think of that time, doctor."

"I know. Tenai, I think you have to." Daniel hesitated. Then he said directly, going for openness and honesty, "Tenai, I'm still convinced your memory holds the key to your emotional responses, whether it's factually accurate or not. And I wonder whether you're refusing to look at it because all that anger of yours is tied up with those memories. And if that's so, the anger is still there. If that's the case, I just don't think you can hold it back forever."

She did not answer.

Daniel said, "Will you please tell me what happened later, after your first attempt to kill Encormio failed?"

"Is this a test you set me?"

"I don't know. *Is* it a test? Is it that difficult?"

A swift, frowning look. "Very well!" she said, just a little sharply. "I will tell you these things if you wish, but they are nothing to do with this land, or with me, now."

"Yes, they are," Daniel said instantly. "We're built of our memories, Tenai. What we do is important. What happens to us is important. Whatever happened to you, your memories echo the past."

Another look, more thoughtful. Tenai made a gesture like a shrug, which might have been surrender or agreement or resignation or something else less recognizable.

Encormio was on his guard, after Tenai succeeded in drawing his blood in his palace and his own hall. She could not pierce the protections that surrounded him. No arrow or crossbow bolt could strike past his guard. Poison whispered in his ear and warned him of waiting death.

Tenai understood, in the end, that there would be no profit to her from continuing in that way, not if she teased the king from just beyond his reach for a hundred years.

"And so in the spring I left Talasayan, and followed the river west into Imbaneh-se," Tenai told Daniel.

Her eyes were not focused on his face. She looked up, but Daniel understood that she did not see the oak leaves, nor the swallows darting above the lawn. It was the past she looked into, not the present.

She said, "In those days, Encormio ruled Imbaneh-se as he ruled Talasayan, and Keneseh in the south: with a steel-clawed whip and a naked sword. But Imbaneh-se never forgot that it once ruled itself. That for many centuries it had been the stronger country and forced Talasayan to yield in everything."

"So you went to Imbaneh-se," Daniel observed, inviting her to continue. They walked out of the shade of the oaks into the warmth of sunlight. Tenai's rich, velvety voice seemed to draw a darkness across the bright sky. It was no surprise she'd captured Michaela with that voice of hers, the stories she'd spun out of nothing for the silent girl ... but *these* stories were serious, Daniel was convinced. He listened with all his attention.

"Yes. I could not lay my hand on Encormio's heart. So I went to Imbaneh-se. If I had too little power of my own, well, there was power in Imbaneh-se that would be ready to my hand."

Daniel did not want to interrupt, and this time made no sound when she paused.

"Imbaneh-se owns a very different country than one finds in Talasayan," said Tenai after a while. "It is a land of broad plains and wide skies. There are trees, but few, and they grow large in their proud solitude. It is from those great trees that the people of Imbaneh-se carve their thrones. I went to Sotatan, to the sea, where the heirs of the oak throne might be found. Encormio did not hunt me into the south ... not then. He thought I had fled. No doubt he believed he would crush me if I returned. Probably I amused him. He did not know what the future would hold, for either of us. Nor did I."

"What did it hold?" Daniel asked, keeping his own voice quiet and matter-of-fact.

"Great armies and terrible wars," answered Tenai, as though not quite aware she was speaking. She was still looking into her memories, her eyes dark with remembered grief. And anger, yes, subtle, but Daniel was sure that was anger in those almond-dark eyes.

"Fields watered with blood. Croplands turned to dust, and forests afire. Bolts falling from the sky like rain ... long decades of struggle and death. I found the heirs to the oak throne. When a line of rule is removed, there are always men eager to claim the empty throne. There were men willing to fight Encormio if they thought there was a chance they would rule. I was that chance."

"All by yourself."

Tenai moved her head, blinking, her attention coming back to the present and the reality of this warm spring day, so far removed from that other place and time. She studied Daniel's face for a moment as though seeing him for the first time. After a while, she smiled ... a bitter smile, not without humor, but holding a great darkness behind the humor. "Doctor, I was Death's Lady. Ambitious men were glad to listen to a woman who held Lord Death for her master, if it meant they might seize a chance to rule." She paused.

"What happened?" Daniel asked, tone hushed.

Tenai looked at him with that bleak amusement in her eyes, in her smile. It was a cold amusement, a hard smile, nothing to do with a peaceful spring day at Lindenwood. "What happened? Why, doctor, there was war. For a little while it seemed that I would win, that I would break Nerinesir's defenses and send Encormio at last to my Lord Death and to the judgment of God. But that was only Encormio believing at first this was a little war, a little army. When he finally believed the threat was real, he put forward his strength and it was Imbaneh-se that was broken."

"Ah."

"Imbaneh-se was always a rival of Talasayan. It had fretted under Encormio's yoke. But this time it had frightened him. To punish Imbaneh-se for its rebellion, Encormio put to death all the men of that country between the ages of twelve and sixty."

"Oh," said Daniel.

"Yes," said Tenai, still with that hard humor. "My name was a curse on the lips of the women of Imbaneh-se for generations. That country took a long, long time to recover from the butchery. But in the end it was Encormio who regretted that order more than I. Those who survived never forgot that it was Encormio's uniform the butchers wore. And I ... I went to Keneseh and dwelt there for a little while, and learned subtlety. It took failure and disaster and a long, long life to teach me subtlety."

"Um," said Daniel, and gathered his thoughts. "You say it took generations for Imbaneh-se to recover. You said, before, you were old. You said you made a bargain with Death so that you would never die. It makes me wonder ... just how old are you, Tenai?"

"Ah." She looked up at the high, cool sky. It was cloudless, so bright it was more white than blue. A sky without end. She said eventually, "Four hundred years and more I battled Encormio. Four hundred years of war and tense peace, of poison in his cup that he yet would not drink, or took no harm of; daggers in the night that went awry in the stroke ... Four hundred years I stalked the king."

Head tilted back to look at the sky, eyes lost in memory ... Tenai looked ageless, not young. She looked to Daniel in that moment as though she had in actual fact lived every moment of four hundred years.

Tenai was going on, still in that dreamy tone. She did not sound angry, not now. It was more as though she felt disconnected from the past she thought she remembered. "Encormio learned fear of me before the end. I came close to his life time and again. He had sons and grandsons and great-grandsons—I killed them when I could not reach the king himself, and so came very near to ending that line. He never cared greatly for any son of his, but he cared that I mocked him so. He did not laugh when the bodies of those sons and grandsons were brought to him one by one, over those long, long years."

Well, that was awful. Daniel said involuntarily, "Good lord, Tenai, what had those boys ever done to you?"

Tenai looked at him, pulling her gaze away from the high, pale sky. "They were his sons. But they were not boys, mostly. Encormio was ageless himself, having made that bargain long ago with Lord Sorrow, but he did not trouble to buy ageless years for his descendants."

"Yes," said Daniel, "but still—" He was silent, thinking this over. Then he said, "You were already angry beyond reason, or you would not have murdered innocent men, would you?"

"Innocent?" said Tenai. "They were his sons."

They looked at one another. Daniel had never felt Tenai's foreignness so clearly. It could not have been greater had she in fact stepped into this world from some other. But he knew he had at last found a lever that would move her from any stability that was not rock-solid. He said carefully, "If Encormio was wrong to kill your son, were you not wrong to kill his?"

This time, the pause grew cold. For the first time in a long while, Daniel felt threat pouring off her. A chill ran down his spine, despite the heat of the day. Oh, yes. That had done it. Tenai did not move, or speak. Daniel knew she burned with danger; blazed like a lightning bolt held still by some almighty hand, to be loosed and fire the world. He held just as still, with considerable effort. "Tenai, are you angry because I'm wrong, or because I'm right?"

Tenai spun and took a step away.

"Is it me you're angry with?" Daniel asked her back, raising his voice a little. "Or memories from the past?"

Tenai turned sharply back toward him, and he went on urgently. "Tenai, all that anger is *still there*. It's always been there. But I'm not the cause. Dammit, woman, stop!"—as she took another step toward him. "Tenai, I know you can break me in half. Is that what you want to do?"

And if the answer was *Yes*, what would he do then?

Tenai stopped. Her breathing steadied, eventually. She did not speak.

"How are you now?" Daniel asked, cautiously.

She blinked, and blinked again. She looked at him. And smiled, with what effort Daniel could not imagine. "Well," she said, "if it was a test you set me, I see that I have failed it."

"There's no failure, no success," Daniel said instantly. "Only knowledge. Self-knowledge: there's nothing more valuable. Don't deny what you find out. You can't walk forward with your eyes closed. Are you all right?"

"No," said Tenai. "No."

"Is this a true thing about you, Tenai? Are you the sort of person who will kill anybody, whether they did anything themselves worthy of blame, just to get at an enemy out of reach? Is that you?"

"I see ... I see what you are saying," Tenai said, speaking slowly, as though not quite sure of her words. "I became that sort of person, I think. Although ..." she paused.

"Yes?"

"There was one child I spared, a boy of six or seven ... Doctor, do you never feel fear?"

Daniel laughed, a little shakily. "God, yes, Tenai. But I thought you wouldn't hurt me, and was I wrong?"

"But you might have been wrong, doctor. How did you know?"

"All I ever do is guess. That's my job. Sometimes I guess right." He hesitated. *"Is all that anger still there?"*

"Yes," said Tenai. "You were right, doctor. It has always been there."

If she was angry, it wasn't apparent any longer in her face, or her voice. There might have been a hint of it in the tension of her hands. Something in her eyes, maybe. Daniel fancied he could see the beat of blood under her skin, along her throat, in her wrists. He said, trying to give her a different means of coping, "Let it go, Tenai." He gestured upward, at the pale sky. "There's the sky, wide enough to take in any amount of rage or fear or grief; there's the wind, to carry it away ... let go. Let it *go*."

Tenai said nothing.

After a moment, Daniel sighed. "Will you walk with me back to the hospital?"

"No," said Tenai. "You go, if you will. I will walk a little and think ... think of many things."

Turning his back on this woman was one of the hardest things Daniel had ever done. But he did it, and walked away, and Tenai stood in the warm June sunlight behind him and let him go.

After that, Daniel was more certain than ever both that Tenai was far from well; and that those fantastic memories of hers held every key to open up all the problems through which she was currently battling. He could not even imagine what Tenai might have done, or thought she had done, or wanted to do, that might have been translated in her mind into the murder of Encormio's sons. That was so much more personal and, well, disturbing, than the broader memories of war. What real actions or thoughts could possibly be concealed behind all this complicated symbolism? He wanted to believe it was nothing worse than the typical homicidal thoughts that OCD sufferers sometimes experienced. But what if it was worse? What then? What was he trying to release into the world?

Dr. Martin, when Daniel described this incident to him, frowned. "Is this progress? You think you've kicked something loose that's going to knock her off balance in a helpful way?"

"I think ... I think any time a patient moves ahead with self-understanding, that is progress. I think we finally have something to work with. I also think ..." Daniel paused.

"Spit it out, man." But the director's tone was not as impatient as his words.

Daniel tapped his fingertips on the arm of his chair. "We haven't quite gotten to the end of her story. But I think we're getting close. Whatever real events her false memories are based on, I think she's finally got a chance to move past them. To move on. But I wouldn't be surprised if she seems more iffy to everyone else now, at least for a while. I think it's more important than ever to handle her carefully. I think if anyone gives her another push right now, they might get more of a response than they want."

"Great advice, coming from you."

Daniel shrugged. "I'm her doctor. If she were going to go after me, I think she'd have done it already. I think I'm all right. I don't know about everyone else. There're a lot of stressors embedded in normal life in a place like this. I mean, I know Lindenwood's right at the top, but—"

"Yeah, I get it. We're still an institution, not normal life."

"Yes, exactly. I'm just saying ... it might be a good thing if we made sure Tenai only had her *own* demons to wrestle with for a while."

"So. Kid gloves for a little while. Probably a good plan." Dr. Martin leaned back in his chair. "Go arrange that, then, Doctor. Keep me informed."

Daniel nodded.

6

The urgent summons of his phone jarred Daniel out of sleep which had been deep. He fumbled after the phone, still half-blind with sleep and fragmentary dreams, and knocked it off the bed table. It kept ringing. He got it eventually, hit the talk button, and mumbled "Hello?" More than likely it was a wrong number ... too late to let the machine pick it up ...

A deep voice, calm but with underlying tension, drawled, "Dr. Dodson? Dr. Martin. Sorry to wake you. Got a situation here."

Daniel tried to focus. "Situation?" Possibilities suggested themselves, emphatically. He said more sharply, "Tenai?"

"Exactly," said Dr. Martin. "I'd really appreciate it if you could come in, Doctor."

"Twenty minutes," said Daniel, and dropped the phone on the bed. Seconds ticked past ... time to throw on clothes, whatever came to hand, time to wake Jenna and bundle the sleepy child into clothing of her own. By the time they were out into the cold air, she was awake enough to be excited and a little nervous at this unusual adventure. Daniel only wished he could feel as cheerful.

The administration wing of Lindenwood blazed with lights; far too many for the hour. "That was quick," said a distracted nurse at the door. "Here, let me take her—you want a pop, sweetheart?—you'd better go, Doctor. Dining hall—"

Daniel arrived at the dining hall out of breath. Banging the door back, he nearly ran into the cluster of orderlies and nurses hovering right inside the hall, as though prepared for a precipitous retreat.

Dr. Martin was standing, big and calm, a little in front of the small group of staff, frowning. It was clear that he, like Daniel, had been hauled out of bed: the director was wearing blue jeans ragged at the cuff and a plaid shirt that made him look more like a lumberjack than a doctor. "Well, Doctor," he said, a little drily, "I think your patient now looks iffy enough to make every single member of the board sit up and notice. Take a look. She's hurting herself and we can't get near her."

"Herself?" said Daniel, startled, and edged through the group.

Tenai *was* hurting herself: she was sitting on a table at the far end of the dining room, lighting cigarettes and putting them out on her arm. It was obvious even from a distance that she had been doing this for some time. She had not looked up when Daniel came in, but what he could see of her expression looked fixed and mad, for the first time he'd ever seen.

The dining room itself looked like a hurricane had swept through it. There were chairs and tables broken at that end of the room, and a large hole through the wall, about the right size to suggest somebody had been thrown through it. Pieces of drywall and boards littered the floor in a broad arc—so whoever it was had broken through the wall from the other side, Daniel thought, and that would have been one of the patient's rooms. He had no idea whose. Not Tenai's, though.

Daniel doubted that another five minutes could possibly make a difference to Tenai, and he had no desire to rush in without thinking this through. He asked instead, "Do we have any idea what happened?"

"I think we do," the director allowed, with an expression of deep disgust. "Looks like maybe one of the orderlies started messing with a patient—the Bowen girl, Samantha, Michaela's roommate. Michaela screamed and Tenai heard her and broke the lock on her own door and got out and beat the living crap out of the orderly—that was Will, by the way. Staff started trying to pull Tenai off Will, and she messed the lot of 'em up and threw Will through the wall into the dining room and climbed through the hole after him."

Daniel was almost afraid to ask. "Ah ... he's still alive?"

"Yep, so that's good. But Richard got in her way, and she broke his arm—"

"Ow." That was much less good. Richard was another orderly, a man with a knack for calming down trouble before it got out of hand. All the patients liked him. This didn't sound great.

"Yeah. So Will crawled away like a slug—I've gotta remember I haven't actually heard his story—and Richard got *back* in her way—good man there—and she stopped, thank God. The ash tray was there, and the cigarettes, 'cause the orderlies had left their stuff lying around when they finished cleaning up in here, and Tenai started in with the burning. Anybody goes near her and she tightens up and looks way too scary. I don't want anybody else hurt. Ideas, please, Doctor, and make it snappy."

"Right," said Daniel, and paused, looking across the room at the woman. Tenai looked calmer to him now, and more intent. There were burns on both arms from elbow to wrist. "Could be worse," he said aloud.

"Doctor?" Martin inquired, in a tone of forceful patience.

"She stopped herself. She was attacking Will, Richard got in her way, she broke his arm, he put himself back in her way, and at that point she turned all that rage inward. That's the flow of events. Right? Yes, I think this could be a *lot* worse." Daniel took a deep breath. "All right. Let's just see what happens." He walked forward.

Tenai did not appear to be aware of him. Daniel doubted this, and then wondered: could she be so focused inward that she actually *was* blind to everything else? He stopped a few paces away. She didn't react to his presence at all. She was moving with fine, careful precision. Light a cigarette. Watch it burn for a minute or so. Knock the ash off the end. Apply the cigarette to some clear area of unburned skin on her arm, and those areas were getting hard to come by, unfortunately. Daniel had no special desire to see what she would try as an encore if she ran out of room on her arms.

The sight made his own arms prickle with goosebumps. He shuddered. It seemed much colder here than back by the doorway. Shock, he diagnosed absently. It was that bad.

The burns looked nasty, black in the center and red around the edges, with narrow white rims. They had to be intensely painful. It was possible that in her current state, Tenai was not feeling the pain. He tried not to imagine what it would be like when—if—she snapped out of it and had all that pain come crashing down on top of her at once. "Tenai?" he said.

There was no response.

Tenai lit a cigarette, let it burn down, knocked off the ash, and moved it toward her wrist.

Daniel reached out and put his hand in the way, between the cigarette and Tenai's arm. He didn't try to take the cigarette out of her hand. He was careful not to touch her at all.

She looked at him, her eyes dark and terrible, opaque with rage, a conflagration of rage that made little cigarette burns look ... trivial. Her whole body, everything about her, expressed an anger so vast Daniel could not believe she could control it. But she did not hit him.

She touched the cigarette to the back of his hand, and whatever shield against pain her fury provided her, that shield was not there for Daniel. The pain was horrible, and shocking even though he'd expected it. He drew in his breath and closed his teeth on a yell, so that the only sound that escaped was a hiss of breath. His vision wavered, darkness pressing in from all sides. It took all his control not to jerk away. But he didn't move.

Their eyes met: hers intense and dark with violence, his, no doubt, wide with shock and pain.

Hers changed. A hint of awareness, of recognition, crept into her face.

"Please stop," Daniel said quietly. He managed a calm, matter-of-fact tone, with great difficulty.

"Doctor?" Tenai said, her tone questioning, as though only now becoming aware of him.

"You're hurting me—" It came out of Daniel's mouth automatically, with a gasp he could not quite control.

Tenai blinked. She looked at his hand, at her own, holding the cigarette—it hurt like hell—Daniel could not tell if it had gone out or if it was still doing damage—she moved her hand, tossing the cigarette away with a sharp, unconsidered motion. The darkness that seemed to loom all around them retreated.

"All right." Daniel's voice had gone a little hoarse. "Are you okay, Tenai? You're going to stop, right?"

Tenai looked faintly puzzled. She studied him, eyes narrow and opaque, glanced down at her own arms, and looked back to meet his eyes.

"Are you ... does that hurt?"

"No." She looked down at her arms again, the puzzlement increasing, lines appearing between her eyes. "Yes. I need—I needed it to hurt, I think."

"Well," said Daniel, "I hope you don't need it to keep hurting. I can't stand even to look at it. Please come down to the nurse's station with me and let's get these burns taken care of, okay?" He shifted back a step, turning to imply invitation.

After a moment, Tenai slid off the table and stood up. For the first time Daniel could remember, she moved as though she had to remind herself how to move each muscle. Daniel was not yet sure that she was quite aware of herself, or of him, or of anything that was going on around her.

Around the door, the small crowd faded into the background. Everyone was prepared to give Tenai room, it appeared. Daniel pretended not to notice. It seemed to him that Tenai herself might really not have noticed—either the staff or their withdrawal.

Dr. Graves, Lindenwood's on-call physician, had already had a much more exciting night than usual. He approached the woman who'd caused all the excitement with a distinct lack of enthusiasm. But Tenai sat with a worrisome passivity, not quite looking at the doctor, or at Daniel.

The doctor tackled the burns with great caution, which wore off as he progressed from one to the next. "You'll be lucky if none of these get infected," he snapped, finishing with the last one on her right arm, too deeply offended by the whole business to worry about any possible danger. "Burns are a bitch and a half. Dammit, woman." The doctor winced in vicarious pain as he got a look at Tenai's other arm. "Why'd you do this to yourself? Never mind, just please don't do it again, you hear me? I have better things to do with my time than patch up damage deliberately inflicted. Dammit."

Tenai did not respond, and the doctor finished and stomped out.

"Wing Five, I think," Daniel told her gently. "Will you come with me?" By then he almost wanted to see a flash of anger, if it came with life and thought. But there was nothing.

Wing Five was the most secure wing of Lindenwood. Daniel installed her in a room with a solid door that had two deadbolts on the outside and bars on the window. Tenai did not protest the move. She seemed ... drained. Hollowed out, all her resources burned to ash in her rage so that she now had nothing left. Daniel had no sense now of struggle within the woman. Nothing seemed left of her but gray exhaustion. He hated to leave her alone. But he also thought time to herself might be exactly what she needed.

The morning shift was starting to arrive, wide-eyed and fascinated by the stories they were getting from the night staff.

Daniel collected Jenna from her emergency caretaker—*she'd* had a great time being made much of by the staff, and somebody had got her a breakfast from McDonald's. Daniel was grateful beyond words. He ate the last pancake himself since it was clear Jenna wasn't going to, coaxed her to finish her orange juice, deflected her questions—What happened to your hand, Daddy? Oh, nothing much, honey, just a scratch—and had her at St. Paul's just barely in time for the bell to ring.

During the drive back, he had finally time to try to get his thoughts in order for the emergency staff meeting that had already been scheduled. It was a small gathering, in Dr. Martin's private office. Daniel was there; and Dr. Christie, head of the wing; and Dr. White, head of Wing Five.

"Okay," said the director, waving them all to seats. "Here's what we know. Will did make a move on Samantha Bowen—"

"Does he admit it? Or do we only have her say-so?" Dr. Christie demanded.

"We have Samantha's word, backed up by Michaela—and—" Dr. Martin held up a big hand, stopping Dr. Christie before he could speak again— "And we have a bruise on Samantha's mouth, *and* yes, we have a confession. I told Will we'd collected a DNA sample from her mouth and if he'd kissed her it would show."

"He bought that?" Dr. Christie demanded.

"Yep. Hell, it might even be true, God knows what they're doing with forensics these days. He believed it. He said he'd kissed her, but it was consensual."

Dr. White snorted.

"Right," said Dr. Martin. "No lawyer on God's Earth would advise him to counter-sue when we press charges. Sexual assault on a patient? No way that would fly in front of a jury."

"Not for us, either, when the girl's father sues *us,*" Dr. Christie snapped. "*We* hired him."

"But we checked him out exactly as procedure demands and he had no record. No reasonable person would expect us to be mind-readers. Just in case somebody *does* feel we should've been telepathic, I ran another complete search last night. His work record is pure as the driven snow. We've had no prior complaints here. The worst we've had is a verbal complaint from a nurse to his supervisor that he got handsy, but his supervisor told him to knock it off and he did."

"He's probably done it before, if not here than elsewhere," Daniel said quietly. "He's nearly forty. A man that age doesn't just start out of the blue."

"You're probably right," the director agreed. "But if he's been trying it here, he's been very careful—and if anybody ever found out anyplace else, they covered it up. His last place of employment was a state hospital. I think maybe I'll call 'em up and ask a few questions off the record. If they covered something up, someone ought to make them squirm. But that's for later. Right now, I'll have a chat with our lawyers and then file charges on behalf of Lindenwood and on Samantha's behalf. Then I'll call her dad, who is, yes, going to be a problem, I expect. You all keep your hands *off* this situation, don't talk out of turn, and *trust me to deal with it.* Right?"

He did not specifically look at Daniel, but that emphasis was unmistakably aimed his way. When everyone murmured agreement, Daniel did too, finding that he actually did trust Dr. Martin to handle this *properly*.

"Good," said Martin. "And if there's something coming down the pike you need to know about, I'll let you know."

There were more nods around the room, including from Daniel. If he'd had to deal with police and lawyers and the whole circus of the court system himself again—he might have quit first, he thought wryly.

"Okay," said Dr. Martin. "That's one thing. Next thing is, how's Tenai?"

Everybody looked at Daniel.

He had to shrug. "She's up in her new room, hopefully calming down."

"Not a peep out of her," agreed Dr. White. "Yet." He looked worried. He said to Daniel, "You stopped her. That suggests to *me* maybe you did something right. If you've got advice, I'm interested."

Daniel shook his head. "She stopped herself. She started self-injuring to stop herself from going after Richard, I think that's clear. That's a very promising sign. Try treating her like she's not dangerous. Be nice to her. She doesn't want to hurt the staff. I think it's a good idea to encourage that."

"And if everybody's being all warm and fuzzy and she goes ballistic?" Dr. Christie inquired, with open scorn. "You won't have any control, you've been so busy playing nice-nice. She ought to be locked down tight. We ought to notify the police and turn her over to *them*. She's *violent,* she's *dangerous,* and we are taking a *completely unnecessary risk* keeping her here."

Daniel nodded. "That's a concern, obviously. But I think if she explodes, it'll be inward, not outward. The risk is mostly to her, not to us. Drop her into the legal system and she'll go up in flames. But I think if we handle her carefully, we can head off any explosions—"

"Oh, head off explosions! We didn't head off this one! The woman's plainly a danger to herself and everyone else—"

"She stopped herself," Daniel repeated, a little too sharply. But it was worth emphasizing, so he said it again, putting some force into it. "*We* didn't stop her. *She* stopped *herself.* We can work with this. If we have time." He looked at the director, not at Dr. Christie.

"Hmm." Dr. Martin stretched out his legs. "I don't see how we can put her out just at the moment. Taking care of women who are a danger to themselves and others is kind of what we're here for, right? On the other hand, if she's not getting better, if she's actually getting worse, this isn't the place for her."

"Then let's give her enough time to see which it is."

Dr. Christie started to cut in, but Dr. White said pacifically, "It's true that patients often look like they're getting worse before they get better. Tenai sinking back into silence and withdrawal isn't what we want to see, either."

"True," agreed Dr. Martin. "True."

"Neither is that woman killing herself, or more likely somebody else," said Dr. Christie.

It was his attitude, reflected Daniel, that made everything he said, no matter how true, sound so *snide*. Daniel looked at the director. "Dr. Christie is right, of course, but we all know Dr. White is right as well. If we let her go, who's going to help her? She can be helped, I think. Can't we give her another month? That's not much. One more month and then see how she's doing? I could come in earlier. Or come back after my daughter's bedtime."

The director tilted his head. "You offering to work with Tenai on your own time, before or after hours?"

"If necessary, yes, sir."

"Good for you, Doctor. That won't be necessary. You've got

your month. In fact, you can have ... say, to the end of August. That's just about nine weeks. Show me something I can use to justify keeping her longer than that, and maybe we'll extend that." His voice gentled. "But, Dr. Dodson, if we're not seeing real progress by then, I do think we'll have to re-evaluate."

Daniel let out a breath he hadn't realized he was holding. "Thank you, sir."

"I cannot believe you want to waste more time on that woman," snapped Dr. Christie.

"We 'waste' time on them all, now and then," said the director. "When no one else will, we do. Sometimes it pays off." He looked at Daniel. "I know we can't make a patient get better on schedule. But, hell, you're creative and stubborn. I won't bet against you." He mimed an underhanded throw, as though tossing something to Daniel. "You've got the ball, Dr. Dodson. Go ahead and run with it. Check in with me tomorrow. Plan to give me weekly updates, minimum. Good luck."

"Thank you," Daniel said fervently.

The end of August seemed way too close. But it was a lot better than the end of June. Two whole extra months. Almost nine weeks. Anything might happen.

The whole ward was tense, picking it up from the staff or the air or the patient's grapevine. Not much useful was likely to go on today, not with that stormy atmosphere hanging over them all. Daniel spent one appointment after another just calming patients down. He let Tenai wait. He wanted to see her. But it seemed to him that giving her a long time to settle down was not necessarily a bad thing. After hours was soon enough for a visit. He'd still get to Jenna's school and pick her up on time. Probably. Nearly. He asked one of the receptionists to call the school and tell them he might be a little late.

Finally he knocked on Tenai's door, unbarred it, and put everything else out of his mind.

Tenai was standing by the window in her room, brooding. Or at least, it looked like brooding to Daniel. Her bandaged arms were folded, her strong-boned face tipped down, her dark eyes blank. It took her several minutes to respond to Daniel's arrival. He waited patiently, sitting in the room's one chair, a heavy metal thing that was, like all the furniture on this wing, bolted to the floor.

At last Tenai turned her head. "Doctor."

"Tenai. You sound tired."

She tipped her head a little to the side. She said, "I am tired, yes. I hurt you. I am sorry."

"Did you know it was me?"

After another long moment, Tenai said, "Yes. I knew you were there. I did not know—I did not know it was your hand I burned, I think. Partly I knew it, and partly not."

"What happened?" Daniel asked gently. "Can you tell me?"

"Michaela was screaming." Tenai looked away, out the window. It was painted closed. Unbreakable glass outside the bars distorted the view just a little.

"Michaela screamed," Daniel repeated, trying to encourage Tenai to go on.

"Yes. So I broke the door and went to her. That man, Will, he was threatening those girls, trying to make them be quiet."

"Why didn't you call staff for help?"

"Doctor, I did not think to do so. I was angry. I wished to—" she stopped, flexing her fine, narrow hands. She said fiercely, "I wished to punish him. To kill him. They are my ... my *kishe-a*, mine to guard, no man's prey. Who else should protect them but I?"

"Tenai—"

"I know," she snapped, looking sharply up at him, "I have no right to lay down justice, here. I told you: I was angry. I understand I am at fault. You were right about me, Doctor. I thought I was less angry. But like a wolf in a cage, the fury only waited to be let out. I hurt you. And Richard. After I hit him, I saw I was too angry. I tried to put down the anger." Her head bowed, the flash of temper fading. "I am sorry I hurt him."

"I know you are. That's not the issue. No one is judging you. You were trying to put down your anger by hurting yourself?"

"Yes," Tenai agreed, and stopped, brows drawn together, thinking about that. "I understood I should not kill anyone. That I have no right to do so, here. So I tried to stop."

"Does it hurt?"

"Yes," said Tenai, looking down at her injured arms before glancing up again at him. She seemed to read the distress in his face. "It does not matter, Doctor. It is only pain. One accepts it, and in time it passes away."

"And it worked? You're no longer angry?"

Tenai thought about this. "Less angry," she said eventually. "I put the anger aside into the pain, and so the anger became ... less."

"It's a frightening strategy. Other strategies might work better. Pain doesn't bother you. You accept it, and it goes away, you said. Why not anger? Isn't anger a kind of pain?"

Tenai stared at him, eyes unreadable, control so tight it was a wonder she could breathe—a tight control that Daniel knew was far more fragile than it looked, or she would not need to use pain to head it off. He said, "Tenai, do you fight the pain?"

"No," she answered.

"No. You let it come, and go. Then why do you fight the anger?"

"I—" There was a pause, that lengthened. Tenai said at last, "I do not want to harm you, doctor."

"Do you think you will?"

"Yes," said Tenai, and hit the wall, one sharp hard blow that thudded harmlessly against the cinderblock. The walls on the secure wing were pretty solid. She was up, moving, the fierce unconsidered movements of someone who *cannot* stay still one more instant.

Daniel leaned back in the chair, trying to look relaxed. "You try to lock all that anger up inside, but it only gets stronger, doesn't it? If you let it go, maybe it'll flow away and be gone. What do you think?"

"I think you are a fool," Tenai said harshly. "It does not go. It does not pass. It is always there. It is stronger than I am—it will outlast me, I think—"

"It can't, you know," Daniel reminded her. "How could it? It's part of you, Tenai. All that anger is part of you, but just a part. You contain it. How can it be bigger than you?"

For a moment they were both still, eyes meeting. Daniel thought of the first time he'd seen this woman, as vivid and dangerous as a frozen bolt of lightning contained by will alone. She was a lot less frozen now. A lot more dangerous? He didn't think so, somehow.

He said, "You've been hurt, I know. Something in your life hurt you badly. And you fought back. You were angry and grieving and you fought back so hard you forgot how to stop fighting, even when you ran out of enemies. Isn't that right? You hated Encormio, didn't you?"

"Yes!" Much stronger this time.

"Well, he's dead." Whatever 'he' actually represented. "He's gone. After you kill a man, there's nothing else you can do. That's all there is. So let it go, Tenai. Let it *go*."

"You do not even believe that Encormio was real."

Of course she'd noticed him thinking exactly that. "Does that matter? Something was real. You defeated whatever it was. That's gone. It's *gone*."

She made a small baffled movement.

Daniel waited for a little while. When she said nothing else, he said gently, "There's a medication I think I will ask you to try. It helps some people. In your case, I've been hesitant. But I think you might be ready to try it now—if you're ready to give up some of that anger. You weren't ready before. Are you now? Will you try it?"

An infinitesimal hesitation. Then, "If you wish, Doctor."

"All right. Good. The idea," Daniel added, in case she did not know, "is to find things that will both help you and protect the staff. The move to this wing isn't intended as punishment. Nor is this medication. Anyway, I think your arms are punishment enough. All right?"

"Yes. You are generous."

"I hope I'm at least reasonable. The medication I'll give you takes about four weeks to work if it's going to, usually." He would cross his fingers he had her for long enough.

"Yes," Tenai repeated, with a slight nod.

"I'm going to leave. I'm going to lock the door." He paused, to see whether she would object.

She said nothing.

He went on. "You can scream and cry and that might help. It can be good to get your emotions out in the open and see what's there. But, Tenai, sometimes the best way to clear anger out of your soul—" Daniel made a gesture like tossing a small captive bird out the window— "is to let it go. Let *go*. Then maybe you can find room in there for other things."

She nodded, but he wasn't sure she agreed or understood; he wasn't even entirely sure she'd heard him. But there seemed nothing else to do, yet. Daniel left her standing in her room. But she was still in his thoughts, even when he left Lindenwood to pick up Jenna.

Daniel felt reasonably optimistic. He'd wanted a crisis. They'd had one—a big one. Now, at last, they could figure out what shape Tenai's problems really took and what might be done to help her. If they only had time.

They had to have time. Nine weeks had to be enough.

Traffic was worse than usual—of course, Daniel realized: he was late enough to have run into real rush hour traffic. He hoped the secretary had made it clear to the school staff that he'd been unavoidably detained by a real crisis. They'd be annoyed, but they knew he was ordinarily on time; they would understand ... but to his surprise, when he at last turned into the school parking lot, he found it crowded with parents and students. Bewildered, Daniel waited for a powder-blue minivan with two adults and four children in it to back out of a parking space. Both parents came to pick up the kids?

It took him longer than it should have to realize the reason for that, and for all the activity in general. Even then, he didn't believe it until he'd checked the date on his phone. Twice. Then, cursing under his breath, he flung himself out of his car and ran up the wide stairs to the school's front entrance. Clusters of noisy children and their parents had gathered on the stairs and in the hallway. Teachers—some secular, and some nuns in blue and priests in black—chatted with parents and smiled indulgently upon the general hubbub.

Daniel wove his way through the crowded hallway and swung around the corner to the principal's office. It was deserted, and he paused in confusion and sudden worry.

Then his name was called from the hall.

Father Wolfe was a tall Jesuit priest with a stern expression and steel-gray hair. He was also principal of the school, and not the sort to take much foolishness from the parents of his students. Now he strode toward Daniel, parting students and parents alike like the razor-edged prow of a ship cutting through the sea. Daniel braced himself.

"Jenna is with Father Hederman," the principal said briefly when he'd joined Daniel. Despite his severe expression, his tone was nonjudgmental. "We made a special point of cheering her performance. She recited 'The Highwayman,' you know."

"I know," said Daniel.

"She recited the whole poem with great feeling and only stumbled once or twice right at the beginning. She did especially well with the part about 'down like a dog on the highway.' I promised her I'd personally tell you how well she did."

Daniel was sure that wasn't the only thing the principal wanted to tell him. He had to admire the man's restraint. "Was she very ... upset?"

"Yes," said the priest, delivering the plain truth in that same neutral tone. He met Daniel's eyes. His own, as gray as his hair, were cool, but not unsympathetic. "In a very quiet way. No doubt losing her mother has made her sensitive to these unavoidable moments."

These moments of abandonment, he meant. "Yes," said Daniel. "I think so."

For a moment the two men continued to face each other, almost like adversaries. Then the principal said in a kinder tone, "These things do happen. We know that. I hope your patient is all right, Dr. Dodson."

Daniel let out a breath, feeling like a boy who'd been generously let off the hook. "Thank you. It's hard to tell yet."

"I'll pray for the unfortunate woman. Your daughter will be fine. This way." Father Wolfe stepped back and opened a hand in wordless invitation.

Daniel fell in at his side as the priest walked with him toward the school auditorium.

Father Hederman was an enormous, good-humored, ruddy-faced man with a booming laugh and a fringe of sandy hair encircling his bald pate. He taught Latin and literature and religion to the older students and music to both the older students and the younger ones. Jenna, still not willing to attach herself to any woman among the staff, adored him.

At the moment, Jenna was perched high up on the priest's shoulder. No matter how upset she had been earlier, he had teased her out of it: she had a hand on top of his head for balance and was giggling as he pretended to be unable to duck low enough to fit through the auditorium door.

Then he made it through and turned, and Jenna saw her father. Daniel winced at the relief that flooded into her face; if she had been laughing, he understood, it had been with bravery and a desire to please Father Hederman as much as anything. Fear of abandonment, indeed. He hastened forward.

The priest put a massive hand up, engulfed both of Jenna's, and swung the little girl down to the floor.

I'm sorry, I'm sorry, I'm sorry, Daniel wanted to say, but he didn't: if he made a huge fuss over having missed the elementary school talent show, would that comfort his daughter or only frighten her? Instinct suggested a matter-of-fact attitude as much as guilt prompted dramatic apologies.

"I thought," Jenna whispered, "I thought maybe you weren't coming." She lowered her voice in shame. "I didn't do the first part right."

And so had wondered whether maybe she'd deserved to be abandoned? Daniel was afraid something like that might be in her mind, though probably not consciously. "Hey," he told her, "Jen, listen: I may be late every now and then, but I will *always* come for you. Every single time."

Jenna, anxious to be reassured, nodded. But he thought she might not quite believe him. The experience of loss was still too raw for her to tolerate anything that felt like desertion.

Daniel said, "I've heard all about your poem. I'm proud of you. Lots of times, if somebody makes a mistake right at the beginning, she wants to stop. It's brave to keep going. Father Wolfe told me you were wonderful at the end. I wish I'd been here to see you. I don't remember how 'The Highwayman' goes for the last bit. Now I guess I'm not going to find out."

The child brightened. "Oh, I can tell you how it goes! Only I have to start at the beginning or I don't do the end right."

"Well, then, let's see if we can go back in the auditorium and you can stand up on the stage and tell me the poem, okay? But if it's sad at the end, I might cry."

This warning made Jenna giggle; this time, Daniel was pleased to note, without the fear underneath. So. Crisis past. Or as past, at least, as anything ever really was.

Daniel had to wonder whether it was possible to concentrate on his patients, all right, on *Tenai,* as he needed to do right now—and still be the father his daughter needed. He'd dropped one ball this afternoon: had there been other balls he hadn't even noticed?

Jenna seemed perfectly fine by evening, but the next morning she was noticeably reluctant to get out of the car when they got to the school—and she'd been eager to run in, before. Daniel bet her a double chocolate ice cream sundae against a pickle that he'd arrive to pick her up at exactly five-oh-three and a half, and she thought that was hysterical and let herself be persuaded that it was okay to leave him. But then it was Daniel himself who had a hard time driving away.

And once he got to Lindenwood, he had trouble losing himself in his patients—which he had not for months. Finally he set an alarm on his phone and *also* asked the wing's secretary to be *sure* to tell him when it was four, so that he could put the time out of his own mind and concentrate. And this became a new part of his routine, because even though he set his own alarm, he found he needed the assurance that others were also tracking the time with him or he could not relax.

A touch of obsessiveness, there. He didn't even care. He would worry about that in a month or so, when Jenna wasn't watching the clock so closely herself.

7

Prozac normally took four weeks or so to begin to show an effect: two weeks to build up to useful levels in the brain and two weeks, for some unknown reason, before it began to affect inward experience. Of course it didn't always prove useful. But Daniel liked it because, although a clean drug in the sense that it affected serotonin uptake almost exclusively, Prozac nevertheless affected an extraordinarily wide range of mild personality disorders, and did so typically with relatively minor side effects. Actual therapy was essential as well, to prepare the ground the drug was to work in. Daniel took it as an axiom that if Tenai was not prepared to give up her rage, there was no chance that Prozac could offer more than a panacea.

But at the same time, Daniel strongly suspected that the fast start and clean intervention the drug could offer might indeed prove very helpful to this seriously disturbed patient. A reminder to her of what health *was*, of what it *felt like* to be well. He strongly suspected now that she had lost that somewhere along the way.

He had hoped to have Tenai back on the lower security wing in a week or so, picking up where she'd left off, coaxing Michaela along and walking on the grounds. He'd been sure he could get Dr. Martin to agree. But in fact, Tenai continued to hurt herself. Sometimes she got her hands on cigarettes and matches, although neither was supposed to be brought onto the secure wing. Several times she stole a pair of scissors from the nurses' station. Some of the resulting cuts might have been dangerous; the hospital's on-call physician snapped that she damned well *ought* to have lost enough blood to teach her better and he didn't know why she hadn't. In frustration, Dr. White banned scissors from his wing entirely, and Tenai stole a nail file from a nurse's purse.

Daniel did not even want to know what she might find next. At last he offered a straightforward bribe. "Look, even if you can stand this, none of the rest of us can. You stop with the cigarettes and the cutting and I'll get you back down on the ground floor, okay? You can go outside ... walk on the grounds, breathe the air, admire the roses."

He thought Tenai looked wistful. But she shook her head. "Doctor, I am not to strike you, not to harm anyone. I understand this. There is no one here I *should* harm. So I do not. I use the fire and the knife." She paused, and added, in a low voice, "I wish ... I would like to have understood this before, that this small pain can bring silence into my heart."

"You're using a small physical pain as a distraction from a greater emotional pain," Daniel suggested, meaning to clarify this for both of them. The self-injury was not really important, he thought. Not really. A symptom. The emotional distress that made it seem necessary to Tenai that she hurt herself ... that was the danger. He asked her, "Is silence really what you want in your heart?" Silence sounded to him a lot like it might be a kind of emptiness, not a kind of peace.

"Silence is better than rage," she said. But too flatly. He didn't like that lack of affect.

Her emotional distress was rooted, obviously, in her confabulated past, which, whatever its origin, must hold the signposts that would match up emotionally with Tenai's real truth. Essential to hear the rest of the story, even if it was hard for Tenai to tell it to him. "You want to get off this ward, back in the fresh air," he said patiently. "I want that for you too. I don't know whether you can move forward until you deal with your past, or what you remember as your past. Please tell me the rest."

She sighed. "You are persistent, Doctor." She was silent for a while. But then she finally said, "Very well. Though I hardly know where to start ... well. Near the end, Imbaneh-se and Keneseh and Tesmeket all broke free of Encormio's hold. All his enemies grew bolder as they saw he could not destroy me. I was telling you—I was telling you of the passing centuries, was I not? Of the armies that tore the country, of the fire that ruined towns and cities, of the blood and the death ... in the end, in the end, there was another army, and Encormio was no longer laughing."

It seemed to Daniel that they might indeed be coming to the heart of this story. Tenai's tension suggested a hard focus on something terrible coming ahead.

"That was the last of my great armies," Tenai said slowly. "Raised of Imbaneh-se and Talasayan. I had men, generals ... some of the great generals of all history. Gomenah Kelabili-go-e of Nerinesir, once of Encormio's own counsels. Maschai of Kaya-sa. Wise old Kapuas of Matakat, who was of such great assistance to me in persuading Tesmeket to cooperate with our strategies. And," she said in a lower tone, "and Sandakan Gutai-e of Patananir." She was silent for a time. Daniel did not interrupt her thoughts, and in the end she went on.

"The army was ... it was a real army. It was a real army and it fought bravely and well. Sandakan took it up the Khadur for me, straight at Nerinesir's walls. There was a woman there, like me to the eye, like me in the voice. Her name was Kinubala Tingar-e. She was a sorcerer, and she hated Encormio, as so many had reason to do."

Daniel nodded.

"So there was this army," said Tenai, gesturing as though showing him where it lay, "And there was I, but not with it. The army came up the river, toward the River Gate. And I—I came into Nerinesir as I had done the first time, through Death's Gate in the south, and no one, no one knew that I was there. Because of Kinubala, all believed I was with the army I had raised.

"So I came for one last time into Nerinesir. It was winter again, bitter midwinter ... all knew that I was in my season and my time. But Nerinesir was the place of Encormio's greatest power, so no one could say how that contest would go. My army came against the River Gate and the river, frozen hard in a cold greater than Talasayan had ever known ... the river itself was the road that lay open for them. There was a battle there in the dark. I saw only a little of it. I know that my army lost to the king's. But my soldiers, my generals, my sorcerer ... they made a show of their blood and their deaths. They made a pageant, to draw all eyes. To draw Encormio's attention.

"I came into his presence by another way, hidden in shadows. He stood on his high tower and watched blood freeze into crimson ice in the cold, and set all his attention and power against my sorcerer on her black mare, while I stood behind him in the dark."

For a while, Tenai was silent. Just before Daniel would have made a prompting sound, she went on. "Lord Death was there.

Encormio had guards, many guards ... but they were cold, taken by my Lord Death, in the moment that the year died. All light died, fire and spell-light alike smothered by the darkness at the heart of the winter. Then Encormio realized I was there behind him and turned. He fled," Tenai said, quietly, in a bright prosaic room that seemed now somehow darker and colder. "When he saw me there, he fled. I pursued. When he knew that I would bring him at last to bay, he turned. He had many defenses. But I had many weapons. And the men of my army, they knew by then they were going to die, and yet they kept on. Kinubala Tingar-e went knowingly and willingly to her death from the very beginning. She made her death a sacrifice, and there is no greater power than that to set behind enchantment. She poured the power of her death into my hands, and I broke every defense Encormio possessed, and in the end he fled into the darkness of death rather than allow me to lay my hand on his soul. He fled to my Lord Death, and past the final Gate, fearing the judgment of God less than he feared my vengeance." She fell silent.

"So that's how it ended. Then it was over," Daniel said at last.

Tenai looked at him and laughed. There was a bitter tone to that laughter. "Over?" she said. "How could it be over? That was not the end. There were Encormio's people: his advisors and courtiers and soldiers, the merchants who made their fortunes under his rule, the farmers who grew his grain. Should they be suffered to live?" She lifted both her hands, fingers spread like the talons of an eagle. "My fury burned across the night. The very snow melted from the flanks of the mountains in the force of my anger."

"The memory of your triumph doesn't seem to be a happy one," Daniel observed. He was not surprised. He had already realized that Tenai had been at war with some aspect of herself and this war had never been resolved.

"Happy?" Tenai lowered her hands and looked at him, dark eyes unreadable. She said after a while, "My sword ran red with blood. In time ... in time my generals came to me and tried to dissuade me from killing. They said, 'Go back to Chaisa. You have won.'"

"Well, hadn't you?"

Tenai looked down, pausing. She said finally, "I think now, I could not see that I had won. My bitterness was too great. I could not put it aside. My army became divided between those who would support me in anything, and those who demanded that I turn aside. I would not turn. I wanted to kill everyone who had ever dared support the king. Encormio had ruled for a thousand years before ever I cared who might hold the throne in Nerinesir. When he was destroyed at last, a hundred little wars arose. I did not care."

Daniel nodded. It seemed reasonable. Chaos after the destruction of the great obsession: that made sense. An internal chaos that undoubtedly mirrored the external chaos Tenai thought she remembered. "What happened?" he asked.

"Nolas Keitah Terusai-e, lord of Terusan, brought out the only remaining son of Encormio—Mitereh Encormio-na, that was, a child of nine or so. Talasayan united behind this boy. I was dismayed: Encormio's son, on the ivory throne! And doubly-dismayed: many people of my army went to Keitah Terusai-e and took his part."

"Um," said Daniel, thinking, *Well, that took guts on somebody's part, I wouldn't have wanted to face this woman down like that.*

Then he remembered the whole thing was symbolic, not real. And then was this Keitah a direct symbol for someone else, or did he represent another aspect of Tenai herself? How interesting that Encormio, who symbolized her obsession, should have been succeeded by a son. And what would that mean?

"I would not accept this," Tenai said, her eyes distant. She was not seeing him or anything here. "My anger burned across all the land."

"You'd been fighting a long time. Perhaps you'd lost the ... knack of stopping."

"I think I had forgotten it was possible to stop. Some of my people tried to tell me. Sandakan tried, I think. I heard nothing but my anger. My fury roared in my ears and would not cease."

"So ... what did you do?"

Tenai smiled, wry and bitter. "I would not stop. My own army turned against me, and I was forced east, away from Nerinesir. I could have fought, but they were my own men! Though I killed them, there was no joy for me in their deaths. I was pressed back again and again. I fled for Chaisa, the heart of my strength, but Kapuas of Matakat was there before me and forced me south. I tried to turn back to the west, but Keitah and Sandakan met me before I could find the shelter of the mountains and forced me south again. At Antiatan, at last I was brought to bay. I might have fought, even then."

"But you didn't?" That was interesting, and probably good. A healthy desire for peace battling a long habit of anger and grief? That might be too simplistic an explanation. He put the questions aside to wait for a better chance to mull them over.

"I did fight, for a little while. It was midwinter, a year since Encormio's death. Lord Death was there on that field, waiting for the men I might send him; I had only to touch a man to send him to that dark kingdom. But I had no heart for their blood. The veil is fragile at midwinter. It was thin enough to tear a way through. I went through it, but not to the country of Lord Death. I sought another place, and found one, leaving Talasayan and all that land. And so I came here, Dr. Dodson, to this other land and to you."

That was a conversation stopper. Daniel cleared his throat.

Tenai paced the length of the room and back. After a little while, she went on. "I was so angry. And so you found me. You have showed me ... you have showed me my own anger, I suppose. You saw that I was mad, which I had not known. You tried to help me. I am grateful. But I see now nothing has changed. The anger is still there, and behind that, there is nothing."

"Hey," Daniel said, startled. "Hey. A whole damned lot has changed, Tenai, and you've got plenty of real solidity in there at the core of yourself. Don't play that game with me, or yourself. You've come a long way since that first time I saw you. Look, put yourself back in those days after you won your war: if a bunch of your men came to you and said, 'You've won, all right? Now let's stop'—what would you say?"

Tenai looked arrested. She said slowly, attention inward, "I think ... perhaps I would stop," and looked at Daniel with widened eyes.

"You see?"

"You are right," Tenai said. "You are right. I am still angry, but even so, I see more clearly than I did in that time. And ... Sandakan was right, Keitah was right. I had not known." She looked as though she'd been struck by a thought she would rather not have had.

"Are you all right?"

"All their trust, all their loyalty, and I failed them in the end."

Tenai bowed her head. "I thought ... I felt that Sandakan had betrayed me, they had all betrayed me. I think now ... it was *I* who betrayed *them*."

There it was.

Daniel had not framed it that clearly to himself, had not precisely expected it, certainly had not expected it right now, at this precise moment. But he recognized it instantly: the heart of the problem and the heart of the cure, bound up together. As always, the patient was the one to find it. *His* role was to help her accept the truth she had discovered.

He said gently, "We all fail. Sometimes in terrible ways. Sometimes we push our failures off onto other people and blame them instead. Sometimes it's just so much easier to do that."

"Yes," she said quietly, head still bent. "Yes, I see that is so. You give me new eyes, doctor, and I thank you, but how am I to endure this new sight you have given me?"

Daniel held out a hand to her in sympathy. The pain she expressed was real, however symbolic the events she remembered, and he answered in the terms she had given him. "Tenai ... you stopped. You chose a different direction. Here you are."

Tenai lifted her head. Met his eyes. "I killed so many."

The way she said it, so quietly and simply, it sounded absolutely true. For a moment neither of them spoke. Daniel lowered his hand. He said after a while, "Don't judge yourself too harshly, Tenai. You were badly hurt. Don't blame yourself for that. Just aim to understand what happened, and why. Then set it behind you and face forward, toward the future and not the past."

"Yes ..." she said, as though she did not quite believe it. "You mean that the name I held at the last is not the name I must hold forever. Or, though I cannot set that name aside, then at least men should not speak it with terror."

"Life exists. The future exists. You can always choose again, and make yourself over into the person you want to be. I flatter myself I might hold up a signpost from time to time, Tenai, but it's you who will have to do the actual work. But I think you can. I'm sure you can. Will you trust my judgment?"

Tenai looked at him with that unsettling intensity. "Yes," she said.

"Will you trust your own? Shall I move you back out of the secure wing yet?"

"Yes," said Tenai, and hesitated, and said more reluctantly, "No. Not yet."

"You are the master of your own treatment," Daniel emphasized to her. "You are the captain of your soul. Anger is part of what you feel, but it's not *you*. You are yourself: Tenai Ponanon Chaisa-e, and *I* trust you to know who you are, and who you want to be. All right?"

He had hope she might be, if not yet, then soon. But, as an orderly arrived to escort Tenai back to the secure wing, Daniel acknowledged to himself that he'd never felt more wrung out in his life.

The self-injury tapered off, returned, tapered again, and finally, in the middle of July, ceased entirely, to everyone's great relief ... apparently as the medication kicked in at last, but possibly because Tenai's understanding of her own emotional state had improved. Or both. Probably both. Some of it might have been because she'd finally brought herself to finish the story for him and thus gained some kind of sense of completion.

Whatever the causative factors, Tenai's anger declined. It seemed to the staff, when Daniel asked, that Tenai seemed to show more spontaneity in her interactions with others, that she had become less focused on her need for constant iron self-control.

Tenai herself found the difference striking. "It is like the difference between ice and water," she said, trying to explain her new-found calm to Daniel. "One blocks you, holds you out. The other invites you to swim. I had forgotten what it was like, not to be angry. It is like ... being hobbled and weighted, and then being set free to walk unburdened."

Daniel nodded, understanding her. "And your memories? Are you easier within yourself for what you did, for what you failed to do?"

This, Tenai did not seem able to answer. Daniel waited. Eventually he said, "I can give you absolution, Tenai. But if you can't grant forgiveness to yourself, in the end there isn't anyone who can do it for you."

The woman gave him a wry look. "But Doctor, neither you nor I has a right to extend either absolution or forgiveness. We were not the ones wronged."

There was that. Daniel cleared his throat.

"But we are here, and those wronged are not," Tenai added.

"Yes, so we have to be satisfied with our own judgment," said Daniel. "Are you more comfortable? More at ease?"

Tenai hesitated. "I think I am. I am ... I feel hollow. Empty." She moved restlessly. "The anger was better than this emptiness."

Daniel said gently, "I think probably that's grief. I think possibly you might not have allowed yourself to feel that in the beginning. You'll find you can handle it, if you let yourself reconnect to the world."

She only looked at him for a long moment. "I do not know how."

"None of us *knows how*. We have to just let that kind of connection happen." Words to live by, for himself no less than Tenai. But he set that slightly too-keen moment of self-assessment aside. He said instead, "I'd like to move you back to the main wing, if you think that's all right."

Tenai inclined her head. "Yes, Doctor."

"If you want to go out on the grounds, go. Invite Michaela to go with you, if you want. Or Samantha. They both might enjoy your company, I think."

Tenai smiled, a little painfully. "Because there is a connection? Very well, doctor." The smile faded. "Samantha is very ... she is weak."

"Vulnerable."

"Yes. Vulnerable. Any man's toy. That is why that one tried to hurt her: he knew she would let him do as he pleased. I would like to teach her how to be a little less vulnerable."

Daniel nodded. "She could use a little of your strength, Tenai. I hope you succeed." He made a mental note to mention this to Dr. Martin, thus demonstrating his willingness to be a team player. "Do you want to continue on medication?"

She shrugged, and again it was a freer, more relaxed gesture than he was used to from her. "I will do as you wish, doctor."

"I'm going to suggest you stay on it for at least a year, then, I think," said Daniel. "Two years is fairly standard. We'll see how it goes." He studied her. Obsessive syndromes normally took somewhat higher doses of Prozac than anxiety or depression to get a good response ... but every patient was different. Unique. He said, "I'll decrease your dose a little. Tell me if you become too angry."

The lower dose seemed to be adequate. Tenai still drew the eye, still had that edge of intensity ... but she no longer set Daniel's teeth on edge with that grim sense of radiating violence she'd carried for so long. She was reliably calm with the most vulnerable of the other patients who had attached themselves to her: Samantha, Bess, Kitty, and of course Michaela. They'd formed a group of their own within the ward, these fragile young women—none was over thirty. Tenai, while not exactly part of their group, was the key to it. Certainly the key to the improvements they all showed.

Daniel cautiously raised the idea that Michaela might soon shift to outpatient therapy with the young woman's brother, her guardian now that their parents were gone. The brother, much older, had been carrying a tremendous burden of guilt for having survived the accident that killed their parents and younger sister and then having—as he saw it—failed Michaela as well. That guilt was just about inevitable, no matter how unfair it might be. Unlike his sister, the brother had had the strength and resilience to cope, plus he knew perfectly well the guilt he felt was irrational. But he'd had a bad time. Daniel had been trying a little subtle therapy with him as well, whenever he came to see his sister. Not crucial, probably, but he wasn't going to leave the man suffering with that much guilt and pain if he could help it.

The brother was elated to think his sister might finally be getting better—and terrified that he'd fail her again.

"We'll take every possible care to help her build up the resilience she needs," Daniel emphasized. "We won't cut her off. In fact, we truly wouldn't want to cut her off because this spring she's finally found the strength to make friends. That's a very good sign." He indicated the view from the window, where they'd both been watching Michaela and the other three young women practice the easy self-defense techniques Tenai had begun teaching them.

"It's been good for all of them," Daniel said, making sure his tone was warm and approving. "Tenai—the tall woman who's teaching—is very important to your sister, but Tenai will be leaving soon. She's a charity patient, but we hope she'll do all right." He added, "Michaela's fortunate you've been so supportive and so patient. Not all our patients have someone who can be supportive both emotionally and financially."

"She looks ..." began the brother, and then shook his head,

apparently giving up on finding words. "A charity patient, you say?"

"Yes," agreed Daniel. "It's difficult sometimes, working with someone in trouble when she has no safety net at all. We can't keep them here forever—and we don't want to, once they're able to move on. But those first months are difficult for the ones without support." He sighed. Then he said briskly, "But we've gotten away from the topic a bit. Let me tell you a bit about what I think we might try with Michaela, if she agrees she's ready." Turning, he led the way firmly back to his desk.

Four days later, when Dr. Christie tried to make Samantha attend her session with him, Tenai got in his way. When he tried to make Tenai go to her room, she refused. She didn't lay a hand on him. She just stayed a couple inches out of reach, like she wasn't quite aware of moving, until he was turning purple. Like she was teasing. Playing. Daniel heard about this after the fact from Dr. Martin, who had gotten an earful from Christie afterward.

"Playful is excellent," Daniel pointed out. "No one really sick has energy or attention to spare for playfulness."

"Yes, please explain that to me," Martin said drily. "No, never mind, that's fine. You're right that Dr. Christie didn't get the joke. Lisa broke it up." Lisa was one of the nurses. "She just came up like she didn't realize anything was going on, and said, 'Oh, Tenai, there you are. I wonder, dear, would you be a love and help Heather into her room? I know she responds so well to you.' Tenai just said, 'Certainly, nurse,' and strolled away, casual as you please. Very helpful, considering how violent Heather can get." He leaned back in his chair. "Dr. Dodson, I believe your Tenai is setting those young women up to be each other's projects. I expect that will be beneficial, but do please keep an eye on the situation. And please ask her to be polite to Dr. Christie for the next few days. He really can be an effective doctor, with the right patients, when he's not being driven mad by deliberate teasing."

"Yes, sir," Daniel agreed, relieved nothing more dramatic had happened and that the director wasn't inclined to take Dr. Christie's temper seriously.

"One other little detail I'm wondering about." Dr. Martin picked up a pen and tapped the top of his desk with it, eyeing Daniel thoughtfully. "You'll be pleased to know Paul Alston approached me yesterday."

Daniel nodded. "He's happy with Michaela's progress this spring."

"Yep, he did mention that, among other things. But it's actually you I'm wondering about." Dr. Martin fixed him with a shrewd look. "You happy where you are, Dr. Dodson? No plans to move back up in the world? That fuss about Belfountaine's died down a good deal, and enough came out about Hinkley that I imagine plenty of top-notch places might be about ready to agree you're being wasted at a small hospital like this. I wouldn't blame you for thinking you could do better. Maybe working for me's not to your taste. Or maybe you're getting burned out on clinical work and you're thinking of an admin position somewhere. A foundation. Or one of the Ivies, maybe. The Ivies love a guy who can hook in the donors. Anything like that in your mind? Cause if so, you might let me know I need to expect a vacancy here."

"No, no." Daniel found himself smiling. "Not much gets past you, does it? But you're off base this time. I like Lindenwood. I like working with our patients. I like the connection with real people. I'd forgotten how important that connection can be." Or he'd been too focused on himself to remember the kind of healing that came from genuine connection. He didn't say that. He said, "I don't mind working for you. You might be the only administrator on the planet who's also a fine psychiatrist."

Dr. Martin smiled. "Flattery, Dr. Dodson?"

Daniel snorted. "I'd have to be a lot more subtle than that. No. An Ivy is not in my future, and I wouldn't touch a place like Belfountaine again with a stick. Admin is not what I want—at all. Fundraising's not something I want to pour time into, believe me. I just saw a chance to give a little nudge where it might do some good."

Dr. Martin studied him for another moment. Then he nodded. "Okay. Good. I'm glad to hear it. I would be damn sorry to lose you. I'll add that if you see a chance like that again, feel free to take it, but you're here to work as a shrink, not a fundraiser, so don't feel compelled to go out of your way. One plus of hooking Paul Alston is, I can guarantee your Tenai a spot in our halfway house for a couple of months if you and she agree that's the next step for her. But first thing is, check on the interactions she's got going with our other patients. Your *professional* judgment, please,

Doctor, not any kind of wishful thinking."

That could have been offensive from someone else. From Dr. Martin, it was just a reminder of an ordinary professional hazard, not a vote of no confidence. Daniel nodded.

"Great. Keep me in the loop." Dr. Martin tossed down the pen as a sign of dismissal and nodded.

"Yes," Tenai agreed, when Daniel asked her about the possible rescue project she'd started. They were, for once, in his office, avoiding a summer thunderstorm so violent that even Tenai showed no enthusiasm for walking through it. Outside, the wind threatened the hospital's power. The lights had flickered once or twice, but hadn't actually gone out. Yet. Not at all disturbed by the storm, Tenai had curled up on the old-rose couch. Her feet were tucked up, catlike and comfortable. She looked far more relaxed than she would have a month earlier. "Do you think this is not wise, Doctor?"

"If I had to guess, I'd say that Samantha has the most dependent personality among all the women on this ward. But the rest of those women are dependent too. I'd worry about that."

"Having no one to depend on is their greatest source of unhappiness," Tenai argued. "Michaela wants to depend on me. She should not. Caring for Samantha and Kitty will make her stronger, not weaker. And Samantha will learn to depend on someone she can trust. Is this bad?"

"It might be, later."

"Later is later. Now the trouble for those women is loneliness, fear, grief, guilt, unhappiness. Am I wrong?"

"Um. No. I think you're right."

"Let the dependence happen. Later it can worry you." Tenai frowned and corrected herself. "You can worry about it later. When they are stronger. *You* will be right. You should take Samantha away from Christie, Doctor." She left Dr. Christie's title off, and gave it to Daniel with some emphasis.

"It's not my call, Tenai. He can be an effective doctor. Martin's keeping an eye on that. I think she'll be all right. What about Kim? I've wondered why you didn't include her in your little group."

Tenai shook her head. "Kim is too much older, and too helpless. The younger women would look to Kim to lead them, but she does not have the strength they need. Anna might, but I think she will leave the hospital soon. Too soon for my young women."

Daniel thought so, too. He hadn't even known Tenai had noticed Anna. He certainly noticed the possessiveness with which Tenai said *my young women*. He didn't permit himself to show that he'd noticed that.

"Michaela is stronger than she understands herself to be. Bess is like Michaela, stronger than she knows. Let Samantha and Kitty trust the strength they find there. Those women will help one another out of the dark in the end."

"You're thinking about what to do with those women when you're gone yourself. Aren't you, Tenai?"

"Yes," she agreed, gravely. She looked at him, calm, reserved, difficult to read.

"And when do you expect that to be?"

She made a little deferential gesture with one hand, like, *What do you think?*

Daniel thought about it. There had never been any sign that Tenai had begun to recover the true memories behind her confabulated past. He was fairly certain now that she never would, and not a hundred percent sure that she would gain any benefit from doing so anyway. He was also more certain than ever that she was prepared to move into the real present, to turn her face toward the real future. That the anger was not only under control, but also actually lessened in Tenai's mind, from an overwhelming and alien force to merely an emotion like any other.

And if whatever violent past was real stayed locked in the past, then maybe that was for the best. If no one had tracked this woman yet, found out who she really was and what had happened to her, then it seemed quite possible no one ever would. She had something, Daniel thought, that no doubt a whole lot of men and women throughout history would have given almost any price for: a chance to break with her past and walk forward into a clean future. If she had gained the strength and health to go out into the real world and build a real life for herself, wasn't that the important thing? Wasn't that what all his patients needed? Whatever the past might have held, or whatever they might remember it holding?

"You've only been on the medication a little more than a month. I'm not even certain we've got the dose right. Do you feel ready to leave Lindenwood? I don't want to rush you. Before the thing with Will, you might have felt ready to leave the hospital. A lot of the staff expected me to suggest it—or you to suggest it yourself. But were you ready?"

"No," agreed Tenai. "Not then, doctor. I understand you. I understand everything you are saying. But that was not the same." She bent her head, thoughtful. "I am still angry, not so much, but it is still there. Still here, in me. But I understand that the past is past. That I am I, and the anger is only a part of myself. Not something different, outside myself, nor something stronger than my own strength. Not something I must have to fill the silence. I believe that now. I think I have learned enough. So I wish to leave."

Left unspoken was her certainty that she could leave, if she wished, whether the hospital wanted to keep her or not. Daniel nodded. "You've learned a great deal about yourself in your time here, I think. But it's hard for me to be certain you haven't just made up a less angry face to show me. It would worry me very much, if you went out into the world still carrying that much anger."

Tenai frowned at him, possibly offended. "I would not lie to you, doctor. You ... I know that you are ..." She stopped again, searching for words. "What you do here, this is not something I knew could be done. This hospital, it is a terrible place. It is also a wonderful place. You ... I wish I had met you, when I was young. Or at least, before I was old. I know I have been mad."

"Tenai—"

The woman lifted a hand, halting his words. Her head was tilted to the side, her eyes calm and intent. She looked out of place, curled on the couch. It would have been easy to believe that she had been born in a different country, a different world.

"I have been mad," she repeated. "I have been angry ... beyond reason. Beyond thought. Beyond hope. It is right that insanity should be called *madness*. And you showed me my face in a mirror, and broke it, and showed me how to put the pieces together again."

"Did I?"

"Doctor, yes, that is what you did. Did you not know?" Tenai looked down, rubbing her hand over the rose cushions of the couch. "You found me where I was lost in madness and showed me the way out. You did not fear me. I did not know ... I had forgotten it was possible not to be feared. And you showed me the suffering of other people. I had forgotten that too, I think; that I did not own all the suffering in the world."

"No one ever born has cornered the market on anguish," Daniel said gently.

"I know." Tenai looked up at him, smiling a little. "You taught me that. You wonder if I hide from you. No, Dr. Dodson. The face I show you is my true face. I wish to leave this hospital. Not at once, but soon. Soon. But I will not go if you say not. I will obey you." She bowed a little from where she sat on the couch, an odd, formal, peculiarly practiced gesture.

Daniel picked up a pen from his desk and turned it over in his fingers. "Where would you go, Tenai, if you left the hospital? You have no money. You do understand the need for money, once you're no longer a patient here?" Ridiculous question, but he didn't catch himself before he asked it. Sometimes it was just easier to act as though he believed Tenai's fantastic past was real.

"Yes."

"You've seen the halfway house where our patients sometimes stay for a while, while they adjust to their new lives in the outside world. It's the brick one that adjoins our grounds here. We could get you a place there for a month or so, probably. I don't think you'd precisely like it there, but I think it might be a good first step for you. You'd need to find a job before you could become truly independent. And you're so proud, Tenai. Would you wash dishes? Flip burgers?"

He absolutely could not imagine it. But Tenai said drily, "I have done worse things in my life."

"Um."

"I have thought about this necessity. I have few of the right skills, I know." Tenai did not sound humble about this. It was simply a fact. "On the television, there is a show where a man teaches a formal kind of fighting. Karate. Do places like that exist, doctor? I could teach at a place like that, perhaps. I could teach fighting with the sword. Are there places for armsmasters in this world? Or soldiers, perhaps."

"We don't usually fight our wars with swords, Tenai." And he would purely hate to see her enter any kind of military type of organization that would take a woman with no on-paper background but Lindenwood. He couldn't think of anything more likely to throw her back into obsessive rage.

Tenai said, reassuringly, "I know. That is as well. I am tired of war. I do not want to take up battle or lead men to war. I will find something gentler, I think. Or wash dishes."

"Well," said Daniel, "Give it some thought. But there's time enough. I'm sure we'll come up with something."

He did not file papers for Tenai's official release from Lindenwood at once. There *was* time: they had three more weeks to sort things out. It was novel to look forward to those weeks rather than dread their passage. There was time for Tenai to spend with her young women, time to see that she'd been right about Michaela, and maybe about Bess. Probably Daniel shouldn't have been surprised. Elective mutes typically did have strong, stubborn personalities, for all they'd sometimes been beaten down by life. And there was the vulnerable neediness of the other girls right there to bring out the best in Michaela and Bess. Tenai began to withdraw herself from the center of that little group, carefully, seeming to have that priceless instinct by which a psychiatrist may be guided to do what is right for a patient, or a parent for a child.

There was even time to get Tenai's sword back from the police, although Tenai did not touch it. Daniel put it away in his office and tried to forget it was there. It was an unusual item for a psychiatrist's office. He expected Tenai to take it off his hands pretty soon, though.

And there was time, finally, with six days remaining til the end of the month, to inform Dr. Martin what was in the air. The director was not surprised. "I thought you were probably planning to cut the apron strings," he said approvingly. "You've done a great job with her, as I'm sure you know. And hey, a whole week to spare, nearly. You're going to put her in the halfway house?" A sharp look. "You don't expect her to stay there long. I'm guessing you have a real good notion how she might be able to get her feet under her in a month or so."

"Maybe," Daniel admitted.

"Taking a lot on yourself," Martin said, amused. "But no one's going to complain about high-handedness this time. I sure won't. Any notion what she might do to support herself longer-term?"

"The longer term," Daniel said firmly, "Will be up to Tenai. If she's not capable of sorting herself out given a month or two's grace, I'll be very surprised."

"Optimist," Dr. Martin said without heat, and waved Daniel out of his office. "I'm sure you've got dragons to slay somewhere. Windmills to tilt at. Go to it."

Daniel grinned, delivered a casual salute suitable for a knight, and strolled out to look for windmills. Or for Tenai. One last official conversation. Just one. He had a pretty good idea that after this, conversations might be a lot less official, with no need to take notes or make progress reports.

"You know," Daniel said, settling down not behind his desk, for once, but in a chair set slantwise to the couch in his office, "You know, doctors and patients cannot socialize. That's an important rule. Ordinarily a psychiatrist won't see a former patient socially for several years at a minimum. I've talked this over with Dr. Martin, though, and he's agreed that we'll let the edges between social and therapeutic contact blur in this particular case." He didn't say, *Because we agree you're potentially too damn dangerous to cut off cold turkey, and thank God Martin's got the sense to be flexible in how he defines 'therapy'*. He didn't say, *I'll be keeping an eye on you*. What he said, stretching the truth, was, "I think you're ready to move out and move on. I don't think you need me as a doctor anymore, but I hope you'll consider me a friend."

"I will always value your opinion," Tenai promised him. She had seated herself on the couch, as usual, but not curled up with boneless informality. This time, she sat straight, watching him with a level gaze. Perfectly well aware what was up, probably. No longer so focused on herself that she'd miss much.

Daniel cleared his throat. "I'm flattered. But that's not, fortunately, the same thing. Tenai, I think the halfway house will do for you, briefly. A week, two weeks, maybe. What you'll need soon is a place of your own, a life of your own, work that pays enough to live on. You need to get on and leave Lindenwood behind. Not that you can't visit, if you like. But I think you're ready to move on. Do you agree?"

Tenai's almond eyes were steady on his. She was smiling a little. "Yes, Doctor. I think that is true."

"Good. So, that leaves one or two practical issues to sort out. Have you thought more about what you might like to do? You said once you could teach the martial arts, or horseback riding."

"Yes."

"Right. So, what you need is a start." Daniel reached down beside his chair and brought out the phone book he'd stashed there earlier. "I've marked here all the martial arts establishments in the city. I've also marked employment agencies in case that idea doesn't pan out. You're smart—you're talented—you're very focused—I'm sure you could learn anything you chose to. There are all kinds of certificates and degrees you could get. You'd need your GED first. You could get that. I've marked a couple of community colleges where you might get a start. Or you could begin with something menial and work your way up, probably fast."

"Yes," Tenai said again, with no hint of which option she might prefer.

"But it's a lot easier to manage these first steps if someone gives you a boost, obviously. Fortunately, Michaela's brother recently decided to establish a grant for women in your position—ready to leave Lindenwood, that is, but without an immediate source of support."

That surprised her. "Michaela's brother?"

"You've met him once or twice, I believe." Daniel kept his tone perfectly matter-of-fact. "He's very fond of his sister, who's told him a lot about you, I gather. It turns out he's also fairly well-to-do. So, a grant, with you as the first recipient, but no doubt not the last. It's not a huge amount. But it should be enough for you to get your feet on the ground. Maybe buy a car—a used car, mind, nothing fancy—pay rent a few months someplace halfway decent so you can get out of the halfway house just about as soon as you feel you're ready. Enough to buy some clothes and some basic necessities, if you're not extravagant. All right?"

Tenai tilted her head in query. "Doctor, did you arrange this?"

"Call me Daniel. You'll need ID. You can get non-driver's ID, that's no trouble, and a driver's license when you learn to drive. And I've been looking into how you can get a social security number even though you don't have a birth certificate. I'll go over the paperwork with you when you're ready."

Tenai said after a moment, "You are very generous. So is Michaela's brother. I am grateful to you both."

"I hope to be repaid many times over, by watching you build a good life. We all hope for that. I think you'll be just fine."

"Indeed," said Tenai. "I think I shall trust your judgment, and expect to prove it sound." She paused. "Whatever life I build ... it will be to your credit, Doctor. Daniel. I will expect ... I will hope for you to be a part of it." Her expression had become just a little wistful.

"I look forward to that," said Daniel, and smiled, unable, at that moment, to maintain his professional doctor's façade. It was obsolete, anyway.

Interlude:

Chase

1

Brian McKenna's first impression when he saw Tenai Chase was, This is a *killer*. He changed it to *fighter* in his mind at once, but he remembered, later, what his very first response had been.

Even recognition that she was a woman was secondary; and he registered her unusual, striking looks only after that.

She wore black jeans and a plain white shirt with a v-neck that showed off her long throat; she was tall; she was dark—black, maybe, but then maybe not; it was that kind of coloring. She moved with a fine, centered balance that was like a neon sign over her head saying This Woman Knows How To Fight. Her hair was long, but knotted at the back of her neck. Her eyes were dark, both almond-colored and almond-shaped, just slanted enough to suggest a trace of Asian ancestry. The quick neutral glance she sent around the dojo registered the mats and mirrors, the canes and swords and knives in their racks and the protective gear in a series of bins, the window that showed the outdoor practice yard and the one that showed the garden. That same summing look assessed Brian himself, and then she shut the door behind her, the bamboo noisemaker at the top of the door chattering softly, and walked over. She was wearing those light ankle-high woman's boots that lace up the front with narrow laces. They didn't squeak on the wooden floor the way sneakers would've. And they'd be all the better to kick you with, my dear, which might be coincidence, but Brian wouldn't have taken odds on that. She had a sword slung over one shoulder like that kind of hardware was perfectly ordinary.

Brian had been sitting behind the counter, looking through the class rosters and figuring out whether he could fit another advanced class into the schedule. But he found he did not want to meet this woman sitting down. He stood up, walked around the counter, leaned his hip against the counter-edge, crossed his arms, and looked at her inquiringly. He did not ask whether he could help her.

"Brian McKenna?" the woman said, not quite a question. Her voice was low and rich. If she sang, she would surely be a second alto. It crossed Brian's mind that if this woman was Catholic and local, perhaps she might be persuaded to join the choir, which, second altos not being all that easy to come by, would be a good thing. At his nod she went on, "I am looking for employment. Emily Hahn sends me to you. She said you are looking for a woman teacher for some of your classes." She spoke with a slight but distinct accent, nothing Brian recognized, a liquid sort of accent, a little like a Welsh accent. Not that this woman looked at all Welsh.

"Yeah?" Brian said, immediately interested. "So is Emily, same as me. Why didn't she hire you, then?"

The woman did not seem taken aback by the question. She said, "Ms. Hahn teaches the style called *karate*. I do not know that style, or any other one style. Ms. Hahn told me you would not care for style."

"That what she said, is it?"

"She said you do not teach for competition, but for survival."

"That's right," Brian acknowledged. "Here at Nighthawk, we believe the purpose of fighting is to win the fights when the bad guys try to pull some kind of shit. We believe everyone ought to be able to protect herself in a pinch. That work for you?"

"Yes," said the woman, in her low, accented voice. "That works for me." The casual slang sounded odd in her mouth. If she was uncomfortable with it, he couldn't tell.

"We teach competition, too, enough of our clients are interested, but it's not our focus. You ever taught before?"

"Yes," the woman said again.

"Where?"

"Not here."

Brian looked at her. She had said that last with a deliberate kind of finality. "You got a past?" And, on her look of noncomprehension—so she was not completely comfortable with slang— "You've been in trouble with the law, then?"

"Ah," said the woman, enlightened. "No. Nothing to regard."

Brian accepted this with a slight nod. "You got a name?"

"Tenai," said the woman, and added as an afterthought, "Chase."

Tenai sounded about right, for this woman's unusual looks. *Chase?* That sounded awfully ordinary. An English daddy, maybe?

Tenai Chase met his eyes levelly. She was almost as tall as Brian himself, built long and lean; small-breasted and narrow-hipped, like a model. Her ears were not pierced. Her cheekbones looked almost Indian—the feather, not the dot. Her complexion and the softness of her hair suggested maybe a black grandparent or two someplace in the pedigree. Maybe. With a mental shrug, Brian gave up guessing. He said, "So, you any good, then, Ms. Chase?"

Narrow eyebrows lifted slightly. "Yes."

Brian knew she was. No novice moved like this woman. "Okay," he said. "No shoes on the mats."

She turned neatly, in balance, walked to the edge of the mats, and placed her sword on the floor. She unlaced her boots and set them aside. She took off her socks and walked out onto the mats, barefoot and graceful, and Brian thought again: This woman is a *fighter*. He barely heard the faint echo of his real first impression echoing behind that thought—a faint sense of unease.

Brian was barefoot himself, as he usually was in the dojo. He walked over to join her, but did not step onto the mats, not yet.

"I want you to show me what you can do," he told her. "This isn't for real, not even real practice, not yet. We take it slow and easy. You do one strike at a time, I do one back and you block, very light contact—aim to barely touch. I just want to see what kind of training you've got. Understand?"

"I understand you." She stood there, hands at her sides, waiting. It was a neutral stance, giving away nothing.

"Okay, then. Show me what you've got."

She demonstrated strikes and steps and blocks for at least an hour, although Brian was involved enough in studying her technique that he couldn't even *think* of looking at the clock. She moved beautifully, as beautifully as anyone he'd ever seen. Her style was not one thing or the other: she had boxing strikes like karate, but not karate; she had wrestling throws like judo, but not judo. Brian saw suggestions of stylized exercises, but none of them was quite familiar.

Tenai Chase did not fight like a woman, sliding a man's strength delicately away instead of meeting it directly. At first Brian thought this was a sign of bad teaching. But then, as he got the measure of her strength, he realized that she did in fact have the sheer physical power it took to meet a man straight on, and that was damned unusual in any woman, no matter how tall. Height, reach, and strength, and a damned great lot of skill to draw on. "Break," he said. "Break—" backing away and showing her his hands, palm out, calling a halt.

She backed off at once, perfectly in balance, not in the least out of breath.

"Where'd you train? Who with? Anybody I'd know?"

She looked back, expression reserved. "Everywhere. No. I would not think so."

"You fight like a man. You think you could teach a woman, a kid maybe? Somebody who wouldn't have your strength or your reach?"

"Yes."

"Yeah?"

"I do know how to match a stronger opponent, a heavier opponent. Shall I show you?"

"Later, maybe. Let's do this for real, then. Practice rules for instructors: take it fast and hard if you're going to hit the protective gear, fast and light if you're going for the legs or the face. The object is to wind up with nothing worse than bruises. Okay?"

"Yes," Tenai answered, very simply once again, which seemed to be her style. English was certainly not her first language, Brian thought, but she did seem okay with it. "Gear's over there. Chest protector, hand and foot gear, helmet—I'll help you with the straps on the chest protector."

Once they were both geared up, Brian brought the woman back onto the mats. He lowered his hands, took a neutral posture, and just stood there. Inviting Tenai to take the offensive.

Which she did, after a few seconds: she stepped in, exhaling smoothly, and kicked—a very simple roundhouse kick, low, for the knee, which was good and showed reflexes trained in the real world and not in a class. And very fast. But not, Brian thought, maybe not as fast as she could have taken it. He had no time to think about it.

He jumped into a kick of his own, a jump side kick, simple and fast, tucking his leg up out of the way so her kick could pass under him. Tenai used the momentum of her kick to pull her body around out of the way of his. Brian threw a punch as he touched the mat, and Tenai blocked his blow with her forearm, leading his hand aside—a woman's move, and no coincidence, he was sure—and opening his guard for her other hand, which stabbed in toward his stomach in a spear hand. Brian stepped sideways out of that strike, pivoted into a back kick of his own—fast, because he was confident she could stop it—and she caught his foot in a judo-type maneuver and threw him. Brian slapped the mats and rolled to his feet and they went on like that for a few minutes. She was very, very fast. There was no time for thought. She had a kick like a mule and a punch like Muhammad Ali, and a very respectable ability to render either feather-light when attacking around the protective gear. She got him in the kidney twice, in the throat once, and across a knee once—each time very lightly. Brian never managed to touch her anywhere except where the protective gear covered her, and had not once landed a full-force blow to the chest or side of the head either. And the woman was still not even breathing hard.

Humbling, was what it was.

When Brian signaled a break, there was the tiniest hesitation. Then Tenai gathered herself and turned, neat as before, and walked to the edge of the mats. Brian followed her, removing the protective gear, then went over to the counter, where he leaned again, studying her while she did the same. He, damn it, was still breathing hard. "You've done it for real a lot more than as a teacher, haven't you?" And what kind of life would lead to that kind of background? But that he didn't ask.

"Yes." She added after a moment, "And your skill is very excellent. It has been a long time since anyone pressed me so hard."

Brian was glad to hear it. "You're good. Real good. Better than me. Isn't that right?"

It wasn't like she could have missed it. She inclined her head, a slight, elegant gesture.

"Uh-huh." Brian gave her a serious look. "Accidents happen. But this is a business as well as a school. If a student, especially a kid, gets hurt, that could get the school in a lot of trouble. A lot. Maybe close us down. Liability is a big deal these days, I expect you know. We do a lot of stuff full-force because you have to train the reflexes right, but it's the students that go all-out, not the instructors. It seems to me you can handle that. You think so?"

Tenai nodded. "I understand you, Mr. McKenna. I would ask you to give me students who are only beginning, if you wish. Until you are certain I will not make a mistake."

It was fair. It was even useful. Beginners were just what Brian wanted to give her anyway, if she could handle them. "Beginners are tough. Gotta start them right."

"Yes." After a moment, when he just looked at her, "I agree. One must set the skills correctly at the beginning. This is important."

"Okay, so you think you know how to do that, then. You're a tough lady, right? Can you take my orders, Chase?"

The woman looked very slightly surprised. Or maybe that was irony. "Yes."

"Contract I use says you have to give a week's notice to quit, but it says I don't have to give you notice to fire you. Which I will, if I think you're a danger to the clients, or the other instructors, or if you're just a bloody nuisance one way or another. That okay?"

"Yes."

"You're not quarrelsome. You don't pick fights. You don't make trouble."

"No."

"We do co-teaching here. One instructor and one assistant instructor per class, or sometimes two assistants team up for a class. If I hire you, it'll be as an assistant. Assistants make shit wages, but some of the assistants live upstairs. There's room up there, if you want. You want to do that, you trade work around the dojo for rent. You buy your own food and stuff, though. If I think you're good enough, I'll bump you up to full instructor. Which I will do as soon as I think I can. That's *good enough* as an instructor, not good enough in your own personal performance. How's that sound? All of that clear so far?"

"Yes. This is all clear. I have a place elsewhere," Tenai added. "But I am happy to work here also."

Brian nodded acknowledgement. "I want you to teach a class for women—that's why I was looking for a woman instructor. This is a special class. A lot of these women have been attacked, some of them raped, and that brought them to us. Some of them were referred to us by the police, or by rape counselors—that kind of thing. Almost all of 'em would do best starting with a woman instructor. Sound like you can handle that?"

"Yes."

"Any questions?"

A slight hesitation. "No."

"Can you teach advanced students? I may ask you to teach instructors' classes. How about that?"

"Yes," Tenai agreed. "I could do that."

"You get paid extra if you can advance the instructors' skills. Including mine. And the opposite: if somebody here teaches you a skill, you pay for his time. If it's a trade, you can trade even with the dojo, skill for skill. Can you use that sword of yours, then?"

The woman glanced over at her sword, lying on the floor next to her little boots. "Yes."

"You as good with it as bare hands?"

She looked at him for a moment. Finally she said, "I am best with a sword."

"Better than hand-to-hand?"

"Yes."

Wow, Brian did not say. He nodded toward the weapons hung on the wall. "Anything else? Or just swords?"

Again that hesitation. Brian waited, eyebrows lifted interrogatively, and at last she said, "Any of those. Or bow."

Carefully, he did not show surprise. "Guns?"

"No. I think I would like to learn ... guns."

"That could be a trade, then," Brian suggested. "Gun for bow. We don't have anybody here who does bows. You can teach that?"

A nod. "Yes."

"Crossbow or long?"

"Either."

Brian stepped back behind the counter and just looked at her for a minute. Tall, yes. Graceful and striking, yes. Good looking ... it hardly mattered ... the way she moved, she would be a handsome lady no matter if she was horse-faced and boy-chested. Well, she *was* sort of boy-chested. Not that anybody would mistake her for a boy. She stood there calmly, relaxed, hands at her sides, barefoot. Solemn as a judge. Not a smile out of her this whole time. Not a mean look, but solemn. "You're hired, then," he said, and tabbed the panic button. "When can you start?"

She looked a little nonplussed. "Today?"

Brian grinned. "Today it is, then. Tenai, right? Or Chase." Tenai was an odd name. He couldn't quite place it. Giving up, he started flipping through drawers, looking for the necessary paperwork. Before he had found it, a rush of thuds down the stairs announced the arrival of Tom and Kim, with, Brian was sure, Dean on his way over from the house.

Tom skidded to a halt right inside the dojo, so suddenly that Kim nearly ran into him from behind and cussed, sharply. She got around him, threw a look around the dojo, noted the lack of anything resembling an emergency, planted her hands on her hips, and glared at Brian. "For God's sake, Bri."

Brian made a show of glancing at his watch. "A minute and a half. Children, children. What was keeping you?"

"Hell," said Kim disgustedly. "If the bread burns, it's your fault, you ass." She looked the new woman up and down. Kim was almost as tall as Tenai Chase, but a lot stockier, a lot blonder, and a lot more American. "New kid on the block?"

"Our newest assistant," Brian said, and slid a contract across the counter, along with a pen. "If she's still brave enough to sign. Right there on the dotted line, Chase."

Most of her attention on the new arrivals, the woman picked up the pen. Across the dojo, Dean slid the glass door open and came in, quietly, from the garden. Tenai looked that way at once, with that quick assessing stare of hers.

"Children," Brian said briskly, "This is Tenai Chase, who will be joining our merry band. Be nice to her. She's better than I am, so I expect she can clean up the mat with any one of you lot. Chase, that big one with the beard is Tom Cox. The loud female is Kim Lehninger. And the little fellow with no beard is Dean Ng, our token Inscrutable Oriental."

Dean instantly put on his best Inscrutable look. Behind that, Brian could tell he actually *was* tucking his initial reaction out of sight. Dean was sharp; he'd picked up the same dangerous vibe

Brian had felt the moment Tenai had stepped into view.

Brian went on smoothly. "Tom and Kim are assistant instructors. Dean is a full instructor and my partner with Nighthawk. Tom and Kim live upstairs. Dean lives next door, with me. Tom, the lady uses a sword. I would like a demonstration. Promptly, please. We have a class starting at six. Kim, love, please go take the bread out of the oven."

"And miss this?" said Kim. She said to Tenai, "Pleased, I'm sure, Chase," and to Tom, "Don't you dare start till I get back, hear?" Then she ran back up the stairs.

Tom looked thoughtfully at the new woman. He glanced over at her sword, sheathed and lying on the floor, and looked back at her. "May I see it?"

After a moment, Tenai said, "Of course, if you wish." Retrieving her sword, Tenai drew the weapon with a smooth practiced motion. She laid the sheath on the counter and turned to offer the sword itself to Tom.

It was black: that was the first impression Brian had of it. It had a dull matte shine, but it was black as iron. The hilt was black, too, of course: shark skin, Brian thought, although he couldn't be sure without touching it. It was long and slim, single-edged, very slightly curved and with that odd squared-off tip that a katana would have. But it was not a katana. Like Tenai's hand-to-hand style, the sword did not quite fit any category he knew.

Tom took it with a polite nod. The hilt was a little small for his hand. He just held it for a minute or so, than took a stance, saluted the window, and swished it through a pattern. When he gave it back to Tenai, his expression was respectful. "Very nice. Very well balanced. It moves like a work of art. What's the alloy? Not plain steel. Do you know who made it?"

Tenai inclined her head. "Thank you. I am sorry, I do not know what metal it is. I do not know what person made it. It was given to me ... a long time ago."

"Um." Tom gestured toward the mats. "Shall we? Are you good enough to use real swords in practice?"

"Yes," said Tenai. "But this one is not for practice." She sheathed it, carefully.

"Um. Can you use an unfamiliar blade? We don't have another sword exactly like that one. In fact, I don't know that I've ever seen another sword just like that one."

"Any sword. You chose."

Kim arrived back down the stairs in time to hear this, and hooked a sword off the wall, not quite at random. She called, "Here, Chase, catch!" and tossed it to Tenai, who caught it effortlessly, of course. This one was a katana, not the best the dojo owned, but a good one. It was a little too heavy and a little too long for most women. Brian remembered the strength he had found in this particular woman, and was not surprised when she hefted the sword and nodded in approval.

Tom had a sword of his own. He didn't get it, which was his sense of fair play: he wouldn't use his if Tenai wouldn't use hers. He took a sword off the wall, a long straight sword—a good match for the one Tenai held. Where Kim might have deliberately tried to give Tenai a challenge, Tom went out of his way to make the contest as fair as possible: in character for them both.

Tenai discarded her sword's sheath and stepped onto the mats, her attention all for Tom, who followed her. Kim leaned against the wall and watched, frowning. Dean came over and jumped up to sit on the counter, which Brian usually didn't like, but he made room without comment this time.

"She can move," Dean commented. "Is she really better than you, Bri?"

Brian leaned his elbows on the counter, staring across the dojo at the mats. "Yep. You know Carlo Martinez?"

"Sure."

"Pretty sure she's better than him."

Dean raised his eyebrows. "Huh."

"You'll get your chance at her."

"You took her on as an assistant."

"Well, now. I know she can move. I know she can fight. But I don't know she can teach, now, do I?"

"You'll put her with beginning classes, I guess," said Dean. "The survivor's class? Of course."

On the mats, Tom bowed, to be echoed after an instant by Tenai. He started a sweep at mid-height, aimed to cut down from her neck into her chest: a serious blow, but very, very slow. Tenai answered equally slowly.

No hiding lack of balance or skill at that drifting speed: no recovering a mistake with sheer strength or tricks of momentum. No. Slow like that, one was either right or very obviously wrong.

Tom looked very good. Tenai looked *perfect*.

Feint. Block, with the soft scraping hiss of metal against metal: no ringing of metal, not as gently as they were moving out there. Guard and strike and feint, and strike again.

Tom took it faster.

Tenai matched him, and stepped up the speed herself, and the metal *was* ringing now, sword against sword full-force. Tom tried a sweep at her legs and Tenai jumped exactly high enough to clear the blade. He spun his sword around to cut at her hip, and Tenai caught his sword on hers, ran hers down along the length of his, and flicked it out of his hand with an irresistible spiraling twist. It fell on the mats, ten feet away, and Tenai stood there, lightly, on the balls of her feet, with the borrowed sword held across her body, ready to go in any direction.

Tom shook out his stinging fingers. He was grinning broadly behind that beard of his. "Break," he said. "All *right*. Chase, is it? Lady, you can be on *my* team any day of the week! Will you show me that move?"

In the face of his enthusiasm, even Tenai was smiling—a cautious, narrow smile. But a smile. "Yes," she said. "If you wish, I will be pleased to show you."

Dean's eyes had widened. "Yep," Brian said to him, quietly. "Beginners."

"Right," said Dean.

Brian grinned at him, took a step away from the counter, and clapped his hands sharply. "Off the mats," he called. "Students will be arriving any moment. Chase, if you've got time, I'd like you to observe this class. Kim, how's that bread?"

"Fine," said Kim. With a frown.

"Beautiful. If you stay, you're working, love."

"I've got prep to do for the seven fifteen class," she said, still frowning.

"Then I'll see you here at seven fifteen, won't I?"

She threw him a sharp look and a casual salute, and walked away, back to the office.

The first students arrived, Katie Smith and her sister Joan, Mary Twist and Jeanne Kurtz. Dean, their instructor, went off to greet them. Brian, ordinarily acting as the assistant instructor for this class, waved Tom off after Dean and leaned against the counter. Tenai stood at his elbow, her manner reserved and watchful.

"This is a tough class," Brian told her quietly. "They're first-session students; clients who are about half-way through our introductory three-month class. They're learning basic technique and very simple falls and throws. They're also learning when to go all-out against a bad guy and when to try to get out of it, or talk him out of it; how to ignore the stuff he may be yelling at them—most of the baddies have foul mouths and I've known women to stop and freeze because they get so scared—how to maneuver him into position so they can take him out. All that stuff. Kim can't work with students like this. She doesn't have the patience. She works with third- or forth-session clients, advanced stuff. It's classes like this one I mostly want you to handle, along with the survivor's class. I'll schedule that to start very soon, if you can handle it."

Tenai was listening carefully. "Yes."

"Dean and I have been splitting the work on this class. Watch how this goes. Dean will direct the whole class, and Tom will work individually with students who need assistance. This class meets three times a week. Students from this class can also join a mixed-level class if they like—the higher ranks can pull the lower forward, there's good energy there." For a little while, they were both quiet, watching Dean welcome students as they arrived and set them to warming-exercises and simple *kata*.

"I do not know those ... patterns," Tenai said quietly.

"Anybody can show you the *kata* we use for the beginners. I expect you're a quick study, yes?"

"Yes."

"You see Jeanne, there, that redhead. That girl hasn't been doing her homework. Not our job to do the work for them. But it *is* our job to see that they have the motivation to work the way they should. Dean's going to make her sweat. There. You see. It's a fine line—push too hard, and she'll drop out and get no good of the class at all. You have to make them feel like you're on their side. Tough, but rooting for them. Nearly all of 'em like a tough instructor. Hardly any of 'em want to take it easy or go slow, though some of them think they do."

"Yes."

"There are four assistants, not counting you. Most of the

assistants work eight or ten sessions a week, not counting the classes they take themselves. There are three instructors: Dean, me, and Dave Lack, who's got a family of his own. The dojo handles a total of twenty-two classes per week right now, most with three sessions, some with two. Weekends are our busiest times, of course. If you work out, I'll add two additional classes right away, that's six extra sessions. You'll work under an instructor or an experienced assistant the first time through."

"I understand."

"The second run-through, I'll put you in as an instructor, but not at instructor's pay until I see what kind of job you're doing. But I won't drag my feet if you can do the job. Ask the other assistants: I'm fair."

That got him a careful look, and a small nod.

"Any questions?"

"No."

"All right. Relax and watch the class. Tell me what you see. In the students, or the instructors. Problems, with solutions, please. Comments, thoughts, questions, complaints—tell me about that black woman, the older one."

Tenai turned her serious, thoughtful stare on the class, busy sparring in pairs. She said, in that calm, neutral tone that seemed habitual with her, "Her stance is too narrow. She can achieve neither steadiness nor power so long as she has so narrow a stance. And she should turn her back foot."

"Yep. How would you fix what she's doing wrong?"

Much later, back in the house and sitting cross-legged on the floor in front of the wall fan, Brian accepted a rum punch and a weary smile from Dean Ng, who settled nearby, leaning back against the foot of the couch. "So, and what do you think of our latest catch?" he asked.

The TV was on, but turned down very low because nothing worth watching was on. One of the cats was lying on top of the set, blinking disdainfully upon the room. He was a big heavy-bodied cat, half-Siamese, white on the chest and belly and feet, toast-brown tabby stripes on the back and legs, with seal-brown ears and tail and mask and bright blue eyes. Brian said, gesturing with his punch toward the cat, "She has about the same expression as our big fellow, doesn't she?"

"I like her," Dean said mildly.

"Do you, then?"

"Sure. Not everybody has to be effusive as the excitable Irish, Bri. She's not American, I can tell you that."

"Yeah, a little bit of an accent there, you think?"

"Sure, but besides that, she didn't get the inscrutable joke. Everybody who watches martial arts flicks gets it. Everybody who doesn't get it is offended. Not her. QED."

Brian nodded, thoughtful. "Moderately persuasive. Okay, I bow to your superior expertise, Master Ng."

"As you should, Grasshopper. She's the serious type, but she moves like a dream."

"She's got a good eye. I think she *can* work beginners."

"You've got her figured to take on instructor's classes?"

"Probably. If she will. She's killed people, I think." Brian let his eyes rest on the flickering near-silent TV screen, but in his mind he was watching that woman move and turn and stand and move again. "She's been a soldier somewhere. I'd put money on it. God knows where. Not American, right, I believe it. Tenai. You ever hear a name like that?"

"Beats me, Bri." If Dean was shocked by the suggestion, it didn't show. "But she's in either way, right?"

"Sure."

"Yeah," said Dean. He lifted his own rum punch in a wry salute. "Here's to taking chances and playing with fire: without risk, where would be the fun?"

2

"Hey, Chase! Guess what?" Kim swung energetically through the main door of the dojo, Brian following more restrainedly behind her.

Tenai Chase had been engaged in developing a series of exercises and *kata* suitable to teach fencing to raw beginners, a job she had recently taken on at Brian's request. She glanced inquiringly over from the mats, dark eyes carrying a startling impact of attention. Even after close to eight years to get used to it, Brian still experienced an instant of discomfort at meeting that dark gaze, as though he'd met the eyes of a wolf or a lion. Something dangerous, and something not quite comprehensible. He admired her, the way a person might admire a wolf or a lion. But splendid as such an animal might be, anybody would be well advised to remember it was a wolf, or a lion, and not a *tame* animal.

Brian dealt with this unwelcome feeling by acting like it wasn't there. Most of the time this strategy worked just fine. Admittedly, when he faced Tenai on the mats, that kind of thing was less successful.

Brian was aware he was not the only Nighthawk instructor who felt this discomfort, this awareness of danger. Kim got it, though it didn't bother her—she liked riding the edge in a lot of ways, and treating Chase casually was one of those ways. Tom didn't get the scary vibes. It wasn't that Tom lacked imagination. Or even perception. No, Tom was just too *nice*, in Brian's estimation, to see danger even when it was there. If there was good in a person, Tom would see that—and only that, blind to anything dangerous. It was his greatest weakness as an instructor. Also, of course, his greatest strength with the shy ones and the children.

Jonnie was blind, too, although not for the same reason. That was pure sex—Jonnie, despite his long-term, apparently permanent girlfriend, was easily smitten by tall lithe beautiful women who also happened to be serious martial arts masters. It could happen to anybody. But, since Jonnie saw Chase through a testosterone haze, naturally he didn't see her very clearly. Not, to be fair, that Chase did anything to lead him on. She wasn't dangerous to the girlfriend, which Charlene had figured out and likely Jonnie knew too, really. Chase wasn't interested, and Jonnie dreamed from afar. Brian could afford to be amused, since nothing about the attraction harmed anybody.

Dean—now, Dean knew just how spooky Chase was. He liked her anyway, but then, Dean had a feel for quality. Besides, Chase was good for Nighthawk. Very good. If Chase left Nighthawk, she'd take half the customers with her, and Brian knew it. So he'd better like her. Not that she showed signs of leaving. Which was good, given the use he wanted to make of her. He looked at her, standing there on the mats with a long, narrow sword in her hand, in perfect balance. When she moved, it was beauty in motion.

That was another reason to appreciate this woman.

Chase lowered the sword she was using and walked over to the edge of the mats, and even then she looked like she was moving to music. She was smiling just a little, head tilted curiously, prepared to be pleased or amused by whatever news Kim brought her. She was always good natured, Brian had to admit it. She simply gave the continual impression that this might change.

Kim, as always, appeared blithely unaware of any possible reason to be impressed. She swung towards the mats with her customary aggressive stride, grinning. "Chase, guess what we've got? Tickets to Blast! at the Fox. You know Blast!, right?"

"No," the other woman said patiently.

"Well, you'll love 'em. These are real good tickets, the best, some people I know were going and now they're not and they gave 'em to me. *Seven* tickets, let me tell you, you don't score like that every day! You've gotta come, you don't get out nearly enough."

Brian put in, "It's a good band. Dynamic. You really will like the show, Kim's got that right. Dean's going. That leaves Tom, Jonnie, and you, if you want to come, plus a guest if you've got somebody you'd like to bring along. Or Jonnie can ask his girlfriend, but it's not really Charlene's thing. She's seriously into opera." He pretended to shudder.

Chase raised an eyebrow at Kim. "You are not asking Peter?"

Kim rolled her eyes. "Good lord, Chase, Pete was two boyfriends ago, thanks for keeping up. You remember Doug, the blond guy with the mustache? You met him a couple weeks ago when he picked me up. Doug isn't into a night at the Fox. He's more a karaoke guy."

"My sympathy," Chase said gravely.

Brian laughed.

"Yeah, laugh it up," said Kim. "But you know what they say about guys with mustaches." She wiggled her eyebrows, and Brian laughed again. Even Chase smiled, which was an accomplishment.

"Show's at nine Saturday, so we'll get a late night, but hell, we're tough, we can take it. Listen, Chase, if you don't have a guy, and when do you ever, ask that kid of yours. Blast! is a great band for kids. She'll love it. You'll both love it."

Chase tilted her head, apparently considering this. She never did 'have a guy,' as far as Brian could tell—Kim was right about that. Chase put out *not looking* vibes through the aether so powerfully, a guy'd have to be a complete blockhead to make a move on her. Not that some guys weren't blockheads, but not with Chase—not twice. But she was friendly with one of the students— well, she was *friendly* with a lot of the students, but this one kid, Jenna Dodson, was different. Chase knew the family somehow, went way back with the dad, treated the kid kind of like a little sister. Brian had always found that reassuring. Woman might have big-time privacy issues, but she *did* have friends.

He said now, "Invite the kid *and* her dad if you want. I can wangle another ticket."

A thoughtful nod. "Perhaps. Are there no classes Saturday night?"

Another eye-roll from Kim. "Where've you been, Chase? Get with the program! This's Easter weekend coming up, no classes for anybody all weekend. I figure we can go out for a midnight snack after the show and sleep in Sunday morning."

"That's why Dave can't go," added Brian. "He's got to hide eggs for the kiddies. No sleeping in for daddies with five-year-old twins. The rest of us are free to go out on the town. Dean and I and Kim'll go out afterwards, drink, carouse, and make public spectacles of ourselves. You're invited for that part too, but not sure it's your speed. But catch the show at least."

"Maybe," Tenai allowed cautiously.

"God, Chase, live a little!" said Kim. She said to Brian, "Of course she's going, Bri, and we'll have a blast, pun intended, but if you make a public spectacle of yourself, Dean and me'll dump you on the street by your lonesome, I swear. I got enough of that from Fred."

"Four men back," said Chase. "You see, I do keep track."

"Yeah, okay, I'm impressed. Honestly didn't think you'd remember that one. I think Fred only lasted, what, maybe three-four weeks."

"Dear, I think he lasted three or four *days*," Brian said, and held out a hand curiously for the sword Chase was holding as Kim sputtered. Chase handed the weapon to him, and he hefted it with some interest. "A little light for you, Beautiful?"

Chase inclined her head. "Very light, for me. I was thinking of Jenna. She might like to learn such a skill."

"Oh, you think? She's a sharp kid, but not real aggressive. Oh, you figure that's why she'd be into fencing? More like a sport, not so much like a fight? How's her daddy feel about her playing with sharp toys?" Kim might seem a shallow, facile kind of woman, but she wasn't. She'd put that together fast.

Chase said mildly, "I think her father will not object to the sword. I will be very careful."

"I should hope so," Brian agreed lightly. "Can't go around cutting up the kiddies. Don't you have a class coming in any time now?"

"Yes."

Kim grinned. "Yeah, the cop class. How's that going?"

This was an advanced class, one filled mostly with police officers who wanted to go beyond the basics offered by standard police training. That was a new market for Nighthawk, and it was Chase who'd given Brian the idea for it. She could teach anyone, and she impressed the hell out of cops otherwise very hard to impress. This was the third cop class offered, and by far the best attended. Nothing like word of mouth.

"Come, if you wish. I would be glad to use you." Chase offered Kim one of her rare smiles "Some of these students are arrogant. They believe they are skilled. They understand that I am more skilled, but they do not believe anyone else is. Men, you know? They must be taught that they can lose even if it is not me they oppose."

Kim grinned, a swift predatory expression that made her look for a second as dangerous as the taller woman. "Hell, I don't have anything much tonight. Sounds like fun. Count me in. This bunch is *all* guys, isn't it?"

Chase smiled again. "Yes."

"Fun, fun, fun. Meet you down in the dojo in ten." Kim swaggered away toward her room to change.

Brian wanted to laugh, and tamped it down to a grin because the first students were arriving right then and bursts of laughter didn't seem the way to greet them. "I'll get out of the way of you ladies, but okay if I watch?"

"Of course."

"Okay. Be gentle with 'em, Beautiful—they don't know what they're getting into."

"They will find out," Tenai said with perfect composure, and offered, with a slight bow, to let Brian precede her to the desk to check in the students.

There were twelve students in this class: all male, mostly big, mostly macho as hell. That they were in this class at all was a testament to the enthusiasm with which earlier students of Nighthawk had promoted it. They greeted Chase and Kim with a series of whistles and cat-calls—teasing, but not unfriendly. Nor disrespectful, not really. Brian knew how cops had to posture: can't let a civilian *woman* break our balls. They'd already found out that Chase could break any one of them in half. They didn't know Kim at all, yet, which Brian was looking forward to watching the women rectify.

"Oooh, look, we've got *extra* help tonight!"

"Chase, where you recruiting from?"

"Hey, baby, I've got some moves I'd like to show you!"

Kim put a deliberate sway into her step and grinned back. "Oh, yeah? Think you've got what it takes to impress me, do you?"

"Oh, yeah, I've got what it takes, all right!"

"Then I doubt I could handle it." Kim pretended to think hard. "—less you're all brag and no *performance*, my man."

Chase smiled, a flash of white teeth in her dark face. She knew the same thing that Kim knew, the same thing Brian, watching from the desk, knew, that these guys were riding for a fall.

Chase wore ordinary clothes: black jeans, a black exercise top.

All the men wore jeans and t-shirts, too: if a cop got up close and personal with a bad guy, it wouldn't be *gi* they'd be wearing. That they were barefoot was only a concession to the well-being of the mats.

"Can I have your number, teach? I might have questions later about the *kata*."

"Can we all have your number?"

"Hey, haven't seen you before—come be my partner," called one man. Kim wasn't by any means petite, but this guy was twice her size.

"Sign my dance card and I'll get back to you," Kim shot back. "—When I'm in the mood to dance. With a bear."

"He'd step on your feet," objected another cop, the smallest guy in the room. "I'm a much better dancer."

"Yeah, but he's so small, if he steps on your feet, you won't even feel it," said the first man. Probably they were partners for real. Partners and friends. The teasing had that kind of feel to it.

"Aw, you know it's not the meat," Kim told the big guy, with the slightest suggestion of a wink and a twitch of her hips. Everyone laughed, and the bigger man came in for his share of the jeers.

"If you please," said Chase, not loudly, but somehow she drew all eyes. "We will begin with simple *kata*. Kim will work with you individually, which I believe you will find is not such a great pleasure as all that."

An hour later, no one had energy left to tease.

Tenai Chase, Brian acknowledged for the millionth time, was a hell of a teacher. She could spot imbalance or a weak stance at a glance, and, even more important, she could see how to correct it and teach the student how to stand and move correctly.

And these men were serious students, a lot more serious than a casual observer might have guessed from the attitude they'd brought in with them. Well, of course they were—a cop usually had a bitch of a schedule anyway, and yet here these guys were on a night off, working their tails off in a dojo.

Kim had shocked them silly when she proved able to toss them around almost as well as Chase. Well, not almost as well, maybe, because face it, who was in Chase's class? But adequately, at least. But the guys had settled down pretty damn well after that surprise. They looked like they were having fun out there. It was tempting to join in, but if Brian went out on the mats, he'd no longer be able to watch the general flow of the class. And that was what he wanted to see tonight.

It was a good class, very good. Serious about learning, but not too serious in attitude.

"Okay," said a man Kim was partnering at the moment—the big guy, in fact, the one who'd wanted to dance. "What the hell am I doing wrong?" He climbed back up off the floor while Kim cocked her head at him, looking frustrated.

Brian had been trying to figure that out himself. It was subtle, something about the way the man moved; he was clearly weaker moving than standing, which was unusual. Kim also evidently didn't know what the hell the guy was doing wrong, either; hence the frustration. Brian was glad to see Kim just shrug at this question and raise her hand. No grandstanding at all. That was a woman-thing, maybe, that willingness to ask for help; damn sure few male teachers would have called for a second opinion so fast or so easily, certainly not a male as prickly as Kim.

Chase materialized at Kim's shoulder barely a minute later.

"Watch this," Kim said to her, and nodded at her partner. "Let's take it from the top, okay?"

"Okay," agreed the man. "Be gentle with me." He pretended to be frightened.

"Why?" said Kim. "It's not your first time." She grinned at him and started the drill, which shouldn't wind up with the guy hitting the mats quite so fast. But there he went: wham! And was up with credible speed—Chase was death on any pause in the advanced classes: you lie there and let the bad guy keep on at you and you'd damn sure pick up another bruise or three, all the time with Chase yelling at you to get back in the game. So the guy was up, but he shouldn't have gone down in the first place, that was the problem.

"Break, break," said Kim, the only way the man could be sure the bout was over, and he straightened up, wincing.

"Well?" Kim said to Chase.

The taller woman tipped her head to one side. "Take your stance," she said to the man, and walked around him in a circle, frowning. She began the same attack Kim had used, but broke off and backed away before the attack was fairly begun, with the cop still on his feet. "Break," she said. "Kim, again, please, but very slow." She walked around behind the man and looked expectantly at Kim over his shoulder.

Kim started the move, in slow motion. It was very much harder to do the sparring drill right in slow motion. The man showed the strain in a stance grown suddenly less secure, in a body less precise in executing the pattern.

"Stop," said Chase.

Kim stopped smoothly—her own skill level had gone up considerably in the past few years, or she'd not have made that look so easy—the man struggled to a halt with more difficulty, now clearly out of balance.

One hand on his shoulder and one on his hip, Chase altered the way the man was standing. She walked around him, studying him, and nudged his foot with her own, signaling him to move his leg further away from his body. His eyes had gone distant, concentrating on the way the new stance felt.

"When you move to the side, to the left, you do not put your foot out far enough," said Chase. "You were injured in that leg once, yes? I thought so. You have the habit still, of favoring that leg. Not always, but sometimes, when you feel strain come on it. But when you do, you lose your foundation, your support. You try to compensate, but you cannot compensate enough. That is why you go down, because you have no solidity behind your block." She glanced at Kim.

"I should have seen that," Kim said, chagrined.

"No," said Chase, very properly preventing her co-instructor from taking inappropriate blame. "The compensation looks right to the eye. That's why you do not see it. But the balance is still wrong. Do you see it now?"

"Well, sure. It's obvious, now."

"Then go again." Chase walked away to work with someone else.

"She's something else, I guess," said the man to Kim, watching the other woman walk away with that cat-grace of hers.

"Yeah," said Kim, "but I warn you, she's an ice queen."

"Yeah, I got that." The cop grinned now at Kim herself. "She's not my type anyway. I like blonds."

"Yeah? What's your name?" Kim asked him, with dawning interest.

Brian, at the desk, hid a grin of his own. Trust Kim. A new

man every month and never serious about any of them, though no one was more good-natured about a casual relationship or a casual breakup than Kim.

Chase, on the other hand ... maybe not exactly an ice queen, but her clear disinterest served Nighthawk well. A woman, any woman, would be infinitely less able to handle men like these if sex got into the equation. Kim couldn't teach a class like this solo, and Chase could ... or a class of shy beginners, or a survivor's class. Anything but the really little kids; she wasn't great there, but then Tom and Dean were both fine with kids. Chase didn't need to be good at everything, right?

"So, Beautiful, mind if I walk you home?" The students were gone; Kim had waved and grinned and departed on the arm of the big cop she'd picked up halfway through the class, likely spelling bad news for the karaoke guy. The lights were on dim and the dojo quiet. There were occasional sounds from the apartment upstairs, peaceful day-is-done kinds of sounds. Brian leaned on the desk and watched Chase complete her after-class notes, which she did with the same meticulous care she brought to everything.

She glanced up, reserved, but not unfriendly. "It is late."
"So it is."
"If you like, then," she agreed, and shoved papers aside. "I am finished with this, I think. The night will be fine. Spring is a good time for walking in the city."

It was. Crisp spring night, clear sky ... too much light at ground-level for the stars to be particularly brilliant, but a pretty night all the same. The great church on the corner was lit up: Holy Week coming up, and special services offered at odd hours. Most everything else was dark ... a peaceful darkness.

Chase's house was an easy mile-and-a-half walk from Nighthawk, up Grand, past the big shopping center and the much more interesting International Grocery, then a block or two off Grand: a little brick house with a tiny sloping yard in a neighborhood of countless little brick houses with tiny yards, most neatly-kept, with a handful of daffodils and a forsythia or two in most of the yards ... Not in any hurry, they only strolled, enjoying the cool spring night.

"A good class tonight," Brian commented, glancing up at the moon, which was bright and nearly full.

"Yes," Chase agreed, and left it at that.

"All your classes go well, though."

That got a thoughtful look out of dark almond eyes and a composed, "Thank you."

Brian shoved his hands in his pockets. "We've got a lot of business, these days. More than we can handle, really."

No comment to that one.

"I've wondered—" said Brian. "I've wondered if you might be thinking of going off on your own, Chase. Setting up your own business. You could do that. Plenty of clients would follow you. You'd do fine. And Nighthawk—we'd be smaller, a bit less busy. But we'd get by. I wouldn't want to hold you back if you wanted to leave us, you know."

For a while they walked in silence, Tenai not seeming in any particular hurry to answer. The breeze teased, cool, but carrying the scent of magnolias: spring, it said. Spring, and winter's over, but maybe a frost might settle out of the sky tonight and kill the flowers ...

"I had not thought to leave Nighthawk," she said, eventually. And after a little longer, when Brian didn't answer, "I think I will not. You do not desire me to do so, do I understand you?"

"No, no, not at all. But you do understand, Chase, you're not beholden to us. To me. So I'm asking. Are you happy at Nighthawk, then? You think you'll be with us, oh, another five years at least?"

Another sideways look, not covert, not exactly secretive, but by no means open or straightforward either. "Who can know what future days may bring? But yes, I think so."

"You don't want to go off, set up your own business?" Brian asked again, to be clear. "Be your own boss, answer to nobody, make all the decisions? You don't want that?"

A thoughtful silence. "I will stay with Nighthawk," Chase said at last, with finality.

"Ah." And after a few minutes, "I don't want you to feel trapped, or badly treated."

"No."

No. No, she did not feel trapped, or no, she did not agree with Brian's comment? But she said, answering that question, "The world is wide, is it not? I could go—" she waved a hand. "Oh, out, away. I could go and never look back. I could do this. So I am content to stay, knowing I am not imprisoned. You wish to know whether you may depend on my presence for the coming years. I think you may."

"All right." After a moment, Brian added, "Good, then. I have a proposal that may interest you."

One narrow eyebrow went up a little and the look she turned on him was inquiring. For her, that was expressive. Brian took a breath and laid it out. "Nighthawk has more business than we can handle. That's your doing, Beautiful. So here's what I've thought of doing: we might buy that paint store behind us. Buy the building and lot, I mean. Rearrange the building into a second dojo, maybe with a couple of studios in the back. Hire a handful of new assistants and maybe one more instructor, double our number of classes, expand the range of our classes, up our advertising budget for the year ... I've made some inquiries and I'm sure I could get a loan to cover the expense. We could have the loan paid back in four years, I figure, even bouncing your salary up by half. Or we could set it up with you as a partner, not on salary but with a percentage. Got any thoughts on that idea?" Brian waited. His stomach was tight, God, he was actually tense ... it had been a long time since he'd been as excited about an idea. She ought to go for it: why not? She wasn't interested in leaving; she'd said so. There was no reason Nighthawk couldn't be the premier martial arts establishment in this city, maybe in the state: again, why not? They could teach specific disciplines, teach for competition, add more fencing or real knife-work or God knows what to the class schedule ...

If Chase agreed. And meant it. Although surely there would be ways to set things up so that it would take more than one car accident to take Nighthawk out of the running, once they got it up ...

"Do it, if you wish," Chase said. They'd reached her house, and she'd turned at the walk to look at him. Wearing black, with her dark skin, she seemed almost a part of the night herself. The light of streetlamps slid across the strong, unusual planes of her face and cast her eyes into shadow.

"You agree? You think this is a good idea?"

"Yes," she said. "Do it. I will sign a contract ... five years. Salary, I think. Probably you may look for me to stay longer, but I will sign for five years and after that think again about partnership. That is acceptable to you? Yes? Then draw up what contract you wish. I will trust you to be just."

Brian laughed. "Beautiful, only a fool would play fast and loose with *your* good will, and my mother raised no fools. I'll draw up a contract and a plan and ask you to look both over, and if you want a lawyer to have a look also I've no objection at all. You're sure, now?"

"Yes," Chase said calmly, smiling just a little. She stepped back, making a slight gesture towards the house. "Will you come in?"

"God, no, it's damned late, Chase, and I know you like your quiet nights all on your lonesome. So, no. See you tomorrow?"

"Of course."

Of course. Just like that. Just like that. Brian was walking on air on his way back up Grand towards Nighthawk.

3

The show was great: all noise and verve and electrifying energy, exactly what Brian liked. He'd seen Blast! before, so he'd known what to expect. The part that was the most fun was watching Chase, who had not: constantly surprised by the band's crazy tricks, absorbed by their energy and sheer fun ... oh, she got into it, he was sure she did. All that channeled verve: what wasn't to like? Plus she enjoyed the kid's, Jenna's, delight. The dad hadn't come, which was fine, he'd sure have been the outsider in this gang, but the kid had been a student at Nighthawk almost since Chase had come on and fit in just fine. Thirteen, but raised right. Nice kid.

Jonnie had grabbed the seat on Chase's other side and spent as much time watching her as watching the performance, thoroughly distracted. He'd have had more fun if he'd just given up, but try to tell a guy he was being a fool. Dean, next to Jonnie, cast the occasional amused glance at Brian, thinking the same thing. Tom and Kim were simply absorbed by the band.

The theater was great, too: all ornate gilt out of a far more baroque era. Blast! was fun and exciting; the late night air brisk enough to keep energy high and lively for the walk back to the parking lot. They'd parked way down from the theater because walking that far let the crowds clear out, a trick Brian had learned long ago. Chase always liked walking in the city at night, and Brian had known that and deliberately played to it when he chose to park so far away, because why not? Besides, a long walk gave everyone time to talk about the show and laugh over the best bits.

It had never crossed Brian's mind that a party like theirs could possibly run into trouble on that walk. Seven people, dressed nicely but by no means richly, they shouldn't have drawn the wrong kind of attention. Oh, Jonnie wore a thick gold chain, maybe a bit ostentatious; and Kim liked dramatic earrings, and they *were* awfully far from the well-policed area immediately surrounding the Fox. It might have been Brian and Dean together, openly a couple; the wrong sort of people might have underestimated them. Jonnie didn't look like much, not to a casual glance, and that left only big Tom Cox to intimidate would-be attackers—assuming they were too stupid or too inexperienced to really *look* at Chase.

These little punks were exactly that stupid and inexperienced. Five of 'em, street thugs, young punks with attitude ... only five. But two of them had guns. If they'd just had knives or something, the situation would have been laughable. Five stupid punk kids against six martial arts instructors: ludicrous. Brian was aware, distantly, that if they let themselves get shaken down they might very well never hear the end of it, in certain circles.

But there were the guns. And a kid to protect.

"Oh, for God's sake, are you *kidding* me?" That was Kim, rolling her eyes.

Jonnie laughed, partly nervous laughter, but it *was* funny, too. Funny and stupid and dangerous.

"Bri?" That was Dean, questioning, willing to take direction, which was more than Brian could say for Kim.

Tom said nothing, but he stepped sideways, covering Jenna. Solid, that was Tom; solid and dependable.

A little to Brian's surprise, Chase had let Tom cover the kid. She herself had shifted forward just a breath, but, good *Christ*, everything about her was suddenly different. The woman *radiated* blazing, brilliant fury. The first moment Brian had ever seen her came back to him in a vivid half-caught memory, a buzz of terror at the back of his skull, as though she were a wolf or a tiger, something unpredictable and dangerous. The punks were focused on Tom, as though *he* were the one to worry about, with danger pouring off Chase like heat off summer blacktop.

One of the punks jerked his gun a little, in a gesture that was probably meant to look intimidating but only served to mess up his aim, if it came to shooting. But *he* wasn't nervous, not that one; he was too stupid or too damned young to understand that violence always carried risk ... if you picked the wrong target, if you screwed up the game, if the target you picked didn't behave the way you expected. That young punk was a fool: he had realized that the reactions he was getting weren't normal, but it only made him mad, not cautious. *And* he liked violence, Brian could see that. Mean and stupid and armed, not a great combination. The other one with a gun did look nervous, maybe not such a fool, but nervousness armed with a gun was just as bad in a different way. The ones with knives couldn't be ignored. They might not be showing more than knives, but that wasn't proof they didn't *have* more.

"Hellfire and damnation," Brian said, but with a little wry calm-down kind of motion that Dean, at least would respect; and Tom, and probably Jonnie ... the women were more of a question.

"Give us everything you've got and nobody needs to get hurt," said the leader of this little rat-pack, with another silly little twitch of his gun.

"God, who writes your dialogue?" That was Kim again, of course.

"Kim," said Brian.

"Well, God.*"*

They *taught* classes for this ... how to handle multiple attackers, how to handle guns. They taught their students that a targeted victim could surely improve her chances, but risk was always there. Always. Giving stuff up was sometimes the best option. Getting away was always the priority. If the bad guys really meant to kill you, though ... in that case, doing *anything* was always better than doing *nothing*. But this wasn't likely to get that bad. Probably. Maybe. Brian said, "For God's sake, everybody take it easy. We don't want trouble. In case, Dean, two, Kim, twelve, Jonnie, nine, Tom, you stay put, Jenna, stay behind Tom. Chase, just *hold it*."

"Yep," Dean said. Nobody else said anything, but they got it, and giving Kim a job ought to steady her down a bit.

Chase was not paying any attention to Brian at all. She was watching the punks, with a cold steadiness that was not even a tiny bit like fear. God. Even now, clearly, the punk kids hadn't picked up on the danger in that woman, not really.

"Hurry up! Hurry up!" snapped the boss. He picked one target and steadied his aim, picking Kim, not a bit to Brian's surprise, with that mouth on her ... the other kid had his gun pointed at Tom, maybe thinking he was the scary one. Kim was *pissed*. Tom just stood there, like a wall. Jenna stayed still, not panicking, thank God. The wrong kind of bullet could go right through Tom and hit the kid.

"Easy," said Brian, still willing them all to be calm, because once things started happening they'd happen very damned fast and there was no telling who might get hurt. "Listen, we don't have a lot of cash—"

"I've got about a hundred," Tom said, calm as a tree.

"You've got to be shitting me," Kim said, anything but calm. "Come *on*, Bri! Punk-ass kids're *begging* for it!"

"Shut your mouth!" snapped the punk-ass boss kid.

God, he was going to *shoot* her, that was suddenly obvious, although Brian wasn't sure exactly how he saw it. He yelled, "Chase!" and dove for the boss punk himself, meaning to take the kid's legs out from under him and get the gun's aim broken.

Everybody moved at once, on both sides and violently—impossible to track everything—impossible to track *anything*. Guns went off, one and then one more shot, and that was all for the guns, thank God, Brian had *no* idea if anyone had been hit.

He rolled to his feet, looking around fast. Tom was on the ground, on top of Jenna, covering her, could've been hit, but Brian didn't see blood, not yet. Kim had got the knife away from one of the punks, Dean and Jonnie another one, everybody was okay, apparently. Brian himself had put the boss kid down with a really brutal blow that had the boy curled up and puking, and not the least sympathy for him.

Chase had already dropped her first target and had one of the others pinned on his knees in the street, his arm twisted up behind his back at an awkward, straining angle. The kid's neck was totally exposed like that, and Brian suddenly understood that she was going to take that target. There was that dark violence about her, trembling in the air, and God, her first target was *dead*, Brian became aware that that boneless limp sprawl was *death*. And this *other* kid was going to be dead, too, in another heartbeat –

"Chase!" he said, urgently.

Tenai looked at him. Although she was looking straight at him, Brian had no sense that she saw him. Her eyes were blank and opaque, utterly unreadable except for the savage rage behind them.

"No!" he said sharply.

Chase slammed an elbow strike down on the kid's neck, no hesitation, no indication she'd heard Brian or cared if she had. She threw the kid's body down in the street and stalked towards the next in line, which was the boss punk himself, and Brian didn't give a damn for the kid, exactly, but he could hardly stand right here and watch a disarmed prisoner murdered in front of his eyes, no.

Besides, he was terrified of what might happen to Chase herself if she did that.

Jonnie was on his cell, calling for help which Brian was by no means sure he wanted in the way, but it was too late to stop him. Dean had his prisoner flat on the pavement, one knee planted firmly on the kid's back, with his attention all for Chase, and no wonder. Tom had let Jenna up and was getting to his feet himself, looked worried. Not his kind of fight, this one; and Kim was bending over the first kid's body, just figuring out, Brian could see, that that one was dead.

And Brian was standing between Chase and her next intended victim. It was not a comfortable place to be.

"Stop!" he said. "Chase, dammit!" Which didn't seem to slow her at all.

Then Jenna Dodson said, "Tenai! Hey!"

That got a response: a hesitation, some small fraction of the woman's attention. Brian took a step closer to her, even though every instinct he owned was screaming at him to back the hell up. Jenna, eyes wide but definitely not panicking, scooted in between them, and he wanted that even less. He grabbed her shoulder. Chase focused on him, very suddenly, not in a friendly way. He let go of the kid in a hurry, shoved her back instead. Jenna took several quick steps, caught her balance, and said "Tenai! I kinda think we're done here! Stop!"

Chase looked at *her* very differently. Like she knew what, who, she was looking at. Then she looked at the next punk in line. A considering look. Cold as ice.

"I am damn sure we're done," Brian said, going for intensity rather than volume. *"Stop it right there, Tenai."*

She heard him, he was sure of it. She was thinking about it. He could not read those thoughts in the least. He said, with as much force as he could muster, "Dammit, woman, it's not your *right* to go killing bad guys—not when they're already down and disarmed. It's not your *right*, it's not your *job*, and it can get you in a *hell* of a lot of trouble, so back it off, you just back it off, you hear me?"

Tenai said something in a language that wasn't English, a language that by the sound of it ought to have flowed and rippled. In her mouth, it sounded harsh.

"I'm okay!" Jenna said urgently. "I'm okay, everybody's okay,

Brian's right, so stop, just *stop*, okay?"

And that did it. Something in there somewhere did the job. Chase shivered a little and suddenly the woman he knew, sort of knew, was standing there, the killer folded up and tucked away, nearly out of sight. In the distance, sirens swelled. Brian drew a breath, and let it out: *It's over.* And it was. Thank God, it was.

A gunshot cut through the sirens like the crack of a whip, and Chase staggered, caught herself, and went to one knee, a controlled motion, not a collapse. A lot of blood, way too fast, but from that terrifying blankness, her expression became a strange mix of surprise, annoyance, and something very like humor. Brian had barely a heartbeat to see that before everyone moved at once. Tom had already flattened the punk and gotten the gun away from him, but everything else was surely bad enough. "Femoral artery," Dean said sharply, and Kim answered, frantically, "I can *see* that, dammit, gimme your shirt—"

It was, yep, the femoral artery. The big artery in the thigh had been nicked, cut, maybe even severed, which was not good. Chase wasn't going to live, Brian knew that, whatever Kim could do jamming that shirt as hard as she could against the wound.

Chase was now sitting on the pavement, weight braced on one hand, letting Kim hold pressure on her leg. Jenna held her other hand, which Chase permitted. Her eyes were closed. She opened them when Brian bent over her. Her eyes were her own again: dark and secret, but no longer dangerously opaque. "Forgive my stupidity," she said.

Her mouth had quirked upward—she *was* amused. There was nothing funny about any of this. Brian touched the back of his hand to her cheek. She was chilled, bad sign, probably shocky, likely bleeding out right here in front of them. From the sound, ambulances were practically on top of them, but they were all sitting in a widening pool of blood and Brian couldn't imagine the EMTs would be in time. He met the woman's eyes and said, trying to believe it, knowing it wasn't true, "You'll be all right. You'll be fine."

Chase half-smiled, that little wry smile of hers that never let go of a secret and never revealed a thought. "Yes," she said. "I will be. Do not concern yourself, Brian." She turned her head toward Jenna. "Do not be afraid. I will not die."

Jenna, white and shaking, nodded. The kid was trying to be

brave, doing a great job actually, but it was a hell of a lot to ask of a kid her age. Especially when all this blood made it obvious Chase was definitely not going to be fine.

Amazingly enough, Chase *was* fine.

Brian followed the ambulance to the hospital, not exactly to wait for Chase to come out of surgery. Honestly, he expected to wait for word of her death, and he didn't expect to wait long. But he had to go. Who else did she have who was closer to a friend? Except Jenna, who was just thirteen, and the kid absolutely *insisted* on going to the hospital. So, then, no way out of the death watch. Brian left everybody else to give their statements to the cops and then go home. He drove the kid to the hospital, expecting all the time that they'd hear, the moment they arrived, that Chase had been dead when the ambulance got there. No way to pour enough blood into her fast enough to make up for what she'd lost. No way.

He could hardly believe it when the nurse said no, she *was* in surgery. He was even more surprised when the surgeon came out to the waiting room to tell them Chase was going to be all right.

"Absolute miracle," the surgeon said. "Just astounding. But she'll be fine." He smiled at Jenna, who was on her feet, gripping her hands together. "She really will. You can go see her when she's out of recovery. Just a few minutes. She was already waking up."

"How much blood did you give her?" Brian asked, because he could not believe it.

"Buckets," the doctor told him with relish. "Gallons. Just about five and a half units. The most inexplicable things do happen every now and then. Somebody upstairs likes your friend."

"Can we see her now?" Jenna asked, on her feet, looking from the doctor to the door. "Please, we want to see her."

A nurse came in right then to beckon them through the door.

Chase definitely wasn't dead. By the time the nurse guided Brian and Jenna to the right room, she was sitting up, calmly alert, in complete possession of herself, as though nothing had happened. She smiled when they came in—smiled at Jenna. Then she looked past them and nodded gravely, and Brian, embarrassed because he hadn't realized anyone had come up behind them, looked around and stepped to the side.

"Here you are," said Jenna's father, Dr. Dodson. "Thank God." He held out his hand to his daughter, and folded Jenna into an embrace when she came to him. He looked down at her for a long heartbeat. Then he looked up, over her head, at Chase. "Thank you."

"There was very little danger," Chase said softly. "I would never have permitted harm to come to her."

"Of course not." The man was smiling, his expression wry. "Harm to *you* is not okay either, Tenai. Next time, try to remember you're not faster than a speeding bullet."

"Next time, I will be very certain to remember that," Chase agreed wryly. "I was careless, I do confess it. That will not happen a second time."

Dr. Dodson made a skeptical sound and went to sit on the edge of her bed, snagging the treatment orders off the hook at the end of the bed on the way, but still touching the back of his hand to her forehead to check her temperature.

Brian had met Dr. Dodson before, several times—first because the man was a student's father and then casually from time to time as the doctor picked Jenna up, occasionally both Jenna and Chase. Brian had wondered from time to time what kind of relationship Jenna's dad had with his instructor—or what kind of relationship the man might want. But that question was answered, now. It wasn't a lover's attitude the guy had. No. The man came off like he was her *father,* like Chase was a kid of his, a hurt child. That was the vibe between them now, Brian was almost sure of it. Amazingly enough, Chase accepted this attitude as though the man had the right to think of her that way.

Brian moved out of the way. He didn't go far. Lots of chairs here and there down the hallway, not real comfortable, but adequate. Picking one not too close to the door of her room, he settled down to wait.

Dodson came out of the room after a while, not so long really, leaving his daughter behind, Brian noted. Everybody else had cleared out. It was very late. Or very early. Dodson looked around, spotted Brian, and headed over. "Thanks," he said quietly. "For taking care of Jenna. And for taking care of Tenai. It was good of you to stay."

"She lost a hell of a lot of blood," Brian said in his most neutral tone. "I guess the EMTs got to her just in time."

Dodson made a dismissive gesture. "Any blood loss you walk away from. That's not what I was worried about. Jenna says she killed a couple of the people who attacked you."

Brian said cautiously, "It was self-defense. They attacked us first. We had to defend ourselves. They nearly killed Chase, obviously."

They'd all agreed on that, right before the first police and ambulances had arrived: The whole thing had been self-defense. It was pure luck they weren't all dead. Tenai Chase's speed and skill had saved them all—they might be martial arts instructors, but they weren't magic and the bad guys were the ones with guns. She'd nearly been killed.

Dodson wasn't buying it, Brian could see. He really, really wanted to ask a bunch of questions about her past, because if anybody knew, Dodson was probably the guy. But he didn't ask. He wasn't entitled, and he knew it. But he couldn't see any reason this guy was entitled to the whole, unadulterated, undiluted truth either. Brian waited.

Dodson raised a skeptical eyebrow. "I heard you'd offered to make her a partner in your school. I heard you were going to double the size of your business and jump her salary to match. Those offers still open?"

It was a question. It was a damned perceptive question. Brian started to say, *Of course*, and couldn't quite make his mouth shape the off-hand words. *Yes, of course*. But *were* those offers still open? Did he—would any sensible man—want Tenai Chase as a partner after he'd seen the darkness looking out of her eyes? The loan had come through, but no work had been started ... there was time to back out, if he wanted to. Or needed to. Or had to.

Brian shrugged, and managed a smile that felt halfway normal. "Your kid is still in there with her, isn't she, Dr. Dodson? That doesn't worry you?"

"Touché," said the doctor. He gave Brian a little nod. "There'll be a hearing of some sort, I suppose. Maybe even a trial."

"You're a clever man, Dr. Dodson. I bet you'd shine on the witness stand, you being a doctor and all. You can tell everyone it's a miracle she's alive in a very sincere tone, if it comes to that. But let's hope for better."

"Under the circumstances, my credentials are only half a blessing," Dodson murmured.

"Yeah? Oh." The shoe dropped, with a heavy thud. "You're *that* kind of doctor, then. Ah, well, we'll hope it doesn't come to more than a little bitty hearing, then, Dr. Dodson."

In the event, there was only a hearing, and it went fast. It might have helped that Tenai Chase was a woman, and so polite and formal and soft-spoken. It certainly helped that she'd nearly died. The surgeon who'd treated her did indeed sound extremely sincere when he said, "I have never in my life, and I mean never, seen anybody survive after their blood pressure dropped that low. Ms. Chase should be dead. It's an absolute miracle she lived."

Everyone likes a miraculous survival. Plus, of all the survivors on both sides of that incident, only one had been badly hurt and that was Chase. At the time of the hearing, she was still using a cane to walk. It wasn't a fake, either. The bullet had taken out a chunk of muscle at the same time it nicked the femoral artery, and the surprising thing was that she was walking at all so soon, cane or no cane. The surgeon pointed that out, too, enthusiastically. He liked Chase, or he liked the paper he planned to write on her, maybe.

So it came to nothing, in the end. Nothing serious. The surviving punks did a plea-bargain based on their ages and the survival of all their intended victims and drew some stupid light sentence, in the standard fashion, and so there never was any trial at all for anyone ... an outcome Brian at least appreciated. Get it over, get it in the background, and move on, asking no more questions of Tenai Chase, who, in his estimation, would do no one any good at all on a witness stand.

Chase was still a Nighthawk instructor.

She offered, on the day the hearing was concluded, to let Brian tear up the new contract. She appeared in the doorway of his office, her cane in her hand, her calm expression revealing nothing of her thoughts.

"Yes?" said Brian, aware he sounded just a tiny bit stiff.

"The contract I signed, and you signed," she said. She was always direct. "If you have changed your opinion, I would understand. I would release you from that contract, if you wish."

Brian put down the schedules he had been working out, and studied her. Her expression gave away nothing. "Why don't you come in, then, and shut the door?"

She did, wordlessly.

"So, do want me to tear that contract up? Do you *want* to go off on your own?"

"No," she said. Simply. Nothing but that one flat *no*, which was her way. It left a man guessing at everything that might be hidden behind that calm face and that simple word. There might be oceans there, but what kind? And made of what?

"You're a killer," Brian said, to have that straight between them. "I've been an American citizen for thirty-three years, but I've been worse places, and glad I was to get out of them. God bless America, I say, because I've seen worse, and I know a killer when I see one. I knew guys in the IRA, and they were killers; those damned punk kids were killers and I'm not one to shed tears for them; and you're a killer, too, aren't you, Tenai?"

"Not anymore," said the woman. "Not here." No excuses, no explanations, no amplifications.

"Yeah, good. But ... dammit, woman, tell me you're not dangerous to my staff or my students. Tell me you've got that temper of yours on a leash that won't break. Tell me you'll be an asset to my business. I'll believe you. I don't *want* to lose you, do you understand that?"

Chase inclined her head in a gesture almost more like a bow, face impassive. Eyes unreadable. "I appreciate what you say. No one here has the ability to touch my temper. I assure you that is true. Nothing has changed, for me. But ... Tom is unsure of me, now. Jonnie was horrified by that night, I think." She gave that minimal smile of hers, wry and amused and hiding ninety-nine percent of what she was thinking. "Kim is all right, Dean is all right. And you, I do not know. You think more widely, because Nighthawk is yours. So I do not know what you will do."

"You did stop."

"Yes," she agreed, and this time there was a little more intensity to that smooth voice of hers. An intensity and a resonance, as though she meant what she said just a little more than she usually did. "I heard Jenna. Then I heard you. I heard what you said. You were correct. I do not have the right to render justice, here."

It was something. Brian knew, hearing it, that it was a lot. He drew a slow breath, thinking. "You're dangerous," he said eventually. "But not to me. Are you?"

"No."

"If I sent you away ... what would you do?"

"I do not know."

"Streetfight? That'd be a disaster for you, you know, get you in with all the wrong people. Become a mercenary? That'd be worse."

"I would find something," she said calmly.

Brian found that he had relaxed, somewhere in there. He wasn't even sure why. "I'm sure you would, Beautiful, but would I want to be responsible for it? Tell me I won't regret that contract we both signed."

"Not by any action I take," she promised, still with that impassive calm.

"All right, then. You're in. Tom'll come around. Be nice to the poor guy, and I'll have a little chat with him. Same with Jonnie. You surprised 'em, but they'll be all right. That contract's still good. If that's what you want."

"Yes," Chase said. Simply. As always. So that was that.

It was a lot of work, expanding a business. There was the lot to clear and fence off, joining it to the original school's lot; the building to refurbish and re-design ... it had two large rooms, one for display and one for storage; and two little offices; and a tiny lounge and tinier restroom for the employees. The two big rooms could be combined into a single bigger one; the wall between the lounge and the office knocked out to make room for a smaller studio. The other office could stay an office, not being conveniently placed for any other function. So. It was a big job, but a promising one. Money could be saved by knocking out the walls themselves and fixing up the new ones; Tom was good with wood and sheetrock and stuff like that, and anybody could fetch and carry. It was even fun, in a way. So that looked good: the business expansion proceeding almost exactly as planned.

There were new instructors to hire, full instructors—Brian wanted at least one more—and assistants who could be brought on and eventually become instructors themselves, as Tom had, and Kim. A little discreet word-of-mouth around town brought in a trickle of applicants for the instructor's positions. Brian had his eye on some of the advanced students for assistants.

In the meantime, the normal class schedule kept up. A bit hectic, particularly because Brian, not making any particular point of it, made sure he was present for all of the classes Chase taught.

Just to be sure. He *was* sure. But he wanted to be surer.

Nothing has changed for me, she had said. As near as he could tell, that was right. She handled students—beginners, advanced, cops, civilians—with exactly the same impersonal, calm competence, and if she noticed Brian keeping an eye on her, she didn't mention it. He was about ready to admit that no student could possibly kick off that dark violence, and give up worrying about it ... but not yet, not quite yet. Even a month after the incident, the memory was still too fresh.

This class, the early-Saturday class, was winding up. It was a beginner's class, mostly kids, a challenge because, as with all kid's classes, there was a scattering of brats who didn't want to be here, whose mothers were making them come ... they were determined to be bored, and bored kids were a pain in the neck. That wouldn't last. Chase would suck them into the game in another session or two, or just possibly boot them out if she couldn't get them interested, although that was rare. They'd settle down. Brian was already picking out the ones he thought might have a knack, and the ones who would get through with hard work. Both types would do well if they could be persuaded to go on past this introductory class. There was one boy in particular who looked like he was going to shine ...

The bamboo knocker at the top of the door clattered gently, and Brian looked that way, mildly curious because it was awfully early for students for the next class to be arriving. Then he smiled. It was Jenna Dodson. Not here for a class; she was in Kim's Tuesday-Thursday-Saturday class. A social call.

Confirming it, the girl glanced over at Chase and the students working on the mats: her half-experienced eye inspected the students with hilarious solemnity, so like an instructor's attitude Brian couldn't repress a grin. Which she returned when she saw him, waving, and walked over to lean on the desk.

"Hiya!"

"Hi, kid. What can I do for you?"

"Tenai's busy? I thought this class was over at ten?"

"It's gone over a bit, but she'll wind it up soon, I'm sure. You two got plans?"

"Yeah." The girl leaned confidingly close. "It's my birthday!"

"Yeah?" Brian looked her over carefully. "I can tell, I think. Yep. You definitely look older."

Jenna laughed at him. "Yeah, since yesterday! No, the thing is, my dad's buying me a *horse* for my birthday! Isn't that the greatest!"

"It's pretty neat, all right." It sure was. The guy must be planning to board the animal someplace out of town, at huge expense. He must be doing okay, but then, the guy *was* a shrink and Brian was sure that was good money. "Chase gonna go help you admire it?"

"She's going to help me pick it! That was part of the deal. I can have a horse if Tenai helps pick it and teaches me to ride. Which she says is *her* birthday present! It's gonna be great. We're going to go around today and look at horses for sale. Look." Jenna pulled a little notebook out of her pocket and showed it to Brian, ruffling quickly through the pages to show him what they held. Each had either a neatly-printed name and address on it, or an add clipped out of a newspaper and taped to the page. "There're twelve places we're going to look. I bet we'll find a good one *some*place."

"I bet you will. Probably the twelfth place you look," Brian agreed solemnly. "Bet it'll be fun to look at the other eleven, though." Girls and horses, yep, the kid was just at that age, and she probably *was* going to have a whale of a lot of fun. "Don't get so wrapped up in the horse-crazies you forget about us, though, kid. We'd miss you."

"You'd nag me 'til I came back." Another flashing grin, full of joy, and the girl whirled and waved violently at Chase, who was just dismissing her students and strolling over to the desk to do the follow-up paperwork. Her return wave was far more restrained, but her smile was almost as happy. That Chase genuinely loved this kid was blindingly obvious.

In the face of that smile, Brian found the last knot of wariness untying itself in his gut. The woman might be a killer. But that wasn't *all* she was. That wasn't what she was to *them*, and Brian knew that he wasn't going to bother sitting in on her next class. He could relax. And he was damned well going to, and get on with other concerns in life. Real concerns, and not general spookiness over Tenai Chase.

4

Jenna was tired, but in a good way, a done-that, been-there, had-a-great-time-thanks kind of way. It was nearly dark, and the weather had changed abruptly, as often happened in spring: a fine mist was in the air, not enough to really use the windshield wipers, but enough for Tenai to flick them on and off from time to time. It was chilly, but pleasantly so, with a fresh, clean ozone-tang to the air.

Tenai drove as she did everything else, with a kind of absent-minded casual skill that suggested it didn't take much of her attention. When they got home—got to Jenna's home—Daddy would have burgers ready, with cake and ice cream for after, and probably some silly game like Pin the Tail on the Donkey. Tenai would win it—Tenai always won everything like that—but Jenna didn't mind. The real party would be tomorrow. All her friends would be there, with lots more cake and presents and everything. But today had been a perfect birthday. Better than a party.

Tenai might have felt Jenna's gaze, because she glanced over and smiled, her quick, slanted smile, before looking back at the highway. Jenna knew her father thought Tenai was a secretive person. Jenna herself knew better. Tenai wasn't *secretive*. She was just ... *selective*. Jenna turned the word over in her mind, liking the sound of it. *Selective*. Tenai didn't casually share every little thing that came into her mind. She never said anything by accident. She always knew what she was going to say and what effect it would have on anybody who was listening, and she never babbled just *because*.

Jenna admired that effortless self-control. She wished she were more like that. But then, she admired everything about Tenai. Her father had warned her about that. *Don't measure yourself against Tenai, Jen. She's been around. Her life hasn't been easy and she's tough. She's a good model in a lot of ways, but don't try to match her anytime this decade, okay?* Jenna knew what he'd meant. Daddy was real perceptive—too perceptive, sometimes. But he hadn't needed to worry. Jenna had always known Tenai was special.

"Yes?" said Tenai, glancing over at Jenna again, her tone very slightly amused. Daddy wasn't the only one who was perceptive.

Jenna said, "I still like the black mare best."

"You do not. You feel pity for the black mare. That is a different thing."

It *was* different. But— "I still want to buy her."

"She is not healthy. She is not strong enough to ride. I think she will not ever be that strong."

"Yeah, you said."

Tenai slid a wry look towards Jenna again. "The mare is not being badly treated. She is thin, but that is her illness. The stable is not ideal, but it is not filthy or dangerous for the mare. Her owner is not unkind. Is it a riding horse you desire, or do you wish a burden that will ride you?"

"Yeah, okay," Jenna agreed reluctantly. She brightened a little. "How about the pinto mare, then?"

"Her head is pretty but she is not well-trained, nor does she have a good temper. I think not the right horse for a novice rider. And her shoulders are steeply set. I would not like to see her jump downhill with you on her back. I think she would fall."

Outside the car, the mist turned to a light rain, and Tenai turned the windshield wipers on low, slid the car into the left lane to pass a slow truck, and tucked them back into the right lane, in no hurry to get home, evidently. Jenna understood that. The day had been very good. She didn't want it to be over, either. "Well, which one did you like best?"

Tenai smiled. "You will not care for my choice, child. He is not flashy or pretty. Is *pretty* not more important than *good?*"

Jenna groaned, theatrically. "Not the brown gelding!"

"That is a good horse. And his price is good. Everyone else likes *pretty*, too. His head is plain, but he is built well. His gaits will be good. He is small, yes. But you are not tall. You do not need a tall horse."

"He's old!"

"Hardly older than you are," Tenai pointed out, with that sly absolutely-deadpan humor most people missed completely. Jenna laughed. "And fifteen is not old, for a horse. Old enough for him to be steady and experienced, not old enough to be *old*. That horse has good sense. I think you would like him."

"Well, I think I'd like any horse, really," Jenna said frankly. "You liked him the best, really?"

"He is the best. The bay gelding, the Morgan, I think he would do, but he is not so good in the, ah, the foot. The pastern. I think in time he will break down in the front. The red mare with the white feet is good, but young and silly. The brown is the best. Of course," Tenai added, "we did not see all those you marked down. We need not decide at once. We could go again and look more. I would have time next week, if you wish."

"Tell me what you like about the brown one," Jenna requested, and settled back as Tenai, half-amused and half-serious, described a list of virtues that would have impressed anybody.

"Well," said Jenna, "he's kind of boring to look at, but you make him sound really good." "You could persuade yourself to like him?"

"Sure, I guess." Jenna brightened. "He's like a secret, isn't he, because he's good but people don't see it. He doesn't get appreciated like he should be. Poor guy."

"Exactly true." Tenai was amused again, but so was Jenna. She knew it was funny.

"Okay. Let's buy him, then. Daddy will be happy because his price is good. You'll be happy because he's your pick. And I'll be happy because he's *my* horse, and so he's special. When can we get him? Tomorrow? When are you going to teach me to ride him? Can we start that tomorrow, too, before my party? When's your last class?"

"Quietly, quietly," Tenai said, raising one hand in a gesture of mock alarm. "My *last* class tomorrow is not finished until nine in the evening, but I have time after lunch, so yes. Ask your father if he wishes to come. We will borrow a trailer and take the horse to his new stable, and yes, I will begin to teach you to ride him."

"Great!" For a moment, Jenna was silent, thinking about this. "What was his name?" she asked eventually, curiously.

She could picture the brown gelding in her mind. Not too tall, but that was okay. Jenna herself was only just past five feet tall. Tenai was right. Really tall was too tall. Not pretty. But that was okay. He'd let her stroke his face and look into his eyes. He was beautiful, really, because he was a horse and horses just *were*.

"His name is Trooper," said Tenai.

"Yuck."

"You can change it. What would you like to call him?"

"I don't know." Jenna thought about it. She'd had names picked out, names to dream about, but those names were all better suited to flashy black stallions or dainty palomino mares. "Not Brownie or Coco or anything stupid like that. What's a good name for him? Do you have any ideas?"

"No."

"Oh, come on. Sure you do. What was your first horse's name?"

It was raining a little harder now, rain spatting down on the windshield. The sun was not down all the way, but the clouds were heavy and gray. It looked cold. It *was* cold. Tenai looked thoughtful. What was the word? Pensive. She looked pensive. She said, "My first horse? I am not sure I remember," and gazed out into the night like she was seeing more than rain out there. Sometimes she was like that. If you ignored the mood, it went away.

"Sam," Jenna decided.

After a second, Tenai seemed to register this. One narrow, elegant eyebrow went up—Jenna wished she had eyebrows like that, but hers persisted in being thick and straight and too blond. "Sam?" said Tenai.

"He doesn't need a pretty name," Jenna defended her choice. "What's wrong with Sam?"

"Nothing at all."

"Hey, *Samuel Clemens*. That was Mark Twain's real name, you know. We just read Tom Sawyer and Huckleberry Finn in school. Mark Twain's okay," Jenna added, briefly diverted. "I wouldn't mind going on a raft sometime. Anyway, that's all literary and stuff. Samuel Clemens. And Sam, for short."

"Good," said Tenai.

"They say we'll read more Mark Twain in high school." That started a different train of thought. "Tenai?"

She didn't answer out loud, but looked in Jenna's direction briefly. They left the highway, merging seamlessly into the slower city traffic. It would be maybe twenty minutes before they got home. The rain seemed lighter, but probably that was because they were going slower. The air was cold when Jenna, testing, rolled her window down a little. She rolled it back up.

"Child?"

Tenai was the only person Jenna didn't mind calling her stuff like that. Well, Kim called her *kid* sometimes, and that was okay. Most of the people at Nighthawk did. The guys at Nighthawk were okay. Kind of fun, actually. Not like Tenai. But kind of fun. Jenna said, "I start high school in the fall, you know."

"Yes, I understood so."

"That's a different school. Daddy wants me to go to this school downtown, a Catholic school. A girl's school."

Tenai did not seem to know where this line of conversation was going. "I am sure it is a good school," she offered after a moment.

"Well, yeah, I guess." Jenna was silent, rubbing her finger up and down on the arm of her seat.

"You do not wish to go to this school?"

"I don't know anybody there. None of my friends are going there."

"You will find new friends."

"Yeah, that's what Daddy says."

Tenai lifted an eyebrow at her, not dismissively. Thoughtfully. "Is he not right to say so?"

"Oh, I guess so." Jenna paused. "I wish I could just be done with high school. And with college. Done with all that and grown up and free to ... to ... I don't know. Travel. Go places. Start *life*."

Tenai gave this a second, still being thoughtful. Then she said, very seriously, "Jenna, this *is* life, and you are living it. You are too young yet to know how the years rush past, how brief they are, how little they are held back by our desires. You should not try to push the years to turn. The past is gone, out of your reach, and all the things you have treasured in those years gone as well."

Jenna was sure this was true. Tenai's low, somber tone made it even *sound* true. But it didn't really *feel* true. She said nothing.

"You will go to this new school. It will be well. You will find friends there. Bring them to Nighthawk, if you wish. Let them join you there. Would that not please you?"

"Yeah, maybe."

"What else troubles you?"

"Nothing," said Jenna. And then, half-reluctantly, "There's a breakfast this summer at the high school. For incoming freshman girls and their mothers. I thought—I wondered—Daddy could go and that'd be okay, you know, but I wondered if maybe—"

"I would be honored to join you at such an event," Tenai said soberly.

"Yeah? Good." Jenna leaned back in her seat again, happy. A perfect birthday.

Death's Lady

Book 2:

Of Absence, Darkness

1

Daniel's first impression of Tenai's world was of darkness.

They had been at Jenna's college graduation, he and Tenai. Jenna had wanted Tenai to come, of course, so she had taken a day off from her job – easily, now that she was Brian McKenna's full partner and the senior master at his third martial arts dojo. Tenai had been gravely interested in the graduation ceremony, as she was still interested in new things she encountered in her life. She had been smiling a little, pleased by the happiness of the young graduates. She knew a handful of them, of course: some of Jenna's college friends, like Jenna herself, were habitués of her dojo. But nothing could make Tenai look like an ordinary parent or friend.

Daniel had been conscious of the sidelong glances Tenai

attracted – tall, with that unusual bone structure; carrying herself with an absolute physical confidence that was clearly out of the ordinary. No doubt some of the attendees thought he and Tenai were a couple and were wondering how a man like him had attracted a woman like her. The thought hadn't bothered him: anybody with an ounce of discernment was going to be struck by Tenai. Even sixteen years after having built a normal life for herself, she still stopped the eye.

As far as he could tell, Tenai hadn't even noticed the reactions she engendered. Well, she was no doubt used to double takes, and she was focused on Jenna anyway, rising to greet her when the young woman tossed her cap into the air and ran back to them, the sun no brighter than her happiness.

They had been heading back toward the car after the ceremony. Jenna had grabbed his hand and then Tenai's. She had pulled them, linked hand-in-hand-in-hand, into nearly a run. They had been laughing, pleasantly guilty because they were skipping out on the reception. Even Tenai had been laughing.

And now they were elsewhere. The change was jarring, like missing an unexpected stair, only more so. Daniel had been holding Jenna's hand, but his daughter's slim hand was no longer linked to his own: they'd both stumbled hard and lost their mutual grip. He knew he yelped, and heard a shocked little cry of surprise from Jenna. There was ground underfoot, not pavement; he had fallen and caught himself on one knee and the palms of his hands, and it was earth and grass under his hands, not blacktop. The very air had changed: much more humid, warm with a moist heaviness not at all like May. It smelled of growing things. He could not see anything.

A long hand reached out of the darkness, closed on his elbow, lifted him back to his feet, and let him go again. From quite near, Jenna's voice, sounding very young in the dark, a child again instead of her almost-twenty-two, said, "Daddy?" in a tentative tone.

"Jenna?" he said quickly. "Tenai?" He took a step, and stumbled again over the uneven ground. It was not completely dark, he found. It was the contrast between what they had been used to and the place they now were that blinded. Overhead, a half-moon rode through torn fragments of cloud.

"Daddy?" Jenna said again, frightened.

"Hush," said another voice, velvet and dark as the night.

Tenai's voice, but her slight accent had taken on a less familiar edge in this place, unutterably more foreign. "Hush, child. There is no danger for you here. See, here is your father." Faintly visible as their eyes adjusted, Tenai led them together.

Even in the dark, even through his own shock and fear, Dodson felt her anger, burning across the surface of his skin as though he stood too close to a fire. He hadn't felt that for a long time. He said, "Tenai?" again, and his voice shook.

"I am well enough, Daniel," answered that velvet voice. Pale moonlight slid down Tenai's cheek as she turned her face toward him. "I am angry, yes, but I have reason for my anger. I am my own master. Do not be afraid."

"Where are we? Where are we?" Jenna's teeth chattered despite the warmth of the air, and Daniel put an arm around her shoulders and pulled her close. He was terrified himself, and fighting it. It was hard to believe that this was real, and for a moment Daniel even thought that maybe it *wasn't* real, that this was a weird and complicated hallucination, probably they were all still running over the sunlit parking lot, with the car just a few yards away – they would bang into it any minute, and that would jar them out of it – jar *him* out it, probably no one else was hallucinating this way, that'd be a mass hallucination, and too strange for belief –

The night was quiet around them, all of them, Jenna and Tenai and himself. The warm humid air was unstirred by any breeze. It carried living country scents that had nothing to do with a large city.

"Where we should never have come," Tenai answered, speaking to Jenna. "Not even I, and certainly not you. This is my world, and I am sorry that it is unlikely to offer you a fine welcome, child."

"You brought us here?" Daniel asked, leaving aside for the moment other questions, like, *You mean this place is real? You mean that everything you told me was true?* Incredulity ran through him like a tide, and certainty, as strong, that it was true. He stood still, caught for a trembling instant between convictions. At the same time, all the stories Tenai had told him of her long, long life in this world crowded at once into his memory, and for a moment he was so frightened he was close to throwing up.

Jenna broke the moment, by asking in her clear, trusting voice, "But where *is* this place? Your world? Tenai, what do you mean?"

"The land is called Talasayan," Tenai answered her. "Once, it was my home."

She was angry, angry, angry. That was unmistakable. Daniel heard other emotions in her voice as well: grief and loss and something very like joy, in a complex tangle. He asked her again, "Did you bring us here, Tenai?"

For a moment, he thought she would not answer. She walked away a little distance, far enough to be lost in the night, but then she came back again, her arms full of branches. She dropped them on the ground and a moment later, fire caught in the center of the pile, golden and homey as any other campfire, utterly welcome despite the smothering warmth of this night. The fire blazed up. The crackle it made against the too-silent dark was comforting as a blanket. Its light showed Tenai's face more, fine-planed and foreign and not comforting at all. She said, "Not I, Daniel. This was never my intention nor my action."

"Then whose?" Jenna asked. She was still shivering, but not so much now, in the light of the fire. She held out her hands to the warmth as though it offered hope of safety.

Tenai glanced at her, a glance so filled with impassioned anger that Jenna blinked and stared and even took an involuntary step back; probably, Daniel thought, without even knowing she had done so. "Not my friends," Tenai said, and turned away to gather another armful of wood.

"Your – enemies?"

"This is my expectation, Jenna, yes." Tenai stirred the fire with her foot. Sparks flared and floated up into the darkness. She spoke without looking at Jenna, at either of them. "This should not have occurred. I did not imagine it could occur. Someone has done this, and because you were holding my hands, this person has done this to you as well as to me. Now you are here. I am very sorry."

"You're serious? I mean, this is a ... a different world? For real?" Jenna turned in a circle, gazing out into the darkness. "I mean ... for real?"

"Can we just ... go back?" Daniel asked.

"Wait, you want to just go *home*? Without even looking around? Seriously?"

"Jenna ..." Daniel let his voice trail off. He had no idea how to say, *This isn't a fantasy movie. Terrible things happened here. Tenai suffered terrible things here – Tenai* did *terrible things here.* He didn't know how to say any of that without frightening his daughter. He said instead, "Tenai, can't we just go home?"

Tenai was gazing at him. Very likely she knew exactly what he was thinking. She said, her voice soft, "At midwinter. At midwinter I will be able to tear open the veil. I am sorry, Daniel. There are ways to open the veil, but it is not so easily done out of season. It would take great power to tear it open now."

"Someone did," Daniel pointed out.

"Yes." Tenai looked into the sky, at the broken clouds. "Someone made a great sacrifice tonight. A sorcerer poured the blood of that sacrifice out upon the earth for this. I have such skill, but whom should I kill, to gather such power into my own hands?"

"It takes *human sacrifice* to do this?" Daniel demanded, shaken.

Jenna, shocked, said, "You do human sacrifice here? You don't, really?"

"Such a sacrifice was made tonight," Tenai answered. "That is the only way to open the veil, save at midwinter. And the sacrifice must go consenting into the country of Lord Death." Her voice was soft and dark as the night that waited outside the small light of the little fire. "I have enemies. Sixteen years ago, I had many enemies, and no friends at all. What sorcerer brought me across the veil into this land … I do not know. Nor for what purpose, though I may speculate. But I very much doubt this was anyone who meant to do well rather than ill."

Daniel touched Jenna's hand; reassurance for them both.

Tenai went on in the same soft voice. "I think it unwise to linger here. I do not trust the intention of anyone who would reach across the veil to bring me back into this world. That there is no one here to meet me suggests either that my enemies did not know precisely where I would be when I came back across the veil, or that they did not care where I would be. I think they did not care. I think they believe my presence will serve their purpose no matter what I choose to do now that I am here. But I may be mistaken. I think it best to walk away from this place, lest someone searches through the night to find me."

Daniel cleared his throat. "Ah. Ah, won't the fire draw searchers, if there are any?"

"Let it draw all eyes." Tenai's beautiful voice was in that moment chillingly angry, a tone Daniel had not heard for more than a decade. "Nothing would please me more," said Tenai, still in that savage tone. "Let the one who called me know that *I am here*."

Stooping, she buried her hand in the heart of the fire and came up again, holding a handful of flame in her naked hand. It blazed up in her palm, bright and eager and far too real for something that should have been a special effect. Tenai threw her head back and said harshly, "Let the taste of my blood wake the fire from its rest! Let the smoke of this burning carry my name on the wind, to the terror of my enemies!"

Jenna made a small wordless sound, and Daniel hugged her hard. He found he was holding his breath.

Tenai stopped, and drew a sharp breath, and went on in an easier tone, "The feel of the wind, the sense of the night, these tell me no one is very close. We will go at once. We will not be here to meet anyone who comes." She had opened her hand, letting the fire drip back down among the branches and burn in a more natural way. Her hand seemed unmarked.

"Can you ... do magic, Tenai?" Jenna asked, voice high and startled and yet somehow fearless. The shock, Daniel could see, was already leaving his daughter. She liked the idea, he understood. She didn't really believe that anyone could have killed someone to do magic—or she was thinking that most magic couldn't be dark and bloody. The sense of unreality was already leaving her. It still held Daniel, typical of a sudden shocking occurrence, of course, victims of car accidents almost universally reported that it took long, long minutes to believe that the accident had happened to *them*. So this was what that felt like.

But Tenai half-smiled, attitude easing a little more as she answered Jenna. "Sometimes," she said. "Depending on what you would call 'magic.'"

"*Damn*," Jenna breathed. With clear enthusiasm.

Daniel, more wary than his daughter and hearing the hidden constraint in Tenai's voice with an experienced ear, chose not to question any of that, not yet, not now. He asked only, "Do we ... have a place to go?"

Tenai tilted her head back, looking at the sky. They were in the midst of a rocky, open meadow, with scattered trees visible as lacy shadows against a slightly lighter sky. She was silent for a moment, in apparent reverie, but said at last, "The taste of the air, the pattern of the stars, the shape of the mountains against the sky, all these things tell me where we are. We are far north, near

Kandun, hard against the heels of the mountains. Chaisa is not very near here, but neither is it so very far away. We will go there." She offered Daniel and Jeanna each a hand, guiding them to turn away from the fire. To walk away, leaving it burning behind them.

"Chaisa is still your land? After so long?" Daniel thought again of the brutality this world could hold, and shuddered, trying not to let Jenna see that.

"Always mine," Tenai said, sharp and definite. "No one will have laid hand to it. There is safety there. I will protect you, I promise you. And that is no careless promise, Daniel."

Daniel found he believed this. He let his breath out and nodded.

"How far is it?" Jenna asked. She had pulled off her graduation gown and bundled that under her arm; beneath that, she was wearing decent slacks and a dark gold blouse—not entirely suitable hiking attire, but at least she'd chosen flats rather than heels for the ceremony. Daniel's clothing was no more suited for walking a long way across country. He hoped Chaisa was not that far.

"A little way. A hundred and fifty miles, more or less, I think it would be."

"A hundred fifty miles!"

Tenai slanted a quick smile at her. "We will do well enough, Jenna. Your *cars* make it seem a long distance to walk. It is not so far, although a lot of the road is through the mountains. Soldiers would walk that far in seven days. Fewer, perhaps, if the road were good. I would like to find the road, the broad road that lies between the source of the Barun river and the Gos ... although I am not certain we should walk openly on so well-traveled a road. Still, we shall see. There will be smaller roads through the mountains that we may find and use more safely."

There was a road, later. Dirt, but rutted with the evidence of wheeled traffic. Jenna swung along with a long, free stride, but Daniel, already breathing hard and wishing he'd worn more comfortable shoes, was wondering whether he was going to make it a hundred and fifty miles. *Go on without me,* he imagined himself saying plaintively, collapsed in the road. He imagined Tenai's nonplused look and almost managed a smile.

At last they built another fire in a sheltered spot a little way from the road, this one far more discreet than the first. There was even breakfast as the sun came up: a rabbit Tenai had knocked over with a well-thrown stone and gutted with a delicate little pocketknife Daniel had not known she carried. Tenai cleaned the knife on the grass. She did not re-fold it and put it away, but laid it aside by her knee.

Jenna shifted a little closer to the fire. "It smells good."

"Your people are right to say that hunger is the best spice. Rest while the meat cooks. We will walk again after we eat."

Daniel stifled a groan.

Tenai slid a glance his way. "You are not so tired that you cannot go on."

Forcing a smile, Daniel said, "I guess not, Tenai. Jenna, are you all right?"

Jenna looked up with a quick frown. "Sure."

"Of course," Tenai agreed, with a hint of humor. "Certainly you will be able to walk your poor father into the ground with your young vigor. I shall try not to exhaust either of you."

"Jen'll be fine," Daniel said. "I'm the one who's going to have a coronary on one of those uphill stretches." He smiled at his daughter and Jenna smiled back. Her smile was a little stiff. She was worried about him, Daniel guessed, and assured her, "I'm just kidding. I'm not *that* out of shape." He felt *that* out of shape, but he was trying not to show it.

He found Tenai's eyes on his face. She did not speak, but met his eyes, when he looked up, with a wry half-smile and a small nod. Feeling obscurely reassured, Daniel leaned back against the bole of a tree and relaxed, muscle by muscle. It was almost impossible to believe that just hours before they had been sitting on hard-backed school chairs, watching young people file decorously up to a stage to receive their diplomas ... and now they were sitting on the ground in a different, God help them, *world,* watching a rabbit sizzle over a campfire.

Taking the rabbit's liver, Tenai impaled it on a separate sharpened stick and put that over the fire as well. "Enchantment is like ash," she said. Although she was not looking at either of them particularly, Daniel thought she was speaking especially to Jenna.

Taking up her tiny knife, Tenai flicked the blade against the ball of her thumb. Blood welled from the slight cut, vivid crimson drops. Tenai held her hand out over the fire, letting several drops of blood fall into the flames and onto the sizzling liver. The fire blazed up, but died back down before anyone could recoil.

"Fire and smoking blood," Tenai said, "and the will of the sorcerer, imposed on the world: a power bought with pain and sacrifice—the sorcerer's own, or that of another. No magic is without price, and it is all, like ash, bitter on the tongue." She slipped the cooked liver off the skewer, dusted it with ash from the fire, sliced it into two portions, and held it out, flat on her palm. "Liver, which is the seat of memory," she said. "Fire, for thought, and blood, to seal the spell and set my will upon it."

Jenna, her eyes steady on the older woman's face, was the first to reach out. Daniel stopped his daughter with a touch on her elbow. "What will this do?"

"Eat it, if you will trust me," Tenai said, unsmiling, "and find out."

The rabbit's liver was indeed bitter, whether that was the meat itself, or the ash, or the blood. When the last piece was gone, Tenai sat back on her heels. She did smile, then. "Trust is a powerful force," she said, but in a much easier tone. "For a great deal of magic, the sorcerer needs the cooperation of the ... one to be enspelled."

"But what did that *do?*" Jenna asked. "It tasted horrible enough it ought to do *something!*"

Tenai tipped her head to one side. "It ... frees the tongue. You will find that you answer every person in the language in which he speaks to you. A far easier method than I was forced to use, for all you will find that you stumble over some words that do not translate well. Language constrains thought; you will find difficulty expressing some of the thoughts to which you would give voice. Still, you are fortunate to have this spell. Your English was a difficult language for me to learn."

"You couldn't use that ... spell for yourself?" Daniel asked.

"It was your trust that gave the enchantment power. To use the same spell on oneself would require a considerably larger sacrifice, lacking that source of power." Reaching out, she checked the roasting rabbit, and picked up her knife again. "So, my companions. I think you will find this meat more to your taste." She added, deadpan, "It tastes like chicken."

Daniel laughed, startled, and Tenai grinned in return, a quick flash of teeth, and set about disjointing the rabbit.

It didn't take that long to eat this peculiar breakfast, and then Tenai insisted on going on.

Daniel suppressed every protest. If Chaisa offered any promise of safety, then he wanted to get there. He couldn't begin to work out how long it would take a middle-aged man of generally sedentary habits to walk a hundred and fifty miles. Quite a few days, probably.

The land grew a little more wooded as they walked, so that it wound now past numerous small copses of trees. *Mountains* might have been a strong term, but the land was hilly enough that half the time the road ran up- and downhill, uncomfortably steep. The little track met a real road, not wide, but at least closer to level. Every step drove home the reality: this was a *real place*, and it was not America. Or Earth. And yet it did not seem an alien place, either. The trees were aspen and birch and maple, nothing especially strange or remarkable. There was both a sense of the ordinary and a sense of the fantastic in every step, which produced an odd dichotomy of feeling.

This feeling intensified as the sun rose higher. The brightening day lent every tree and grass-blade and rut in the road a solidity that nothing had possessed until the sun created it. It was very quiet, except for the wind through the grasses and the occasional cry of an unseen bird. It was warm enough to be uncomfortable already, promising real heat later in the day.

Jenna swung along with her long-limbed young energy, pointing out soaring hawks and the occasional scuttering lizard, still too interested in their adventure to mind the lack of normal breakfast foods and baths and the other comforts of civilized life. They might have been on a normal camping trip.

Except that vacations were planned in advance and had delineated endpoints. Daniel didn't like to think of the surprise and worry of friends and colleagues when he and Jenna vanished literally off the face of the Earth. They couldn't go back until midwinter, Tenai had said, and from the feel of the air it was now surely the height of summer. Months, then. Well, there would be months to think of some story to explain this abrupt disappearance. It would *take* months, to come up with something plausible. Maybe Jenna could come up with a good story. She read adventure novels. She'd probably be better at it than he was.

Meanwhile ... he really didn't know what Dr. Martin was

going to think when he failed to turn up at Lindenwood on Monday. Or Tuesday. Or at all.

Thinking about his patients was worse. Barbara Ridenour ... Barbara suffered from chronic and deep depression, unrelieved by antidepressants, which for her produced only side effects. Her sister had at last brought her to Lindenwood. At least Barbara had listlessly cooperated, permitting herself to be admitted. Daniel had hoped that he might find a way to help her. Now who would find the time for the protracted, unrewarding work that might eventually commute this woman's suffering? Anne Felton—perhaps borderline, perhaps schizophrenic, with some subtle hints of rapid cycling, Anne didn't trust doctors. She had—the work of months—just begun trusting him. Now he'd vanished without laying any groundwork for his absence. She was going to fall apart. Daniel closed his eyes in pain, imagining this. Perhaps Dr. Martin would pick her up fast enough to prevent too deep a crash.

All those patients who needed him. And he was here.

Daniel could do nothing about that. He glanced up the trail. Tenai walked with a long, easy stride, expression calm and abstracted and closed. Certain she could protect them—or putting on a confident manner so that they wouldn't be too frightened? He couldn't tell. She probably really could take them home again, or she wouldn't have promised that. But not until midwinter. Midwinter! And, all his abandoned patients aside—what might this strange, dangerous country hold for Daniel and his daughter in the intervening months? Would they ever get back at all?

Daniel cleared his throat.

Tenai sent him an unreadable look in response. "Daniel, my friend?"

"What's going to happen?" he asked Tenai, watching Jenna shove her hands in her pockets and stride ahead of them. His heart twisted with love and fear for her. "Do you know? Can you guess?" He tried to smile. "I know when I'm out of my depth, Tenai."

She gave him a serious nod. "Yes," she said. "The great thing is not to let anyone else know it. To smile while you are drowning and trying to learn how to swim. We will go to Chaisa, my friend, and draw its walls about us in safety until I can tear open the veil again and send you home. I have every hope that this will be a simple exercise."

"And your enemies will wait for all that."

"I do suspect the intention was only to bring me back, and let my very presence act in some way to fulfill their will. If that had not been so, if my enemies knew where I was and wished to take me up, I think we would have met them before this. I have every expectation I will indeed be able to bring you to Chaisa. The distance is not so far. Unless an army lies between, I think I can bring you there. Once I have had a chance to set myself there, not even an army would be glad to assault me."

She added a moment later, "However, bandits on the road, ignorant of my name, may be less wise. Jenna!"

There was time to call Jenna back, time for Daniel to catch his daughter by the hand and throw a panicked look at Tenai.

She seemed quite calm. The men she had spotted, a dozen or so men mounted on horses, had gotten quite a lot closer in those few minutes. They spread out a little as they came, and picked up the pace of their approach. Several of the men called out, whoops of delight that were not at all reassuring. One man with two women, all on foot and no one armed—the approaching band saw no threat there. It was perfectly clear what they wanted. The creaking of saddles, the jingle of bits, the thud of hooves on hard-packed earth: all ordinary sounds, but carrying extraordinary menace. Everything seemed to be happening very slowly.

Daniel said, "Tenai—"

"Only stand here and be still," Tenai told him. "You will be safe, I promise you. After this, we will have horses, so that will be useful." She looked carefully at Jenna, touched the young woman's shoulder. "Have no fear," she said. "If men come past me—as they will not, but if it should happen—then trust your training, my child. You have been well taught. Defend yourself and your father. Yes?"

"Yes, yes, I will!" agreed Jenna. She was up on her toes, her eyes wide with terror and excitement.

Tenai nodded and walked away from them, toward the bandits. Tall as she was, she seemed tiny against that whole mass of men and horses. Her hands were empty. She was not even holding her little knife.

The first man to reach her had a sword naked in his hand. He did not strike at Tenai, but reached with his other hand to grab her. Daniel did not see what happened; it was too fast. The man was on the ground, sprawling, and Tenai was in the saddle, with his sword in her own hand. She no longer looked tiny. The other riders kept coming, but Tenai gathered the horse with experienced hands. It spun in place, half-staggering as it reared. Tenai balanced it with hands and legs and leaned far forward, shouting, her voice high and piercing. The animal came back to the ground and lunged forward, surging into a charge against the rest of the riders.

There wasn't even time to think again that Tenai was far too outnumbered, that she couldn't possibly beat back so many men. One man hurled himself to meet her; Tenai's sword swept down and across, cutting across the man's chest. He fell, not screaming: dead, or at least too badly hurt to scream. Tenai's horse flung its head up and leaped over the toppling body, and Tenai swept her sword around without looking to block a crossbow bolt. It shattered against the blade of the sword.

That was impossible. All of this was impossible. Maybe Daniel hadn't seen what he thought he'd seen.

Jenna hid her face against his chest for a second, and then looked back at the fighting as though she could not look away. Daniel knew how she felt. He felt the same way. Ten seconds into this battle and he already knew that *battle* was the wrong word. This was a *slaughter*. Half of the outlaws were already dead, and Tenai was untouched. There was blood on her hands and arms and face, but Daniel was fairly certain that none of it was hers and completely sure that if she took any wound, it wouldn't slow her down.

Her face showed both savage rage and a kind of dark exaltation. She looked like a Fury, like a dark Valkyrie, like nothing human. As Daniel watched, she tossed her sword up in the air, caught it by the blade in front of the hilt, and flung it impossibly hard, like a spear, at a man who was running for all he was worth for the brush at the side of the road. It slammed into the man as he fled and knocked him flying into the shelter he had tried to reach— impaled back-to-front through the torso, and, *God*, Daniel hoped he was dead, but he heard the man's gasps, nearly screams, from thirty feet away.

Tenai did not even look to see that the man had fallen. Her horse tucked back on its haunches and spun, and there was a knife in her hand from somewhere, not her tiny pocketknife, but a dagger as long as her hand. She hurled her horse forward at a tight group of three men with crossbows.

They did not break, not quite. Tenai and her horse were the target of three bolts at once. The horse went to its knees, screaming in a high-pitched voice for all the world like the voice of a little girl. But Tenai was no longer on its back. She had dropped off and left it. She'd been struck in the chest by one of the bolts, but she simply wrenched it out, not even changing expression. That crossbow bolt ought to have taken her instantly out of the fight; from the angle and placement and depth of that injury, it had obviously hit her lung. But she didn't fall. She didn't even slow down. She no longer held the knife. Daniel hadn't seen her throw it, but after a second, as one of the bandits crumpled, he realized it was standing in the man's throat. Tenai had a crossbow in her hands now, with the previous owner of the bow dead at her feet. She shot a man, rewound the crossbow and shot another. No one even returned fire. They were trying to run, that was all.

Tenai was not going to let them go. She had caught another horse, this one smaller and faster than the first; and she had found another sword, snatched up from the reddened earth of the road, and another half-dozen crossbow bolts retrieved from a dead man's body, and the few remaining men didn't have enough of a head start to matter. She jumped the horse neatly over one still-twitching body and shot a man scrambling into the trees, then bypassed a groaning man bleeding out from the stump of his leg and rode down the last, who struggled with a horse in the middle of the road. He fell, screaming, and she reined her own horse about and ended his screams with a short thrust of her sword. For a moment Daniel saw her face, before she turned her horse again, and she looked cold and focused and furious, all at once.

"Oh, my God, oh, my God," Jenna repeated, too stunned to know that she was speaking; and Daniel tucked her close to his body and just held her, tight. Almost twenty-two was much too young to have to see this kind of blood and violence. Hell, fifty-two was much too young to have to see this.

The road had become a battlefield, and a charnel-house. The bodies of men and horses lay scattered, blood clotting on the ground. Flies were already gathering, a muted hum quite audible from where Daniel stood with his daughter. Wounded men groaned and screamed, horrible sounds. The smell, of blood and ruptured bowels, was worse than the sounds.

Quite near, someone moaned, and then screamed, a raw, weak

sound. Jenna pressed close to her father, flinching. Daniel held her tightly and looked for the injured man, dreading what he would see.

A man knelt by the side of the road, half concealed by the carcass of a horse. He faced them, about thirty feet away. He was not the one that had cried out, although there was blood on his face and his chest. He supported another man, hardly more than a boy, across his knees. It was the boy's blood and the boy's voice they had heard. A crossbow bolt stood up from his stomach and another from his chest. His face was bloody, and Daniel, in the relative quiet, heard the wet sound of his breathing and knew that one of the bolts had pierced a lung. Unlike Tenai, he was not proof against such injuries. The older man cradled the younger, murmuring too quietly for the words to be distinguishable.

Daniel shifted, thinking that he should go look at the wounded boy, reluctant to move. His daughter, shaking, clung to him. Nervous horses wandered among the trees at the edges of the road. The dirt surface of the road reddened as great pools of blood soaked into the earth. Flies hummed. From the trees a crow, first on the scene, called harshly.

Tenai returned, her horse's hooves raising little puffs of dust from the road, except where they squished in the blood. She had not gone far. None of the fleeing men had gotten very far. She rode now through the carnage without sparing a glance for the tumbled bodies, except for the briefest pause to finish a groaning man whose intestines were spilled out across the road. Her arms, her hands were covered with blood. There was blood in her hair and in the mane of her horse. It did not seem to trouble her. There was a hole in her shirt where she had torn out the crossbow bolt. That injury didn't seem to trouble her either. She was not looking at Daniel or his daughter. She was looking past them, at the man who held the wounded boy. As though pulled by that pitiless gaze, the man raised his head and looked back.

Tenai rode toward him, in no hurry. Her sword dripped blood. The sun was at her back. Daniel could not see her expression. The man had none. His face was set and blank.

"Emel," the boy said, choking a little. "Emel."

The man said gently, "Hush, boy. You'll be well enough." His voice was deep and harsh, not quite steady. He tipped the boy's head against his chest, so that the boy would not see Tenai approach, then looked up at her with resignation as she drew up her horse. She sat on the horse, her sword slanted across her thighs, and studied him, not speaking.

The man said to her, in his deep, gritty voice, "He will die in a very little, Nolas-Kuomon. Will you not wait?"

"What is this man to you, that you should care for him?" Tenai's own voice, inexpressive, held neither anger nor even any perceptible interest. If that bolt really had hit her lung, there was nothing to show it. It would have been easy to think he'd hallucinated her being struck by that crossbow bolt, except for the hole in her shirt. Besides, Daniel knew what he'd seen.

"Nothing," said the man. He continued to hold the boy's face turned away from Tenai, with her bloody hands and her sword and her pitiless eyes. "A boy. A companion of the road. Should one die alone, when one can die under the eyes and hands of a companion?"

Tenai backed her horse a step, her hand light on the reins. "I do not care," she said. "Do as you please. But put me to no trouble, man. Do you understand me?"

"Nolas-e," answered the man, bowing his head.

Tenai came to Daniel, leaving the horse with its reins dragging on the ground. Jenna was quiet, with the quiet of shock. Daniel had no idea what his own face showed.

"You are well?" she asked him in a low voice. Daniel, searching her face, saw the echo of black rage. But she was calm now, or at least she seemed calm. Looking at her, looking at the carnage she had made out of a dozen armed men, he could not believe what Lindenwood had thought it held. Probably Brian and the other martial arts people would have been less shocked.

Patient, Tenai asked again, "You are not hurt?"

"No," said Jenna, and cried, "You killed them all!"

Tenai answered, without anger or impatience, "Your world is so gentle, is it? No one dies there?"

"Not like that," Daniel answered. "Not for most of us—not in my life. Or Jenna's. We don't see—" His voice shook, and he stopped, tightening his arm around his daughter's shoulders. She leaned against him hard.

Tenai lifted one shoulder in a tiny shrug. "Battle is difficult, perhaps, for those unaccustomed. But spare them no pity," she added, speaking directly to Jenna. "Or pity them, if you choose; that's well enough. But they would have killed your father and used you as their common toy, if they had overpowered you. As they would, had I not been standing in their way. All the men would have been at you. If you lived, you would have been kept to please the men, or sold to a river-house."

"I will pity them anyway," Jenna said, with admirable dignity.

"Gather the horses," Tenai told her. "Tie them over there, where the ground is clean. They will be frightened and hard to catch. Can you do this?"

"You don't have to, sweetheart," Daniel said swiftly.

"It's all right," Jenna said, and picked her way into the woods after the nearest.

"A task to do is better than quiet," Tenai said to him, not without pity of her own. "Being brave for frightened animals is better than being fearful by yourself. And you, Daniel. Gather the dropped bundles, if you will, and assist your daughter to catch the horses. I will ask you stay in sight. Will you be well enough?"

"I'm fine. But that boy—I should look at him—"

"He will die. There is nothing you can do now."

"I could at least look—"

"Daniel," Tenai said, lifting her hand to stop him. "He is at the very Gate. He has one foot already on the other side. There is nothing you can do."

"All right," Daniel said. He knew it was true.

"Take what you find back where the earth is clean. And keep your eye on Jenna. She is the one who may profit from your care now."

"And you?"

"I?" A moment of incomprehension. Then an ironic tilt of the head. "The crossbow bolt." Tenai sounded as though she had forgotten about that entirely. She lifted a hand to the long rent in her shirt. Then she shrugged. "Never fear for me, Daniel. The injury is nothing. Lord Death will not lay his hand upon *me*. He does not trouble himself over cuts and bruises, but mortal injuries he lifts aside at once."

"I—all right. But I—" Daniel thought it was going to take some time to accept *any* of this.

"You will do well enough," Tenai promised him.

"I guess so. I hope so." He rubbed a hand across his mouth. "That man. The one who isn't dead. You're going to kill him?"

"Certainly."

A chilling indifference in that casual answer. He said carefully, "Will you please not? I don't think I can take it. I don't want Jenna to see you do it. And ... I would prefer ... may I say, as a friend, that I wish you would show mercy to an enemy, even if he doesn't deserve it?"

A pause. One that stretched out.

Jenna had caught one horse, and another, leading them to the side of the road and tying their reins to branches. She avoided going among the bodies, keeping her eyes resolutely on the horses. Daniel didn't watch her. He was worried about his daughter. He was worried about himself too; he felt seriously off balance. But he kept his eyes on Tenai's face. A thoughtful expression had seeped into her eyes in place of that chilling indifference. "I cannot set a brigand loose to prey on travelers. But as you ask it, Daniel, I will consider what other choices I might have."

Daniel let out a slow breath. "Thank you."

A small, curt nod. Tenai walked away. She found a water flask tied to somebody's saddle. She washed the blood off a horse's shoulder and inspected the deep cut that ran across its neck and withers. The horse stood still under her firm touch. Tenai went through saddlebags, found the tools she needed, and began to stitch the cut.

Before she was finished, the surviving brigand lowered the body of the boy to lie back on the earth, got to his feet, and came slowly toward her. She glanced at him, and he stopped, but then came forward again when she did not move. He was not armed, so far as Daniel could see.

Tenai finished with the horse and turned to face the man, crossing her arms over her chest. She tilted her head to the side. Sardonic. Cool. Remote. She was not quite as tall as the man, but somehow seemed taller. If Daniel hadn't known her ... he hoped he did know her. He thought he did.

The man went to one knee on the rocky ground, resting his hands on his other knee. He was a thick-set man with shoulders like an ox. His long hair and short ragged beard were dark. He didn't move like an old man. Probably still on the right side of forty, Daniel guessed. He was dark-skinned, but not as dark as Tenai: his complexion might have been the result of a deep tan. His eyes were an almost golden brown, the color of dark honey. His appearance was powerful, the bones strong and even harsh in his face. Although he looked nothing like Tenai, Daniel could see that there was somehow a certain cast of features they had in common.

"You have been a soldier," Tenai observed, studying this man. It was not a question.

"Years ago, Nolas-e."

"How is it that you came to be riding with these curs?"

The man risked a glance up, then dropped his gaze to the ground. "Nolas-e, there was trouble in my company. I killed an officer. I did not want to die for it, so I ran away."

"And thieved for your bread."

The man's mouth tightened, but he said only, "Yes, Nolas-e. I came to that."

"And now, do you still not want to die?" she asked him. "Even now?"

There was a slight pause. Then the man said, "Yes, Nolas-e. I would rather live, if you will have it so."

"So you would neither lift your sword against me, nor run."

The man looked up again. "Well," he said, his deep voice almost apologetic, "Sixteen years ago, I was at Antiatan. I knew you at once, Nolas-Kuomon, when you laid your hand to sword."

A pause. Finally Tenai said, "I happen to have need of a servant. You may therefore serve me, if you choose."

Daniel sighed in relief. That wasn't a solution he had seen—he didn't know enough of this world to guess what possible solutions existed. He'd sort of thought of tying the man up and reporting him to the authorities, though, yes, that had probably been an unrealistic idea. He couldn't exactly imagine this man as anyone's *servant*. But whatever Tenai had in mind, this was far better than watching her carve the man up in cold blood. Far, far better than *Jenna* watching her do that.

The man ducked his head. "Nolas-e."

"What is your name, man?"

"Emel. Emelan, Nolas-e."

"Only that?"

"I would not ask any family to own me, Nolas-e."

One eyebrow rose. "Well, I should understand that. Emelan, then. Do you fear me, Emelan?"

"Yes. Nolas-e."

"So you should. Will you serve me?"

A slight hesitation. Then the man bowed his head again.

"Yes," he repeated. "Nolas-e."

"Drag the bodies out of the road. Find a sword for yourself, and one for me, better than this." She waved a dismissive hand at the sword she had stabbed into the ground a few feet away. "Get the coin and any decent food and bring it to me. Also anything else I might wish to see."

"Yes, Nolas-e." The man waited a beat. Tenai, ignoring him, went back to caring for the horse. The man gathered himself to his feet and backed a careful step back, then another, before he turned to go back to the scattered bodies.

"We will go on from this place as far as we may before dusk," Tenai stated, not quite looking at Daniel. "We should not like to sleep near this place, I think. There will be no need to hunt, if the food we find here is acceptable. I think we will ride until full dark. I would like to get closer to the mountains, if we can go so far."

Daniel nodded. "That sounds good. Thank you, Tenai. I mean … thank you."

A cool, dismissive nod. But she had become … at least somewhat familiar once more. More the woman he'd known for sixteen years, and less the terrifying figure out of history, Nolas-Kuomon, who savagely dealt out a death she had long ago given up for herself.

2

The road did not seem the same after that. The world did not seem the same. It was hard to believe that just an hour ago they had walked along as freely as though out for a simple hike, that only a day and a night ago they had been innocent of the smell of blood and the screams of dying men. Jenna did not chatter now, nor point out the occasional flutter of a bird. Her new constraint was almost painful to Daniel. He couldn't think of anything to say to break the silence. Nothing useful. Nothing even possible.

They all rode horses, unkempt scrawny-looking animals. That was a distraction, at least. Especially for Daniel, who barely knew how to ride and had his daughter to thank that he could stay on at all: Tenai had taught Jenna, and Jenna had made him learn well enough that he could go on the occasional trail ride with her. At first he was glad to sit in a saddle and save his feet. Then the saddle grew uncomfortable, and at last painful—acutely so, after the first couple of hours. Daniel tried to stretch his knees out without losing his stirrups and gritted his teeth against any complaint.

Jenna, on the other hand, loved horses and could go all day without a twinge. Probably she was missing her own horse, a brown gelding Daniel had bought her for her fourteenth birthday, though she said nothing about it. From among the outlaws' horses, Tenai had chosen for Jenna a small mare that would be pretty once she was in better shape. The mare had obviously been badly treated for a long time. Fresh cuts and old scars from spurs and whips marked her sides and hips. Jenna was a good rider and loved to be needed. She handled the mare with the gentleness she would have shown any injured creature.

Tenai herself rode a tall bay mare, which, Jenna assured her ignorant father, was a really good horse. She rode in front, pressing them all with a cold disregard for any discomfort or weariness, seldom glancing back to check on them. Or perhaps with a considered intention to exhaust them all past dreams. Daniel, though he longed to stop, would not have argued with that.

The native—the local—the ex-brigand, Emelan, rode a little behind the rest, and a little to one side. He led a spare horse as well. From time to time, Daniel glanced back at him. The man rode most of the time with his eyes fixed on his horse's ears. Once, Daniel caught his glance, and the man dropped his gaze immediately. Plainly he feared Tenai. Just as plainly, he did not know what to think about her companions.

They made a camp in the dark, as Tenai had said. Daniel dragged his leg over his horse's rump and clung to the saddle to keep from collapsing to the ground as he dismounted. His effort to be subtle didn't fool Tenai, who came over to take his arm and help him sit down by the fire she'd already started. "It is hard for you," she said. "I am sorry."

"I'm all right," Daniel said. "I'm too old for this, I suppose." Not that he'd ever been up for a trip like this, even in his thirties. "I'll keep up. You set whatever pace you think is best."

"I will. I must. I am sorry for it, Daniel. I promise you, it will become easier for you in a few days. And I promise you as well, you may rest once we are in Chaisa."

Daniel—though he wanted to wail *A few days?*—nodded without comment and gingerly stretched out his legs. Ow. With luck he wouldn't need to move again for a long, long time. He felt he could quite easily sit right here without moving for several days. Or lie here. A blanket would be nice, though. He glanced up and tried to smile as Tenai brought him one. It had been claimed from the outlaws and was none too clean, but it was softer to sit on than the bare ground.

There was just enough moonlight so that everyone else could go about the necessary tasks. Tenai and Jenna unsaddled the horses and took them to a small stream to drink, while Emelan began to cut up dried meat for soup. The outlaws had contributed bowls and spoons as well as a couple of small pans, which, like the blanket, were not very clean. Jenna, discovering with loud disgust that there was no soap, washed the dishes and pans in the cold water of a small stream near the camp. She scrubbed them with a handful of grass and only then let Tenai show her how to make soup out of dried meat and almost nothing else.

Daniel was exhausted. Jenna was in better shape, but, though she did not fall asleep over her soup, he suspected that she was, like him, running on nerves and not much else. As he looked at her, she yawned and covered her mouth belatedly, looking embarrassed.

"Sleep, if you will," Tenai told her. "Dawn will see us on the road again."

"Should ... one of us keep watch?" Daniel wondered. He was glad—deeply relieved—that Tenai had spared that one outlaw. But he would have been a lot more comfortable with the man locked up somewhere, not sitting a few feet away. Besides, who knew what other outlaws might be out there in the dark? Or wolves, maybe. Or dragons; he had no idea. Or, probably more likely and possibly more dangerous, whatever unknown enemies had pulled Tenai back to this world.

Tenai made a dismissive gesture, appearing wholly unconcerned. "I will watch." She smiled suddenly, a narrow, edged smile, but with real humor. "It will not be the first night I have spent sleepless, I assure you. I, too, will rest at Chaisa."

Daniel hesitated another minute, and then sighed. "All right. Good night, Tenai." He picked up another blanket Tenai had dropped near him and tossed it to Jenna, hoping it did not harbor fleas from its previous owners. "Go to sleep, kid."

Jenna didn't argue, but Daniel himself, though he lay back and pillowed his head on a saddle, found that not only did every muscle he owned hurt, he also could not close his eyes without seeing screaming men and flashing swords. He stared into the fire instead.

"The shock will fade, in time," Tenai murmured. She was sitting near him, her back turned to the fire, her head bent a little. The firelight drew a high-angled cheekbone out of the dimness, the arch of a winged brow: bits and pieces of her face, lacking all expression. "The strangeness of events troubles you, I know. That will ease as you become more familiar with this land."

Daniel made himself smile. "Yes, I know."

"Of course you do, Daniel."

"Are *you* all right, Tenai? I know ... that is, it must have been a shock for you, too. You didn't expect to ... ever come back here, did you? Or did you?"

She turned her face away. Firelight slid down the elegant line of her cheek and jaw, and he thought again that she looked foreign. Out of place. But she wasn't. Not here. This was her world.

She also looked, and was, very dangerous. The tension that in recent years had eased out of her body was visible now. She said, "Memory plagues me. I have no doubt I am not alone in that. I meant to wait a hundred years, until memory faded from this land. Then, once I had passed out of the memory of living folk, perhaps I might have returned across the veil."

What an incredible thought. Yet her tone was perfectly matter-of-fact. "Would it help at all to talk about ... anything?"

"Not now. No. Do not press me, I do ask you. This is not the time." Tenai glanced away, out at the dark, and back to Daniel. She said, tone somber, "This night echoes too many of my memories. There are too many paths I do not want my thoughts to turn down, not tonight."

That seemed very understandable. "All right."

"Rest, if you can. I trust God will grant you gentle dreams. I will watch. Have no fear. Rest."

Daniel sighed, leaned his head back against the saddle, closed his eyes, and was gone, out, like that.

It seemed like just a moment later that Tenai was waking him with a touch to his shoulder, but a bleary look around showed the traces of dawn on the edges of the mountains. His daughter was up, and busy—making tea, her attitude cheerful, undoubtedly for his sake.

Emelan was saddling the horses, silent, as he had been silent all the previous night, watching all that went on and volunteering nothing of his own.

Tenai brought Daniel a cup of tea and a piece of the hard biscuit the bandits had carried. She sank down to sit on her heels at his side as he pried himself, groaning, off the ground, and met his eyes with a direct look. "Are you awake, Daniel?"

"More or less," he muttered, taking the tea and wishing desperately for coffee. But at least the strong, astringent tea made his mouth taste cleaner and took the fuzz off his teeth.

"If danger will come at our heels, it may come so early as today. Men with bows, disciplined men, I would fear that. Men seeking me, I would fear that. I would not be able to take such men unawares. It is unlikely I should myself be put in danger, but it would be hard for me to defend you and Jenna."

Daniel looked at her. "Now I'm awake."

"I should know it, if such a company were to approach. There are options. We might outdistance them or avoid them; I might send you on ahead and ride back to face pursuers. They would not wish to face me, unless they were very unwise. A great deal would depend on the specific circumstances, which cannot easily be anticipated. For your safety, for the safety of your daughter, you must be prepared to obey me at once if there should be danger. May I expect your obedience, my friend? I do not ask this lightly."

"I assure you, Tenai, if it comes to danger, then I'll do anything you say. And I'll speak to Jenna, if you haven't yet."

Tenai nodded. "Please do that, Daniel. Your trust is a treasure beyond price. I shall hope not to test it too far. Also, I have told the man Emelan, if I should be forced to send you ahead of me, he is to go with you, and protect you, and guide you to Chaisa. He will obey me, I think. My name will gain you respect and shelter there."

"Can *he* be trusted?" Daniel didn't believe that for a second.

Tenai smiled, a slight curve of her narrow mouth. "This is a man who was at Antiatan. He will not lightly disobey me. Only if he is certain I am dead need you fear him—and he will know very well that I may step into the kingdom of Lord Death and out again. No, he will do as I bid him. He was not born a cur on the road. This man remembers better manners; clearly so, or I'd not have him near you or Jenna." She stood up. "You should get up, stretch, walk a little. It is a long ride we will have today."

The fire was smothered, the cups put away, the gear stowed. Tenai gave Jenna a leg up onto her little mare, and then came over to help Daniel heave himself up into his own saddle. All the muscles that had complained the previous night screamed anew. Daniel set his teeth and pretended he was fine.

Even the previous afternoon, unpleasant as it had been, had not prepared Daniel for the unrelenting torture of an all-day ride. Tenai, expressionless, began to schedule more frequent rest breaks as the day stretched on. This did not help. Nothing, he thought, would help except stopping long enough to allow abused muscles to rest. Say, a week. Somewhere with a hot tub. Which was not going to be provided anytime soon. And, just to finish things off, not only was the heat uncomfortable, but Daniel could also tell that he was picking up a nasty sunburn on the top of his head and ears.

But Tenai did not suggest halting for the day, and Daniel did not protest. He thought about who-knew-what enemies possibly searching for her, and didn't say a word.

Jenna didn't complain either. Sometimes she rode next to him, darting occasional worried looks his way, so that he couldn't even groan when he tried to change position. It was better when his daughter rode next to Tenai. Jenna wanted to know all about this world, which was perfectly understandable. She asked about the land, about the trees and animals—no dragons, apparently, but occasional wolves—and about ancient history. The Martyr's life and death made a fascinating, disturbing story.

Somehow Jenna had figured out that she shouldn't ask about Tenai's own personal history; that nothing about the past four hundred years was fit for casual conversation. Daniel wasn't even sure how she'd caught on to that. Something in Tenai's manner, maybe—or in his own.

At last Tenai let them all stop for a real rest. The trees were closer together in the country they had come to, almost a real woods. Tenai had stopped them in a meadow by the banks of a stream. "We will eat and rest," she said, "and then go on for a little, I think, once the moon has risen. The horses should rest, also. Emelan, unsaddle them and slip the bits. Check their feet."

The man bowed his head and went to do that, while Daniel just managed to stop himself uttering a low moan at the thought of going farther in a mere few hours. Jenna was beside his horse, offering him a hand down from the saddle. Daniel, beyond pride, accepted his daughter's help to dismount and stagger a few paces away to a nice flat place where he could let himself collapse.

Tenai came over and knelt down beside him. He was grateful that she refrained from comment about his condition. She said instead, "We have adequate food, but fresh meat would be welcome. I will hunt a little, I think. I will look at what lies around us, listen to the wind, see what messages it carries. Make a fire, if you wish, but have a care for the smoke."

Daniel levered himself up enough to lean against the saddle Jenna brought him for a backrest. "You don't think anyone is about, then?" he asked, trying to be interested in the answer. At the moment, that took real effort.

"I think not. I will not go far."

"There aren't many people on this road," Jenna commented, with a diffidence unlike her.

"Fewer than I would have expected," Tenai allowed. "But this land is less crowded than yours, and we are far from the most frequented ways. I would not expect our luck to hold for very much longer, but we shall see. We shall see. Make tea, Jenna, and rest."

"All right," Jenna agreed.

"I will be back in a little time." Tenai walked into the woods and vanished from sight without a breath of sound.

Daniel looked warily at Emelan, but the man kept his gaze down, mending a frayed bit of tack. Occasionally he glanced up, at Jenna, or Daniel. When he happened to catch Daniel's eye, he looked away again immediately, letting his long hair shield his face. Apparently Tenai was right that he was no threat now—that he was too afraid of her to be a threat. While Jenna made a fire and laid out supplies—a pan for tea, a few pieces of dried meat, more of the hard biscuit—Daniel massaged his legs. It didn't help.

Tenai came back out of the woods about an hour after she had left. It was sunset by that time, with the western sky gone crimson and purple over the mountains. Her step as she returned was so quiet she did not even startle the horses. She carried a small wild turkey by the feet. With her angular face and dark coloring and arrogant grace, she looked like some Hollywood producer's idea of Pocahontas. A whole lot less cute and cuddly than the Disney version, though.

She gestured Emelan back down when the men would have risen, tossed him the bird, gave her crossbow into Jenna's hands, and came over to clap Daniel on the shoulder

"All peaceful, all peaceful hereabouts," she said. "I find no trouble near us. We will take the time to cook that bird, I think. By that time it will be moonrise, with light enough to keep to the road. Are you rested? Are you well?

Daniel grimaced. "I guess I can stand it."

Tenai smiled. "You will do well enough. The stiffness will ease in another day or three."

She seemed to think this was comforting. *It's only pain,* Daniel remembered her saying, and something about how you accept it and it passes. He tried, not very successfully, to capture this feeling for himself.

Tenai sat down by the fire with a slight sigh, and he remembered that she had not had time to rest yet herself, nor slept last night. But she looked only a little weary.

The turkey, even without stuffing and cranberry sauce, was

wonderful. They cooked pieces of the meat on skewers over the coals, wrapping some of it in leaves to keep for later. Daniel wouldn't have thought that would work, but if one didn't have plastic wrap, then apparently layers of oak leaves would do. He'd never really noticed how big some sorts of oak leaves were.

Tenai did not seem in any special rush to go on after they'd eaten, for which Daniel was grateful. She sat by the fire with her legs stretched out, leaning her back against a saddle, and let Emelan gather up their supplies to pack away.

Then she said, "Emelan. Come face me."

Daniel glanced from one of them to the other, startled. The man's broad shoulders had tightened, visible even in the poor light, when Tenai said his name. But he stood up came back to the fire, and sank down in front of Tenai, on his knees. "Nolas-e."

Tenai looked down at him. Her expression was unreadable. "Who rules now in Talasayan?"

Emelan met her eyes, though with obvious reluctance. "Nolas-e, it is Mitereh who rules there, as he has ruled there since you ... left."

"So," Tenai murmured. "The boy has ... twenty years, now? No, he must be nearer twenty-five, is that so? And does he do well enough, on his father's throne?"

Emelan bowed his head. He said, his rough voice careful on the words, "The king has recently come to his twenty-seventh year, Nolas-e. It is said that he takes after his mother, not ... the old king. Even a cur on the road knows Mitereh is a reasonable man. Nerinesir is a city that men do not fear to visit, in these years. Nolas-e—you do not aim at the king's blood?"

Tenai lifted dark eyebrows, regarding him with cold surprise. "Man, do you question me?"

Emelan bent, touching his forehead to the ground at Tenai's feet. "Nolas-Kuomon, forgive my impudence and allow me to ask: is it Mitereh's blood that called you back across the veil? I swear the king does not deserve your anger, Nolas-Kuomon. Forgive my presumption, I beg you."

Daniel sat up straighter, distracted from his discomfort by fascination. That was not at all the sort of speech he would have expected from any outlaw.

After a moment, Tenai reached down to lay one hand across the back of the man's neck. She lifted her hand. "Up."

Emelan straightened. His harsh, lean face did not readily express apprehension, but he might have paled. Or that might have been a trick of the uncertain firelight.

"Well," Tenai said drily, "you did not learn such manners among the road-curs you have recently kept company, I think. In whose house were you a soldier, Emelan no-man's son?"

"Nolas-ai Keitah Terusai-e," the man answered, after a moment.

"Keitah," Tenai murmured. "Indeed. Nolas-ai, is it? When did that elevation take place? After Antiatan, I presume? By Mitereh's hand, is that so?"

"Yes, Nolas-e."

"Yes. And he holds ... what estate now? Shall I guess? Not merely Kandun; that is not so high a grant. Bangan? Even Patananir?"

"Kinabana, Nolas-e."

Tenai lifted her fine eyebrows, evidently surprised. "Kinabana. Indeed. Keitah has moved up so far in the world, has he?"

"Keitah Terusai-e has been very useful to the king, Nolas-e."

"Yes. You once served in the Terusai house guard, dare I guess so? Yes. I do not ask concerning your birth, though I see your family could not have been low. Yet you came down to ride with curs on the road? I confess I am amazed."

Emelan bent his head, looking suddenly older, and worn.

"Well ... life brings us all to unexpected places, perhaps," Tenai said, a shade more gently. "It is no intention of mine at all that brings me back across the veil, Emelan no-man's-son. Assuredly it is no dream of the young king's blood. I have no intention whatever to take up that old battle. By my Lord Death himself, I do swear it. And will this satisfy you?"

"Nolas-e, how can I do anything but believe anything you tell me?"

Tenai regarded him with an ironic tip to her head. She asked after a moment, "What other men advise Mitereh now? Are you aware of the names? Mikanan Chauke-sa, Gomenah Kelabili-go-e?" She paused. "Sandakan Gutai-e?"

That last was a name Daniel recognized. And he thought he heard something in the way she pronounced it. A slight pause, as though speaking that name cost her something.

The man said softly, "Yes, Nolas-e. All of those. None of

those people deserve your anger, Nolas-Kuomon. Forgive my impudence that I say so."

Tenai looked down at him for a little while, her expression unreadable. Finally she said, "You do test my patience, man. What coin will you pay me for it?"

Straightening, Emelan looked at her wordlessly.

"Your loyalty," Tenai suggested. "Your honor. Your life's blood."

The man's breath caught. "Nolas-e—I *have* no honor."

"Will you break your oath to me if you give it?"

"I *have* broken it, Nolas-e!"

"To be sure," Tenai said softly. "But if you give it to me, will you break it?"

Emelan looked at her helplessly, and Daniel, watching, thought, yes, he could see how this woman might have led armies.

"No one can go back through the gates he has passed through," Tenai said, her expression unreadable. "All doors lead only ahead, into new country. One has no choice but to go forward. You choose how that will be. You choose what honor you will carry with you."

It was near enough to something Daniel had argued to her, in earlier years. She brought out that argument now as her own weapon.

"I ask for your oath," Tenai said, her tone not loud, but intense. "I ask you, Emelan no-man's-son, if you give your oath to me, will you hold to it?" Behind her, the last fingers of blood-red cloud stretched across the sky.

"Yes," the man said, barely above a whisper, and cleared his throat and said again, "Yes, Nolas-e. I will.

Tenai offered him the little American pocketknife, blade open. "Then give it."

Emelan drew a slow breath. He took the knife out of her hand, set the edge of it against his left wrist, and drew it sharply back and down. The cut was not deep, barely through the skin, but it bled abundantly. Jenna, next to her father, whispered under her breath, as though to herself, "Blood to set the spell?"

Daniel touched her elbow, and his daughter darted a look at him and shushed.

Emelan gave the knife back to Tenai with a hand that trembled a little.

She did not reach at once to take it. "What is it you offer me, man?"

"Loyalty and obedience, Nolas-e," Emelan said, his harsh voice also shaking a little. "Before God, I swear to you: I give my life and my honor into your hands."

Tenai inclined her head. "All these things, I accept." She took the knife back and put it away. Then she stood up and stood for a minute, looking down at the man who still knelt at her feet. "Organize your thoughts," she told him at last. "Plainly you have attended to important events. I will wish to know everything you can tell me about events that have occurred here in the past sixteen years."

Emelan looked up at her. "Yes, Nolas-e."

"For now, however, time is passing. Saddle the horses." Tenai picked up the nearest saddle herself and went to help do that.

During the new hours, Tenai kept Emelan beside her as they rode. She spoke for a long time with the outlaw—the ex-outlaw—extracting a long tale chock full of unrecognizable names. Daniel was too tired even to try to follow that. He was also too tired to stay awake very long, listening, after they finally stopped again to rest for the last few hours of the night.

They began to meet other travelers on the road the next day; not many, but a few. Tenai possessed astounding skill at detecting these other travelers at a considerable distance, and she would turn them all aside into the woods and let the strangers go by. Several times she went back to the road alone to watch them pass.

"A man with a load of charcoal," she told them one time, and again, "Several men, going out to hunt, I think."

On the last day's ride out from Chaisa, they encountered travelers less harmless. Tenai paused, putting up her hand to halt the others, looking with sharp attention down the road that rolled out in front of them.

Uneasy, Daniel tried to hear whatever she did. He heard nothing. "What is it?" By this time he had finally become accustomed to sitting in a saddle all day; as Tenai had said, the pain and stiffness had passed. The relief of this was so great that, if it had not been for the tension that rode with them, and the lack of running water and other amenities, he would almost have begun to enjoy the ride. But now tension heightened into real nervousness.

Tenai glanced at him, face abstracted and calm. "Not farmers or villagers," she said. "Soldiers, I think. Closer than I would like. Do you hear the bits jingle?"

Daniel did not, but Jenna said, "I hear it."

Tenai spared her a quick, affectionate smile. "The young have the keen ears of mice. Yes." She reined her horse off the road, into the trees, gesturing to Emelan to take the lead.

They waited, back among the trees as they had waited before. Eventually Daniel could himself also hear the jingle of metal and the creak of leather. It was a distant sound, but not distant enough to let Daniel feel comfortable.

The noises seemed to linger, and Emelan, who stood at his horse's head with his hand over its nose, looked at Tenai. "They have left the road," he said in a low voice.

She nodded. "Yes, I think they have. They saw our tracks, I expect. Several horses, turning into the woods to avoid meeting soldiers. They think they have discovered brigands." She touched her sword hilt. "If they will come, then they will."

"You aren't going to *kill* them!" Daniel said urgently.

Tenai spared a glance his way. "No," she said. "I think it most unlikely. Emelan."

"Nolas-e."

"You will speak to them. Perhaps they will not recognize me. Say that we feared they might be outlaws, and so hid off the road."

"Nolas-e," Emelan acknowledged.

They listened to the men approach. The soldiers advanced along a wide front, a dozen men. They spotted Tenai's party a few seconds after Jenna nudged Tenai's arm and whispered, "There!"

"I see them," Tenai answered, in a low voice, but not a whisper. "Only wait, Jenna, all of you. They will come up to speak to us."

She was right. The soldiers paused, evidently surprised at what they had found at the end of the tracks they had followed, and then came forward much more quickly.

They were dressed much as the brigands had been, but these men were in uniform, and in far better order. Metal mail glinted at their throats and wrists, but brown shirts, laced at the throat, hid most of the mail. Their trousers were also brown, but each wore an ivory-colored vest over his shirt, and a badge showing a spiraling blue pattern against a brown background. They had swords over their shoulders, and crossbows holstered at their knees, and sober, wary expressions.

"Captain," said Emelan to the man in front, with a slight inclination of his head. He still looked like a brigand, he couldn't do anything about that, but his diction was precise and formal. "We are pleased to see king's men. We had feared worse."

The man looked at him for a second, and then at the rest of them, regarding the American clothing a couple of them wore with wonder. His eyes went to Tenai without recognition. "Fortunately not," he said, with a courteous little nod. "Do you require escort? We are going west."

Emelan smiled, the expression just a little stiff. "No, thank you, captain. You are kind to offer. We haven't far to go now, and our own road lies east."

Behind the captain, a soldier caught his breath with a hiss.

Emelan's shoulders twitched. He didn't glance at Tenai. But the soldier was staring at her. The captain glanced at that man. He looked at her again himself, his attention sharpening, and his eyes widened. His hand moved toward his sword.

Tenai lifted her own hand, forbidding, and that movement stopped. All movement stopped. She did not step forward, did not do anything more to draw notice, but all eyes were on her. "We have no quarrel, captain," she said softly. "Pass us by."

"Nolas-Kuomon," said the captain, in clear amazement.

"Captain. I have no quarrel with you. Do not press one with me. Pass us by and go on your way."

For a long moment, the man simply stared at her. Then he drew a sudden breath and lifted his hand in a signal to his men. The men reined back, turning their horses awkwardly amid the trees, and retreated back toward the road. It was clear from the sound that once they reached the road, they pressed their horses into a run.

Emelan glanced at Tenai, and then away. "Word will be in Nerinesir in a week. Sooner, if they have a sorcerer in that company."

"Yes," Tenai agreed, gazing after the departing soldiers. "But we will be in Chaisa today. Mount. Mount up. We will press the pace a little."

They pressed the pace a lot, until Daniel, who had thought nothing about horses or saddles could bother him any longer, found he had run out of comfortable positions on his horse. His daughter, younger and more resilient, fared better; but even Jenna was flagging before, by midafternoon, they came around a curve of the mountain and out of the woods, into open land.

"Chaisa," said Tenai, in a voice so blank that Daniel gave her a sharp look. Her hands on the reins were white-knuckled. But she started her horse walking again before he could decide to speak, and the rest of them fell in behind her.

3

Chaisa, it became clear, was a term that encompassed a large area. The woods gave way to cleared land, gently rolling pastures that draped across the foot of the mountains. Neat stone walls began to cut the land into orderly blocks as the road curved around toward the south-east. Cattle, tawny-red or rusty-black, grazed behind the walls. Boys watched over some of the herds with big shaggy dogs; the boys stared in evident surprise at the travelers, but none of them came up to the road.

Orchards and fields of grain began to be interspersed with the pastures as they rode onward, all well-kept. Tenai studied it all with a blank expression that might have concealed any emotion. Once or twice she seemed surprised, as though the land had changed its character since she had seen it last. But all she said, running an experienced eye across fields where grain bent in the light wind, was, "The harvest will be good this year."

"The weather has been good all through the north," Emelan said, a little hesitantly. It was almost the first time he had spoken to any of them without being first addressed himself, the first time he had ventured an unnecessary comment. Daniel thought he braced himself when he spoke, as though he anticipated a cutting response.

But Tenai, glancing over at him, only said, "Not in the south?"

The big man relaxed minutely. "Too little rain in the south, Nolas-e."

"Well, the year is not so far along. They may yet receive enough to serve."

"Yes, Nolas-e."

The first houses came in view, small but neat stone cottages with thatched roofs, scattered at first and then more crowded, each with its little garden for vegetables and herbs, and, Daniel saw, flowers in abundance. Hens pecked about in the dust of the road, and there were a startling number of goats loose among the houses as well. They were much taller and shaggier than the little black animals that Daniel recalled from trips he had once made to the zoo with his daughter; most of these goats were a warm coppery color, and their horns looked like they could be dangerous.

Again, Tenai seemed a little surprised. She drew breath, as though to speak, but then did not. Dogs came out from the village, barking, and heads turned. Men and women and dozens of children suddenly appeared, all distracted from whatever mysterious tasks they had been about by the approach of travelers.

"This village is new," Tenai commented, in a tone that gave away nothing.

"It seems ... prosperous," Daniel observed. He wasn't actually sure what this sort of village ought to look like, but everything looked orderly and well-kept, at least.

Tenai seemed to find nothing odd about this comment. "Yes," she said absently. She rode straight forward, at a walk, so that the rest of them necessarily followed. She paid no overt attention to the people, although Daniel and his daughter studied them with great interest that seemed returned in full measure. It was clear when they recognized Tenai, from the sudden burst of whispers and the swift, startled wave of obeisance that passed through the crowd. Men bowed, and a few even went to their knees. Women in long skirts lowered their eyes and curtsied as Tenai rode past them, but looked openly at Daniel and Emelan, and especially at Jenna. Boys ran forward to take the dogs out of the way, women shooed younger children back from the road, and it was all an odd experience for an American of no particular importance. No one got in their way, and although the villagers spoke to one another in a low uninterpretable susurrus of sound, no one had the temerity to approach the travelers.

There were about a hundred houses in the village. Tenai rode straight through without turning her head, but Daniel, looking around, saw several boys on ponies burst out from among the houses and tear away across the fields. He could guess everyone would know Tenai had come back soon enough. Tenai did not seem to see the boys go, but Daniel would not have bet a penny that she was as oblivious as she appeared. Emelan turned his head to watch them race out of sight, but made no comment.

On the other side of the little community, the road turned around a low curve of the mountain and then opened up at last to show a huge sprawling manor—or castle, Daniel supposed—set high on the slope of the foothills. The castle or manor or whatever it was must have been a mile from the village. A wall, a great stone affair at least twenty feet high, was set below the great building. Its forbidding height curved right across the road ahead of them, which ran straight through broad iron gates. At the moment the gates were standing wide open.

Two soldiers stood at the gate, one to each side of the road. They stood perfectly still, at stiff attention, as Tenai and her party approached. Their trousers were brown, their shirts dark blue, their vests a tawny lion-color. Each man wore, over his heart, a badge showing a simple silver half-oval against a brown background. They wore swords, and each held a kind of long spear or pike upright in his right hand. They looked sharp and professional, but Daniel saw the effort that went into their slow smooth breaths and attentive poses. He thought they had only just got to their places, and in a tearing hurry. Those boys had probably gotten up here just about in time to enable this show.

The soldiers pivoted simultaneously to face the road as Tenai passed them—again, she did not acknowledge their presence by so much as a flicker—and tilted the spears they held to form the suggestion of an arch. Tenai rode between them, down the exact center of the road, her eyes set straight ahead. Definitely a show, on both sides.

Jenna had flushed. Daniel couldn't blame her. He felt horribly conspicuous himself. Wearing the same once-nice shirt and slacks he'd been wearing for days made the feeling even worse. He fixed his own gaze straight ahead, just like Tenai's. Pride expresses itself in unusual ways, he thought wryly, but he was not going to stare about and gape like a country hick come to the big city.

Past the broad gates lay an immense courtyard, and within this courtyard were numerous outbuildings of all descriptions, a central well with wide flagstone paving surrounding it. Also, he guessed, the entire staff, drawn up in careful order to meet the lady of the manor on her return. There were dozens and dozens of them, men and women and children, right down to babes in arms.

Tenai rode straight up to the gathered people and stopped her horse right there in front of them. Her face was perfectly calm, but

Daniel observed the tightness of her back and knew her apparent calm was not entirely real. What must it be like, to come home … to return to a long-abandoned home … after so long? After, perhaps, becoming resigned to the idea that she might never return? Or, at least, not for a hundred years or more?

The people all bowed low as Tenai drew her horse to a stop; and they stayed down, waiting … for acknowledgement? Permission to straighten? For disaster to strike? What sort of disaster might they anticipate? They seemed terrified of Tenai, and that was disturbing.

There was a man, standing to the fore of the people, older than most of those gathered there, who did straighten cautiously. He said, in a husky voice, "Nolas-e Tenai Ponanon Chaisa-e."

Tenai tilted her head to the side, regarding the old man. She made a little gesture with one hand, and the people all straightened, with a low whisper of sound. The sound was only cloth rustling; none of them had yet dared to speak. She said, in her most neutral tone, "Penon. Is all well with Chaisa?"

"Yes, Nolas-e," the man said, in a voice that was not quite steady. He was not as dark as most of these people. His hair, probably no darker than bronze when he'd been younger, was now grizzled throughout; he had cut it short, which seemed uncommon here. His face was fine-boned, with deep eye sockets and lines at the corners of his eyes, which were dark and shrewd.

"And with my house?"

"Yes, Nolas-e."

Her eyes lifted, passed across the faces of the people who faced her, and returned to the old man. "I will see you in my study at once," she said. "And the captain of my house guard; and my steward. Have my rooms turned out and aired, and an adjacent apartment opened for my guests. Have someone look out appropriate clothing, for my guests and myself. Is Demera still here?"

The man spread his hands. "I regret, Nolas-e, no, Demera married and moved away, up-mountain."

"Then find another woman to serve me, and staff to attend my guests. And send someone to the armory to see if my sword has yet come to his place there."

"Yes, Nolas-e." The old man waved a hand, and men ran forward to take the reins of the horses.

Tenai swung down from her tall horse with unthinking grace and glanced over at Daniel, who was clambering down more awkwardly. She extended a hand to help him without comment, glanced at Jenna, who'd bounced effortlessly down from her saddle to the ground, and swept them both with her past the gathering and into the manor.

The formal doors that led into the house were twenty feet high and bore ornate carving. The hall beyond was large enough to use as a roller-skating rink. Daniel couldn't help but stare around. The manor was a great echoing edifice of stone. Rugs, yes, big ones. And a huge tapestry on one of the walls. High, narrow windows let in slips of afternoon light, which lay in warm bars across the flagstone floor. The overall impression was luxurious and yet somehow harsh. Maybe *castle* was in fact the right term. Daniel discovered that he wasn't exactly sure what defined a castle. Except maybe a moat. There hadn't been one of those, at least. Fine, he would think of this as a really big house.

Tenai strode through the hall as though she owned it, which, Daniel supposed, she did. She paused at the foot of a broad staircase that swept up and around the corner of the vast hall, and beckoned Daniel and his daughter to join her. Emelan trailed them, looking wary and uncomfortable.

"I will see you settled at once," Tenai told Daniel. She touched Jenna's hand, a light, reassuring gesture. "I know you are weary. You may rest safely here. Be patient only a little while longer; your rooms will soon be made ready. Come with me now." She led them up the stair and along the hall at the top—this one was floored with polished wood—and into a large room. Generous windows on two sides of the room admitted the heavy golden light of the late afternoon, illuminating a wide desk, several chairs, and a broad fireplace. A rack along one wall held what appeared to be scrolls. Daniel touched one, slipped it out of its place and unrolled it a little, angling it toward one of the windows. Disappointingly, the harsh angular letters of the writing were nothing he could recognize.

"You will need another spell to be able to read that," Tenai said, with a faint touch of amusement in her tone. "I shall attend to it later, if that would please you."

Daniel replaced the scroll in the rack, smiling. "Yes, please, Tenai, if it's not too much trouble."

She inclined her head. "It is no trouble, my friend."

There was a quiet rap at the door, and the older man from the courtyard entered. There were two other men with him, neither of whom Daniel recalled from the courtyard, although he supposed it might have been easy enough to miss a couple of men in that crowd. The first was tall and bearded, dark-skinned and black-eyed, probably somewhere in his fifties. His beard was streaked with gray. His face and hands were weathered, as though he'd spent most of his years out of doors. He wore a sword at his hip, but he was carrying another sword in his hands.

The other man was much younger and even taller, though not nearly as muscled. Nor was he as dark—his coloring was more like Emelan's. He had a thin, bony face and big, capable-looking hands gripped together before him. He looked to be caught somewhere, as nearly as Daniel could tell, between terror and resignation.

The level of tension in the room had risen markedly at their entrance. Daniel put one hand on his daughter's arm, but did not know whether he meant the gesture to be for her comfort or his own.

Tenai turned to face the men, an arrogant tilt to her head; even in American dress she looked entirely at home in this foreign room, this foreign castle, this foreign land.

"Penon," she said, looking at the old man; and to the soldier, "Beres. And who is this? Where is Hacara?"

"Ah," said the old man, "Ah—your steward, I regret to inform you, he died four years gone, Nolas-e."

"How?"

"Ah—he choked, Nolas-e. On a bone."

Tenai regarded him. "Thus Lord Death dismisses our wish for dignity," she observed. "I am sorry to hear of this loss. Very well. And this man, then, is acting as my steward now. How did this come about?"

The old man looked uncomfortable. "Nolas-e, this is Galt, son of Nesuka Tantukad ... someone had to take the place ... " His voice trailed off.

There was a pause. Tenai studied the young man, who took a step forward. Unlike the rest of her people, he did not just bow, but went clumsily to one knee, bowing his head.

"So I am to understand that you usurped my authority in this house," Tenai said to him, her tone neutral. "You have claimed my authority to made decisions regarding Chaisa's affairs, yes? I saw as I came through Chaisa that many changes have been made here. Changes to the rules of pasturage, I believe, and to well-rights and wood-rights. I recall only one village so near my house, and that to the west. Now that one has been razed, and there are three new villages in this immediate vicinity. All three clearly took considerable resources to build. Am I to understand that the decisions leading to all these things were yours?"

Galt looked up. He half-lifted his hands, and then dropped them. "I was ... I was presumptuous, I know. Someone ... someone needed to ... " his voice trailed off. Looking up, Galt met Tenai's eyes with a desperate kind of resolution that had, Daniel saw, taken him beyond fear. He said firmly, "You were not here, Nolas-e, and Hacara was dead. Someone needed to take charge of Chaisa's affairs."

"And so you chose to do so. This was indeed presumption."

"Nolas-e—" Penon began, coming a step forward.

Tenai stopped him with a look. She said to Galt, "I shall speak to you at greater length. Until then, I shall reserve my judgment. Go and find for me all of Chaisa's accounts and records for the past years of your stewardship. Gather these and wait for me to call for you."

The young man bowed. Then he got awkwardly to his feet and took a step backward toward the door, his eyes on Tenai's face. Then, when she did not pay any further attention to him, he retreated. He stumbled at the door. Beres made a little move as though to help him, but then glanced at Tenai and changed his mind. Galt steadied himself with a hand on the doorframe, cast one last apprehensive glance over his shoulder, and vanished down the hall.

"Nolas-e—" the soldier began again, sounding tentative.

Tenai, ignoring the question in his voice, held out her hand to him. "My sword."

Beres hesitated, but then stepped forward and offered her the sword he carried.

Tenai took it. Daniel craned his head forward covertly for a look, and Tenai glanced at him and smiled, an edged smile as sharp as the sword.

"Yes," she said, "this is the same sword, Daniel. Gomantang will always find his way into my keeping, and we will seldom know the paths he may take: they are not the paths men may travel. As I believe I told you once before, Gomantang is not from this mortal land, but from the dark kingdom of Lord Death. He is more than a sword. He remembers that dark kingdom, and is himself a gate one may use to enter it ... if one should be so desperate."

She had probably explained that before, yes. At the time, Daniel had thought the whole thing metaphorical. He wasn't entirely sure he wanted to know how a sword could be literally a gateway to the kingdom of Lord Death, in some way other than the obvious, but he was fairly certain that was somehow exactly what Gomantang must be.

Tenai set her sword aside and looked again at the bearded soldier who had brought it to her. "And *your* sword, my captain? Will you offer that to me as well? You were my man once, Beres. Are you still?"

The man's eyes lifted, unwillingly, to meet hers. For a moment that seemed to last for a long time he did not move. Finally he said, "Nolas-e. Forgive my presumption and permit me to ask: Have you returned to take up steel and fire against Mitereh Sekuse-go-e? Do you mean to raise up an army to that end?"

"If that is indeed my intention?"

The man met her eyes. "I will not set my sword at your service to that end, Nolas-e."

Tenai smiled, barely. "Bravely declared. But that is not presumption, Beres. That is defiance."

The man knelt. From him, the gesture was not awkward at all, but practiced. He said steadily, "I would never defy the lady of Chaisa. I am the captain of her guard."

The older man gripped his hands together tightly, hardly breathing, watching Tenai and Captain Beres.

"Indeed. I perceive that it is Nolas-Kuomon you defy. Indeed, I understand you perfectly." Tenai held out her hand. "Your sword," she commanded, and waited, her hand extended in steady, patient demand, for a long, long moment.

Finally Beres took his sword, still sheathed, from his belt, and held it out. When Tenai drew it, with a soft scraping of steel against leather, he did not flinch, but only waited.

Tenai drew the edge of the blade across her own palm, delicately. A little blood welled up; just a drop or two, but shockingly crimson. She said, her tone perfectly level, "I have no intention of taking up any violent cause. I have no quarrel with the young king. I have no desire to begin a second war—or continue the first. I am satisfied to let the past lie. I swear this by Lord Death and before God. Let my blood seal the oath."

Daniel drew a slow breath of relief. He had almost expected— not that, exactly. But something *like* that. Something calculated to reassure, but something suited to this world. That sounded about right. Captain Beres was staring at Tenai in absolute shock. Emelan was smiling a little in wry amusement, no doubt recognizing that emotion.

Tenai offered the bloodied sword back to the captain of the guard. "Well?" she asked.

Without a word, he took the sword back from Tenai. His gaze never leaving her face, he closed his left hand over the blade. Blood welled between his fingers—again, just a little. But carrying as much meaning, certainly. "My life and my honor," Captain Beres said. His voice, so steady a moment before, was a little ragged as he went on. "Loyalty and obedience I swear to you, Nolas-e. I am your man. I beg your pardon for my earlier hesitation."

"I grant you pardon," Tenai said softly. "I take your loyalty. Now that you have returned it to me, I will expect you to set no other lord before me, my captain."

Beres bowed, rose to his feet, sheathed his sword, bowed a second time, and backed away two precise steps.

"Penon," Tenai said.

The older man took a breath, cleared his throat, and rallied. "Yes, Nolas-e."

Tenai indicated Daniel and his daughter. "These are my guests. You will show them all possible courtesy, Penon. Inform the staff of this house. See that all those hereabout are informed."

"Yes, Nolas-e."

Tenai made another small gesture, this time indicating Emelan. "Captain Beres, this is a man I happened to take up along my way. He has been a soldier, and in a lord's house guard. Now he shall be again. See to it."

Beres gave Emelan a quick summing look and said, "Yes, Nolas-e." Emelan returned the captain's glance without expression and said nothing at all.

"Keep a watch on the south roads," Tenai added to Beres. "If men or news comes this way from Nerinesir, I wish to know it. I do not expect to hear anything from that direction so quickly, but events may yet surprise me."

"Yes, Nolas-e."

Tenai dismissed both Captain Beres and Emelan with a nod and glanced at Daniel and Jenna. "If you will come with me, please, I shall make you at home in my house."

Tenai's own apartment turned out to include fourteen beautiful rooms, including an elegant little greenhouse, complete with a tiny fountain and colorful fish. Jenna exclaimed over it. Her mother would certainly have enjoyed it. Daniel only wished Kathy could have lived to be here with them and to see this.

"My lord husband loved this sort of folly." Tenai gave a glance around, half-fond and half-dismissive. "It would have been a shame to let it fall into disrepair. And the staff is proud of it." There was no grief in her manner or voice, no sense that she felt the loss, only that faint fondness. Daniel was reminded that she *really was* hundreds of years old. Even after nearly seventeen years, he could not quite imagine ever thinking of his own wife with that kind of dismissive indifference. He didn't *want* to imagine that.

The apartment allotted to Daniel and his daughter was not quite as large as Tenai's own, but it was generous enough. There was a door by which they could have private access to Tenai's rooms, if she chose to allow it. All the locks were on her side of doors.

"The arrangement is meant to allow a lord to install a discreet mistress," Tenai explained to Daniel, a touch drily. "A close friend may occupy such an apartment, or a foreign lord with whom the lord of the house wishes to make private arrangements. There are multitudinous uses. I trust you will find it sufficient for your comfort."

Daniel glanced around at the elegance. "I'm sure we will."

"Among other things, it will make clear your status to my household."

"Yes, and about that, Tenai—"

A door opened and closed, in some outer room, and someone clapped hands, somewhere quite close by.

"Come," Tenai called, with no evident surprise.

The someone proved to be three young women and a pair of young men, all in light robes suitable for indoor wear. They stood in a row, eyes modestly lowered.

"Your names, please," Tenai requested.

They gave them, in a soft chorus: the girls were Enera, Setai, and Melesa. The young men were Tebin and Dart.

Tenai studied them. "Enera. You are, perhaps, Demera's ... sister?"

"Cousin, Nolas-e," murmured the girl, whom Daniel judged to be a bit younger than Jenna.

"There is a resemblance. Are you afraid of me?"

The girl glanced up through her lashes, a shy look but not a fearful one. "No, Nolas-e. Demera told me—nothing about your private business, Nolas-e, but she told me you were kind."

Tenai laughed, though without discernable humor. "It's just as well I spent so little time here at the last. Very well, Enera. You may serve me, if you will, and I shall endeavor not to contradict your cousin's good opinion. You others: my guests are foreign, wholly unaccustomed to our manners. You will find them good-hearted, however, and willing to learn. I am confident you will not shame my house."

The young people murmured assurance.

Tenai glanced at Daniel, swept her gaze across his daughter. "Be at ease," she requested. "Jenna, Daniel. These people will assist you in everything. You have had many questions, I know. You may speak to these persons quite freely. Is this well enough?"

Jenna nodded, looking, to her father's experienced eyes, a little frightened and lost.

Setai came half a step forward and bowed, a tiny gesture, just a bob of the head. "There are baths ready—" she made a slight bend of her body to the right, and she and Melesa went off that way, taking Jenna with them. Jenna threw one look over her shoulder toward Daniel, but she was already relaxing, responding to the obvious friendliness of the other young women.

Tenai smiling, nodded to Daniel. "And these young men will see to your needs. I trust you will be comfortable. I ask you will bear with any awkwardness, as I know many of the customs here will be unfamiliar. Please be patient with everything. Rest well, my friend. I will see you in the morning." She turned toward the door that led into her private apartment.

Daniel took a step after her. "Tenai—"

She stopped and turned back. Her smile was wry, but seemed to him to express genuine humor. "All will be well. You have had a difficult and tense introduction to Talasayan, but truly, you will be safe here, Daniel. Whatever may come, no peril will attend you tonight. You and Jenna will be quite safe. This is my house. Fear nothing. We shall all rest this night, and I shall see you when the day brightens tomorrow."

If someone had twisted Daniel's arm, he'd have had to admit that just at this moment, a hot bath with plenty of soap was indeed looking more desirable than practically anything else in the world. Two worlds, possibly. Sighing, he nodded and let her go, turning at last toward the waiting young men and his own bath. With supper no doubt to follow, he assumed, and a real bed after that. All but limp at the thought, he allowed himself to dismiss all less-immediate concerns.

Undeniably odd to be attended by quiet, earnest staff, but then they probably found him odd and foreign too. Fortunately, they were willing to leave him alone in the bath. With soap, thank God, and warm towels and a soft robe. He hardly noticed anything about the bedroom, when he finally found it down a short hallway from the bath, except that it was warm and the bed was luxuriously soft. It was impossible to hang onto worry after that, impossible even to wonder if Jenna was all right. He knew his daughter was fine. He knew they were safe, both of them, at least for tonight, because Tenai had promised it was so.

4

In the morning, when Daniel worked his way reluctantly out of the very soft and comfortable bed, Tenai had already gone out. Galt, Tebin explained, had gone with her. So, to Daniel's slight unease, had Jenna. Though he knew his daughter would be perfectly safe—though he knew Tenai would look out for her no matter what—he would still have liked to just check in with his daughter.

He had to acknowledge, however, that he was glad he hadn't been awake to go with them. Ah, the resilience of the young! Not that Tenai was exactly young. She was merely ... not aged. He wondered, now, how he had failed to notice that sixteen years hadn't changed her at all. He truly *hadn't* realized that, until now, when he finally had the leisure to think back over everything that had happened and notice that. Surely before another sixteen years had passed, everybody would have noticed. He wondered what Tenai would have done then. Probably she wouldn't have explained that she'd surrendered mortality to a literal incarnation of death as the price for his help against an immortal king.

Or maybe she would have explained it exactly that way. In fact, she *had*. Daniel just hadn't believed her.

The young men brought a generous breakfast, laying out the dishes on the apartment's wide balcony. This included a kind of rice porridge with bits of pork, not actually bad, but odd to American tastes. Daniel was relieved to find that breakfast also included eggs, peaches, and very good bread, with butter and tart black jam. No coffee, more's the pity. But there was a kind of sweet, spicy tea that wasn't bad.

Daniel watched butter melt into the warm bread and thought wistfully about toast. It would have been a little too dark—the spring on his old toaster always stuck a little and so the toast always was a little dark, even on the lightest setting. Jenna had told him he should get a new toaster, but Daniel was used to the old one and thought he would miss the faint taste of charcoal if he got a new one.

Toast and microwaved bacon and orange juice and coffee. And maybe a Danish or two, though Jenna didn't like him eating junk food and would give him a look if she saw the pastries. She would have orange juice and a whole-grain bagel with cream cheese and lox. Daniel hadn't ever understood how she could eat lox for breakfast. Probably she had liked the rice porridge.

He had always cherished their mornings together. Though he'd encouraged her to go out of state to college, though he'd told her she ought to try dorm life and get a taste of independence, he had in fact been almost painfully relieved when she'd chosen a university close enough that she could continue to live at home. Which, he knew very well, she had done for his sake. He had meant to make her get an apartment once she'd been accepted into graduate school—make her spread her wings, since she was born to fly.

And now they were here, instead.

When midwinter arrived, would Tenai want to return to … he couldn't quite help but think *the real world*. Or would she remain here? He had a hard time imagining her leaving this world, now that he'd had a chance to see her fitting herself back into it. She had so obviously come home.

Maybe the king, what was his name, Mitereh something, maybe he would force Tenai to leave again. Maybe he wouldn't want to wait till midwinter. Maybe he'd be willing to start a war to force her out of this world, even if she wasn't.

Probably Daniel could borrow a whole lot of trouble if he tried. That did not actually seem a useful exercise.

If Tenai did want to return along with Daniel and Jenna, or decided she had to return … hmm. Explanations of what had happened might be tricky. Maybe they could tell something of the truth. An enemy of Tenai's had tracked her down and … and what? Daniel—or more likely Jenna—would need to think of a brilliant bit of fiction.

He gazed over the edge of the balcony to the village below Tenai's manor. The neat fields stretched out beyond the village, with darker woodlands beyond. The whole scene looked very … quaint, he supposed. Not quite real. Rather like a painted backdrop.

It had felt *much* more real when he'd been riding through it for day after day.

One of the young men had brought clothing for him. Not actually too different from American clothing, which made things easier. Brown trousers, a cream-colored shirt that laced up the front, and a brown vest with blue embroidery down the front. Daniel dressed carefully. The trousers were meant for a man with longer legs and somewhat less bulk. Daniel fastened them with a certain amount of difficulty, grateful for the vest that disguised his too-ample midriff. He looked at himself, a little uneasily, in a tall mirror. He still looked like an ordinary middle-aged psychiatrist of generally sedentary habits, only dressed a little oddly. He still looked like himself. After he had lived in this house, in this world, for the months that led up to midwinter ... he wondered whether he would still recognize himself then.

The house was beautiful. Daniel wandered through it for a while, admiring and a little uneasy, hoping he wasn't annoying the staff. He wound up, frankly bored, in a comfortable chair in the apartment he and Jenna had been given, waiting for Tenai and his daughter to return. He wished he could read the script in which all her scrolls and books had been written. Since he couldn't, he found himself dozing again. He dreamed of Tenai as he had first seen her, striking and dangerous, caged by walls of silence she had built around herself: he dreamed she spoke, but the words that came out of her mouth were swords whose blades ran with blood. He woke, jerking upright, his heart beating hard. The breeze that stirred the sheer draperies at the window was slow and hot. Midafternoon, maybe. He pushed himself upright, gingerly because he'd stiffened up again. Not young enough to fall asleep in a chair. He should go walk around the house or something, work the kinks out of his neck and back. Maybe one of the staff would tell him the titles of the books. Even knowing that much would be interesting and informative.

Jenna found him not long after that. She was perfectly safe and happy. Obviously. She was bubbling with enthusiastic descriptions of villages, of flocks of cream-colored sheep and a stream with a wide bridge just below a wild little waterfall. She also informed him that there would be a banquet that evening in honor of Tenai's return, and, ignoring Daniel's groan at the thought of attending a no-doubt formal event, insisted on showing him the clothes Tenai had sent for her. All in shades of blue, embroidered with tiny pearls over the bodice and at the hem.

"And she sent this for you," Jenna said, bouncing on her toes and waving a hand at another outfit. Daniel groaned again. Blue and brown, and not quite as fancy as he'd feared, once he'd gotten a good look at it. No pearls, at least. But, unlike the clothing he was wearing now, the vest was stiff with embroidery: abstract wave-like shapes in dark blue over the lighter blue of the cloth.

"Melesa's going to help me do my hair," Jenna said, still in that bright tone that implied nothing could be more fun than a banquet. "She's going to be playing—she plays something called a *kithe*, she showed it to me, it looks kind of like a guitar, but not as big and a lot rounder. It sounds kind of like rain falling."

"How nice," said Daniel, not really listening. "Listen, where's Tenai now, Jen?"

"In her study, with Galt," his daughter informed him, not in the least concerned.

When Daniel found Tenai, indeed, she was in her study, with what looked like *all* the province's records for the past sixteen years piled around them on tables and on the floor. What kinds of records? Daniel wondered. Records about cattle, maybe; about crops and the grinding of grain and the building of houses. Enough to keep plenty of accountants busy. If they had accountants here. Maybe they'd just had Galt.

The young man looked exhausted. Tenai did not. She was as cool and untouchable as ever. She sat at her desk, leaning back in her chair, regarding Galt expressionlessly. Galt stood in front of the desk, his big, bony hands clenched together in front of him, white-knuckled with tension. Tenai gave Daniel a slight nod of recognition—not, he thought, welcome—when he came in. Galt didn't even glance his way, as though he didn't dare look away from Tenai. Daniel slipped into a chair to one side and folded his hands in his lap.

"Yes," the young man said to her, in response to some question Daniel had missed. His voice was as tense as his hands.

"Why?" Tenai asked him, her manner neutral. "My previous steward found the original village sufficient."

"Hacara—Hacara was a good man, Nolas-e. But he was ... he had become rigid in his outlook. Sometimes—sometimes he did not see clearly. The houses of the old village were not in good repair. They were cold in the winter, and unclean in the summer. They brought too much illness and discomfort. Folk who are content work better for their lord, Nolas-e. The new villages cost to build, but the cost—the cost—" For a second, Galt seemed to lose track of his argument. He blinked, collected himself, and finished, "The cost was recovered over the next seven or eight years, Nolas-e, in higher yields in other areas."

"Perhaps those areas would have yielded well anyway. Perhaps the link you try to draw does not exist."

"Nolas-e, your folk worked longer hours because they were sick less often, and worked more effectively because they were content. At least part of the increase was due to those differences."

"In your judgment."

"In my judgment, which I had to depend on, Nolas-e, because neither you nor your lawful steward were—were available."

"And Penon agreed with you."

Galt hesitated, probably not knowing what response Tenai wanted to that. She did not help him, either, not with her neutral tone and cool expression. He said finally, "Yes, Nolas-e."

"I see you also removed the post, and the block."

"Hacara—in my judgment, Nolas-e, your steward had come to depend on those things too much. The people feared him too much. They were ready to fear anyone set over them."

"You courted their favor. One might expect a slack attitude to result."

"I courted their trust, Nolas-e, and their pride. If the people do not trust the judgment of their lords, they are afraid. If they are afraid, they look over their shoulders too often. A man looking over his shoulder can't plow a straight line, Nolas-e. And a man who feels no pride in his work will not care whether the line is straight."

Tenai looked more sardonic than ever. "No doubt these changes also resulted in a clear increase in profit, yes?"

The young man shrugged, a small movement. "Yes. In fact, yes, Nolas-e. The accounts are clear. I could show you. Or Penon."

"I should trust these accounts?"

"It's clear how your lands have prospered. I, or Penon, could show you—"

"I need an escort to perceive my own lands?"

Galt blinked at her. It took him a few seconds to answer, and no wonder, when clearly no answer he gave was going to please Tenai. At last he said, "To provide prompt answers to any questions you might have, Nolas-e."

"You are slowing down, man," Tenai observed. There might have been a hint of satisfaction in her tone, or a trace of humor, Daniel could not decide.

There was no answer Galt could make to that. He only bent his head before her unrelenting gaze. Daniel took a slow breath and let it out, torn between interrupting for the young man's sake and staying out of this.

"Go," she said then, with a curt wave of her hand, and when the young man stared at her in seeming disbelief, "Go on. Go. I shall send for you."

Bowing low, Galt backed a step, another step ... reached the door and escaped through it with obvious, and understandable, relief.

The young man shut the door quietly as he went out, leaving ... not peace behind him, Daniel thought, but a kind of fraught stillness. The window was open, the rich golden light of late afternoon slanting through it. A breeze stirred the fine curtains. Somewhere not far away, a bird was singing—a liquid trill that danced upward in quick phrases, each ending in a high-pitched buzzing whistle. In the distance, Daniel could hear a bucolic sort of moaning sound that he thought was probably made by cows. Perhaps the cows were being brought in to be milked. Although, no, didn't one get up at dawn to milk cows? Being brought in for the night, then.

Daniel leaned back in his chair and gazed out the window at the passing clouds.

Tenai stood up. She went to the window, studied the scene for a few moments, then turned. She answered the thought he hadn't voiced. "Daniel, I must be harsh with this young man before I may be kind. He was rash to take power in my name without my leave. He knows this, and he is afraid of me. I do not know yet whether he has the courage necessary for the station he claimed. Nor does he. We must both see that he does, or in time his fear will break him."

"Ah," said Daniel. "You do mean to be kinder, eventually?"

"He has been diligent, that is plain. I do not disapprove his work here. I will not punish his temerity. I will undoubtedly confirm him in his place—so long as he possesses the strength of will to take that place from my hand." She paused, almost imperceptibly. Then she added, "To give the grant of my authority, I have no choice but to take up the name I had laid down."

"And you're not sure you're exactly happy to do that. Is it different than you expected? It seems to me it must be very different, after all this time and … after everything."

"I was so brief a time in your country. And yet … "

Brief for her, Daniel supposed. But sixteen years had been time enough to build a complete new life for herself. Find a role for herself that did not include the blood and rage and violence of Nolas-Kuomon, Lord Death's Lady.

Tenai had fit herself into her new life—or expanded out into it—and now, perhaps, found herself at something of a loss when faced with her old persona. Rather like a man shattered by war, and then returning to his hometown to find himself surrounded by family and friends who remembered the boy he had been and did not understand that he'd become someone they didn't know. Only more or less in reverse.

Tenai turned again to the window, looked out across her lands. She ran a hand along the stone windowsill. The delicate curtain fluttered as a breeze made its way along the face of the house. She made a little gesture which Daniel read as confusion. "This is *Chaisa*."

"You always loved Chaisa," Daniel said, which he knew was true: during her long war with Encormio, Chaisa had been for Tenai more an ideal of home and peace than a real place. She had seldom lived here, and never for long. He suggested, "But now you aren't sure how you feel about actually being here."

"I have regained my name. This is my home. These are my people."

And yet she did not fit back into her name, back among her people; yes. Daniel understood that very clearly. "You'll find your balance here soon. A new role. A new life, even. You've done it before, Tenai. Surely it was much more difficult to adjust to a whole different world."

Or maybe not. Maybe when *everything* was different, it was easier to build a different life. Thrown back into a home she had known when she was *actually* young … he could see how that might actually be *more* disorienting.

"People here don't know you now," he observed. "They remember the woman you were. I guess it will take time for them to see that you've changed." He couldn't help but be a little concerned about the weight of expectation coming down on Tenai. Four hundred years of expectation would definitely be a heavy weight.

"Yes. Well, eventually everyone will understand I do not wish to take up the old war. I have sworn it, and it is true. The king will surely send to me. He will send soon. We shall see whom he chooses to send, and what manner that person shows, and what message that person brings. When I see all these things, I will know better how I should respond, I hope. I will decline again to take up the old war. Whatever question or demand Mitereh Encormio-na presents to me, I will return a gentle answer. That should calm fears everywhere. No doubt that will also disappoint whatever enemy brought me back across the veil."

She was no longer by the window, but had moved back yet again to her desk. She took out papers, scrolls—glancing at each item impatiently and setting it aside. She spoke to Daniel, but he had a sense she was talking as much to herself as to him. "Mitereh will move cautiously. I would expect caution. Whomever Mitereh sends to me, I will give that person the same message. I will say that I do not mean to remain."

So she had already made that decision. "Will it hurt you, to leave again?" Daniel asked her. "I'd be sorry for that, though … I understand it would probably be difficult for you to sort things out here well enough to remain. Yet. You did say you might have returned in another hundred years or so."

Tenai did not look at him. Nor did she answer right away. She sat down in the chair at the desk, shifted papers from one pile to another; found a blank sheet and a pen, dipped the pen into a jar of ink, wrote for a moment, and set that paper aside as well. She still seemed impatient. After another moment, she stopped, sighing. Then she faced Daniel. She met his eyes. "Once I was young and new-wed. I remember that time, but as though another woman lived that life. Later I raised my first army and broke it against Encormio's walls. That time, also, was long ago. That woman is also gone. Later still I gained the victory, but I was consumed by fury and hatred and my enemy's defeat did not satisfy me. That is the woman you met. I remember that woman, but I do not clearly recall how it was to feel as she felt." Tenai paused and lowered her head, studying her hands, which lay open, flat on the surface of the desk. "I remember … everything that woman did. What I did. To all those who followed me."

"Now you intend to choose again, differently. Are you worried about whether you can make that clear to the king? Is that something I might be able to help with? I'm no part of that long history. I'd be glad to speak with whomever the king sends."

"Perhaps. Perhaps this is a wise suggestion, Daniel. Anyone will surely be intrigued to hear of your world. As you say, the history there is nothing to do with me. Nothing to do with Encormio." She was silent for a little while. Finally she said, "I think your suggestion is very likely useful. Thank you, my friend. Whatever message I return to him, Mitereh may believe me, or otherwise. Greatly would it benefit Mitereh Encormio-na to believe everything I say. For that reason alone, he must surely be wary in accepting my word that I will retire once more. But whatever words you speak … he must listen carefully. You are foreign and mysterious. Yes. Your suggestion may well be wise." She paused, smiling a little. After a little while, she added, "Mitereh will ask his advisors for their opinions. Some will likely advise caution. Sandakan Gutai-e … may advise otherwise. If the young king sends anyone against me, that is the man whom he will send."

"Ah." Daniel had a shadowy picture of the man in his mind. Sandakan had been important to Tenai; perhaps the most important person in this world other than Encormio himself. And in a wholly different way. "You definitely won't fight him."

"I certainly do not wish to."

Daniel nodded. "If Sandakan were sent against you, Tenai, couldn't you talk to him and explain? You worked together for a long time. He was your most important general. Wouldn't he listen to you now?"

She looked at him, her expression closed, hard to read. But after a moment, she said, "Perhaps. Perhaps he would."

Daniel waited a moment. Then, when Tenai showed no sign of following this rather limited response with anything more elaborate, he said, "I do wonder a bit that a man who was so firmly on your side, almost to the very end, should wind up a close advisor to Encormio's son. Or do I misunderstand?"

He saw at once he had hit an unexpected, or only half-expected, nerve with that remark. Tenai's expression, never open, closed down as though a shutter had come across it. She seldom made extraneous gestures. But now she shifted her weight, began to stand, changed her mind, and settled back into her chair. "Mitereh would have been a fool to discard the sharpest-edged sword that offered itself to his hand. He had a kingdom to rebuild, a hundred little warring lords to bring under his banner, Imbaneh-se and Keneseh to hold quiet, Tesmeket to lesson in respect. All those goals, Gutai-e would have shared. Nothing would be more likely than Gutai-e offering fealty to the boy. He would understand that Mitereh could not achieve these things save if he might hold the fealty of strong men."

"But it bothers you anyway."

"Perhaps," Tenai acknowledged, which from her, like this, certainly meant *yes*."

"Well, that seems natural to me. Anybody would be upset when a friend switched loyalties like that. Even if he didn't, exactly."

"Perhaps," Tenai said again. She went on after a moment. "Sandakan belonged to Encormio, at the first." The flickering light of the candle flames leant a dream-like quality to her fine, angular face and drew an opaque veil across her dark eyes. She spoke now as though she had half-forgotten Daniel's presence. "We met at Gai-e. That would be, oh, thirty years past. Something close to that. I was coming out of Imbaneh-se. I meant to destroy all the harvests in the east of Talasayan, around Gai-e and Kinabana and Patananir, and inland toward the mountains."

"The harvests? Why?"

Tenai brought her eyes back to his face. After a moment the corner of her mouth crooked upward in a wry little smile. "To starve the people in that region and make them a burden to Encormio. That is war. So, if he would prevent me, Encormio must send an army after mine. This would bring his army away from the heart of his strength at Nerinesir. I meant to destroy that army, if I could. Then later I hoped to take the southernmost region of Talasayan, all the land below Ipos that thrusts down along the Bari-e River, and occupy it. Thus I would gain the grain produced there and further weaken Encormio, so that in the next year I might have a better chance if I came against him directly. It was a complicated business, and more difficult in execution than in conception, for Encormio understood much of what I intended."

Daniel nodded. "An ugly business."

"Of course," Tenai said, but with chilling indifference.

She had fought that war, or different iterations of that war, for *four hundred years*. Of course all that seemed natural to her, all that suffering unimportant. Daniel nodded. "And Sandakan was one of Encormio's officers, in the army he sent?"

Tenai smiled, this time with true amusement. "No. He was the commander of the garrison at Gai-e. He was young. That was his first real command. He had been ordered to hold me at the river long enough that the main army could arrive, come against me, and throw me back. But he was a clever man, and saw a greater opportunity. He pretended incompetence and pulled half my army into a trap."

"But it didn't work?"

"I saw his trap when time just remained to avoid it. For an hour, only God knew which way the battle would tip from that knife-edge, but in the end it was his garrison that was defeated."

"Poor Sandakan."

"Indeed. In those years, it was the custom to kill freely when one defeated an enemy. Bitterness ran in a deep river between men who had been enemies for generations. There were practical considerations also: any man spared would be a drain on your resources, for you must feed him and guard him. Or if you permitted him to be ransomed, you would face him again on another field of battle, for this was not a war that would end. Thus men fought fiercely, for they did not expect quarter."

An ugly business indeed. Daniel tried to keep his mind focused on Tenai, on the story she was telling, but it was hard not to think about side issues, about the coarsening of men's sensibilities in war. Daniel kept his breathing even with an effort. He said, "But you spared the garrison?"

"I had seen that their commander was a skilled tactician. Such are always valuable," Tenai said. Her dark, smoky voice seemed to belong to the night, to the candlelight, to the air, scented with the distant pine and snow from the high mountains, that moved the fine curtains by the windows. "Once it was clear I would win the field, I offered quarter. Gutai showed his quality again, for he saw I had won and did not try to deny it. He yielded quickly when I offered the chance, though the offer must have surprised him. I was gracious in victory: I allowed the garrison's physicians to tend their wounded, and I did not permit my army to plunder the captives or the town. Then I had Sandakan Gutai-e brought to me."

Sandakan Gutai-e had come into the black tent of Nolas-Kuomon with a firm step and a calm expression, which together almost served to conceal his apprehension. He had been very young then: twenty-four or twenty-five, something close to that. He had been allowed to see that his wounded men were tended; he had been allowed to bathe and given clean water to drink and hard army bread. He had not been bound: it was presumed he was not fool enough to lift a hand against his captors. From all these unexpected kindnesses, he undoubtedly understood that he was being courted. Even so, he could not help but be apprehensive—the more so, if he did not intend to be won.

Tenai waited for him alone, her officers being engaged upon their various duties. Gutai-e walked before his guard until he came near her. Then he went formally to one knee and bowed his head.

"What is your name and your family? What is your city?" Tenai asked him.

He told her these things in a steady voice.

"You may stand," Tenai told him, and, more generously yet, "You may sit." She indicated a chair drawn up by the long table that occupied the center of her tent. She poured him wine with her own hand—well watered, for he would not trust strong wine. From a captor to her captive, all these gestures were courtesy.

Sandakan took the offered chair and the cup and drank, which he, as her prisoner, was constrained to do. He would not look at her face, however, but studied the fine grain of the table.

Tenai leaned her hip against the edge of the table and examined him with a like intensity. She asked him, "Whose man are you, Gutai?"

He did look up then, and met her eyes. "Nolas-Kuomon," he said respectfully. "I am sworn directly to Encormio." That he thought he might die for this was clear: he had braced himself to meet her anger.

Tenai only said mildly, "Yet you are from Patananir. Then why are you not sworn to the lord of Patananir?"

"So I was, Nolas-Kuomon, until the battle at Kelabili late last year."

Tenai knew the battle he meant. She had not been there. Kapuas of Tesmeket had fought for her there. The engagement had been inconclusive and, as no decisive victory had been won, tension had flooded down the Bari-e all winter as Talasayan and Imbaneh-se faced each other from opposite banks of the river. She said, "And it was after Kelabili that Encormio made you his and set you at Gai-e?" She received the young man's nod without surprise. "Well," she said, "If Encormio was ever a fool, it was so long ago that the memory has been lost in the gray kingdom of Lord Sorrow. Of course he would want you. You are clever. You were clever today."

To agree would have been arrogant; to disagree, insolent. Sandakan wordlessly bowed his head.

"Forswear Encormio," Tenai said to him. "Swear to me in his stead, Gutai. I swear before the Martyr and by Lord Death, I would use you well, and toward a better end than the one you now pursue. You cannot love Encormio. His very existence is an offence against God. God will surely forgive you the broken oath in this cause."

The young man met her eyes again. "I owe the king fealty," he said, and after a moment, "And if I did not ... my family is in Nerinesir."

"Ah." Tenai was silent for a moment, regarding him. "Gutai ... if you will set your banner beneath mine, I will spare all your men who follow you. All those who will not, I will spare also, because they were yours." She did not have to say what she would do if he refused. Thus Tenai set the lives of his remaining men—there were hundreds even after their defeat—against the lives of his family. It was cruel. But it was one of the few prizes she was able to offer.

Sandakan took a quick breath and let it out again without speaking. Then he said formally, "Nolas-e, I am grateful for your care of my men. You offer me a great concession—one beyond my small worth to you. I regret I cannot do as you wish."

"You may have seven days in which to consider," Tenai said to him. "No, do not tell me that you will not fail in your resolution. Whether you will or no, you have seven days." And she summoned his guard and sent him out.

"But you didn't actually kill all your prisoners," Daniel

protested, appalled at the idea. "No, of course not—because he did join you, in the end. How did that happen?"

Tenai, recalled to the present, looked at him and offered one of her narrow secretive smiles. "He had a stern heart even then, Daniel. I do not know that he would have yielded to me, save that I went quietly into Nerinesir. I slipped beneath Encormio's notice into his city. And when I left, I brought away with me Gutai's mother and his two young brothers. This was a complicated exercise—not for my part, but because Encormio's forces wished to take Gai-e back from me. I had not sent my army farther into Talasayan, you understood, but rather set my people to hold all the land about Gai-e, along the river and all along the coast. Encormio's forces, uncertain of my intentions, did not even attack my positions, but delayed to consider."

"I thought your objective—"

"My objectives changed at Gai-e. I had perceived a different path. Gutai was astonished, I believe, when I brought him to me again after seven days had passed and he found his family there in my hand."

"I should think so!"

Sandakan Gutai-e had been very much astonished, and as much alarmed. He had stared, eyes widening, at his mother and at his brothers seated there. His mother rose quietly from Tenai's black table, but did not try to go to her son. Nor had he tried to go to her, nor even to speak to his family. Rather, he had turned at once to Tenai and said bitterly, "You have gained a sharp-edged weapon, Nolas-Kuomon, but I confess I would have thought it a weapon better suited to Encormio's hand than to yours."

For a man in his position this was insolence; even as he spoke, he clearly realized that punishment might not fall on him alone. He would have caught back his words if he could. He knelt at once, ashen-faced, and drew breath to beg her pardon.

"I had intended to send these folk to Chaisa," Tenai told him, cutting off whatever he would say. "There in the heart of my own land, they would be safe. But I see that if I made that disposition, you would believe I had taken them as hostages. Fortunately another option presents itself. You did not tell me that your mother is a woman of Tesmeket."

Sandakan, speechless, had only stared at her.

"Once of Tesmeket, always of Tesmeket. I believe," Tenai said, "that your family will find safety and some measure of peace in the mountains around Katet, where perhaps they may locate relatives who will welcome them. Or if that hope fails, I know people in Mataket who will make a place for them."

"My grandfather will welcome us, my dear," said Sandakan's mother, with quiet confidence, when her eldest son looked her way. "We will not require to impose on—on Chaisa's hospitality."

Tenai gave the woman a little nod and continued to Sandakan, "I am sending one of my own ships to take your family south, as I believe the sea will be less perilous than an overland journey. You may choose one or more of your own men to accompany them, if you wish."

There was a short pause. Then, without rising, Sandakan offered Tenai a slow, profound bow. "Forgive my hasty words. I am grateful beyond expression for your generosity." He hesitated and then added with the air of a man forced despite his better judgment to be honest, "I am still—I beg you will forgive me, Nolas-e—sworn to Encormio's service."

"This service is not contingent on your compliance. I offer it freely." Tenai clapped her hands and said to the soldier who responded, "My guests may retire. I am certain they are weary. Please escort them to their quarters. Gutai-e will wish to join them later. He may. All their ordinary requests may be granted."

The soldier bowed and led the woman and two boys from the black tent. Sandakan's mother looked back once as she left, her forehead creased with worry.

Sandakan turned his attention back to Tenai. He said after a moment, "You have put yourself to some considerable trouble for my sake. I confess I do not understand why."

"Forswear Encormio," Tenai said to him. "You alone I would gladly take into my hand, but I ask for more: Bring your men to me after you. They need not fear Encormio's retribution against their families here. If they will give me their loyalty, I will take Gai-e and make it my own."

Sandakan was silent for a long moment, contemplating the enormity of this suggestion.

"Do you doubt my ability to hold Gai-e?"

"No more," answered Sandakan carefully, "than I doubt your ability to hold any town."

Tenai smiled. Indeed, all the towns on the border had been battered by the changing winds of this long war. But she only said, "Once Gai-e turns from Encormio to come to me and men see how I welcome it, other towns may turn. I will hold it, that all those who watch may witness my strength and know they will be safe to come to me. Do this for me, Gutai, and thus your service to me may become the falling leaf that turns the age."

Sandakan considered this.

Tenai said, with rising intensity: "I shall defeat Encormio in the end. Why should it not be during your lifetime, Gutai? Why should it not be now? Your service to me may turn the age at last—or if it achieves some lesser outcome, is that not even so of value? Will you declare Encormio the victor and the battle without hope, without even testing the field? How long must this age of war stretch out, before men of resolution act to turn it?"

Sandakan lifted his hands and let them fall again, a gesture eloquent of confusion and distress. "For seven days I have known what I would say to you. I have all my life been a man of my word."

"Yes. You are young. You yet own a purity of heart. I ask you to surrender that purity," Tenai answered, but gently. Then she waited, watching her prisoner with a terrible patience.

Sandakan braced his shoulders back. "And if I will not, even now?"

"Then you will die here, and all your men," Tenai answered. She stood still, her hands resting on the plain surface of her black table, regarding the young man, remorseless as death. She went on, "And I will give Gai-e back to Encormio in smoking ruins. Then I will go to, oh, perhaps Kelabili. There I shall make the same offer I have made here to you. With the example of Gai-e before Kelabili, I think perhaps the answer there will be different than yours." She added into the small stricken pause that followed this, "But Gai-e would serve me better as a gentler example, Gutai. I still look for that."

Sandakan did not answer at once. He had turned his head, to gaze out of the open door of the tent and out into the camp. The lines where the prisoners were held were visible, and beyond that Gai-e itself could just be discerned. He said at last, not quite to Tenai, "And yet you need not attach me personally to your banner to achieve your aim, Nolas-e. There must be a double handful of men of Gai-e who would serve your purpose as well as I."

"I might find another to serve my purpose. But not as well as you would, Gutai." Tenai paused. She said, much more gently, "A man of proven integrity who comes to my banner is more valuable to me than a man of lesser reputation. It is you and no other I wish to attach to my service."

"Integrity," Sandakan said, his mouth twisting. "How, if I should turn to you? How shall you trust me, if once I am forsworn?"

Tenai laughed outright. "Men have betrayed me in the past, and others will assuredly betray me in time to come, for such are men. But you will not be among them, Sandakan Gutai-e, or I know nothing of men. Nor do I believe you will find your men renounce you." She offered him a knife, hilt first across her forearm.

Sandakan took it, slowly. He looked at it for a long moment as though not quite certain what it was or what he should do with it. Then he drew the blade across his palm in one quick motion. A thin line of blood ran down his hand, coiled down his wrist, and dripped slowly to the floor of the black tent.

He said to her, "Nolas-Kuomon, before God and the Martyr, I swear to you obedience and loyalty. My life and honor I set in your hands, renouncing all other fealty I have owed elsewhere. I swear that all my life I will do good to you and not evil. That I will listen for your voice and take your commands. That for all my years I shall speak truth to you and never falsehood." He hesitated, and then added, "I will bring you Gai-e, and trust you to hold it safely, Nolas-e. All the cities of the coast and the border I will help you take into your hands."

"I think you will," Tenai said, and laughed, for she saw how discomfited Encormio would be for this day's work.

"And that was the beginning of the end," Daniel murmured.

Tenai rose and went to the window, looking out at the black sky. "Yes. So it was. Encormio's final defeat came very soon after that. I think it was not more than fifteen years. I did hold Gai-e, as I had sworn. Later I took other towns along the border, Ponos and Kana-e and Kelabili and all the land south of Ipos. On the coast, Kinabana saw my strength and found the courage to become neutral, though it would not declare for me. I took Patananir and

Bangan. Encormio held less and less, and became more and more desperate—though even in his waning he remained very strong and dangerous. I could not hope to break Nerinesir. You will remember that at the last, I took that city by means of subterfuge."

Daniel remembered that story very well. "And Sandakan never did betray you," he said gently.

"He was true to me when I betrayed myself," she agreed, turning back toward him. Candlelight turned her face to a mask, unreadable.

"So it's only natural you don't really like knowing that he's probably equally steadfast now on behalf of Encormio's son."

"Should he have wasted his heart and will in obscurity, when Talasayan needed him so desperately? Should he offer himself elsewhere but to Mitereh, when the boy alone might be the shield that could be raised up to protect Talasayan from continuing devastation?" She paused, and sighed. "Yes, Daniel, so I may well understand this new loyalty of his and yet find it difficult to forgive."

"Grief and loss are ... ephemeral. You told me that once, I believe."

Tenai gave him a sharp look. She began to speak, paused, and said after a moment, slowly, "I had not thought of it as a grief."

"Well, it seems like that to me."

"Yes, Daniel. I believe you see clearly, as is your custom." Tenai laughed a little, without much humor. "I knew already that Sandakan Gutai-e remains important to me. So he has, and so he will. Perhaps I may hope that you are correct. Perhaps he will regard my word, though I send to him across all the river of blood and betrayal that lies between us now. That may be so."

"I think he might. I hope he will. I think ... I think you'll end up defining a new role for yourself here, either way, and eventually everyone else will figure that out. But you do need to make sure it's a role that meets your own needs, and not just the needs of this place. Even if everyone here treats you as though neither the role nor you has changed. Eventually everyone *will* realize you've chosen a different role, if you commit to that."

Tenai listened to him carefully. Her mouth crooked in a wry smile. She said, "I did not know how free I was to become a different person in your country, Daniel, until I heard my name spoken again in this one." Her expression turned a little inward.

Listening, Daniel thought, to the way her name—all her names—echoed in her heart.

The great hall was a huge, vaulted, rectangular room that offered ample space for every member of the castle staff and most of the villagers. They all seemed to be present, as far as Daniel could tell; some seated at the long tables and the rest standing. The murmur of their presence was like the murmur of the sea: undecipherable white noise with a sense of massiveness behind it. It was an uneasy murmur. Daniel had no doubt that Chaisa would have been more comfortable going on for another dozen years without its ruler turning up. He had been placed at the high table, set off from the rest of the hall by a four-inch dais. The table offered room for a dozen places, though not all were occupied. Tenai was not yet present.

Penon sat just to the left of the head of the table. Daniel was next to Penon. Jenna was on his other side, looking startlingly grown-up in the blue gown Tenai had sent her, with her hair gathered up into a complicated coil behind her head. She wasn't chattering as she might have under more usual circumstances. Tension ran through the hall, like electricity before a storm. No doubt Jenna felt that. Everyone must feel that.

Porcelain lamps poured their warm flickery light in pools along the hall. There were so many lamps that it was, in fact, fairly well-lit. The floor, quite bare, was flagstone. But the hall was softened by cloth hangings on the walls, most in natural wheaten or gold shades, with subtle abstract patterns in the weave.

Jenna's friend Melesa wasn't the only young person who had brought an instrument, Daniel saw: there were two other young women with instruments like hers. Daniel wouldn't have thought of the sound of rain himself, but he could see what Jenna had meant by her description. The stringed instruments had a kind of peaceful swishing sound to them. There was hardly any other sound in the hall. Everyone was waiting, Daniel thought. For Tenai: for whatever she would say, or do, that would show them how she meant to unroll Chaisa's future.

The musicians faltered and drew to an abrupt close. Daniel saw why at once: Tenai was finally coming. She entered the hall through the broad double doors that led in from the inner courtyard, and it *was* an entrance. She did nothing so obvious as stop and pose, but it was definitely an Enter, Stage Left moment. She was dressed formally, in brown and blue, with the silver half-oval over her breast. She wore her sword, in its plain black scabbard. *His* scabbard, maybe. Tenai had always spoken of her named sword as though it—he?—were a person. Her hand rested on the hilt of the dangerous, ambiguous sword that had followed her from one world to the other and back again.

Those seated rose to their feet, and the gathering parted for her like water. Tenai walked down the exact center of that hall like she was the only person in it, turned, and stood before the chair at the center of the high table. She said nothing. She didn't need to say anything to take control of the hall and the gathering. Everyone was silent, waiting for her.

Daniel and his daughter stood with Penon, close to Tenai's chair—close enough to hear Tenai easily, if she spoke; in fact, the acoustics in this hall made it possible to hear from one end of it to the other. But she still did not speak. The men of the house guard had come in after her and were now drawn up in neat ranks to one side of the hall. There were only a few dozen men in Tenai's guard. Emelan was among them; Daniel saw him, a few down from the end of the last rank, and wondered how he was getting on with the ordinary guardsmen. A pause stretched out. Daniel couldn't guess what they were waiting for.

Captain Beres came in, not entering by the same door. He escorted Galt, a hand under the younger man's elbow. The two men walked the whole length of that hall under the eyes of the crowd. The captain's face was blank. Galt's was set and rigid. Daniel closed his eyes briefly in sympathy, imagining how that walk must feel.

Once they reached the high table, Beres stepped aside. Galt glanced after him, took a breath, and came forward alone. He went to one knee before Tenai and bowed his head. The gesture this time was smooth; Daniel guessed he had practiced it in the hours since Tenai's return. The silence in the hall deepened.

"Galt, son of Nesuka Tantukad," Tenai said. Her voice was clear and cool. Dispassionate. "You took the place of my steward without leave from me. Using authority I never granted you, presuming to speak with my voice, you made many broad decisions concerning my affairs. What punishment is due this effrontery?"

Galt answered, his voice admirably steady, "As I acted in your name, Tenai Ponanon Chaisa-e, so I will submit now to your judgment."

"So. That is as well." Tenai rested her hand on the hilt of her sword. "Galt Tantukad, I have reviewed your use of the authority you took so presumptuously. I find you have used it well. I approve everything you have done. Thus, I confirm you as my steward for all Chaisa. My voice and my authority are yours."

Galt looked stunned.

The corner of Tenai's mouth twitched upward. She held out her hand without looking, and Captain Beres stepped forward at once, drawing his sword. He put the hilt into her hand. He stepped back again, and Tenai rested the tip of this more ordinary sword on the gray flagstones. She said, almost kindly, "Well, man? Four years ago you took authority in Chaisa without my leave. Will you take it now when I offer it freely?"

Very slowly, Galt reached out and took hold of the sword-blade. A thin line of blood made its way down the blade. "Before God," he said, and cleared his throat. "Before God, I swear, I will set you and Chaisa before any other loyalty, Nolas-e. I will answer your voice and obey your commands. My life and—and my honor, I set in your hands, Tenai Chaisa-e."

Tenai gave him her hand, and he touched his lips to it, looking dazed. "Good," she said, and stepped back, handing the sword back to her captain and seating herself.

Behind her, the silence in the great hall swelled into a pleased murmur: nothing so gauche as cheers. Tenai did not acknowledge the sound by so much as the flicker of an eye.

It was quite a way to start a banquet.

5

Four days after Galt had been confirmed as Tenai's steward, at roughly the time that Daniel had almost begun to feel, if not at home, then reasonably comfortable in Tenai's house, the soldiers that Beres had posted to watch the road brought word of an army coming up the road toward Chaisa.

Tenai took the report in her study. The captain of the house guard was present, and Penon, and Galt, summoned in a hurry from the village smithy, where he had apparently been discussing the smith's need for a better grade of metal. Daniel was there by chance. Tenai had been looking through old scrolls and discussing history—old history, of eras before Encormio had ever been born. It made fascinating listening. Daniel wished she would get around to doing the literacy spell she'd mentioned, but apparently setting it up was difficult or complicated or something, for some reason he didn't entirely understand. And she was genuinely busy; he did understand that.

Now, with this report, nobody was interested in ancient history. Only in Tenai's own personal history. That seemed all too relevant.

"How big is this troop?" Tenai asked. Her voice was quiet. She did not seem worried at all.

"About two hundred men," her captain answered, as though the number held intrinsic meaning that should be clear to all of them.

Tenai had been running the feather of a quill pen through her fingers. She put this down. "Well. Interesting. This is not someone who plans an attack."

"No," agreed Beres. "I thought I might hear reports of other forces maneuvering in the vicinity, but nothing of the kind has as yet become apparent. Two hundred, and no more, or so it seems now."

Tenai nodded thoughtfully. "What banners?"

"Only one," answered the captain. He stopped there, as though the meaning of this was obvious.

"The king's own," said Tenai. The way she said it, it was not a question. Captain Beres did not answer. For a long moment, no one spoke. Then Tenai glanced up and around the room, taking a second to catch each man's eyes in turn. Her own gaze was calm and secret, holding unguessable thoughts. She said, "Close the gates, my captain."

"Shall I call in the villagers?" Galt asked her. His voice was low, deferential ... wary. But determinedly steady.

"No," said Tenai. Galt moved as though he would protest, but she raised one hand a few inches and he stopped. He did not drop his gaze, but from the tightness of his shoulders, it might have taken an effort. "No," repeated Tenai. "The *villagers* are not in danger. We shall not have a war here; or if we do, certainly not yet. Let the young king see that I take no measures to protect my people. He will understand the meaning of my restraint. Beres?"

The guard captain said quietly, "I agree. The king certainly hasn't come to Chaisa for war. Our people are not in danger. Nolas-e, as Mitereh plainly poses a question by coming to you in this way, are you certain you will close the gates in answer?"

"Yes," said Tenai.

Beres hesitated. Then he nodded. "Very well. As you command, Nolas-e."

Tenai said softly, "We will find out what measure Mitereh will choose for this dance. Let us go up to the walls and watch it begin."

The two hundred men made quite a crowd, spread out along the wall before Chaisa's gate. They had come up very close, and set their tents in the shade of the walls. Where, as Captain Beres pointed out to Daniel, who had not thought of it, they would be vulnerable to anything dropped from the top of those walls. Boiling oil, for example. Large rocks. Crossbow bolts.

"The king has already made his wishes clear by coming himself to Chaisa with so small a company," Beres explained. "Now he sets his camp beneath our walls, as though he were an ally; as though he has no fear he may be met with anything but courtesy. This, in the face of closed gates. Nolas-Kuomon is certainly correct. Mitereh has not come here to fight." He glanced sideways at Tenai, who stood nearby on the battlements, studying the army at her feet.

"Has the king actually come here himself?" Daniel asked, looking with fascination at the men and banners and wagons and horses. It was all like something out of a history documentary. Or a fantasy movie. But the arrows and swords down there were really sharp. Really meant to kill enemies.

Enemies actually killed each other, here. This was all absolutely real.

"Yes." The guard captain nodded toward the largest of the tents, where a banner flew. A blue spiral wound across that banner, the same complicated spiky pattern the soldiers had worn. "That young man, there, do you see?"

"Ah," said Daniel, surprised. The king was one of those men who look younger than they are: he could have passed for twenty. But a second look showed that he stood with the confidence of a man, not a boy. That he was the center of attention in that gathering, as Tenai was, among her own people. Daniel studied him uneasily for a moment. Then he asked Beres, "What do you think he'll do?"

Tenai, standing a little distance away, turned her head. She said, her tone abstracted and just a little amused, "Mitereh Encormio-na has set out a challenge. He is inviting me to match him." Behind the humor in her tone, Daniel wasn't certain she was actually amused at all. She was gazing down toward the small army. Toward the king. She said, "When I do not give him any answer, he will not withdraw. I do think not. No, he will challenge me again. I think … I think he will come to the gate alone, or with only one or two guards. When he does, Captain Beres, let him in and bring him to me. With all due courtesy, to be sure."

"Nolas-e," acknowledged the soldier. "In your study, Nolas-e?"

"The library." Tenai turned toward the stair that would take her back into the main house. She added over her shoulder, "Penon. Daniel. Accompany me, if you will." Daniel wouldn't have missed this for the world. He took several running steps to catch up.

Seen up close, the king did not appear quite as youthful as he

226

had at a distance. There were fine lines at the corners of his eyes and a faint weathering to his dark skin. He also looked more, well, kingly. He was good-looking, but that wasn't the source of his presence, Daniel judged; that was something else. Experience. Poise. Something.

The king paused for a second in the doorway of Tenai's library and looked at them all, his own expression neutral. His glance paused for an instant when it came to Daniel, but his expression did not change. He was not accompanied, and he was not armed. Alone and unarmed, he had come into this lion's den. Yet there was no trace of fear in his face or bearing.

He was dark-complexioned, as most people seemed to be in this country—a shade darker-skinned than Tenai. He had something of her angular cast of features as well. His hair, a very dark brown, was long and caught back at his neck with a clasp. His eyes were almond-shaped and darker than Tenai's: true black, at least in this light.

Tenai had risen when the young king entered. She stood behind the table, her fingertips resting on its smooth surface. It was a big room, one that offered plenty of space for people who were not too friendly. There were chairs around the table, enough for everyone present plus several extras, if they ever chose to sit down in them.

Like the king, Tenai showed no readable expression. Captain Beres, who had escorted the king to this room, stepped to one side and stood there at a relaxed kind of attention. Penon, more obviously anxious, gripped his hands together and stood with his eyes going from the king's face to his lady's. Daniel, behind Tenai and a little to the side, trying to look like he belonged there, was impressed with the king's poise. The young man walked forward and stood in front of her, on the other side of the table, his hands at his sides and no suggestion of discomfort anywhere about him. He was just a fraction the taller. He did not bow.

Neither did Tenai. After a moment, her expression cool, she inclined her head just a little. "Mitereh Encormio-na."

The king returned the gesture, to the exact degree. "Tenai Nolas-Kuomon. I go by my mother's name now." His voice was cool; not hostile, but inexpressive.

Just as formal and reserved, Tenai inclined her head again in acknowledgement. "Sekuse-go-e, then. Permit me to be direct. I had thought we had an understanding, Mitereh Sekuse-go-e. I would not return, and you would not pursue me. I perceive I was mistaken."

The king answered steadily, "If we had such an understanding, it was you who broke it. I did not pursue you, and yet here you stand."

"You brought me back. Or had it done."

There was a short pause. Then the king said, "No."

Tenai regarded him thoughtfully. "It was not by my doing that I returned across the veil, Mitereh. Another's will took me from that other world and set me here. I take that act as an offense and an insult. I will not be used according to the will of an enemy. I do not intend to take up my sword and my name and my war. All that is ended. I swear this by Lord Death."

The king nodded. "I am glad to take your word. Nor was it my doing that brought you through the veil, nor do I have knowledge of it. Which I will willingly swear to, and do, by my mother's name and before God."

"Then I must take your word," Tenai said, and lifted one hand toward a chair. "Will you sit? There is wine. Will you drink from a cup I offer?"

"Without hesitation." The king took the indicated chair with a grace that Daniel supposed had been trained into him as a child. Tenai sat down in her own chair. No one else made any move to sit, so Daniel didn't either. Galt poured wine with hands that trembled, offering the straw-pale liquid first to the king and then to his lady. Tenai took her goblet in her hand and sat there, watching the king.

Who, his eyes on her face, lifted his goblet in a gesture like a salute, and drank about half the wine all at once.

For the first time, Tenai smiled: a thin, ironic smile, but a smile. She said, "You are safe here in my house, Mitereh Sekuse-go-e."

"At least," murmured the young man. "I do not believe you would use poison in a cup."

He swirled his remaining wine gently around the goblet, gazing down at it, then lifted his eyes again to meet hers. "My advisors are concerned."

"Do you wish to go out to them, to reassure them?"

"No. They will wait. They have their orders. The persons who opened the veil for you ... I wonder whether *they* are worried."

"I should think it likely. Why would anyone have taken this chance, if not to bring down the son of Encormio?"

The king lifted one shoulder in a minimal shrug. "I see no other reasonable possibility. Any man might well have believed Nolas-Kuomon would resume the war she had once pursued so relentlessly. I might have expected that myself. Except I remembered a garden on a fair spring evening, and a moment when Lord Death's lady chose to hold her knife. Except that I felt we had reached an understanding: that you would not return, nor would I pursue you."

"And then I did return," Tenai said, with the slightest glint of humor in her dark eyes.

The barest hint of a smile. "Just so. This created great consternation in Nerinesir, and in me, I do confess it. That you retired at once to Chaisa ... I took that as possibly a sign you did not desire to resume your war. But I was by no means certain of this surmise."

"And so you came here. To me. With no guard worth mentioning, and then alone into my house. A great burden to set on one moment in that garden."

The king's gaze remained steady. He said, "I came because I held to hope that you might not have returned in order to take up your sword against me. I came because my death would create difficulties for Talasayan, but not so much as setting the whole of the land once more at odds in a war between Encormio's son and Nolas-Kuomon."

"You think your death would have returned peace to the land?"

"I might have hoped for that."

"Ah. Once, I might have looked for any reason to continue that war. Or no reason. Your death would not have prevented me." For a moment, there was silence. Then Tenai moved a hand a little, dismissively. "Well, no longer. Whatever plan it was, misconceived in whatever mind, it has surely gone awry. I am here, but I bear you no ill will, Mitereh Sekuse-go-e. Or if I do, I will set that aside. You might have raised an army for fear of me, but you have not. Clearly an enemy has aimed at you. But the fire this person thought to set alight has guttered and gone out." She opened her hands, a gesture of relinquishment. "Let us not strike further sparks upon the kindling your enemy laid ready, Mitereh. Give me until the year dies. I will depart, and not return a second time to trouble you."

The king set his goblet on the table and folded his hands. He raised his eyes to Tenai's face, but said nothing.

"Well?" Tenai asked him. Softly.

"In sixteen years," said the young king, just as quietly, "I have created peace throughout the land. When you were forced through the veil, I was eleven. When you were defeated at last, the remnants of your army surrendered at once to mine. You will guess what men had charge of the kingdom in that time: Unyatan Kayalaran, Madai Simpana-e, Keitah Terusai-e, Embadau Penad."

"Yes," agreed Tenai, in an utterly neutral tone.

"I was eleven years old, Tenai Chaisa-e, and a child, but I knew my own will. That, at least, is one thing my father taught me."

Tenai inclined her head.

"In five years there were two rebellions from within Talasayan. Imbaneh-se tried to break my hold four times, once compelling me to actual war. There were continuous raids from out of Tesmeket for all that time, which grew worse when Imbaneh-se pressed Talasayan the hardest. The men who ruled in my name put down the rebellions, forced Imbaneh-se to the uneasy submission in which I now hold it, and persuaded Tesmeket to a greater courtesy. I still knew what it was that I desired. When I was sixteen, it had been achieved: there was peace in all the land, and I had learned enough to hold it in my own name. My father's partisans were gone ... or at least quiet. Neskiku was dead. So was Emsamta Nesuke-sa. Benkayan Tana-ai was gone, exiled beyond the sea. The Geraimani of Imbaneh-se were quiet at last. Keitah and Mikanan are my advisers, now, and Unyatan. For ten years, I have worked to secure the gains we have made. I think we have done well."

"I rejoice to hear it."

"I hope you may find peace pleases you. Yet in a handful of days, you have done more to threaten this peace than the Geraimani, Benkayan, and all of Tesmeket could have done among them."

"Not by my will."

The king regarded Tenai steadily. "I am satisfied that you did not return in order to resume your war, as you assure me this is so. I accept that you did not return of your own design. I think we both understand that I am grateful beyond words that you destroyed my father. No one else could have done it. I would forgive you any crime and any sin as fair return for that one great service, if my forgiveness were something you desired. For that, I would give you anything in my power to give, including time."

"And yet—"

"And yet, I will not allow you to destroy the peace that has at last been wrought in this land."

Tenai lifted one narrow eyebrow.

"If you had come back to kill me, I would not have fought you. Four hundred years of battle were enough. I think—I hope—that you would not be able to rouse an army against me in Talasayan. But I know you could, in Imbaneh-se."

"I understand you, Mitereh."

"Whether you go to my enemies or whether you do not, your presence alone will create an army in Imbaneh-se, which has never yet been content to be ruled by Talasayan."

Tenai put her hands flat on the table. For the first time, Daniel knew he saw opponents sitting there: one on either side of the table, striving to win ... something. Tenai said sharply, "Yes, I understand."

"Imbaneh-se has partisans all through the west, and more than a handful here in the north. Men who strove to use my father's death to break Talasayan apart down the middle. Men who do not serve me, or even Imbaneh-se, but themselves and their dreams of power. Those who fought under you at the last. Men who would rise again, if you should once again lift your banner on the wind, hoping to ride that wind to their own victory, caring for nothing but their own power—"

"I said, I understand."

"Then what," asked the king, "what will you do, Tenai Nolas-Kuomon, lady of the dark kingdom, lady of the long departed years?"

"I am certain you have a suggestion."

"Even if you went back across the veil, that would not serve. Not now. Not when all men understand you may always return. Imbaneh-se will not be quiet now. There are always pretenders in Sotatan to claim the oak throne. The Geraimani will cry your name and set the hilltops alight with their beacon fires. They will bring out your banners, whether you will or no. If Imbaneh-se should rise, Tesmeket will likely take the chance to challenge my hold. If Talasayan should be challenged by both Imbaneh-se and Tesmeket, then there will be trouble from Keneseh as well. Kaitre Umangse has come to his power there, had you heard it? He wishes to test me. He will, if he sees my strength is divided." The king stopped, and looked at Tenai.

"If you are going to ask something of me, then ask it," she said. For the first time in this tense interview, Daniel heard the echo of old anger behind her words. He winced inwardly.

The king said quietly, "Swear to me, Tenai Ponanon Chaisa-e, Nolas-Kuomon. Set your banner beneath mine on the tower. Let all men see that you are mine. Then their violent tongues will cleave to their teeth in fear and they will be quiet and stay in their homes."

Tenai looked at him for a moment in silence. Then she stood up and walked away, as far as the opposite wall. Mitereh did not move. Turning to face him, Tenai smiled, a cold and deliberate smile with no humor in it at all. "Do you know what it is you are asking, Encormio-na?"

"I know well. I am perfectly aware. I still ask."

"I intended to kill you once. Or, no. I intended that twice. Both times, I gave this over. Was this not generous of me?"

"I acknowledge it was generous."

"Encormio destroyed all I held dear. In my despair, I declared that God had mistaken his way. I forswore all masters save one, and that one I served for four hundred years. And you would ask me to serve Encormio's son? Last of that cursed line?" The tension of gathering rage sang under Tenai's words, hidden beneath her passionless tone, and yet not hidden at all. In that room, no one moved. No one would have dared.

Mitereh met her eyes. "I do not ask it lightly."

"I confess I am astonished that you ask it at all."

"Nolas-Kuomon, I have no choice. All the choices in this room are yours."

Tenai stood still for a moment. Then she came back to the table and stood there, quite near the young king, the fingertips of one hand resting on its surface, looking down at him. He tilted his head back to continue meeting her eyes, but he did not speak.

She said, "I see alternatives you have not given breath. I could kill you, and take the ivory throne of Talasayan myself. Talasayan would have no choice but to accept me. Keitah and Mikanan and Unyatan would be too wise to fight me. Imbaneh-se would not dare rebel against me; they would not carve another throne of their own."

She did not mention Sandakan Gutai-e. Daniel noticed that, and wondered if the king noticed it too, and what that omission meant. He would not have dared interrupt.

Tenai was going on. "I could force them to support me, all three. Keneseh would come into line, and then I could set Tesmeket down with merely a look. There would be no war then. Am I not correct?"

"Likely," answered the king. "Likely you could do that. If you kill me, Talasayan would surely go to the strongest lord. If that should be you, Tenai Nolas-Kuomon ... if you should be still alive and on this side of the veil by midsummer next, with your banner flying ... then I would count *you* my heir. I left that command with all my people: to yield to you if that should come to pass. I think they would obey ... after a year, seeing that you were determined. If you wish to rule."

There was a tense pause. Then Tenai laughed, a curt sound without much humor. "You have learned a bold strategy, Mitereh."

"Yes. I learned it of you."

"You do not tell over the faults with this plan?"

"You hardly need me to number them for you, Nolas-Kuomon."

"True," said Tenai. The tension in the room was brutal. "Do you know why, when you were a child and I found you in that garden, I let you live?"

"No," answered Mitereh, in a low voice. "I have never known that."

"Nor have I." There was a grim silence. Tenai broke it. "And yet you put yourself now into my hands, unarmed as that child."

"I told you, all the choices here are yours. Will you murder me?"

After a moment, Tenai said, "No."

"Then yield," said the king, as quietly as ever.

"Nor will I set my hand under your foot, Mitereh Encormiona. I am disposed to favor you, Mitereh. I will not kill you in my house. I will permit you to go freely. Go, and leave me in peace. I will not set foot beyond the borders of Chaisa, and at midwinter I will depart. Count that as enough."

"I will not. I cannot."

Tenai laid her hands flat on the table, leaning forward toward the king. "Go, or I will disregard your pride and cast you forth. I will not serve you, Encormio-na. The very suggestion amazes me. If there is war, it must pass me by, for I will care nothing for it. I tell you again, at midwinter I will depart. If you are wise, you will not involve me in the affairs of Talasayan at all."

The king gazed into her face. No longer quite expressionless, he looked tired. He looked, Daniel thought, like he had come to Tenai with only faint hope and had now lost that hope and was trying to resign himself to what would follow. He said, one last effort, "You *are* involved. Whatever I do, wherever I turn, you are on the road before me, Tenai Chaisa-e. Will you not aid me to make that road a bright one?"

There was a cold, hard look to Tenai now; not just to her face, but emanating outward from her, Daniel thought, like heat from a fire. Except that her coldness was the antithesis of fire: there was no promise of passion and life to it. She had shut out the young king's words, the plea behind them. How much of what he was asking was she even hearing?

He cleared his throat.

The small cough drew everyone's attention, even Tenai's, which was so intense as to be uncomfortable. For a moment, he hesitated. But he had not been afraid of Tenai for years. If he said nothing, whatever was getting ready to happen would happen. Whatever that was, it would be partly his fault. He said into the teeth of that cold intensity, "Tenai ... are you the kind of person who would start a war and let hundreds, maybe thousands of people die, in order to protect her pride?"

There was a pause. The king leaned back in his chair and looked at Daniel with deep curiosity. Penon was staring at him with something that resembled horror, Beres with an expression that might have been hope. Galt was watching the king, and Tenai. Tenai's eyes were on Daniel's face. He could hardly guess what she was thinking.

Or, no. He could make one obvious guess.. He said, "This isn't Encormio, Tenai."

"It is his *son*."

"So what?"

Everyone stared at him. Daniel looked only at Tenai. "It was Encormio who was your enemy. You went to war against Encormio. You won. It's *over*. It's wrong to visit the sins of the father on the son. Everyone seems to agree this young man is a good king. No one wants to go back to war—except, I guess, your enemies, whoever they are. You don't want to do what they want, so … don't do what they want."

There was another, longer, pause. At last Tenai said, "You cannot be aware what Mitereh Encormio-na is asking."

"True," Daniel conceded. "But you are. And I've never been through a war—not a serious war. You have, and I thought you were tired of it. Is your pride worth starting one now? Or is there something else at hazard here? Something worth resuming the war you agreed was ended sixteen years ago?"

Rage, no longer frozen into silence, glinted in Tenai's eyes and thinned her mouth. She turned her head back to regard the king. He met her eyes with no shadow of either trepidation or triumph. Daniel could not imagine what effort that neutrality took.

She said, "Perhaps I might agree to a pretense."

The king hesitated. Then he said in a low voice, "A pretense would not suffice."

"Do you think I will offer more? What I *will* offer, must serve. Accept what I will grant you, Mitereh, and be satisfied."

"I cannot. Tenai Nolas-Kuomon … it cannot serve. Your banner must fly beneath mine; all men must see it set so on the tower. I must trust you at my back; all men must see that trust." The king paused, then added steadily, "I will beg, if that might sway you." He rose, and began to kneel.

"Cease!" Tenai snapped, bringing her palm down on the table with a sound like a gunshot. Everyone flinched—at least, Daniel knew *he* had jumped, and was certain he wasn't alone.

Though his expression still did not change, Mitereh stopped. After a second, he sat back down in his chair and folded his hands on the polished table. For a moment his gaze rested on his hands. He took a long, careful breath. Another. Then he lifted his eyes again to meet hers. He said, "All the choices here are yours, Nolas-Kuomon. You must yield to me, or there will be war—war to no purpose; war with no good ending for any land. Those are the choices. I see no others. That is why I came."

Tenai stared into his face. "Will you guarantee me Chaisa?"

"I will guarantee nothing."

Tenai's head went back a little, as though this refusal had not been expected. The anger had settled; to Daniel she seemed more exasperated now than furious. It was a vast improvement. She folded her arms, frowning at Mitereh, who was completely still.

"I promise nothing," said the king. "I guarantee nothing. I will accept no conditions. Did I not say that it is the reality I must have? I will beg you to yield to me, Tenai Ponanon Chaisa-e, but it is a true yielding I must beg you to give me."

A pause spun itself out.

Mitereh broke it. "Must I remind you that events do not hesitate on the fears of men?"

The corner of Tenai's mouth turned up, for all the hard look to her face. "Impatient youth."

"Then be wise with the wisdom of age," said the king, not backing up at all.

Tenai glanced at Daniel. When she spoke, her tone was not cold, only sober. "If I do this, both you and Jenna will be in this man's hands. Not in mine. That is indeed a hazard beyond my pride, which I confess, I do value. But I promised you both the safety of Chaisa. If I give you now into the hands of Mitereh Sekuse-go-e, this is far from what I promised you."

Daniel hesitated. He hadn't thought of that. He hadn't thought *nearly* so far as that. He glanced at the king, who looked back at him with a dark, intelligent gaze. Mitereh Sekuse-go-e didn't *look* like a crazy sociopathic killer. But he was a king, here in this still largely unknown world. Daniel couldn't guess what this young man might do. He had no idea. He asked Tenai. "Would we be in danger?"

Tenai opened a hand in a gesture like a shrug. "This is not the child I remember. This is a man who has learned to be ruthless, with himself and doubtless with others."

Mitereh leaned back in his chair, watching Tenai and Daniel with undisguised curiosity.

Tenai added, "I think a man who came to me as this man came, who has spoken to me as this man has spoken, is far too wise to offend me lightly. But I cannot say there is no peril for you or for Jenna."

Daniel looked at the king, who met his eyes, waiting quietly. Daniel thought about the courage it must have taken, for this young man to walk into this house and make the demand he had made. About the courage it took to wait now, without a word, without any sign of impatience. He thought about the stories Tenai had told him, of her long, long life. It seemed obvious that the horrors and desolation this land had known while Tenai and Encormio fought had given way to a far safer and more prosperous peace. Everyone from an outlaw to the captain of Tenai's own guard had obviously feared Tenai might set herself against the young king. No one had wanted that.

He had seen himself, it was obvious, that Mitereh Sekuse-go-e was a man willing to die for his country. That seemed … like enough to go on with. Facing Tenai again, Daniel said, "I would never ask you to set any peaceful, well-governed country at war. Not for me, not even for Jenna."

Tenai inclined her head. She glanced around the room, at Penon, at Beres. She looked for a long moment at Galt, who was very pale. There was a knife in her hand. Daniel had not seen her draw it. She took a step toward the king, who rose to face her.

Tenai studied him for a moment. Then she went to one knee. After the smallest hesitation, she drew the knife across her palm, her eyes not flickering when blood ran down her hand and dripped on the floor. When she offered the young king the hilt of the knife, her stare was as blank and cold as Daniel had ever seen it. But she said, "I will serve you, Mitereh Sekuse-go-e."

"What do you offer me?" asked the king, in that quiet, steady tone he had used all through this whole brutal interview.

Tenai inclined her head. She answered without a hint of emotion, "Loyalty and obedience, Mitereh Sekuse-go-e, and what honor I may have." Behind the inexpressive face was that harsh, terrible self-control Daniel had learned to recognize sixteen years ago. Beyond that … hopefully not the conflagration of anger she had once carried. He wasn't certain. He couldn't tell.

"Your life?" asked the king, as neutral in tone and manner as Tenai.

"Promised to Lord Death long ago, and I advise you respect that other service of mine, Mitereh."

The king took the knife she was holding out. He said with grave formality, "I accept everything you offer, Tenai Nolas-Kuomon. You may stand."

Tenai rose, expressionless. Mitereh stood an arm's-length

from her. His expression revealed nothing. But his voice held … barely perceptible relief, perhaps. Or barely suppressed terror. "I will return to the capital at once, Chaisa-e. You will accompany me."

"As you command, I will do," she acknowledged.

The king's drew in a slow breath and let it out. His eyes went to Daniel. "Who is this?"

Daniel, despite himself, found himself holding his breath. He wondered what the king saw, what he thought: no local clothing could possibly let Daniel look like he belonged to this house, to this land. He suppressed a nervous urge to run a hand across his smooth scalp.

Tenai answered, "A chance companion, Mitereh, a man of that other land beyond the veil, who had the misfortune to be near me when the veil opened. His name is Daniel."

"But not a companion of one moment."

"No. Of the years. The man is a physician of the … mind. I was fortunate to find myself … under his authority, in the country of my exile."

Mitereh examined Daniel thoughtfully. He asked, speaking directly to Daniel for the first time, "What is this, a physician of the mind?"

Daniel wondered whether he should equivocate. He said, "I try to heal the sick."

"The sick?"

"The mad," Tenai said, more plainly than Daniel would have.

"Ah." The king did not seem shocked. He added, still to Daniel, "And the other? Jenna? That is your … wife, perhaps?"

"My daughter," Daniel said, and was shaken by terror in case he'd made a mistake after all. But Tenai did not seem concerned, when he looked at her. She didn't seem much of anything, actually, but, well, that was Tenai. Having no choice, he trusted her. Determinedly.

"Ah," said Mitereh again, drawing Daniel's gaze back that way. "Danyel. Will you hold yourself under my authority?"

Daniel looked at Tenai again. She gave an impatient little nod and said, "Yes, of course. You have no choice now. All the choices now are his."

"All right. I guess. Yes," Daniel said.

The king said, "I take both you and your daughter into my

hand. You, also, will come with me to Nerinesir."

Daniel, feeling thoroughly out of his depth, nodded.

Mitereh turned and walked to the door. And turned again there, to glance back at Tenai. He said, "Chaisa is yours. Leave it in what order you see fit. We will leave for Nerinesir within the hour."

6

The room seemed larger after the king had gone: larger and far more comfortable. But not much safer. Daniel looked at Tenai, who was looking at nothing. Her expression was … different. Blank and hard. Her awareness was turned, he suspected, toward the past. But as he watched her, she turned her head to look at him with a more specific attention. "Daniel."

"Tenai. Are you all right?"

A grim species of humor touched her mouth. "I will do, my friend." She looked at Penon, who stood with his hands clutched together, gazing at Tenai as though she was his hope of heaven. Then she looked at Galt, who dropped his eyes. "Well," said Tenai, "This is nothing any of us had looked for, I think. Penon."

"Nolas-e," answered the old man, with a worried dip of his head.

"It seems that you and Galt must order Chaisa again, as before. I have no doubt of you." She glanced at Galt again. "Either of you. I do assure you."

"Nolas-e," murmured Galt.

"Then go set matters in order." Tenai waited until they had gone, the older man and the younger, and then turned her formidable attention to Beres. "Captain Beres."

"Nolas-e."

"How does the man I brought you, Emelan? Does he sit well with your guard?"

The captain shrugged, a minimal movement of his shoulders. "Not so easily, Nolas-e. I have brought houseless men into this guard on occasion, you may recall. It does take a little time."

"I will ease your burden by taking him with me, then," said Tenai. "In any case, I should have a man of mine in that camp."

The soldier nodded. He said, Daniel thought with some reluctance, "You should have more than one man, Nolas-e, for the honor of your house. You should take dependable men, men you would be able to trust."

Tenai said, "No." And then, more kindly as Beres flinched and dropped his gaze, "No, I do think not. Men of mine, dependable men—we do not know what the future may bring us. You may need those men here."

"As you say," agreed the captain, with possibly some relief.

"Horses I must have, however. The best in the stables. A black horse for me, or gray would do. Bring my sword. He would follow, but I prefer not to put him to the trouble; the means Gomantang takes to come to my hand may be uncomfortable."

"Indeed, Nolas-e, I will bring the dark sword to you myself."

"Good. Go see to these things. Send Jenna here to me. Tell Enera to pack everything I will need."

Captain Beres bowed, received a curt nod of dismissal, and went out.

There was a silence. Daniel looked at Tenai. Finally he asked, "Would you really have started a war, if you had tossed that young man out on his ear?"

She smiled. Daniel could not tell whether there was any real humor behind that smile or not. "Shall we say, I should not have liked to test the chance, Daniel. As well you prevented me from doing so. I hope we may come to be glad of that. Should events prove otherwise … I will tell you something I will not say before others: I will keep my eye on you still. You may count yourself still within *my* hand. And Jenna, to be sure. I ask that you do trust me. If this young king has mocked me … which I think unlikely, very unlikely, Daniel … but if that is *in truth* the very son of Encormio, I will not leave you in his hands. I would be forsworn rather than abandon you. You may assuredly trust me for that."

Daniel nodded, relieved, though actually he'd assumed that. "Can you give me any idea what Jenna and I should expect?"

"Ah. I strongly suspect Mitereh will take you both into his own household. He will do it to show you honor, and to have you under his eye. He will be very courteous. That, I certainly expect. He will not wish to offend me. He is aware he has pressed me hard."

"All right. I guess that sounds all right. He won't take *you* into his household?"

"He would never dare." Then Tenai thought again, and

smiled. "Or perhaps he might. He is certainly bold enough. But I think not. He will give me leave to establish my own household, either within his or adjacent. That is what I expect. First he will test me. My oath. He has no choice in that. He will make a display of me, to show all his people that I am in his hand. A display, indeed. This will be a *pageant*." In a way, the idea seemed to amuse her, an amusement with a dangerous edge to it. But she added, "Have no fear for me. Do you?"

"If I were you, *I'd* be angry," Daniel admitted.

For a moment, Tenai's eyes hardened and seemed to glint like metal. "Oh, yes. I am indeed angry. But I know very well Mitereh Encormio-na has not earned my anger. I shall save that for my enemies … and his, as seems likely."

Daniel nodded.

Tenai went on, her tone now thoughtful. "Many, many years have passed since I last owned a master. Any master but Lord Death. A very long time." She met Daniel's eyes. "But I owned *you*, Doctor. Not with the fealty Mitereh would have of me, certainly. Still, no. I do not have so much pride that I must set it as a bridge over an ocean of blood. You were wise to ask me that. I think Mitereh will be wise. He does seem so, to me. He was wise to leave me Chaisa."

"*After* he got your oath."

"He does know his own mind." Tenai seemed to approve this. "I think you will find Mitereh certainly finds a place in his household for you, a place of honor. Likely he will elevate you. You have no estate, and he is not likely to grant you that. But likely he will set you among the ranks of nobility."

"*There's* an odd thought." It was definitely odd. But Daniel thought that sounded just as well—for Jenna's sake especially. If those kinds of rankings existed here, he wanted Jenna high enough up that she'd be safe. Safer. Though he knew she wouldn't take anything about that very seriously.

"I think you will find Mitereh is curious. About you." She gave him a close look. "About me."

"Doctor-patient privilege. Plus the privilege of friendship." Which he'd just made up on the spot, but was willing to solemnly invoke if necessary. "I won't discuss you with him, Tenai."

Tenai nodded, smiling, but she said, "This is not your gentle America, Daniel. I think Mitereh will respect your loyalty. Press his patience as far as you think fit, this would please me; but if you must protect yourself, by all means do so, and trust me that I will protect myself."

"All right."

"I think this young man will not take that turning, Daniel. I do think not. Bloodlust is not what brought him into my house—" There were footsteps outside in the hall, and Tenai broke off. Jenna came in, and Emelan behind her. Jenna came directly to Daniel and put an arm around his waist, tucking herself close to his side. Daniel hugged her, hard, trying to put confidence into that gesture.

Emelan gave a small bow, saluting Tenai. He looked like one of the regular house guards: thinner than he should be, but now resembling a soldier far more than a brigand. He wore the house uniform as though already accustomed to it. His beard had been shaved off, and his newly-trimmed hair had been braided and clubbed at the nape of his neck. He looked younger now that he was better groomed—Daniel thought he might be closer to thirty than to his first guess of forty. Still, for all the improvements, Daniel thought he would have still been able to pick the man out of any lineup by the uncertainty hidden in his eyes.

Tenai said, "Beres told you what passed?"

"Yes, Nolas-e. I will ask … Nolas-e, permit me to remain in Chaisa. I do ask you. I should not—it should not be I whom you choose to accompany you—"

Tenai dismissed this request with a slight gesture. "What lies in the past, lies there. You are my man now. I expect you to make yourself a new history."

"Yes," said Emelan, but looking distinctly like he would have wished to make it *No*.

"Well?"

The man lowered his head, took a breath, and lifted his gaze again to meet her eyes. "Keitah—Keitah Terusai-e will know me. I do fear so. Even if it has been years. Even if no one else should. And he would know me for an oath-breaker, Nolas-e. Forgive my presumption to ask whether you will want it known what you have brought into your house—"

Tenai made a dismissive gesture. "I am not accustomed to allowing my decisions to be questioned. By Keitah Terusai-e or anyone else. Set your mind at rest, Emelan no-man's-son. You may be certain that if I attach you to my company, I shall not look for shame to come of it, whatever is known or not known."

Emelan said nothing.

"Go. Inform Beres he is to see to your kit. Choose a horse from the stables. Grey or black. Then wait for me in the yard."

Emelan hesitated. Then he went to one knee. He said, with the air of a man forced against his will, "Nolas-e, forgive my impudence to ask again—"

"When I have already made my decision known?" Tenai said with sharp impatience. "This is indeed impudence. No. Enough. I am unconcerned with the opinion of Terusai-e, or Nerinesir entire. Nor do I permit you to concern yourself with either. Earn my regard, and I assure you, no other opinion need signify."

Daniel thought that Emelan might protest again. The man drew in his breath as though he would speak. But then he only let his breath out again and got to his feet. His expression was hard to read, his face blank, all thought and emotion hidden. He bowed again, and went out without another word.

"Will he be all right?" Daniel asked her in a low voice, looking after the man once he was gone. He was disturbed by Emelan's evident distress, and more disturbed at Tenai's apparent indifference.

"I must trust that he will," Tenai answered. Her tone was quiet. She glanced at Daniel and opened a hand in a gesture like a shrug. "He is ashamed of his past. As well he should be. But I have seen shamed men before. You will agree with me, I think: there is no way out of that shame save to go forward. A man cannot hide from the world forever. The longer he is permitted to hide, the more difficult it will be to come out into the light. And he will likely be hard-used if I leave him here: curs off the road are not easily granted honor by honorable men."

Daniel nodded. "All right. Yes, you're probably right."

"I think I am. Now. Jenna." Tenai turned to young woman. "Are the horses ready, child? My kit, and yours, and your father's? My household?"

"Enera said she would have everything in the courtyard before you got there, Tenai."

"Good." Tenai's eyes rested on Jenna's face for a moment. "You are not afraid?"

Jenna lifted her chin. "Not me, Tenai. Not much! I trust you.

I'm looking forward to meeting the king. Melesa says he's very handsome."

Daniel choked, but Tenai smiled, much of her chilly distance disappearing. "So he is. Likely married. Never yet in the history of the world has a king come to his twenty-seventh year unmarried. His advisors would never permit such a thing."

"Oh, well," Jenna said philosophically.

"He will admire you, nonetheless," Tenai predicted. She was still smiling. "He will be greatly taken with you, my bright child. All his young men will be. You will come among them as a golden cat among—"

"Hounds?" Jenna interrupted, laughing.

"Mice, bright child. Assuredly a golden cat among so many mice. If you feel out of place, remember that you are beautiful as a rare bird. Your coloring is sweet as the sunrise; your face catches the eye with its unique beauty. All the young men of the court will fall in love with you. All the women will watch your steps with envy."

"If you say so." Jenna was still laughing.

His daughter, Daniel saw, was pleased and excited and ready to be reassured. But she hadn't been present for that excruciating interview with the king. Daniel was very certain that young man would never, ever forget for one second that his foreign guests were important to Tenai. He was positive Mitereh Sekuse-go-e—Mitereh Encormio-na—would never lose sight of the possibilities inherent in that kind of connection.

For a moment the world seemed to shiver with unseen threat. Daniel longed to turn and beg Tenai to find some way to keep them here in Chaisa, immured safely away from this dangerous land, until midwinter arrived and they could run back to a sane and civilized country that *had* no kings and no hidden enemies and no bloody history come to life around them. But he said nothing. The moment for that particular cowardice had passed.

The courtyard seemed crowded, with people and horses everywhere. But Daniel noted that all of people were Tenai's. Outside the gates there might be a crowd around the king, but it was quite clear that no one of that gathering but the king himself had dared intrude. Or would that be Mitereh's own act of sensibility?

Tenai appeared. She was wearing black—black shirt and trousers, black vest, black boots. She ought to be terribly hot in this weather in that outfit, but she looked cool and comfortable. Possibly her oath to Lord Death made her immune from heatstroke as well as crossbow bolts; Daniel wouldn't have bet against that. Her hair had been fixed back in an intricate braid that swayed when she walked. She stood with a hand on the hilt of her black sword, as naturally as though she had never spent a moment of her life without a sword at her hip. She looked tall and dangerous and every bit like she belonged to this world.

A girl led up a horse for Tenai: a black mare, neat-footed and delicately boned, with black ribbons braided into its mane and tail and crystals set into the fittings of its tack.

Emelan, pale and strained, rode up on a gray gelding. He was leading another gelding, also gray, for, Daniel presumed, himself. Galt, looking worried, was there, on the outskirts of the little group, listening. Penon stood beside him, one hand on the younger man's arm in a gesture of support or restraint.

Tenai said to Penon, with all the formality that seemed customary in this country, "I have trust in the officers of my household. You will do very well."

Penon bowed in response. "Have you orders, Nolas-e?"

Tenai met his eyes, and Galt's. "Follow your inclinations and you will have no reason to fear my return. Which I do expect, in rather less than sixteen years."

The young man bowed without speaking, but Daniel thought there was less tension in his face.

Tenai laid a hand on her mare's neck and swung, graceful as a dancer, into the saddle. Jenna jumped up on her own horse. *Hers* wasn't a gray. It was a lovely golden animal that Daniel was certain had been chosen to complement his daughter's own fair coloring. It seemed an unnecessarily tall horse, but Jenna was effusive in her delight with it.

Smothering a smile, he heaved himself up onto his plainer horse. He made it into the saddle on his own, but it took two tries and wasn't graceful at all, so, well, he had to hope that in fact no one had been watching.

Tenai swept a look across Daniel and Jenna and Emelan once they were all mounted. "Be proud," she reminded them. "Represent yourselves with pride. This is a *show*, and we are all players in the light; but we choose our own lines. Remember it."

"I'm a doctor, dammit, not an actor," Daniel said. He wasn't quite joking, but he said it under his breath so no one else would hear him. Then he followed Tenai, as she led them all out her gate.

It was, indeed, a show.

Tenai set her black mare into a brisk trot and led them out through the gates of her house without any glance back to see if they were following. She looked straight ahead, like any Evil Warrior Queen from any made-for-TV fantasy movie Daniel had ever seen, but carrying it off a lot more effectively. Jenna rode directly behind her. She was nervous and excited, but plainly determined to carry everything off with flair. Daniel might be biased, but he thought his daughter carried her central role off well.

Daniel hoped merely not to look too ridiculous. He rode next to Emelan, who had covered probable nervousness with a thin-lipped calm. Daniel made a deliberate effort to keep his face as blank as Emelan's.

The king had his two hundred men drawn up in order outside Chaisa's gates: soldiers, a lot of soldiers; and a few men with different dress and manners. Nobles, probably. The king's advisors, most likely. The soldiers stood in long ranks with Mitereh himself and his nobles at the end of the line, waiting for Tenai. Daniel knew without turning his head that Chaisa's walls would be just as crowded with Tenai's people. It was a longish way to ride, on display like this. No problem for Tenai, but a test for the rest of them.

For so many men, there was remarkably little sound. No one spoke, or coughed, or sneezed. Tenai rode straight up to the king, who stood with his nobles to one side and his banner to the other and waited for her. Everyone else followed her. When she halted her horse, when they all halted theirs, the tense hush deepened.

For a long, long moment Tenai just sat there in the saddle, looking the king in the face. He looked back. Neither of them had any more expression than carven statues.

Then she swung her leg over her horse's shoulder and slid to the ground. She walked forward, the few steps necessary to bring her to the king. She stood there for another heartbeat, looking at him eye-to-eye. Nearly of a height. Both tall and slim; both with dark coloring and even, angular features; both proud. The king was twenty-seven. Tenai was four hundred years plus, but since her years didn't exactly show, they might have been brother and older sister.

Then she took Gomantang from her belt, still sheathed, and knelt. She made that a neat and graceful gesture, going down on one knee and offering the young king her sheathed sword, lifted in both hands in a dramatic gesture of surrender. She did not bow her head, but looked up into his face.

A sigh went through the observers: both the king's men and Tenai's people, like a wind through branches. For another long moment, they held that scene. Then the king reached forward with one hand to touch her sword. He did not take it, but only rested his hand there, on the sheath between Tenai's hands. He said, his voice not loud but pitched to carry, "Tenai Ponanon Chaisa-e, are you mine?"

Daniel could see no anger at all in her neck, her back. This is a *show*, she had said, and she had meant it. She said in a clear voice, "Yes, my king. I yield my loyalty and my honor into your hands, Mitereh Sekuse-go-e."

The king lifted the sword. Tenai let it go with perfect equanimity.

For a moment, the king held the sword up, so everyone could see it. Then he drew it. Light slid greasily along the black blade. It seemed to Daniel that smoke might drift from the sword as it was drawn, though he couldn't be certain. Turning it in his hand, the king brought the blade down, gently, to rest along Tenai's shoulder, next to her neck. She didn't move.

"Are you mine?" he asked a second time. Again, he let his voice carry.

Tenai answered, "My life belongs to Lord Death, to God, and to you."

The king lifted the sword. He said, "You have put me to some trouble, Tenai Ponanon Chaisa-e, in your return and in your retreat into Chaisa. You should have come to me in Nerinesir. You may beg my pardon."

Tenai didn't even blink. "I beg your pardon, my king."

Mitereh stood there, Tenai's black sword in his hand and no expression at all on his face. He said, "You may bow by my feet."

Daniel blinked, and controlled his own expression. Jenna, just in front of him on her little mare, hissed between her teeth, but that was all. Emelan didn't react, as far he could see.

After the very briefest pause, Tenai went from one knee to both. She bent, placing one hand flat on the ground for balance, and touched her forehead to the ground by the king's boot. She stayed there, holding that pose. For a long moment, the king let her. At last he lifted the black sword, naked in his hand, and held it poised for an instant. He brought it down fast in a blow that went past Tenai's unguarded neck to strike against the ground with a ringing sound that seemed unreasonably loud for metal against earth. Tenai did not even flinch, but Mitereh's mouth tightened and his eyes narrowed.

Then he said, his tone level, "I grant you pardon." There was absolute silence from the audience. Daniel found he was holding his breath and let it out; around him, he rather thought he heard other people doing the same.

Tenai, face composed, straightened again to kneeling. The king sheathed the sword and turned it to rest point-down on the ground. He offered Tenai his hand, Daniel thought at first to help her stand, but she kissed it instead in a gesture of fealty.

"You may stand," the king said after that, quietly.

Tenai rose.

The king gave her sword back to her. She took it, expressionless, and hooked it back on her belt.

For the first time, the king turned a look on the men around him, gathering their attention with his eyes. It was hardly necessary. No one was looking anywhere but at him and at Tenai. Bringing his gaze back to her, the king said with curt decision, "We will leave for Nerinesir immediately. Mount. You will ride last, Chaisa." He turned away and put out a hand, and a man brought up a horse and put the reins in his hand.

Tenai stood still, face calm, while the king mounted and rode out. He went without a backward look. There were plenty of looks from other men: from the young king's nobles, from the soldiers ... sidelong and uncomfortable, most of those glances. Daniel, taking his cue from Tenai, waited, trying to look unconcerned. Only when the last of the soldiers had passed did Tenai move, lifting herself back into the saddle and sending her horse after them.

Riding through the village was a different experience at the tail-end of a bunch of soldiers. People still bowed and stared, but it wasn't the same. Daniel felt his face heat: he was embarrassed, he diagnosed. And *he* knew it was a play. Drawing a breath, he guided his horse past Enera's and up to Tenai's side.

She gave him a curt nod. "Daniel."

"Are you all right? Was *that* all right? Was that what you expected?"

She smiled. Her expression was a little stiff, but not angry. They were just past the village and riding past the rolling pastures. Dust kicked up by the horses ahead of them hung in the heavy air. "I told you he would press me," Tenai said in a quiet voice, not to carry to the men ahead of them, Daniel understood that. "So he did. But he did well. He understands how to hold the eye. He has skill, this young king. Everyone was impressed, I have no doubt of that. But you may be easy. He challenged my pride a little there, but he will not press me too hard, Daniel. I do think not."

Daniel let out a breath. "All right. You *did* expect all that ... business, then."

"Something very like."

"He touched your sword. He *drew* your sword." That had seemed fraught, somehow. It still did, even in retrospect.

Tenai smiled, a swift expression, not especially kind. "I doubt he enjoyed the experience. Gomantang is not a kind sword. Mitereh managed to strike near me without touching me. Then he sheathed Gomantang again without drawing blood. That speaks well of him ... though, to be sure, he has already showed he is uncommonly determined to have his own way in everything."

Jenna nudged her mare to come close beside Tenai, on her other side. "Tenai, I know no one else is supposed to draw your sword, and now I guess I know it—he—is from Lord Death's country. But what does that actually *mean?*"

Daniel had forgotten how little his daughter knew about Tenai and her past.

Tenai was smiling a little. "Between life and death there is the Gate, Jenna, and Lord Death is the Gatekeeper. This you know, yes?"

"I guess so," Jenna agreed doubtfully, while Daniel realized, again, that she meant this was *literally* true. She must. He was once again struck by the sheer horrifying danger underlying the fantasyland prettiness of this country.

"Before the Gate is the dark kingdom of Lord Death," Tenai was saying matter-of-factly. "For the dying man who fears the Gate and the judgment waiting beyond, for the one whose hand slips at the last from the lintel, for the cursed and the damned, for the man desperate not to die and fool enough to hope for better, there is the kingdom of Lord Death. That is the place in which Gomantang was forged. A man who dies by Gomantang's blade goes not to the Gate, but to the dark kingdom. It is not God who judges such a man, but Lord Death, who may keep Gomantang's dead for his own or allow him to pass the final Gate, as he pleases."

"Oh." Jenna sounded a little uncertain.

"Gomantang has a soul and a will. His desires are not the desires of a man. He will twist in the hand; he will try to kill—both his wielder and the enemy of his wielder. He is hard to use gently. So I say, Mitereh did well enough." Tenai seemed amused, but there was a bite to her tone. "I think he will not wish to lay his hand to my sword again. He is young, but one sees he is not a fool. He returns Gomantang into my hand, he gives Chaisa back to me … he puts me at the foot of the company—to try my pride, yes, but that is not all."

"No?"

"Daniel. No soldier would be so lost to pride as to turn his head and stare over his shoulder at me. Therefore I am not the target of attention. That is a kindness. Although Mitereh has gathered both you and Jenna into his hand, he leaves you in my company—and sets me at the rear, where you may speak to me freely. That is a second kindness, and never think Mitereh did not intend it." She paused, and then added, "Emelan."

"Nolas-e," said the man, in a quiet voice.

"My position will improve, and with it yours. I bid you have patience and wait for that. By the time you must draw pride from your oath to me, I will have pride to give you."

There was a short pause. Emelan answered at last in a low voice, "I have faith in everything you tell me, Nolas-e."

"As you should," Tenai responded, tone a little sharp. "Hold to that, then."

Emelan made no answer. They rode in silence after that, while the afternoon shadows stretched out away from the sinking sun. Daniel had hoped they were finished with long horseback trips, but at least this time he was not so out of shape. The Talasayan Health Spa, he supposed: horses and endless roads, and the threat of violence to sweat off weight. He would have traded it in a heartbeat for the comfort and safety of home. Jenna … probably would not.

And Tenai? Looking at her sidelong through the lengthening shadows, Daniel wondered whether she, too, might prefer obscurity and a calm life and the absence of any reminders of her long, vengeful past, over home and hearth and her own people. But the calm planes of her face and her dark secretive eyes gave away nothing, and he was not sure.

Eventually, the king must have given the order to stop for the night and make camp. By that time, scattered trees had given way to little groves. Ahead of them, the road ran into the forest and vanished from sight. Tents went up, on either side of the road. Fires sparked to life ... unlike Tenai, men seemed generally to light them with actual matches. Daniel found that Tenai had a tent of her own: small, but large enough for three people, if they were friendly. It had traveled, bundled up anonymously, across the hips of Emelan's gelding.

There were blankets as well; light things that would probably serve more to muffle rough ground than to provide unnecessary warmth. And stools to sit on, provided by the soldiers. The scents of cooking food: some kind of stew, sausage, and toasting bread. It was a far cry from the luxury of Tenai's house, but fortunately even farther from the discomfort of their first night in this land. Daniel took a bowl and spoon Emelan brought him, and sat on his stool with a sigh. In the darkness, horses shifted quietly and made peaceful little horse noises.

A man came out of the orderly camp and presented himself at the edge of light from Tenai's fire: no one Daniel recognized. A soldier. A king's man.

Tenai had been kneeling by the fire, feeding twigs one by one into its heart. She stood up when the man appeared, looking at him with calm attention.

The soldier bowed, eyeing Tenai with professional caution. "Nolas-e, the king desires the presence of Nola Danyel and Nola Jenna."

Daniel put down his bowl. Jenna stopped with her spoon halfway to her mouth. Tenai merely nodded with no evidence of surprise. Firelight glinted in her eyes. She said, "I did tell you that the king would likely bring you into his household. There is nothing to fear. He will do you honor. You hear he has granted you each a title. Accept this grant from the king's hand. Go with this man. Remember that you represent me as well as yourselves. Stand up straight and speak honestly, or else declare honestly that you will not speak." She paused. Then she added, speaking English—Daniel hadn't realized until that instant that she hadn't been, before—"If there is need, most unlikely, but if there *is* need, by all means call me by name. I will certainly hear you."

"All right," Daniel said, and was glad that his own voice was steady. He tried, experimentally, to say it in English. He could tell he succeeded by the feel of the words in his mouth, not so much by the way he heard them.

Jenna tilted her head, intrigued. She said, also in English, "From all the way over here? I mean, you really would hear if I said, 'Hey, Tenai, help!' and you were someplace a long way away?"

Tenai smiled, swift and warm. "I would indeed. Perhaps not across many miles; I would not claim so much. But, indeed, certainly so far as this. I would come at once. Various persons might find that disconcerting, so I will ask that you do not make the test. But if there is need, then call."

"Right." Probably things would get awkward if Tenai *disconcerted* the wrong people, but nevertheless, that was reassuring. Daniel took a deep breath. Then he stood up and held a hand down to Jenna, who took it to humor him even though she certainly didn't need the help.

"You will do very well," said Tenai, both reassurance and, if Daniel understood her correctly, an order. He nodded.

Tenai stood by the fire and watched them go.

7

The king's tent was not like Tenai's, nor like a soldier's. It was big, big enough for a crowd: made of heavy creamy-white panels that seemed to glow in the firelight. An awning stretched out to shelter the doorway, which was tied back with braided cords and guarded by a young man with a serious expression. A carpet lay outside that doorway; other carpets, in rich deep colors, covered the floor of the tent.

The king and his guests did not have to eat outside perched on stools; there was a table inside the tent with ample space to seat a dozen men. Only two men sat at the table: the king himself and an older, bearded man. They sat in real chairs: high-backed and made of intricately-carved wood, with cushions on their seats. It might have been hot and airless, except there were windows of fine muslin set into the sides of the tent to let in the breeze. Ornate lanterns, hung above the table, cast generous pools of light across the scene.

Two more young men stood in alert attitudes near the table, behind the king. They measured Daniel, dismissed him as a threat, and turned with much more interest toward Jenna. Daniel, though he didn't exactly blame them, was not entirely happy with that.

Jenna's eyes were wide and fascinated; she pressed forward with a fearless eagerness that for a moment strongly recalled her mother, in the good years before her illness had changed her so bitterly. Daniel was swept by a sudden intense awareness that, indeed, Kathy would have loved this tent; would have loved to meet this reserved young king; would, like Jenna, have regarded this whole thing as the best kind of adventure. Kathy had always longed to travel—to Africa, to Asia, to any destination out of the ordinary for a couple of people who had never once left the States. They had always thought there would be plenty of time for that. For a moment, as though her wretched disease and her ... death ...

had only just happened, Daniel could hardly bear her absence.

The king rose to his feet, and Daniel tried to focus on the moment. Daniel, feeling like he was performing a role in a play, bowed, the way he had seen other people do here. He was aware, beside him, of Jenna following his example with considerably more grace.

"You bring honor to my house," said the king. "Nola Danyel. And Nola Jenna. Be welcome to my household." He met Daniel's eyes, glanced at Jenna, and inclined his head just a little, black eyes intent and curious. "I invite you, share my table. Sleep tonight in my tent."

"Thank you," said Daniel, hearing the stiffness in his own tone but not able to prevent it. He would have liked to ask about the exact meaning of the title, but probably this was not the right time to ask questions. Or the right person to ask them of.

"What about Tenai?" Jenna asked, obviously feeling no such wariness.

"Ah," said the king, still in that soft tone. He did not seem offended. "You are concerned for the lady's honor? When we enter Nerinesir, I will bring Chaisa-e up to ride by my side. Provided she proves compliant until that time, as I have no doubt she will. Will that satisfy you, Nola Janna?"

The bearded man stirred and began to speak, and the king glanced that way at once and said, without raising his voice, "As I have said, so I will do."

The bearded man closed his mouth.

The king smiled and said, "Everything in life is a risk." He turned his dark eyes back to Daniel and lifted an inquiring eyebrow.

Daniel said, speaking for both himself and Jenna, "I don't think we know enough of your customs to know whether to be satisfied. Tenai—" he hesitated.

"Yes?" said the king, still not showing any trace of offense or impatience. "You may speak, Nola Danyel. I declare that I will not be offended."

All right. All right, then. Daniel said, "Tenai refers to all this as a *show*."

"Ah." The king glanced at the bearded man, not quite smiling. "A wise and perceptive woman, Chaisa-e. Did I not say so? A great treasure in my hand."

"If she is," said the man, frowning back at him.

"Just so. Yet I say she is, and will be." The king turned back to Daniel. "Yes, Nola Danyel; a show indeed. I have some hope word of Chaisa's submission to me will run to the ends of the world before ever any of us set foot in Nerinesir, to confound my enemies. Our enemies." He lifted a hand in a gesture that might have been invitation or command. "You are welcome within my household. Sit, if you wish. Eat with me."

Daniel touched his daughter on the arm. Jenna, eyes brilliant, ready to be pleased, took the seat a servant held for her. Daniel took the chair next to her. The king's young guards did not sit at the table, but stayed where they were, standing attentively behind the king.

The food was not simple stew, as the men outside were eating. Daniel could see sliced meat, whole stuffed mushrooms, and something mounded, pureed and golden, in a bowl. The scents were inviting. Platters and plates and cups were all made of wood, like the chairs, but they were not in any sense plain: the rims were as ornate as the chair legs, and the cups, taller and narrower than Daniel was used to, had elaborate inlay in dark and light woods on their sides. Daniel sipped from his. The drink was hot and sweet, tasting a little like chocolate and a little like oranges, but mostly like something flowery and less familiar than either.

The king held his own cup in both hands, long dark fingers cradling its warmth. He said, nodding toward the bearded man but with his eyes on Daniel's face, "Nolas-ai Mikanan Chauke-sa. He does not trust Tenai Nolas-Kuomon, but perhaps that may change. You know her well, perhaps, Nola Danyel."

"Fairly well," Daniel admitted.

"And you are a *physician of the mind*. Chaisa-e was a patient of yours, perhaps?"

"For a little while, a long time ago. And then a friend, for many years."

"A friend." The king seemed amused again, or surprised, or both. "A wonder of the age. A *friend* of Nolas-Kuomon, before God. And is she now *your* friend, as you are hers?"

"Yes," said Daniel, still wary. But it was the truth.

"Doubly a wonder," said the king, and slid a glance at the other man. Mikanan Chauke-sa. The man grunted and lifted his cup, avoiding that glance.

The king returned his gaze to Daniel, curious and intent. He said, "Eat, I do ask you," and made a slight gesture toward the filled plates. "You will injure my cook's pride if you decline. Try the pastry. It's very fine. It is a difficult time you are having in Talasayan, I fear. The land is fair, I promise you, in ordinary days. Is it like your own land at all? Mind, there is more to Talasayan than Chaisa, fair though Chaisa is."

The pastry, which proved to contain small whole boiled eggs wrapped in a layer of sausage, was delicious. Daniel wondered when exactly the king's cook had found time to prepare something like this. There hardly seemed to have been time since the company had broken its march. "It's pretty country," he said. "It seems very ... peaceful."

The king gave Daniel a steady look out of his dark eyes. "Yes. Talasayan is peaceful, now, and may remain so, perhaps due to your influence with Lord Death's lady. We treasure that peace, which was not easy to win. Is this a contrast, with your own land?"

"Ah," said Daniel, surprised. "Not really. My country has been at peace for a long time."

"One wonders what Nolas-Kuomon found to do there," said the bearded man, Mikanan Chauke-sa, in a dry tone.

"She became a teacher," Daniel said.

"A teacher," said the man, even more drily. "Of what? If I may ask, Nola Daniel?"

"Tenai taught fighting with bare hands, and the sword and other weapons."

"Ah," said the man. "A teacher of the arts of war, then. *That* I understand."

Daniel met his eyes. "It was something she knew how to do. Tenai said she was tired of war. She said she would rather do menial work than fight. What she taught was *defense*—to women."

"Among other things," Jenna murmured, but in English. Daniel hadn't realized how odd it would sound to hear English and this other language—he didn't know its name—at the same time. Both sounded right, but in different ways. He wondered how that actually worked, how magic made the brain interpret the unknown language as familiar and comprehensible.

Over the king's head, the two young bodyguards were exchanging a bemused glance. Mikanan Chauke-sa also looked nonplused. "To women?"

"My country is a safe place to live, but no place is *absolutely* safe. A woman alone may sometimes be at some risk. So Tenai taught women who wanted to learn how to protect themselves."

There was a thoughtful pause. It seemed a foreign notion. "To protect *themselves*," the king repeated. "Do husbands not defend their wives in your country, Nola Danyel? Do fathers not defend their daughters?"

Jenna, at Daniel's side, rolled her eyes and answered, this time in the language of Talasayan and with some heat. "Why should a woman have to depend on men for protection? What if she isn't married? What if her father isn't with her when some—" whatever word she reached for obviously didn't translate and she floundered for a quarter of a second. Then she found words that satisfied her and went on. "What if some horse's rear end decides not to take no for an answer? A woman ought to be able to handle that kind of thing herself. Why should she limit herself by needing somebody else to protect her?"

Mikanan Chauke-sa looked a little shocked, either by what Jenna had said or just because she had been the one to say it. The young bodyguards might have been as shocked, but certainly not in exactly the same way as the king's advisor: they both stared at Jenna in obvious admiration. One of them murmured under his breath, clearly not meaning to be overheard, "A golden lioness!" The remark wasn't under his breath enough; they all heard it. The young man realized this at once. A flush rose into his face, dark enough to show even with his warm skin tone and even in the lantern light.

"Ranakai!" Mitereh said, turning sharply.

The bodyguard bowed his head. "Forgive my stupidity, my king."

The king lifted his chin, his expression austere. "You need not apply to *me* for forgiveness."

At once, the young man moved a step toward Jenna and dropped to one knee, bowing his head again, this time to her. "I beg you will forgive my insolence, Nola," he said to her. "Though my foolish boldness was inexcusable, yet I have no recourse but to beg you will be kind to forgive it."

Jenna obviously did not know what to say. The tense sincerity of the bodyguard's attitude implied that her response was important, probably because the king's own response was going to depend on hers. She looked at her father for suggestions.

Daniel crooked a finger across his mouth, trying not to smile, and let her decide how to handle this situation. Now that it had happened, he thought it was a good thing that the king had been put at a disadvantage by his bodyguard: if Mitereh was moved to lay down the law to his men regarding his young female guest, that was fine.

At last, Jenna turned back to the king and said, "I don't know your customs. I'm not offended. That was hardly an insult! What should I say?"

The king's glance at the young man was severe. "Nola Jenna, it was indeed an insult for any man to speak so freely in your hearing and in mine. If you were a Talasayan lady of rank, you would certainly dismiss so impudent a young man from your presence. You are not of Talasayan, but you are a lady of rank, and a lady of my own household. If you wish me to dismiss Ranakai, I grant you leave to make the demand. If you are indeed so kind as to forgive the impudence, he must count himself fortunate beyond his deserving. And I as well, as his behavior reflects upon me."

"Oh!" said Jenna. She paused for a moment.

Ranakai bowed his head a little lower and murmured, "Be gracious, Nola, I beg you."

"I forgive you," Jenna said after a moment. "You don't need to leave on my account." She added, with what Daniel thought was an admirably severe tone considering she had probably *loved* being called a golden lioness, "Don't do it again."

"Indeed, no, Nola," the young man said, with an earnest bow. Rising, he looked at the king.

Mitereh made a small, curt gesture, and Ranakai, clearly distressed, bowed once more, turned, and left the tent. The other young man, expressionless, gazed straight ahead.

Jenna frowned at the king. "I *said* I forgave him," she pointed out. "I said he didn't need to leave! That wasn't fair."

Daniel felt strange addressing kings and nobles, but he suspected his daughter didn't really believe in them. Or at least not in their rank. He leaned back in his chair and waited to see what the king would say to this.

Mitereh regarded Jenna with evident approval. "You are generous, Nola Jenna. But even an ordinary soldier would be held to a higher standard, and the men of my own guard are not ordinary soldiers. It is my honor they uphold. You are a lady of my household, and you are a friend of Tenai Nolas-Kuomon. For both reasons, you are due courtesy and respect. If you are over-kind, I will punish insolence on your behalf. However, as you have chosen to be generous, I will not dismiss Ranakai from his post, merely set him at a distance for a little while."

The other young man's expression didn't change, but Daniel saw him let out a long breath. The whole thing must have been more serious than he'd thought. What *he* thought was important was the king's evident determination to treat both his guests with serious, careful courtesy. That was definitely reassuring.

Mitereh turned back to Daniel. He said, "Before she was your friend, Tenai Nolas-Kuomon was your patient, Nola Danyel, or so I have understood. If I may inquire, as you treat the mad, what did you find in Nolas-Kuomon?"

Daniel answered, "A physician of the mind, in my land, takes an oath before God to protect his patients' privacy. I can't discuss anything about that." Then he waited to see what the king, balked, might do or say.

"Ah." Mitereh made a little gesture that stopped Mikanan Chauk-sa's swift and probably heated answer before the man could quite begin it. The king himself merely regarded Daniel for a thoughtful moment. "Then I shall not ask; or if I do, I shall not press you. Nola Danyel, you are quite safe in my hand. I tell you so, as you may not know. Permit me to ask a different question. Has Nolas-Kuomon given you her name to use?" The king paused then, waiting for an answer.

After a second, Daniel nodded. Then he said, "But of course, we won't need to use it, will we? Since we belong to your household." He felt he should say *sir,* or maybe *your majesty,* but no words of that kind presented themselves. He hoped the king wasn't a stickler for formal courtesy.

The king leaned back in his chair, smiling, with no evidence of offense. He lifted his cup toward Daniel in a kind of salute. "Indeed, you will not, Nola Danyel. Very well. I shall not press you for that answer. Nor your daughter—" with a glance at Jenna. "I shall not press you at all. Either of you. Certainly not until you have become more confident that you may answer as you wish, without hazard. I am aware you do not know me; I am aware you have heard tales of my father from Chaisa-e. Are you able to trust me when I tell you that you are safe?"

"Maybe," Jenna murmured in English. "Soon."

Those were actually good answers. Or at least, accurate answers. At least, Daniel hoped so. He said in the language of Talasayan, "Tenai said we should trust you. I trust her. So …" He opened a hand."

"A wonder of the world," murmured the king. "But, indeed, that will do. I ask you, be comfortable in my house. Such as I may offer, while we travel in this manner, but I ask you to tolerate these rough conditions. Allow my servants to prepare places for you to sleep."

"Yes, of course. It's a beautiful tent. We're honored to be permitted to share it." Daniel was quite clear about that and thought it better to make it clear they understood it.

"Good." The king lifted a hand, gesturing to servants who came forward to clear the table and carry it out of the tent. Thin mattresses were laid out along the sides of the tent, screened from one another by sheer curtains hung from the sides and roof of the tent. The king rose and offered a small bow, first to Daniel and then to Jenna, who blushed in confusion and returned the bow.

"We shall be on the road at dawn," the king said, speaking now in a more formal tone. "Rest, I do suggest it. No one will trouble your night. I shall hope God will send you both pleasant sleep."

"Thank you," said Daniel, and thought, wistfully, of Tenai's house. And his own.

The mattresses were thin, but they were more comfortable than they looked and, Daniel realized after a moment, perfumed with some subtle musky fragrance like incense. Jenna gave hers an experimental bounce and said, in a low tone because the tent was not that big, "Smells nice. I wonder what they stuff them with."

Daniel shrugged. He and Jenna shared a corner of the tent with those sheer curtains separating them from the main part of the tent and more curtains that could be pulled down between their mattresses. The king had a sleeping area that was close by, though screened by extra layers of curtains. Guards stood outside the tent; one of his young men—not Ranakai—sat on a mat inside the tent. The chairs were gone. The lanterns remained; they had all been put out except one, a small white lantern that was evidently going to serve as a nightlight.

"I'm never going to be able to sleep," Jenna said in English, with assumed, dramatic gloominess. She touched the wall of the tent with the tips of two fingers, glancing sidelong at Daniel. The creamy canvas dimpled under the pressure.

Daniel had to concentrate to make sure he answered in the same language. "I think you did very well tonight."

Jenna gave him an ironic look. "I don't want to make a lousy first impression. But, damn. Yes, right, I know this isn't twentieth-century America. Kings and queens, lords and ladies, soldiers and guards, servants to *help you dress,* my God! It's all fine when you're reading *history,* but I'm not going to put up with medieval nonsense about *protecting the little ladies* if I don't have to."

"You aren't likely to change this society all by yourself, Jen."

"Hah. Watch me. No, I know. But if Tenai gets to be an exception, then so do I." She sounded quite fierce.

"I think you've got a good start on that," Daniel agreed, not quite smiling.

"Damn right. Though men could say *lots* worse things than *golden lioness.*"

"I knew you'd like that."

"Anyone would like that! Only now I'd like to get to know Ranakai, only he's going to be afraid to say *word one* to me. They're all going to be afraid to talk to me. You're laughing."

"A little, yes. Sorry."

"Sure, sorry! Like I believe that," Jenna took off her boots—low boots, a little over ankle high, travel wear for women; men's boots were higher—and her vest. Then she reached up and pulled down the curtain, letting the sheer cloth fall between them. "You just wait," she added, now mostly hidden. "I'll get those guys chatting in twenty-four hours. Even Ranaki. Forty-eight at the outside. I'll get them to tell me all about the king and what he's *really* like."

Daniel cautioned her. "Don't push them against their loyalty to the king. They won't like that—and they'll probably lose respect for you if you try."

"I know that!" Jenna answered, her tone scornful. "Anybody could see that. That's not how I'll do it. I'll ask them about themselves—about growing up here. That'll do the trick. They'll like that—and I'll learn a lot about them, and about Talasayan, and about the king. I bet you."

Daniel couldn't help but smile. "No bet."

"What I want," Jenna added, her tone now resigned, "is a bath. Camping, ugh. Oh, well. Good night, Daddy."

Silence fell across the tent. Daniel heard his daughter's breathing deepen and smooth out almost at once. It left him on his own, lying on his back and looking into the dimly-lit half-hidden darkness. A soft breeze stirred the curtains, bringing in a scent of pine and woodsmoke to mingle with the faint incense fragrance.

What a long and strange road they had come. And a longer road still lay before them: in a few days, they'd be at the capital. Nerinesir. The seat of the royal court. What would that be like? Jenna would love it, Daniel decided as he drifted slowly downward toward sleep himself. She'd carve out a place for herself that was exactly the shape she wanted: he bet she could do it. He slipped into dreams of his daughter, in a black karate *gi*, with white flowers in her hair, a lioness at her side, walking amid the spun glass towers of a fairy-tale city, and smiled in his sleep.

8

They passed through Goshui-sa-e four days after leaving Chaisa. This was one of the larger cities between Chaisa and Nerinesir. A city of white houses with elaborately carved doors, set in a country of a thousand rivers: that was how Tenai had described Goshui-sa-e to Daniel, back when he had thought her description symbolic, or displaced from the real world to an imagined world. It had been a city where, in her youth, people had loved poetry and birds, so she'd said, and he'd wondered what the birds had symbolized.

A city destroyed by Encormio. He'd thought he'd understood the symbolism behind *that* memory: a life ruined by something unknown, a past ruined by unbearable memories.

No. It had in fact been Encormio to blame. The countryside still showed the scars of that war: many of the thousand little rivers that wended through the salt marshes had bridges that showed signs of having been torn down and then re-built. Many of the houses and barns they passed had been burned long ago and had still, sixteen years later, never been rebuilt. The remnants of a defensive wall still stood around the city itself, Daniel saw, though many of the stones had obviously been carried away to build newer structures and those that remained were tumbled and broken.

The marshes stretched off beyond the town, away toward the sea, and Daniel could see that several rivers, contained behind broad levees, ran through the town itself. A crop—rice, possibly, or something less familiar—grew in terraces between the rivers.

The houses and buildings strung out away from the town were a warm creamy white. Plaster, maybe. The roofs were thatched or, closer to the center of town, made of gray wooden shingles.

Tenai rode through the town with a blank, inward-turned expression that did not invite comment. Daniel watched her, wishing for a chance to speak privately with her, but there were always too many other people about. Besides, usually he and Jenna rode toward the front of the column, and Tenai toward the rear. It was hard enough even to catch a glimpse of her as they traveled. Daniel had to take it on faith that she was all right. He didn't like this, but there seemed no good way to change the situation, yet.

They stayed for one night in the house of Nolas-e Tantana Sintai, lord of Goshui-sa-e. Daniel noted the family name. Tenai's family had once ruled Goshui-sa-e. Not a single member of the Ponanon family remained in the province, one of Mitereh's men explained later.

The man, Apana Pelat, was captain of the king's personal guard. He was older than the young men the king kept about him. No doubt he was meant to leaven their youth and high spirits. Daniel understood better, after these days of travel, how Ranakai could have made his mistake with Jenna—the young men were at least as much companions as guards, and most of the time their manner with the king was easy and familiar. But whatever their ordinary manners, they were all now extremely formal and polite in their manners with Jenna and her father. Ranakai hadn't yet been re-admitted to Mitereh's presence. Jenna hadn't yet gotten any of them to relax enough to chat with her, though she refused to admit she'd lost her bet, pretending that the few words she'd pried out of one and another of the young men counted.

Apana Pelat was a different sort of man altogether. His black hair, clipped back at the nape of his neck, was streaked with gray. His short beard contained a good deal more gray than his hair. He had a strong, angular face; a steady, calm disposition; and a contained, formal manner. But he was not afraid to speak to Daniel or his daughter, even after the younger men had become almost painfully cautious.

Encormio, he explained, had hundreds of years ago given every member of the Ponanon family he could find to the fire and the sword. Only a few were left, and those scattered everywhere but Goshui-sa-e. But the Sintai family had also stood with Tenai at the end. Or almost to the end.

Jenna, sitting between her father and the captain, shivered. She said, not a question, "You mean, until Antiatan."

"Where did you hear about Antiatan?" Daniel asked her, but then waved a hand, resigned. It was a grim story, but anybody might have told it to her. No doubt a dozen people had. His daughter always made friends easily. Who knew with whom she might have struck up a friendship, or what tales they might have told her?

"Yes," Apana said quietly, answering Jenna. "I was at Antiatan myself. It was a terrible day." Then he was silent.

Daniel frowned. "But Tenai told me she barely fought at Antiatan. That she had no heart for fighting, and that was why she fled to my world."

Apana glanced at him, quite clearly startled. "It was from *Nolas-Kuomon* herself you had that tale?" He shook his head at Daniel's nod, not in disbelief, Daniel thought. In something like awe. "I would not have thought that she would speak of Antiatan. You are right that the fighting there did not last long. But it was not the battle itself that made Antiatan terrible. It was at Antiatan that Sandakan Gutai-e came face to face with Tenai Nolas-Kuomon and lifted his sword against her. At the end of that battle, Nolas-Kuomon laid open the veil and rode out of the world, and we thought ... we thought it was over."

"Somebody *beat* Tenai?" Jenna asked, her tone expressing open disbelief.

Apana looked at the young woman, but Daniel thought he didn't see her. His eyes were dark with memory. "Oh, no," he said, very softly. "No one mortal ever defeated Lord Death's own lady in direct combat. Not even Sandakan Gutai-e."

Not even Jenna found anything to say after that.

It was a hundred miles or so from Goshui-sa-e to Nerinesir, much of the journey through the mountains.

"Eight days more, nine days," Apana Pelat said, when Daniel asked him. "We will come to the mountains soon. Then it will only be six days more. It is not so far."

Daniel groaned, and Captain Pelat grinned, a brief flash of white teeth in his dark elegant face, and rode away up the column.

Jenna gazed after him wistfully. "He looks sort of like Sean Connery, doesn't he?"

That took Daniel aback. "No?"

"Well, not *really*," Jenna conceded. "But he's got that same sort of extra-sexy older guy thing going." She gave her father a teasing sidelong look. "If you don't see it, you can trust me on this one."

"The extra-sexy older guy thing, right."

Jenna grinned. She wasn't serious ... Daniel was almost certain. She was teasing. Of course she was. He decided nevertheless that they couldn't arrive in Nerinesir too soon.

It took two more days for the mountains to come in sight, and another day after that for them to reach the rolling foothills where the road divided. They were not tall mountains, though Daniel supposed that, compared with the flat lands they were leaving, these hills were mountainous enough. The roads became broader and better-trafficked than the ones further down toward the coast. Other travelers always made way for the king's party. And they always stared at Tenai's banner, set under the king's, and then at Tenai herself, and whispered. By this time, Mitereh had brought her up to ride near him, often directly at his side. She rode by the king with a closed, still face, turning her most opaque gaze back on those that stared at her. Daniel could just imagine the rumors that must be spreading.

They passed villages from time to time. The king sometimes stopped in one or another, if there was a village handy as dusk was falling. His people always put their own tents up to stay in, but they accepted food the villagers brought and once a man from one of the villages joined the king's table for supper.

Jenna and her father always stayed in the king's tent. Tenai did not, though now a tent of her own was always pitched near his. The king went out of his way to speak to her from time to time. As far as Daniel could see, her manner was always civil. She did not have that look of a barely contained conflagration which Daniel remembered from her early days with him. But her manner *was* certainly contained. It had to be tough, being a person everyone else tiptoed around all the time.

It took nine days from Goshui-sa-e to reach the walls of Nerinesir. But they came around a long slow curve and into sight of the city late in the afternoon of the ninth day. And they found waiting for them, drawn up before Nerinesir in endless ranks, thousands and thousands of men.

They drew up a little, Tenai slowing her horse, and the king his—they had been riding nearly side by side, and which of them had reined back first Daniel did not know. The company bunched up a bit and then drew rein behind them.

"You have surprised me," Tenai said to Mitereh. "I do confess it." Her tone was neutral, but Daniel thought she was laughing that hidden laugh of hers behind her sober face. He was relieved to hear that edge of amusement in her voice.

"I made you my heir ... after a year," Mitereh answered, without expression. "Did I not say so? I would not see Talasayan torn by endless ages of war ... but neither would I lightly see my own murderer acclaimed to the ivory throne. This is the hand I held out of your sight, Chaisa."

Ah. Daniel looked back at the army. The ranks of men stretched out of sight around the curve of the city's wall. He wondered what resources the king had expected Tenai to find, that would have made an army like that necessary.

"With orders ... not to attack," surmised Tenai.

"To contain. To hold you apart from any who might be your allies. And at midwinter, to drive you back across the veil, if they could."

Tenai lifted her hand to shield her eyes and scanned the long ranks. "They might have done it. I do think they might. A potent weapon you hid in your left hand, Mitereh, while you offered me your own life's blood with your right. On such short notice. I am very much impressed." She gathered up her reins. "Shall we go on, and show them what you have wrought?"

The king did not move, and Tenai checked her black mare before it could go more than a step or two forward. She turned, frowning, to study the king. Then she asked, in a tone that was not the same, "Who commands this army of yours, Mitereh?"

He answered steadily. "I left these men in the hand of Sandakan Gutai-e."

There was a pause. Eventually, Tenai broke it. She was not laughing now. Her tone was absolutely neutral, her face blank, but now she looked dangerous. She said merely, "A wise choice, my king. No one could be more likely to succeed at the task you thought might be laid down for this army."

"Chaisa, whose are you?"

"Yours, my king. Nothing has changed." Tenai answered. But that cold edge of danger was still in her voice, in her manner.

"Then let us go on," said Mitereh, ignoring that tone. He gestured to the standard-bearer, who held both his standard and Tenai's, with hers set lower.

Sandakan Gutai-e had been more than Tenai's most important general and her right hand during the last part of her war with

Encormio. Daniel had gathered from things Tenai had said and things she had not quite said that he had also been almost like a friend ... perhaps the closest approach to friendship she had managed, during those last years of her war.

And then had come the ending of the war, and Antiatan.

Jenna leaned close and asked him in a low voice, "Were they lovers?"

Daniel gave his daughter a startled look. "Jen—"

"I think they were," Jenna said. "Lovers, I mean. They met on the field of battle with swords drawn, and unable to face killing him, Tenai fled the whole *world*. Wow."

"A little romantic, Jen, don't you think?"

"Well, don't you think so? Look at her—she's gone awfully cold. And the king knew she was going to. Poor Tenai! I wonder if Sandakan is still in love with her? Or if she is, with him?"

If Tenai and Sandakan Gutai-e had been lovers, she'd never mentioned it to Daniel. Jenna was such a romantic: of course she would think of something like that. But it didn't seem likely. Daniel glanced at Tenai, riding ahead of them, at the king's shoulder. She didn't look like a woman thinking about meeting her estranged lover after a sixteen-year absence. But Tenai wouldn't show anything she didn't want to show. That didn't necessarily—or ever—mean it wasn't there. Perhaps Jenna was right.

The actual approach to Nerinesir and the army seemed to take a long time. He'd thought they might have put their horses into a trot, at least, but no—a slow steady pace, no different from the pace they'd kept through all these mountains.

Even as they at last drew close, Daniel couldn't distinguish Sandakan from the rest. There was a banner—the king's banner, and another that he didn't recognize, a red shape on a cream background. And a third, black lines on a toast-brown background. He found, at last, a dark man on a bay horse just behind the banners. The horse fidgeted, tossing its head and fussing with its feet. That horse's rider wasn't fidgeting. He sat perfectly still. Daniel thought this might be Sandakan Gutai-e.

Beside him, Jenna asked Emelan, who was riding near her. The man pointed out the man Daniel had chosen. "That tall man there. That is the general."

Sandakan Gutai-e looked older than Daniel had expected, as they got close enough to see one another plainly—but of course it had been sixteen years. Sandakan was probably in his fifties—close, in fact, to Daniel's own age. There were lines at the corners of the man's eyes and his thin mouth. He had the sharp look-of-eagles features common to people here, but more so, maybe. His lean, strong-boned face gave him a saturnine look.

Arriving at last before the ranks of men, with the long outer wall of Nerinesir stretching away on his right hand, the king drew up and lifted his hand to halt the much smaller company he'd brought with him.

For a long moment, the king let them all look at him, and at the tall woman who rode at his side. Everyone obviously recognized her. The silence was stunning. Not a single man anywhere shuffled his feet or dropped something. Nobody even coughed. When somebody's horse shifted its weight so that leather creaked, the sound was startling enough that Daniel twitched. His own horse dropped her head and mouthed the bit and Daniel realized he was gripping the reins too tightly. He tried to make himself relax.

"Rejoice!" said the king, in a loud, formal voice. "I have brought Tenai Ponanon Chaisa-e to my hand. She has sworn to me in the sight of men and God. Let all men be made aware that Chaisa's banner flies with mine on the tower! Let this word be passed to the west and the north and the south: let all men know that Chaisa-e and Sekuse-go-e ride together on this road!"

A reaction passed over the gathered ranks of men and over the face of Sandakan Gutai-e. Daniel could not read it. He thought there was relief in it, but he also thought the reaction he saw was more complicated than that. He thought the man had been glad to hear what the king said, but that maybe at the same time maybe Sandakan didn't actually believe it. It was like being braced for news of a terrible disaster and then finding out everything was all right: It wasn't possible to let go so fast. You would keep waiting, expecting to find that somebody had made a mistake and everything you were afraid of had happened after all.

Then Sandakan Gutai-e brought his horse forward a few paces, and bowed. "All men will rejoice to hear the words of the king," he said formally, not looking at Tenai at all. His voice was quiet. His manner went beyond contained, to tightly controlled.

"My general, I thank you for drawing up these men in this fine display. They may now be dismissed." the king answered, almost as expressionless. "You may accompany me now."

The general bowed, his manner still absolutely neutral, and signaled his captains to pass this command on. The king inclined his head in return and started his horse moving forward again. Most of the men with him turned aside, moving to join this much larger company camped outside the city. A handful came with him ... his young men, a few soldiers, Daniel and his daughter. Tenai, of course, and Emelan. And Sandakan, who still had not looked at Tenai, though her gaze, ironic and unreadable, had rested on him for a moment as he turned his horse to ride at the king's side for this last little distance. Jenna gazed after the general and frowned.

"What?" Daniel asked her.

"Nothing," said his daughter, still frowning. She added in English, "He really *is* good-looking, isn't he?"

She was, Daniel concluded, probably trying to decide whether Sandakan and Tenai looked like estranged lovers. He thought, watching them, that while it was just possible that Sandakan might, Tenai did not. Sandakan had turned against her, at the end. Along with nearly everybody else. But he had meant more to her than everybody else.

Tenai had told him something about Antiatan. They had discussed forgiveness ... of herself, for her terrible mistakes. Of Sandakan? Perhaps, but Daniel remembered no such discussion. And now? Even if Tenai understood—believed—that she had herself been in the wrong in the first place, would she be able to forgive her most important, most trusted general after he had turned against her? Daniel found he could not guess.

It seemed to take forever to ride through the city—and all the longer because of the tension that rode with them. But it was a huge city. They came in by an entrance evidently called the Sunrise Gate, where the road was broad enough to let ten men ride abreast. Great gray and black stone blocks made a forbidding outer wall for the city; houses of the same gray and black stone stood in scattered clusters away down the hills below the wall.

The buildings of Nerinesir were tall and crowded together, made of stone the colors of ash and charcoal. The streets were narrow, cobbled with more of the gray and black stone. The effect was heavy and somber. The wood trim was painted in sober shades of gray or green that did nothing to relieve the heaviness of the city. The people, gathered on rooftops and balconies, seemed strained and worried. They whispered to one another as the king's party passed, a low susurrus of sound, like the sound of the sea.

"They are afraid of you," the king said to Tenai, who rode close by his side. Nolas-ai Mikanan Chauke-sa rode at his other side, with Sandakan Gutai-e beyond Mikanan Chauke-sa.

"I know," she agreed, her tone distant. "For us all, sixteen years gone is as a breath."

There was a slight pause.

"Declare a day of celebration at dawn," Mikanan Chauke-sa advised the king. "Announce to the people they have reason to rejoice."

"Is there a reason to wait for dawn?" Sandakan asked. His deep voice was still quiet and expressionless. He went on. "Do not wait for the dawn. That is my advice, if you will hear me, my king. Everyone is afraid now. This afternoon, at once, send someone to the Martyr's Cathedral. Have them ring the bells for rejoicing. Have the priests announce to their people at every church that all is well."

"Well thought," Tenai said, her tone just as neutral. "Indeed, Mitereh, I agree. This is wise advice. Let the priests pass the word that I have set my banner beneath yours. People will believe what they hear from the priests."

"Well thought," agreed Mitereh, and signaled Mikanan, who reined aside to give those orders.

They came to a sinuous wall of green-shot black stone, neither as high nor as thick through as the first wall. The gate to this wall stood open, but it was guarded by men with the king's badge. Past that gate everything was black stone. Buildings here were more graceful, and set further apart than those in the outer city. Here, too, people gathered to watch the king pass. These were the wealthy of the city: they wore beautiful clothing, and the women wore intricate jeweled nets over their hair.

"This is the nobles' city," Apana Pelat murmured, riding near at hand. He had seen Daniel look one way and another.

Daniel had actually already guessed this, remembering Tenai's descriptions of Nerinesir. "And there in front of us, that must be the court, surrounded by the Martyr's Wall?" He nodded toward the intricately carved wall that swept out to either side before them.

"Yes," agreed Captain Pelat. "It isn't meant to guard against enemies so much as show where the boundaries of the court lie."

The white mansions beyond this inner wall were all anyone could ask for in the way of palaces. All the stone here was white, seeming almost lit from within. The road, covered with white chips of stone, unwound ahead of them like a glowing ribbon to a final wall. This one seemed made of crystal. Jenna would love it, Daniel thought, and looked for his daughter. She was gazing up at the wall in awe. Perhaps feeling his gaze, she looked around at him and grinned, opening her hands and tossing her head back in a gesture of delight.

The gates that stood open to let them through this glass wall seemed to be made of silver. And on the other side of *those* gates was, finally, the true palace.

Before it, all the lesser palaces of the court seemed almost plain.

"Wow," Jenna murmured aloud, looking up, and up, at the spreading wings of the king's palace. "Wow. *Damn.*"

Daniel, though he said nothing, agreed with the sentiment.

The king's palace was beautiful and incomprehensible: high towers made of white or pink marble rose toward the sky from among a confusion of walls and balustrades and lower towers. A broad crystalline staircase spiraled up one of the nearer towers and stretched out into a wide balcony high above the ground; the same crystal opened out in a fan-shaped patio before the main doors, which were probably fifty feet high.

There were elegant people everywhere, hurrying—they all seemed to be hurrying—about mysterious tasks.

Daniel thought he would need a real night's sleep in a real bed, and then maybe he would be able to face it. At the moment it filled him with a feeling that made him want to take Jenna, crawl into a hole, and hide. He felt exactly as grubby and disheveled as nine days on horseback without a real bath could make somebody. Jenna's obvious delight at the palace didn't help.

To his surprise, while his daughter whisked off in one direction with Tenai, when he took a step to follow, Captain Pelat turned up at his elbow and indicated a different direction.

"You have been taken into the king's household," he said, to Daniel's querying look.

"But ... hasn't Jenna?"

"Yes," the man said, with evident surprise. "Thus the king shows he favors Chaisa-e." He must have seen Daniel's confusion because he added, "It is more proper for your daughter to go among women. The king might give her into the keeping of women of his household, but he shows his favor for Chaisa-e."

All right. Daniel thought he understood that. He, at least, was a lot more comfortable knowing Jenna was safe with Tenai. There were doors and hallways and more doors and the occasional room that looked like a museum gallery. Captain Pelat turned suddenly through one more doorway and into a set of luxurious rooms that sprawled along the west wall of one level of the palace.

Late sunlight poured through wide windows, giving a golden tint to the rooms' fittings; appropriate, Daniel thought, to their opulence. Rugs in brilliant blues and greens covered tiled floors. Furniture was ornate: rich fabrics and wood carved and inlaid with mother-of-pearl.

And everywhere was the bustle of dozens of men about urgent and mysterious business, none of whom Daniel knew and none of whom acknowledged his presence with more than a distracted glance.

Captain Pelat might have recognized Daniel's pause as the sudden attack of nerves it was. "Here," he said kindly, "this way. You will want to bathe."

He separated one of the hurrying men out the crowd with a jerk of his head and showed Daniel a luxurious bathing room larger than his own generous living room at home. "Tipana will help you," he told Daniel, indicating the young man he'd pulled out of the other room. Tipana dipped his head, shy, but smiling in a way that seemed friendly. "You need not hurry, Nola Danyel," Captain Pelat continued. The king is also bathing. There will be a supper later, I am certain. I will see that appropriate clothing is sent to you."

"Thank you. I know you must be busy."

"The comfort of the king's guests is also within my duty," the captain answered, inclining his head in a formal nod that was almost a bow.

Tipana fetched fragrant soap and warm towels for Daniel, and laid out an outfit of brown and ivory.

Daniel was not at all comfortable having servants hover around while he bathed and dressed, but on the other hand, the outer garments involved some mysterious ties he would not have figured out without help. Mitereh's spiraling blue sigil was embroidered on the collar of the shirt.

Daniel fingered this, thinking about identity and affiliation and how clothing might indeed, in some circumstances, make the man.

9

Mitereh, when Daniel found him again, was pacing. The king was ignoring the attendants who tried to adjust his embroidered vest and braid his still-damp hair. Daniel knew no one in the room except the king himself and stood to one side, trying to sort out who might be whom. He found his eye caught particularly by one man who had settled comfortably in a chair to one side, legs stretched out and crossed at the ankle, chin propped on his palm, watching with a wry amusement as the king impatiently waved away a man with an ivory ribbon in his hand. "Let it be," he snapped.

The man with the ribbon snapped right back, "And let you go out among your court like that? I would die of shame. Will you stand *still* for one beat of time?"

Mitereh made a little sound of impatience, but he actually did stand still, allowing the ribbon to be threaded through his hair. The attendant rapidly braided his hair in a way too complicated for Daniel to follow, then said, "*Thank* you, my king," in a surprisingly sarcastic tone.

Mitereh, far from taking offense, grimaced and answered, "Forgive my impatient manner, Perau."

"Yes," said the attendant, much more gently. "You shall honor your household, Mitereh."

"If I do, it is all to your credit, Perau," said the king and resumed pacing, although not with quite so much energy this time.

The relationships between the king and his guards, and now between the king and his servants, was well outside the normal American experience. But the complete lack of, for a better word, servility, made the whole concept of staff and servants less uncomfortable than it might otherwise have been. Still, Daniel wondered whether he might possibly be able to find a Talasayan version of *Miss Manner's Guide to Excruciatingly Correct Behavior* or something similar that would explain how people were expected to behave toward one another.

"Patience, Mitereh," advised the man in the chair. "Settle, if you please, before we all grow nervous."

This man was not young, although not old. He was somewhere above fifty, Daniel judged, studying him again, but probably not much above. There was gray in his hair, but people in this country sometimes seemed to gray early. The man had the air Daniel would have expected from a tenured professor or senior administrator: calm and authoritative. His powerful shoulders and arms suggested a background as a soldier, whatever position he now held. His bones were powerful rather than delicate: he had a straight broad nose and wide strong cheekbones rather than the hawk features common to so many of the people in this country. His eyes were dark, glinting now with humor. He spoke to the king with casual, wry amusement, in the familiar tone of a friend.

The king ignored this advice. He paced the length of the room and back. He was waiting for something or for someone, Daniel surmised, and wondered who. He did not sit himself. He felt too out of place and uncomfortable to sit down, restless despite his tiredness.

A woman entered the room. She, too, might be somewhere near fifty—mature enough to be comfortable and confident, but not old. Her dark hair, threaded with gray, was caught back in a net of silver and amethyst. The silver of the net brought out the color of her eyes, a pale gray startling in her dark face. There was more silver in the embroidery on her vest and the hem of her skirt, both of a rich color that matched the amethysts. And yet she brought with her an air of brisk, cheerful warmth that somehow seemed at odds with her elegance.

"Taranah." Mitereh turned in obvious relief, holding out his hands to her in welcome.

"Mitereh," answered the woman, her manner both casual and warm. Taking his hands, she let the king draw her into a brief embrace. "Well, my dear, and so you have brought a falcon to perch among the cooing pigeons. I confess you have surprised me." She stepped back, smiling.

"I believe all the court is likely astounded, and all the city; but you, Taranah? You must forgive me if I doubt your word." Mitereh, smiling also, drew the woman around and added to

Daniel, "Nola Danyel, may I make known to you my mother's sister, a jewel of my court, Taranah Berangilan-sa. Taranah, allow me to present to you Nola Danyel, a friend of Tenai Chaisa-e."

Danyel blinked. He had gotten the impression that the young king had no relatives, probably because he didn't on his father's side. It took him by surprise to find otherwise. And how were introductions managed here? He bowed and said, "I'm pleased to meet you, uh, would it be Nolas-e Taranah?"

The woman returned his interested look with a smiling nod and a straightforward curiosity of her own. "Nolas-ai, Nola Danyel; and you are a friend of Nolas-Kuomon? How interesting that must be for you."

Her tone wasn't in the least sarcastic and didn't seem to contain any hidden meanings; Daniel thought she meant simply that it must be interesting for him. Her pale eyes ought to have looked cold, but instead seemed to express friendly warmth. She was not beautiful, but so comfortable that Daniel found himself returning her smile with genuine warmth of his own. He liked her already. He imagined almost everyone probably liked this woman immediately; she had that kind of gift.

Turning back to the king, she said, producing a little scroll from the pocket of her skirt, "You may find this useful, my dear. This is a list of men for Chaisa-e to meet as publicly as possible: various of the cardinals, various of your lords, the Imbaneh-se emissary and the one from Keneseh, Belagaiyan Tenom-e and Tantera Turoh-e—it would undoubtedly be best for Sandakan to clear the way there. I have been so bold as to arrange suitable appointments with all these persons. Now, I think it likely you will want to have a procession through the city tomorrow, yes? So I have arranged an appropriate route that should do for the purpose but avoid disarranging the ordinary business of the city; that is included."

Taking the scroll, Mitereh said with real warmth, "Taranah, you are the seventh wonder of Talasayan."

The king's aunt smiled. "Everyone made plans in the case you should fail, my dear. I thought it would not be amiss to make a plan in the case you should succeed. I believe I have been told that Nolas-e Tenai came to Nerinesir without proper attendants? Your staff will be all in a flutter for nervousness. I have therefore been twice bold and sent three women of my household to hers. If they have not come there yet, they will soon. Calm, sensible women. They may draw upon my resources to make Nolas-e Tenai comfortable. Comfortable women are so much less irritable, I have found. And I will ask Nolas-e Tenai to supper in my apartment in three days, or four. Perhaps I will invite another woman or two. I have one or another in mind who might benefit from such an encounter."

Mitereh grinned, captured the woman's hands again, and lifted them for a moment to his forehead. "My aunt, you are more splendid than the sky. I approve everything you have done."

Taranah patted him on the cheek. "I confess you amaze me continually, my dear. I shall await tomorrow's pageant with the keenest expectation." She gave the older man a smile and Daniel a friendly nod, and departed. The room seemed at once a touch cooler and dimmer. What, Daniel wondered, had it taken to survive a life of war and the knowledge that Tenai might at any time come after anyone even tenuously linked to Encormio, and still have a personality like that?

Then Tenai came in. The focus of everyone in the room shifted at once to her, and Daniel forgot his curiosity about the king's surviving relatives. Emelan, at her back, peeled off at the door and took a silent post there as though familiar with the duties of a guard, which Daniel supposed he was. Compared to Tenai, he was almost invisible. The king turned to Tenai with impatient briskness, so that Daniel guessed he had been waiting for her. He met her eyes with a slight, arrogant lift of his chin that, to Daniel's experienced eye, might have suggested an underlying uneasiness.

Tenai focused first on the king, but Emelan, Daniel noted, barely glanced that way and gave most of his attention, covertly, to the seated man. Daniel formed an obvious surmise, and watched both of them with covert and sympathetic interest. He was fairly certain one or the other was going to have a tough time in a moment. Maybe both.

Tenai herself seemed perfectly at ease. She and Emelan were both armed. No one else in the room was except two of the king's personal guard. By this time Daniel knew their names and knew that one was named Inkaimon and the other Torohoh. Both had been standing in relaxed, alert poses. That relaxation had disappeared when Tenai entered, though neither young man set a hand on a sword hilt or anything like that.

Tenai nodded to Daniel and inclined her head in a minimal bow to the king, but she spoke to the seated man. "Keitah Terusai-e. You hold Kinabana, so I have been informed. I gather Terusai has prospered in these years. I am not surprised to find it so."

Daniel was not at all surprised when she gave the name of the man whom, of everyone in all Nerinesir, Emelan had feared would recognize him.

Keitah rose at once when Tenai spoke. He was taller than Daniel had guessed, and not quite as broad as he had appeared when seated. He bowed, a slight inclination of his body, hands at his sides. "Chaisa-e," he said. He was smiling, but it was a cool smile. "Living still, and submissive to a son of Encormio. Thus we see that all surprise is not lost from the world."

He had not looked twice at Emelan, and obviously did not recognize him. But then, with Tenai there to draw all eyes, Daniel supposed he could understand the lord's failure to recognize a man he'd not seen for ten years.

Tenai chuckled, but to Daniel's experienced ear, there was little humor in her tone or her manner. She looked ... maybe not quite hostile, not quite antagonistic, but not exactly friendly. She said to Daniel, "Nolas-ai Keitah is one of those who found it possible to remain neutral in the war. I counted such men as almost my allies, for any power lost to Encormio in those years was as strength given to my hand."

Daniel noticed the "almost." He made a noncommittal sound.

"Keitah is no longer neutral," the king said impatiently. "He is my man, as you are mine, Chaisa. It is my desire you shall make your bow to Keitah, as to me."

Keitah added, with a wry tilt of his head, "Not a moment I had looked to see, Nolas-Kuomon."

Tenai half smiled, not in amusement. Her dark eyes were opaque and hard, holding no trace of humor. She said, "And how do you find Kinabana, Terusai-e? Is the sea to your taste?"

"At times I find it so," Keitah answered mildly.

"Pay Terusai-e all due courtesy, if you please," the king snapped, with a hard look at Tenai.

"As you will have it," she said, not quite looking at the king. She removed her hand from her sword-hilt and bowed to Keitah, much lower than he had to her. "Accept my service, then, Terusai, and I trust you will find this, also, to your taste."

"I have no doubt of it," the man said, imperturbable, and Tenai, rising from her bow, almost smiled. Again, Daniel could find no humor in her expression.

"So, my friend, here is Nolas-Kuomon to bring into my court, and so set back Imbaneh-se as hard as may be," said the king. "Are all matters in hand for this?"

Keitah inclined his head. "Give me until dawn. I shall present a plan for your consideration, my king."

"Until dawn, then."

Tenai tilted her head. "And I? You might have commanded me to go aside to establish myself within the city, but instead of setting me at a distance, you have given me a place in your house. Shall I understand that you wish me to establish my own household within yours, in the sight of all?"

The king looked at Tenai, expression thoughtful. "I do wish that. Yes. Do so in the sight of God and all men. Is Nola Jenna comfortable with you?"

"She is. You are courteous to allow me her company."

Mitereh nodded. He said to Daniel, "You understand, Nola Danyel, I would permit you to choose to go into either household, or to establish your own. In time, I shall. For this little time, I believe it best the court see you are in mine."

Daniel had learned just enough about Talasayan customs that he wasn't surprised. He nodded.

The king shifted his attention back to Tenai. "I shall send for you at dawn, Chaisa. A progress to the Cathedral will be necessary. You have sufficient ceremonial garments?"

Tenai bowed and murmured that she was certain she could contrive.

Mitereh regarded her, frowning. "Apply to my aunt for assistance in all such matters. Or pass requests to any servant of my household. But my staff cannot supply every lack. You should have more men in your household. I credit your sensibility, that you brought only one. But you should have more. Perhaps some number of my personal guards might be so courteous as to allow me to reassign them for a little while."

"Mitereh!" Inkaimon exclaimed. Then, as the king raised an inquiring eyebrow, the young man sighed and bowed. "We would consider it an honor, of course, my king."

"Of course," murmured the other young man, Torohoh.

"Indeed." He made absolutely no effort to sound sincere, but he did add to Tenai, in a much more carefully respectful tone, "It *would* be our honor, to be sure, Nolas-e."

Tenai smiled, this time with genuine humor. "I must be grateful for the offer. However, permit me to decline, my king. For the moment, Emelan will suffice." Her eyes as she said this were on Keitah Terusai-e. Daniel also watched Nolas-ai Keitah, curious to see whether the name would strike a familiar note with him.

Emelan himself glanced, helplessly, at Keitah. Without that glance, without the sudden currents in the room between Emelan and Daniel and Tenai, who knew whether Keitah would have made the catch, even with that name dropped into the conversation? But the lord looked first at Tenai, and then, with surmise growing in his eyes, at Emelan.

Keitah's eyes, meeting Emelan's dark-honey ones, widened and then narrowed. The lord looked the younger man over from head to foot, his gaze lingering for a moment on the other man's hands before again returning to his face.

Emelan did not move. He had gone as pale as a man with his coloring could manage. But he met the lord's eyes without outwardly flinching.

"Emelan?" Keitah said, not quite a question, not exactly a statement. He did not look happy to recognize the younger man. More ... astonished.

"Nolas-ai," Emelan said. Not quite expressionless. He could not manage that.

"Emelan?" the lord said again, both certainty and disbelief in his voice. He took one step forward, regarding the other man with stiff amazement. And, thought Daniel, not a little dismay.

"Keitah ... " said the king, looking from one of them to the other. "Who is this?"

Keitah Terusai-e did not answer. He might not have even heard the king speak. Daniel thought Emelan hadn't. Neither man had any attention to spare at the moment for anyone else.

Mitereh settled on Tenai and repeated his question, a little plaintively. "Chaisa, what is this man you have brought into my house?"

"I am uncertain," Tenai admitted. "I had expected nothing so dramatic from it. Emelan. What secret have you guarded so assiduously from me?"

Her voice broke through Emelan's focus where the king's voice had not. He turned his head.

"Well?" demanded Tenai. "Is it obedience you owe me, man, or is it not? What is this defiance?"

Emelan answered at last, his deep voice rougher than ever with anguish he could not quite hide, "I should have let you kill me on the road."

"Your hand was a mere breath from the Gate. But that is no choice you have now, Emelan no-man's-son. Whose son are you?"

Keitah Terusai-e twitched at this question, and was still again.

Emelan looked at Keitah, and then at Tenai. His tawny eyes were bleak. He said, "As I owe you all obedience, Nolas-e, so I hear your command. My father was Tohoris Terusai-e. Keitah Terusai-e ... is my brother."

For a long moment, no one spoke.

"It was not that I strove to hide this from you," added Emelan. Half-lifting a hand that, Daniel saw, trembled, he made a small gesture like a man casting something away. "I think ... I think only, I have been hiding from the world for so long ... I tried to hide from you out of that habit. I should have known," he finished, a tired look in his eyes, "that mine was a foolish silence."

"Well," murmured Tenai. She glanced from him to Keitah Terusai-e and back again. "You have thoroughly surprised me, I confess."

Emelan flinched a little. He said, "You should have permitted me to stay quietly in your house, Nolas-e."

Tenai tipped her head to the side, regarding him. "No. I think that would not have served," she said, almost gently. "Ten years you stayed nameless and aside from the world, and still God threw you at my feet the moment I returned through the veil. And you think you might have turned away, Terusai? Or that I should have dared allow you to try?"

"Don't call him by that name," grated Keitah. Looking at them now, Daniel thought he could in fact see some resemblance. Keitah was a good deal older—the son of a first wife? Could they be half-brothers? But there was indeed something in the set of his strong bones ... in the shape, if not the color, of his eyes; in the timbre of his voice, maybe, that the younger man seemed to echo.

But where Emelan was upset, even distraught, because of this encounter ... his brother, Daniel thought, was *furious*. Daniel, an only child himself, had no brothers. But if he had a younger brother, he wondered whether he would have been less than delirious with joy if the brother had turned up alive after a decade lost and presumed dead.

Maybe. Possibly. He had observed a lot of complicated family relationships over the years.

Emelan did not look at Tenai or move toward her, but Daniel nevertheless got the impression that he had appealed to her for help. Tenai might have picked up on the same notion. Though she did no more than shift her weight, there was suddenly an unmistakable edge of aggression to her attitude. She drew all eyes instantly, despite everyone's understandable focus on Emelan and Keitah.

"He is mine," Tenai said, deliberate and cold.

Keitah took a breath. "How?"

"In the usual way."

The king made a sound midway between a cough and a laugh; not amused, Daniel thought, so much as shocked.

Keitah took a step forward, toward his brother. He was taller than Emelan, several inches taller, but the younger man looked to be more powerful. Physically. In terms of attitude and manner, there was no question which man was more authoritative.

"How?" he asked again, this time of Emelan. His tone was lower, this time, making the question seem almost a plea. "Where were you? How have you been living?" His voice rose. "I thought you were dead!"

"I was dead," Emelan said, not quite evenly. "I had no name and no memory. I still have no name. I ask for nothing. I will not take anything you try to give me."

Keitah brought a hand down in a sharp gesture of denial. "That won't do."

"It will have to do, Nolas-ai."

"No!" Keitah turned to Tenai, an abrupt gesture. "Release this man to me, Chaisa."

"After God cast him at my feet?" Tenai asked in a dry tone. "I should hardly think so, Terusai. I should not think that would be wise. I have taken him in. All else is gone into the kingdom of Lord Sorrow. I advise you, Terusai, let the dead past go."

Keitah turned to the king. "Mitereh—"

The king held up a hand, stopping the other man's words.

"You should know better," he said. He sounded sympathetic, but decisive. "It is certainly not my place to command any such thing, Terusai, as well you are aware." He turned to Emelan. "Emelan. Is that your name?"

Emelan bowed, with evident relief because he could now turn away from his brother. "Yes, my king."

"I don't recall you."

"I was a boy when I was last in Nerinesir, and not much in your way, my king."

"How old are you now?"

"Thirty-two, my king."

Daniel was surprised. He'd been revising his guess about Emelan's age downward for weeks, but he would still have guessed the man years older. Thirty-two, and on the run ten years? He'd been hardly more than a boy when he'd committed his crime and run for his life. A baby. Christ, he'd been just Jenna's age.

"What did you do, that you became outlaw?"

"Killed an officer, my king, and I in Nolas-ai Keitah's house guard." Emelan stopped, and then added, "The man was hardly fit to be a soldier at all, far less an officer, and I had a fierce temper in those days. But I had no right to strike the blow, and knew it at once"

"So you ran. And then?"

"I was dead, my king, for all I had not ... not the courage to face the knife. I would not remember my name. I was nothing." Emelan fell silent, a silence hard with bitter memory.

"And then fell into Chaisa's hand. As she said. Nolas-Kuomon stepped across the veil, and at once took you up. I agree I see God's hand there. Or, indeed, more likely the Martyr's hand, who grants us less mercy when we would turn aside from a difficult path. So." The king was silent for a moment, studying the other man. "And so you will not now recall your name?"

"No," Emelan said fiercely, an echo, Daniel thought, of the temper he must have had as a boy.

"And have no desire to renounce your service to Chaisa, now that you are attached to Nolas-Kuomon's name and household?"

"No."

"And you, Chaisa, knowing this man's history, you will not turn him off?"

"No," Tenai agreed. "What would Terusai do with him? I, at

least, have a use for him."

"And God or the Martyr cast him at your feet."

"So it would seem, Mitereh."

"I confess I don't believe so," Keitah snapped, furious.

Tenai turned dark ironic eyes his way. "How not?"

The king said, gently, "I see no possible way recognizing this nameless man could be to your good, Keitah. Or his." He opened his hands. "Let him go, Keitah. By his own word he is none of yours. How could you possibly improve what Chaisa-e gives him? Let him go to find his own path."

Keitah was silent.

"I take him to be yours, Chaisa," the king said to Tenai. "Nor am I curious about anything of yours. Nor do I ask concerning any disposition you may make within your establishment."

She offered a minimal bow. "You are generous."

"I recognize an intractable situation. But, Chaisa ... if you have other surprises for me, I will ask you make them known to me now."

Tenai barely smiled. "I have no other, so far as I am aware, Mitereh. But I did not recognize this one until this moment."

The king looked skeptical, but gave her a slight inclination of his head. "So, well. Take *this* surprise out of my presence, Chaisa, and yourself, and all connected to your household, and restore mine to peace, if that is possible. Nola Danyel ... I find I must ask you after all to go, for this little time. I will send for you tonight." And, turning last to Keitah, he added very gently, "Keitah, my friend. Please stay."

Tenai gathered up both Daniel and Emelan with a glance, and retired quietly from the ... field of battle, Daniel thought, was not an inappropriate phrase.

10

Tenai's apartment fell short of the king's by only a hair. The main entrance led first into a large and richly-furnished reception room, which gave onto an even larger study with a single broad table and a dozen ornate chairs and, on the other side, a small but no doubt fascinating library, which Daniel regretted he would not be able to examine properly because Tenai had not yet gotten around to her literacy spell for him. Granted, a lot of events had interfered. Plus apparently it was just a more difficult sort of spell, for reasons that no doubt made sense if you were a sorcerer.

They didn't exactly tour the place, but Daniel saw all that as Tenai led the way through the suite from the front rooms to a dining room at the rear. This room offered a long table suitable for seating a dozen people. Bread and bowls of fruit had been laid out on that table, in case anybody couldn't wait for supper. The opposite wall consisted of a single great window that stretched from floor to ceiling and let out on a small balcony and a splendid view. The sun, sliding down over the city, poured light thick as honey across the gardens of the court and turned the white mansions of the nobility beyond to warm ruddy gold. A breeze wandered through the window, carrying the wild scent of pine off the mountains and the pungency of horses. Somewhere not far away, Daniel could smell fragrant smoke and roasting meat.

Jenna was already in the dining room, along with three attendants who must, Daniel realized at once, be the women the king's aunt had sent. Like the king's attendants, these women seemed reassuringly unintimidated, if in this case less ... casual, for want of a better word. His daughter had had a chance to clean up, and somewhere she'd found an outfit of tawny gold and creamy ivory. Both skirt and vest swept down in sheer lines that showed off her lithe height. She looked, with her fair coloring, rather like she'd been made out of gold and ivory herself. Her hair was up and pinned with an ivory comb. She looked very adult and, to her father's admittedly biased gaze, extremely beautiful. He wondered how many young men were going to look at her and exclaim, *Ah, a golden lioness!* Plenty, no doubt. She would undoubtedly enjoy it.

"Daddy!" she exclaimed, catching his hand to draw him forward. "This is Paninah Meden-sa, Kitanan Tondut, and Inaseh Suaneni. The king's aunt sent them—she's asked me to supper later. Do you think it would be all right if I went? Inaseh gave me this dress! Wasn't that nice of her? Isn't it beautiful?"

Of the three women, Inaseh Suaneni's complexion was the closest to Jenna's—not close, but the woman's tawny coloring was about as fair as people in this country seemed to get, and her hair was a beautiful tawny bronze that wasn't exactly blond, but not exactly dark either. "A generous gift," Daniel agreed, nodding to Inaseh. "Thank you—I'm grateful for your kindness to my daughter."

Inaseh Suaneni smiled and bowed and murmured that she was honored to be able to serve the king's guests—not Tenai's guests, Daniel noted—and Tenai stated that she was indebted to Taranah Berangilan-sa for the loan of women of her household and would be grateful for their attendance in the morning. As hints went, this was fairly direct. The three women bowed and retired gracefully into the farther reaches of the apartment, leaving Tenai alone with Daniel, Jenna and Emelan.

"So, do you think I should go?" Jenna asked, bouncing on her toes—asking Tenai more than her father. Daniel looked at Tenai as well. He was almost certain, even having barely met her, that the king's aunt was exactly the woman he'd like his daughter to meet.

"You must certainly attend Taranah Berangilan-sa, as she has done you the honor to request your company." Tenai gave Jenna a short nod. "She is both clever and wise. Remember she is the king's aunt, and a subtle woman. I advise you be both courteous and prudent."

Jenna looked a little startled, and then thoughtful. Daniel, reassured by the thoughtfulness, added "I just met her, Jen. I liked her, and I think you will—but remember we're not at home." He felt drained by the mere thought; he found he longed to be at home, leaving the king and his aunt, Emelan Terusai and his brother, to sort out their lives without involving him or his daughter.

Jenna, picking up at last on Daniel's tension—or on the distress pouring off the silent Emelan like a dense, angry fog—fell silent. She looked from Emelan to Tenai and then, eyebrows raised, back to her father.

"It's a little—" *complicated,* Daniel had intended to say. But it wasn't actually complicated. It was just difficult.

Tenai had turned to face Emelan. For a long moment, she studied him without speaking. Looking, Daniel wondered, for traces of his brother in him? For noble birth and gentle rearing? Daniel found little of Keitah's suavity and class in this rough man.

Not quite returning her gaze, Emelan went to one knee. This took Daniel aback; then it occurred to him, for the first time, that the man might well be in trouble with Tenai. He had let her walk into that little encounter almost as blind as his brother.

Jenna looked much more openly surprised. Daniel realized she still knew nothing about all the recent soap-opera encounters and revelations. But she didn't ask. Eyes wide, she perched on the edge of the heavy dining table and watched. Daniel found he was glad his daughter was present; Tenai was not, he thought, nearly as apt to let her anger loose with Jenna here as a witness.

But in fact Tenai did not seem angry, though Emelan lowered his head under her continuing regard. She said, "You made some effort to tell me. I do recall it."

Not looking up, Emelan said, "It is not that I ... I did not intend to hide from you, Nolas-e. I thought ... I hoped nothing would come of my fears."

"And this seemed more likely if you did not tell me." Tenai folded her arms, tilting her head. "You should have told me. As you know very well. I count your failure in this matter as defiance. But this once ... I forgive it."

Emelan flinched ... as much from the sting of Tenai's unexpected gentleness, Daniel estimated, as from the reprimand.

"If there were any possible way to return you to your brother, and if you should wish to go, I should release you."

Another flinch. That was not what Emelan wanted at all. Daniel thought he understood: one goes last for judgment to the person whose opinion one most values. More than one patient he'd known had shown him how much courage it takes, to do that.

Jenna was looking both disturbed and mystified. Daniel joined her and murmured in her ear, "He's Keitah Terusai's brother.

Keitah is an important advisor or something. Emelan committed a crime ten years ago and became an outlaw."

Jenna's eyes widened. She looked back at Emelan, intensely curious.

Tenai was continuing, her tone matter-of-fact. "The first shock is the worst. Keitah will accustom himself to the idea. The word will make the rounds of the court, but as they have no reason to care one way or another, other gossip will supersede this."

"Yes," Emelan said, not quite looking at her.

"So. Up, then, Terusai, and we shall consider your place in my household."

"Don't call me by that name," Emelan said fiercely, jerking his head up. He sounded, in that moment, exactly like his brother. Daniel blinked in surprise.

"Ah." Tenai moved a step forward and put out a hand, capturing Emelan's jaw and turning him back to face her when he tried to look away. "Is there a thing in this world you cannot endure? I think not. I do think not. If there is one strength you have in abundance, Terusai, plainly it is endurance. So. Set yourself to endure. If you fear your pride cannot bear what it must, I bid you recall it is *my* pride you hold."

Emelan, Daniel was surprised to see, actually looked somewhat reassured by this.

"Up," Tenai repeated.

This time, the man got to his feet. He wouldn't look at any of them, but stood in their company, like a prisoner hauled before a court. And in fact Tenai's gaze was calm and assessing, much like that of a judge.

Daniel said, "Tenai ... is Keitah Terusai-e your enemy, now?"

Her dark eyes turned to him at once. "I should not imagine so, Daniel. Though I understand why you inquire. But once Terusai-e has opportunity to reflect, I believe he, too, will perceive the hand of God in the remarkable chance that set his brother in my way. Indeed, one could hardly mistake it."

Jenna made a little sound, and, when Tenai's attention turned to her, asked, "Do you really think God made your paths cross?" Clearly she wanted the answer to be *Yes.* Daniel could see that his daughter found the whole story terribly romantic—a tragic romance: the mistake made in youth followed by ten years in exile, and then—one presumed—redemption. Only, Daniel knew, as his daughter had not yet discovered, that redemption is not always so easy to come by. And that the real world does not always feel compelled to follow the desired storyline.

"Or the Martyr put his hand out, perhaps, who has little pity for any of us, when we try to turn from the path we know we should take to find an easier way." Tenai sounded quite matter-of-fact. "Emelan ... I understand you may not perceive so. I bid you have patience."

Emelan bowed his head. He said nothing.

"You must have a place in my household. This must be a place of honor. Nor may it be a place hidden away in the shadows. I will not have a man of mine cower from public attention." Tenai paused. Then she glanced sideways at Jenna and continued, still speaking to Emelan, "This guest of the king's. Clearly Mitereh means to leave her in my household. As she must have a guard, I give this duty to you."

Jenna looked startled. "I need a guard? What, because I'm a woman? Is this some kind of sexist thing? Because if that's what this is, I *don't* need a guard!"

Emelan looked taken aback too, at least as much by the original proposal as by Jenna's vehement response. He looked at the young woman, blood rising in his face. He looked away, started to speak, and then did not.

Daniel found he was just as uncertain about this particular idea. He said, "Tenai—"

Tenai said, "Jenna, my bright child, this is not your home. You must have a guide and a guard. Ladies of the court must, if they would go out into the city. If you do not, you must be imprisoned in this court as surely as though in a cage."

"Yeah? *You* don't have a guard, I bet. And *you* aren't imprisoned."

Tenai barely smiled. "So, well. But I am an exception to many rules. In time you may be also, but I should be failing in my duty toward you if I suggested you emulate my example just now. You must first learn the customs, my child, so you may discard them to purpose."

The rebellious look eased. Jenna even seemed entertained by this last comment. "Well ... I still say it's stupid. But okay. For a while."

"Very good," Tenai said with grave approval. "So. Mitereh

might assign a man of his personal guard to the duty. That would show you honor. But setting this duty upon Emelan will allow him a place of honor. I have as yet few enough to offer. You would be kind to allow this one." She was speaking to Jenna but also, obliquely, to Daniel.

Jenna said, "Well ... all right. I guess." She looked at Emelan, more curious than annoyed by the idea, Daniel thought. The man dropped his gaze at once, obviously uncomfortable, and Jenna's expression at once became sympathetic. It occurred to Daniel that he might want to have a word with his daughter about bad-boy romances at some time in the near future.

"And if you will permit it," Tenai said to Daniel.

"What?" Recalled to the immediate question, Daniel glanced back at Emelan, who ducked his head, his expression hardening. The man expected ... what? Daniel wondered. Contempt? Disgust? Distrust, certainly. Daniel wasn't even certain what he felt, but he knew he showed none of those emotions. He'd been drawn straight into clinical neutrality by the other man's emotional vulnerability, he realized, as his daughter was drawn to sympathy.

Daniel didn't want Jenna wandering about this city on her own, regardless of how his daughter felt about the customs here. Emelan was a big, tough-looking man, just the sort punks and riff-raff would hesitate to mess with. Jenna could indeed take care of herself, more or less, but he would prefer she didn't have to. And he could see Tenai's point about Emelan needing an honorable post. That, perhaps, most of all. "Well ... I suppose he'll be a pretty effective guard. If you're sure."

"I am quite certain, Daniel." Tenai gave Emelan a little nod, settling the matter.

Emelan glanced at Jenna and then away. His manner had eased a little. A job to do, and trust that he would do it, Daniel thought; and they all had to hope Tenai was right that the man was a reformed character. But Daniel, too, thought it might be all right. Change the situation, change the expectation, and the man, too, changed. That was no surprise at all.

It had been that way, hadn't it, for Tenai herself? At McKenna's dojo, surrounded by men and women who expected a gifted and agreeable woman with a civilized distaste for real violence, that was what Tenai had become. Or nearly. Most of the time.

Brian McKenna had come to see Daniel right after Tenai had applied for an instructor's position at Nighthawk—Daniel had been her main reference, of course. Daniel remembered McKenna's wary questions, half-suspicious of what had walked into his dojo and applied for work. That was why he had come in person to see Daniel.

"So you'd recommend this woman, would you, to teach children?" McKenna had asked toward the end of that interview, still faintly skeptical.

Daniel had glanced out the window to where Jenna was playing in the yard with two other little girls. "I'd trust her with mine," he had said. "How old does a child need to be to start classes at your, um, dojo? How much is it to enroll a child in one of your beginner's classes?"

McKenna had been convinced. And eight years later, his dojo flooded with more business than he'd ever expected, Brian McKenna had made Tenai a partner, added a second and then a third dojo, and tripled the number of advanced and self-defense classes he offered.

The question recurred, as it did at odd moments, of what McKenna and the Nighthawk staff and students had made of Tenai's disappearance. And Jenna's. His own, he supposed, would hardly have been noticed at the dojo. On the other hand ... he winced, thinking once more of Lindenwood, and tried to put all that out of his mind. Nothing to be done about the hospital, his patients, about any of that. Russell Martin would cope. Of course he would. Lindenwood's director could cope with problems much more serious than the unexpected disappearance of one of the hospital's doctors. This night, this present, this was the important time and place.

There was a soft handclap outside the door of the dining room, and everyone jumped and looked up. Well, everyone except Tenai. "That will be a servant of Taranah Berangilan-sa come to summon you, my child. I believe you will find that Inaseh Suaneni wishes to escort you. Emelan, you will also attend Nola Jenna through the evening."

Emelan bowed, his expression determinedly blank. Jenna looked startled, but nodded after a moment.

But in fact, when the door opened, it was not on any servant of the king's aunt. It was Sandakan Gutai-e.

Jenna, surprised but no doubt positive this was some kind of romantic moment, looked from Sandakan to Tenai and back again, plainly ready to smile and be pleased for them both. Daniel, after the first moment's startlement, found that he was not surprised at all by the man's appearance at Tenai's door. But he did not expect an easy reconciliation. Laying a hand on his daughter's arm, he drew her quietly aside, out of the way.

Tenai herself might have been surprised. Or not. It was hard to tell. Her face had gone still, her eyes opaque and secretive. Her posture suggested challenge or even repudiation more than welcome. But Sandakan stepped through the door without hesitation. Although his eyes flicked across the others in the room, his manner dismissed them all. All his attention was for Tenai.

They were much of a height: Tenai was tall for a woman and Sandakan not especially tall for a man. They also shared a similar cast of features, though more angular and almost harsh in the man. His coloring was darker than hers. Sandakan's eyes were true black, darker than Tenai's. His hair was very dark, but not quite black. Up close, he looked older than Daniel had first guessed.

"Tenai Chaisa-e," he said, calling Tenai by name, as so few people here ever seemed to. His voice was rather harsh. He sounded somehow tense and neutral at the same time, as though he was trying not to show what he felt but not quite able to hide everything. He came forward one more step, eyes on Tenai's face, and stopped.

Tenai stood, her arms folded over her chest. Her expression was calm, but to Daniel her pose looked less forbidding or closed than self-protective. She inclined her head just the smallest degree and answered, "Gutai-e."

Sandakan said, eyes searching her face, "I serve the king, now."

"Indeed."

There was a little silence.

Tenai broke it, her tone hard, even curt. "Ask me, Gutai, if you will ask."

"And you, Chaisa? Whom do you serve?" His harsh voice made the question sound almost like an accusation, but his eyes were not accusing. They met hers with what seemed a plea, behind the mask of formality.

Tenai answered with a formality that came across as cold. "I have no intention to strike at the king, Gutai. It is he whom I serve. I have no thoughts of fire or of blood. I have no desire to bring an army forth from the land. I have no designs to bring men back to my service. I have said all this to one man and another since my return. Now I tell you the same. If these fears have been in your mind, then be at ease."

The man bowed, hands at his sides, and straightened. "I am glad to take your word, Chaisa."

Again there was a pause, somewhat fraught. There was a lot going on, Daniel knew, that he wasn't catching. This was something with history behind it, more history than Tenai had ever revealed even to him: something long and private that didn't need an audience. He thought about signaling his daughter and Emelan and retreating. But any movement anyone else made now would probably only make their intrusion worse.

"Well?" said Tenai impatiently.

Sandakan took a breath. He came forward a step, hesitated for just an instant, and dropped to one knee with the grace people here often seemed to give such showy gestures. He said, pain audible in his harsh voice, "I betrayed you."

For once, Tenai was visibly nonplused. She started to speak, stopped; started again, and just shook her head instead, a tiny motion. She put out her hand as though she would touch the man's cheek or shoulder; but then did not complete the motion.

"I had to do it," Sandakan said, eyes on her face. This time there was no mistaking the plea. "I still consider so. But it was betrayal still, and sometimes that is the hardest sin of them all. I do not ask for forgiveness, but for …" he hesitated, searching for words. "I ask for forbearance, if any plea of mine can move you to offer that much. It would serve neither the king nor Talasayan for us to be at odds. As we are both servants of the king, can we not be at least tolerant of one another? Or, if you cannot bear my presence near you, I ask you to be plain in this regard. I will offer Mitereh my resignation and retire to Patananir. Or farther, to Pitatan, if that will satisfy you. Or only tell me what you will accept, and I will do it, Chaisa, whatever you would have of me."

When Sandakan stopped speaking, the quiet seemed profound. Nobody rushed to fill it. Daniel found himself holding his breath, and let it out covertly.

After that brief moment, Tenai came forward the necessary

step. She laid her hand on the general's shoulder, close by his neck. "Gutai," she said, and stopped, and began again. "Sandakan."

The man closed his eyes, looking shaken.

"It was I who betrayed you," said Tenai. She lifted her hand, but did not move back. "I have had years to remember those last days. Years to remember the words you used to try to persuade me to turn aside. Years to remember your face, when you lifted your sword against mine at Antiatan. Years in which I have wished to meet you, so that I might say that I was wrong, wrong at Antiatan and wrong before that at Nerinesir, when you told me the war was over. I should have listened when you told me to put away my sword and let the living tend to the grim harvest we had reaped for them."

Sandakan looked up at her. "Chaisa—" he stopped. And began again: "Tenai Chaisa-e. Do you mean what you say?"

Tenai met his eyes. "Should I mean other than what I say? Sandakan Gutai-e, the king is fortunate in your service. I have no claim and no complaint. I swear by Lord Death and by the Gate: I mean everything I say."

The man drew a hard breath. He looked, to Daniel, like a man who had expected to die, and been reprieved at the very last second. Beside Daniel, Jenna swallowed and looked away, embarrassed to witness what she had no right to see. He touched her arm, and his daughter leaned against him. He hoped she drew comfort from the contact. He did.

"I feared—I thought—I was afraid to face you, Tenai," Sandakan was saying. "Even when I saw you had come in company with Mitereh. Even when I saw that it would not be across a battlefield that I would face you, this time. Even then. I came here in fear, because I thought—I thought—"

"You thought I would hate you," said Tenai, her own voice quiet. "Even though you knew you had been right. Even though it was I who had forged the dark knife of bitter rage and thrust it into my own heart."

Sandakan met her eyes wordlessly.

"I remember you only kindly, Sandakan, and that, too, I swear by Lord Death and by the Gate. You turned against me. I am grateful. You stopped me when I did not know how to stop myself. Mitereh gained a great prize when he took you into his service, as who should know better than I? It is least of all my desire to deprive him of your service now, or you of the place you have gained in his hand. Will you ask now for my forgiveness?"

"Now I will ask," the man said, his rough voice sinking almost to a whisper.

"It is yours, given gladly. Please, rise."

Sandakan got to his feet. He began to speak, but then plainly did not know what to say.

Tenai spoke instead, softly. "I have more hope than you. I will ask for your pardon, as you were always more generous than I, for Antiatan and for what came before, and I hope you will give it."

"You have it." Sandakan seemed at last to draw a full breath. "Indeed, you have it."

"And in time, perhaps, your trust, which is not so easily repaired." Tenai moved a hand when he would have spoken. Her tone seemed dark with memory. "It has been sixteen years, but I have not been here, Sandakan. For you it is still Antiatan. For you, I am still Nolas-Kuomon, who tried to burn all this land to ash, a pyre for Encormio. How else could it be? In sixteen more years, perhaps, you will have learned to see past those memories."

The man looked at her, his black eyes unreadable, shadowed with memory. "It will not take sixteen years. Even at Antiatan, I think I waited only for some paltry shadow of a reason to trust you. And found one, when you chose to run and leave me still living behind you."

Tenai turned her face aside, not answering.

After a moment, when she did not speak, Sandakan bowed his head. "With your leave?"

"You do not need leave from me to come and go in this house, Gutai."

"But I still ask it," Sandakan said, his tone harsh.

Tenai turned back to him, meeting his eyes once more. "Then I give it."

Sandakan bowed again, turned, and went out. The silence he left behind him was profound. No one, it was clear, wanted to be the one to break it.

It was Jenna who did, in the end. Brave and empathic and trusting: of course it would be Jenna. She crossed the room to Tenai's side and put a hand on her arm, looking into her face.

Tenai did not like to be touched. But she had always made an exception to this rule for Jenna. Now awareness of the present, of this room and her companions, seeped back into her face. She touched Jenna's hand with just the tips of her fingertips and moved away. But she stepped away with a back-to-business attitude.

The next handclap, thankfully, was nothing more alarming than the woman from Taranah's household. Jenna, looking pleased and excited and a touch nervous, went out. Inaseh Suaneni and Emelan went with her.

Daniel turned back at Tenai after the door closed behind his daughter. He tipped his head after everyone who had just left them. "You're sure that's a good idea."

Now, in private, with only Daniel to see her, Tenai permitted herself to look tired. "I know Taranah Berangilan-sa only very little. I know nothing about the queen's sister to alarm either of us. But she is royal, and thus one is wise to be cautious."

Daniel had meant sending Emelan with Jenna. He paused now. "Does she outrank you? Does anyone? Keitah Terusai-e, I gather."

A tiny quirk of one eyebrow. "Let us say, I would not attempt to issue a command to Taranah Berangilan-sa or Keitah Terusai-e. Nor, despite their higher rank, would either of them be comfortable to command me. We shall walk carefully with one another in the coming days, you may be certain. So we see how useful a man God or the Martyr has set into my hand: Emelan will know very well how to understand everything that passes at the table of the king's aunt. He will advise Jenna, if advice would serve her."

Daniel pulled a chair away from the table for himself, and one for Tenai. "I gather a supper invitation from the king's aunt is a command performance."

"No less than from the king, whom I expect to send for you in a very little. Thus he will signal his favor. I will remain attentive to both you and Jenna, I do assure you. In the unlikely event you find it necessary to call my name, I shall hear you. That has not changed. A good many miles would have to lie between us before your voice would fail to carry to me." Tenai seated herself and leaned back in her chair, resting her hands on the table and gazing between them at the polished wood. She looked up after a moment. "And are you well, Daniel? I have hardly seen you to speak to these past days."

Daniel shook his head, then held up a hand when she tilted

her head in concern. "I'm fine. As fine as can be expected, I suppose. I admit, I can't help but be nervous. I do actually like Mitereh. I think I do. Not that I actually know him well, obviously, but he seems …" he thought about that and said finally, "He seems an earnest young man. I'm less worried than I was at first, I can tell you that." He paused, thinking over the past days. "Your world certainly seems a good deal more real now that we've ridden through part of it. Your history seems far more real now. I'd really like to dig into that a little, if there's a library around here somewhere, and if I could read."

"The library is no difficulty. There are two within the palace. Or there were." Tenai tapped her fingertips restlessly on the table. "The enchantment to open your eyes to our writing … that may be more difficult. Mitereh will not wish me to work any true sorcery without his leave, which he may prefer not to give. Or not yet. I know you will not wish to wait. I will ask him. Or you may do so, Daniel. He would not be offended by the request. He may ask you to permit someone else to work this spell upon you. Some among his personal guard must be at least minor sorcerers. Taranah Berangilan-sa certainly is."

Daniel nodded. "All right." He might have been a little uncomfortable at the idea of anyone but Tenai working any sort of magic around him, or on him, but maybe he wouldn't mind if the king's aunt did it.

He was also thinking about history, and how much more real it seemed when one met figures who might as well have stepped directly out of the pages of dusty history. He said, "And how about you, Tenai? Are you all right? That might have been … a little too much history this evening."

She knew what he meant. She gazed down at her hands where they rested on the table. "Sandakan remembers the ferocity of those last years. How could he not? That dark fury eclipsed the sky for us both."

Daniel nodded. "In Chaisa … you seemed to me to be regaining your balance. Even on the ride here, I don't know, we didn't have much chance to talk, but I thought you seemed … if not comfortable, at least still maintaining your balance. This has been a tough day for you, I know that. But … I'm glad you had a chance to make a peace with Sandakan. I know he's important to you."

She did not deny it.

"It seems to me, though maybe I'm not the best person to judge, that you handled Keitah Terusai-e with some skill in a difficult situation. And Emelan with restraint, even with kindness. And Sandakan Gutai-e with grace and honesty. I think you left something there that will have room to grow. Is that not how it seems to you?"

Tenai rose and moved across the room, to the window, as she always tended to move toward windows when disturbed. The rich light of the low sun silhouetted her, cast her face into shadow when she turned back toward him, struck dark bronze highlights from her hair and skin. She looked foreign in that light. Almost unrecognizable.

Then she shifted out of the sunlight and became at once herself. Familiar.

She said quietly, "I have long wished to say to Gutai-e the things I said. But I ..." Her voice trailed off.

Thought that it would feel different? That giving, and asking, forgiveness would give a different, or greater, sense of closure? That Sandakan would somehow be able to offer her a kind of absolution she could not give herself? Daniel could imagine all those reactions.

"I am a fool," said Tenai. "It was not Gutai-e who accompanied me through the veil."

Daniel waited, but she did not elaborate. He suspected he knew what she'd meant. He was fairly certain she meant *Lord Death* had accompanied her. That was a fraught idea. But ... he could think of one or two things that really made him think she must mean that.

There was a handclap outside the door before he could decide whether to ask.

It was, this time, a servant of Mitereh's, summoning Daniel back to the king's apartment for the long-promised supper. Because he was part of the king's household now, and not Tenai's. Probably Keitah Terusai-e would be there, too. Wonderful.

He gave Tenai a last look, trying to communicate—what? Trust, he decided, because that was what each of them needed from the other now. Then he followed the king's attendant.

In the event, Daniel found, when he'd made his way once more through the somewhat complicated hallways between Tenai's apartment and the king's, that Keitah had gone. To re-write his will or the Talasayan equivalent, possibly, one way or the other. Daniel could hardly guess whether the man might decide to reconcile with his brother or disinherit him or what. Regardless, his absence probably lowered the tension level in the king's apartments by, oh, a thousand percent or so.

The king, alone except for a couple of his guards and various attendants, welcomed Daniel with a little nod. "Join me, Danyel. We shall have a quiet evening, I hope," he said kindly. "Come; sit with me. I trust you have not been too much discommoded by all these events." Then, as he guided Daniel into a different room, he added with more focused intent, "Nor has Chaisa found herself discommoded, I hope."

The other room proved to be a surprisingly casual space; a comfortable room with couches and low tables arranged in small groupings, and, more to the point, a large balcony where a small table had been laid for supper. Only two chairs had been set at this table. Daniel was fairly certain he was being offered a significant honor. He wished again for a handy etiquette guide, but also assumed the king did not intend to take offense at anything but truly egregious blunders.

Declining to answer leading questions hopefully wouldn't count. Saying anything like *Actually, whatever's going on between Tenai and Keitah and Emelan, that's not as important as her working things out with Sandakan* would be a definite breach of Tenai's privacy.

He decided finally on a mere statement of observable fact that therefore definitely could not constitute a breach of privacy. "Tenai appointed Emelan as Jenna's bodyguard. I think that may have been ..." a bit optimistic? Just what the man needed? "A reasonable option," he concluded. He hoped. He took the chair toward which the king nodded and added, a cautious probe of his own, "I hope, ah, Nolas-ai Keitah finds that acceptable."

"He will become accustomed," murmured the king. "He was surprised, of course. Who would not be?" He sat down himself, not facing Daniel across the table, but at an offset angle. An etiquette book would probably explain that choice. He went on, "That appointment should serve, so long as this man has recovered any measure of honor in Chaisa's service. By making such an appointment, she declares that he has. By declaring so, she makes it true—unless the man she takes up should prove cur enough to bite the hand that she has held out to him."

Daniel nodded, thinking about this. "I don't think that's likely."

"I think it most unlikely. Nolas-Kuomon cannot be a poor judge of men. I should be astonished if that were so."

Two of his young men had taken positions behind the king: Torohoh and—apparently finally restored to the king's favor—Ranakai. They looked relaxed, but attentive. Torohoh gazed out across the garden below the balcony; Ranakai kept an eye on the door that led back into the apartment. Bodyguards added a certain something to a private supper. So did the quiet attendants, who brought covered dishes from some unseen kitchen and deftly slid these onto the table without any clinking of porcelain or metal.

Sliced meat of some sort, in a creamy sauce with tiny green seeds or something; the golden puree, which Daniel knew now was made of a vegetable similar to beets; a whole fish with its scales replaced by overlapping slices of some other kind of white vegetable; a roasted chicken, exactly like any roasted chicken, a note of familiarity amid the other dishes. Far too much for two men, obviously. Perhaps the guards or the servants would get the vast amount that would be left from the king's supper, and that was another strange and uncomfortable thought to a man unused to this sort of hierarchy.

And definitely unused to small, intimate suppers with kings.

"I am aware you must prefer the lady's household to mine," Mitereh said, his manner entirely matter-of-fact. "I cannot permit that for some time, but I wish you to be at your ease, Danyel. Tell me, if you would, whether there may be some other small accommodation I may make for your comfort here."

That was unexpectedly direct—and unexpectedly kind. Almost certainly, the king would like to be asked for something easy, something safe to offer. Daniel had no trouble thinking of one thing that ought to fit that description. "Well ... if it's not too much trouble ... Tenai said she would do a literacy spell for me, as she did a spell to permit Jenna and me to understand and speak your language. She didn't have a chance to do it before ... before you arrived at her doorstep and things got complicated. She said you wouldn't want her to work any kind of sorcery. But I'd appreciate being able to read."

"Ah." The king looked thoughtful. "Indeed. A simple request

in every way but one. Nolas-Kuomon is correct: I would prefer that she work no sorcery for the next little while. Someone else might assuredly fulfil your request. My aunt could do so, or Keitah." He smiled suddenly, obviously pleased by this thought. "Indeed, that might do well. Let Keitah Terusai-e work this sorcery for you, Danyel, and let Nolas-Kuomon permit him to do so. That would be useful in every possible way."

Daniel nodded, cautiously pleased—although he would have preferred the king's aunt to work the spell, if it couldn't be Tenai. But he was distracted by another detail. The king was addressing him by name, with no titles; it had taken him a few minutes to realize this and now he wasn't certain how to respond properly. He asked directly. "I'm not certain how I should address anyone, or speak of anyone. Chaisa-e, Chaisa, Tenai? I think that's most formal to least, but I'm not certain which mode to use when. I also haven't understood how to address you. I'm sorry; I should have asked before, but I haven't found the chance. I hope I haven't given offense."

The king smiled. "I understand your customs are different, Danyel. I would not and shall not take offense at any trifling errors. Though you are a member of my household, I am not your king; you have taken no oath to me. Nor do I ask it, as I am aware you must owe fealty elsewhere, to a king or lord of your own. Thus, you may call me by my name. You should *certainly* call Chaisa-e by her name, as she has clearly given you leave to do so. Indeed, that will be useful."

Useful. Because some people would find it shocking, or perhaps reassuring, that anyone at all addressed Tenai by name? Even people from a different world, evidently.

"*Chaisa-e* is not more formal than *Chaisa*, precisely," Mitereh added. "It is more, ah, more elaborate. It is a term that indicates that Nolas-Kuomon is not merely a lady of that title, but *the* lady; the head of the ruling house. There is no other lady there, to be sure. If there were, that lady would never be addressed as Chaisa-e. She might be addressed merely as Chaisa, or, if she were in the direct line and one wished to indicate an understanding of this, Chaisa-na."

Daniel nodded. "Tenai addressed Emelan as *Terusai*."

"Did she so?" Mitereh regarded Daniel with a thoughtful expression. "I am glad to know this. Nor am I entirely astonished.

Chaisa-e has never been over-fond of Keitah Terusai-e. If he had supported her during the last years of her war, she might take a kinder tone now, but he did not. I think you heard her explain that Keitah was one of the few so adroit as to manage to maintain a neutral pose at that time. After Encormio was finally forced through the Gate, Keitah ceased his pose of neutrality. He brought me the whole of the east and a large part of the north. His support then was important, perhaps crucial, but one is hardly surprised if Chaisa is little mindful now of his pride. She means to force Keitah to recognize his brother. She intends that all men recognize that what Keitah discarded as irretrievably flawed, she has taken up and restored."

"That's good for Emelan? Or bad for Keitah? Or both?"

"Good for Emelan, embarrassing for Keitah, and a declaration of confidence in her own power." Mitereh appeared faintly amused rather than offended. He added, "Tell me something of your world. Anything you wish, Danyel. I shall be interested in anything you tell me."

"I hardly know where to start," Daniel admitted. "For one thing, we don't have kings. Not in my country, anyway."

"Indeed?" The king tilted his head. "By what title do you know those men who rule?"

So *that* was going to take them right through supper, obviously. Daniel found himself smiling, suddenly looked forward to explaining exactly how that question was based on three different faulty premises. Though as politely as possible, not necessarily trusting *too* much in the king's promise that he wouldn't take offense. He wondered if Jenna might be explaining exactly this kind of thing to Mitereh's aunt right now. He wouldn't have laid any odds against it. Taranah would probably be amused and interested, a lot like Mitereh himself. What was the other part of her name ... Berangilan-sa? He wondered what the -sa suffix indicated. He would ask someone when he got a chance.

He felt a little better about kings and courts, remembering the warmth between the king and his aunt. A little better about this whole business of being taken into someone's household, of the subtle—or at least unseen—political winds undoubtedly blowing all around himself and his daughter. Tonight seemed all right, at least. Though after this night, the morning—coming if anything too quickly. Dawn. And a progress to the Cathedral. Daniel found himself looking forward to that, to seeing more of the city. He was feeling more confident of the king's good will, he realized. The young man had gone out of his way to show personal warmth, not merely polite courtesy … that was part of it. The rest … he got it after a moment. Mitereh was pleased that Tenai had taken up Emelan, even if the act embarrassed one of his important advisors. Daniel was almost sure the king truly was genuinely pleased, for Emelan's sake and not just because of a careful political calculation about where advantage might lie. He liked that. It made him feel better about the young king. It made him feel better about everything.

11

The next morning, Daniel had a chance to really take a look at the palace. Seen by daylight, it was ... magnificent. Too much so for Daniel to easily imagine people *living* in it, making it their home, thinking it was ordinary. Almost everything in the public areas seemed to be grand scale. Rooms were vast, with fluted columns supporting arching ceilings. They all seemed to have complicated mosaics of stone tiles on the floors or stunning murals painted on their walls. The ceilings were sometimes painted, too: with pale fiery colors broken by unexpected geometric rings and squares in red or blue or black. Kathy, Daniel thought, gazing up at those shapes, would have loved the ceilings. He wondered what the shapes were meant to symbolize.

Then there were the people crowding all these rooms. The nobles of the court were clad in jewel-toned fabrics: shimmering blues and violets, or garnet, or vibrant yellows. Both men and women wore rings and necklaces and earrings, but only the women tucked their hair up into fine jeweled nets. There was a scattering of older children, in or at least close to their teens. The children already had the same air of self-possessed restraint as their elders.

Daniel himself had been given clothing of rich royal blue and teal to wear and had felt himself overdressed until he'd gotten a good look at the court. Jenna was in blue and amethyst, setting off her blond good looks to lovely effect. It was not, Daniel thought, his imagination that made it obvious she drew plenty of attention.

It seemed that every single member of the court was present. Even tucked into the background, Daniel seemed set to meet hundreds of people. He was not going to remember one name in twenty. Jenna, near him, was making more of an effort—she'd always been good at this kind of thing, and he saw the crease between her eyebrows that meant she was working to bear down hard and remember.

"Why are you bothering?" Daniel asked his daughter, during one lull when everybody appeared to be waiting for some signal to begin doing something.

The look Jenna returned was startled. "But isn't it interesting, Daddy?"

Well, no; it was in fact deathly boring, to someone who had no idea who any of these people even were. Wasn't it?

"Oh, no, Daddy," Jenna protested, wide-eyed. "Emel is telling me who everyone is and all about their families and everything. I met a few of them last night—Nolas-ai Taranah was so kind—look, there's Sandakan Gutai-e. I bet the king is arriving."

Daniel had missed all Emelan's flurry of helpful clarification, probably because he kept concentrating on Tenai—on her reactions to everything, which were not obvious; and on everyone's reactions to her, which were revealing. But no one could have missed the king's entrance: Mitereh was clad all in white: white trousers, white shirt, white vest with shimmering white embroidery, with a loose white robe over it all. White, white, white—Daniel did not know what kind of statement the king was making by that, but had no doubt that some kind of statement was intended.

The king's arrival seemed to have been a signal, for everyone now moved in a bewildering number of directions. There were more rooms and more hallways and a lot of people departing and a lot more arriving, and then everyone poured through a huge doorway where massive double-doors had been thrown wide, and out into a courtyard. Or a street. The distinction did not seem to be too clear. If there was a distinction. On an ordinary day it might have been possible to tell.

It was oven hot, although a high haze blocked direct sunlight. It was not as humid here as it had been in Goshui-sa-e, thank God for small favors, but it was still hot. The point of the thick, heavy walls of the palace suddenly became clear: it had been much cooler indoors.

On foot and in daylight, it was much easier to get a real impression of the city. The court. The white stone was all but blinding in the sun. The brightly-clad nobility seemed even more vivid surrounded by all that white, which might have been the point.

There was nothing resembling an American lawn. Everything was stone and gravel, with tall graceful trees planted to accent the sweeping white walls. Silver cages holding small, colorful birds hung from the branches of the trees and from the edges of balconies. Daniel recognized neither the trees nor the birds, but roses bloomed crimson and gold and white all along the edges of the courtyards.

Horses were brought—white ones for Mitereh and those of his household. Some of the noblewomen rode in litters. One of Mitereh's guards, Torohoh, turned up at Daniel's elbow, guiding him to a spot where a grave-faced boy held a tall white horse, its saddle tooled with silver,. Torohoh's own horse was also white—definitely the king's personal guards counted as members of his household, then.

Tenai rode past on her black mare. She barely glanced at them, but she somehow swept Jenna up in her train while Daniel was still struggling to get up on his tall horse. Emelan flung himself into his saddle and rode after the women. *They* were all mounted on black or gray horses. All part of the pageant, probably.

Another white horse came up beside his. Taranah Berangilan-sa smiled at him from its back. Sunlight glinted across her gray eyes like light on water, rendering them almost colorless and giving them an unusual depth.

"Nola Danyel," she greeted him, with a cheerful nod. "Ride beside me, I do ask you. I would be pleased by your company."

Daniel was certainly happy with hers. Though the roads were packed, no one crowded the king's aunt. It wasn't just the presence of the king's guards, though Torohoh stayed at Daniel's back. Nolas-ai Taranah was surrounded by ladies in jeweled gowns and then by guardsmen of her own, clad in gray and white, an entourage that enforced Taranah's status and, possibly, Daniel's own.

The horses were suddenly moving, caught up in the king's procession, but with Mitereh's aunt next to him, at least Daniel didn't have to worry that he'd miss some signal. He asked Taranah, "Nolas-ai Taranah, why do some of the women ride in litters?"

"A remnant of manners from Encormio's age," she answered, with a dismissive wave of a hand. "Some ladies are reluctant to relinquish privileges. Even those that were always meant to bind rather than loose. Sekuse, now—my sister never mistook bonds for freedom, for all she yielded gracefully to her prison when Encormio required her to become his queen."

Taranah's tone was perfectly straightforward, despite the rather appalling topic. Daniel couldn't quite recall whether anyone had explicitly explained previously that Encormio had taken Mitereh's mother in what sounded like a forced marriage. Not exactly surprising, but ugly. He said after a minute, "Some people adapt to whatever life throws their way, while others, I suppose, give up and fall into despair when faced with real trouble. And others fight and fight and, if they are overpowered, finally become bitter."

Taranah gave him an interested look and a smile, and he found himself certain that she was the first kind of person. At least, he doubted very much that she was much inclined toward either despair or bitterness. She was the sort of person who brightened the emotional landscape wherever she went. He found himself smiling back.

"Sekuse accommodated herself to everything," she said after a moment's reflection. "She was too wise to waste her strength in anger, but she never despaired, though she feared Encormio more and more in those latter years."

The procession streamed out through the silver gates of the court and turned to take a direction that, Daniel estimated, would probably lead all the way around the nobles' black city. The streets were lined with people, at ground level and leaning from windows and balconies. Nobles in Nerinesir wore colorful clothing, but in shades darker and more muted than those worn by the court.

"So were you a member of your sister's household, back then?" Daniel asked Taranah. "Or Encormio's? Or neither?"

"Ah," she answered, her cheerfulness dimming. "I was at that time married to Bintatang Neranani of Pitatan. Sometimes we lived in Pitatan, but Encormio sometimes called my lord husband to Nerinesir. He died there. Not by Encormio's hand, or at least not directly because of Encormio's intention. My lord was among those who raised up a banner in defense of the king, and died on the field. He was loyal … reluctantly loyal, but to the end." She was silent for a moment, her round face uncharacteristically somber.

"I'm sorry. I shouldn't have asked."

Taranah gave him a shrewd look, and after a moment a smile. "By no means, Nola Danyel. Of course you are curious. You wish to know the age which birthed Tenai Nolas-Kuomon. How strange it seems to me—a man my own age who does not remember the age of Encormio! It was an age of death and sorrow, to be sure, but it was long ago, as mortal men measure the years. Not every story that came from that age ends unhappily. I will tell you a story if you wish—a story of Sekuse and Mitereh and Nolas-Kuomon. This is a tale that may please a man who calls Nolas-Kuomon a friend."

"Yes, please. By all means."

Taranah smiled again. "There came a time, near the end of the age, during which my sister Sekuse and her son Mitereh were in Kinabana. That is an estate which can be strongly guarded, and Encormio sent them there to guard them, for by then he had few sons still living. Mitereh had, oh, six years, seven, perhaps. Nolas-Kuomon found him there. My sister told me later that Mitereh did not try to run away, but stood up straight and very bravely declared to Nolas-Kuomon that his death would only hurt his mother and not his father and that it would not be fair for her to hurt his mother, who had never done anything to hurt her."

"She listened to him?"

"She did. Perhaps she was amused by my nephew's courage, or perhaps she admitted the simple justice of his scolding. Or perhaps she chose to hold her hand for some other reason. She gave Mitereh the knife she had meant to use to kill him, and went away. She told him to give the knife to his father." She added, no longer smiling, "That is the part I witnessed, later."

The hoofbeats of the horses rang against the stone of the streets; people crowded on both sides of the procession, cheering and calling out phrases Daniel could not catch. Yet he was much more interested in Taranah's story. The heat of the sun, the brilliance of the day, the clatter and noise, seemed almost like a movie backdrop. The scene Taranah was spinning for him seemed somehow more real.

Taranah went on after a moment. "Encormio took this mercy as an insult. Perhaps it was; Nolas-Kuomon might have intended it so. She might as well have declared, 'I can destroy anyone you would protect, but see, your son is of so little importance to me I will not even trouble myself.' Encormio was very angry. He sent for them. He meant to kill Mitereh himself."

That idea wrung an involuntary exclamation from Daniel. He'd heard references to this incident before, but Tenai had never mentioned this part. Perhaps she hadn't known.

"Oh, he did not say so, Nola Danyel," Taranah told him. "But what else would he do? By such an act, he would show Tenai Nolas-Kuomon that she had spared nothing he valued. That was precisely what he meant to do. Sekuse was quite certain when she told me what had happened, and I am certain she was right."

"But Encormio obviously changed his mind."

"He did. Sekuse asked him if he would show all the land that Tenai had touched his temper. She said perhaps he might show better indifference if he did not react at all. Then she asked him whether he would not at least wait to get a second son from her before discarding the first. That was Sekuse: brave and quiet-voiced and willing to court what she feared. And, indeed, Encormio liked to please my sister, as a man might cast a tidbit to a favored hound. He was so old, I think he had by then begun to see men and women as ordinary men see dogs or falcons. But something my sister said made him think again, and he relented. He took the knife and said that he would return it to Tenai himself. But she killed him instead. Fortunately Sekuse and Mitereh had returned to Kinabana then, and I to Pitatan. Though my lord husband was in Nerinesir, with Encormio. He died there. But Sekuse and Mitereh were spared."

"Surely," Daniel began, and hesitated. Then he went on, with resolution. "Surely *Tenai* did not kill your sister, later? I always assumed, I guess I always assumed, that Encormio killed Mitereh's mother. But it sounds like that didn't happen."

This time, remembered grief shadowed Taranah's face. "The king did not mean to kill my sister, Nola Daniel, though if Encormio had not worn out her strength she might have lived. She died of the second son he got on her. Sekuse was a small woman, and not strong when she conceived a second son. The birth was difficult for her, and the baby too large for the birth to be easy. So his mother lived to see Encormio torn down and the new age dawn, but died before she could learn to live in it."

Daniel wasn't certain whether that was much better than being deliberately murdered by Encormio. He said, "I'm sorry. Did the baby—?"

A slight pause. Then Taranah answered, "The child lived, and thrived. My sister lived long enough to know her second son would not follow her at once into the dark kingdom."

Daniel said gently, "Then at least she lived to hope that her sons would inherit a quieter age."

Taranah gave him a thoughtful look. "Yes, Nola Danyel; you are wise to say so. That was a comfort to her, I believe."

"That's not wisdom. I've got a child of my own, you know." Daniel glanced ahead, looking for Jenna in Tenai's train. He found her almost at once: the only flaxen-haired woman in all the city. She had gotten some of the other women near her talking and looked like she was having a great time. As Daniel watched, she tossed her head back and laughed delightedly at something one of the others had said, and after a startled moment the other women laughed too.

"She is a charming child. She has a gift for joy," Taranah observed, following his gaze. "A wonderful gift. One of my own sons is like that: he wins the hearts of men wherever he goes. Your daughter is a lovely girl. Such unusual coloring, and so lively a manner. And a *friend* of Chaisa-e. Indeed, now that I have met Nola-e Jenna, I have been greatly reassured of Chaisa-e."

Daniel hesitated. After a moment he said, "I doubt Jenna remembers a time when Tenai wasn't an important part of her life. Her mother ... died ... when she was a little girl."

Taranah made a sound of sympathy.

Daniel cleared his throat and went on, "For Jenna, for years, Tenai has been sort of like a mother and sort of like a sister, and always somebody to look up to and trust. And if you trust somebody, you know, they tend to become trustworthy, if they're at all decent."

"So they may," she agreed.

"I'll tell you a story, if you like, about my daughter and Tenai, in return for the one you told me. This was when Jenna was thirteen or fourteen. She and Tenai and some other people had gone to see a performance. When they left the theater, most of the ..." the words *parking area* did not work in the language he was speaking now, and he said instead, "It was late at night by then, so everyone had to walk some distance. A gang of young, um, brigands, ambushed them. They must have thought they had easy prey."

Taranah looked amused. "And they faced Nolas-Kuomon."

"Right." Daniel's hands pricked with sweat, though, even remembering the incident. He understood why it seemed funny to Taranah. Even to him it seemed funny, in a kind of horrific way.

But it could so easily have turned into every father's nightmare. Except for Tenai. And she had made it ... a different kind of nightmare. A better kind, absolutely. But still ...

He cleared his throat and went on, "Everyone with Jenna was a, um, they were all trained to fight. Plus Jenna knew, or thought she knew, a little about what Tenai could do. She told me later, it was so stupid and funny and dangerous that when the leader of the, ah, brigands, said, 'Do what you're told and nobody gets hurt,' she actually wanted to laugh. She said she couldn't help herself; that it was just like bad dialogue in a, a show. She was scared, but at the same time, she knew—she *knew*—that Tenai would never let anyone hurt her. She knew Tenai could stop them, and she knew she *would* stop them."

"Yes," murmured Taranah. "And so Nolas-Kuomon killed all those people to protect your daughter?"

"No, actually." That was the point Daniel wanted to make. "Jenna told me Tenai just *radiated* danger, it came off her like flames, but the bad guys were too stupid or too blind to feel it. It was the first time Jenna had seen Tenai truly *on*, probably. She hadn't been like that for years, but I can imagine exactly what it must have been like. I can't believe the bad guys didn't realize they'd grabbed a ..." there was no word for tiger, apparently. "A lioness by the tail," he said instead. "But it actually wasn't a good situation at all, because one of the bad guys had a, hmm, a weapon that's like a bow, but more dangerous. Anyway, Tenai took out three of the bad guys, even though she was shot—the doctors said later the bullet had nicked her femoral artery and her blood pressure had dropped so low it was a miracle she didn't die. Now I guess I understand that it wasn't exactly a miracle. Or not the way we thought then."

"No," agreed Taranah. "God does not hold His hand above Nolas-Kuomon. She is Lord Death's lady; it is his hand that ceaselessly guards her and his will that permits her to dismiss every dire injury. Even in your world, this must have been so."

"Yes, apparently that's true. But before that, when the danger was over, Tenai started to kill the bad guys. She wouldn't *stop,* even when people, friends, yelled at her to stop."

Taranah said, "Were these not brigands of the road? Why should she not render justice upon them?" Then she added, "No, I see. In your country, Chaisa-e had no standing to do so."

"That's right." Daniel went on. "We really don't like killing people, even people who are attacking you, once they're down. And you're right, Tenai didn't have the right to, well, execute people there, as I guess she might in Chaisa."

"All decent people have the right and, indeed, the duty to put down any brigands who prey on travelers. For a lord or a lady to decline to do so would be a dereliction of responsibility to their people."

"Well, that may be so, here. Anyway, Jenna was shocked and upset, and *she* shouted at Tenai to stop. And my point is, Tenai *did* stop."

Taranah nodded at this and looked ahead to Jenna, where she rode talking and laughing with the other young women.

"Jenna told me Tenai was like a lion or a wolf: like some dangerous animal that could never be *tame*. She was so angry it was scary. But even injured and furious, she stopped when Jenna shouted at her. It was all pretty horrendous," Daniel added. "Jenna felt horrible because, if this makes sense to you, she hadn't tried to stop Tenai more quickly. Two of the bad guys were dead before she figured out she should even try. But ... you have to understand, there is no one, no one at all, I'd rather have with Jenna in a dangerous spot. Because I trust her to do whatever's necessary to protect my daughter. And then I trust her to stop."

Taranah nodded again. "I understand, Nola Danyel. I am happy to hear this, that Nolas-Kuomon has learned to love. This is a great thing that you and your daughter have given her. And given us. A great thing."

"Well—"

Taranah peered ahead. "Ah! There is the Cathedral. At last. I am not so young as I once was, to enjoy a long progression."

She was hardly *old*. Merely ... attractively mature. Daniel didn't say so, for several reasons. He turned his attention instead to the Cathedral.

Set among the heavy, low buildings of the outer city, the Martyr's Cathedral seemed doubly splendid: a great gray towering structure that reared up to the sky, powerful rather than graceful. Square towers were set at each corner, with a far greater tower centered in the front and vaulting arches linking all the towers to the sweeping domed roof of the main structure. Immense bells hung in that highest tower. They began ringing now in great glad brazen voices—it might have been the cheering on all sides that made the bells too sound joyous.

Mitereh rode his white horse right up the broad sweeping steps of the Cathedral and reined it about on the wide landing, beside a white-robed man who stood before the great doors at the top—doors so tall his horse might have reared beneath their arch without endangering its rider. These enormous doors were carved with intricate images Daniel could not make out. The king leaned from the saddle and spoke to the man, and then straightened, still without dismounting, and made a speech. Daniel couldn't catch one word in ten past the ringing of the bells and the constant murmur of the crowds, but he understood the tone of it just fine, and so did the assembly. All the women in litters put back the concealing curtains and knelt at the edges of their litters so they could see, and cheered along with everybody else.

People cheered the king at the beginning of his speech and again at the end, and cheered a third time as he held out his hand to Tenai, who dismounted from her black mare and came up the Cathedral steps on foot to kiss the king's offered hand. Then she turned and knelt to the white-robed man, kissing his hand as well. Everyone cheered yet again, with still greater enthusiasm.

Tenai rose again and moved to stand, dark and dangerous, before the king's horse. He drew his sword and held it up for everyone to see, then tossed it to Tenai, who caught it and turned to take the reins of her horse when someone led it up the stairs to the landing. She swung up into her saddle and brought the sword the king had given her up and around in a wide circle, ending with it held crosswise before her body, the tip slanting away from the king. There was a breathless pause, and then a final cheer. Horns sounded, not quite like trumpets, not like anything Daniel recognized. Their rich, mellow notes rose above the cheers and rolled out across the city.

All in all, Daniel thought, this was surely a successful day's work.

"Let the swallows carry word of *that* south," Taranah said, with considerable satisfaction. *"That* will strike terror through the hearts of all those who would challenge Mitereh. A gift for show, has my nephew."

Her confidence was reassuring, even contagious. Daniel found himself smiling back at her. "So that's done the job, has it?"

"All the city will rejoice, and very many of the dangerous whispers will be quieted, or so I should expect, Nola Danyel. All have seen Mitereh make Nolas-Kuomon his champion. His enemies, if they are wise, will understand from this hour that they have made a dire mistake in bringing Lord Death's lady back to Talasayan."

Jenna swept through the crowds on her pretty black mare and rode up to them. Emelan trailed at her heel, looking professional, like a real guard. Jenna's eyes were snapping with delight and excitement.

"Wasn't that beautiful, Daddy?" she said to him, and then at once turned and bowed to Taranah. "Nolas-ai Taranah, wasn't it beautiful? Tenai's going to ride with Mitereh on the way back; can I ride with you? Emel said it was proper to ask," she added to Daniel.

From her tone on that last, she had forgotten her earlier doubts about being guarded. He really did need to remind her that bad-boy romances seldom worked out well.

Taranah gave Jenna a warm smile, and nodded to Emelan, who flushed and looked aside. "Of course it is proper, and I should be pleased by your company, Nola Jenna. We need not ride in such strict order now. Let us take a more leisurely route through the city, if that would please you."

"Oh, yes!" Jenna agreed. "This is such an interesting city! Emel's been pointing out things to me, but it would be nice to be able to look at everything a little bit instead of just riding past. And it will be nice to ride through it like a normal person and not like, you know, an ornament in somebody's procession."

The king's aunt laughed out loud. "Sunlight child, you would ornament any procession! But yes, we will dismiss most of our entourage, shall we, and ride unencumbered."

His daughter was right, Daniel found: it was more comfortable to be just people and not part of a parade. He and Jenna attracted curious glances, but the restrained manners of Talasayan—and perhaps the inhibiting effect of Taranah's guards—served as a welcome buffer against people's curiosity. No one was so presumptuous as to point or yell. This gave them the freedom to see the sights.

Taranah Berangilan-sa provided not only the names of some of the landmarks of Nerinesir, but also offered little anecdotes that brought the landmarks to life. There was a tall straight-sided tower, a lot like the Washington Monument, but of black stone shot through with white veins; narrow windows spiraled around it from top to bottom, sunlight flashing from them like so many jewels. At the top, barely visible, a slender balcony wrapped around the tower. At the tower's base stood a doorway, but with no door.

"Encormio made that tower to imprison nobles who had displeased him," Taranah explained. "He made the windows that his prisoners might look out upon the homes they had lost; he made the balcony that they might stand in the wandering breeze and know they could not follow it. None who entered that tower ever left it, until Chaisa-e broke its lock and shattered its door."

Jenna shivered. "Aren't there any *happy* stories in this city?"

"Ah, well, Nola Jenna, Encormio ruled for a long time. Many stories of distant ages when he did not rule have been lost to the gray past."

Daniel wondered if the old king had helped them be lost. That seemed like something a tyrant might do: eliminate all signs of former ages and raise up monuments to his own grandeur.

Emelan, riding near Jenna, began to speak, hesitated, changed his mind, and was silent. Intimidated by his company, Daniel assumed. He gave the man a nod. "Yes?"

Emelan hesitated a moment longer, but at Jenna's expectant glance he said at last, "There is the Martyr's Cathedral, which you have seen, Nola; and the Martyr's Wall, which I think you have not examined. And the Badan Kulirang, the House of the Oak. I do not know ... I do not know if the stories they contain are happy, Nola, but they are nothing Encormio made."

"Nor would have made," Taranah agreed, with no sign of offense that Emelan had joined the conversation. "Encormio resented the limitations the Martyr imposed on the world, but even he could not tear down the monuments raised to the Martyr's glory."

"So what did the Martyr do, exactly?" Jenna asked, and gained a raised-eyebrow look from Taranah and a shocked one from Emelan. "Tenai told me a little, but as important as the Martyr is for everyone here, there's got to be plenty she didn't have time for."

"Indeed, we must assuredly take time to show you some of the panels of the Wall," the king's aunt said. "The Triumph and the

Reign and the Martyrdom."

"He sacrificed himself," Emelan explained. His tone was reverent. "In the name of God, he sacrificed himself to set into the world his great spell of redemption, that limited forever the ill that could be done by magic. The willing death of the Martyr, willing for all three days that he hung on the oak, gave him at the moment of his death the power to bind all magic. Thus he reshaped sorcery so that no unwilling or unknowing sacrifice could yield benefit to the sorcerer."

"Oh," Jenna said, in a small voice.

Daniel hoped she was thinking about a world where an unwilling sacrifice could give power to a sorcerer: she was too interested by half in the magic here and he wanted her to understand that it was dangerous stuff. A question struck him, and he nudged his horse to come up with the others. "Was this before Encormio, then?"

Taranah answered, "Oh, no, Nola Danyel. The Martyr died a thousand years before Encormio became king, but Encormio was older than the Martyr. Encormio was already a great sorcerer before the Martyr died on his oak." Her voice lowered, but she went on, "Encormio was a sorcerer of blood and death, until that great death. It is said that Encormio was so angry at the Martyr's sacrifice that he made his bargain with Lord Sorrow, to gain the power of unending years and so replace some of the power the Martyr had taken from him."

"Lord Sorrow?" Jenna asked. "So is that like Lord Death?"

"Very like, Nola," agreed Taranah. "Lord Death rules the Gate between life and death. Lord Silence is lord of all unspeakable truths; he holds memory and the shadow of time. Lord Sorrow is the lord of all that is departed."

Emelan added, "That is the darkest of all the Lords under God; the Lord of all that fades and is forgotten."

Daniel, reminded somehow of a line of poetry he'd once heard somewhere, said, "'The years like great black oxen tread the world, and God the herdsman goads them on behind, and I am broken by their passing feet.'"

Both the king's aunt and Emelan looked at him in surprise. Then Taranah said, "Yes, Nola Danyel, just so," and Emelan bowed his head in agreement.

"Oh, *that's* cheerful," said Jenna. She was trying to keep her tone light, Daniel thought, but she hadn't quite succeeded. "What's that over there, Nolas-ai Taranah?"

"That" was some kind of enormous cupola, maybe a quarter-mile away, just across the black wall that separated the black noble's city from the common city. One evidently reached this cupola by riding across a long slender bridge that arched over a deep steep-sided canal. Both the bridge and the canal were made of black stone, but the road that led to the bridge was made of the plainer gray stone of the outer city. Even from this distance, it was easy to see that both road and bridge carried plenty of traffic: brightly-clad nobles as well as ordinary people streamed in both directions.

"Ah," said Taranah Berangilan-sa, following Jenna's gaze. "That is the Badan Kulirang, the House of the Oak. That is the oldest of any shrine dedicated to the Martyr himself. The oak there is not the very one on which the Martyr made his great sacrifice, but it was grown from an acorn of that tree. Today—" she broke off.

Emelan said, his tone curt, "Today, folk go in gratitude to the feet of the Martyr because Nolas-Kuomon came in peace with Mitereh into Nerinesir. It was a sacrifice of pride from him, and then from her, and all great sacrifice is loved by the Martyr. So it is said."

Daniel looked at the steady procession of people crossing that bridge. How strange it still seemed that Tenai could be the cause of such alarm, that her peace with Mitereh could be the cause of such an outpouring of relief.

"You should also show your regard for the Badan Kulirang," added the king's aunt. "I must return to the court, but I perceive no pressing urgency requiring your presence, Nola Jenna. Your man is certainly able to advise you regarding propriety." She turned to Daniel. "Nola Danyel, you would do very well to cross the bridge and lay your hand on the Martyr's oak. I am entirely certain Mitereh would agree with me."

Her expression had become, not less warm, but faintly calculating. She obviously meant that the king's foreign guests—or Tenai's foreign friends—ought to visit the House of the Oak as a political gesture, though maybe she also thought it was just the right thing to do. He would have preferred, say, a little snack and a soft couch, but it didn't seem politic to say so. He said instead,

"I'm sure we'd be happy to visit the, um, Badan Kulirang."

"Oh, yes!" Jenna was sparkling with enthusiasm, more than ready to play tourist.

"And you must certainly grace my apartment tonight, Nola Jenna. And you, Nola Danyel. Indeed," Taranah said thoughtfully, "I believe I may be able to choose one or another guest who might benefit from becoming acquainted with friends of Chaisa-e. Yes. I do request you attend me this evening, Nola Danyel, Nola Jenna—unless Mitereh requires your presence elsewhere, as he may."

Daniel had no idea how the king or Tenai meant to parcel out his or Jenna's time, or for what effect. That all sorts of people must be calculating the political effect of each step they both took, he was now certain. He closed his eyes briefly, wishing that it was midwinter and all the maneuvering over, and Jenna and himself back home where they belonged. What had kings and high-level politics and deified martyrs to do with either of them?

"I'd love to! We'd love to!" Jenna assured Taranah, glowing with enthusiasm. She, at least, suffered from no such doubts. "Thank you!"

The king's aunt reached across the small distance that separated their horses and patted the girl on the hand. "My dear, you are as a breath of clean air from the high mountains. I shall inform my women; they will admit you whenever you arrive. Do go make yourselves known to the Martyr's oak, and I shall make you welcome within my household this evening." She gathered her entourage around herself with a wave and rode away toward the white city of the court.

"If you would," Emelan muttered, nodding toward a different road.

12

It turned out that even though the bridge had seemed fairly close, to reach it they had to backtrack far around through part of the outer city. This part of the city was the first neighborhood through which they'd passed that gave Daniel the impression of having grown up organically; the haphazard placement of structures required one detour after another. Tall, narrow, gray buildings leaned close together with no room between one and the next. They were not actually *ugly,* Daniel decided. The construction was too solid to be ugly. And the tiles on the roofs were handsome. But everything looked rather as though it had been built by people who hadn't much cared if it were attractive or not. And all this only a stone's throw from the Serpentine Wall that delineated the noble's city; it was a more abrupt transition of style and tone than Daniel was yet used to.

The streets were narrower here, too, and the traffic was of a less formal kind: carts and wagons and people on foot. For the first time there were more women on foot than riding. Children appeared—toddlers and young children with their mothers, older children in small groups. And for the first time some of the people they passed looked like they were poor—though, to Daniel's surprise and relief, he saw no one who looked starving and they passed no obvious beggars. The interest the people here showed in Daniel and Jenna was still polite, but far more overt than it had ever been in the inner districts of Nerinesir. Now and then, someone even pointed.

Wheeled booths appeared along the sides of the street, selling fruit, bread, roasted chickens, fried pastries—enticing smells filled the air. Daniel and Jenna looked at each other, and then at Emelan. The big man's mouth crooked in wry humor, and he reined his horse to the side for a moment and came back with a pair of fat flaky turnovers that proved to contain a spicy filling reminiscent of

Indian samosas. They were delicious.

"Wait, Emel, didn't you get one for yourself?" Jenna asked him, surprised.

Emelan shook his head and said, "I will eat later, Nola."

"But—" she began. Far off in the distance, bells began to ring, long mellow notes that spread out across the city and lingered on the ear, and she paused.

Emelan explained. "That is the Cathedral. The bells are to mark the hour. Ordinarily there would be a service now, but not today. The cardinals held a service this morning before the king came there with Nolas-Kuomon and again after they had departed. At midnight there will be another service, but now it will be quiet. But they still ring the bells."

"There's a service at midnight?" Jenna asked. "Always, or because today's special?"

"Today, it is because of Nolas-Kuonon. Midnight is the time when the dark night breaks and turns toward day. On occasions when special thanks are owed to God, there is always a midnight service."

They had come into an area of narrower streets and fewer carts. There were still people, though. They turned to watch Daniel and Jenna, or leaned out of windows or came out onto balconies, craning for a glimpse. Celebrity status felt very strange.

Somewhere close at hand, people were playing some kind of stringed instruments and something like a flute, the music distinctly audible between the ringing tones of the bells. A woman was singing in a high clear voice.

Jenna smiled, tilting her head to listen. "That's—" she began.

A scattering of quite young children ran out into the street in front of Jenna's horse, waving to make her look at them. They waved at Daniel, too, but he was only foreign and interesting, whereas Jenna was beautiful and radiated friendly good humor. They called out, words Daniel didn't catch.

"Far too bold," Emelan said, and started to ride forward.

"Oh, don't!" said Jenna, waving back at the children, who were delighted and pressed forward. Two of them—girls in brown and tan, with plain nets over their hair—threw handfuls of flower petals over her as she rode past them. The horse laid back its ears at the shower of petals. Jenna laughed and leaned forward to accept a flower from the hand of one of the girls.

Something *whicked* through the air right behind her. At first Daniel thought one of the children had thrown something, or that some kind of large insect had zipped past. He didn't understand right away, even when Emelan leaped out of his saddle and swept Jenna out of hers: he turned in the saddle, staring, and a crossbow bolt went past him with a startling sharp buzz and buried itself in the neck of his horse. The horse reared, screaming, and Daniel immediately fell off. This saved his life, as the next bolt cut through the air right where he would have been, if he'd stayed in the saddle.

Children were scattering all around him. One of the little girls had fallen in the street, horribly close to a plunging horse. Somewhere people were shouting. Daniel scrambled to his feet, caught the girl up and ducked for the protection of a doorway—then wondered if he'd done the child a favor when he'd grabbed her: whoever was shooting hadn't been aiming at *her*.

The door he found was locked. Daniel tucked the girl behind him, against the door, and turned to look for Jenna. His heart all but stopped when he didn't see her—then he did, hidden behind Emelan in a narrow alley between two buildings. Only a bit of her hair and part of her face was visible behind the big man.

But, thankfully, there were no more crossbow bolts. There was a lot more shouting. The door behind Daniel opened abruptly and hands dragged him and the little girl he still held into the building and slammed the door again.

"My daughter—" Daniel gasped, turning to the man who'd pulled him inside, and couldn't get anything else out past the urgent terror that closed his throat. He meant that he wasn't going to be able to stay in safety and leave Jenna out there where he couldn't even *see* her.

There were two men and a woman in the room. The light wasn't good, as all the shutters had been slammed shut, but Daniel could see that the woman had gathered up the child he'd grabbed and was comforting her.

The men, both built big and broad, looked reassuringly able to handle trouble. One had a close-trimmed beard; it was this one who gave Daniel a hard assessing stare, nodded, and ordered, "Stay there. I'll check on the bright lady." He glanced at the other man, who lifted the bar on the door and opened the door just enough for the one with the beard to slip through. There was shouting, indistinguishable and alarming.

But the man was back in moments. "Safe behind her guard," he told Daniel. "The assassin will be long gone," and he gave a grim little nod that said, *He'd better be gone.* "But just you wait a little, Nola, so we may all be certain. Guardsmen will be coming. The king will send men of his own personal guard, I've no doubt of it."

"You're certain Jenna's all right?"

"So her guard promises," the man assured him, and then caught Daniel's arm when he swayed, dizzy with terror and relief and fury.

There was a chair in an inner room—Daniel was illogically reluctant to go even that much farther from his daughter, but the men insisted, and he needed to sit down. The floor would have done, but they insisted on the chair. Men came and went. Someone came in and muttered something to the bearded man, who nodded; someone else, a younger man, came in and bowed low to Daniel, taking his hands and pressing them to his forehead. Daniel blinked, trying to understand; he gathered at last that this was a brother of the little girl he'd picked up in the street.

"She was only in danger because of us," he protested.

The brother bowed again. "But when she fell, Nola, it was you who protected her," he said, and went away again. Daniel gathered there were passages between the buildings and that people were coming and going through them. And if that was so, where was *Jenna?*

On that thought, she arrived. A lean man with a nose like a blade and the white streak of a scar through one eyebrow led her in. She ran across the room. Daniel stood up to catch her, but she hit him with such force that she knocked him back into the chair. She didn't speak. Neither did he. He simply held her, bending his head over hers, feeling his heartbeat slow as he absorbed at last the visceral fact of her safety.

When he looked up, Emelan was watching them. His expression was neutral, yet there was a kind of bleak wistfulness to him. A wistfulness for families lost and not regained, Daniel understood, and looked down at his daughter again. He said, "Thank you."

"It was my duty," Emelan said harshly, and went to consult with the bearded man.

Apana Pelat arrived soon after that, with two of the king's own guards, plus a largish troop of soldiers.

"Nola Danyel, Nola Jenna," Captain Pelat said, bowing to each of them.

"We're all right," Daniel said.

"I want to go home," Jenna said, in a small voice. Daniel knew she meant *home* and hugged her, wanting to take her there immediately, knowing it was impossible.

The captain missed the subtext. "We will escort you back to the palace at once, Nola," he assured her, and offered them both tiny knives made out of some white material, alabaster or porcelain. They were much too small to be weapons.

"Nolas-Kuomon sends these from her own hand," Captain Pelat explained. "The king did not wish her to come for you herself, and so sent me in her place. Yet Nolas-Kuomon sends you her own protection in these charms. She asks you to take these from me as from her hand and bids you keep them close: they will turn the point of a bolt or the edge of a blade."

"Sounds like a plan," said Jenna, recovering herself a little. She took one of the knives and tucked it away in the sort of small soft pouch ladies carried here in interior pockets of their vests.

Daniel took the other. He had the larger sort of pouch men carried, but no money in it; even if he'd had money, he was afraid it might not be suitable to offer it to their benefactors. He turned toward the bearded man, searching for words to express his gratitude.

The man bowed at once. "Nola ... we think you are safe to go out, and wish you good fortune and the protection of God and the Martyr." Then he turned to Captain Pelat, offering him a much more profound bow. "Captain, my name is Menai. I can show you the house from which the bolts came. The assassin shot from the roof of my cousin Laitan's house. I swear before God and the Martyr, neither my cousin nor any of us was complicit in this wickedness. We are offended, we are most seriously offended that an assassin would attempt Godless murder against the king's own guests here from amongst our houses. There are many ways to flee from that roof, that is why the assassin was there, the only reason, Captain. We pursued this assassin at once, but he fled and evaded us."

Captain Pelat returned a grave nod. "I have no doubt of you, Menai. I believe everything you tell me. However, I must ask this cousin to present himself to me."

In the end, Laitan was asked to accompany the troop back to the palace. He turned out to be a big man with broad shoulders and thick, powerful arms and an air of quiet competence. He had showed the king's men his house and his roof. Two of the king's young men, Ranakai and Iodad, set up a spell meant to trace the path of the assassin's flight, but came back shaking their heads; Daniel gathered they had found some kind of counter-spell in their way.

Menai, on his own request, came with his cousin. The cousin was, Daniel understood, actually under a kind of polite not-quite-arrest. He didn't believe for a moment that the cousin, or any of the people of that neighborhood, could have been involved. But when he said so, Captain Pelat merely answered, "The king will wish to make that determination himself, Nola Danyel," as though the statement had the force of natural law.

The king was waiting for them in a room Daniel hadn't seen before. It was a large, square room at the western edge of the palace. A mosaic of gray and white marble and turquoise swirled like water around the walls. A wide low-silled window was set into the center of three of the four walls, looking out onto the palace gardens or out over the white and pink walls and crystal rooftops of the lower wings of the palace. A single table occupied about half the floor space. A map, probably hand-drawn, was pinned out on this table, held flat by six-inch-high marble pyramids. More maps—Daniel presumed the scrolls were maps—occupied racks in each corner of the room.

There was one chair in the room, drawn up close to the table. Mitereh was sitting in it, but he wasn't looking at the map. He was watching Tenai. She had been pacing, but spun round to face them when they came in. The king didn't move, except to turn his head to watch them enter. His arms rested along the arms of the chair; he was, in fact, almost ostentatiously relaxed. Daniel got the impression he'd been using his own stillness as a foil against Tenai's violence. Because Tenai was absolutely furious.

Mikanan Chauke-sa and Keitah Terusai-e were also present, along with several young men of the king's guard. They all looked much relieved to see Apana Pelat and his party arrive. Everyone looked stiff and worried. Given Tenai's demeanor, Daniel couldn't blame them.

"Daniel!" Tenai exclaimed, and came forward to take his

hands in a strong grip. She looked into his face and then turned to draw Jenna into an embrace. "My bright child. Are you well? You are not harmed?"

"We're fine," Jenna assured her, making a brave attempt to look as fine as possible.

"When I heard—" said Tenai, and drew a hard breath. "I would have come after you myself. I wished to." She shot a savage look at Mitereh.

Daniel, not wondering at all that the king hadn't wanted Tenai out on the streets of his city with that kind of rage radiating off her, said, "Emelan protected Jenna. I think he saved her life. Neither of us understood fast enough what was happening."

"Next time you say I need a guard, believe me, I won't argue," Jenna said fervently.

Tenai blinked, and blinked again. The dangerous blankness eased from her face. Redirected from her fury, she turned at last to Emelan.

Emelan flushed and bowed his head. He did not look at Keitah, who spared his brother only a brief glance.

"Tell me everything," Tenai said to Emelan.

"I should suggest we rather hear the account of these men, as it is they whose neighborhood was the site of ambush." Keitah nodded toward the two men. "We do not know what they may have seen or heard that may be of urgent use."

Tenai turned toward Keitah, a sharp movement that suggested barely-contained rage.

The king lifted a quieting hand, palm out, toward each of them. "Peace, peace. We shall hear all accounts. Each seems urgent to me. My captain, you have an investigation begun, may I assume so?"

"Well begun, my king."

Mitereh nodded. "Then we will first hear Chaisa's man."

Hearing everything described from Emelan's point of view gave Daniel an odd feeling of both immediacy and distance, as though he had shared the other man's desperate lunge to get Jenna out of the line of fire and back against the protection of stone, as though he had covered her there with his own body, and from that position watched himself snatch the fallen child up from the road and disappear into the blackness of an unknown house.

Mitereh, now freed from the necessity to counter Tenai's

violent rage with his own calm, had shifted to prop an elbow on the arm of his chair. One of his feet swung, tapping one heel against the leg of his chair. It was a restrained sort of movement, but the anger in that motion, Daniel thought, might almost match Tenai's. The king rested his chin on his fist. He asked no questions. He merely said, at the end of Emelan's story, "And if you would be patient, Nola Danyel, may I ask that you also tell this tale?"

That was worse than listening to Emelan tell it from his side. Daniel made sure to give due credit to Menai in his account, but what he recalled most clearly was being jerked out of sight of Jenna, of the terror that had consumed him until she'd been reunited with him. He was sweating by the time he got to Captain Pelat's arrival. He folded his arms to conceal his shaking hands. No one asked questions: that did not seem done. Maybe all the questions were reserved to the end; maybe everyone was waiting to see how all the accounts matched up. It made sense to get as clear as possible a picture, he supposed, before deciding what you knew and what you needed to know.

"And now, you, if you will," Mitereh said quietly to Menai, when Daniel was through.

The bearded man took a small step forward and told the story for the third time, putting in a lot Daniel hadn't known about or understood at the time. Menai described the hidden movements of the people of the neighborhood—through the alleys, through one another's houses, over the steep tiled roofs—as they had tried to figure out where the assassin was and get Daniel and Jenna under cover. This had apparently been more complicated than it should have been, because some of the connecting doors between the houses had been locked because so many people had been gone—to the Badan Kulirang, to the Martyr's Cathedral, and, it turned out, to a neighborhood party in honor of the reconciliation between Tenai and the king.

"My brother and uncles, and my cousin here, they tried to apprehend the man, once we knew where he must have been standing to shoot," Menai concluded. "He fled, but we were afraid there might be another. I went through the houses to open the door for Nola Danyel, and my friend Bataran went to bring Nola Jenna to safety, but there was no door right in that alley, so it was hard to come to them."

"They stood around us," Jenna put in. "That's how they did it, finally. I mean, that's how they kept us safe— Laitan and a lot of other men surrounded us and made themselves into a shield so we could get to a door." She gave Laitan an admiring look. "It was really brave. Please tell everyone who helped me how grateful I am."

The big man ducked his head. "We did very little, Nola. We thought the assassin was gone. Bataran thought it would be safe, and it was safe. So it was not so much."

"Well, hey—it was to us, you know." Jenna impulsively crossed the room and took the man's hands in hers, smiling into his face. "Thank you so much."

Tenai lifted one hand a few inches, drawing all eyes. She said to Menai and Laitan, "Nola Jenna quite properly acknowledges the debt. I also acknowledge a debt upon which your neighborhood may draw."

The men, looking even more embarrassed, ducked their heads. "The assassin used our houses, our neighborhood," murmured Menai. "We are grateful, exceedingly grateful for your gracious forbearance, Nolas-e, but we understand only your kindness forgives our foolishness in allowing this man a place to stand for his Godless attack."

"I see no error in anything *you* did," Tenai said, in a flat tone that produced a moment of silence.

After a moment, Laitan took up the story. "We tried, Nolas-e; indeed, we did try, but we could not come up on the assassin. He was too quick. He went south over the rooftops, which we didn't think of at once because there's no good way down from the roofs that way. Only he had a rope in place there. So he eluded us, to our shame."

"It was your house from which the assassin made his attack, do I understand so?" Tenai asked Laitan. "How did he come to his place on your roof?"

The man, much less nervous now, answered quietly. "Yes, Nolas-e, to my shame. I believe he climbed up where broken stone provides handholds—that is the way errant children climb to the rooftops—and came to my house in that way. My roof offers the best view of the street."

Mikanan Chauke-sa lifted a hand an inch or so, halting this recital. "For a man who knew the direction of his quarry, mark you," he said to the king.

"I do mark it," Mitereh acknowledged. He rubbed his chin, looking troubled.

The king wasn't alone in finding that particular fact troublesome. Daniel took a breath, trying to decide how to put the obvious conclusion they should all have drawn. No matter how obvious it seemed, it was not the sort of thing anybody was going to want to hear.

To Daniel's relief, however, before he could figure out what to say, Keitah Terusai-e took a step forward and put the same thought into words: "And yet the decision to go to the Badan Kulirang was made of a moment, do I understand so? So a man who knew of that decision ran ahead and found the place."

Mitereh brought both his hands down hard on the arms of his chair. He moved as though he would stand up. "It was never a man belonging to Berangilan-sa! Never say so!"

Keitah held up both his hands in immediate placation. "Not as Taranah Berangilan-sa would know, indeed, I would never believe so, Mitereh, I earnestly assure you! But I think this was not Imbaneh-se at all. This fills my mouth with the bitter taste of treachery closer to home. It was clearly an attempt by some lord of your court, one placed to listen closely to Nolas-ai Taranah. One of her entourage may indeed have been suborned; we do not know otherwise. They must all be examined."

"This is correct," Captain Pelat agreed, frowning. "Though I confess even now I should more readily believe this was the act of an Imbaneh-se agent, one hidden in your court."

Tenai had folded her arms and now stood with one hip leaned against the edge of the table. It should have been a relaxed pose, but it was not. She said, "I agree with your captain, Mitereh: I believe it would be unwise to discount an Imbaneh-se connection; indeed, I find such a connection almost certain. But Terusai is also correct: a man of your court has clearly been suborned. At least one."

The king eased back into his chair and inclined his head in wordless assent to all of them. He waved a hand toward Captain Pelat, who said, "We were not able to trace this agent, whatever his fealty." He glanced at Iodad, who gave a brief account of their failed efforts to do this by magical means, which Daniel couldn't follow but everyone else accepted with grim little nods.

At the end of this, there was a silence. Then Mitereh rose

from his chair. He said, "I am satisfied, Chaisa. And you?"

Tenai uncrossed her arms and straightened. She looked stern, but no longer furious. "I am *far* from satisfied, Mitereh. But I agree you may dismiss these men."

The king nodded. "With my thanks for your efforts on behalf of my guests. Inkaimon, if you would see to that."

Inkaimon inclined his head and beckoned to Menai and Laitan, who bowed low to the king and followed him out.

"This attempt was, if I do not mistake it, meant to set Chaisa once more at odds with you, my king," Mikanan Chauke-sa said, after the two men were gone. "This is a continuation of your enemy's initial plan: he attempts to retrieve what has gone astray."

"Clearly so." Tenai made a curt little gesture. "The error was mine: I should have foreseen this tactic. I beg your forgiveness, Daniel, and yours, Jenna, that I so carelessly sent you into peril."

"Oh, no!" Jenna exclaimed, a hair before Daniel could object. "Nobody could have expected anybody would aim at *us!* That's just too weird."

And too dangerous, Daniel thought but did not say. He didn't *think* Tenai would have snapped and gone after Mitereh if he and Jenna had been murdered. She would have gone after the assassin.

On the other hand, he doubted Mitereh would have been able to stop her, or even direct her. And if the king lost control of Tenai, would he think of that as the same as her actually turning on him? Whether he took it that way or not, what would he do, and how would Tenai respond? Daniel had a sinking feeling that the spiraling violence that might have resulted from that kind of scenario might in fact have been exactly what the king's enemy had hoped for. If that were so, that hadn't been as clumsy an assassination attempt as it initially appeared. The whole operation might even have been precisely calculated.

"On the contrary, I should indeed have anticipated exactly this," Tenai was saying, and Daniel wondered whether her thoughts had traced out the same pathway as his. "From the beginning, I have been meant to serve as a tool. This hidden enemy is determined I should be a weapon in his hand. I am offended, I am *profoundly* offended to be so used."

"You must not allow it, then," Daniel said to her. "Even if we had been—been killed, I hope you would not have allowed it to shake your judgment."

Tenai glanced at Mitereh, who lifted his chin and returned her gaze. Daniel saw that the king had wanted to say just that to her, but of course he, of all men, hadn't been able to. He couldn't even openly agree with Daniel. He didn't say a word. But he was too proud to flinch or look away from Tenai's hostile glance.

There was a brittle tension in the room which Daniel thought hadn't been there previously: anger, yes. But this was something else. Tenai said, cold as ice, to the king, "I will not. You may be sure."

"I am confident of it," answered the king, with a courtier's smooth manner.

Tenai made a sharp gesture, nothing Daniel could interpret, except it did not express acquiescence. She turned to Daniel. "I shall bring you back into *my* household."

Daniel started to say *Whatever you think best*, but stopped before the first word was out: Mitereh had gone, not stiff, but very still. It was a fraught kind of stillness. Daniel said instead, "I don't know, Tenai. Is that the best thing to do?"

There was a pause. Keitah Terusai-e turned his face away, a graceful refusal to be drawn into the quarrel, so that told Daniel he'd been right to think something was wrong about Tenai's offer. Mikanan Chauke-sa glanced worriedly from Tenai to Mitereh. Emelan folded his arms and looked down. Apana Pelat dropped a hand to the hilt of his sword in what seemed an involuntary gesture and then set his jaw and took it away again. The king's young men watched Tenai, their faces blank, but the muscles of their arms and backs rigid.

Jenna, feeling the undercurrents that had sprung up but not understanding them any more than Daniel did himself, pursed her lips in a silent whistle and raised her eyebrows at her father.

Mitereh met Tenai's eyes and said not a word.

"You have offended me intolerably," Tenai said at last, speaking now straight to Mitereh, no longer using Daniel to aim indirect blows against the king.

The king didn't waver. "Yet as I have had no choice, I will ask you to tolerate it." His manner was not arrogant, but it was not hesitant either. 'Authoritative' wasn't really it, either. 'Resolute' might have been closer.

There was another pause. Tenai's jaw tightened, and relaxed. She said to Daniel, "If you are willing to remain in Mitereh's household and under his protection ... this would perhaps be better, Daniel. But only if you are willing. I do assure you, under my hand you will be *safe*."

The tension in the room did not break, but it eased. Daniel said after a moment, "Jenna and I will both do whatever you and Mitereh think is best, Tenai. I'm sure either you or the king can offer a guarantee of safety. After all, the, uh, problem this afternoon wouldn't have come up, would it, except none of us expected it."

"You are generous, Nola Danyel," Mitereh said in that smooth courtier's tone, and rose, holding Tenai's cold stare without apparent effort. "I will ask that all arrangements remain as they have been, and that all declare themselves satisfied with this."

And so Daniel found himself still within the king's household, while Jenna remained a guest of Tenai's household. Daniel would much rather have had them stay together ... he thought he might never willingly let his daughter out of his sight again ... but clearly some kind of political necessity dictated otherwise. He didn't understand it. But he didn't have to understand it to see that the fragile peace between Tenai and Mitereh had come very near fracturing, and that this arrangement was somehow necessary to brace the weak point in that peace.

"Chaisa—Nolas-Kuomon—is not accustomed to yielding her will to another when she would not," Mitereh commented. "I am grateful for your support, Nola Danyel." He had dismissed most of his attendants and guards and now gestured in invitation toward a small grouping of chairs near a window.

Daniel couldn't say to the king that he only hoped he'd been right to support him over Tenai. He said instead, "She was understandably upset. But I gather she didn't actually lose her temper."

"She held to her oath to me. For which we may all well be grateful to God and the Martyr." Mitereh glanced at an attendant, who crossed the room and poured spiced wine out of an earthenware pitcher into a pair of glazed cups. The attendant began to offer a cup to Daniel, but the king intercepted him and took both cups, then turned and gave one to Daniel himself. Undoubtedly an act symbolic of royal favor, Daniel concluded, and took the cup with a nod of thanks.

"So we may all see that she will hold to it. Thus my enemy is again confounded. And once more, that you asked her to do so. You were gracious in that," added the king. "I did not mistake it. Your continual care for a country not your own does you credit, Nola Danyel. You bring honor to my household. You are safe here, I do assure you."

Daniel murmured that he was sure of it. On impulse, he added, "I understand—I think I understand that you left Jenna with Tenai to show you trust her; did you want to keep me with you to show everyone else she trusts you? Or did you want—" he hesitated, not certain now to phrase this question.

Mitereh moved a hand in a weary little gesture. "Indeed, we must be perceived as close allies. I believe this day will serve to strengthen this impression. Although, I confess, I would not have chosen these precise events to serve this purpose."

"How close did she come, to ..." he did not want to say, *turning against you.* He was fairly certain that was exactly what had come near happening.

"Slipping my hold? Close enough, Nola Danyel. To the very edge of disaster. Yet not past that edge, so we may bring yet another day forward out of the dead past and cast it into the unrolling future." The king lifted his cup in a small salute. "For which I am assuredly grateful." He rose, and inclined his head to Daniel. "May the good God send you peaceful rest, Nola Danyel; and a gentle dawn before a peaceful day."

That was a prayer Daniel could really get behind.

13

Much later that night, he woke with that sharp jerk that meant *something* had awakened him—that jerk that brings parents awake when the baby fusses at night; that startled abrupt awakening that means some noise in the house does not belong.

For a moment Daniel had no idea where he was: the low bed made no sense to him. The sheer curtains at the window moved in a slight breeze, startling him as though they had been ghosts. Even the smells were wrong: incense and pine, smoke and horses, like a strange cross between a church and a campsite.

He sat up, and as he did memory returned in a rush: this was Talasayan, the city of Nerinesir, the palace, the king's own apartment. He felt now that it was quite late. What had woken him? As soon answered as asked: Jenna was with Tenai and he was here. That had been the cause of his unease: Jenna's absence and the lingering worry that resulted. But she was safe with Tenai. Daniel let his breath out and, after a moment, lay back down. All was well. He could relax.

But in fact he couldn't. A tension somehow filled the air, though he had no idea why. Just the unfamiliarity of this room? Just Jenna's absence? Or something more?

Somewhere not far away he thought he heard the soft whisper of cloth against cloth. No doubt it was someone who had legitimate business to be up—somebody with an urgent need for what they called here, elliptically, the accommodation. Or some guard about normal rounds. Maybe it was even time to get up, and the servants were stirring. But somehow none of those explanations *felt* right.

There was dim light in the apartment: one small lantern left burning out in the dining hall. It was just enough to let dark-adjusted eyes see. Daniel rose from the bed and eased across the room to his door, which had been left ajar, to look out into the main sleeping chamber where Mitereh had his own curtained bed.

And what he saw in that room, near the main door that led out into the hall, was Tenai. Daniel frowned, trying to imagine a reason for Tenai to be here, like this, in the dark. But he was not mistaken: he recognized her tall elegant body in the dark before the dim light slid across the elegant bones of her face. Besides, he recognized the way she moved.

Pitagainin and Ranakai, the two young men who had been standing at the door of the king's bedroom, were slumped over, unconscious. But strange though this was, Daniel found he could not truly be alarmed by Tenai; whatever she was about, he trusted her. Blindly? No, he decided: he might be worried about her, but he just couldn't believe she would actually, irrevocably, slide over the edge into murder and mayhem. He just didn't believe it. He made no sound.

Tenai crossed the room to where the king lay sleeping and brushed aside the curtain that screened the young man from the rest of the room. Daniel let his breath out and shifted his door open a hair more so he could see better.

With the bed-curtain pulled back that way, it was possible to see what took place: Tenai sank to one knee, drew a knife, and laid the edge of the knife across the king's throat.

Mitereh woke instantly. Daniel saw the shine of his eyes in the dimness. Aside from opening his eyes, the king neither moved nor made a sound. Daniel didn't blame him.

Tenai spoke in a low voice: "In a moment, I will set aside the knife. I have laid sleep across this apartment; I admit that. But I have done and will do no harm to you or your people. I ask you to be quiet, Mitereh. Be quiet for just a little. Hear me. I went this night to the house of Laitan and looked there for what I might find." This news might have offended the king, by the impatient little snap that entered Tenai's tone. "I went there, I say! I have only just returned. I came thus to you, Mitereh, because of what I found there. Will you hear me?"

She must have received some signal, for after a second she lifted the knife, turned it hilt-first in her hand, and laid it on the mattress.

The king closed his eyes, took a breath—Daniel could see the deep rise and fall of his chest—and opened them again. He sat up, a swift movement, ignoring the knife. But his body was rigid with anger, and his voice, although no louder than Tenai's, held considerable intensity. "Another time, Chaisa, wake me *without* the knife."

"I feared you might rouse your household."

"I know what you feared! Another time, leave aside the knife."

Tenai, still kneeling by his mattress, turned her hands palm up. "Another time, then, I will leave the knife undrawn. Forgive my impudent caution."

The king let out a breath, raked dark hair back from his face, and put anger aside by an obvious effort of will. "Well ... well, Chaisa, I will hear you. What did you find at that house?"

"Sorcerous traces, left by a hand half-familiar." Tenai paused, regarding the king with narrow intensity. "Mitereh ... you have sorcerers among your house guard?"

The king, face cold, made a short little gesture of repudiation. "This was no man of mine, Chaisa. Never say so." His voice rose. "It was my house guard that tried to trace the assassin; of course you would find their signs!"

"That was not what I perceived. You think I would not be able to distinguish the signs of the assassin from those of his pursuers? Do you believe me so lacking in skill? I tell you, Mitereh, it was a man of yours who meant to deal out treachery and death. I have become familiar with your house guard, do you think not? I could hardly mistake the trace of royal fealty betrayed."

"And yet, my own sorcerers mistook it?"

Tenai lifted her chin, as coldly arrogant as Daniel had ever seen her. "If your young men are blind to what they would not see, well, I am not; do you think I am so inexperienced I may be misled by either familiarity or slanted expectation?"

Mitereh began to speak, but let his breath out without saying anything. The familiar mask of strict impassivity closed over his face. He lifted an inquiring eyebrow. "So, then, the man you accuse?"

"I cannot be so exact."

"Oh, to be sure! You cannot be exact!"

Tenai sat back on her heels and waited.

Mitereh took a breath. Another. He said more moderately, "Very well, Chaisa; and so perhaps I shall take your word: what then would you have of me? I have several sorcerers among my guard. Shall I set them all aside and leave myself with none? Shall I put you in that place and draw your skill about me as my shield, do you so advise me?"

Tenai might have smiled; in the dark it was hard to tell, but there was something about her voice that made Daniel think so. She said, "It seems perhaps more prudent to let this assassin show his hand. That would be a thing we would both be interested to see, provided we might be assured his blow fails."

Mitereh's eyebrows rose. "Indeed; and am I to perceive you would expect such a blow to come down this very night?"

"I do not know your enemy. Our enemy. But I believe I begin to perceive the shape he draws in the world. Indeed, all my long years inform me of a blow waiting to fall tonight—perhaps against you, and the blame to come to me; or perhaps against Daniel, to set us two at odds. I think that might well suit the evident preference of this enemy for indirect action. Not against Jenna; no one would raise a hand against anyone in my close keeping. But here, in this household, the protections are all woven by mortal hands. You are vulnerable. Those in your keeping are vulnerable. Will you say I am mistaken?"

There was a little pause. The king did not answer.

"I confess I should prefer to set my own hand between my friend and the knife of our enemy, Mitereh," Tenai said. "I have slipped your defenses because they are Encormio's defenses, and familiar to me; an assassin tonight may slip them because your trust is a weapon in his hand. But whoever this man should be, I think he will not expect to find me in his path."

"And so I shall permit you to draw shadows about yourself and wait in the dark. Here in my very apartment." Mitereh paused, and then went on steadily, "Is this wise? You may advise me, Chaisa. This past day you drew the traces taut. And this evening you went into the city, disobeying my command—well, Chaisa, my clear expectation, then; let us not equivocate! And this very night you come here to me, slipping all the defenses of my house, and tell me to set you before the men of my house guard, men I have known for years! Shall I hear you?"

Tenai said nothing, but glanced at the knife she had laid down next to the young king.

Mitereh's mouth tightened. He demanded, "Whose are you, Chaisa?"

"Do you ask me?" Tenai inclined her head. "Yours, or I assure you I should not be constrained, Mitereh. You do constrain me. Do you imagine not?"

The king reclined on his bed again, supporting himself on one elbow. "You disobeyed me tonight, and now you say you are constrained?"

"Command me to leave this apartment and I will do so, Mitereh. I will take Daniel with me rather than leave my friend at hazard. Your enemy is not a patient man. That is what I see in all these events."

"Constrained, is it, Chaisa?"

"Or I would command *you,* Mitereh Sekuse-go-e. I ask. I ask most firmly. But this is still a request. Permit me to set this snare where the attack is most likely to come."

The king studied her. Finally he said, "Very well. I take your word. And your advice, Nolas-Kuomon, I will take also. Remain, then. And we shall discuss your manners and your actions at dawn, if the night passes to daylight without event."

Tenai inclined her head, looking faintly amused at this prospect. She drifted away, tucking herself in among the folds of hanging curtains. Once there, she grew still enough to become all but invisible.

The king lay back down. The knife Tenai had left lying by him disappeared under his blanket. Quiet enveloped the apartment. The king closed his eyes. That was trust, to lie there like a goat staked out for the lions and wait for a possible assassin, after your putative protector woke you up with a knife at your throat.

Daniel stood very still. Eventually, stiff and tired, he sat down on the floor of his room and leaned against the doorframe. Nothing happened, for a long time. This created the oddest effect: he half-expected a violent, dangerous event to take place and yet suddenly found sleep a hundred times more alluring. This must be, Daniel thought muzzily, what carries children off to sleep on Christmas Eve. Something like this. But without the fear. Probably Tenai was wrong, so he sat up for nothing. He'd feel a fool in the morning if he was wandering around comatose for lack of sleep and nothing had even happened.

The faintest rustle of movement brought him awake again, his heart racing. He blinked into the shadows, trying to see. He found he was sure this newcomer *was* an assassin: this cautious and secretive intrusion brought an aura of danger with it that, Daniel now realized, Tenai's own arrival somehow had not. It might have been merely his long and trusting relationship with Tenai, but he thought it was rather some subtly menacing quality of the intruder.

Daniel did not immediately recognize who this was. Then the man eased forward, past the sleeping guards at the door, past the one lit lantern that first cast its delicate light on his set face and then stole all detail as it silhouetted him. It was one of the king's young men, Iodad. The knife he held was black, except for a silver edge along the blade.

Iodad glanced across the room toward the king's bed ... then turned smoothly and came toward Daniel's door instead. Daniel flinched backwards, reflexively slamming his door closed and bracing it with his weight. No assault came; instead, there was the scraping ring of metal against metal. Of course. Daniel opened his door again, just a crack.

Tenai, still half-hidden in the shadows, had her sword naked in her hand. Iodad's knife had been flung across the room, so that he stood empty-handed. The king himself was up, guarding himself with the dagger Tenai had given him. Mitereh wore nothing but a twist of white cloth around his hips. Even so, he did not look like anyone's easy target. But his face was tight with the pain of betrayal.

Iodad did not glance aside at the king. He drew a second knife, but he did not lunge forward—or back. He slashed his own palm. In the dim light, the blood looked black.

Tenai did something fast and violent, and Iodad made a muffled sound and went down hard. He rolled and tried to get to his feet, and Tenai kicked his feet out from under him and brought the point of her sword down to brush his throat.

Iodad lurched forward, trying to drive his own throat against Tenai's sword—Daniel only understood this after the fact. But Tenai flicked her blade out of the way and hit the man in the face with the hilt. Then she hit him again, quite hard. He collapsed.

Tenai bent over him for a moment, and then straightened. She was not breathing fast, Daniel noted. He was panting enough himself for them both. Tenai glanced his way and said, "You are well?"

Words were beyond Daniel. He managed a nod.

The king walked forward. He had tossed his knife down on a table and stood unarmed and nearly naked. He did not look harmless. Or undignified. He looked ... grieved. He stood for a moment, gazing down at the fallen man, his expression unguarded.

Tenai said with a kind of distant sympathy, "Those close to us are best able to strike us down, Mitereh, for how shall we choose to guard against them?"

The king lifted his chin, flat neutrality settling over his face. He said to Tenai, ignoring the issue of the assassin's identity, "Why are the rest of my people not roused *now*?"

Tenai opened a hand. "*I* cast no such spell."

"Iodad, of course, possessed the capacity to do so," Mitereh acknowledged. "I would not have thought he ... how could he do what he has done?"

Daniel thought the king had begun that sentence meaning simply *I wouldn't have thought he could do this spell*. But by the time he finished the thought, Mitereh was thinking of the betrayal: the end of the sentence was an open cry of pain.

Tenai appeared unmoved. "This man is not your true enemy, Mitereh. He has been set to this use by another. He must be questioned. Will you allow me to do it?"

The king shut his eyes for a moment. Then he drew a hard breath, gathered himself to face this necessity, opened his eyes, and said grimly, "Yes."

Tenai gave a little nod. "If you wake your men, Mitereh, that would be safer than for them to wake by my hand. You, they will trust."

"Except for any other of them that betrayed me tonight," answered the king bitterly, and walked over to touch the men by the door.

Tenai came over to Daniel's room. "Did you never sleep, my friend?"

"I woke up when you came in, I think. After that I didn't want to go back to sleep. Why on Earth would Iodad come after me?"

Daniel found he was shivering. And not wearing nearly enough. He backed hastily into his room and reached for his clothing. "Poor Mitereh."

"Yes. This may be the first real betrayal that has befallen the boy." Tenai's tone was a little abstracted. Usually Daniel could not think of her as four hundred years old, but tonight those years showed. The young king's pain did not move her.

She went on. "Iodad is, one gathers, an accomplished sorcerer. Yet when he drew blood to strike at you, Daniel, his malice passed over you without doing any harm. Nor did my little spell of sleep touch you, nor the larger one he made. That is a thing worth remembering. Though the ash on the tongue gave you words to speak, enchantment imposed on you unwilling did not touch you."

"What?" Then Daniel nodded understanding. "He tried to do, um, magic? On me? You mean magic doesn't work on me?"

"Unless you accept it freely, Daniel, yes. This seems likely, for you and for Jenna as well, or so I should expect. Your world is one where sorcery is unknown, or so rare as to be unknown. I suspect now that this may be why that is so. I gave you language, so a spell you accept willingly touches you. But other sorcery, I think slips aside.

Daniel nodded again. That sounded like a good thing, probably, but, distracted by more immediate concerns, he couldn't summon much interest. "You're sure Jenna's safe?"

"I promise you. I laid protections over my apartment; and I warned Emelan to guard her sleep ... but more than any of that, Daniel, she is my guest and within my protection. A mortal king is not proof against malice. But no one will lightly offend *my* lord."

"All right." That actually *was* reassuring. In a way. "Um ... you're going to question that man? What does that ... entail?"

The king had woken his guards and sent one of them out to rouse anyone he thought needed to be informed of what had occurred. Now he accepted a robe from an attendant who had hurried in and came back to join them before Tenai could answer. He nodded to Daniel and said to Tenai, "All my people fear that you might set yourself against me ... and among them all, you are the *only one* who could not have been behind this attack tonight. Even if you had wanted to design such a thing, you have hardly had time to suborn any man of mine since your return."

Tenai inclined her head.

A handful of the king's young men had come in by this time: Badayan, Torohoh, Ranakai and Inkaimon. They all looked ashamed and uncertain. They took places around the king; he welcomed them with a glance. Inkaimon started to speak. Mitereh moved a hand to stop him. "There is no fault for you in this, Inkaimon. None of us could reasonably have expected this. Nor is it your duty to deal with either treachery from within or hostile sorcery." The young man hardly looked comforted, but he took a place at the king's back without further protest.

Sandakan Gutai-e arrived in a rush, his saturnine face set in an uncompromising expression that was no doubt meant to hide terror. He caught the king by the arm, giving him a little shake—needing that contact, Daniel judged, to be sure the young man was indeed alive and well—then gave him a quick head-to-foot inspection. Though they were nearly of a height, the king looked younger than ever beside his general. The difference in their ages might almost have made them seem father and son, except that even now, in the midst of alarm and turmoil, Mitereh looked like a king. Daniel wondered how he did it, and if it was a conscious effect or a quality that Mitereh had simply absorbed with time.

"I am perfectly well," Mitereh assured his general.

Sandakan seemed at this to realize he was gripping his king's arm. He let go at once and took a step back with an embarrassed air. But as he stepped back, the king touched his shoulder with his fingertips and gave him a little reassuring nod. Some of the terror went out of Sandakan's eyes, and his expression eased.

From her place near him, Tenai said, "Gutai, I hold my hand between the king and every enemy."

Sandakan turned to her at once. A faint confusion had come into his dark face. Daniel thought maybe he had been set off-balance because he had been so slow to recognize and respond to her presence; that Sandakan expected to orient toward Tenai regardless of whom else might be nearby. He might be wondering now whether it was the shock of the threat to the king or the passage of time which had weakened that tropism.

Or maybe he was just surprised to find her in the king's apartment.

"Chaisa's perspicuity confounds my enemies," Mitereh said, sounding a little bitter about it. "Whomever they may be."

Sandakan gave a small nod, to Tenai as much as to the king. Tenai returned it with a regal inclination of her head. Where in the privacy of her apartment the tension between the two of them had been striking, in this fraught moment that tension had become muted. Sandakan respected her promise, clearly; and clearly that promise made him feel better regarding the threat to the king. He started to speak, but then Mikanan Chauke-sa, tousled and bleary-eyed, entered. He came in with less drama than Sandakan, shook his head over the unconscious assassin, conversed low-voiced with the king, and went out again.

The king's young men, still very obviously tense and uncomfortable, stood guard: Torohoh at the door and Badayan over the bound prisoner, who lay unconscious on the floor. Ranakai was at the door. Inkaimon held a post behind the king. Attendants moved around the room, offering hot spiced wine to everyone. The king waved it away impatiently. Tenai took a cup and tossed its contents down her throat like she wasn't quite aware it was there. Daniel sipped his. He was shivering a little, which wasn't due to cold: adrenalin, excitement, fear ... all of those. He felt he was dreaming; he half-expected to wake up and find out the whole evening ... the whole past weeks, even ... had been a dream.

Keitah Terusai-e came in, looking grim, a moment after Mikanan Chauke-sa had left. He spared the assassin barely a glance before moving to join the king. Like Sandakan, he looked the king over quickly, though, unlike the general, he didn't touch him. "You are well, Mitereh?"

The king gave a short nod. "I was a fool. Fortunately Chaisa redeemed my foolishness."

Keitah gave Tenai a hard stare. "For which we must be grateful," he said at last, in a brusque tone.

Mitereh made an impatient little gesture. "Peace, Keitah. Chaisa is not at fault because she perceived a risk neither you nor I had considered."

Keitah let out a hard breath. "True, my king." He nodded to Tenai.

Tenai returned his nod, but not as though she cared for his opinion. She stood with one booted foot propped on the seat of a chair, her hands resting on her raised knee, watching everything with unmoved calm.

Taranah Berangilan-sa entered quietly, with a muted rustle of skirts. She had taken time to dress, but her hair fell loose down her back rather than being gathered up beneath a jeweled net. She had beautiful hair, longer than Daniel had guessed, nearly black, discreetly streaked with silver strands here and there. She took in the growing crowd with one comprehensive glance: her nephew and Tenai, Sandakan and Keitah, poor Iodad, bound now, but still limp on the floor, with others of the king's young men standing watchful guard over him. A small line appeared between her eyes. "My dear," she said to Mitereh. "I am so sorry. How difficult a situation this is. Though the return of Chaisa-e certainly prompted an enemy to move, we must be grateful that her presence also thwarted this enemy's will."

She was certainly fast on the uptake. Daniel had stayed where he was, near the doorway to his own room, out of the way, but he was glad she'd come. Even from his position on the periphery, he could see how Mitereh had finally relaxed a little, just for her presence.

The king held out his hands to her, and his aunt crossed the room at once to take them. She touched her nephew's cheek first, a light, affectionate touch. Her manner was sober, but warm. That gesture said more clearly than words, *Don't worry, I'm here, I'll help.* Mitereh relaxed a little more. He said, "Indeed, this is so. But the blow was not aimed for my throat. Or not directly."

Taranah's eyebrows rose. But almost at once she said, "Ah, I see," and turned to nod politely to Tenai, who returned the nod with, as far as Daniel could tell, cool indifference. Then the king's aunt regarded Daniel. Her pale gray eyes met his, and she said, almost as warmly as she had spoken to her nephew, "Nola Danyel, we must all be grateful indeed that this blow went awry."

Daniel cleared his throat, uncomfortable to be the sudden focus of attention. "Thank you," he said. "I'm certainly grateful for that."

Taranah smiled at him. Then she said to the king, "My dear, perhaps you might permit me to examine poor Iodad. His breathing does not sound quite as it should to me."

"Yes," the king began, but just then the outer door opened

once more and Apana Pelat came in. Despite his dark coloring, the captain was practically gray with distress. He went to one knee before Mitereh, offering the king his sheathed sword across both hands, as Tenai had done in making her formal gesture of submission when she chose to acknowledge the king's authority. Daniel surmised, wincing, that it had been *his* job to deal with treachery from within and hostile sorcery. The depth of the captain's distress now was painful to witness.

The king looked soberly down at Captain Pelat, not reaching to touch the offered sword. "Well?"

The captain laid his sword on the floor at the king's feet and nodded toward the assassin. "My king ... Iodad Sonnas-na seemed to me a loyal man and a useful member of your personal guard. So far as I am aware, he has no connections in the south. I am astonished by this event. I would not have said that my eyes were blind, but in this they have been. I also would not have said any man could cross so many lines of protection drawn by my hand and my order so as to strike at you, but Iodad himself laid down many of those lines and knew well what they comprised. My error permitted an assassin to draw his knife against you in your own chambers."

He paused, and then went on, bowing his head, "I have not betrayed you, my king. But even if you believe me innocent of this treachery, I am aware you will have to dismiss me. I ask to be spared the disgrace of dismissal without honor. I would prefer to go to Lord Death rather than return to my father's house bearing the mark of shame."

Sandakan Gutai-e had withdrawn to one side. His expression took on a grim stillness at the captain's stark plea, but he did not speak. Keitah Terusai-e had found a chair and sat in it, his elbow leaned on its arm. He looked profoundly disgusted. But he said, "You will indeed have no choice but to dismiss your captain, Mitereh."

"No," acknowledged the king, his tone bleak.

"Apana Pelat," murmured Tenai, her dark-velvet voice soft and unreadable. She took her foot off the chair and strolled closer, studying the captain. "How long have you been captain of the king's personal guard?"

"Seven years."

"Seven years. You should know your men as you know the fingers of your hand."

Color rose in the captain's face, a warmth under his dark skin. "Before this, I would have said I did. I confess I must have been blind."

"Well," said Tenai. She turned her head to catch the king's eye. "Well, and have we not all been blind? And do we not all continue so? There is more than this one assassin, we may be sure. Who else bears the stain of treachery upon his heart? Captain Pelat? Indeed, that is possible. Another of your house guard?" Her eye went to the young men at the king's back. They looked stricken, but she was already going on. "One of your attendants, made free of your person? And behind the assassins with their blades and their sorcery and hidden treachery. Who could this be? One of your lords of this court? Some agent of Imbaneh-se? Would you wish to guess, Mitereh?"

"No," answered the king quietly.

"I am your man," Captain Pelat put in. "I failed you, my king. But I swear before God and the Martyr, I did not betray you. I beg you will be wary of the man who seems faultless, but yet may hide treachery behind smiling teeth."

"I do not doubt you," Mitereh told him. "But ..." He paused, irresolute.

"Mitereh. You must permit me to question this man," said Tenai.

The captain did not protest, but his gaze went to Tenai with trepidation.

"I recognize the necessity," said Mitereh reluctantly. He gestured to the assassin. "However ... first the man whose guilt we know."

"To be sure." Tenai walked over and knelt down by the assassin. She studied him. "I fear Berangilan-sa was correct. This man's breathing is not as it should be."

"You hit him hard," the king observed.

"Not so hard as this." Tenai reached out and touched the prisoner's forehead. Drawing her fingers down his face, she touched his eyelids with the tips of her fingers. "Nolas-ai," she said to Taranah. "My skill to heal is not as finely honed as yours may be. I ask your opinion of this man."

The king's aunt had already been moving. She knelt across from Tenai, bending to examine the stricken man. Her expression intent, she held one hand out, palm down, above his face. Then she looked up, not at Tenai, but at the king. "He is dying, Mitereh. His hand is on the Gate."

"Chaisa, where was your skill?" the king demanded. "My aunt, can you bring him back to us on this side of the Gate?"

Taranah sat back, shaking her head, spreading her hands in regret. "His heart beats far more slowly than it should. He will assuredly go into the hand of God, and that soon. The blow that struck him down could not do this. I think—I am certain—that this is sorcery. Another man's intent closes around this man's heart." She looked up at Tenai. "If I may ask, are *you* able to free him from your lord's hand, Nolas-Kuomon?"

Tenai met Taranah's pale eyes. Then she turned to Mitereh. She said her tone flat, "He is beyond my recall. I think, beyond any mortal recall. If we had tried at once ... but we delayed. I think death lies now before this man's next step. He cannot be saved." Tenai rose, glancing at the king. She turned a hand palm upward. "But whether he has passed entirely beyond my lord's call ... that, I do not know. With your leave, my king, I might discover this."

There was a slight pause. Then the king inclined his head a little, giving permission, Daniel was not quite sure for what, but something dangerous. Something magical? Or, what, somehow questionable? Tenai was looking very, well, very *contained*, in a dark kind of way. Taranah had risen to her feet and now moved back, withdrawing with a swiftness that showed that whatever might happen next, it would not be something *safe*. Daniel wanted to ask Tenai if whatever she meant to do was something she was certain she wanted to do, but he wasn't quick enough.

Rising, Tenai drew her sword, hesitated a bare instant, and drove it into Iodad's chest. His body arched and spasmed. Daniel jerked back. He wasn't the only one who flinched: the king's young men twitched, and one of them, Badayan, stepped between the king and Tenai.

Daniel hardly had attention for any of that. His eyes had gone to Tenai's face, assessing. The smooth assured violence of the blow had been very disturbing.

Then the body seemed to fold weirdly in upon itself, into a

tight dark knot of shadow. Smaller, smaller. And then gone.

"Christ!" Daniel exclaimed, quite involuntarily.

"Martyr's blood," Apana Pelat muttered, sounding just as shaken.

The king did not move or speak, though his eyes had narrowed. Nor did Keitah. Sandakan looked grim, but also said nothing. None of them looked at all surprised, and Daniel realized they'd all expected this.

Well thought, said a voice that was nothing like a human voice, from the far reaches of the king's apartment.

Tenai turned to look across the room. She seemed to find someone there, in the far spaces of the bed chamber, although with all the lanterns lit there were few enough shadows for anybody to hide in. Following her gaze, Daniel almost thought he might be able to make a figure out there ... faintly. A shadow where there shouldn't have been any shadows.

Mitereh's gaze was on Tenai. Taranah shifted forward a step, resting her hand on her nephew's arm, a supportive gesture. Apana Pelat caught up his sword, jumped to his feet and moved to face this new presence; the young men of the king's guard quickly followed his example. Attendants, eyes wide, backed away toward the other side of the room. Keitah stood up, looking grim. Sandakan did not move, but the strong angular bones of his face seemed suddenly stark.

Tenai took a step toward that half-present shadow and said, in a perfectly ordinary tone of voice, "My lord."

The presence there shaped itself more clearly into the form of a man. The light of the lanterns seemed to fold back away from the form, as though darkness rather than light was necessary to reveal what was there.

It was Lord Death. He was absolutely real. Tenai had described Lord Death to Daniel. Descriptions did not do him justice. No description could. He was like ... nothing on Earth. Shaped like a man, yes, if a hole into midnight darkness could be said to have a shape, yet he was not like a featureless silhouette, either. He had too much solidity and presence for that. He seemed to look for one instant directly at Daniel, who met his hollow gaze and found he could not move or breathe. Then Lord Death looked away with perfect indifference and the moment passed.

Tenai showed neither surprise nor fear. She walked forward, putting out her hands to Lord Death, who took them in his and drew her forward. She came freely.

You have returned, said Lord Death. Daniel shuddered at that voice, which was nothing like the voice of a man.

"I did not depart willingly, my lord," answered Tenai. "Forgive me. I knew my departure from this land would bend the oath I swore to you."

There is nothing to forgive. I waited for your return to this land, said Lord Death. **But I watched over you in that one, though you could not see me. I was prepared to wait a long age, if required. Sixteen years is only a moment. You are here, returned. Does this please you?**

"It pleases me, my lord."

Lord Death slid hands like holes in the dark up Tenai's arms to her shoulders. He was taller than she, and bent to kiss her forehead. Tenai accepted this gesture as though it was completely normal. **You have regained your balance in the world,** he said.

"Does this please you, my lord?"

You properly belong to life as well as to my domain. That you have remembered this pleases me. Releasing her, Lord Death turned his attention to the young king and said, in that bodiless voice that had nothing to do with the voices of men, **Mitereh Sekuse-go-e, Mitereh Encormio-na, have a care for what you do. Would you challenge my right and my bond?**

Mitereh touched his aunt's hand, a light, reassuring touch, and she let her hand fall. Then the king parted the men of his guard with a slight gesture. He came forward a step and bowed. He had paled. But he said, "Never willingly, lord," in a steady voice. "Driven by necessity, I asked Tenai Nolas-Kuomon for obedience and loyalty in the mortal realm, but I do not seek to come between you and your lady."

Lord Death came forward a little, moving without sound. **Your father evaded my touch for many years.**

The king bowed acknowledgement.

You, now, Encormio-na, I have been close to you, from time to time. From time to time you might have touched my hand if you had reached out.

The king offered another slight bow. "If I have offended you, lord, I beg your pardon and ask how I may make amends."

Lord Death smiled a terrible smile. **Ah,** he murmured, in that bodiless voice. **Have you offended me, Encormio-na?**

Keitah shifted, as though he might move protectively forward. Before he could, Tenai stirred. She was half-smiling, a far more human expression, but seeming strange in the company she was keeping. She looked comfortable standing by that terrible man-shaped shadow. "My lord is jealous of his precincts," she said casually, tone almost dismissive, "but he is aware he has had no cause for offense from you, Mitereh. The choice was mine." She walked a few steps away from Lord Death and folded her arms over her chest, frowning and glancing back with her eyebrows raised. "I was not quick enough? The man did not come to you, my lord?"

He had his hand already on the Gate, answered Lord Death, sounding almost regretful. Daniel had not seen him move, but he had somehow joined Tenai. **It was not my country he entered, but the far country of God. He is beyond my eye and does not linger within my hand.**

Tenai inclined her head in understanding. "It was to you I hoped he would go. But I knew the chance was small. Can you tell me then whose hand it was that sent him to the Gate before you could gather him into your country?"

I perceive only the dying, said Lord Death, still regretful. **And you. The murdered and not those who do murder present themselves to my attention. I would hold him for you if I could. But once his hand is on the Gate, he is no longer mine to hold. I am able to tell you this: he came to the Gate unwillingly.**

"Ah," breathed Tenai. "He did not consent? That ... that, at least, is well worth knowing, and I thank you for bringing this word."

It is a small thing. I would do more for you, if I could.

"Ah, well ... as you are come into this place, my lord, I would indeed ask a second favor." Tenai glanced at Captain Pelat, who shifted an involuntary step back before he could stop himself. But he did stop after only that one step. His breathing had quickened. He slowed it deliberately, an exercise of sheer physical courage Daniel had to admire. Then he gave his sword to Inkaimon and answered Tenai's gesture to come forward.

"Speak truth to me," Tenai said to him. "Apana Pelat of Kaya-sa: what is the truth of your heart? What is the truth of your hands?"

Lord Death lifted a hand and settled a gentle grip about the captain's throat. The spread of his strange, dark fingers against the man's skin made Lord Death seem less human than ever, less real. At the same time, he seemed more solid and far more terrible.

Apana flinched from that touch, but did not attempt to struggle against it. He lifted his own hands to his throat, but arrested the gesture before he touched the dark hand that held him. Then he moved as though he would try to push himself away from the force that held him. But he did not actually fight Lord Death's grip. He looked into those hollow eyes. Whatever he saw there turned his face stiff with horror.

Apana Pelat. I know you. On your death, you will come to me. Surrender to me now the truth of your heart, Lord Death demanded, echoing Tenai's question.

The captain answered with obvious difficulty, "I have been true to my king's trust. Neither with ... neither with my hands nor my heart have I ... *God* ... have I done treachery. *God and Martyr!*" He began, helplessly, to fight against the inhuman grip that held him.

Ignoring the man's struggles, Lord Death brought up his other hand, shifting his grip so that he held Apana by both shoulders. Gasping, the man tried once to wretch himself free and then went still. He closed his eyes: Lord Death shook him once, not hard, and he made a muffled sound and opened his eyes again.

You maintain you are not at fault?

The captain was shuddering, long slow tremors that passed through his whole body. "My fault ... my fault lies in error. Never intention."

Lord Death let him go. He turned his head, regarding Tenai from his empty inhuman eyes.

Apana Pelat collapsed to his knees at Lord Death's feet. His hands went first to his throat where Lord Death's dark hand had gripped him; then he wrapped his arms around himself like a hurt child who has no hope of comfort and huddled down against the floor.

"I am satisfied," Tenai said gravely, not glancing down at the stricken man.

To Daniel's astonishment, the moment Tenai made that declaration, Taranah Berangilan-sa moved softly forward. She bowed her head deeply to Lord Death, murmuring, barely audible, "Let thy gaze not linger, O Death, lest it strike to the heart." Then she drew Captain Pelat to his feet and a little distance away. He moved like a blind man, following her gentle, silent urging. Daniel thought he might not have ever seen anyone do anything braver. Embarrassed that he hadn't even thought of doing anything of the kind, he moved quickly to take the captain's other arm, steadying him, guiding him to a nearby chair. The captain sank into that chair, as though blindly. He was shuddering, long tremors that shook his whole body.

Lord Death did not deign to notice any of this. He had turned his terrible gaze to Mitereh. Now he said, somehow imbuing the simple question with profound threat, **And are you also satisfied, Encormio-na?**

The king bowed, hands at his sides. He chanted in a clear, low voice, "O Death, turn thy gaze from us and pass by! Our swords do not mark thee; our shields do not stay thy hand; only thy good will may spare us! O Death, turn thy gaze from us and so pass by!"

For a moment longer, Lord Death continued to regard him. Then he asked, **Is it my good will you desire, Mitereh Encormio-na?** He held out a bodiless dark hand to the king, palm down.

After a second's hesitation Mitereh strode forward, and okay, fine, that set yet another standard for courage; Daniel hadn't seen much resemblance between the king and his aunt until that moment, but now he did. Mitereh waved his young men back with a curt gesture when they would have prevented him, and stopped Keitah Terusai-e with a look when the older man showed the same impulse. Going to one knee before Lord Death, the king took the dark hand in his own. He did not flinch visibly, but he took a short breath. Then he touched his lips to the back of that dark hand. "Lord," he said, and lifted his gaze to meet the hollow, empty eyes.

Encormio-na, though my lady may have been so generous as to declare she considers your offense against me slight, *I* consider you have trespassed.

Mitereh answered in a steady voice, "I acknowledge you have cause, and beg your forgiveness of mortal necessity, Lord Death."

For my lady's sake, I shall forbear. Lord Death withdrew his hand and moved back a step, regarding Mitereh without favor, but also without obvious hostility. **Twice in this past year, young king, I have reached out my hand for you and only turned aside at the last instant of time. Your breath has warmed my face. Your hand has brushed the very lintel of the Gate. You are brave, but it is not my mercy nor my good will you should seek, for even were I to give them, they will avail you nothing.**

Mitereh looked up again at the terrible face, not moving, face blank ... hiding surprise, or fear, or some other emotion he did not intend to show. "Nevertheless, I am grateful for your mercy, as all mortals must be. Thank you, lord."

Nothing I do is for you. Do not offer me thanks, Lord Death answered, with frightening coldness. He stepped back and said to Tenai, **Do not wait for the year's ending. Do not wait for your power to wax with the lengthening nights. I fear you will find you do not have so much time.**

Tenai inclined her head. "I hear your warning, and thank you for it, lord."

Lord Death did not tell *her* not to thank him. He inclined his head minutely, took another step back, and folded away into darkness and shadows and the thin air. He was gone, leaving behind a profound silence and a sense of cold hiding behind the sultry heat as though the summer was only an illusion, and light and warmth had never truly existed.

14

The first to move was Tenai. Of course. Daniel watched her. Where the rest of them were fighting shock and lingering horror, Tenai was untouched by either.

Mitereh got to his feet, moving a little stiffly.

Tenai said, her tone cool, "You did well, Mitereh Sekuse-go-e. Lord Death is jealous of my service. You see why I took care what I would offer you." She regarded the young man with a certain satisfaction.

"Yes," said the king. He shuddered a little, unable to hide that simple physical reaction. He drew a breath and looked around, as though reaquainting himself with the mortal world. Finally he nodded to Taranah. "Please, my aunt, another time, do not take such risks."

"I took no risk," Taranah answered. "I have not offended Lord Death—nor Chaisa-e."

"True," said Tenai, smiling a narrow, unfriendly smile. Most of her attention was still on Mitereh. But she added, "Altogether true, Berangilan-sa. That was well and kindly done."

"It was," Mitereh conceded. He stepped to Captain Pelat's side, laid a hand on the man's shoulder, and took his arm to aid him to stand. "Forgive my doubt."

The captain shook his head, not in refusal, but as though trying to shake off the lingering effects of Lord Death's touch. He let the king help him to his feet. His shivering had abated now that Lord Death was gone from the room, but he still looked gray and shocky. Daniel couldn't blame him.

"So I may trust your heart," Mitereh said to him. "I had no doubt, but I declare I am glad that your loyalty has been made clear to all and everyone. I am more glad of that than I can well express."

The captain gave a little nod, but did not yet try to speak.

One of the young men, Inkaimon, said hesitantly, "My king ... of all men, our captain is proven to be true. None of us guessed Iodad's duplicity. How is Apana Pelat more at fault than any of us? The men of your guard desire no other captain. We ask that you hold his honor to be clean and return him to us as our captain."

Badayan and Torohoh both nodded, their faces earnest.

Some of the color came back into Captain Pelat's face. He drew away from the king, reclaiming self-possession. He said, "My king, I commend Inkaimon to you in my place. He is young, but he will do well."

"But—" Inkaimon protested.

Mitereh lifted a hand, silencing Inkaimon. "I have no choice but to dismiss him," the king said gently. "You know that is true."

The young men showed open distress, but did not seem to disagree. Tenai merely watched, unmoved. Keitah Terusai-e gave a small nod of grim agreement. Not even Taranah said a word of protest, so whatever law or custom governed here, apparently it was not something the king could flout.

Captain Pelat said quietly, "If you will permit my presumption in twice making the request, my king, I would prefer death to such shame."

Given that they all seemed to agree that Apana Pelat was not really at fault, death seemed a little extreme. Daniel drew breath to say so. He did not know how he was going to put it, which might have been why Sandakan Gutai-e beat him to it.

"If you were to turn this man away, my king," the general said, his tone harsh, "perhaps there might be one outside your household who would be willing to take up even a man of ruined honor into her hand and thus moderate the shame of the dismissal."

Everyone in the room regarded the general with astonishment, but no one more so than Captain Pelat himself. Sandakan folded his arms over his chest and stared back at the captain, more saturnine than ever. "Shame seems unendurable when it is new. But with time, it ages and dies and passes at last into the bleak kingdom of Lord Sorrow, unclaimed and unremembered. You are not a young man, Pelat. You should not mistake this truth."

The captain did not answer, but he bowed his head a little.

Tenai said after a moment, "So, well. Would you hurry your steps toward the dark kingdom, Pelat? All that Gutai has said is true. Indeed, I have been long accustomed to taking men where I find them, asking nothing of birth or background. In my service, sometimes a man may regain honor he once believed irretrievably lost." To Daniel she seemed to be referring to something, some incident, that was common knowledge. Even though he didn't understand the reference, everyone else seemed to. Significant glances passed around the room.

The king nodded, a short decisive gesture. "Indeed, Chaisa. So they may. I declare I would approve this." Turning to Captain Pelat, he added, "Apana, you must make your own decision. But this would please me very much, my friend."

Taranah Berangilan-sa, watching the captain closely, said gently, "It is a hard thing the king asks you to endure. Everyone is aware this is a hard thing. But I think I may say that my nephew would be pleased if your loyalty were so great that you could bring yourself to endure even this. Let us note that of all those persons of rank and position, Chaisa-e is perhaps the *least* likely to have been suborned by a secret enemy. In serving Chaisa-e, you yet serve Mitereh and Talasayan entire."

The king repeated, "I would approve it, Apana. Please do not demand the knife. If you make that request a third time, I will accede, but please, remember that Lord Death is endlessly patient. I ask that you do not to hurry your journey toward that dark kingdom." Without waiting for an answer, he turned both his hands palm upward in a gesture of release and went on. "Apana Pelat, I return your oath to you. I set you aside. You are not mine. You are free to take service elsewhere. I ask, I earnestly ask that you do so."

For a moment longer, Apana Pelat hesitated. Then he turned toward Tenai. Inkaimon came quietly forward to give Tenai his captain's sword. She took it without a word, and offered it, flat across both hands, to Pelat. He knelt and bowed to the floor, rose again to kneeling, and reached up to accept his sword from her hands.

"I take you up. You are my man," Tenai told him.

"My obedience and loyalty are yours, Nolas-e," Apana

answered, bowing his head. Then, looking rather stunned, he got to his feet and slung the sword into place at his belt. He looked at the king, and made himself look away; took the few steps necessary to put himself at Tenai's side and a step behind her.

"So," said Tenai, evidently dismissing all this. "If we may now turn our attention to a different question of some importance. Who is your enemy, Mitereh?"

"What inhabits your enemy's heart? Is it ambition, or mere hatred?" Sandakan Gutai-e added. "Political maneuver, or malice? The knife will have a different poison on the edge for the one or the other."

Metaphorically, Daniel wondered, or literally? He didn't ask, being out of his depth in any case.

There was a brief silence as everyone thought about this question. "Hatred could lie behind any sugared smile," Keitah commented eventually. "But the shining teeth of ambition are more difficult to conceal."

"True," agreed Tenai. "So. Who would gain from your death, Mitereh? If you have no heir of your body ... to whom would Talasayan go if you were put out of the way?"

There was a brief silence. Keitah looked forcefully neutral. Sandakan had also gone even more dourly expressionless than usual. Apana Pelat glanced at the king and then down at the floor. It was plain no one wanted to answer this question. Tenai saw it, too: her smile grew edged. She tilted her head in an attitude of exaggerated patience.

At last Mitereh said reluctantly, "I indeed suspect that Talasayan would go in the end to the strongest. As ... as my heir is yet young."

"Your heir," Tenai repeated. One elegant eyebrow lifted.

Mitereh met her gaze with, most uncharacteristically, obvious uncertainty. "It is true that I have no heir of my body ... but I wonder whether you ever knew, Chaisa, of my mother's second son."

Tenai regarded the young king with a certain irony. "No. I did not know. And I perceive you were not at pains to tell me. This boy is, do I surmise correctly, Encormio's son as well? And sixteen years of age, or perhaps a little more? A well-grown boy, am I to understand so?"

Taranah murmured, "Tegaitan is a fine, clever boy, with a kind and loving heart. He favors my sister."

Tenai studied her for a moment. Finally she said, "I take your assurance, Berangilan-sa." She was smiling, with, so far as Daniel could tell, real amusement in that smile. "Very well, Mitereh. I assure you in turn, I bear this brother of yours no ill-will. If I bear none for you, how should I resent this boy? Indeed, you are surely correct: with so young an heir, Talasayan would go to the strongest. Fortunate boy, that you stand between him and that melee. However, surely you mean to get an heir of your body?"

Another hesitation. Mitereh braced himself visibly and admitted "I have been trying to get an heir. My wife has not borne a son."

Daniel thought, surprised, *wife?* No one had mentioned a queen, not that he could remember; not the king and not any of his young men and not any of Tenai's people. No one. But now he remembered that Tenai had said no king even as old as Mitereh could be unmarried.

"Your wife?" Tenai echoed that silent surprise, and then moved a hand in a swift gesture that dismissed surprise. "I see. You have not wished to mention your wife to me. You had no need to be so careful, but of course the caution was wise. Who?"

Mitereh inclined his head. "I confess I had not cared to have you know her name. I will tell you now, Chaisa. Niah Madalan Kuyad-sa, of Antiatan. My wife of six years gone." The king studied Tenai and added, in a level, expressionless tone, "She gave me a daughter swiftly, but does not quicken again. My advisors urge me to take a second wife, and I have agreed to the necessity." The king said this with care, as though there was a great deal more he was not saying. "Negotiations are ..." the king hesitated, and finished the sentence with the faintest edge to his tone, "Constant."

Tenai half-smiled. "None of my people mentioned either your brother or your wife or her daughter to me, which may well please you. So I would see, if I had not understood it before, that Chaisa is not displeased by your rule, Mitereh Sekuse-go-e. No heir of your body, indeed. Only a second son of Encormio and Sekuse, and a daughter of your own. Where are they, these children? In Nerinesir, perhaps in this very house? In Antiatan?"

"Tegaitan is in Antiatan, with our mother's family," the king answered deliberately. "Keitah Terusai-e was kind to offer hospitality to my wife and my daughter during this ... uncertainty. As I thought Kinabana best for the purpose."

Tenai inclined her head. She was not smiling, but behind that sober face Daniel had the impression she was laughing. "With someone you trust prepared to take your brother and board a ship for Tesmeket—or Keneseh?—if I should draw steel and come that way. A good choice. And your own child in Kinabana. Another good choice. The gardens in Kinabana are beautiful in this season."

"I have always thought them so in all seasons."

"So, well. I am no longer inclined to make war on children, Mitereh. No matter their parentage. I swear this is so, by—" Tenai hesitated. "By my own children, long given to Lord Death and to God."

The king gave a reserved nod. Although nothing in his expression changed, Daniel understood that he was intensely relieved at this reaction.

"So you are taking a second wife. My king, if I may ask, when was this decision made public?"

"At the dawning of the year," Mitereh answered, and paused.

Sandakan shifted forward a step. He was frowning. "But does your enemy wish to prevent the getting of a son ... or the passing of the direct line away from Madalan, or Kuyad, perhaps?"

Tenai glanced at him and nodded. "Sixteen years gone, and I no longer know how the lines of power run in Talasayan. I will learn. You will teach me, I trust so, Mitereh. Or is this only happenstance?" She lowered her voice. "Mitereh ... do you trust your wife?"

Daniel blinked. Taranah Berangilan-sa coughed, hiding a smile with a lifted hand. Keitah lifted an eyebrow. Sandakan, like the king's aunt, merely looked amused, but blood rose to Mitereh's face, swift and hot, touching his strong features with sudden arrogant temper. "You do not know the lady, or you would not ask, Chaisa. Put that out of your mind. Whoever may work against me, it is not my *wife*."

Tenai made a little pacifying gesture, although to Daniel's experienced eyes she didn't appear very worried about the king's temper. "Forgive me, then. I suspect everyone."

"Well ... well, as you should," the king conceded. His tone

firmed. "As assuredly we all must keep in mind. Though Niah is hardly suspect," added Mitereh. He glanced around the room. "One must trust *someone*."

"One assuredly must not," Sandakan returned curtly. "I shall watch, of course. I should choose soldiers to guard your rest in the coming days, my king: plain men of unexceptional birth, men who have never come to your notice and are unlikely to have been suborned. If you have an enemy among the men of your personal guard, you are in danger every moment; and worse danger for being forced to dismiss your captain."

The young men didn't look offended at this assessment. They looked grim, and ashamed.

Apana Pelat said sharply, "Yet the danger is all the greater if the men of your guard lose your trust, or become unable to trust one another."

"True," Sandakan agreed at once. "That is also true. Thus your enemy weakens you, my king—weakens all of us. In all truth, we can hardly expect many of your house guard to have been suborned. Probably Iodad was alone among them in his treachery. Your true enemy will be a man directing others in their deaths and looking with foresight to shape what he desires. This will not be any young man. He will be a lord, and he will be someone you do not wish to suspect."

"You?" asked Mitereh.

"Perhaps," said Sandakan. "Neither I nor anyone else will attend you alone, my king. Two soldiers and one of your personal guards at all times." He looked at Tenai. "Better if we had all been set to the question by Lord Death."

Apana Pelat shuddered and turned abruptly away from them all to hide his reaction. Everyone else pretended not to notice.

The king shook his head. "It was concession enough Chaisa won from him. Nor am I confident—" he hesitated, glanced at Apana, and changed what he had intended to say. "No, Gutai. You, I trust." He looked around the room. "All of you, everyone here. How shall I do otherwise? Still, I will follow your advice, that we may all have trust in one another. Yes, my general: find soldiers for me. I will trust them because you have chosen them. And you, my companions," he looked at each of his young men in turn, "I will ask your forbearance in this extremity. Accept these soldiers and let them share your duty. Be gracious to them. It is my hope that in their presence you may trust one another as I will always trust you."

Inkaimon murmured, "My king." Plainly none of the young men was happy about this plan, but they looked resigned.

Mitereh glanced around again, sighing a little. "The night is all but past. And there will be the court to face in the coming day."

"Handling the court will be like juggling knives, Mitereh," Keitah said. "This night has been hard. Would it be better to set all ceremony back another day?"

Taranah said mildly, "There will be no good in waiting, Keitah."

The king gestured agreement. "My aunt's words are correct. I will juggle knives, since I must. Indeed, Nolas-Kuomon will be the blade I toss into the brush to see what birds fly up."

Tenai tilted her head at this, plainly amused.

"Apana ..." the king hesitated. "Inkaimon. Find Nolas-ai Mikanan Chauke-sa, if you would, and ask him to come to me here, if he is ready to make his report to me. My aunt, design a statement regarding these events that will serve to reassure our people. Keitah, my friend, consider, if you will, the design of the defenses laid upon this apartment and this palace. Where weaknesses have been found or made, better defenses must be raised up."

Then the king turned away, as though that series of orders closed the matter, closed down all the weird and dangerous events of the night. Everyone else seemed to take it that way, too: heading out about various tasks, or bending to clear away the signs of the struggle and its ... aftermath. Except Tenai, who only moved a little aside and stood there, speaking quietly with Apana Pelat, who listened silently, his head bowed.

Daniel sank into a chair and shut his eyes. He felt a little stunned, like he was coming up short in his attempt to sort through everything that had happened. He would have liked to be able to come up with something pithy and insightful to help with that. Nothing brilliant was coming to mind.

What a world, with such darkness and such, what?—proof of mortality?—so close beneath the surface. Was that so different from home, though? Well, yes. It *was* different, not merely on the surface, but all the way down to the deep reality hidden beneath the surface of things. Unless that deep reality was just a *lot* better hidden at home. Daniel shuddered, remembering Lord Death's terrible blank gaze and strange empty voice. But maybe it was not entirely a bad thing, to have the darkness so blatant and personified? Maybe that made people value light and life more. Maybe it made people braver. Certainly Mitereh had demonstrated both courage and kindness—and Taranah—and Sandakan. Even Tenai, in a way. He had certainly seen a great deal to admire in all these people.

Even so, thinking of his daughter, Daniel would have given anything to take her back to an understandable world without assassins or magic or dark personifications of death and loss.

"Come," Tenai said softly, having come close without him noticing. "Daniel. I am aware everything tonight must have been disconcerting. Come, if you wish. I will take you back into my household just for the rest of this night and the coming day. I have ordered Pelat to stand guard here."

That was a surprise, briefly. Then Daniel smiled, realizing he should have understood that she would do exactly that. Probably everyone else had understood it. "Good."

Tenai's mouth crooked a little. "Yes," she said. "His loyalty should come to me, but if I command him to guard the king and Mitereh accepts my presumption in issuing that command, then we may all regard the coming day with a little more equanimity. But I am certain you will wish to observe with your own eyes that your daughter remains well and safe and well-guarded."

"Yes," Daniel said. "All right. Good. It won't be a problem if I go back into your—your household?" But he didn't really care. The moment Tenai said her name, he felt a desperate need to check on his daughter. He started to get up, suppressing a groan. He was amazingly stiff, considering he hadn't done anything but watch all those terrifying events unfold.

"Not for the present, no," Tenai told him. "For this next little time, I will take you back under my protection and no one will question this." She offered him a hand to help him to his feet. Daniel cast a look toward Mitereh, and the king gave him a little nod and a gesture of permission. So that did seem to be all right.

In the morning, over breakfast, once she finally heard about everything that had happened, Jenna was fascinated to hear about the eventful night. Daniel's description of Lord Death didn't frighten her: words couldn't describe the being Tenai had called into Mitereh's apartment. "It's like something out of a story," she declared. "I can't believe I missed everything!" She seemed to have forgotten the piece of nut bread she held in her hand.

"A horror novel, maybe." Daniel himself had no appetite. "Tenai's sword doesn't kill someone—it sends him to Lord Death. That is actually, literally true. You can't imagine, Jen. It was exactly like a weird special effect, but it was real. Lord Death is truly, actually a ..." *person* seemed both accurate and wholly wrong to describe that ... entity. "Lord Death is actually real," Daniel finished, a little lamely.

"This is so, so neat. Like stepping into a real, no-kidding, honest-to-God fantasy movie!"

She had absolutely no idea. Daniel couldn't imagine how to make her believe that magic was terrifying, or that the ... being ... to whom Tenai owed her first and greatest allegiance was even more terrifying.

"And the assassin's spells didn't work on you," Jenna went on cheerfully. "We're immune to magic, huh? Or at least you are for sure, but probably me too. That's also neat." She remembered the bread she held and took a bite.

"Some kinds of magic," Daniel cautioned her. "Maybe. Apparently we might be able to let it work or not. Tenai doesn't understand the rules—and neither do you, Jen, so don't get carried away. We don't really know why Iodad's spell didn't work on me."

"Of course not, Daddy." Jenna was humoring him, but then the other implication of the night's events seemed to dawn on her. "Wait, now. Did you say Iodad? Iodad was the assassin? But I liked Iodad!"

"Sweetheart, you like everyone."

"Well, Daddy, everyone's likable, usually." Jenna put her bread down on the table, looking really upset for the first time. "But usually they don't sneak around trying to murder people." She shook her head again and repeated, "I can't believe the assassin— okay, all right, *one* assassin—was one of Mitereh's own guards. That just seems so weird. Emel, why would he do that?"

Emelan had been standing quietly against the wall, so still

Daniel had almost forgotten his presence. Jenna plainly hadn't. Now, addressed directly, he turned his hands palm-up to signify puzzlement. "There are many possible reasons he or any man might betray a trust. Perhaps he acted so because he was an agent of Imbaneh-se, Nola. Or because he hated Encormio with such passion he would pretend to serve Mitereh Encormio-na in order to destroy this son of the old king. Or because he gave his true loyalty over to a lord who would bring down Mitereh Sekuse-go-e for political gain. Or because he believed that striking down the king's foreign guest would serve some end we do not know."

Jenna stared at him. "The king's foreign guest. Wait, you mean Iodad was after Daddy? Daddy, specifically? Not the king?"

Daniel had tried to gloss over this detail. Now he had to admit it.

"Well, why?" Jenna stood up and paced, far more disturbed by this than by his stumbling descriptions of magic and swords and Lord Death. "Why?"

Unable to provide an answer, Daniel shrugged.

"This was a blow aimed to strike at Chaisa-e and at the king," Emelan explained quietly. "This was a move in a long, wide game, and Iodad merely a piece in that game. The king is surely the eventual target, but the king's enemy seeks still to use Chaisa-e as another piece in his game. By reaching through the protection of the king to strike against people Nolas-Kuomon values, this enemy strives again and again to turn her against him. Or so I surmise."

Daniel leaned back in his chair, studying the other man. It was reassuring to have a younger, fitter, tougher man standing between Jenna and every possible assassin. It struck him for the first time that, of everyone in the court and the city, Emelan was the single person they could be absolutely certain was not working with or for the king's enemy. He'd been too far outside normal life to possibly be involved. Hadn't the king said something like that to, and about, Tenai? And for something like the same reason. He said, "This all seems strangely indirect. Who do you think is behind all this?"

Emelan shifted uncomfortably in his place against the wall. "Nola Danyel, I would say Imbaneh-se. But I know nothing of the court of these years."

"Um."

"Imbaneh-se, or an ambitious man of the Talasayan court, or both, or neither," Tenai said, entering the room and taking up the conversation as though she'd heard everything. "We cannot yet determine the source of this malice." She had gone away again for some time, working with the king or with someone else to deal with all the problems and complications of the night. But here she was, back again, as imperturbable as ever.

She gave Emelan a little nod that apparently relieved the man of duty, as he at once moved aside and dropped into a chair. Tenai turned to Daniel. "Well," she said, "my friend. Mitereh and I and half a handful of his advisors have discussed these very questions all the morning, and have arrived at no definite conclusions. I have a proposition for you, however." She glanced at Jenna. "For you both."

"Oh?" From Tenai's tone, Daniel thought she might not expect them to approve of this proposition, whatever it might be.

"Oh, yes?" Jenna said, in a much brighter tone, ready to be pleased at whatever suggestion Tenai might make.

"Yes." Tenai leaned in the doorway, her expression bland. "Mitereh proposes sending you both to Kinabana, to the grant Terusai-e holds there. There you may join the boy's wife, under the protection of Terusai and of Kinabana itself. Thus you will both be removed from the risk that attends us all here in Nerinesir."

"Could be fun," said Jenna, her tone just a little dubious.

For a beat, before he achieved impassivity, Emelan looked dismayed. It took Daniel a moment to understand that if he and Jenna went to Kinabana, Emelan would probably go with them—and that would put him in his brother's unavoidable company. No wonder the man didn't like that idea. Daniel was disturbed himself, but not for the same reason. He said, "Wait, Tenai, do you mean we'd go to Kinabana, wherever that is, without you?"

"Oh." Jenna stared at Tenai. "We would what? I don't know, Tenai ..."

Tenai turned a hand palm-up. "Jenna, my bright child—Daniel, my friend—there is no question but that I must remain in Nerinesir for this present. You are manifestly unsafe here. While Mitereh's house guard is unsettled this will be doubly true. I would send you to Chaisa, save that everyone would believe hostility had prompted me to reclaim you from Mitereh's household. They would understand the boy to be weak that he would allow it, and they would believe me to be preparing for war that I would do it. Thus Mitereh suggests Kinabana."

Daniel looked at her closely. "The *king* suggests this, does he?"

"I might have prompted the suggestion," Tenai admitted. "Balancing one likely enemy against another ... I think, indeed, you will find a greater portion of safety in Kinabana." She came into the room and settled at the table, crossing her hands on the table's dark surface. Slim and almost as dark as the polished wood, her hands might have been made by the same carver who had lent ornament to the table's edge. But those hands could hold a knife or a cursed sword, or willingly be lifted to touch the face of Death ... Daniel brought his gaze back to Tenai's face.

She leaned forward just a little. "Daniel, who is this enemy who strikes at Encormio's son? Is it an enemy who hates him for the memory of his father? Possible, but then why wait sixteen years to strike? Further: why layer the blow through intermediaries? Would hatred not suggest a more personal attack?"

Daniel nodded. "I'm with you so far. Go on." Jenna had leaned forward, too, and even Emelan drifted toward the table to listen.

"If not an enemy who acts from the memory of hatred, is this person then an ambitious lord of Talasayan? Again, possible. Ambition turns readily to the black knife and the poisoned cup. Who, then? Sandakan Gutai-e? He might indeed hold Mitereh's armies if the king were cast through the Gate of Lord Death, but I do not believe the guilt is his."

Jenna gave an emphatic nod. "Right! No way!"

"Mikanan Chauke-sa? Gomenah Kelabili-go-e? Belagaiyan Tenom-e? Kanantan Tondut?" She glanced at Emelan. "Keitah Terusai-e, perhaps? Each is possible; all lords of this court are alike possible. Any of them might believe he might take the throne should Mitereh fall. But which of these men would be arrogant enough in himself that he would believe he might make Nolas-Kuomon his dupe? All those men remember me too well. I do not believe any of them would be such fools."

"Yes," Emelan said earnestly. "Yes, Nolas-e. They never would."

Tenai spared a nod for him and went on. "An agent of Imbaneh-se? Such a person might well fear me less than a lord of Talasayan. I do regard this as far more likely. But Iodad Sonnas-na had no ties to the south. All his knowledge is of Talasayan and of this city. Would a man of Mitereh's own personal guard turn willingly to Imbaneh-se? Or would a man of that company readily be suborned or deceived to the violent causes of the south? I confess I cannot well consider so. The boy does not choose so ill for his companions. So this again suggests a closer enemy."

Again, Emelan murmured agreement.

"So, who else is there?" Jenna asked. She had moved the platter of bread to one side and was now leaning forward, her arms crossed on the table, absorbed in the whodunit Tenai was spinning. Daniel, more of his attention on Tenai herself than on the argument she was laying out for them, found a chill creeping down his spine. He could see, not what was coming, but that it was something bad, something ugly.

Tenai answered Jenna, the corner of her mouth crooking upward, but not with humor. Perhaps with irony. "Why, my bright child ... Mitereh revealed his vulnerability himself. 'One must trust someone.' Was this not his very phrase? Thus he reveals his blindness."

Daniel remembered the context of that particular statement. The sensation of cold increased. "You don't think ... not his wife, after all?" It was an appalling idea, but it did make some sense. "He did say, didn't he, these assassination attempts began when he decided to take a second wife. And divorce the first?"

Tenai tilted her head to one side and opened a hand, expressing measured uncertainty. "He would not go so far, Daniel, I do believe not. But a second wife would threaten the standing of the first even should she not displace her entirely. Assuredly so, should the second wife bear the necessary son. Such a son would at once supplant the daughter thus far produced. Niah Madalan Kuyad-sa cannot be pleased at this prospect. Yet Mitereh will not suspect her, nor hear a word of suspicion against her. Thus others must consider whether she may be his enemy. She would be uniquely well-placed to be so."

Daniel sat back in his chair, frowning.

"She is said to be a gentle girl," Emelan objected.

Tenai made a dismissive gesture. "All daughters of good families are described so. When they are offended, some become less gentle. Or perhaps she is indeed a tender child, and Mitereh's enemy wears a different face. Perhaps that of Tegaitan Encormiona."

There was a brief silence, as they all turned this second appalling idea over in their heads. Daniel ventured at last, "Isn't he about sixteen?"

"A blood prince of sixteen years is not a child. Young enough, however, that, like the little queen, he will not remember me. He would not know," she touched her own chest, "in his heart, why he should be cautious of me. He would know only tales. And then, many persons so young are impatient and foolish. If this prince should also be also clever and ambitious, well, young princes have been known to strike down their brothers before this. And, mark you, this *is* a son of Encormio. Perhaps he has more of his father about him than is commonly recognized."

"That's horrible," protested Jenna. "This is all horrible."

Tenai glanced at her, the patient glance of a woman who has seen everything and has long since stopped being horrified by any of it. "But both possibilities nevertheless remain."

"Yes, but ... would either Mitereh's wife or his brother have the—the resources, to bring you back here?" Daniel asked. "Young people like that? Wouldn't the king's enemy have had to—to *kill* someone, to bring you back?"

Tenai half-smiled, again with irony rather than amusement. "A wedded queen and a blood prince? I do think either might contrive. Both must have been accustomed to the ways of power from their most tender years. Both must have partisans. Or either might have become the tool of ambition. Indeed, someone must have willingly surrendered his life's blood for this cause. If the young king's enemy is working with Imbaneh-se, no doubt many men there would gladly lay down their lives if by doing so they might drive a mortal blow against the son of Encormio and so perhaps raise up a king from among their own people."

Jenna was frowning. She asked, before Daniel could, "If this other country, Imbaneh-se, wants that badly to be independent, why not let them go?"

Tenai lifted one shoulder in a minimal shrug. "In the days

when Imbaneh-se was ruled by its own kings, that country struck again and again against Talasayan, as the king of the oaken throne wished to bring all lands under his sway. That is not a peaceful country. The boy does well to hold Imbaneh-se in a stern grip. If he were to gentle his hold there, likely enough the peace he treasures would be lost as well. But that is why, if a young queen or a young brother or any enemy of the king looked about for allies, why, allies would surely appear. I am certain Imbaneh-se has placed agents here and about, waiting with smiling teeth for any hint of dissatisfaction they might turn to their gain. Perhaps ready to nudge some young queen or young brother into dissatisfaction, if the chance should come."

Ugly indeed, but not necessarily implausible. Daniel said, "So ... you think Mitereh's wife might be behind all these assassination attempts, so you want to send Jenna and me to, uh, Kinabana, where she is? Does anybody else see a problem with this?"

Jenna raised her hand.

Again, Tenai showed them her narrow smile. This time, Daniel thought it held amusement. "I think the danger is slight, and the possible advantages compelling. I do not trust Mitereh's word of his queen's gentle heart ... but, Daniel, I would accept *your* word."

"Oh." Daniel absently picked up one of the slender three-tined forks provided with breakfast and turned it over in his hand. After a moment, he put it down again. The small click the utensil made against the wood of the table was distinct in the quiet. He looked up at Tenai. "You want me to assess Mitereh's wife for you, and decide whether she's behind all this? That's putting a lot of trust in my personal opinion. Too much trust, Tenai. What if I'm wrong?"

"There's no way he's going to Kinabana!" Jenna put in. "We're not going! You're not thinking of it, Daddy, are you? Honestly, Tenai!"

"Peace, peace, child." Tenai gave Jenna an absent smile. "I would count it a great favor," she went on to Daniel. "I trust no other opinion more than yours, Daniel. But, I assure you, the proposal is not so perilous as you take it to be." She held up one slender finger. "First, recall that I am not fixed on this interpretation. Indeed, by no means does my *first* suspicion fall on the young queen. I believe she would have some difficulty acting from the distance of Kinabana, or from within the close guard of the Terusai. Someone closer to the king might be more likely. Someone older; someone long accustomed to power; someone more able to come and go as he pleases. *Perhaps* the queen may have acted in this, but more likely you will tell me she is not at fault. I *would* accept your judgment, Daniel. I do not think that is too much weight to place on your opinion. But I would listen to everyone's judgment." She looked deliberately from Daniel to Jenna and then Emelan and then back to Daniel.

"Second?" said Daniel.

"Yes. Second." Tenai lifted another finger, "Should this indeed be the queen's hand behind the knife and the bow, well, she must be a fool to strike at you in Kinabana, when everyone must think of her should you die there. For all it seems unlikely, I judge you will be safer close to the queen, if she is indeed our enemy." Yet one more finger lifted. "Third, no one is aiming at you. Emelan is correct: all blows directed toward you are truly meant to strike me. These blows have now been seen to fail. Further, I have taken steps to make it clear to our enemy that no such blow will have the intended effect."

"Assuming that the intended effect is to make you break with the king," Daniel said. "What if that assumption is wrong?"

"I see no likelihood that it is wrong, Daniel. Do you disagree?"

"Well ... no," Daniel allowed.

"No. The intent is clearly to send me mad, that I may fail to consider what I do and thus act as a weapon in the hand of my enemy. I shall not act without due consideration, and this I have sworn even this morning—publicly, before the Martyr's shrine here in the palace. I am persuaded that word of this oath will have spread at once even to the farthest reaches of the city."

Daniel was sure it had. But he was not as sure that any such oath would be enough. Would everyone believe it? Was he even sure he believed it himself?

"I have also put out the word," Tenai added, "that whosoever should spill your heart's blood shall earn the profound enmity of Lord Death. That word, too, our enemy will have heard. This person may hope to evade mortal eyes. But this person will know that he must in the end come before a colder eye that cannot be blinded."

All this was delivered in a calm flat tone that was thoroughly persuasive. Jenna said, "Well, if I were the bad guy, I guess I'd find a different line of work."

Daniel remembered the dark inhuman form that had come into Mitereh's apartment at this woman's call, and nodded. *"That should work."*

"I think it should," Tenai said, in a tone of satisfied malice. "I think my enemy, whosoever this person may be, will yet learn to regret summoning me back to his game-board. Or hers." She gave a little nod and went on, more briskly, "You may consider for some little time whether you wish to go to Kinabana, Daniel. Mitereh desires this and will not hear suspicion of his queen, but he will not *require* anything of you. You may stay here in Nerinesir if that pleases you better. But I think you will likely be safer in Kinabana. Likely our enemy is not the queen. Then you may reside wholly safe in Kinabana, for there is no house so well-guarded as the one held there in the king's grant. And, on your return, you may bear me word of the young queen."

There was a little silence. Daniel said at last, "And if I don't think the queen is the bad guy, will you send me next to have a chat with Mitereh's brother, Tegaitan?"

He thought he was joking. But Tenai said, unblinking, "If I can contrive it, Daniel, I will," and Daniel understood that it wasn't a joke at all. She truly did trust his opinion more than anyone else's. That ... that was a weight he was afraid might prove heavy indeed.

15

Four days later, Daniel and Jenna found themselves back on the road, riding toward the distant coast, escorted by Keitah Terusai-e and a dozen of his men. For the first time since they'd fallen into Talasayan, Tenai was nowhere in reach.

Daniel felt creaky and old and far out of his comfort zone. Lack of sleep no doubt contributed to this, for he had slept badly since the assassination attempt. He would have given a good deal for a car rather than a horse. Better yet, an easy chair rather than a saddle. Best of all, *his* easy chair, in his own living room.

Jenna looked bright, fresh and irrepressible. And how much of that insouciance was real, and how much put on to reassure him, Daniel could just about guess. Probably about fifty-fifty.

High mountains spread away in front of them once they were out of the city. They would follow the river almost due west for a while, then turn north-west once they were out of the mountains and go on to Kinabana. Seven days, maybe as many as nine or ten. Daniel tried not to groan out loud at the thought. No one, not even men his own age, seemed to think anything of a week's ride. A few weeks just weren't enough to knock a sedentary American into shape. And it added insult to injury that the men here *never* seemed to go bald. Daniel ran a hand over his own smooth scalp and sighed.

This was all steep, rugged country. Snow glittered on the tallest peaks. Though along the river it was hot, the breeze that came down from those mountains was cool against the face. The sky past the mountains was a pure, clean blue. Despite himself, Daniel felt his spirits lift.

Jenna might have felt the same way. She began to hum under her breath.

Keitah looked at her sidelong, but two of his men—there were eight altogether—rather shyly taught her a catchy little number that was, Daniel suspected, the clean version. It was all about the nine districts of Nerinesir by torchlight, and it had a lot of repetitive bits that probably had alternate wording. A wink his way told him Jenna also guessed there was a different version.

Then one of the men sang a song about the way the road rolled away from the city and his girl. He had a good, clear tenor voice. Jenna sang some pop song Daniel didn't recognize. She sang it in English; it took Daniel a moment to understand why it sounded strange to his ear. The men were all orienting toward her now, just as inevitably as flowers turning toward the sun. Jenna was enjoying the attention. Emelan looked thunderous.

"Not many travelers," Daniel commented to Keitah.

"Not in these years," Keitah answered, his tone wry. "The ages of war took their toll on the country, you understand, Nola Danyel." He gestured broadly. "All this country is little settled now."

"It's beautiful country. Does the snow ever melt up there?"

"Ah, no, Nola Danyel. Not even in the most brilliant summer. The winds that come down from those heights cool Nerinesir all the year. Kinabana is much warmer. There, flowers bloom in every season."

"Nice," said Jenna appreciatively, drawing her horse closer so she could listen. She raised her voice to speak to Emelan. "Did you grow up in Kinabana, Emel?"

Emelan hesitated.

Keitah answered instead, his tone harsh, "He has never been there. Kinabana was granted to Terusai only after Mitereh became king."

"So families move according to grants from the king?" Daniel commented, stepping in to defuse the sudden tension. "That must be difficult, if you love the house and country where you grew up."

Keitah turned a hand palm-up. "Kinabana is a powerful grant. By custom it is held by the king's close ally, or by his brother or a near cousin, or by a prince when he comes into his majority. I am glad to hold it. In time it will go elsewhere. Perhaps to the king's brother. Terusai's accustomed grant is Kandun and I expect Terusai to seat itself there again one day. That is country more like this." Keitah glanced around, and up at the glittering peaks. "I confess, sometimes I miss the mountains."

Emelan seemed about to speak, but said nothing.

Jenna, evidently giving up on him for the moment, chattered brightly about the quick river and the high mountains and the small twisted trees that grew, bonsai-style, out of the sheer cliffs. Keitah's men taught her two more songs and she taught them a folk song about blackberry jam, translating as she went, that made them laugh and even Emelan smile.

It took nine days to make the journey to Kinabana, traveling at a comfortable pace. Daniel was ready to admit, after the first night's restorative sleep and a good breakfast of bread, bacon and fruit, that with good company and beautiful scenery, he might after all enjoy the trip.

This was especially true as Daniel found that Keitah was often willing to discuss history—both what Daniel had come to think of, with deliberate melodrama, as the Dark Age of Encormio and what he'd tagged Pre-Encormian history. The history of Talasayan and Imbaneh-se and the other, smaller countries here seemed to go back a long way, right back into this world's Bronze Age. "I wish Tenai had worked her literacy spell for me," Daniel said. "There never seemed to be time, and then I gather something about it became politically awkward."

"Indeed," Keitah answered, smiling. "A trifle awkward, for Nolas-Kuomon to work sorcery upon a man in the king's household. Mitereh mentioned this problem to me. I am not such a sorcerer as Nolas-Kuomon; I would never say so. But I have some small skill, Nola Danyel. If you will permit me, perhaps I may work that spell for you once we have come there. Though—no—perhaps not, as our sorcery passes you by, or so I have heard."

"Tenai's gift-of-tongues spell worked fine," Jenna said cheerfully. "Apparently if we say yes, then the spell takes. That's the theory. I'd like to try that literacy spell too."

"Kinabana is a place of calm and quiet. We shall have leisure there for any trials of sorcery you might wish to permit," Keitah promised.

Apparently Kinabana was always the retreat of choice for anyone the kings of Talasayan wished to protect: even Encormio had used it that way when hard-pressed by Tenai.

"Thus Mitereh sent his queen there as soon as word came that Nolas-Kuomon had returned. Niah will wish to rejoin Mitereh as soon as she may," Keitah explained. "Yet no one would wish to be hasty when assassins strike here and there. I regret that a swift return to Nerinesir will likely prove impossible for the queen—though, Nola Jenna, I hope your presence and bright spirits will console her."

Daniel, listening closely, discerned no trace of suspicion in the other man's voice or manner. "I'm sure she's very nice," Jenna said, her good cheer sounding, to Daniel's experienced ear, rather forced.

Keitah made a little dismissive gesture. "Niah is a well-mannered, dutiful child, a good queen for Mitereh. It is most unfortunate she does not quicken with a son."

"Because naturally her only worth is in the children she bears," Jenna said, with a sudden edge. "Excuse me—the *sons.*"

Keitah gave her an uncomprehending look.

Daniel said quickly, "I gather the king can have more than one wife at a time if necessary. Is that something ordinary men can do?"

Jenna rolled her eyes. "Can women have more than one husband at a time?"

That prompted raised-eyebrows look among the men, some of them shocked and others admiring. Daniel suspected at least a few of them were thinking about golden lionesses, although no one uttered the phrase. Keitah, diverted, asked, "And may they so, in your country?"

That was one to keep the conversation rolling for hours, especially as Jenna was perfectly willing to go out of her way to shock the Talasayan people—though she never actually *lied*.

They halted that night only when shadows were stretching out long and the very air itself had seemed to dim. The long curves of the river, scrolling away to the west, still held a little of the sunset light: glints of red and orange and, where it flowed into the shadow of the mountains, violet. Keitah had strolled a little away from the rest of them and stood with his arms crossed, staring out over the river. Emelan, sitting near Jenna, looked that way, and then away. And then back again. Daniel wanted to say, *Go on, then!* But that would certainly be too intrusive. He said nothing and pretended not to watch.

At last Emelan got to his feet and went over to his brother. Keitah turned his head, not otherwise moving, and Emelan hesitated. Then he took the few remaining steps.

"I hope they're okay," Jenna said to her father, watching. Her expression was one of both exasperation and sympathy.

"So do I."

"They ought to be. Poor Emelan. If *I* had a brother—or a sister, I guess—if I'd lost somebody and got them back, *I* wouldn't be snarky about it."

Daniel considered how to reframe the problem for her. "What if you'd had a sister who murdered somebody and had been in prison for ten years? How would you feel then when you saw her again at last? How would you expect your sister to feel?"

"Ah," said Jenna, absorbing this scenario. "Um. Well, yes. That might be pretty uncomfortable."

"It's not easy to build back a relationship that's been broken." Daniel watched the two men. They were standing a few feet apart. Emelan's head was bowed. Keitah said something to him, and he shook his head and turned partly away—then, with obvious reluctance, back.

"And if you did something so awful you wanted to die, something so awful you let your family think you were dead—" he stopped, left it there.

Jenna nodded, looking serious. "I could have asked Tenai to keep him with her."

Daniel picked up a stick and stirred the fire. "No. No, she was right to send him with us. What with ... everything ... I'm just as glad you have a guard, Jen. He's proven himself, more or less. But besides that, well, when you're offered an easy way out, sometimes you just don't have the strength not to take it. If he'd been left in Nerinesir, I don't know that he'd ever have had to force himself to face his brother." He glanced toward the two men again. "I think it's important he did."

It was full dark now, but the fire cast enough light to see Keitah put out a hand toward his younger brother, and Emelan take it, slowly. Keitah drew him forward, not into an embrace, but close enough to grip him by the arm. He said something. Emelan answered, and then they both turned at last to come back to the fire. They didn't sit together, and neither one looked happy, but there was, at least, not quite such an air of stiff constraint between them.

This new ease stayed with them after that. The weather continued fair. The mountains thinned out and opened at last into gentler country; sparse woodlands thickened to real forests, the temperature climbed, and travelers became more numerous.

On the sixth day, the road ran into a broad sparkling bay and divided, the upper branch turning to run along the northwest shore toward Kinabana and the lower diverting off south toward Gai-e, on the border with Imbaneh-se. Emelan unbent enough to draw Jenna a map in the ashes of one cooking fire. Daniel looked over his daughter's shoulder, and Keitah leaned over from his place and drew another line, showing how the river they'd followed the long way from the capital divided to make both the lower Khadur and the broader, slower Tese.

Emelan did not reject this overture from his brother, but added, "The Tese links Talasayan with Imbaneh-se and makes a country that is both at once; the people that live along the river have made a peace of their own and would never welcome conflict."

"We'll hope none of us need endure it," Keitah said quietly.

Late in the afternoon of the ninth day, they finally saw Kinabana ahead of them. It was a comfortable city of white plaster houses and milky-pink and gray tiles. Farms and estates stretched out along the road. Sails were visible out on the water beyond the city. Four ships were anchored near the shore; big ones, with three masts each. Daniel wondered where they went, what they did there, what they saw ... what the shape of this world would look like from the deck of a ship that sailed around it.

Jenna stood up in her stirrups, eager to see everything possible. "Can we see your house from here, Nolas-ai?"

"Nearly. We can see the edge of the estate's grant. You see the line of trees that runs there? That is the lake."

Keitah's house proved to be huge. It sat way off the road, down a long track that curved around through the woods. Then the woods opened out to broad fields or pastures, heat shimmering over the open land. There was a high wall surrounding the house, rooftops just visible over it.

Everything looked bigger the closer they got, the wall going out and out to both sides, the rooftops seeming to spread out and recede at the same time. It seemed to take a long time to come to the gates. The house was all creamy stone, golden in the last slanting light of the afternoon. Jenna slid off her horse without waiting for a mounting block; Daniel pried himself stiffly out of his saddle with a groan and was grateful the block was there.

Keitah waved a hand at servants who seemed to Daniel to have been spontaneously generated from the crushed white stone of the courtyard. "Bathe, rest, ask for any service you desire," he told his guests. "You are weary, I know. I will order a light repast served in your apartment, Nola Danyel."

Daniel nodded.

"Emelan—" Keitah added. But then he paused.

His brother looked back at him. He said after a moment, "I will attend Nola Jenna, Nolas-ai. That is my charge."

"So, indeed. You may do so, if you feel it necessary," Keitah said, with a dismissive little wave of his hand. Emelan's mouth tightened, but he said nothing.

The house was grand outside—and twice as grand inside. The floors were polished marble, the ceilings painted pale blue with birds skimming across them or dark azure with stars. Rich tapestries and graceful abstract statuary adorned the halls. Daniel wondered how the queen's little girl liked this house: it wasn't a place that invited running or shouting. The house itself seemed to whisper a scandalized "Hush!" to the mere thought of any such childish behavior.

Servants guided Daniel and his daughter to adjoining suites of rooms on the second floor, where investigation found steaming tubs of scented water in each bath and an elaborate supper already being laid out in a sitting room shared between the suites. Other details blurred in the face of these attractions.

After her bath, Jenna wandered into the sitting room wearing a robe of pale blue, with pearl buttons all down the front. "Do you have a view from your bedroom?" she asked Daniel, who had just arrived himself. "You can see all the way to the lake from mine. The sunset is great tonight." She hesitated. Then she added, "Emel's insisting on standing guard. Inside my apartment, right by the door."

"Not inside your bedroom."

"No—that would be way too weird. This is weird enough. All these servants! There are guards outside my apartment too—and outside yours. I looked. Keitah thinks there's enough danger from *someone* to make that necessary."

"Hmm." Daniel hadn't realized this. He said after a moment, "I expect he doesn't want to take any risks. Think of the explanations he'd be making if anything happened to us."

"I guess," Jenna conceded. Coming to the table, she took a cover off one of the platters and sniffed appreciatively at the rising steam. "I don't know what this is, but it smells great."

"Duck, I think, in some kind of fruit sauce." Daniel settled into a chair opposite his daughter. His robe was dark gold, with real gold embroidery at the cuffs and around the hem. He said, "No sunset from my windows. But you can see part of the city. It's a pretty town."

"We can ride down to it tomorrow, maybe. After we meet the queen." Jenna sent him a sidelong look and lifted an eyebrow, meaning, *As long as she's not an evil genius. Then we might be in trouble, huh?*

"I doubt it, though," Daniel said, answering that look rather than what she'd actually said out loud. "Tenai didn't actually think it was likely." He began taking covers off the remaining dishes. Everything—tiny dumplings swimming in broth, vegetables carved into flowers, something savory wrapped in leaves secured with bronze skewers—was elaborate, beautifully presented, and delicious. After the meal, servants brought in hot spiced wine. Why they always served hot drinks in a country as warm as this one was a mystery. Though the wine was perfect for relaxing into deep, dreamless sleep when he finally retired to his own room. The soft beds, the first they'd seen since Nerinesir, didn't hurt either.

16

Breakfast the following morning was served in an intimate dining room with a sliding door of woven wood all along one side. The door had been opened wide to let in the morning breeze, fragrant with the scents of honeysuckle and green growing things. The gardens spread out beyond that door, riots of flowers contained by tall evergreen hedges.

As Keitah had promised, both he and the queen joined them for breakfast. Niah Madalan Kuyad-sa proved to be as graceful as a fawn, an impression encouraged by her huge long-lashed eyes and delicate build. She was timid as a fawn, too—or that was the impression Daniel had of her: all eyes and nerves. It was not easy to picture her as an evil mastermind. He felt the knot of tension he'd carried from Nerinesir begin to relax.

"Welcome," Niah said to them both, glancing briefly down and then lifting those beautiful eyes to meet Daniel's. She seemed to flinch a little from his attention, transferring her gaze instead to Jenna. "My women have told me of you." She had a woman with her now, an elderly attendant with suspicious black eyes and a severe expression. "I am so glad you have come here," the queen continued, "though, indeed, I am sorry for the reason. You must tell me all the news of my husband. All the news of—of Chaisa-e. She is your friend, is it so?"

Jenna answered readily, "Yes, Tenai's been a friend of my father's practically all my life." Jenna also glanced at Daniel, eyes a little wide: *This* is supposed to be a bad guy?

"Friends of Nolas-Kuomon! A wonder of the age!" Niah exclaimed in her soft voice, and made a place for Jenna beside her at the elaborately-carved table by the window. Jenna settled into that place with only a trace of self-consciousness. Keitah took a seat on the opposite side of the table, gesturing for Daniel to take the remaining place. Niah seemed shy of Daniel, and, if anything, shier of Keitah. Daniel found himself feeling charmed by and protective of the young queen. He wondered at the feeling: it put him on his guard, because normally he felt that way toward those among his patients who suffered from minimal depression. Could this young woman herself be somewhere in the penumbra of depression? Or was it possible this image was something she deliberately projected? But he didn't really believe that. He was already all but convinced she couldn't have anything to do with the clever, ruthless enemy who had tried, was still trying, to use Tenai as a weapon against the king. He could be wrong, obviously. But he would be very surprised if he were wrong.

The table was laid with graceful wooden utensils as ornately carved as the table, and with square porcelain plates and shallow bowls painted with flowering twigs. A sideboard a few steps from the table held the breakfast offerings. These included a platter of moist nut bread, sliced and drizzled with honey, and one of tiny pastries filled with custard. There was a plate, shaped and decorated to look like a nest, that held dozens of tiny hard-cooked eggs, much smaller than hen's eggs, each stuffed with a sweet creamy filling. A wide, shallow bowl with painted fish swimming around the outside held broth with savory little meatballs. Another plate held little iced cakes decorated with tiny candied flowers. Daniel wondered how early the cooks had been up.

The older woman attending the queen withdrew not quite out of earshot and settled down in a stiff-backed chair at the edge of the room. Emelan retreated similarly, leaving the field to young women who whisked around, serving the amazing food and offering tall narrow cups of a sweet musky herbal tea.

"The view is wonderful," Jenna said to the queen. She gestured to the wide windows. "I've heard so much about the gardens of Kinabana. They look lovely." With an apt instinct, she added, "Your daughter must love them. She isn't here this morning?"

"Inana is with her attendants," Niah answered. Her smile had softened at the mention of her daughter. She added, her shyness easing as she thought of her child, "She does love the gardens. She falls in the lake. She must enjoy it, for she falls in every day. She would be taught to swim if she were a boy. I think indeed that she needs little teaching."

Jenna smiled. "I look forward to meeting her."

The queen glanced at Keitah and then down at the plate in front of her, looking shy again. "Her attendants will bring her to me later in the morning."

Daniel sipped broth from the bowl, as Keitah was doing, and ate a meatball. It was delicious. Both he and Keitah seemed content to let Jenna carry the conversation—maybe they both saw how much easier the young queen seemed with Jenna than with them.

"I'll be glad to meet her, then," Jenna said, happy to chat away about anything with anyone.

Jenna, Daniel thought, had already ruled the queen out as a suspect in convoluted plans to trigger Tenai's rage, assassinate Mitereh, and seize power for herself. Jenna had good instincts about people. He added another tick mark to his mental *not an evil genius* column.

"Does your daughter like it in the city?" Jenna asked the queen. "I don't suppose there are so many lakes to fall into there. It seems so quiet and peaceful here. Do you look forward to going back to Nerinesir yourself? Or will you miss Kinabana?"

There was a slight hesitation, hardly noticeable, and then Niah answered softly, "Kinabana is beautiful, and Nolas-ai Keitah looks after us very well here, but I would be happy to join my husband again in Nerinesir."

"Soon," Keitah assured them all.

"Yes, of course," murmured the queen, eyes on the table.

After breakfast, Niah showed them part of the gardens. They seemed to unroll forever, stretching back away from the house along pathways that ran through a series of clever hedges that drew the eye further into the distance. The lake, Daniel gathered, was outside the main gardens. But there was a pool, with bright little fish flickering through the water. Niah seated herself on the rim of the pool and trailed her hand through the cool water. Sunlight struck bronze highlights from her dark hair. Jenna sat on the gravel path, leaned an elbow on the rocks that edged the pool, and drew the queen into describing the differences between the clothing styles of Kinabana and the capital.

Daniel found a bench a little way from the fountain and settled down to watch the two young women. A persistent aura of sadness clung to Niah. He truly could not believe this was an act. Again it occurred to him that though the little queen might not necessarily be clinically depressed, she might fall under the shadow of the condition. He felt more and more strongly that she was exactly what she appeared: a timid young woman skirting the edge of emotional illness. He wondered whether there was any such profession as psychiatrist here—anything remotely the same—anyone who could help those suffering from real emotional distress. He hadn't wondered that before, but now the question troubled him.

So did the question of whom Tenai's attention might fall upon after he passed this impression of Niah on to her. The king's young brother, of course; and after that? Maybe by then she'd have discovered a more credible suspect.

It was not until a young woman servant brought Inana out to her mother that Niah truly seemed to become happy. The child was a cheerful little thing, nothing pensive or sad about *her*. She was a tomboy, and broke away from her nurse to run and show her mother the bug she'd found crawling on a flower. Niah exclaimed and laughed, but drew back fastidiously when her daughter tipped the bug out on the rim of the fountain. Daniel was too far away to see it clearly, but caught a glimpse of a blocky gold and green form; some kind of beetle, he thought.

"Pretty," Jenna commented, leaning forward to study the insect. She nudged it onto her palm and immediately found herself the recipient of an intense stare by the budding naturalist.

"You could have it," Inana informed Jenna, with hilarious solemnity. "They eat leaves. You could keep it in a wine cup and give it leaves to eat."

"Yes, but," said Jenna, "do you know what kind of leaves it would want? Because usually they only eat one kind and if they don't have that kind they starve."

"Oh!" Inana gave her beetle a worried look, then transferred the look to her attendant. "What kind of leaf?"

"I fear I did not notice," confessed the girl. "We could go look and see if we can discover more such creatures, young Nolasena."

Inana contemplated this prospect. "We could feed it to the fish," she proposed, with quite cheerful bloodthirstiness.

"We could just let it fly away back to its mother," suggested Jenna, stifling a grin. Daniel could see indications that the beetle was preparing to do just that. It had climbed by this time to the uppermost tip of his daughter's finger. And, yep, there it went.

"Bye!" cried Inana, waving. "Back to its mother!"

She was a charming child. It was clear Niah doted on her. Inana darted through the garden like a fish in its pool, but always circling back to her mother. The expression on the queen's face as she watched her daughter was one of the most intense tenderness—quite a contrast to the shy but guarded smile she turned to Jenna or the caution she showed the men. Jenna obviously had picked up on the same thing: she was using the child as a conversation piece, drawing Niah out with a handful of comments and questions about the little girl. How sweet, how busy, did she ever settle down? How intelligent, how curious about everything, did she always bring bugs and twigs and flowers to her mother? What, surely not *every* bug?

"Many insects," said the queen, laughing a little. "But only few flowers. That is Inana: she likes things that move and crawl. She brings me frogs also. She brought me a fish once, in a cup of water. And once a little bird that had fallen out of its nest." She mimed her own cautious, distant admiration of this find. "It did not even have feathers! I did not know little birds could be so ugly! I, too, told her it must miss its mother. So I persuaded her to allow one of the men to put it back."

Jenna laughed, and Niah rose, inviting her for a stroll with a little gesture. Daniel, who could take a hint, made his excuses and let the two young women go off by themselves, which from her shy relieved glance must have been what the queen had hoped for. Well, almost by themselves: a couple of woman attendants and Emelan followed them at a discreet distance.

Daniel would be interested to hear his daughter's opinion of the young queen, later. In the meantime, well, there was this splendid house to explore. He turned back toward the cooler, more comfortable environs of the house to see what interesting things he might turn up there.

One could get used to this life, oh, yes, Daniel concluded. It was a bit like staying in a luxury hotel. Actually, it was a lot like that. Indolent garden strolls in the cool morning, fabulous food, staff to make the beds and lay out towels by an amazingly luxurious tub.

Emelan drilled with Keitah's house guard in the mornings, while Jenna slept in and then breakfasted with Daniel. He hovered a bit when Jenna left their apartment, but not all that closely—another indication that they were expected to be safe here. That, too, made it easy to relax.

The house here also boasted a small but apparently high-quality library. That was almost as welcome as the sense of safety.

Keitah, as the king had suggested, worked the literacy spell himself, for both Daniel and Jenna, early in the morning of their second full day at Kinabana.

"I have many obligations of my own, as I have taken up residence here for only a short time," Keitah explained to them. "I must return to Nerinesir soon, so I must dispose of all my obligations quickly. I will have no choice but to leave you much on your own. Let me do this small service, and then you may avail yourselves of any of the books and scrolls here."

Keitah had already arranged a small but heavy bowl of black iron and a tiny round one of white porcelain on a table in the library, along with a sheet of fine, heavy paper, a jar of ink, a genuine feather pen, a fat white candle in an ornate holder, and a long silver needle. To one side, he had set a white stone ornament. This was oval, about the size of Daniel's thumbnail, with a hole pierced through it as though it was meant to be strung on a chain. To the other side, he set a leather-bound book with a lot of gilt on the embossed cover. The title of the book was, of course, incomprehensible, but pretty, the writing long and looping, with little dots and other symbols above and below the letters.

"Only a little blood is needed for this sort of magic. A drop or two," Keitah murmured, picking up the needle and setting the white bowl down in front of Daniel with a tiny click of porcelain against the polished wood. Daniel and Jenna were both sitting across from him. Emelan was not present; this was the time of day during which the house guard trained and sparred and drilled and so on; early in the morning, before those they guarded required their attendance.

Keitah went on. "Nearly all magic requires blood, as perhaps Chaisa-e explained to you."

"She hasn't explained much about how magic actually works," Daniel began.

"But she's explained that much," Jenna interrupted. "Blood to set the spell—only it's not exactly the blood itself, isn't that right, Nolas-ai? It's the sacrifice."

"The willing sacrifice, indeed," Keitah agreed. "For you and for Nola Danyel even more than for a person of this world, that aspect may perhaps be key. You must be willing to take the spell upon yourselves; is that not the surmise? That is not unlike the limitation the Martyr set into the world, but stronger or sharper or more absolute for your people. So Taranah Barengilan-sa surmises, and I believe she is very likely correct; she is a sorcerer of some subtlety herself."

Daniel hadn't guessed that.

Keitah must have seen his surprise, because he smiled. "I assure you, Nola Danyel. Subtle and powerful. I am a lesser practitioner, but I think my skills should suffice to open your eyes to writing. I give you my word that this working will give you that and nothing else." He was smiling, a wry, somewhat cool expression, but not unfriendly. "If this does not work, then no harm will have been done. If you cannot read written language after today, I shall assign some young person with a pleasant voice to read to you, Nola Danyel, and you may ask Berangilan-sa or, if Mitereh thinks that may do, Nolas-Kuomon, to work this spell for you once you return to Nerinesir."

Requiring someone to read to him would be quite an imposition. Daniel would certainly prefer the spell simply work as advertised.

Keitah took Daniel's hand in his, pricked the tip of one finger with the needle, and caught three drops of blood—four—in the white bowl. Then he carefully tipped one drop of blood out onto the white ornament, then at once the rest into the flame of the candle. To Daniel's fascination, *all* the blood ran out of the bowl, leaving it as clean as though Keitah had poured out mercury rather than blood. The little flame sputtered and burned up. The candle, which had been white, turned red. The white stone of the ornament had also become streaked with crimson.

Keitah took up the feather pen, dipped it into the ink, and wrote several words across the paper with a flourish. "Understand," he murmured. "Comprehend. Let what is written be recognized and known and become familiar." He tore off the part of the paper on which he had written and held the paper to the candle flame.

Then he caught the resulting ash in the iron bowl, crushed this with his thumb, and brushed a smudge of ash across each of

Daniel's eyelids. "Thus the eyes are freed to perceive the written word," he murmured. "If this spell takes hold, you will comprehend the language that burned to make this ash. Here, Nola Danyel, regard this book." He picked up the heavy, leather-bound book "What is the title?"

The scrollwork of the title now made perfect sense. "Being an Account of the Life of the Martyr and His Reign and His Sacrifice," he read out loud. "Wonderful!"

"Indeed," Keitah agreed, smiling. "Well done, Nola Danyel. You have wished to pursue an understanding of our history. This work is largely accurate, or so we adjudge it today. It is yours; I make you a gift of it and the words it contains."

"Thank you, Nolas-ai Keitah." Daniel took the book, which was beautifully made. He was very much tempted to open it at once, but made himself set it aside as Keitah turned to Jenna.

"Nola Jenna, let us make use of the candle while it still burns high and red." He first passed the tip of the silver needle through the candle flame and then held out his hand to Jenna.

Eyes wide with fascination, she gave him her hand. Another little needle prick. Again, Keitah poured a single drop of blood on the white stone ornament, which this time immediately turned black. "Good," murmured Keitah. He repeated the part with the ink and paper and candle. He brushed the ashes across Jenna's eyes as he had Daniel's. Then he pressed out the candle flame between thumb and finger and leaned back in his chair, smiling.

"Thus you are made free of language both spoken and written," he said to them both, and stood, capping the ink and gathering up the bowls and needle, the candle and stone ornament. "I must leave you much to your own amusements this morning and today, and likely tomorrow and perhaps for some few days longer, but now perhaps you may find more to please you in my house. Make yourself quite free of this library. Ask my staff for whatever you wish. Go anywhere you please within the protection of the estate walls. Nola Jenna, I think the queen might be pleased by your company at breakfast this morning." Inclining his head in polite dismissal, he went out.

Daniel re-read the title of the book, then opened it at random and read a few lines of the beautifully handwritten text within. *Thus the Martyr went from that place to Lahara, the land beyond the sea, seeking the teachers of the way of long silence* ... plenty he wouldn't understand until he'd built up more background understanding of history, obviously. But the *words* made sense to his eyes.

Magic was a wonderful thing. This kind of magic, at least. He nodded absently when Jenna explained hurriedly that she'd better hurry if she was supposed to meet the queen for breakfast and dashed out. For himself, he was happy to settle down in a comfortable chair in a corner of the library and turn to the beginning of the book. He suspected strongly that they were wasting their time here, that the trip to Kinabana had been pointless ... but he did feel safe here, even though Tenai was nowhere nearby. Libraries and gardens and far, far less political tension of all kinds. Though it was a shame Taranah hadn't come along on this little trip. Her calm, warm social ... *finesse* was close to the right word ... she was the sort of person who would, just by stepping into a room and murmuring some perfectly ordinary social niceties, smooth out the tension between Keitah and his brother and settle the queen's nerves and so on.

Taranah Berangilan-sa. Mostly the names here were easy enough to pronounce, but difficult to remember. But that one, multisyllabic though it was, stuck in Daniel's mind. He liked the sound of it.

Maybe he could find a dictionary in this library, find out what the -sa suffix meant. That would be nice. An etiquette book, not the first time he'd thought of that. Preferably one that explained all the titles and modes of address and so on. Setting the history of the Martyr aside, he stood and moved to the shelves, scanning the titles. This library wasn't massive, no surprise if books were hand-copied, but he estimated that about three hundred titles occupied the shelves. That would certainly be enough to keep himself occupied for this ... strange sort of vacation, was perhaps a useful way to think about Kinabana.

Jenna also settled in happily, though with much less attention for the books and much more for the young queen. Niah struck Daniel more and more as a young woman who struggled with feelings of loneliness and isolation; who would not argue with or criticize her husband's decision to send her here to Kinabana, but was nevertheless deeply unhappy. Most likely the problem wasn't that Mitereh had sent her here—it was the king's decision to send her here *and* take a second wife. Or that was Daniel's best guess.

He was *certain* Niah could not possibly be any sort of evil mastermind. Especially not when Jenna agreed with him. His daughter liked the queen and felt sorry for her.

Niah gave Jenna a net of pearls and pale amethysts for her hair. "It's not for the country," Jenna informed her father, modeling it for him. "But Niah says I should wear it when we go back to Nerinesir. She *really* wants to go back to Nerinesir." She frowned at Daniel, not angry, but thoughtful. "Big bad guy, yeah, sure. No, there's no way. Niah's sweet, but not, you know, that awful saccharine kind of sweetness, if you know what I mean."

"Barely," said Daniel.

"She's pretty quiet," Jenna added. "Really reserved, you know how people are here. She's different when Inana's with her, though. It's kind of strange how Niah doesn't keep Inana with her all the time."

"Local custom," Daniel offered. "Custom, as they say, is king." He rolled up the scroll he had been reading and began to search through the rest he'd piled up on the table for the second part of the history.

"But she's a queen. You'd think she could break the custom if she hates it." Jenna leaned forward with earnest concern. "And I think she does hate it. But she sticks to it anyway: a visit in the morning and one in the afternoon, and that's it. Niah hates it, but she never tries to keep Inana with her. She just seems resigned to it."

"Mmm." Daniel was listening, but he was also rolling out the next part of the scroll.

"That's actually a good word for Niah," Jenna went on. "Really, if you had to pick just one word for her. Resigned. You know, I wouldn't have thought it of Mitereh. I mean, I liked him. But what does it say about a guy if the one word his wife most brings to mind is 'resigned?'"

"I gather he really doesn't have much choice but to take a second wife," Daniel said. He tapped the scroll. "Uncertainty in the succession can definitely be bad news. You should read this section here."

"Whatever." Jenna dropped into another chair and tapped her fingertips on the table, restless. Not exactly bored, but not happy with Niah's situation, not impressed with questions about the succession, and probably thinking of a handful of choice words to explain her opinion to the king.

"I also found a book on courtly etiquette," Daniel told her. He pointed to the slim volume, which he'd set aside. "You might like that better—and you'd better read the section on royalty before you tell the king what you think about polygyny and privilege." He added, tapping the scroll he'd been reading, "It could be worse. It says here that Encormio sacrificed *his* first wife to Lord Sorrow. That must have been back when human sacrifice would get you power. I don't imagine she was resigned to that."

Jenna said with tart scorn, "You notice it's always the wives who get sacrificed," and went away to rejoin the queen. Emelan, her constant and silent shadow, followed her.

Daniel, his attention caught for a moment by an entirely different concern, glanced after them. What one word would capture Emelan? Quiet? No. Perhaps ... *guarded*. More so here than even back in Nerinesir. His brother's constant presence, maybe. Or Tenai's absence. And how *was* Tenai doing, and when *would* they be recalled to the capital? Maybe Keitah could get them news. Surely he had some kind of magic mirror or crystal ball.

He did—not a mirror nor a crystal ball, but a glass bowl filled with water. "I speak to Mikanan Chauke-sa every day," he told Daniel, showing him the small wrought-iron table on which the bowl was set. "All is well in Nerinesir. Chauke-sa believes the assassin who attempted your life has been apprehended; Chaisa-e is satisfied it is he, so the court is also pleased, though the man does not appear to know who set him on his target. This man has clear ties to the south, so that is as well. I should not have liked to think of Mitereh's heart, had the man been another of his companions."

Daniel nodded. "Has anyone discovered why Iodad might have turned on him? Did this man explain that?"

"Alas, Nola Danyel, evidently not. The man knew little. I think it most likely that Iodad Sonnas-na possessed hidden ties to the south as well. But whomever our enemy may be, he must have few men remaining in Nerinesir, I think."

"At least not so well-placed as poor Iodad," Daniel agreed. "So are we planning to return soon, then?"

"Perhaps. Chaisa-e has assisted Mitereh in gaining assurance for his house guard, and no other men of the guard appear compromised, so all are relieved on that account. I believe that investigations are still progressing in several areas. Still ... yes, perhaps soon."

Daniel nodded and wandered back into history, then found himself diverted by a footnote into a complicated but fascinating treatise on ethics, religion, magic, and madness written by some Talasayan philosopher who'd lived a thousand years ago. A few more days or a week in the warm, comfortable security of Kinabana would be fine.

But a mere two days later, Keitah told them they would leave for the return journey. "Soon," he assured them, smiling. Daniel and Jenna and Emelan were with him in the garden nearest the house; Niah had not come out this morning. "Perhaps even before this morning is wholly past." He laid a hand on Daniel's arm, drawing him aside for what was evidently meant to be private speech.

"So quickly?" Daniel asked, puzzled. "Is there some new problem in the capital? Or here?"

Jenna had run ahead to look at the fish in the pool, and Emelan lengthened his stride to catch her up. Now Jenna was pointing at something in the water, the man leaning over to see. Jenna looked happy, Daniel saw. Carefree. And Emelan was smiling.

Keitah smiled, too; his wry, charming smile. He looked a little tired, and a little distracted. "Not for me."

"I beg your pardon?"

The other man lifted one hand in a gesture like a shrug. "You have no need to do so, Danyel. And it will bring you no benefit."

His tone seemed no different. Yet Daniel halted and turned to face Keitah, the crushed shell of the path gritty under his feet. He was aware, abnormally aware, as though all his senses had been heightened, of the heat of the sun against his shoulders, of the feel of the ocean breeze on his face and the smell it carried, of salt and fish. He knew, as though the other man had dropped a mask he'd been holding up over his face, that it was not the queen they should have suspected. He knew that Keitah Terusai-e was not a friend. Not a friend to any of them.

"Trust is a very powerful thing," Keitah said softly, meeting Daniel's eyes. "And a very dangerous thing. It does not give you power, but gives power to those whom you trust."

Daniel said, not moving, "The king trusts you." He could feel his heart hammer in his chest.

"So he does. Thus he gives me power. But power gained by strength is better than power given by gift, for what is given may be withdrawn, but what is won—" he closed a hand into a fist, "is owned entire. I have now an opportunity to win what I could not have gained under Encormio, Danyel. Though it will be simpler if Mitereh sires no sons. You will assist me in ensuring the young king dies before complicating the matter of the inheritance."

"Mitereh's brother?" Daniel asked. "Isn't he the heir?"

"Tegaitan is a boy. He will require a regent, whom he need not live to supplant. Thus he will become another stepping-stone. As Inana will be useful to me when she is grown, the boy will be useful now. You will also assist me, Nola Danyel."

"Will I?"

Keitah lifted his hand and closed it, hard. Forty feet away, turning happily to say something to Emelan, Jenna suddenly threw back her head and staggered.

Emelan caught her, and then instantly let go, clearly aghast, as she screamed. But letting her go did not help: she was screaming and screaming, as fast as she could draw breath, staggering in blind circles until she fell.

Daniel threw one incredulous look at Keitah and started to run to her, only to find his arms caught from behind by one of the soldiers. "Stop it," he said urgently. "Stop it, please, stop it—" Keitah was just standing there, watching him, and Jenna was still screaming. Daniel, with an enormous effort, stopped fighting the grip of the man behind him and forced himself to meet Keitah's eyes. "Please, Nolas-ai," he said, much more carefully. "Please!"

The soldier released him when he stopped fighting, and he dropped to his knees on the path, wracking his brain for anything he could say, anything he could do, anything at all that would make Keitah stop doing whatever he was doing to Jenna. "I understand, I understand you, Nolas-ai, you don't have to do this, stop it, please stop it—" Daniel's voice rose again, out of his control. He found himself fighting to get words out past sudden, wrenching tears, and his daughter was *still* screaming –

"What will you do for me?" Keitah asked. His voice hadn't changed; he was as calm and pleasant in manner as though they were still strolling at ease in this beautiful garden.

"Anything," Daniel shouted at him, and heard it come out as a whisper. "Anything—"

"Yes." Keitah opened his hand, watching Daniel with narrow concentration. The cessation of the screaming was as shocking, in its way, as its beginning had been.

Daniel lifted his head, scrubbing a shaking hand across his face. Jenna was half-lying on the stones around the pool, Emelan supporting her weight across his knees. She was crying, out loud like a child, in shock as much as pain, Daniel thought; she was not yet aware of where her pain had come from. But Emelan knew. He was staring across the garden at them, horror in his wide unguarded eyes.

Daniel started to get to his feet.

Keitah said mildly, "Did I give you leave?" and began to move his hand.

Without even having to think about it, Daniel flung himself back down to kneel at the other man's feet. He thought bleakly, through the shock that lay like a fog over everything, *So, this is how long it takes to train a man out of thinking he's the equal of kings.* He did not even dare look up, although he wanted more than anything to see Keitah's face, to see if he could read there what the other man's intentions might be. Even knowing he would see nothing there that Keitah did not want him to see. He had never once thought of Keitah as the enemy. No one had. That argued a formidable ability to conceal the mind and heart.

"You may stand." Keitah studied Daniel as he cautiously rose. "You are an interesting man, Nola Danyel. I thought you useful primarily as a tool with which to prod and control Chaisa-e. How greatly mistaken I was! Neither magic nor sorcery touches you, save you give it leave. Yet if you accept it freely, a spell may bind you. Do you even remotely comprehend how great an advantage that could be to you? Or, at least, to me?"

Daniel said nothing. He wanted to grab his daughter and run for the horses. He wanted to hit Keitah. He wanted, with an intensity that was almost pain, to open his eyes and find out all this world and all that had happened in it had been a vivid dream.

"And Chaisa-e sent you to me with a will," Keitah added. "It took very little prompting. A small suspicion, gently sown, to turn her mind toward Niah—that child!—and away from me." He half-turned. "Walk with me, Nola Danyel."

Daniel flung a quick glance toward Jenna. Emelan had helped her to sit on the rim of the pool. She was bent over, her elbows propped on her knees and her face hidden in her hands. Even forty feet away, Daniel could see she was shaking. Emelan was standing at her side, one hand on her shoulder. But Emelan was not looking down at Jenna, but still staring across the garden at his brother, and his face now was blank and careful.

Daniel looked away. He fell into step beside Keitah at the other man's gesture. He did not ask any question, make any plea, shout any denunciation. He did not trust himself to speak at all. He was aware, distantly, that his hands were trembling; that he was trembling all over. He kept his eyes on the path under his feet and tried to steady his mind to some semblance of order.

"You," said Keitah Terusai-e, "Will do a small task for me. Take this from my hand."

He offered Daniel a familiar little ornament, made of black, polished stone, now strung on a thin gold chain. The ornament had been white before Keitah had let fall on it first a drop of Daniel's blood and then a drop of Jenna's blood. Daniel had never even wondered why Keitah had done that. The man had offered no explanation regarding any part of that spell. The part with the words written and burned had seemed plausible, and Daniel, assuming magic was obscure and puzzling, had not asked about the rest.

Even if he had asked, he knew he would have believed whatever smooth assurance Keitah provided. He had never met a man who lied so effectively and so comprehensively.

"Take it," Keitah said softly.

Daniel held out his hand and let the other man tip the little ornament into his palm.

"So long as you wear this pendant, Nola Daniel, I will hear every word you speak and every word said to you or in your hearing. That is what you gave me, when you gave me your blood and accepted the words I set within the pages of my gift to you. Do not think to write what you would say; I will hear words you write as though you spoke them. Show it to no one; I will know if any gaze but yours falls upon it. Put it on."

Daniel obeyed. His fingers felt stiff and clumsy; it was hard to fasten the catch. Keitah waited patiently. Daniel felt no different after the pendant was on. Though the chain felt cold against the back of his neck, the slight coolness of the stone warmed against his skin and became unnoticeable. He asked, "What is it you want of me?"

The lord of Kinabana smiled. "Danyel. Can you not guess? I want you to kill the king. If you do so secretly, that will do. If you strike him down in the sight of all men, that will also do well."

The hot air seemed very still; the morning breeze had died. Somewhere a bird called. The splash of the fountain was just audible in the distance. Jenna was not, thank God, crying any longer—at least not loudly enough for Daniel to hear her. None of Keitah's men were within earshot. Keitah himself was standing with his hands tucked into his belt and an attitude of perfect composure, watching Daniel.

Daniel knew he himself did not look half so self-possessed. He said at last, "Even if I would—stop, please, don't hurt my daughter!" Keitah, looking at him narrowly, lowered his hand, and Daniel said as earnestly as he could, "Nolas-ai, I'll try. Of course I will. I'll *try* to do anything you want. But I'm not a ... a soldier, not any kind of ... of assassin." The idea was so utterly ludicrous that Daniel could hardly make himself say the words.

Keitah smiled. "Anyone can kill a man who trusts him. This is not a difficult task for a man of reasonable wit. I am quite confident you will contrive. Consider, Nola Danyel: all Mitereh's magical and sorcerous protections are for you less than cobwebs strung across your path. He favors you—he is curious about you for his own part, and he favors you both for your sake and to please Tenai Chaisa-e. He has permitted you to enter his presence freely; that will assuredly continue. I am certain you can contrive."

Daniel was certain he could, too, if he had to. He felt ill—literally sick, as though he might throw up. Pride he had not even known he possessed made him clench his teeth. He found himself putting on his blandest, most professional face, and was surprised he could.

"You will return to Nerinesir. Tell Mitereh that the little queen is ill—nothing dangerous, but a cough and a touch of heat in the wrists and forehead. Your daughter stayed with her, and both lingered in Kinabana to wait for the queen's vigor to return. Your daughter will come to Nerinesir in a handful of days. The king will be patient."

Daniel nodded. He understood that Keitah meant that he'd

better deliver the news in a way that ensured Mitereh would indeed be patient.

"You will do your task; and why not? What is Mitereh Encormio-na or Talasayan to a foreign man who owns no king? Chaisa-e is your friend, you aver; well, she will not mourn a son of Encormio, and why should you care one way or the other? Do this for me and I will pardon you, should you yet live, and at midwinter I will escort both you and your daughter back to your proper domain. I will fill your hands with gold from Kandun and your daughter's hands with pearls from Patananir. Or fail me, and I will put your daughter's voice into that stone you wear so that you may listen to her scream her way into Lord Death's kingdom. *That* was the spell she allowed me to set upon her."

"I understand." Daniel's own voice sounded distant to his own ears.

"Of course." Keitah nodded down the path to the gate, where, Daniel saw, men waited with horses. "Go, then. The weather is fair; the roads will be good. You will have a pleasant seven-days journey on which to decide what you will do."

Daniel took a step backward, and paused. "You don't ... you don't have doubts about what I'll do?"

"No," said Keitah, smiling. It was hard to decide whether the smile actually looked harder and more ruthless than it had previously, or whether that impression was due simply to a better understanding of the ambition that lay behind it.

Daniel turned toward the gate, and then hesitated. He glanced at the fountain where Jenna still sat—her head was no longer propped in her hands, though, and she had uncoiled from her hunched posture—and then at Keitah.

"No," said the lord. "You need not delay. Your visit has honored my house. I have delighted in your company. But I must insist that you allow neither the bonds of hospitality nor the beauty of Kinabana to delay your anticipated return to Nerinesir, where I know both Mitereh and Chaisa-e wait impatiently to receive you. You will see your daughter again the sooner if you are prompt about your task. Indeed, I shall expect no less."

Daniel wanted to protest, argue ... at least delay. He did not dare. He bent his head to hide his face because he could feel the professional bland expression he wore wanting to crack and fail. He said helplessly, "Don't hurt her. Nolas-ai. Please."

"Give me no reason to doubt you, Nola Danyel," said Keitah Terusai-e. "Be discreet, and then be swift."

Daniel cast one last look at his daughter—he could see that she had turned her face his way; he saw her start to get to her feet—if he hesitated at all he knew he would try, despite Keitah's plain order, to go to her—he turned sharply back toward the gate instead and walked away. Leaving his daughter behind, in the hands of an enemy. The chain weighed against the back of his neck as heavily as though he bore a great weight at his throat and not merely a little stone pendant.

The road south along the coast and then inland to the Khadur river and up into the mountains to Nerinesir was exactly the same: plenty of spectacular scenery and comfortable inns. Keitah's men were perfectly polite … but they were his guards now. Daniel wondered whether they knew what Keitah Terusai-e meant to do. Was doing. Most of these men were old enough to remember the great wars that had stretched on and on until the old king's death; they had enjoyed sixteen years of peace since. They had names and families and lives; did they know their lord was angling to start yet another war to try to take power in this land? Would they approve, if they knew?

Some of these men probably had daughters. Would they approve of torturing young women to force men to do as their lord demanded? Daniel remembered, bleakly, the stories Tenai had told about this land and all its wars, and thought they might. Men in those years had been so accustomed to brutality. Had sixteen years of peace taught them to let go of those memories? To be kinder in their dealings with the world?

Not that he could ask them in any case for help against Keitah. Or ask anyone. Daniel rested his hand on his shirt above the pendant Keitah had given him and tried not to shudder. He could not forget for a moment that Keitah might be listening to anything he said. It was incredibly inhibiting. Was he going to be able to act normal in Nerinesir, wearing this chain? Well, he would have to. No choice, no way to bear failure, with Jenna still trapped in Keitah's house. He closed his eyes for a moment, consumed by a wave of longing for home, for a safe civilized life in a safe civilized nation that had never heard of magic, never endured a centuries-long war between an immortal king and his remorseless enemy …

he almost imagined he could open his eyes and find himself in his own house, waiting for Jenna to slam cheerfully through the front door and shout a greeting. But no. Unlikely as it seemed, they were both really here in Talasayan, caught between their friends and their finally-recognized enemies, with no hope of getting out any time soon.

What would Jenna be doing now, prisoner as she was? At least Emelan was with her—*was* Emelan with her? The man had been shocked and horrified at what Keitah had done to Jen; Daniel didn't think he was wrong about that. Emelan couldn't be deep in his brother's plans or confidence or whatever, could he?—because he'd been completely estranged from Keitah for the last decade. So *Emelan* at least had to be sincere in everything he'd said and done right from the beginning.

Daniel had believed Keitah intended to try to build a new relationship with his brother. Daniel had thought *well* of him for it. He tasted bile, and thought he might throw up. He wanted to spit on the road and didn't dare, because it might raise the wrong kind of questions in the minds of his escorts.

Might *Niah* be able to protect Jenna?

The two young women had seemed to become friends. How much of that had been sincere? Daniel tried to remember every nuance and shading of meaning and inflection in Niah's manner, in her conversation. Had there been any special secrecy, any hidden tension there? He could not tell. All his memories were colored by his current knowledge; he doubted all his previous assessment of the little queen.

Was it possible that Niah was not even Keitah's hostage and prisoner, but his willing partner, and Tenai's first guess about her at least half-right? Keitah had implied otherwise. But Keitah might have meant to deceive Daniel on that point. If Keitah had lied about that as about so much else, Daniel probably wouldn't have been able to tell. Whether Niah was imprisoned or duplicitous, Jenna probably could look for little help from the young queen.

Daniel shuddered again. He remembered Tenai describing how she had heard the voices of her husband and son screaming for days out of a letter the old king had sent her. And he had thought her description of that horror *symbolic*. Symbolic, hell.

Immune to magic. Except magic specifically accepted. Daniel had been glad he and his daughter had that protection. Protection, *hell*. Keitah had certainly had no trouble getting Daniel to accept the literacy spell, and everything else that came with it. How *easy* everything had been for him.

They traveled fast enough this time that Daniel ought to have fallen into exhausted sleep every night. Instead, he lay awake for hours in unfamiliar beds when they stopped for the night at an inn, or wrapped in blankets under the stars when there was no inn. He would stare into the shadows under a roof or into the depths of the sky, equally blind in each case. The bone-deep weariness of too many days' travel in a row was first endurable and then actually welcome: his exhaustion prevented him from thinking about killing the king. About walking with an actor's smile past all of Mitereh's guards, through all of the king's magical wards and protections. With what? A knife?

The king was probably a trained warrior. A young soldier. And Daniel himself was no longer young and never athletic. He had never in his life even been in a fist-fight. He rubbed his hands hard across his eyes, and then his forehead and smooth scalp, wanting to swear. He didn't dare do it, even in a whisper.

If Mitereh were truly taken by surprise, if an assassin were quick enough, then neither his youth nor his training might matter. Daniel imagined the feel of flesh parting under the point of a knife, of bone grating against metal. He imagined the astonishment in the young man's eyes as the knife went home. Could he do it?

He knew, with a surety as complete as his love for his daughter, that he could not.

That surety came to him like a gift. Like a kind of inward freedom.

He did not have to plan an assassination. He did not have to imagine how a knife would feel in his hand. It was not necessary to imagine the shock Mitereh would feel as he died, because Daniel was not going to kill him.

How many days until he arrived back in Nerinesir? Daniel had lost track. It seemed this road had been rolling out under the hooves of his horse forever, with all his companions men he did not know and could not trust.

Four more days, five? Four or five days to plan—not an assassination, but how to avoid doing one. With a constant spy he did not dare remove hung about his own neck like an albatross, and everything to lose.

But he knew with absolute certainty that he was not going to murder Mitereh. He wasn't going to let that smiling bastard Keitah Terusai-e torture and murder Jenna either.

There was a third choice. And he was going to find it.

Death's Lady

Book 3:

As Shadow, a Light

1

The pain was so strong, so intense, and so unexpected that when it hit, Jenna lost all thought and awareness. She did not know she was screaming; if she had known, she would not have tried to stop because the pain drove her past caring what impression she made or whom she frightened. She was not conscious of pain as a thing outside herself; she was not really conscious of herself as a person at all, with a past that went back before pain began and a future that might extend somewhere outside of pain. All that existed was pain and terror.

Then it was over. Jenna found herself limp on the paving stones, with a man's broad shape bending over her and her head cushioned on his knee. She clung to him in mute desperation, shaking—she was crying like a baby and could not stop—the man was not her father. For a long moment, she didn't know who he was. Then she knew, in a vague way. Emel, right, this was Emelan Terusai, whom Tenai had set to guard her. But she wanted her father. She tried to get up. Emel held her. He was saying something to her. She didn't understand him, but there was an urgency to the way he held her that made her stop fighting him. She let him gather her up—he was very strong, big, his hands went almost all the way around her arms, she hadn't realized before how strong he was. He set her on the edge of the fountain, and splashed her hands and face with the cold water.

"Emel," she said. Tried to say. It came out in a cracked whisper. They had been in a garden. In Kinabana. At Keitah's house in Kinabana, in Talasayan. She knew that. She remembered that. What had happened?

"Hush," Emel was saying. He sounded upset. Well, she'd been hurt somehow. She didn't remember how, but probably that had upset him. She was still shaking. The sun on the back of her neck felt strong enough to press her down to the stones again. The cold water helped. She rubbed her wet hands across her face. Was she still crying? She thought she wasn't. She tried to speak. Where was her father? Her vision seemed uncertain. She peered around, looking for him.

"Hush," Emel said again. "Hush. Nola Danyel is over there, with ... with Terusai-e. Try to breathe a little more deeply. You are well. It is past."

There was her father. With, right, Keitah Terusai-e. Jenna tried again to get to her feet. Again, Emel wouldn't let her. She stared at him, at last feeling her wits jar sharply back to order.

There was no pain now. She couldn't even remember what it had felt like. Just that it had been awful. But it was over, leaving her wrung out and exhausted, but fine. She was stiff all over. But basically she felt okay. And her father was talking to Keitah, over near the gate and now that her vision had cleared, she could see he didn't look happy. He looked *awful*. He kept looking over at her, quick little glances like he didn't dare take his eyes off Keitah for more than a second.

"Emel," she said, and was startled at the fragility of her voice, "what happened? What happened to me?"

The man answered, his rough voice sounding strained, "Terusai-e put pain on you. It is something he can do. He does it sometimes to punish. This time ... it is clearly Nola Danyel at whom Keitah strikes."

Jenna stared at him. "Why?" That had been a stupid question. Pieces were falling into place, inescapably. "I guess we know now who the king's enemy is. Not Niah. Obviously." The young queen had struck Jenna as timid and sad from the first moment she'd met her. She'd immediately decided the suspicion that Niah might be working against her husband was ludicrous. But she sure hadn't jumped from that to suspecting *Keitah*.

As far as she knew, *no one* had suspected Keitah Terusai-e. Not her father, not the king, definitely not Tenai, because there was no way Tenai would have sent Jenna and her father to Kinabana if she'd guessed. No *way*. He must have covered his tracks *really* well.

Jenna looked at her father again, where he stood with Keitah. She swallowed hard.

"Nolas-ai Keitah will be angry if you foul his fountain," Emel said, his tone flat.

Jenna took this as simple advice and nodded. She hadn't thought herself still so badly thrown by ... the thing Keitah had done to her. The thing that ... if he had done once, he might do another time. She swallowed again. "I thought we were immune to magic," she said in a small voice. "Daddy and me."

"Yes," Emel agreed, his tone flat. "Save enchantment you accept freely. I think my brother may have offered you some small enchantment, a kindness, something you took willingly from him, from his hand ..."

"The *literacy* spell." It wasn't a question. The second she thought of it, Jenna was sure. She'd thought that *was* just a kindness, offered because things had gotten so rushed and weird and Tenai hadn't had the time or opportunity to do it. She hadn't thought anything of it.

Keitah had worked that spell on both of them. On her father as well as Jenna herself. She stared across the garden. Her father looked all right ... upset, scared, but all right. But who knew what Keitah had done to him? Or might do, later?

Emel rubbed a hand across his mouth. Then he dropped his hand and straightened his shoulders, bracing himself. "I failed you."

That made Jenna look at him. "You didn't. You weren't there. You were ... I think you must have been drilling with Keitah's guardsmen that morning. My father thought it was all right—he said the *king* told him it was all right. He *said* that. He said Mitereh said Keitah could do the spell for us."

She tried to stand up. It took her two tries, and even then she might not have made it except that Emel set a hand beneath her elbow. Jenna felt sick. Not from what Keitah had done to her, not from the pain. From ... just everything.

As soon as she was steady, Emel let her go and answered, his tone bleak. "And so I failed you. Had I been standing at your back as I should have been, I would never have let you take enchantment from my brother's hand."

"You wouldn't? You *knew?*"

"No—I did not know, but I should have thought of the possibility there might be peril for you in such an offer—"

"Well, I don't know why you should have been so special. If the king didn't guess and Tenai didn't and my father didn't, why should you? You hadn't been anywhere near your brother for *ten years,* Emel!"

He started to say something else, some kind of protest, but Jenna didn't listen. She was staring at her father, who, as she watched, turned and walked away, quickly. Stiffly. Toward the gate, where horses were ready. Most of the men were already mounted and waiting. Her father didn't even look at her. One swift glance, but then he looked away again and let one of the men hand him the reins of a horse and offer a knee to help him mount.

Her father rode away, out the gate and down the road and away, leaving Jenna behind, in this sunlit garden that no longer seemed at all peaceful or pleasant. She watched him go, feeling stunned in a way the pain alone had not produced.

Emel said, tentatively now, "He would not leave you freely."

"No," Jenna agreed. She didn't try to explain that this made it worse.

Keitah was coming toward them. Jenna braced herself. She had no idea what to say. She felt fragile and stupid and frightened.

She didn't have to find something to say. Emel spoke first. This time he spoke in a cool, hard tone that was nothing like his usual manner. "I believed you a friend of the king's, Nolas-ai."

Emel looked, Jenna thought, ten years older than he had ten minutes ago. More like his brother. But a lot grimmer. Keitah never looked grim. He always looked smooth and calm and thoughtful and thoroughly civilized. Even now, it was hard to believe he was a bad guy—*the* bad guy—the enemy who had brought Tenai back to this world in order to use her as a weapon against the king. Who now obviously meant to use Jenna's father as a weapon, somehow.

Keitah merely answered, his tone mild, "He believes so as well. Tell me, Emelan, what opinion does Nolas-Kuomon have of me? Does she also trust me? She must, surely, to send these people of hers into my keeping. Or is this some manner of ruse? Tell me everything you know."

"I am her dog, not her confidant, Nolas-ai."

"Ah." Keitah was silent for a moment. He said then, "You are my brother."

"No."

Keitah said pleasantly, "Repeat that statement, and I will take you at your word."

"I am no brother of yours, Terusai-e."

"I agree, then. You are nothing of mine and nothing to me." Keitah turned his attention to Jenna as though that exchange had been completely unimportant. He *still* seemed for all the world like a perfectly friendly, civilized person. He said, "Your father will do a small task for me, Nola Jenna. You are here to see that he does it. But so long as he obeys me, you need have no fear. I have no desire to harm you. Indeed, I find you most interesting and pleasant company."

Jenna began, "I think I would prefer to spend time with—" Emel closed a hand on her arm so hard it hurt. She stopped.

Keitah lifted an eyebrow at his brother.

"Forgive the young nola," Emel said, still in that flat tone. "She is young and impulsive, and she has been raised to be bold, Nolas-ai."

Keitah studied him. "You protect her?"

"As is my duty, Nolas-ai."

"Should the young nola require protection from me, *you* assuredly cannot provide it."

Jenna thought she had better step between them right this minute. She said, as politely as she could, "Nolas-ai, please. Could you tell me what you did to my father?"

Keitah made a dismissive gesture with one hand. "Did to him? Very little. Frightened him. It is what he will do for me that is important to me."

"Murder the king," said Emel, not quite a question.

"Yes, I know that." Or if she hadn't exactly guessed, it was obvious the instant someone else put it into words. "But why my *father?*"

Behind Keitah's back, Emel made a small gesture at her: do something, Jenna thought. Do what? Oh—do something distracting. She was perfectly willing to, and took a step forward and sideways to draw Keitah's eyes. Keitah was saying, "Because Nola Danyel can, I believe—"

"You God-damned evil bastard," Jenna said distinctly, and spat on the ground by his feet.

Keitah stopped dead.

Behind him, Emel flicked a sharp little knife from some hidden sheath into his hand, took a step, and delivered a short hard blow up toward his brother's kidney. Jenna heard his grunt of effort as he made the strike, and the way the sound changed when the knife hit something other than cloth or flesh and skidded off sideways. Keitah, twisting around, caught his brother's wrist in a firm grip and turned, using his body and hip to force the younger man down. Emel, on one knee, struck hard with his fist against Keitah's leg, a blow which skidded off just as the knife had. Rather than breaking his brother's wrist, Keitah let go his hold and stepped back, lifting his hand. Emel, still on one knee, checked himself and froze where he was.

Jenna, perfectly placed to deliver a kick, only just managed to stop herself from trying it.

"I confess I am astounded," Keitah said, sounding no more than exasperated. "A man once of Terusai, striking at *me* in favor to an Encormio scion! It is a wonder of the age. Surely God in his brilliant Kingdom is amazed at the happenstance! Renounce your oath to Chaisa. Give over this strange enthusiasm you have for unsuitable loyalties. I will permit you to bind yourself again to this house—your own house!—and to me. Would this not be preferable?"

Jenna said tartly, "Preferable exactly how? *Tenai* doesn't slink around betraying people who think they're her friends!"

Keitah, eyes narrowed with anger, began to turn back to her. Jenna glared at him. But whatever Keitah might have done, Emel interrupted him by getting swiftly back to his feet, saying harshly, "Surely God in his Kingdom is indeed amazed at the sight of the Terusai. Oath-breakers both, men without honor in their words or—"

Keitah's mouth tightened. He made a slight movement of his hand, and his brother stopped at once, dropped back to his knees, and said quickly, but even more harshly, "Your prisoner begs you will pardon his insolent tongue, Nolas-ai."

"Prisoners of mine would not dare speak so," Keitah snapped, biting off each word. "So I see you still consider yourself my brother at the end of all."

"You mistake me. I am Chaisa's dog, and none of yours."

Emel got back to his feet once more, color high in his face—pride, Jenna thought, or fear? He was terrified of Keitah. She was sure he was. She thought now Emel had always been afraid of his brother. Probably he'd said, like the rest of them, that as the king trusted Keitah, so he must be trustworthy. Probably he'd wanted to forget any doubts. In fact, Jenna thought, he had been *ashamed* of his doubts. So of course he had not said anything to her or her father or even Tenai. He had probably not even admitted his fear to himself. But she was sure she saw that—now that it was too late.

Keitah said, biting off each word, "Shall I then have you chained in the kennels with my hounds?"

There was a pause, during which Jenna gradually realized that Keitah meant the threat literally. Then Emel bowed his head and said in a much more subdued tone, "Forgive my unwise temper, Nolas-ai. I ask you to relent."

Keitah let his breath out and made an impatient gesture. "You are grateful to the one who found you in your chosen death-in-life and lifted you out of it. I understand this. But to strike at me! I will not have a dog of Chaisa's here in my house save in chains!"

Emel nodded as though this made sense. He tilted his head toward Jenna. "Then say I am hers, Nolas-ai. Why not? You have shown I am no threat to you."

Keitah stared at him a moment, and then laughed. "As indeed you are not. Very well. That will do." He sounded now considerably amused. "As you say. Dog you may be, but dog of this foreign lady. Very well! Show Nola Jenna back to her apartment and stay with her there, if that pleases you, Emel. I shall send for her later. Or for you."

That last sounded like a threat to Jenna, but Emel murmured "Nolas-ai," very meekly, took Jenna by the arm, and led her firmly toward the house.

She went, not without a backward look. "What about my father?" she asked under her breath.

Emel gave her a little shake. "Forget impatience. Forget pride. Think carefully what you would know and think again what you dare to ask, and then ask *very courteously*. If Keitah has a use to make of you against an enemy, he will be ruthless. Remember always that he does not permit defiance."

"I get that," Jenna muttered. And then, *"You sure defied him."*

"I thought I might have a chance to end everything with one stroke. I was twice a fool. I had forgotten he would be warded against steel, against violent attack. Come inside, Nola. Better if you are out of his sight."

"Better if *you* are, I bet! After what you said to him. Fine, we both said stupid things. You because I did first, I know that, and you were protecting me. Thanks." And, at Emel's startled look, "I'm not *blind,* you know. It's obvious you said those things to him to get his attention off me. That was dangerous, I guess. I mean *obviously* that was dangerous, so thank you."

"I—it is my duty to protect you," said Emel.

His tone was strange: angry and subdued at once. Jenna thought he was probably still in shock. *She* sure was. "And a bitch of a job that's turned out to be, huh?" she said.

They entered the house and Jenna headed without argument back toward the apartment in which she had stayed quite happily just last night, when everything had been *fine*.

Two guards stood before the door, as they had since Jenna and her father had arrived at this house. She had learned to barely notice them. She'd taken them for a courtesy. Their presence no longer seemed like a courtesy, that was for sure. She lifted her head and walked straight between the men, pushing open the door and stepping into the pretty sitting room. They let her in, but stopped Emel and searched him with thorough care, taking his sword and several little knives. From his stiff calm while they did it, that might be an insult. As well as potentially inconvenient.

Emel came in at her back afterwards and shut the door. He stood in front of it, looking stiff and cold and maybe uncertain. "I must beg your forgiveness," he said at last.

Jenna stared at him. "Why?"

"I will not be able to protect you. I will try, Nola Jenna. I will advise you and guard you as well as I can, but my brother will do as he pleases and I will not be able to prevent him."

"No, how could you? No one could. Unless Daddy slips a message to Tenai." *That* would sure take care of Keitah. Jenna would *love* to see Tenai ride into Kinabana like the Dark Queen and stab Keitah about a million times with that sword of hers. Obviously Keitah must think he could stop her father from telling Tenai anything. Probably by threatening Jenna. That was a depressing thought. She said instead, "I thought you weren't his brother. Aren't you my dog? Why 'dog' anyway?"

Emel grimaced and rubbed the back of his hand across his jaw. He seemed even bigger than usual in this pretty room with its delicate chairs, but it was the hard despair in his eyes that made him really look out of place. He said after a moment, "I misspoke. As for the other ... brigands on the road are called curs. Such a man might get a master and reclaim honor, if he is fortunate, and then he would be a dog. So I am Chaisa's dog. Or yours." He held up a hand at some expression Jenna hadn't even known she was showing. "Nola—if I am your dog, I am nothing to Terusai-e. I ask you not to deny me."

"No," Jenna agreed. "All right. I get that. I don't like the term and I won't use it and I wish you wouldn't either, but fine. You don't owe me any kind of apology. I get that too. Of course you can't protect me, not when we're stuck here, his prisoners. He's too powerful." So they had to get out of this house and out of Kinabana. That way Keitah couldn't do anything to her and couldn't threaten her father with her. Getting out was absolutely crucial. As fast as possible.

Jenna walked across the room and looked out the wide window. Opened its shutters. Looked down. It was a long way to the ground. There was a ledge one might put a foot on, but it was a pretty narrow ledge. She asked, "If you hadn't distracted him, would Keitah have hurt me again? Because I was rude to him?"

"I think he might have done so, Nola."

"Huh." Jenna wandered away into the next room, which was a

dining room. There were several windows in this room, one with a big tree outside it.

Emel had followed her and now stood in the doorway. "There will be enchantments on the windows, Nola, so that no one may climb through without raising an alarm."

"Oh." Jenna turned and studied him. "I bet I could. But, yeah, not you, I guess. How about the doors?"

Emel was looking thoughtful, reminded again that most of the time, Talasayan enchantment wouldn't work on Jenna. "There are men on the doors. The windows might provide a better manner of exit, Nola. But they would come after you at once."

"You can't go through the windows. Only two men on the door. Or would they be impossible to attack, like your brother?"

"Unlikely, Nola. That is an enchantment one is not likely to find on common soldiers. I do not know that I could defeat two well-trained men quickly and quietly enough. More would come if an alarm were raised. The gates will be well-guarded. The walls will be tightly warded, but again, Nola, perhaps not against you."

"Huh." Jenna glanced at the angle of the sun. Early. Hours of daylight yet. She wondered how long it would take her father to get back to Nerinesir. And what he would do once he got there. What *would* he do, to protect her? Surely he wouldn't actually try to kill the king.

Jenna wandered away again, further into the apartment, into another sitting room. The windows here were higher and offered nothing better than the ones she'd already checked out. She turned back to Emel. "Look, if we got out of this house, could we get back to Nerinesir without being caught, do you think?"

"If we could escape from this estate, and from the immediate area of Kinabana ... perhaps. Nola Jenna, I cannot battle a way out for us through all the guards and wards of this house!" Emel leaned forward earnestly, his deep voice dropping further. "You saw them disarm me! And I am only one man. I would be caught, probably killed. Then *you* would be caught, and I warn you, *Keitah is a ruthless man*. You do not want to incur his anger. Nola Jenna, you would risk more than pain. I have seen him cut the foot off a man who tried to run from him. I have seen him chain men in his kennels—did you think that mere threat? It was not. The man was left with the hounds for more than a year."

"I didn't think it was just a threat." Jenna wanted to know why the man had tried to run from Keitah, but she didn't ask because she didn't want to encourage Emel to dwell on it. She said instead, "Look, Emel, that's *my father* he's sent off to *murder the king* for him, or if that's not the plan, then it's probably something even worse! There's *no way* I'm going to let Keitah do anything awful to Daddy! My God, do you think I'm just going to sit here and wait to see what happens? That's *Tenai* in danger and *your* king and I know you're scared of your brother, I understand that, I'm scared of him too, but don't you see we can't just sit around and be captives and wait to be *rescued?* Because what if nobody rescues us, what then, huh?"

Emel looked away from her. He weighed twice what she did and he was nearly ten years older, but he was scared. So scared he wanted to curl up into a little ball and wait for things to get better all by themselves. She understood that perfectly. Only she didn't think they *could* do that. She knew she couldn't.

But then he turned back to face her. More, he came close and dropped down to one knee. "You see more clearly than I," he said, his gritty voice low. "Very well, Nola. I am willing to try. I will accept the risks attendant on the trial. I can take a sword from one of these men at your door and kill them both ... maybe I can do that. But there will still be many other men. I cannot fight them all, Nola, and when Keitah comes, I can do nothing against him."

Jenna sat down in the nearest chair, finding her knees suddenly shaky and her hands trembling. "All right. All right, then. Look, why don't you sit down and tell me about this house. The whole estate. Just what are the obstacles in our way? Come as close as you can to describing absolutely everything. All right?"

There was a clap outside the door, dimly audible even from this interior room. Jenna leaped to her feet.

The clap proved to be one of the guards, looking impatiently polite and bearing a message from Niah Madalan Kuyad-sa.

Jenna glanced at the message and looked up again at once. "Of course I'll come," she declared. She wanted to speak to the queen, in fact. She wanted very badly to know whether the queen was also a prisoner. And if she was, whether she knew it. And why in *hell* she had let Keitah get away with whatever he was doing—for what, months? At least months, instead of doing something useful. She was the *queen*, and she hadn't been able even to slip Jenna or her father a note under the table? She waved briskly for Emel to come and headed for the door.

"Nola—" he started.

"The queen asked only for Nola Jenna," said the guard.

"So? Nolas-ai Keitah specifically acknowledged that Emel is mine, so what's the problem?" Jenna tried to sound brisk, and snagged Emel's arm on her way to the door, at which he yielded and came with her. The guard shrugged and evidently decided not to worry about it, which was a relief. Emel was her ally, probably the only one she could find in this house, and she wanted him with her.

Up three flights of stairs and down the long gallery to the very end—just yesterday, Jenna had lingered in this gallery to admire the porcelains displayed here and the huge painting of Kinabana that hung above them. This time Jenna barely noticed either. She was interested only in the apartment at the end of the gallery. There were guards on that door too. Like the guards on her own apartment, they'd always been there, but she hadn't really noticed them before. She noticed them now. They looked stern and professional. Each had a short sword and a knife; normal equipment for the house-guard. How many guardsmen did Keitah Terusai-e have, anyway? Lots, probably.

Within the apartment, Niah Madalan Kuyad-sa was sitting, surrounded by her women, in her accustomed chair by the wide windows. The view over the gardens was, as always, beautiful. Today Jenna noticed mainly that the windows overlooked the fish pool with its fountain, and that they gave one a fine view of the main gates. She crossed her arms and gave the queen a narrow-eyed stare.

Niah rose to her feet and came half a step forward. She was wearing a silvery-gray gown that fell straight down to her feet and a belt set with pearls and lapis; her fine dark hair was dressed with more pearls. She looked beautiful and distressed and very young. "Nola Jenna. I beg you will forgive my weakness."

"You were watching," said Jenna. She didn't feel very forgiving. "You knew what he was going to do. You really did. And you sat and chatted with my father and made friends with me and *never let on at all what he had in mind*. My God."

"Please," said Niah, coming forward a small step and holding out her hands, "you must understand, Terusai-e made threats. Against my Inana. He said he would cut off her hands and her feet. What was I to do? All these women are his spies." She rounded abruptly on the ladies, who were looking shocked at all this open truth. "Go away! Go out! What is there to report now? Everything has been done according to the will of your master. There is nothing left for you to do."

The women fluttered out, and for the first time Jenna was able to see—or thought she was able to see—the falsity they were hiding behind their looks of distress. Only one remained: the stern older woman called Merai, who had always been with the queen. She gave Jenna a forbidding look and Niah a stern one and settled in a chair almost far enough away to be out of earshot. Jenna had thought her a particular friend of the queen. She saw now that the look was not the look of a friend. And Niah did seem desperately in need of a friend.

Jenna said, "Cut off her hands and feet? He wouldn't really do that to a little girl?"

The young queen drew a shuddering breath. "He said that he would. I thought that he would. So he said I would have to deceive you for days. So you would trust everything he said and give yourselves into his hands. What else could I do?" She was gripping her hands together tightly.

Well. That was awful. Jenna leaned against the windowsill. "We think he probably sent my father to kill your husband," she said, watching the queen's face. "Emel thinks that's probably the plan."

Niah seemed to take this in rather slowly. For a moment she only looked at Jenna without apparent comprehension. Then she said, "It is as well, then, that I wear the ashen colors of mourning. But ... but Mitereh is a man grown, and Inana is only a baby. My husband must look after himself. Inana has only me to keep her safe. So." She rubbed the tips of her fingers delicately over her eyes. Then she looked up again and added, "And your father ... I am sorry. If your father does as Terusai-e demands, he will surely die, and if he refuses, you will probably die, and indeed, I am very sorry, Nola Jenna. But I must protect Inana."

Niah *ought* to take her daughter and run—or stab Keitah in the kidney when he turned his back on her—but Jenna sighed because obviously both ideas were hopeless. Actually, she couldn't think of a lot the queen could have done. Except surely there must have been a way to *warn* them.

"Why does Terusai-e make your father his weapon?" Niah asked.

"We think, because magic doesn't affect us the way it does you."

"Does it not?" Niah nodded, looking very tired. "Yes. He would find a way to use any such difference. He is clever, is Keitah Terusai-e, and turns everything to his hand. And everyone. Will he do it?"

This time she meant Jenna's father. Jenna shrugged. She was sure he wouldn't.

"Of course he will," said Niah. "Terusai will tell him he will cut off your hands and feet. So he will see his only true duty is to you."

That ... could be true. Jenna said nothing.

"They let me see Inana in the morning and in the afternoon."

Niah veered back to thoughts of her daughter with the inevitability of a compass pulled to the north. "The girl who looks after her is kind. Inana is not frightened here." She herself was clearly very frightened. "Is it true what the women say, that your servant is also a Terusai? Keitah's brother?"

Jenna glanced over her shoulder at Emel, who stood expressionlessly just inside the door. "Yes."

Niah reached out and took Jenna's hands in her own; her hands were slender and graceful, but her grip was urgent. "Please," she said in a low intense voice. "If he asks his brother, surely Keitah will let me see Inana more frequently. Even let me keep her with me. Now that he has made your father do as he wishes, perhaps he would promise not to harm her? Can you not ask your man to beg this for me? Would he do it? Keitah might listen to him where he will not hear me. I would be so grateful."

This, Jenna realized, was why the queen had asked to see her. She said gently, "Emel isn't on good terms at all with his brother. I don't think you want him putting your case to Keitah. I'm really sorry. Really," she added, seeing the desolation in Niah's dark eyes. "I'll ask him to do it if he thinks it might work. I'll do it myself if I think I can get Keitah to listen to me. But I don't think you'd better depend on it."

"I would be so grateful," Niah repeated, but not as though she expected anything, now, to come of it. Wretched exhaustion hid behind the smooth façade of her delicate well-bred face, perfectly obvious once you knew it was there.

They did not stay long after that. The young queen had made her plea and that was all she had wanted to say. Jenna didn't want to linger; Niah's desperation was painful and anyway Jenna wanted to think.

2

Once she and Emel were back in their apartment, Jenna told him, "I don't think you can ask Keitah any favors. I told her probably you couldn't. Surely he wouldn't really cut off Inana's hands and feet, though?"

Emel was standing near her chair—standing because apparently it was not right for a man like him to sit with a woman like her, and Jenna didn't know how to make him forget all this stupid propriety stuff and sit down like a normal person. "Would he?" she added uncertainly.

"At Antiatan," Emel said slowly, "I was a young man in my brother's house-guard. I was rising seventeen, and he near forty—you understand, my mother was our father's second wife. I admired my brother fervently. Antiatan was my first taste of war. Terusai was still in Kandun then, not Kinabana, but men already looked for greatness from Keitah. He was ambitious. He had won respect from Encormio and from Tenai Nolas-Kuomon both. He spun an important part of the web that drove Nolas-Kuomon out of this world and into yours." He paused.

"But?"

"But I saw him do that to a man, during the campaign to drive Nolas-Kuomon to Antiatan. The man had a woman, a woman of no family ... the man failed of his duty. He did fail," Emel added. His gritty voice roughened further with the memory of horror. "He failed to obey orders. He was an officer and his whole company failed to hold where they should have held, and Nolas-Kuomon nearly broke away to the west. Keitah ... Keitah had the woman's hands and feet cut off. The officer was not married to her, but ... well. So." He looked up, met her eyes grimly. "So Keitah might do such a thing. Inana is only a child, but the woman was innocent of wrongdoing also."

Jenna took a breath. "What happened to the woman?"

"Ah." Emel looked down, and then up again to meet her eyes. "The officer sent her to the dark kingdom of Lord Death, and then himself followed her. The army mustered by Terusai was renowned for its good order."

"I bet." Jenna thought about this. "We can't leave her here. Either Niah or Inana. We have to take them with us."

This statement seemed to strike Emel voiceless. He stared down at her.

"How can we leave them here?"

"Even allowing we can escape ourselves," Emel said harshly, "we surely cannot do so with a three-year-old child, even leaving aside the queen. Niah is not strong. Did you not see how worn she has become? But she is like an eagle on the fist compared to her child." *Are you a fool?* he did not quite ask.

Jenna knew he was right. She scowled. "She might not agree to try, anyway. She's all wrapped up in trying to, I don't know, placate Keitah, keep a low profile ... she's so afraid for Inana it hurts. But ... I can't stand to leave them here."

"Unless you have a way that we may fly from this house as eagles fly, I cannot regard the matter as urgent," Emel said, in about the first sarcasm Jenna thought she had ever heard from him. She scowled some more.

He stared back at her, brows lifted over tawny eyes. "You declare you will try to escape. Well, I will help you as well as I can. I think the effort will fail, but perhaps God will favor us. Should that be so, you will serve the queen as well as anyone could if only you carry word of Keitah's treachery to the king. We can pray to the Martyr to give her a shadow of his strength, and to God to protect her. There is nothing else possible to do."

"How many men between here and the main gates? Or the garden gates?" Jenna demanded, tacitly conceding the point. How could they leave poor Niah here with her little girl? How could they take her? What if they left them here and Keitah cut off Inana's hands and feet? What if they tried to take them and got caught, would Keitah cut off everybody's feet?

"Two on this door, two at the main stair, two at the main door of the house, four at the main gates, four at the garden gates," Emel answered promptly. "The main gates offer a better chance to obtain horses, however." He tilted his head at her, challenging her to come up with a way to do it.

"The main stair isn't the only stair," Jenna said aloud. "And the main door isn't the only door. Right?"

Emel opened a powerful hand, conceding the point. "Two at your door, and the ones at the main gate. All armed and well trained. And I unarmed."

"But you can get a sword or whatever from one of the guards on the door," Jenna said thoughtfully. Four guards at the gate, though. Four was a lot.

"Or perhaps we may try a different way, so that I do not need a sword," Emel said, "Enchantment does not touch you. You, if not I, can go through a window. You do not need to go through the gates—you can go over the wall. Thus you will find no guards in your way. Steal a horse from some farmer, or trade a bauble for one, and ride across the land as the falcon flies. Cover your hair and stay away from the eyes of men—you can be in Nerinesir in ten days, twelve days, even if you keep off the roads. Then Mitereh will know what goes forth from this house and Keitah will be faced with both his king and Nolas-Kuomon, armed with understanding, and all will be well."

What breathtaking optimism. Jenna said tartly, "You might ask yourself how I'm supposed to avoid people for twelve days as I flounder around in country I don't know. In case you haven't noticed, I'm the most recognizable woman in the whole country. At least, I sure haven't noticed anybody else with really light blond hair! Do you think I can keep ahead of Keitah's men? He'll have people way out in front of me in hours because they can use the roads and I can't and the first person to see my face, never mind my hair, will know exactly who I am. Well?"

"Tell the people you meet who you are, then, and ask for their aid."

"Sure," said Jenna. "I've always wanted to depend on the kindness of strangers while I'm running away from a crazy man who'll cut my feet off if he catches me."

There was a stiff silence.

"I alone cannot fight a way for us out of this house," Emel said, enunciating very precisely; his harsh voice gave the words a tone of finality. "I will try, Nola, if you wish it, but I warn you a second time and a third, the chance is very small."

Jenna blinked. "Ah. Well. Actually … Emel, I think maybe there's something you haven't quite realized. About me. Um … you do know my father's been friends with Tenai all my life, almost, right? Don't you know she's been my martial arts teacher since I was about six?"

This time the silence was not stiff. "You can use a sword?" Emel asked at last.

"Um. Tenai started me on swords when I was thirteen. I'm not … she said I would never be really good, but that I wasn't likely to meet anyone really good either. In my country, she meant. People don't fight with swords there. She showed me knives. I've never … you know, actually *used* a knife. I mean, to cut somebody. But I *could*," she added fiercely. "A sword or a knife or whatever it takes."

Emel regarded her, his expression unreadable. "From six to thirteen, what did you learn, if not the sword?"

"Martial arts, of course! You know. Martial arts! Karate and stuff?" Some of those words were coming out in English, which Jenna hadn't realized at first. Those words didn't translate, obviously, which explained why he didn't get it. She went on, listening to herself to make sure she spoke the right language. "I mean, a kind of fighting without weapons. Look," she jumped to her feet and held out her left arm, "Grab my wrist. Or throw a punch. Go on, go on!"

Emel rubbed a hand across his jaw, where the faintest shadow of beard-stubble was starting to show because he hadn't shaved this morning. "Nola—" he said. Then he lifted one shoulder in a minimal shrug and threw a punch, just as she'd asked.

He made it fast and hard, but the only thing that made the blow difficult to handle was that he was aiming to miss her face by a *mile*. So instead of stepping well inside the punch and getting in close, Jenna followed the punch to the outside, caught Emel's wrist in an X-block, folded his hand into an inside wrist lock while twisting around under his arm in a move that put her behind him, and kicked him behind the knee. It was almost a simple self-defense number thirteen except for the first block, very quick and easy. He wound up on one knee on the floor with his right arm pinned behind him. Jenna brought her left elbow down sharply to touch his neck just behind his head and whispered, "Kia! You're dead." She let him go.

He got to his feet slowly, rubbing his wrist—Jenna had tried to be careful, but wrist locks were dangerously easy to overdo; she'd never had her own wrist broken but she'd seen it happen twice to other people. Then he just looked at her silently for a moment. Finally he grinned, an unexpected expression that lit up his honey-colored eyes and made him suddenly appear much younger. "By God and the Martyr! No one will expect *that* of you, Nola! I see we may indeed do as you say and fly this house. Tonight—this evening."

"Wait." Jenna stared at him. "Tonight?" She had imagined they would spend a day or so getting ready. Somehow. Collecting supplies. Hiding food. Stuff like that. She found that the idea of trying to put her plan into action this very night terrified her. What if they hadn't thought of something important? What if Keitah were coming to talk to her and happened to be in the hallway? What if she couldn't actually do what she'd promised Emel she could do? It occurred to her for the first time that when she'd whispered *you're dead* she had been promising to actually *kill* somebody. She swallowed, and sat down quickly.

Emel didn't seem to notice her sudden attack of conscience. Or was it nerves? "Yes," he said. "Tonight. Keitah will not expect that at all. He will think we are huddled in the dark thinking of him and being afraid. He has set guards, he has set wards, he will not think we will try them. Probably he will be scrying to watch your father. Nola Danyel is important to him. Not you, nor I. So, tonight. I will distract the guards at the door and you will strike with the speed and skill of Nolas-Kuomon—"

"Wait," said Jenna. "I have a better idea. In fact," she felt herself starting to smile and could not stop even though she was trying to be serious and conscientious, "in fact, I think we can use this particular trick twice."

It was a good trick, Emel agreed. Once he'd said so, Jenna immediately found herself doubting it would actually work. There were a lot of men in this house, trained men, soldiers. Against just her and Emel, and they didn't have the strength of ten even if their hearts were pure.

Jenna paced from window to window, studying the gardens visible through them and the plan of the house, as well as she could make it out. She tried to think through the plan and find a way they could get Niah and Inana out, too. She and Emel were the good guys, right? Good guys ought to be able to come up with a way to rescue a maiden imprisoned in a tower—wasn't that what good guys were *for*? She paced some more.

"You will tire yourself," Emel pointed out, which was true. "We cannot make the attempt until close to dusk. You should rest." He had overcome his scruples about propriety enough to sit down on a low couch. He looked calm. He couldn't be as calm as he looked, surely.

Jenna sat down in a chair that had seemed comfortable yesterday, squirmed, tried to relax, and jumped up to pace again. "I can't," she said to Emel when he looked at her.

He got up and walked away, into the bedchamber, and came back with a pillow, which he tossed onto the couch. "Lie down."

"I can't *sleep!*"

"Try."

He looked so patiently expectant that Jenna felt compelled to at least sit on the couch. But she couldn't lie down. She was too tense. She kept listening for voices, for steps. She kept thinking Keitah was going to come in and know everything they'd been planning because he'd had the room magically bugged—she ought to have thought of that earlier.

"Chaisa taught you to fight?" Emel asked her.

"It was mostly just for fun," Jenna said nervously. What if she couldn't do it for real? Emel would think she could, she'd said she could, what if she froze up at the last minute?

"Surely there could be no a finer teacher."

"What? Well, yeah, she was ... "

"You will do well. All will be well. Be still. Think about your breathing. Think about training, the steps, the patterns."

"Like counting sheep," Jenna said skeptically. But she swung her feet up onto the couch and thought about basic form one. Downblock, punch, downblock ... she ran through the sequence in her mind, from the beginning to the end, and then started on basic form two. Emel was right. She could feel tension easing out of her shoulders and neck. Basic form three ...

A touch on Jenna's shoulder brought her awake and she sat up, blinking around in alarm even though she didn't immediately remember why she should be alarmed. Emel was standing by the couch, not looking at her. He was looking out the window, where the sun was sliding down toward the horizon. Jenna remembered everything all at once and bit her lip.

But she could hardly back out now. Sighing, she climbed to her feet.

She slipped through the window in the first sitting room just at dusk, when shadows would confuse the vision of anyone who happened to be watching. The ledge was awfully narrow. But the carving along the window sills gave her something she could cling to. Just. She edged along the ledge, wishing rock climbing had been on her list of hobbies for a few years. The evening that had seemed so still from inside the apartment seemed much breezier from a perch thirty feet up. She tucked her face down against the wall and edged a step along. Another. Reached for a bit of carving. Touched it with the tips of her fingers and hopped quickly along the ledge to get a hand on it, and then clung for a moment to recover her balance. Negotiated the corner—that wasn't so bad, actually, because there was a lot of carving at the corner. Almost there. She was so glad there wasn't far to go. Just ... there.

She clung to the next windowsill along with relief, wanting to wipe sweat off her face but not daring to take a hand off the sill. She bent her forehead against the sill and listened instead. She couldn't hear anything. Emel thought there shouldn't be anybody in this antechamber. It was one of the rooms that belonged to the next apartment along and nobody was in it—they were pretty sure. She still couldn't hear anything. The shutters on this window were hooked on the inside. A credit card would have been handy to slip through the crack and lift the hook. She used a stiff pin Emel had found instead. It was meant for ladies' hair, he said. There had been some in the dressing room, fortunately, since Jenna didn't wear her hair in a style that required pins. For a moment she thought that either the pin would bend, or that her grip on the sill would fail and send her toppling backwards. Then the pin caught on the hook and she lifted it quickly and shoved the shutters back.

She did not breathe again until she was over the sill and tucked down on the floor of the antechamber. Then she did nothing *but* breathe for what seemed like an hour but was in fact probably only a minute or so. That had been a lot worse than she'd expected. And this was only the very first step in their daring escape. She'd have been tempted to call the whole thing off and creep back to her room to wait for the rest of the world to solve their problems for them, except that would have meant a trip back along the window ledge and no way was she up for that.

All right. Forward. Gathering herself to her feet, Jenna tiptoed to the door. It wasn't locked. Or guarded. Because the guards were down the hall and around the corner at *her* door. So this was fine.

She strode boldly down the hall and around the corner.

She was wearing the kind of boy's clothing women here wore if they wanted to go riding or whatever. But she'd made sure the clothing was on the tight side, and left her shirt unlaced. Jenna wasn't all that well-endowed, but she was pretty sure that if she lifted her chin and took a deep breath nobody would mistake her for a boy no matter what kind of clothing she was wearing. And men were so distractible. She lifted her chin, took a deep breath, and walked straight up to the guards, who stared at her in deep startlement.

"Nola—" one began, undoubtedly meaning to go on, *How did you get out here?*

"Good evening," Jenna interrupted him. "Would you get the door, please?"

The guard, still bemused, turned and put his hand on the door latch.

Jenna took one sliding step closer to him and did a jump side kick right into his exposed kidney. And pulled the kick, reflexively, just as though she was doing exchange fighting against a partner who wasn't wearing protective gear. The kick still landed, but without the snap that would have done real damage. The guard grunted in pain anyway—or surprise—she'd been precise, just not powerful. Too late to do it over—you could never do it over—she let the impact bounce her back, spun, found the other guard stepping toward her, and did a jump back kick that he walked right into. This kick *was* right, and he folded up and went to his knees, the breath well and truly knocked out of him. Then the door was open and Emel was there, but Jenna was already spinning to deliver a simple roundhouse kick to the side of the guard's head, since he was on his knees and an easy target. She thought the kick might knock him out, but she felt it break his neck. Her stomach clenched. Oh, *God*. That was what it felt like to break somebody's *neck*. She hovered, unable to move forward or back, but then Emel hit the first one in the throat and it was over.

So fast. Jenna, panting with exertion and shock, took a step away and turned her back to the man she had killed. He was dead. She had *killed* him. She was shaking. Two men. They hadn't known they were going to die, they had thought they were going to stand their shifts and go home to their wives, and they were dead. And if she dwelled on it, the whole thing might well be all for nothing. Oh, God. Keitah would catch them and cut off their feet. *And* make her father try to kill the king. No way to stop. No way to change her mind.

Emel had dragged the men into the apartment and shut the door again, which might buy them a few seconds if somebody came by. He had a sword at his belt now, and a sheathed knife, which he put into her hand. He looked grim. "Stairs," he said, and nodded down the hall, and Jenna ran after him when he headed that way, hooking the knife to her belt as she ran.

The staff used a steep narrow stairway that ran down along the west wall of the house and came out near the kitchens. There was a girl with a tray on the stair, who stared at them in shock as they ran past but didn't try to stop them.

"Will she give an alarm?" Jenna asked Emel as they ducked across a landing and ran down more stairs.

"Probably not at once," he answered, and they caught their balance at the bottom of the stairs and strolled boldly right through the kitchens like they had a right to be there. Jenna snagged a round of cheese as they went past one table, and Emel grabbed a couple of soft rolls and grinned at the baker as though this theft was their whole purpose in coming to the kitchens. He lost the grin as they slid out the kitchen door into the side yard. He murmured, "Keitah's guests are certainly free to come into the kitchens if they please. But they may know we are no longer guests. Along here, Nola, quickly."

Emel had tossed his rolls into the bushes to free his hands, and Jenna reluctantly threw the cheese after them. She bet they regretted the loss of the food later. She hoped they would have a chance to regret that. They ran side by side along the hedge that lined the kitchen yard. Then quick through a gap in the hedge and out into the gardens proper. The gardens seemed a lot bigger at night. And they seemed to have a lot of things to trip over. It was really dark. The moon wasn't even up yet.

"The wall," Emel whispered, grabbing Jenna's arm suddenly and drawing her into the even darker shadow of the main wall. "Do you know where we are? The main gates are *that* way, the main courtyard *that* way, the barracks over there, the formal gardens there …"

"Right," Jenna whispered back, nodding as she got everything sorted out in her head. "How far away are the gates, do you know?"

"Eighty rods, a hundred perhaps."

"Whatever," Jenna muttered. "How high is this damned wall? Give me a boost."

The big man knelt and put his hands together. Jenna put her foot in his palm.

"Ready?" Emel saw or felt or intuited her nod, because he stood up smoothly, throwing her upward. The top of the wall was perceptible, barely. Jenna's hands smacked down across its broad flat surface and she thought much too late about broken glass and barbed wire, but the top of the wall was smooth. Right. Right, because people couldn't come over it, because it was warded. Yeah. She swung herself up to lie along the top of the wall and looked down the other side, where the drop looked twice as far as it had coming up. Great. Down anyway, to hang by the tips of her fingers, and a quick push outward, and let go.

She dropped, hit the ground, and let herself fall onto her back, tucking her chin and slapping the ground with her arms to help absorb the impact. It still hurt. She swore softly as she got back to her feet, but everything seemed to be working. Okay. *Which* way were the gates? Right.

Inside the wall, Emel would be heading that way. How long would it take him to get there? Four guards. With horses. But not mounted or anything, Emel had assured her. Trust an ex-brigand to notice details about how a house was guarded. No, the guards would be standing, two on each side of the gate, with the horses saddled and bridled and tethered near at hand. Which would be handy. If they could get them.

Jenna slid up to the gate on her belly for the last twenty yards, got a good look, and muttered a soundless curse under her breath. There were five guards. Well, probably five wasn't much different than four? Two were standing alertly on the far side of the gates, the other three talking together on the near side.

"God," she muttered, and then changed it to "God and Martyr, look after desperate fools," on general principles. Well, at least the gates were standing open. Emel had sworn they usually were and probably still would be. Keitah was being a bit overconfident. She *hoped* he was overconfident.

Then she slipped backwards far enough to get out of sight, stripped down to her underwear—the undergarments here were a bit more modest than normal American underwear, so that wasn't too bad. She dropped the rest of her clothes where she hoped she'd be able to grab them again real quick, pressed through the bushes, and ran down the road toward the gates.

She knew when the guards saw her because of the sudden silence. Two of them stepped out in front of her and she ran right into one of them, forgetting until it was too late that she was supposed to try for an officer if there was one—she hadn't even tried to look. Oops. She clung to the man who'd caught her and threw a frantic look back over her shoulder.

"Nola—" said the man, in a tone of considerable confusion, pushing her away with one hand and peering into the darkness behind her.

Jenna hoped Emel was in place. No time for second thoughts, no time for fear, no way to change her mind, too late to do anything but go all the way and do it right—Jenna grabbed the guard's hand in both of hers, turned to set her elbow against his and hyper-extend his arm, twisted her body to force him to his knees—the only sound he made was a startled gasp of surprise—and drove her elbow down against the back of his neck, just as she had demonstrated for Emel. Only this time she overrode all her trained reflexes and did it *hard*. The shock jarred all the way up to her shoulder and the man crumpled without a sound.

"Oh!" she exclaimed, jumping to her feet and stepping toward another of the guards. "He fell! Is he all right?"

This actually stopped them for a second. None of them had yet tried to draw a sword. They looked startled, bemused, faintly alarmed, but not yet really upset. All four of them were still there—nobody had tried to go for help. They didn't yet think they were going to need help. Two of them were still looking at her *breasts* instead of her face. Men were such *boys*.

It was easier to kick barefoot than wearing boots, as she'd had to earlier. She'd trained both ways because Tenai had insisted, but mostly barefoot because of the mats. So when she kicked a man in the knee, it hurt her foot, but it was a good, precise kick. It was weird not having an opponent simply step back from a plain side kick, but he didn't at all, he just fell, and she kicked him in the throat as he went down, a roundhouse kick, and let the impetus of the kick spin her around. It would have put her in a great position to do a jump back kick, but nobody was close enough, so she did a really aggressive wheel jump back kick instead because there was a man in front of her in range for *that*. Her aim was a little off, she got him in the hip instead of the belly, and he staggered but didn't fall, and she heard the scraping sound of swords being drawn, finally, and she landed and spun and punched the man in the chest, which was totally useless except he grabbed her wrist, *thank* you, and she did self-defense number three and slammed her elbow against the back of his neck, not hard enough and she did it again and he went all the way down and didn't move.

It took a moment to get up again and turn back to the fight, and then longer to figure out what was happening, and by that time, Emel was killing his second guard and there was nobody left to fight. The horses were pulling at their tethers and rolling their eyes and Jenna ran to get her clothing, leaving Emel to check the three guards she'd hit because she didn't want to know whether they were alive or dead, she really didn't. She got the pants on, and her boots, and ran back to the gates still pulling on her shirt. Emel was up on one horse and had another by the reins, and God, he'd *killed* the other two horses, which she hadn't expected and maybe that was why it bothered her more than seeing the men lying there. He had a pouch in his hand, she didn't know what, but he tossed the contents across the road between the gates and reined around, bringing her the horse he led. It was a scramble to get in the saddle, the horse was a tall one, but she flung herself belly-down across the saddle and heaved herself up and grabbed the reins and then it was down the road and she found she was laughing wildly. Or crying. Or both. She couldn't tell.

There were no shouts behind them.

3

The journey from the coastal estate of Kinabana to the capital city of Nerinesir took about a week. Six or seven or eight days; maybe more. Daniel had lost track. He had been too angry and terrified, and then too exhausted on top of the anger and terror, and those days blurred one into the next. The pendant Keitah had forced on him never screamed aloud in Jenna's voice, but Daniel couldn't help but listen all the time, straining to hear anything from the pendant. He couldn't help but listen even though Keitah had absolutely no reason to torture her. Daniel was doing exactly what he'd been told, so far.

In Nerinesir, in the court, in his tightly guarded palace, the young king waited. Mitereh Encormio-na—Mitereh son of Encormio. Mitereh Sekuse-go-e, who had taken his mother's name, rejected his father's history, and set his own life at hazard to make a fragile peace with Tenai Chaisa-e, Nolas-Kuomon, lady of Lord Death. Mitereh knew he had an enemy. He knew that Tenai was not that enemy. He certainly knew *Daniel* was not his enemy. He trusted Keitah, too, unfortunately. He would never in a hundred years suspect that one of his most trusted and important advisors and allies had set Daniel up as an unwilling assassin.

Daniel hardly believed that himself, even now.

He'd had a week—six or seven or eight days—to come up with a foolproof plan that would let him fake an assassination attempt. Something realistic enough to fool Keitah and keep Jenna safe, but subtle enough that the king wouldn't realize anything had happened. Poison in a cup that accidentally got knocked over before the king could drink from it; that seemed possible. Or adding something to a cup that might seem like a poison to Keitah, but was actually just a mild emetic. That was about the best he'd come up with so far.

If Daniel had access to a reliable pharmacy, that might have been easier to arrange. Since he didn't, he would have to make careful inquiries about available medicines and poisons. Keitah would hear any such inquiries through the pendant, as he would hear anything Daniel said and anything anyone said to him, see anything he wrote. The thing was a kind of magical spyware as well as a threat and a goad, but in this case, that might be useful. Daniel needed Keitah to believe in the veracity of the attempt, so asking about poisons might be useful. But he would also need to keep his questions subtle enough not to make his guilt obvious after Mitereh fell ill. That part would probably be difficult.

Other possibilities seemed even more difficult.

Perhaps Daniel might get Mitereh out on some balcony and fake a stumble that threw the king toward the edge, make it look enough like a deliberate push to fool Keitah, but like an accident to everyone else. Balconies tended to have railings, so that was a problem. A rooftop might be better. If he could somehow get the king to join him on a rooftop. Making absolutely certain Mitereh didn't actually fall … Daniel would have to just make sure of that. Somehow.

Probably faking a push would be safer than feeding the king poison and risking a more violent drug reaction than anticipated. A little safer. Maybe.

Thoughts like that, plans like that, did not make the journey to Nerinesir more comfortable. Even though he never heard his daughter screaming through the pendant.

Then they were there, riding through the outer city and the inner city and the court, right to the palace. Daniel was glad to lose the guards with whom Keitah had surrounded him, but keenly aware that those guards had never been necessary. The pendant was all the guard Keitah actually needed. That was true even when he let a young man escort him directly to the king's personal apartment, then into an antechamber, and finally—only moments later—into the king's presence. That pendant was like having Keitah looking right over his shoulder every minute.

Mitereh looked well—bearing up under the pressure of knowing enemies plotted against him. He was obviously pleased to hear that his young queen had become friends with Jenna, and plainly suspected nothing at the news that Daniel's daughter had just voluntarily decided to stay with Niah in Kinabana.

"No doubt you consider this cautious choice wiser, in these troubled days," the king said. "I believe your daughter would be safe to return to court, but I cannot disapprove your caution, Nola Danyel."

Mitereh had been at a table, examining papers; Daniel was not surprised to find the king's aunt Taranah Berangilan-sa present as well. He knew Taranah was an important figure in Mitereh's court. The first time Daniel had met her had been within moments of the king returning to the capital with Tenai—here remembered almost solely as the terrifying lady of Lord Death—in his train. Taranah had instantly laid out all sorts of political maneuvers to help Mitereh persuade people to accept Tenai. Probably she had prepared the majority of these papers, whatever they were about.

Taranah smiled a greeting of her own, her silvery eyes warmer than seemed likely for eyes of that odd color. But then, Taranah's warmth would shine through any chance of nature or rank. Daniel found himself almost more off-balance facing the king's aunt than the king: Taranah was at least Mitereh's equal in perceptiveness, and old enough that she was probably even harder to mislead. Daniel made himself meet her eyes and smile in return. He hoped necessity and will would make his own expression seem natural rather than strained.

"We have found the assassin who so outrageously struck at you and Nola Jenna," said the king. "And I believe we have confirmed the loyalty of all my personal guards. So I am increasingly confident of your safety, Nola Danyel, or I should not have permitted your return to Nerinesir."

"Keitah and I thought—it occurred to me that my presence here might be helpful. In bringing any other assassins out into the open, maybe."

This halting speech did not sound convincing to Daniel, but Taranah said, "Bravely thought, Nola Danyel," and the warmth of her smile increased a notch.

"Indeed," agreed Mitereh, nodding to his aunt. "But, I do believe, unnecessary. We must await developments, but I suspect we shall find no further difficulty. There cannot be a great many assassins remaining in the hand of our enemy; indeed, the man we seized was aware of no others. Nevertheless, I do urge you to remain constantly under the eye of either my guards or Chaisa-e."

Daniel nodded, although he must now be the absolute last man any assassin would attack.

"Kinabana is beautiful, is it not?" Mitereh was clearly in a mood to be pleased; he seemed far more cheerful than when Daniel had left him in Nerinesir; readier with a smile or a nod of favor. It must have been a tremendous relief to have the rest of his guards cleared, after Iodad's treachery. Those young men were more than the king's guards; they were his friends, as much as a king could have friends. At least his companions. Daniel had understood how that suspicion must have weighed on the king; he saw proof of that weight in the evidence of its removal.

"I spent some years of my childhood in Kinabana, in the same house that Terusai holds now," Mitereh added. "The gardens there are splendid. A good place for children. I am glad my Inana has those gardens to explore. She is very quick with her feet!"

Daniel agreed, with as bland an expression as he could manage, that the whole estate, both house and gardens, were splendid, that Inana was a delight and reminded him of his daughter at that age, that Jenna loved Kinabana, and that everything was *perfectly fine*. "Jenna particularly admired the fountains. And the pavilion in the little hidden garden, you know, the one with flowers growing up the trellis at its back. Inana insisted on showing her every single flower back in the secret garden. And every insect hiding in them."

Mitereh smiled; Taranah laughed and said, "She is a charming trial to her mother."

"Jenna always liked butterflies, but she stopped there. Though she brought me a little brown snake once. It didn't bite her."

"And Inana's small creatures never sting her: how forceful is gentle expectation!" agreed Taranah.

"Tenai's doing all right?" Daniel hoped it was safe to turn the subject, because he could not stand to think of the children trapped at Kinabana. "No problems there?"

"No, no." Mitereh gave his aunt a sidelong smile and went on, "Tenai Chaisa-e has been as splendid as the sky. She has been seen everywhere in Nerinesir in these last days—with me, with Sandakan Gutai-e, with Barihutan Anasad-sa—you have not met Barihutan, Danyel. He is a particular partisan of mine, from Antiatan. Chaisa has met the ambassador from Imbaneh-se, and set him down firmly! She has gone three times to the Martyr's Cathedral, once to the Badan Kulirang, and once to the Basilica of Tantukad. She has been seen by the people to be pious and sincere and approved by the cardinals. No, all is well with your friend Tenai Chaisa-e Nolas-Kuomon. I confess I had expected far greater difficulties." He nodded to his aunt, recognition of who deserved the credit for this list of accomplishments.

Taranah looked pleased and satisfied. "I only arranged a few comfortable little suppers, my dear."

"She made the ladies of Nerinesir open their homes to Chaisa-e," Mitereh said to Daniel. "That, more almost than the cardinals, made the city easy with her. Come, look here." He rose and led Daniel through wide glass doors that let out onto a broad balcony.

A balcony. Within minutes of coming into the king's presence. Daniel took a deep breath, measuring the chance. The railing was too low to provide real security against a fall. He could easily— well, relatively easily—stand beside Mitereh and just tip him right over. Mitereh was even leaning over the railing already, pointing out whatever he had brought Daniel out here to see. Fortunately, the presence of the king's aunt made the idea a little more difficult. Even so, Daniel had to stand still a moment, breathing deeply, before he could make himself believe Keitah might not punish Jenna for failure to act, that Taranah's presence ought to be acceptable as an excuse—that Daniel could plausibly argue he hadn't had a real chance. That Keitah might be open to argument.

That last didn't seem likely. Maybe he should try a little push of some kind. If he stumbled, maybe he could make that look persuasive to everyone in just the right way. He joined Mitereh at the railing.

The balcony looked over a broad grassy courtyard in which two dozen or so young men were practicing sword-fighting. Tenai was among them—indeed, the center of the group: correcting, explaining, demonstrating ... she'd been a very good teacher at the martial arts school, while she had been—exiled, free?—in America. If she looked even better here it was probably because the sword was her preferred weapon. Or because the young men with whom she was working were already exceptionally skilled, a fact which gradually dawned on Daniel as he watched the practice.

"I have joined them there on several of these past mornings," Mitereh said. "I wished to demonstrate that there is trust between Chaisa-e and myself and to encourage my personal guards to offer her some measure of trust as well. She has returned trust to them, for which we must all give thanks to God. Or to Lord Death."

"I was happy to hear they'd all been cleared of suspicion," Daniel said sincerely. "Tenai ... how did Tenai clear them?"

"Ah." At this question, Mitereh took on a grimmer look, but he inclined his head, acknowledging Daniel's right to ask. "That was unpleasant. But it had to be done, as all men could see. It was a thing of magic, Nola Danyel, dark enough that each man must accede to it. That all my guards could submit willingly, this alone made me trust them. That each then satisfied Chaisa-e, this merely confirmed what had already been demonstrated."

"And they don't—" Daniel hesitated, looking for a way to ask. "They don't seem to mind training with Tenai now."

"Inevitably some of my guards resented the necessity, though all that was done was done by my word," Mitereh allowed. "But all also understand that renewal of trust in their company came from what was done. Now Chaisa-e teaches them a little of her skill, that by her teaching they may know her more clearly."

"Um." Daniel had a brief, powerful vision of getting the young king to show him a few tricks with a knife or a sword. A slip, an accident ... he put the vision out of his mind. Too deeply stupid for words. He was not the kind of man who could make anything like that look at all persuasive.

Mitereh clapped a hand down on the railing and whistled. Down in the courtyard, practice halted as men turned to look upward. The king waved. "We will go down and join them," he said to Daniel. "We have all been working hard this morning. We will go hawking this afternoon, if that would please you, my guest. Hawking, coursing, hunting the wild deer, as you please."

Daniel would have much preferred to settle down to a long hot bath. He said truthfully, "I have no preference."

"I confess in your place I should desire nothing but a gentle couch," Taranah murmured, with a shrewd glance his way.

"Ah." Mitereh, looking faintly chastened, gave Daniel an inquiring look.

"I know nothing about hunting," Daniel admitted, but then inspiration struck and he added, "But I would be happy to learn. You might teach me a little."

Mitereh was cheerful again at once. "Yes. Hawking, then," he decided. "That is not too strenuous. I will find you a fine falcon. Or you might carry a light bow if you are not accustomed to falcons. Yes?"

The bow, which Tenai found somewhere and presented it to Daniel, proved to be a small crossbow. "As simple to use as a gun," she told him. "One merely points it and pulls the trigger, here."

Daniel nodded, taking the crossbow. He was trying hard to forget all about Kinabana and Keitah and Jenna. Just an ordinary afternoon. An ordinary afternoon learning to use a crossbow so he could go hunting in the company of a man he was supposed to murder. Tenai could be exceptionally perceptive. She knew him well. He would have preferred to avoid her entirely—well, he would have *preferred* to tell her everything and let her take over. He said, trying to make himself sound casual, "Are you coming?"

"I must be about other tasks this afternoon, Daniel. I must go into the city and be seen with certain noble persons. I will return this evening." Tenai sounded faintly wearied by the whole business. She shifted a hand toward her belt, then rested her palm instead on the windowsill. She did not have her black sword at her hip, or plainly she would have set her hand on the hilt. That she had put that sword aside … probably that was a statement of some kind. That sword had a name and a history: Gomantang had been forged in Lord Death's dark kingdom. Daniel had been happier about that story when he'd thought that sword's history was purely metaphorical.

He eyed Tenai, thinking. He had expected this first encounter with Tenai since his return from Kinabana to be difficult. But now he saw she was absorbed enough with her own affairs that she was going to overlook the strain he knew had to be in his own manner and tone. In a way, this was a relief. In another way, it was worrying. "Are you all right, Tenai?"

"Of course," Tenai said, just a little sharply. "How not, surrounded as I am on all sides by my supporters?" But after a moment, she sighed, and even smiled a little. "The business of the city is perhaps a little tedious. But in truth Mitereh does well enough by me, and for himself, and all becomes smooth under his hand. And the hand of Berangilan-sa. That is a formidable woman, I think."

Tenai sounded as though she approved of Taranah. She probably did. She appreciated competence in all its forms. "Did you know the king's aunt … before?"

Tenai's smile became edged. "Oh, no, Daniel. As Encormio did not care for her, I did not. Fortunate woman. I cared only for those that mattered to the old king, that I might discommode him by their deaths."

Right. And no doubt they would both be more comfortable if Tenai didn't dwell on those kinds of memories. Daniel cleared his throat, hefted the bow. "You just point this, do you? If this thing here is the trigger, what's this bit?"

Tenai took the crossbow back and demonstrated its mechanisms. "You cock the bow—thus. We shall leave this bow cocked. The better to shoot a bird that starts from cover—or an assassin. Take care you do not touch the trigger without intention." Tenai gave him a frowning look. "I am satisfied we brought down the man who previously attempted your life and Jenna's. I confess I am not perfectly certain there are no more such men. Nor are you, I should think: this is why Jenna remained in Kinabana?"

"Partly. She made friends with Niah, and wasn't in a hurry to return. But I did suggest she might stay there, where it's safer." Daniel delivered that line in an amazingly normal tone. He'd never thought of himself as an actor. At the same time, he turned over possible ways to warn Tenai. Without speaking or writing. Charades. Had she ever, even once, seen anyone play Charades? If he drew a square in the air, she would probably either ask what he was doing or say, *Sounds like?* Either could be disastrous. Keitah would almost certainly realize Daniel was trying to signal her.

Tenai nodded absently, apparently hearing nothing suspicious in his tone. "And, Daniel, your impression of Niah Madalan Kuyad-sa?"

Daniel shrugged. "A child. An innocent, I believe. It would be hard to imagine a woman who seems less worldly and ambitious."

"Seems?"

Daniel inwardly cursed his slip. "I've no reason to think Niah's anything but what she seems," he said honestly. "Really, Tenai, I think you guessed wrong on that one. Jenna liked her from the first moment they met. So did I."

This last, perhaps because it was the strict truth, satisfied Tenai. She gave a little nod. "Very well, Daniel, as you say so."

"I think the real bad guy must be somebody else—some lord of Talasayan." This was as much of a hint as Daniel dared to give. He saw no sign that Tenai picked up on it. There must be some reference to something that she'd recognize and Keitah wouldn't. Something that signified *betrayal* or *duplicity*. Or *caution*. He could draw a caution sign—no, of course he couldn't; Keitah would see it and instantly know, not what it meant, but that it meant something.

To give himself time to think, he asked, "Didn't you learn anything from the assassin you caught?"

Tenai gave an exasperated little flick of her hand. "The man was the mere tool of some master he did not know. I should have far preferred to question Iodad Sonnas-na. Our enemy is a man of both skill and luck. Well, Daniel, we shall look elsewhere, then; but I should not expect yet another assassin to strike out of the shadows. No matter how clever, our enemy cannot have an infinite supply." She frowned over this, but then shrugged. "Well, as long as no other strikes at you, Daniel. I confess, I am tempted to ask you to return to Kinabana. How did you find the city and the house?"

"Beautiful," Daniel said truthfully. "We didn't get into the city, just rode past it, but the house is lovely."

"Yes," Tenai agreed. "Kinabana is a beautiful city, and the king's grant there the jewel of it. I am certain Jenna finds it so as well. She proved an agreeable companion for the queen, you say?"

"They're nothing alike. You wouldn't think they'd have anything to talk about, but they seemed to find something." And all the time, Niah had been hiding Keitah's treachery. Daniel deliberately put this thought out of his mind. He said instead, "And I think Jenna liked having a kid around—as long as it wasn't hers and there was a nurse to do the hard part."

"Yes. A clever child, is she?"

"Clever, sweet, talkative, and very, very active." Could he possibly say something about Inana that might carry a warning? Maybe refer to a kid's show Tenai might recognize? He couldn't think of anything.

Tenai smiled. "Jenna may give her an outlet for that energy. Forgive, me, Daniel, I must go, but I think you will find Mitereh is ready to go out also. I told the men to give you an easy horse. Do well. I shall see you this evening, if it would please you to come to my household for the night? I believe Mitereh will permit that. I think he will find it useful for several reasons. He will wish to demonstrate the close ties between my household and his; sending you to me for some days will do that. I regret that you must be used in this way, Daniel. By rights, you should be permitted to establish a household of your own."

"I wouldn't know the first thing about it. I don't mind being, ah, shuffled back and forth, if it helps somehow." He particularly didn't mind being told to return to Tenai's household right now. He had to think of a way to warn her—and he definitely preferred to have an excuse to stay away from the king.

Tenai seemed to hear nothing strange in his tone. She merely nodded. "You are most accommodating. Thank you, Daniel. I shall see you tonight, then. For the present, I hope you will have a pleasant afternoon. More pleasant than mine is likely to prove." She glanced toward the hook on the wall where she had hung her sheathed sword, but left it where it was. She only gave Daniel another nod and strode away, having discovered, apparently, no reason to suspect that he might have a problem. Or have become a problem.

Daniel watched her go. Then he touched the smooth shape of the pendant hidden under his shirt, ran a finger along the cold length of the chain—then lowered his hand with an effort. He knew he didn't dare let her see the pendant; Keitah had been very clear about that. *I will know if any gaze but yours falls upon it.* But maybe Daniel could have drawn her attention to the chain. Might that have been warning enough? But if she'd said, *Ah, a chain, what do you have there,* that would have been disaster.

He found himself looking across the room at Tenai's sword. Gomantang could open a gate directly into that kingdom, tear a man out of the real world, the mortal world, and drop him into

Lord Death's hand. In America, if Daniel had felt the sword's uncanny nature, he'd dismissed the impression. Now he knew that, as with every other poetic thing she had ever told him, that had been exactly true.

Daniel paused.

That … was just possibly the beginning of a real plan. Something like a real plan. A terrifying plan. But … maybe. Maybe that was something to think about.

The hawking party would be leaving soon. Daniel forced his attention away from Tenai's black sword and went to find the king he was supposed to murder, so that he could spend the afternoon pretending everything was perfectly fine.

4

Emel turned out to be a font of unexpected skills. Very useful skills if you happened to be on the run cross-country. Which should probably not have been all that unexpected, Jenna reflected. Ten years with outlaws probably taught you a lot. He'd started the fire with a drop of blood and a murmured word and said, surprised when she asked, "But anyone can light a fire, Nola Jenna, and, you are aware, fire is an ally of blood and wood." Oh, sure, everyone knew that, she didn't say. But even after that, Jenna hadn't expected him to be able to boil water in a leaf. Granted, it was a big leaf. He'd fastened the edges together somehow and suspended it, still attached to its twig, over a small fire.

"Why doesn't it burn up?" she asked, crouching to study this arrangement. It had burned right down to the water's edge, but no further.

He glanced at her, and away again. It was strange for a man like him to look shy. But he managed it. "The water keeps the leaf from burning, Nola." He cut a root he held into small slices and dropped them into the water, which immediately turned the color of strong tea.

"Is that for my skin or my hair?"

Emel cut up another root. "This is for your hair. That," he nodded toward a cluster of unappetizing-looking shriveled mushrooms, "will make the dye for your skin."

Jenna nodded. Neither dye would wash off, he'd told her. The one on her skin would wear off in a few days, especially on her fingers, and he'd have to make more. Because it would take more than a few days to get to Nerinesir and Tenai. If they weren't caught. "I guess they're still looking for us," she said.

"I think they are," Emel answered, stirring the dye. They both knew that Keitah would look for them. Obsessively. So they were hiding, though Jenna could hardly stand it, knowing how desperate her father would be feeling. But, no matter the need for haste, the first need was not to be *caught*.

They had ridden fast along the road for only a few minutes before Emel had taken them off cross-country, pausing only long enough where they left the road to make an interesting trap with a sapling, some cord, and a spare knife. "It will slow them when they find our trail," he had explained. He'd seemed pretty sure the bad guys would find their trail. Jenna hadn't argued. Slowing down the bad guys seemed like a good plan to her, even though she didn't like the idea of flinging that knife at anybody, even a bad guy.

Then they had ridden through the countryside, which got pretty wild sooner than Jenna would have expected, but Emel said that was all right, that if they tried to ride fast for very long the horses would be ruined, so they had to go slowly anyway. He'd found rough tracks for them to follow once they were well away from the city. Deer tracks or farmer's paths, Jenna hadn't known and by then hadn't had the energy to ask. Once they'd ridden along a muddy-bottomed stream for a while, which the horses hadn't liked much. The land around here was at least pretty flat, not like the country closer to Nerinesir. That was especially good when you had to ride across country at night. At least the moon had been pretty bright.

Jenna had at first expected any moment to hear sounds of pursuit, but that hadn't happened. A little before dawn they had stopped to rest the horses, for which Jenna had been very grateful. As soon as they'd stopped she'd discovered she was so tired she could barely dismount. And her ankle hurt. She'd probably hurt it when she dropped over the wall. Her foot hurt, too, where she'd kicked that one man in the knee, but she was trying not to think about that. The fight came back to her in flashes when she started to fall asleep, but she'd been so tired she'd fallen asleep anyway. When she'd woken up, the sun was high and Emel was boiling water in a huge round leaf.

"Here," he said now, gesturing toward the dye in the leaf. "There is not much. Not enough for ... Nola Jenna, I must ask you ... you understand, Nola, few women among the road-curs keep their hair so long ... "

"Sure," said Jenna. She ran a hand through her hair. It *was* kind of long. She'd been thinking about cutting it ... a long time ago, before graduation. She'd thought of going for a different style, something short and sporty. "Are we going to pretend we're outlaws?"

"We cannot easily pretend to be honest folk," Emel answered gravely. He had a beard again—just stubble, but a beard. There was grime across his strong-boned face and dirt on his clothing, and a grimness in his eyes that actually made him look the part of a bandit outlaw. A cur. Was a woman brigand also a cur? A bitch, maybe. Jenna suppressed a smile because it wasn't funny, really.

He got a knife out of one of the soldiers' kits they had acquired along with the horses—Jenna flashed again on the fight and flinched instantly away from the memory—and knelt by the fire. "Perhaps later, when we are further from Kinabana. But probably, traveling by the ways we will go, we will encounter brigands. I am ashamed to suggest you should endure the company of such rough folk, Nola, but I think it would be best. Keitah will be searching for a man and a woman alone. Staying near other folk will baffle that manner of sorcery. Also, outlaw curs will know every good path that stays away from the eyes of decent folk." He offered her the knife.

"You'd better do it for me. You can see what you're doing." Jenna stood up, crossed to the fire, and sat down cross-legged on the ground with her back to Emel. There was a short pause. Then he touched her neck, gathered a handful of her hair together, and began carefully to cut it short.

At the first touch of his hand, Jenna found herself unexpectedly dealing with a sudden startling awareness of Emel, not just as a companion, but as a man. This reaction took her entirely by surprise. She had thought the young king wonderfully good looking, Captain Pelat dreamy, Sandakan Gutai-e splendid. But she had hardly even thought of Emel as male at all. And then had come the desperation and the escape and the long night's ride together, and now they were alone on the bank of this stream and he was cutting her hair. She let her breath out slowly, hoping she hadn't flushed.

She didn't even know whether she actually liked him. Well, she did, of course, but she liked most people. What she didn't know was whether she *ought* to like him. He had been an outlaw for ten years. He'd done awful things—he'd as much as said so. It wasn't okay to ... to hurt people, to murder people, just because you were poor. She was definite in her own mind about that. No. Some things were just wrong.

For God's sake, he wasn't even very good-looking. She'd never had a boyfriend in her *life* who was so, so coarse-looking. Or so much older than she was.

And yet the brush of his fingers against the back of her neck had become suddenly riveting. She might have made some sound, because he stopped cutting and said, "I have not hurt you?"

"No," said Jenna, through a constricted throat.

Tenai had trusted him to be her guard. So had Daddy, and he was usually right about people. Then Emel had tried so hard to build a new relationship with his brother it had almost hurt to watch him. That's what she knew of him.

He'd renounced his brother and helped her escape from Kinabana. He'd killed men to help her. Plus he treated her like she was something precious and said he was her dog, and showed no awareness of her as a woman at all. Which was *good*.

She shut her eyes and concentrated on relaxing, on showing nothing of her confusion, and he went back to cutting her hair, a little tentatively. Then he got her to lean back further and scrubbed the dye through what was left. The warm liquid ran through her hair and over her scalp. Emel put the leaf aside and rubbed her hair with a cloth he'd gotten from somewhere.

"Don't touch your hair until it is dry," he warned her at last, and went to get more water out of the stream. Then he knelt by the fire again, patiently arranged the leaf over the coals, and began to chop mushrooms.

Jenna sat with her arms wrapped around her knees and watched. He moved well, she thought. Not gracefully, exactly. But economically. Like he was comfortable in his own body. She cut that thought off, blushing as her witless mind tried to expand on the theme.

She'd had a steady boyfriend her senior year in college. But she had known even then that had really just been because you were *supposed* to have a boyfriend. You needed one to go on dates with, and boyfriends were a handy source of conversational material when you went out with your woman friends. She'd seen Jeff just a few weeks ago, during graduation. She hadn't thought of him once since, and hadn't realized that until now. She was surprised to realize she couldn't remember the exact sound of Jeff's voice. Had his eyes been blue or gray?

"I will make tea in a little," Emel said, looking up at her. Jenna instantly found herself blushing. She pretended hard that she was perfectly at ease. At least Emel didn't seem to notice anything. He said, "The soldiers had a little food in their saddle-bags. There will be enough for a breakfast. There is a small crossbow for hunting rabbits. We may hope for luck as we ride."

Jenna nodded, tried to gather her scattered wits, and said, "Um ... how long do you think it will be before we get to Nerinesir?" If they weren't caught.

Emel was paying more attention to the mess he was stirring than to her. It was a thick black goop, a lot less appealing than the stuff he'd made for her hair. "Ten or twelve days, Nola Jenna." He glanced over at her again. "Forgive my impudence, Nola. For these days, you must not be a lady."

Jenna nodded. "Should you be Emelan? Or should you change your name? I should change mine, I guess." Would she remember to answer to a different name? She found she had no doubt that Emel would not forget to answer to his false name. She resolved to remember hers flawlessly.

He gave her an approving nod. "I will be Bukitraya. That was ..." he paused. "That was a friend, once," he finished in a low voice.

A friend Tenai had killed? Or from before that, before Emel had killed somebody and become an outlaw? Jenna didn't ask. "Bukitraya," she said, trying it out. "Bukitraya. Okay. Pick one for me."

He sat back on his knees and regarded her with sober intensity, as though trying to come up with exactly the right name for her. She thought she might have blushed again, though she tried not to.

"You ..." he said slowly, "you will look a little like a woman from the far south, I think, when your coloring is darker. Your name will be Asih. Will that please you?"

"Sure."

"You are from a small village near Tapad. Your father ... you do not speak of your family. You speak very little. Forgive me, but your speech is not like the speech of women from this land. You should not be mute. But you should be quiet."

Jenna nodded reluctantly. "I guess so. I could try to talk the way Niah does?"

"You should not," Emel said quickly. "Niah is a ... a woman of good family and great refinement."

"And I'm not?" But Jenna added quickly when he stumbled over words, "No, I'm sorry, I shouldn't joke. I understand. All right. I'll be quiet. I *can* be quiet when I try. Where are you from? Are we—" she hesitated. "Are you my brother, maybe?"

Emel tipped his head back, meaning *no*. He looked uncomfortable. "You will be ... you must be my woman. Not precisely my wife. Forgive my insolence to suggest the necessity, Nola."

She tamped down a smile at the shy way he tiptoed around the suggestion. "All right. Your woman. Tell me how I should act."

"I will try. Here. This is ready." He took the leaf bowl off the fire. "There is only a little, but it is strong."

"All right." Jenna took the goop dubiously. It smelled kind of like swamps ought to smell and kind of like laundry that'd been left lying in a damp pile a little too long. It was black as tar. "It won't make me too dark? It won't make me smell bad?"

"It will make you a little darker than Nolas-Kuomon, I think. On me, it would make me ... as dark as Sandakan Gutai-e, perhaps. It is a useful thing if one is closely hunted. I will use a little also, but you are far more noticeable than I. The smell is much less after it sets and you wash in clean water."

"Uh-huh." Jenna was still dubious, but she took the bowl and retired into the bushes. A little did go a long way, she found, and if there wasn't quite enough, nobody should get a look at her actually nude unless things went *really* wrong. The color was really dark, though, and didn't look all that real. "I should bathe in the stream?" she called.

"Gently," Emel called back.

She wanted to scrub, but she washed gently in water that was surprisingly cold, and found the color mellowed a lot as she did. When she was done, her skin was a smooth brown color, not too dark at all, and the color did look pretty natural except, she thought, around her fingernails. Should that be so dark? Well, probably people would only think the darkness was grime. In fact, probably there *would* be plenty of grime around her fingernails pretty soon, since they didn't have any soap. She grimaced. But she was clean now, at least mostly clean, and dressed again in clothing that she would gladly have washed by hand, if they had had soap. Well, no doubt brigands were not usually clean. She shook her head experimentally. It felt light and strange with her hair so short. The air felt cool against the back of her neck. She ran her fingers through the wispy bits that were left and wished for a comb. And a mirror. Definitely a mirror.

Alas, no mirror. She went back to the camp site and struck a pose. "Well?"

Emel looked her up and down carefully, not smiling. "Good.

You look very much a woman of the south."

"You like it?"

Not-smiling turned into a frown. "You look like a woman of this land, but you act like yourself. Asih is your name. You are from a village near Tapad—"

"And I don't speak about my family," Jenna interrupted, slightly hurt by this attitude. She wanted him, she realized, to think she was pretty. How silly. She said sharply, "I get it. I'm your woman and I'm not respectable. At least, not if we meet, um, curs. If we meet ordinary people, can I be respectable?"

"If we are so fortunate as to fall in with ordinary folk, you will be my wife. But we will not travel by usual roads or among ordinary folk until we are a long way from this place." He stood up, kicking dirt over the fire. "There is a cup of tea there," he added, indicating a thin metal cup perched on a rock a few steps away. "There is a little bread for you. We will go soon. We will ride quietly, but I think we must press the pace."

Jenna thought of her father, on his own road ahead of them. "God, yes."

Emel tipped his head back slightly, cautioning. "We must take care, so we cannot go so quickly as we might wish. Terusai-e must have cast a broad net to find us."

Jenna nodded, accepting this because she had to. "As long as we go as fast as we can."

They had left the trail to rest, and Emel did not pick it up again, but led them east and, Jenna estimated by looking at the sun, a little north. Not south. The horses were not close enough together for her to ask. She supposed he knew what he was doing. There was no sign of pursuit, nothing that suggested the two of them weren't alone in these woods, but she could not resist the impulse to glance over her shoulder about twice a minute just in case.

The woods here had bigger, older trees than the woods closer to Keitah's house at Kinabana, with less underbrush. But the horses didn't seem to have any idea that whacking their riders' knees against trees would be bad, so she had to keep alert even though her horse was just following Emel's. The snap and whish of branches as they moved through the woods seemed loud to Jenna. The hooves of the horses made dull, quiet sounds mostly, but sometimes their hooves rang on stones. Twice she saw deer, standing poised and alert back in the woods, watching them pass. Once Emel shot at a squirrel, but it dodged around its tree and the bolt missed. Jenna had never wished harm to any squirrel or bunny in her life, but she was hungry enough now to look after the little animal wistfully while Emel went to find the bolt.

After what seemed like hours of riding, both bored and tense at once—which, Jenna reflected, she'd never before known was possible—Emel suddenly put up a hand and drew his horse to a halt. Suddenly she was not bored at all. She eased her horse up beside his at his gesture and found that they had come to a road—not a real road with paving stones, not even a really serious dirt road. But not just an animal track. This was the kind of path people took to go somewhere. She looked at Emel questioningly. Bukitraya, she reminded herself. He didn't look like a Bukitraya. It was hard to imagine what a Bukitraya would look like. Jenna smiled. Then she remembered that the real Bukitraya had been a friend of his and stopped smiling.

There was no one on the path. Emel didn't seem to trust it. At least, he didn't seem in a hurry either to lead the way out onto that path or to cross it. Jenna hoped he would decide it was safe to ride along a real path. It would be nice not to have to dodge branches for a while. In fact, she thought after a while, it would be nice if he would decide just to get moving again, in any direction at all. The look she gave him was probably more impatient than questioning. What was he waiting for?

Whatever it was, he must eventually have seen something that made him cautious, because he glanced at her briefly and nudged his horse into a turn and led them quietly back into the woods the way they had come. Jenna rolled her eyes. If they'd been going to go back anyway, had they really needed to wait so long before doing it? But she didn't say anything. Not until they finally stopped to rest, hours later, in the middle of a swampy area with thick tangled brush. And bugs. Jenna slapped one and rolled her eyes. "Why *here?*"

Emel methodically checked his horse's feet, slipped its bit, and tethered it where it could reach some of the wiry swamp grasses. Then he started to do the same for Jenna's, only she got hurriedly to her feet and beat him to it. He sat down on a relatively dry clump of grass instead and began to look through one of the saddlebags. But he explained as he examined its contents, "Men are only men. When their officers say 'Search everywhere,' they will say to themselves, 'Everywhere includes that clean, dry slope where the breezes blow away the biting flies.' Then they will search there and not here."

"Oh."

"Of course, any men who want to avoid notice, any men experienced in slipping quietly past official attention, will certainly also know this."

Jenna nodded, enlightened. "That's why you think we're going to run into brigands."

"Yes."

"All right. So that makes sense. But why are we going north?"

"If we went south, we would come to the great road that runs along the bay and turns for Nerinesir. Look." Emel picked up a stick and began to sketch in a patch of mud. "Here is Kinabana. Here is the bay. The road that we took from Nerinesir to Kinabana is here. There is another road that goes south around the edge of the bay and then more south, to Imbaneh-se—to Gai-e and beyond. At Gai-e the road meets the Khadur River and from there one may follow the river toward Nerinesir from the west, or cross it and go deeper into Imbaneh-se. We may be certain that my— that Terusai-e will have both roads watched. So we do not want to ride along those roads. So we go north a little, as well as east. Soon we will turn more directly east, and then south, and come down to Nerinesir through the mountains."

"You think he had even that little road watched?"

"I could not tell. But he will know of all the roads and paths near Kinabana. Keitah is always thorough. But he cannot search every rod of land from the bay to the mountains. I think we shall slip his search. But I would prefer to travel with outlaws experienced in slipping every search."

Jenna had to admit, falling in with outlaws did sound like a good idea, if they bumped into any.

Emel got some strips of jerky out of the saddlebags and passed a few of them across to her.

Jenna took her share, inspected her grimy hands with dismay, shrugged, and bit into a piece of jerky. It wasn't spicy, but it had a smoky taste that was all right. She ate it slowly, trying to pretend there was more of it. Then she leaned back against a tree that was only slightly damp and shut her eyes.

"Forgive the necessity," Emel said, before she could fall asleep. "We should go on."

It was hotter now. Hot and humid and there were more of those biting flies, which made moving on sound good even if she was tired. Emel gave her water in a cup, but there was no tea. So they didn't dare make a fire, Jenna supposed. She yawned and stretched and drank the water and watched Emel erase the signs they had been here. He did an amazing job. He couldn't get rid of all the hoof-prints, but it was surprising how little like hoof-prints they seemed when he was done. Then he got the horses ready and cupped a hand for Jenna to put her knee in to help her mount.

She flushed. "I can get up all right," she snapped, and Emel looked stiffly hurt and went to his own horse, leaving Jenna to hers. They rode in silence through the afternoon. East, and a little north. Everything seemed asleep in the heat. There were no deer, no rabbits, not even birds. Just the bugs, although as they left the swampier ground behind even those grew fewer. Jenna was glad to get out of the mud, but Emel grew visibly more wary as they moved into higher, more open woodlands. Twice they crossed small dirt roads, very carefully, once after riding some distance parallel to the road. Jenna couldn't see anything different about the place Emel finally chose to cross it.

Once they passed some pigs foraging loose in the woods. Jenna thought maybe Emel would shoot a small one—she could have *died* for some roast pork—but he didn't. Once they heard voices, and dismounted to wait quietly, hands on their horse's noses, as the voices got more distant and eventually faded from earshot.

Shadows grew longer, and it began to cool off again until it was actually comfortable; by then Jenna was too tired to appreciate it. Running for your life from the bad guys, she thought with a certain irritation, seemed to involve a lot more boredom and physical discomfort than actual running, and to take absolutely *forever*.

Finally Emel found them a sheltered place tucked in among a stand of big trees. There was no grass for the horses in among the trees, but there was a glade not far away where Emel cut armfuls of forage for the animals. And there was a small pond nearby for water, though Jenna watched the frogs jumping into it when she got water and wondered how clean it was.

"We will wait until the moon is well up," Emel said. "Then there will be enough light to go on. It will be safer to ride at night. We may chance a path if we come to one." There was a strip of jerky for each of them, a piece of hard bread, and then they were out of food. Emel sat down wearily at the base of a tree near the tethered horses and shut his eyes.

Jenna felt as tired as he looked. But she knew Emel was the one whose judgment had to be sharp. "I'll watch," she said, and got to her feet so that there wouldn't be any risk of her falling asleep.

Emel must have been tired because he didn't object. He only gave her the crossbow and said, "Wake me when the moon is above the trees, or if you hear any sound that is not the wind in the leaves." Then he laid his sword where he could get to it and stretched out on the ground without even taking off his boots.

Jenna stood for a while, then sat down cross-legged with her back straight. It was boring at first. Then it got really dark, and all kinds of little noises began to pop out at her from the night—twigs cracking, leaves rustling. It was easy to imagine hordes of soldiers from Kinabana creeping up on them from all sides. She was pretty sure it was only mice or something. What kinds of animals came out at night? Foxes? Wolves? Would wolves attack people? She was almost sure she'd heard that they wouldn't. Did that apply to two people by themselves at night with no fire?

Then one of the horses shifted its weight and blew through its nostrils and Jenna looked at its relaxed posture, dark against the slightly less dark woodlands, and let her own breath out. The horses would know if anything dangerous was around. They were calm. So everything was fine. The noises were just noises. She could go back to being bored. And, now that she thought about it, sleepy. And stiff. She wanted a chair. With cushions. And a footrest. She looked at the indistinct shape on the ground that was Emel and added beds to her mental list of things the woods were woefully deficient in.

As though temporary freedom from personal fear allowed her thoughts to turn in alternate directions, Jenna found her thoughts shifting toward her father. What would he be doing tonight? Oh, he'd be on the road still. It seemed like they'd been traveling for a long, long time, but it was only one day. Well, one night and one day. Still, Daddy would be a lot closer to Nerinesir than she was. He'd get there way before she could.

What would he thinking about tonight? Probably about her. Was Keitah really trying to get him to kill Mitereh? Emel thought so. Probably he knew what he was talking about. Her father wouldn't do it. Of course he wouldn't—she was absolutely *sure* he wouldn't. But she had better get back to Nerinesir as soon as possible to make certain he knew she wasn't Keitah's hostage, knew he didn't need to worry about Keitah doing anything to her.

Maybe Daddy would tell Tenai what had happened. What would Tenai, do, if she knew? Jenna wondered, for the first time, what Keitah had done to her father to stop him telling. Something involving a threat to her, probably. If he was really afraid for her ... he wouldn't be able to tell Tenai, would he? He'd be all alone.

The thought closed her throat. Jenna stared into the dark and longed for dawn, and light to travel, and wings for her feet.

5

Handling a crossbow and reins at the same time turned out to be awkward. Daniel played up the awkwardness a little and accepted good-humored comments about his clumsiness with a smile. Some of the king's young men had hawks—or maybe falcons; Daniel had no idea what the difference was. The king himself had an elegant tawny-gold and chocolate bird on his gloved fist and rode one-handed like it was the most natural thing in the world. About half the young men carried birds; the others carried crossbows. Everyone carried a sword, except Daniel.

The company rode out of the court through the silver gates of the Wall of Glass into the white city of the court, then through the carved gates of the Martyr's Wall into the city of the lesser nobility, and finally through the open gates of the green-shot black Serpentine wall into the main city. But at least this time they didn't ride through the whole city, because it wasn't too far from there to the Gate of Pearl that let them out at last into the countryside. They immediately turned off the road into rugged hills that led up to the mountains to the south and fell away in steep folds to the west. The country around Nerinesir was apparently much rougher on this side of the city; all the farms, Daniel gathered, lay to the other side, along the Khadur river, in the flat floodplains. It was hot, but not as hot here as at Kinabana or even Chaisa; the breeze off the mountains was cool. Tattered clouds caught around the highest peaks, which glittered white even in this season.

The horses jogged through a sloping pasture and in among stands of young trees, crossed a quick little stream at the bottom of the slope, and climbed up into the shade of an older wood. Sunlight stippled the earth between the trees and gave the shadows a greenish tint. They came out at last upon a wide path and followed it.

"Much of the forest was burned or cut during the war," Mitereh commented, bringing his horse alongside Daniel's. "We replanted extensively afterwards. Aspen and birch in the high meadows, oak and hickory near the city, beech and black maple along the river."

"Why did you bother? So that people would have wood to burn?"

Mitereh laughed. "Burn wood! There would be no trees left anywhere in the world if men were required to burn wood! No, there are charcoal-burners who dwell in the great forests of the mountains. They make the charcoal we burn here, setting the spells that cause the charcoal to burn hot and long. We planted the trees to bring back the game." He added after a moment in a lower voice, "And to hide the scars of war, perhaps."

"Ah." Daniel could understand that. "You were how old when the war ended? Ten or so?"

"I had eleven years."

"And the war had been raging as long as anyone could remember and had bent your whole life out of shape. Everyone's lives. No wonder you wanted to hide the scars."

The king gave Daniel a faintly startled look. He said, changing the subject, "Here, we are come to the meadows. This is good land for rabbits and deer. You have never seen birds flown at rabbits?"

Daniel admitted that he never had.

"The birds are beautiful to watch. My falcon is very beautiful. You have your bow? Likely you will have no chance to use it, but keep it ready. A rabbit deep in the brush may still be prey to a bolt, though out of reach for a hawk or falcon."

Daniel nodded.

The party had spread out a little once they had come out of the woods into this series of rocky little glades. The young men called to one another, cheerful and lighthearted. A rabbit startled from under the hooves of one of the horses and everyone shouted.

Mitereh unhooded his falcon with practiced speed and threw it into the air. The bird fluttered upward, caught the breeze in its wings, spiraled higher—then folded its wings and dropped like a stone. It struck the rabbit with a violence that made Daniel blink and tumbled over with its prey. The king, whooping like a boy, raced his horse to it and swung down to collect both falcon and rabbit. He rode back to Daniel grinning, his unhooded bird crouching with spread wings on his fist and the rabbit in a pouch slung behind his saddle.

"Is she not beautiful?" he demanded. "Is she not a prize worthy of a king? She was a gift sent to me from Keneseh, from Kalamantan—there is not another of her kind in any mews in Nerinesir!"

Daniel agreed the bird was lovely. She was: tawny feathers outlined her eyes and barred her elegant chocolate-colored wings. Her eyes were fierce and golden, her beak edged like a knife. She shifted feathered feet on Mitereh's gloved hand and straightened into an arrogant, graceful form, turning her head to scan the meadow for any small movement.

Others among the young men were riding forward again, waiting for more small animals to be startled out of shelter. Someone else flew a big broad-winged bird twice as large as the king's falcon at a rabbit that dodged away at the last moment into the shelter of thorny brush. The man coaxed the bird back with a furry little lure, swearing as it bit his hand instead. Other men laughed. They left that glade and rode through a wood, where someone flew a smaller hawk at a large grouse-like bird that whirred away from the hooves of their horses. The hawk was no more than half the size of its prey, but it brought it down, and the man who had brought it rode out with a triumphant shout to collect his prize. Then there was another, larger, meadow, where someone's falcon earned shouts of derision when it caught a mouse rather than the rabbit at which it had been loosed.

It was not, Daniel thought, a terrible way to spend an afternoon. If he had been younger, and more athletic in general, and not specifically tired of horses. Pleasant weather, plenty of company, a bit of excitement, a few rabbits for the table. He supposed they were for the table. He had been duck-hunting once or twice as a young man, and this was far more pleasant than sitting for several hours in the freezing pre-dawn waiting for ducks to fly over.

If he hadn't had serious complications hanging over his head, he might have enjoyed it.

He was, he acknowledged, putting off the necessary act as long as possible, because he was scared to death. Scared he might miss by too much—or not miss at all. Just how easy was a crossbow to use? What if it wasn't easy enough? Sweat streaked his back and his face at the hairline, but then it was a warm day. No one would notice that. He tried to decide if he should be talking more and could not decide whether that would have been normal for him or not, so he didn't try to force it.

And at last, as shadows lengthened and the company worked its slow way back to the city, Daniel found a moment he recognized, with a sinking feeling, as ideal. One of the young men, Torohoh, was joking that Daniel hadn't even pointed his bow at a rabbit once all afternoon and must be waiting for deer or boar. They were riding through the woods. There was plenty of brush, and Torohoh was breaking dead twigs off trees he passed and pitching them into the brush, trying, he claimed, to scare out a beast worthy of the king's guest.

Mitereh was riding back and forth, joining first one man and then another, laughing and talking like a boy without a worry in the world. And if Daniel was going to do it, what moment would possibly be better? *God help me,* he thought, with an automatic glance upward. And then, deliberately, because it might actually help, *Lord God and Martyr, help me do this right.*

He said something to Torohoh, he never remembered what—he'd meant to say "There!" or "Hear that?" or something, but in the heat of the moment he thought he only made an inarticulate sound. And as the king rode by once more, he lifted the little crossbow he'd carried all this time and fired into the brush beyond him.

It worked even better than he'd ever thought it might, because he was very lucky. Daniel had aimed further from Mitereh than he'd wanted to, because what if he actually hit him? The thought made Daniel feel almost physically ill. He'd wanted to come just close enough to make the subsequent upset persuasive to Keitah Terusai-e. But either the king was riding faster than Daniel had thought, or else his horse jolted forward a step at just the wrong time. Or maybe the Martyr really did nudge the bolt; Daniel wouldn't have ruled out a divine miracle. For whatever reason, the bolt whipped by so close to the king that it tore his shirt and drew a thin line of blood across his chest before rattling away into the woods.

The king reined back at once; everyone drew up. When Mitereh turned to look at Daniel, his stare was simply astonished. He lifted a hand to touch the cut, glanced down at the smear of blood on his fingers. Most of the rest of the young men were plainly struggling between astonishment, terror and anger.

Daniel hoped that he'd gone appropriately pale. Images of what might have happened if his luck had been worse presented themselves forcefully, and then he was sure he had. He felt cold. His hands seemed oddly stiff. When he lowered the crossbow, he felt as though he could perceive every shift of bone and muscle in his arm and hand. He was vividly conscious of the breeze through the leaves, of the creak of harness, of the shift of weight underneath him as his horse fidgeted.

Two of the men—Torohoh and someone else—made as though to ride to Daniel. The king put up his hand and they stopped again.

"Danyel. Dismount, and face me," the king ordered.

Daniel took a slow breath. Then he swung one leg awkwardly over his horse's back, gripped the saddle, and lowered himself to the ground. He wanted to sit down. He wasn't even sure his legs were going to hold him. But he turned to face the ring of still faces that surrounded him, and his knees didn't give. Someone took his horse's reins. Somebody else took the crossbow.

The king also had dismounted from his horse and given its reins and his falcon to one of the young men to hold. Now he stood with one hand resting on his sword-hilt and the other tucked into his belt. His shirt flapped in the breeze, sliced as neatly as though someone had taken scissors to it. There wasn't a lot of blood, but more than a drop or two. One of his men tried to examine the cut, but Mitereh waved him back. The king was frowning. Daniel could not decide whether that was better or worse than the cold, blank stillness that people here seemed to retreat into when they were upset. The king certainly had every reason to be upset. Daniel said nothing.

"Approach," the king commanded.

Daniel walked forward, stopping about four feet away.

"I made you a member of my household," the king said to him. "As a courtesy. Because you are foreign and have loyalties and manners of your own, I have asked little of you—far less than I would have asked of any man of this world. I must now ask more." He held out his hand, and one of his young men put a knife into it. "Kneel," he ordered.

Daniel went awkwardly to one knee and then to both. He found he didn't know quite what to do with his hands. He closed them into fists and rested them against his thighs.

"Do you recognize the great God? Do you recognize the Martyr who died to free men from the tyranny of dark sorcery?"

Daniel could recognize a rote question when one was presented to him on a platter. This didn't seem like a good time to quibble about beliefs. He'd already seen Lord Death; as far as he could tell the Martyr was a historical figure. Plus he'd just been thinking about miracles. He said carefully, "I do."

"Say these words after me. 'Before God and the Martyr, I vow to you—use my name—obedience and loyalty. My life and honor I set into your hands, this fealty to supersede all others I may owe elsewhere.' Do not hesitate. Speak firmly."

Daniel repeated this formula in as clear a voice as he could manage. The king's face was quite sober. All the young men stood in a semicircle, their expressions just as serious. It might seem to Daniel that this was a moment from a play, from a novel, but unreal as it seemed to him, he knew it was quite in earnest. He did not need to be warned that everyone here took this oath very seriously. He even found that he did himself.

"Now this: 'I will do good to you and never evil, all the days of my life. I will answer to your voice and obey your commands, all the days I shall live. I shall speak truth to you and never falsehood, for all the years that turn and depart. All this I vow before God and the watchful Martyr.'"

This, too, Daniel recited. It had a rhythm to it that made it easy enough to remember.

Mitereh nodded, and gave him the knife. Understanding after a moment, Daniel set his teeth and drew the edge of the blade carefully across his palm. The cut was not deep, but it stung, and bled freely. He looked up at the king, blood dripping from his hand into the leaves, and waited.

"Now answer this: did you choose your aim well? Did you mean to strike me with your bolt, Danyel? Swear before God and the Martyr. I am your king now; address me so as you answer."

Daniel thought that, possibly by the grace of God or the Martyr, he had in fact chosen his aim very well indeed. He certainly couldn't say that. He couldn't answer that question exactly as the king had phrased it. He said instead, carefully sticking to the exact truth, "I would never wish you harm. Um. My king. Before God and the Martyr, I swear I wish nothing but good for you and for Talasayan and all this world. I would never want to shoot you. I'm so sorry. Truly."

"Tenai Chaisa-e Nolas-Kuomon did not set you to kill me. Swear by God and the Martyr."

That, Daniel could swear in exactly those words, and did, adding, "Nor, by anything I know, does she wish for your death. Uh, my king."

"You have never used a crossbow before this day? Do I understand you correctly?"

"Yes," agreed Daniel. "I mean, no. I never have."

There was a small pause. Finally the king said, "I forbid you to carry a bow of any kind, save a captain of my guard or Chaisa-e swears you able."

Daniel had no trouble agreeing to this.

The king sighed and looked up, glancing around the watching circle of his young men. He held out his hand for the knife, which Daniel gave back to him, but the king made no sign that he should get up, so he stayed where he was, kneeling in the middle of the path.

Bringing his attention back to Daniel, the king said, "You have, in vowing fealty to me, given your life and your honor in my hands, Nola Danyel. I have both the right and the obligation to render judgment on those that are mine. Do you understand?"

Daniel nodded. After a few seconds, when more seemed required, he added, "Yes, I understand."

"To shoot your king with a crossbow bolt is not permitted," Mitereh said, quite seriously. "To shoot at all when one does not possess the experience to do so safely is not wise. Will you accept punishment from my hands? Or will you choose to appeal to the cardinals, as is any man's right?"

It was abundantly clear what answer was expected. "Yes," said Daniel. "I mean, I'll accept punishment from you."

The king nodded. "Carelessness does not befit a member of my household. I rebuke you." Lifting his free hand, he hit Daniel across the face, not very hard. The blow was startling and embarrassing, but it didn't really hurt. The king hit him again, somewhat harder. Then, taking a short step back, the king tossed the knife back to its owner and lifted both hands palm up. He declared, "If any witness is not satisfied with the justice I have rendered today, let that man speak."

None of the king's young men said a word.

The king gave them all a moment. Then he nodded and said,

his tone not quite so formal, "You may stand, Nola Danyel. Retrieve your horse from Badayan."

Daniel got stiffly to his feet. The cut on his hand hurt, and he felt flushed and awkward. But also, beyond any emotion of the moment, deeply satisfied. If he'd stage-managed the whole thing, assigned every line to everyone present, he didn't see how this could have gone better.

"Torohoh," said the king. "Dismount and face me."

Daniel blinked, startled. He'd thought the whole incident finished, but the young man swung down from his horse, tossed the reins to a companion, and came forward. He didn't look happy, but he certainly didn't seem surprised. His ordinarily expressive face had become still. He bowed, then went to one knee and waited.

The king said, his tone mild, "I do not rebuke you. I heard your words and did not think any harm would come of them. But another time, perhaps it would be better not to tease a man so inexperienced with a bow, unless it is quite certain his field of fire should be clear."

Torohoh answered, "For my part, I consider that I deserve your rebuke, and must count myself fortunate you forgive my stupidity." He stood up, turned to Daniel, and said, "I apologize for my thoughtlessness, Nola Danyel."

"It was hardly your fault," answered Daniel, genuinely embarrassed. "No, really—it was my fault. I should have known better than to shoot without looking, Torohoh!"

There was a general murmur around the company and several of the young men made little uninterpretable gestures toward Daniel, seeming pleased.

"Mount up, mount up," the king urged. "The night's darkness will not wait for us. Nola Danyel, will you ride at my side?"

For a while, riding beside the king in the middle of the strung-out file, in the deepening dusk, neither Daniel nor Mitereh spoke. Daniel could not imagine what he might say. Mitereh thought Daniel had just come very close to killing him, or at least badly injuring him, through sheer careless stupidity. Daniel fervently hoped that Keitah Terusai-e, wherever he might be, thought Daniel had just barely missed doing purposeful murder.

Daniel himself knew that he had come closer to accidental murder—what would that be, manslaughter?—than he had ever meant. He felt a strange conviction that his guilty knowledge was emblazoned on his forehead; a certainty crept over him that Mitereh would be able to read the whole story in his eyes. Even though he knew this wasn't possible, he fixed his gaze on the mane of his horse so that he would not have to look at the king. He felt a strong urge to blurt out the truth to Mitereh—was this what criminals felt when faced by the police? The ones that weren't hardened, he thought. The men who murdered their wives in jealous fits and then turned themselves in. He could imagine they might feel like this.

The smooth shape of the pendant Keitah had given him weighed at his throat, and he set his teeth against the urge to say anything at all. This silence on his part ought to look exactly like embarrassment. Since this was precisely the impression he wanted to give, he made no attempt to look up.

"I shall have Torohoh teach you to shoot," Mitereh offered at last, in a tone that suggested he, too, was embarrassed.

"Please don't. I have no desire to ever pick up a bow again," Daniel said, quite sincerely.

"Ah."

Daniel tried to think of something else to say. "The birds were beautiful. Watching them is enough for me."

"Ah." The king sounded more cheerful at this. "Well, then, I shall have Torohoh teach you to fly a falcon. I shall give you one. No, Nola Danyel, of course I shall. You came into my realm by chance and into my hand by chance and by your own grace, and now I have forced you to forswear any loyalties you properly owe. I did not intend it, and I am sorry for the necessity. Please allow me to bestow this small gift upon you, that men may see I value you."

This take on what had happened had not occurred to Daniel.

"All right." He was silent a moment. "I didn't owe that kind of loyalty to anyone," he said at last. "We don't swear that kind of fealty to anyone."

"Do you not? Yes, I recall. You explained this to me, but I think I did not wholly understand. How strange a land, where no man has a master. But if this is so, then I am glad, for I feared I had been compelled to do you a serious wrong. I was even afraid you might refuse, and then I must think of another way to satisfy my guard and settle my own mind. You understand ... you have sworn to put my word above that of even Chaisa-e. I shall try not to put your loyalty to the test, Nola Danyel."

Daniel tried to think of something intelligent to say about this. "I never ... Tenai is my friend, Mitereh, but since she's not your enemy, there's no problem."

"Let us pray to God and the Martyr your loyalty remains undivided. Indeed, I *shall* pray for that." For a little while, the king rode without speaking. Night had all but fallen; Daniel could not see the trail at all, but kept his rein loose and let his horse choose its own way. Eventually the king spoke again. "Two times Lord Death has reached out his hand to me this year; at least twice. And then through simple mischance your bolt possibly sent me closer to the Gate than any purposeful assassin has done. So we see that God loves irony."

"You must have been living with fear since Tenai returned," Daniel said, almost at random. But he realized at once it was true, must be true. "Of Tenai in case she changes her mind, of assassins; fear for yourself, fear for what would happen to this land if you were to die. And then I showed you that ordinary life can also hold plain bad luck that can hit you just as surely as deliberate malice."

The king looked at him, clearly startled. Daniel surmised that this was not the sort of thing people ordinarily said to him. He seemed caught between affront and surprise. "Do you say so?"

Daniel realized, belatedly, that a comment about fear might be construed as an accusation of cowardice. On the other hand, that was ridiculous. "The important thing, surely, is not to let fear choose your actions for you. I think you must have learned that growing up—Encormio's son and then made king of a broken land when you were still so young."

Mitereh answered after a moment, in a low voice, "It is true that fear makes a bad master. And it is true that I was very much afraid when I knew Nolas-Kuomon had come back across the veil. I thought she would go to Imbaneh-se. Imbaneh-se has always hated the rule my father and then I imposed."

Daniel seized willingly on this new topic. "Yes, I've never quite understood that. I mean, I understand why your father conquered Imbaneh-se in the first place—because he could, basically—but what I don't understand is why, if Imbaneh-se wants so much to be free, you don't just let it go."

"Ah," said Mitereh. And after a pause, "My father did not conquer Imbaneh-se only to expand his power. Imbaneh-se was a threat to Talasayan first. Too many of the families of Imbaneh-se were ambitious. They wished always to press their borders up past the Khadur. To have peace, conquest was necessary."

"Oh." Daniel thought about this. "It seems a little extreme," he concluded.

"It was not. My father was powerful, and jealous of his power; cruel and perilous to cross, yes. He used his cruelty as a tool, yes. But he was also clever, and he understood how to make men and countries do as he wished. Chaisa remembers him as striking random blows against the world, as a mad fox will bite any creature that comes near, or the very earth or trees if there is nothing else to attack. But that was not the way it was. He had reasons for what he did, and none of his blows was random."

This was a new view of Encormio. So Mitereh had admired his father as well as loathed him; loved him as well as feared him ... nothing unexpected in any of that; Daniel should have understood such obvious subtext without being bludgeoned over the head with it. Yes, and that must also be one of the motivating factors behind Mitereh's uncommon devotion to peace: a distancing from his father. Even a kind of reparation for the sin of being his father's son. And perhaps also for the greater sin of loving his father, or wanting to love him. Daniel made a wordless sound, encouraging the king to go on.

Mitereh gazed into the darkness unrolling before his horse's hooves. He seemed untroubled by the dark; no doubt he knew this trail by heart. His tone was abstracted, as though he was speaking half to himself. "My father had reason for everything he did, even every terrible thing." Then he glanced at Daniel and began again, speaking with more animation, "You know how Chaisa lies in relation to Goshui-sa-e. And Antiatan a little more south." The king drew the jagged coastline in the air with his hand. "Kaya-sa on the other side of the point of Batur, and Terusan and Ipos as you continue south, until you come at last to Tapad and Pitatan in Keneseh."

Daniel had seen maps, but he couldn't actually visualize the landscape very well. He said, "Yes?"

"Tesmeket is here, off the coast a hundred miles or more, but that is not so far for their ships." The king drew in the myriad islands of Tesmeket with a flurry of his fingers. "Tesmeket is always trouble. Those islands are wild country, the mountains impossible to subdue. But the blood of Tesmeket has mingled again and again with the blood of the coast all along the east. Many of these coastal people have cousins in Tesmeket, which they always remember. Most of all in Chaisa there has been a great deal of influence from the islands."

"I see," Danyel said, trying to feel out the way this was going.

"So, then, my father decided that it would be good to have Chaisa ruled by a woman, and not only for one generation, but for two or more, because that would weaken Chaisa as an ally for Tesmeket. It is quite certain, you understand, that the people of Chaisa were favoring Tesmeket when they could. Tenai Ponanon Chaisa-e would not have said so to you: likely she would not even have known. Indeed, my father meant to remove the men of that family as a warning to Goshui-sa-e, and to Antiatan; and it did serve so, because while Tenai Ponanon Chaisa-e went into the country of Lord Death and became Nolas-Kuomon, his dark lady, there were years of peace when Tesmeket was very quiet, very polite. They could not persuade Goshui-sa-e or Antiatan to favor them, because those cities were afraid of my father. As they well should have been. I do not," the king added, "justify my father's choices, which were needlessly cruel, but I understand what he meant to do, and possibly Chaisa never has. She lost her family, her husband, her children; what mother would see anything but that?"

It chilled the blood. Politics with torture and murder as primary tools ... Daniel said after a moment, "But you see it. And you weren't even born at the time."

Mitereh smiled. His eyes held a depth of experience beyond what a young man his age would ever have been expected to show. "Not for hundreds of years after that time, no. But I have studied all my life, how to compel peace from lands whose lords might rather desire to raise up banners and march to war."

"And you fear you won't match your father in his ability to do that," Daniel said, bringing this idea gently out into the open in order to let Mitereh hear it. "As you don't match his cruelty." He made his tone mild and just a little dry, dismissing the idea even as he put it into words.

There was a silence. Mitereh gave Daniel a sidelong long. He said at last, "You hear ... more than I had thought to tell you, Nola Danyel."

Daniel shook his head and said more explicitly, "Mitereh, I've never met anyone as likely as you to know his own mind and do exactly what it takes to get where he wants to go. Whether you'll match a thousand-year-old king for sly cunning, I don't know, but I think you'll manage to make your mark. And it'll be yours, and nothing like your father's, thank God."

There was a pause. "I had thought Tenai Chaisa-e my great prize," Mitereh murmured at last. "But I see I may also learn to value you as well, Nola Danyel."

"Usually I just need to point out a truth that somebody already knows." Daniel shut his eyes, resting his hands on his horse's neck. He desperately needed this day to be *over*. And the worst part still lay in front of him.

But when Daniel finally gave his horse to one of young men with a groan of relief and went wearily to the apartments assigned to Tenai's household, he found her there before him. Her presence effectively prevented him from going on with the second part of his … hard to call it a *plan*. His enormously risky, terrifying, half-framed thought.

Fortunately Tenai seemed almost as distracted as Daniel felt. Unable to muster the energy to explain or even mention the crossbow incident, he pleaded exhaustion—quite sincerely—and retired to the rooms allotted for him. There, without really noticing anything about the rooms or its furnishings, he let one of Tenai's attendants draw him a bath, refused offers of soup and bread, and sank gratefully into the privacy and quiet of his bed.

He dreamed that night of shooting Mitereh, of a crossbow bolt that fell out of the sky with the scream of a falcon, of a short black barb standing out of the young king's chest as Mitereh turned toward him with a look of astonished accusation and fell slowly away into darkness. A rabbit tumbled over and over in a rocky meadow, limp, its eyes glazed with death. A falcon stooped, slashing its talons into Mitereh's face—no, into Niah's face, and the young queen cried out with a sharp piercing cry like a struck rabbit. Daniel turned, holding a bow, lifting it with a feeling of inevitability, and as his finger touched the trigger he saw that his target was his own daughter. He cried out as the bolt left his bow, and woke sweating in the dark. The shutters were open to the night air. Through them he could see stars, and a half-moon riding past broken wisps of cloud.

Sinking back against the sheets, Daniel touched the pendant he wore. It was cool to the touch, even against his skin; the chain was cold where it lay against his neck. He wanted to take it off, cast it out the window, be done with it. He took his hand away from it and lay back down, deliberately. He would have liked to pray, perhaps because in this country God was taken so seriously. But no words came to mind. If you killed somebody accidentally because you were trying to make it look like you'd attempted to kill him on purpose, was that murder or just stupidity?

Self-murder was no better. Accidental suicide wouldn't be much of an improvement. If his so-called plan didn't work, if his *incredibly stupid* plan went wrong and he wound up dead, Jenna would be stuck in Keitah's hands, and Tenai and Mitereh would still ignorant.

But going on as he'd started, trying to make Keitah believe he was trying to kill Mitereh, while pretending to everybody else that everything was just fine … how long would that last? How long until Keitah figured out that, despite first impressions, he wasn't trying very hard? Daniel wondered what it would be like to hear his daughter screaming through the pendant he wore, and shut his eyes. How long could it be until dawn?

6

Jenna found herself perilously close to dozing and got up, glancing at the horses to make sure they were still calm. They looked like they were asleep. She wished she were asleep, like Emel. In a bed. Not the *same* bed. Of course not. She rolled her eyes at herself, irritated that an idea like that could even cross her so-called mind when she ought to be focused on the journey before her.

One of the horses shifted its weight and sighed, and Jenna glanced over at it. Could sleeping horses hear wolves sneaking up on them? With relief, she noted that the moon was about ready to rise above the tops of the trees. She went to wake Emel.

Except when she actually came to it she hated to wake him. The moon showed her lines around his mouth that she hadn't noticed before, drawn there by tiredness and worry. He was lying tucked up on his side in a protective, wary attitude, as though expecting attack even in his sleep. The moonlight in his face hadn't woken him, but, as she watched, his brows drew a little together in a look of strain or anger. If he was dreaming, she thought his dreams could not be pleasant ones.

Kneeling, Jenna laid a hand on his shoulder.

He came up fast, reaching for the knife at his belt. It was in his hand before he stopped, looking embarrassed.

Trained reflexes had sent Jenna scooting sharply backwards. "Sorry. Next time I'll just toss pebbles at you until you wake up."

Emel still looked embarrassed. "I should have told you to be careful. Forgive my thoughtlessness, I beg you."

Everybody was always so earnest and flowery here. A moment before, Jenna had hardly been able to bring herself to wake him, and now she was just annoyed. *"Forget* it, will you," she muttered, and went to get her horse ready. She wanted her own room and her own bed, and her father downstairs in his bedroom, both of them safe. She wanted not to be wandering around in the woods with a man she didn't even really know, who had been a brigand long enough that he woke up reaching for a *knife*. God. What was she doing here? Feeling sorry for herself made her cross with her horse, who had his ears back because, no doubt, he wanted his warm stall and not to be saddled *again* after working all day already. Jenna sympathized with his grumpiness. If she'd been him she would have tried to bite, but he was too well-bred for that, at least. She lifted herself into the saddle and looked around.

Emel was already up and waiting. She didn't get how he could be faster into the saddle than she was when she'd started first and he'd had to put together the saddlebags that had been opened, but he was. It irritated her. To be fair, she was ready to be irritated by just about anything at the moment.

Emel nodded to her curtly and led the way, back to their slow careful one-step-after-another nighttime progress. Jenna banged her knee on a half-seen tree and hissed under her breath, wanting a trail. But when they eventually came out on one and turned along it, Emel was so clearly tense and unhappy that she wanted to shout at him that if he hated trails so much he could damn well stick to the woods. She restrained herself with an effort, then realized it was her father's voice she heard in the back of her mind: *Your temper is your problem. It's not fair to take it out on anybody else, Jen.* That made her grit her teeth against the prickling threat of tears more than against the original annoyance.

Emelan nudged his horse into a trot, so Jenna did too, even though her butt and legs protested at the new effort. They followed a deer trail for a little while. Then Emel reined back to a walk and led them off the trail again and up a slight rise to their right. Then it was down the other side of the slope and nearly into a sleeping hamlet of five or six cottages, but not even a dog barked as they rode carefully away again. And halted, to Jenna's surprise. Emel dismounted, so Jenna slid down from her horse too.

He handed her his reins. "Wait here," he said, not whispering, but quiet, and slid back the way they'd come, heading for that hamlet. Jenna bit her lips and shifted from foot to foot and finally sat down on the ground with a set of reins in each hand and let the horses snuffle her hair. It seemed like hours, but the moon barely moved, so it hadn't been more than twenty minutes or so, probably, before he was back. The horses knew he was coming before Jenna did. They jerked their heads up and stared into the dark woods, so she was on her feet and looking alert when Emel came back through the trees. He was carrying a bundle under his arm and looked satisfied, but he went straight to his horse and reached for the reins, so Jenna didn't ask questions. Her horse seemed taller every time she climbed up on his back. Probably not much fun for him either, all this riding on and on with no grain or stable or pasture. She patted his neck in commiseration.

After that they went on for what seemed like a long time. They found another path and followed it for a while, then skirted the marshy edge of a small lake. A smoke-pale fox paused in its hunting to look back over its shoulder at Jenna, then slipped into the reeds along the lake shore and vanished. Probably it had a snug den to go back to when the night's hunting was done. She wished they had one. The moon settled at last behind the trees and after that it was too dark to travel, thank God.

Emel unsaddled the horses in the lee of a stand of slender young trees while Jenna wordlessly investigated the bundle he'd been carrying in front of him, by touch as much as by sight because she could hardly see anything now that the moon was down. The bundle proved to contain three small rounds of cheese, a loaf of bread, and a whole pie wrapped in cloth. A meat pie, from the smell, and still warm from the oven.

Emel came to sit near her. He broke the pie in half and gave Jenna her share. She suspected her half was bigger than his, though in the dark it was hard to tell. It turned out to be beef, though heavy on the turnips and light on the meat, but she licked the crumbs off her fingers and wished for another just like it. She looked wistfully at the bread and cheese, which Emel had already wrapped up in the cloth and set aside.

"We will need that later," Emel said, which she knew very well. And, "Rest. Let me watch a little," which was much more welcome. Jenna lay down at once and was instantly asleep.

She woke slowly, blinking with bemusement at light flickering through leaves. Her head was cushioned on a saddle, and a spare shirt had been tossed over her like a scanty blanket. She pried herself off the ground, groaning as she rediscovered one ache after another. She wanted, in the worst way, a hot bath, and a toothbrush, and a huge platter of eggs over easy and sausages and French toast with lots of syrup. What she had was a slice of heavy bread with sharp yellow cheese and a cup of water, both laid out for her on top of a saddlebag. Emel was nowhere in sight, but the horses were pulling half-heartedly at leaves a few feet away. Hers tipped an ear at her and whickered and she went over and patted it.

Jenna ate the bread and cheese—the horses looked at her reproachfully, but she ate the last crumb herself—and sat in a patch of sunlight, trying to decide whether the other shirt was cleaner than hers or not. Eventually she decided that it was, but that she wanted a bath before she put it on. Then she just sat in the sun and didn't think about much of anything.

When the horses suddenly turned their heads and pricked their ears, though, she got to her feet and peered through the trees. At first she couldn't see anything. But finally she spotted movement. She was surprised at the relief she felt, since she hadn't been aware of being nervous. But she was glad Emel was back. If he'd shot a rabbit or squirrel, she would be even more pleased. She patted her horse and went to gather the saddlebags together. Probably she shouldn't saddle the horses yet, in case Emel thought there would be enough time for them to linger here a little while and cook a rabbit.

Only it wasn't Emel. She discovered this when she finished putting things back in the saddlebags and looked up toward the woods, and found not Emel, but three strangers.

She knew at once they were brigands. Curs. She hadn't liked the word before, but these men *looked* like curs: rough and grimy and hard-worn. They all had long hair, tied back with bits of cord. Two of them had beards. One of those had a dark narrow face with an angular chin and a scar across his forehead. The other, lighter-skinned like Emel, stared at her with an ugly salacious expression—he made her think of the gang that had tried to attack her and Tenai and the others that time, that exact same expression. She wished fervently that Tenai was with her now. Or Emel.

The one without a beard had a lot of gray streaking his black hair, and a wintry look in his eyes. His eyes were like Taranah Berangilan-sa's, that really pale gray they called silver. He had a sour expression that suggested he wasn't thrilled to find her here, or more likely that he wasn't thrilled with life in general. But he didn't somehow have that ugly, sly look. He looked dangerous, but not really vicious. He had a crossbow that was a lot bigger and nastier-looking than Emel's. All three had swords and knives, but the crossbow worried Jenna more.

She straightened slowly, trying hard to look harmless. A visceral memory of how it felt to slam an elbow down on the neck of a man, how it felt to kick somebody for real, ran through her, and she felt suddenly like she might throw up. Well, vomiting would sure make her look harmless. Though she would rather not.

"You alone?" asked one of the men. The nastiest-looking one. The only word for his expression, Jenna decided, was *leering*. She had never truly *known* what that word meant, before. She would have been happy not to know now. She didn't like him, and she was scared of him, with a tremor in her stomach that had nothing to do with the likelihood she could beat him up if she needed to and everything to do with a gut-deep certainty that he *wanted* to scare her, that he probably wanted that more than he wanted to rape her. And she knew, no question, that he wanted to rape her. She stared at him, at all of them, with the best approach to blank neutrality she could manage.

"She's not," said the older man, the one with the silver eyes.

He was a tall man, not as broad-built as Emel, but he looked strong. There was a note of cold disdain in his voice. He said, "Two horses. Are you blind?" in a tone that implied the rest of the question was, *Or just stupid?*

"Oh, well," said the first man, not taking obvious offense. He grinned at Jenna, nastily. "Is the other one as pretty as you?"

She wasn't supposed to talk. She didn't seem to have a lot of choice. She looked the man straight in the eye. "No," she said. "But he's a lot bigger."

The man looked disappointed and sneering at the same time. The narrow-faced man with the scar smiled, a smile that seemed to Jenna to be malicious. The silver-eyed man lifted one eyebrow and started to say something. Then a short little black bolt went *thwip!* through the air and buried itself in the leaf-mold at his feet. The man hadn't been moving anyway, but suddenly he was standing still in a much more decisive *This is me standing still* kind of way. The other two men jumped, and the nasty one jerked around to face the woods.

Emel was right there. Jenna hadn't heard a thing. No one else had either, obviously. Emel's crossbow was aimed steadily at the older man with the silver eyes and the big bow, but his gaze was on the nasty one. "You want her?" he said, straight to that man. "You want to say so to me?"

"He doesn't," said the older man. He looked thoroughly disgusted. "He can always make do with a goat. No reason we should disagree."

"Put your bow on the ground," Emel said shortly, and the man let the weapon fall and took several steps away from it. Jenna scooted forward to get the bow, then backed off and took it to Emel. He traded it for his light one with economical speed and had his aim back on the outlaws before any of them could move. None of them tried to move, actually. Jenna inspected the crossbow she now held. It *looked* simple to use. She wondered if she could hit the broad side of a barn with it. She looked at the men. Well, if they were close enough to touch her, she could probably hit them. She tried not to think about what a crossbow bolt would do, slashing into flesh and bone.

"Well?" said the older man. "How shall we settle this?"

"Walk away," said Emel.

The two younger men both looked at the older one, nodding they thought that was a fine idea. But the older man didn't move. "Leaving you alone? Just the two of you, are there?"

"We do well enough," Emel said shortly.

The man looked him up and down with his cold, pale eyes, not like he was trying to be insulting, but measuringly. "I see you do. Still, it's hard for a man alone. Even an experienced man. You'd do better to join a pack."

Emel stared at him with a grim expression. "The woman is mine."

"Oh, no question. No question, man. That why you left your last pack, is it? Trouble over the woman?"

"Yes," Emel said, still curt.

"Indeed. Are you the sort sees every glance as an insult, who starts a fight when your woman passes a man too close or smiles at anybody but you?"

"No. I didn't start the fights."

"You won?"

"Yes. But it was trouble and enough."

The man looked him over again, thoughtfully. "Yes," he said. "Well, fight once to show you can and that will do. The woman is yours either way, no question."

"Your word, is it? Do you offer that?" Emel didn't sound doubtful, exactly. Or hostile—exactly. "I've got the bows, I've got the horses, I've got the woman. Why should I take the risk?"

The man nearly smiled. "You have been aside the world ... how long, man? Years, yes?" He nodded at Emel's shrug. "Then you know why. I have five men besides these, and three women. The men are experienced. The women are no trouble. Especially as you have your own."

Emel grunted. He slid a glance toward the creepy guy.

"If Tantang bothers your woman, you have my permission to kill him," said the older man, ignoring the sound of protest the other man made.

Emel lifted his eyebrows. *"Your* permission, is it?"

"If you will own me."

That was the odd phrase people here sometimes used for *accept my authority;* Jenna knew that. So this guy was in charge, or thought he should be. It was Emel's turn to look the man over. So did Jenna. He stood there calmly and let them look. He was, she thought, at least brave. And not stupid. If they had to join up with outlaws for a little while, maybe this guy would be all right. But she sure didn't like the idea of sharing a campsite with The Creep.

Emel finished his own inspection and glanced at Jenna. She shrugged: how was *she* supposed to tell?

"I keep the bow," Emel said to the silver-eyed man.

"When I tell you to return it, man, I will expect you to give it back to me with no argument."

If the silver-eyed man was bothered about laying down the law to a man who held him at bow-point, it didn't show. Jenna was reluctantly impressed. She couldn't tell what Emel thought. But he said, "When you do, I might obey. The horses?"

"We keep no horses. We go by ways horses cannot go. We'll sell those. The coin—you keep half."

"Three-quarters."

"Two-thirds."

Emel nodded slightly. "What is your range?"

"From Kinabana around the eastern edge of the bay, shifting south or toward the coast when we are pressed. We work the roads between Kinabana and Nerinesir; the road to Nemesen and the road up to Sambutan toward Patananir. Occasionally the little roads between. If we're far enough south, we work the road to Gaie, but we take all reasonable care. We don't draw punitive patrols and we don't want ambushes. The take is divided in an eighty-twenty split. The eighty is even."

Emel grunted skeptically.

"It works for us. And your previous range was ... where?"

"East of Kandun," Emel said, in a tone that did not invite more probing questions.

"As you say," said the older man, calmly. "Well?"

Emel scowled, then nodded shortly and pointed the bow he held down at the ground.

The other man had not seemed tense to Jenna, but now she saw he had been because he relaxed. His eyes were still wintry, but he seemed pleased. He said to The Creep—what *was* his name, Tantang?—"You have your use, but I expect you to obey me. That means I'll permit him to kill you if you touch his woman. If he can't, for whatever reason, I'll kill you myself. So keep your hands off the woman."

Tantang's expression was sullen. He didn't seem to dare glare at Emel, but the look he gave her was unpleasant.

Then Jenna blinked. The older man had moved so fast that, not expecting it, she had almost missed the blow which sent The Creep sprawling in the dirt. The narrow-faced man, who hadn't yet said a word, laughed. Emel had put on his most blankly neutral expression. The leader said to Tantang, "Do not even *look* at the woman. Am I clear?"

Tantang gave the older man a look of deep dislike and fear. "Yes," he muttered, and got to his feet to stand with his back ostentatiously to her. Jenna closed her mouth and looked at Emel for what she should do.

"Saddle the horses," he told her, and said to the leader, "How shall I call you?"

The man gave him a brief nod. "I am Kuomat." He nodded to the narrow-faced man with the scar. "That is Gerabak."

Emel gave their false names while Jenna silently heaved saddles up onto tall horses and buckled the girths. "The horses are stolen," he added.

Kuomat nodded as though this went without saying. "We know a man who knows a man who will take them quietly and see that they are sold at last far away. They are plain animals. There should be no difficulty. And you, man, are you hunted closely?"

Emel hesitated. "Maybe," he said at last.

The leader seemed unsurprised. "You have the look. Gerabak will take the horses, then. You and your woman ... you will come with me by other ways. Yes?"

Emel shrugged. "You go in front," he said.

It was amazing how much less flat the land seemed when you were walking over it, Jenna noted, not much latter. She grabbed a sapling to help pull herself up a slope. Maybe these special ways the brigands knew took advantage of what hills and gullies there might be. How nice. The ground seemed rockier, too. You had to keep looking at where you put your feet and that made it hard to keep track of, for example, the men you were traveling with but didn't actually trust.

She was last in line. Tantang went first; Kuomat, then Emel, and then her. The men were carrying the saddlebags slung over their shoulders. Jenna wasn't carrying anything but the light bow, and she found that awkward enough. None of the men seemed to have the least trouble. Well, all of them had longer legs. Maybe that was why they seemed to swing along so effortlessly while she struggled to keep up. On the other hand, Kuomat had to be at least her father's age, and it was just embarrassing if she couldn't outwalk *him*.

They stopped at a stream to drink. Jenna noticed that Emel moved well away from the other men before he put down the bow and stooped to cup water in his hands, and that he glanced at her first, too. So she waited, her eyes on the men, for him to be done and pick his bow up again before she got her own drink. Emel didn't exactly give her an approving nod, but he met her eyes briefly and the corner of his mouth twitched upward, so she thought she'd done it right. They rested briefly. Emel shared out their bread and cheese without comment. Kuomat handed around strips of tough jerky and little crumbly cakes with a warm nutty taste. No one spoke. Tantang looked ostentatiously everywhere but at her. Jenna sat near Emel and wished they were alone again.

Then they went on, tending downhill now, over ground that grew gradually more broken. Yes, Jenna decided, grabbing a young tree to steady herself as she came down a sharp slope, horses probably wouldn't be very good in this area. The trees were bigger at the bottom of the slope, and the ground softer and wetter. There was more underbrush, including something with long thorny branches that seemed to reach out and bite you when you ought to have been far enough out of reach to be safe. Jenna was the only one who had trouble. Everyone else seemed to avoid the spiny plants without effort. It made her want to bite, too. She was tired. It was hot. Sunlight poured like molten gold through the heavy air, and bugs buzzed in green shade. They began to pass pools of open water. Kuomat and The Creep threaded their way confidently through what had unambiguously become a marsh. Emel followed them carefully. Jenna followed Emel, slapped bugs, and thought wistfully about horses and dry roads.

Finally the ground tended upward again, and became drier. The trees became smaller and closer together. They picked a way through a tangle of thorny shrubs and thick vines with big heart-shaped leaves and little white flowers, and suddenly the woods opened up and there were canvas lean-tos, and one big one made out of wood, and a fire-pit with a big pot over it, and people. Armed people, with swords and knives and more of the big crossbows. Jenna looked in alarm to Emel, who didn't seem surprised. He still held his bow, but he wasn't pointing it at anyone.

"We have a double-handful of campsites," said Kuomat to Emel, his tone a bit dry, as though he expected some kind of negative reaction from the other man. Emel only looked at him without expression, and he went on, "We move around. This is a good place. There's marsh all around. We try not to make trails leading to it. The trench is over there. The fire pit is over there, where the branches above will break up the smoke. You can set up a tent anywhere you want. If you haven't got canvas, we have some held in common. Yes?"

The other men—and one woman, Jenna noticed—had come up in a close circle. There were three men. She wondered where the others were. Off robbing people, maybe. All the people here were dirty and thin and ragged and one of them looked ill. None of them was as old as Kuomat. Maybe outlaws didn't usually get old. The woman, not young, had her hair cropped short and an angular face. A small scar twisted her mouth into a permanent sneer. She looked away when Tantang looked at her.

Not much like Robin Hood and the Merry Men. Not much like anyplace Jenna wanted to be, or anyone she wanted to be near. She found she was edging closer to Emel and made herself stop.

"An experienced recruit," Kuomat said to his people, still dry. "And his woman." His mouth crooked slightly on that last. "We'll make them welcome. Imbutaiyon."

The man he had named cocked his head to the side, his expression mildly interested. He had a friendly face and very dark eyes. Unusually for these people, he had cut his bronze hair raggedly short. Of the rest, only the woman had hair that short. He held a crossbow, but like Emel he wasn't pointing it at anybody.

"He says he can fight," said Kuomat. "Let's have a show."

"Can I have his woman if I win?" said the man, in a perfectly straightforward way, like *Can I have his knife?* or *Can I have his dessert?* Jenna blinked and risked a glance at Emel, who didn't look mad. He looked as calm as the other man. And he didn't answer, but lifted a brow at Kuomat instead.

"No," said the leader. "The woman's not up for claiming unless he's dead. If you kill him, that would annoy me. Besides, you already have a woman."

The woman with the frightened eyes and the scarred mouth? Jenna wondered. That woman was looking at the ground, not at Imbutaiyon. Maybe Kuomat meant some other woman.

Kuomat looked at Emel. "And if you kill *him,* that would annoy me, too."

"Yes," said Emel briefly, and gave his crossbow to Jenna.

If he *was* killed, she would probably be able to shoot at least a couple of them ... and then they would probably shoot her. "Don't die," she muttered to him, and he patted her on the shoulder reassuringly—exactly like he might pat a horse on the edge of spooking, exactly like that—and started to take off his vest and his shirt. His expression was abstracted. He hadn't exactly forgotten she existed, Jenna realized, but he was tightly focused on the fight instead of on her. She took the sword he handed her and stepped awkwardly to one side, burdened with more weapons than she knew what to do with. She put the light bow and the sword down at her feet and kept the big bow in her hands in case she did wind up needing to shoot somebody.

Emel had his knife in his hand, which dismayed her. She'd thought they were going to fight with their fists. Nobody was likely to get hurt in a fistfight. In a knife fight, who knew what might happen?

The other man ... Imbutaiyon ... had also stripped to the waist, and he also had given his bow to somebody else to hold. He had a lot of scars on his body. A lot. Probably he liked to fight. Probably he was really good at it. He was taller than Emel, but not as broad across the shoulders. And thinner, like he never got enough to eat. But he looked tough. Maybe that was what they meant when they said somebody looked tough as whipcord. She'd never understood that phrase before. She thought she did now.

In contrast, Emel looked strong. And fit. But he didn't look like he'd be as fast. He had a long thin scar that ran across his chest and halfway down his stomach. He didn't have any hair to speak of on his chest ... neither man did ... and his stomach looked like an ad for weightlifting. She found she was blushing. What a way to get a man to take off his shirt.

Imbutaiyon walked forward. Emel did. Both men moved properly, on the balls of their feet. Jenna experienced a brief intense wish that she was out there instead, getting ready to fight Imbutaiyon herself, and told herself she was being silly, but really, it would have been a lot less nerve-wracking.

Imbutaiyon made a pass with his knife, low, aiming for the

gut, not too fast. Emel caught it with his and it occurred to Jenna that they'd had days and *days* for her to teach him the ways Tenai had showed her to disarm an opponent with a knife and what had she been *thinking?* She wanted to close her eyes but she couldn't.

Imbutaiyon attacked again and Emel defended, and then Emel had a red line across his forearm, but it wasn't bleeding very much and Jenna resumed breathing. The men closed again and Emel came out of it with a shallow cut across his chest, but this time he'd kicked Imbutaiyon in the shin, like a kind of modified low side kick, and Imbutaiyon staggered, and Emel moved in on him, using his greater weight to force the other man back. A knife went flying and at first Jenna though it was Emel's, but it was Imbutaiyon's, and then Emel flung his after it and then it *was* a fist fight and Emel was faster than he looked, but it was a pretty dirty fight and again Jenna wished fiercely that it was her fighting. Emel grunted as Imbutaiyon slammed a knee into his belly—it had been aimed lower—but then Emel did a foot sweep and kicked the other man in the hip as he went down—he'd been aiming elsewhere too, Jenna was pretty sure—but for a moment Imbutaiyon was wide open and Emel started to kick him again and stopped with the toe of his boot touching the side of the other man's head. And then it was over.

Emel walked back to Jenna and picked up his shirt. Jenna shook her head at him and gave him the spare shirt instead so he could wipe off the blood and sweat. Her hands were trembling and she felt sick, which was stupid because it was *over* and he was *fine*. She'd been so tense that now she was almost as tired as though she *had* been the one fighting.

He was still bleeding, but not very much. Jenna cut a strip off the shirt and used it to bandage his arm. It would have been harder to bandage his chest, but luckily that cut was bleeding even less. He totally looked like a brigand, though, with not only grime but blood on his shirt now, and his hair damp with sweat. But he looked less abstracted and gave her a tired smile like he knew she was there again. He turned back to face Kuomat and the other outlaws.

Somebody else—one of the other men—had helped Imbutaiyon to his feet and brought him his shirt. *He* wasn't bleeding, Jenna thought resentfully. But he did have some good bruises, which was satisfying. "Go, team," she said, but very quietly so nobody would hear except Emel. He glanced at her and half smiled.

"You only cut him twice," Kuomat was saying to Imbutaiyon in a severe tone.

"Should I annoy you?" Imbutaiyon said. He grinned at Emel. "Besides, I already have a woman."

Emel did not smile back. But he gave Imbutaiyon a curt nod like he wasn't angry.

"So I see you can fight," Kuomat said to Emel. "You can use a sword?"

"Yes," Emel said.

"I think we need not examine this claim. I would not wish to lose a man proving it."

"I confess I'm glad to hear it!" said Imbutaiyon. He clapped the man nearest him on the shoulder and grinned.

"I hope there is food ready," the leader said to him, even more severely than before, and Jenna thought, *Why, they're friends.* It was reassuring that the cold, bleak-eyed Kuomat could have friends.

"There is," Imbutaiyon agreed. "Enough for our recruit and even for his woman. Medai shot a deer today, and Katawarin brought bread from the village at the ford yesterday, so we have a wealth of nourishment. So you see we all had luck, if not to match yours."

Kuomat nodded. He said to Emel—not to Jenna—"Partake freely of what we have, man, and be welcome among us."

The food was a stew, with venison and some kind of crunchy white root vegetable in it. The outlaws had wooden bowls and spoons that she was afraid to inspect too closely. You put the bread in a bowl and ladled stew over the bread. Jenna pretended she'd never heard of germs and ate her share with appetite dulled only by exhaustion. She sat on the ground with Emel, who had found a place a little way away from the outlaws. Everyone seemed tired, even the people who had been in the camp and not hiking all day. Although maybe they'd been out, but not with Kuomat. No one talked much. Imbutaiyon and one of the other men exchanged a few words and laughed a little, glancing occasionally toward Jenna, who pointedly shifted closer to Emel. The sick man ate a couple of bites and went away to lie down. Tantang watched the woman with the scarred mouth. Kuomat sat on a stump by himself and watched everybody.

Emel watched everybody, too. He didn't look very happy. Jenna asked him quietly, "Are we all right?"

"I've seen worse," he muttered. He gave her a sidelong look. "I had forgotten ... not precisely forgotten, but set aside the memory of how rude such company may be. We are safer in this company, I do think so ... but I ask your forgiveness that you must endure it."

"Yeah, well ... if somebody gets particularly, uh, rude ... would it be a good thing if I beat him up, or would that be a bad thing?"

Emel half smiled. "If it did not look too practiced, it would be very good. You would say I taught you. You would not want to kill the man."

"Unless it's Tantang."

"Yes," Emel conceded. "It would be as well to kill Tantang." Jenna had been joking, or mostly joking, but Emel sounded absolutely serious. "He has some skill Kuomat values, clearly so. Kuomat ... I have seen indeed seen worse."

"I don't think he's stupid. He asked if you were being hunted. What if he's heard Keitah's looking for a man like you and a woman my age?"

"Possible. I do not think so, however."

He didn't explain why not. Jenna nodded doubtfully. "He has silver eyes. Can't people like that see into men's hearts or something?" In this country of magic and immortal kings, maybe this was literally true. She thought that if Kuomat couldn't actually see into people's hearts, he was still perceptive enough to see a lot that they might not want to have seen.

"So it is said." Emel sounded noncommittal. "He will not see the details we would wish to hide."

"All right. You think he's dangerous?"

"Perhaps. But not tonight. Sleep."

She *was* really tired. But ... "What about you?"

"I will watch."

"You need sleep too."

"I will wake you," Emel assured her.

Jenna gave him a suspicious look. His expression was perfectly bland. "You'd better," she muttered, and stretched out on the ground ... was the ground getting more comfortable, or was she just getting more tired? ... and rested her head on Emel's leg. She could hear Imbutaiyon saying something, not far away. Not far enough away. She wished they were alone ... with no outlaws anywhere within miles ... if The Creep touched her, she really would kill him ... she was gone.

7

Daniel felt stupid with exhaustion in the morning, bright sunlight notwithstanding. Fear for Jenna was a constant, but besides that fear, the tension of the previous afternoon clung to him. The thought of what he meant to do this morning, what he meant to do if he couldn't think of anything better, was worst of all. He already knew he wouldn't think of anything better. The strange, suicidal idea he'd already come up with was just too compelling. The thought of it was a continual, surreal kind of pressure in the back of his mind.

He refused, with tired revulsion, the sweetened fruit and bread the servants offered, though he accepted a cup of tea. Then he went back to his room, and sat on the window-ledge, eyes closed against the morning light. After a while he dressed with uncharacteristic attention to detail and a feeling he recognized, with bleak humor, from job interviews and board defenses he'd once done. That felt like a lifetime ago. But it was all one life, and he had no assurance his own cleverness wasn't going to cut it short before another night fell. Though if death let him avoid another night of dreams like the last, that wouldn't be all bad.

Black humor as a defense mechanism, he diagnosed wryly, and went out to see if Tenai were still in the apartment.

She wasn't. So there could be no excuse for putting this off. No delays.

"I'll just wait for her, then," Daniel told one of her attendants, and put his hand on the door that led to her private rooms. The attendant, one of the women Taranah had sent to Tenai's household, protested, "Forgive me, Nola Danyel, but no one is supposed to enter that room when Nolas-e Tenai is absent."

"Good," said Daniel without thinking, and added quickly, "It'll be a private place for me to catch up on my reading while I wait, then." He brushed past the woman and into Tenai's private apartment as though he had no idea anyone might possibly object, and shut the door behind him.

There was no sitting room, which Daniel knew now was customarily the outermost room of any apartment. This was a study, and it was dark. Daniel opened a shutter and looked around in the light thus admitted to the room. A desk. Chairs. Scrolls. Ah. Yes. This had been a sitting room, but Tenai had been treating it as a study. Amazing how much paperwork crept into everybody's daily routine, in this world or any other.

More important, far more fraught, Tenai's sword still hung in its place. The sword's black sheath and dull black hilt were hardly visible among the shadows. But it was there.

Daniel took a slow breath. He stood still for a moment, listening. The sounds of human activity came to him, dimly, through the closed door. No one opened it. Probably no one would. Which was good, because there would be, he knew, no way to lock it from this side. There were supposed to be wards that prevented unauthorized persons from intruding, but if there were, they hadn't touched him.

So. A third path, the one that led directly between murdering Mitereh and sacrificing Jenna, the only plan he'd been able to think of that stood a real chance of thwarting Keitah entirely. Daniel stepped across the room and lifted the black sword from its hook. He'd held it before once or twice, but it didn't seem as heavy as he remembered. Awkward in the hand, though. The hilt was cold. Unsheathing it, he held up the sword. Light slid greasily along the black blade; faint wavery lines ran along it. Its edge shone silver. A shudder went through him at the feel of it in his hand, though he could not put a finger on why it felt so wrong. Gomantang. *He,* Tenai said, of the sword. He loves death and destruction, blood and destruction ... something like that. Daniel felt that. He *felt* the sword in his hand, wanting to turn and cut ... he was unreasonably convinced that if he dropped it, it would twist back and pierce his foot.

A gate that led into Lord Death's dark country. If he had the nerve to use it. If Daniel hadn't seen Tenai use it that way to send a dying man directly into Lord Death's country, this would have been impossible. As it was ... it was merely horribly frightening. And awkward. The sword was too long to comfortably hold reversed. In the end, Daniel removed his shirt, braced the hilt against the back of the chair and placed the tip of the sword over his heart, carefully aiming between two ribs, steadying it with his hands wrapped in his shirt. And paused, getting up his nerve. Just how hard did one have to lunge, to get the sword through the chest wall and into the heart? Wasn't this the sort of thing that Antony had botched in *Antony and Cleopatra?* It would be worse than embarrassing to lunge forward and impale himself the wrong way. He could be lying on the floor gasping when Tenai came back, and how exactly would he explain that? *He loves death and destruction.* Well, good. Let the damned sword do the job right, then.

In the end, he found the sword went in very easily, slipping between his ribs with hardly any sense that he was being cut. There was not nearly as much pain as he had expected, but there was an ugly sense of invasion, of spreading cold. Daniel's vision went dark, not gradually, but all at once. He thought he heard a voice whispering, but did not understand what it said. There was a grating, malevolent tone to it that frightened him so that he did not want to understand it.

It was dark. Blind, Daniel was aware only that he did not seem to have a sword stuck into his chest. He moved a hand across his ribs, encountering nothing ... he had a body, then. As he thought this, he found he had a sense of his own body; that he knew he was standing, not lying down. Standing on something ... not earth or stone, not a rug. A surface like ice, absolutely smooth, stretching out in all directions. As this occurred to him, he understood that he could see this ... place, this plain of ice. Despite the dark. That he could perceive it, perceive himself.

It was cold, terribly cold. Daniel felt the cold, yet did not shiver. He was still dressed as he had been for his death, he realized; trousers and low boots, shirtless. The stone pendant Keitah had forced him to take still hung on its chain around his neck. He could not tell whether it was cold to the touch; here, everything was cold. He should have been freezing, but he was not. There was no blood on his chest, on his hands. There was no sign of Tenai's sword. But ... it seemed to him that there was a ring of tall stones or pillars before him.

The stones pierced through the smooth ice without, somehow, seeming to disturb its featureless expanse. The stone circle was at least something that offered direction. Daniel took a step in that direction, and paused. It seemed to him suddenly that a great number of people were pouring along with him toward that circle, that he could hear their voices, though he didn't understand what they said. Mostly he thought they sounded sad. Sometimes they sounded angry. Once or twice he thought a voice that went past him sounded glad, joyous. These voices did not frighten him. He wanted to hear them more clearly, even the sad ones, even the angry ones, and so took another step along with the rushing people, toward the stone ring. It seemed suddenly urgent he should go to it, step into its unseen center. He took another step.

And found his way blocked. It took him a moment to understand that. There was a bar, some kind of narrow barrier made of solidified shadow, laid across his path. So he could not go to the stone circle, though all around him he thought that hundreds, even thousands, of other people were rushing toward it. He touched the bar curiously. It was cold. Cold radiated back from it through his hand, striking upward toward his shoulder. It should have been an unpleasant sensation, but it was not. Still, he had a sense that he should take his hand away from the bar. That to touch it was wrong somehow, almost immoral. That it would be somehow worse to try to get around the barrier, or duck under it. He looked along it instead, peering along what seemed the great length of the bar, into the distance.

And saw that the barrier which had seemed so long was in fact a staff, and that Lord Death was holding it out to block his way.

He wore the form of a man, if a man could be made of darkness and ice. He was much easier to make out here in this blind darkness than he had been in the king's apartment, when he had come at Tenai's request to question a dying man and then a living one. Here, he looked a lot more like a man. His features were strong. Harsh. His mouth was thin, hard—even cruel. His eyes were hollow, so that Daniel felt he was looking through them into the depths of night. He seemed to be simultaneously very far away and near enough to reach with a few steps. Daniel wanted at once to flee from him and to crouch like an animal at his feet. Every thought, every rational reason he'd had to pick up Tenai's sword and deliberately come to this place, fled from his mind.

It was a faint memory of Jenna that brought reason back. The memory of her voice … oddly, he thought of her first as she had been the year his wife had died, as a child. She had had nightmares, and called out to him in the night … he thought of her as she was now, a bright, bold young woman … he thought of her screaming, collapsed on the ground in Keitah's garden in Kinabana, and it was this memory that brought back his own courage. Meeting Lord Death's hollow eyes, he took a step forward.

He stood at once in a great echoing hall, in a palace with walls of black glass and a floor of flawless black stone. The vaulted ceiling arced overhead like the night sky. Chandeliers overhead bore hundreds of candles that burned with black flames and cast darkness like light, in a strange kind of reverse illumination. Long ornate tables lined the hall to either side, each with perhaps a thousand chairs, but no one sat at them. A throne of black ice stood on a low dais at the far end of the hall, and Lord Death sat in that throne, staring out over the hall with unreadable hollow eyes set in a blank and inhuman face. Behind his throne, a simple door stood half-open. This door was not set into a wall. It stood on its own, a plain framework of smooth black wood containing a simple wooden door, also black. Though it stood half-open, nothing was visible through this door.

Daniel took a step toward the throne, and, though it had seemed far away, discovered that he had come, in that one step, right to the foot of the dais. Lord Death looked out upon his hall. He might not have even known Daniel was there. This lack of attention might have been a pretense, a way to make the lowly feel lower still. Daniel did not for a moment think this ... being ... would trouble with such pretense. He stood for a moment, confused, staring up at the throne. Then he put a foot on the dais, meaning, as he had come this far, to go all the way to the throne if he must and set a hand on Lord Death's foot.

But instead of stepping up on the dais, he found himself at once in a frosted winter pasture, with the wide sky overhead blazing with dark stars and a single black candle as tall as he was, set directly into the frozen earth and burning with a long black flame. Lord Death stood only a yard or so from him. Only now Lord Death was looking at him with close attention. He did not look in any sense welcoming, but neither did he seem precisely hostile.

"Lord," Daniel said to him.

Daniel, said Lord Death. **For your kindness to my lady while she dwelt in your land, I am grateful. Yet seldom do men presume upon my gratitude. Why are you come here to my kingdom before your time?**

Lord Death's voice was not like the voice of a man. Nor was it like the voice Daniel had remembered from Mitereh's apartment. It was heavier here, more fraught with power. It contained the withering chill wind from the heights and the slow tolling of leaden bells. It made Daniel want to cast himself to the ground and beg Lord Death to turn his attention away. To curl up in a ball and scream and weep. He set his teeth hard and tried to take a deep breath, except he was not breathing. Yet he found he could speak. That, with effort, he could almost speak without his voice shaking. "Lord. Your lady is in danger. I know she is. I know who her enemy is, but he ... in the, the other kingdom, he listens to every word I say and I cannot warn her."

But you can tell me, said Lord Death. **Trusting to me to warn her. You came here to me for that purpose?**

"I couldn't ... I couldn't think of anything else to do. Please, Lord. Am I right that no one living can hear me, here?" Daniel touched his chest, where Keitah's pendant still hung. The chain felt like ice against his neck and chest.

The living have no congress with the dead, answered Lord Death. **He cannot hear you here, whatever spell he set upon you in the outer kingdom. I would know this name. What bargain would you make with me for the name of my lady's enemy?**

Daniel almost laughed in astonishment and terror. "Lord ... I'm a stranger in Tenai's land and in yours, but I don't ... I don't believe it's at all wise to bargain with you. I ask. That's all. I only ask. I know you can send me back to ... I know you can restore me to life. If I'm found dead, probably Tenai's enemy would understand what I did, what I tried to do, so it would ... I think it would be better for everyone if that didn't happen. You gave Tenai a horse, long ago, when she first left your kingdom. You restored it to life when you did that."

I did. A pause. Then Lord Death said, **You were eager for the gate, when you saw it waiting.**

The stone circle, Daniel realized. "You stopped me then, Lord. Thank you. I would like to ... to live. If you will. The enemy is Keitah Terusai-e. He ... I was to murder Mitereh, he took Jenna for a hostage to make me do it. But I only pretended to try. Please, Lord. It's very important to me that Tenai know that it was only a ruse, that I never intended to kill Mitereh, that I was only pretending in order to fool Keitah. That if I have to pretend to do it again, I will, but it's all a pretense."

That is two favors you ask of me.

"Yes," said Daniel, realizing this was true. "Please, Lord."

Lord Death held out one hand. Above him, dark stars

wheeled through a measureless sky. **Approach,** he said.

Daniel stared at Lord Death's dark hand for a moment. Then he took the necessary step and reached out to touch the offered hand.

Lord Death's hand closed around his in a hard grip. **You may ask a third favor of me. Remember,** he said. He drew Daniel close, and then flung him away. Darkness whirled about Daniel, and dazzling light. What felt like a succession of silent shocks jarred all through his body ... utterly disoriented, Daniel lunged to his feet, staggered, and found himself standing in Tenai's study with her sword lying, clean and unbloodied, on the floor behind him.

Fortunately, Tenai did not come in at that moment. Daniel had time to put her sword back where he had found it ... picking it up with his hands wrapped in his shirt, flinching from the cold that seemed to radiate from its black hilt. He put his shirt back on. His fingers were stiff and clumsy on the laces at the throat, so that in the end he gave up and left the shirt unlaced. Then he moved a chair over to the window and sat down in the sunlight, looking out over the slanting white and pink rooftops and crystalline towers and broad gardens of the palace.

He longed for the world he'd lost, less lovely and far less dangerous, where a dark kingdom didn't underlie the real world, where you couldn't drive a sword into your own body to go there ... where, most of all, no sorcerer had kidnapped his daughter and forced him to personally experience such things. *Oh, Jenna.* Surely Keitah hadn't hurt her. Surely he hadn't. He wouldn't, couldn't know about Daniel's visit to the underworld, or wherever he had gone. Jenna would be safe. She *would* be safe.

Daniel found he was shivering, fine tremors that seemed to radiate from the core of his body outward. The real world somehow seemed strange. Not brighter, exactly. And not more real. In fact, it seemed in some strange way to *lack* reality. It seemed to Daniel that the real world lay stretched out like the skin of a soap bubble on top of a vast depth of dark strangeness. And as though he had somehow become able to see its ... thinness. Its fragility.

Darkness edged Daniel's vision. He seemed to catch glimpses of Lord Death's kingdom out of the corners of his eyes, as though it pressed against the edges of the world of the living. Shadows seemed to have acquired a frightening kind of depth. They showed a disturbing tendency, if Daniel looked into them for too long, to creep out sideways and begin to nibble away at the bright areas of the world. He shifted a little further into the sunlight streaming through Tenai's window, trying to drown himself in light. An aimless thought about skin cancer drifted through his mind, ludicrously out of place.

That thought should have carried humor, but it didn't. The trembling was passing off at last, but he still felt cold and ill. He found himself touching his own chest, and the touch brought back a memory of Tenai's sword sliding into his body. For a moment, Daniel thought he might throw up. He leaned his head on his hand and shut his eyes—then opened them again quickly and tilted his face to the light. He wanted to drink the light; he wanted to wrap himself up in it, absorb it through his skin and let it run through his veins ...

There was a sound at the door. Daniel shut his teeth hard against a gasp. He'd expected to be able to hide what he'd done, if he lived through it. He'd *counted* on being able to hide it. But he knew he wouldn't be able to. At least not right now. Not from Tenai. He stared helplessly at the door, feeling like a rabbit caught in headlights.

But no one came in. Thank God for small mercies. Daniel tilted his head back against the back of his chair and stared again into the light.

He dreamed of a falcon that flew in long circles through an empty sky, only he slowly realized that the sky was cut from a single great clear stone and that the bird's flight traced a vast circle through this stone. The circle was a gateway. A river poured and poured through this gate, only the water was so clear it could not be seen, but he knew it was there. The river was made up of a thousand voices that called to him, many grieving and some joyous; he heard Jenna's voice amongst the rest and jerked sharply upright, choking back a gasp.

"You have not been sleeping well, I perceive," Tenai said quietly. She was sitting, booted feet stretched out before her, at her desk. She had been reading through a long scroll, but she let it roll up now as she turned toward him. She added, "You are suffering from dreams. I am sorry you have found Talasayan a frightening and difficult land."

"I—" said Daniel. "What time is it?" The quality of the light in the room had changed. Tenai had opened all the shutters on all the windows, but the sun had shifted so that Daniel was no longer sitting in a flood of light. He got up and, trying to make the move look casual, repositioned his chair in a pool of sunlight by one of the other windows.

"Well past midday. You are cold?" said Tenai. "Sometimes dreams leave us chilled." She rose and went to the door, calling for hot spiced wine. Then she turned and stood in the doorway, her arms folded over her chest, observing him with uncomfortable intensity. "Mitereh is not angry with you."

For a long moment, Daniel could not imagine what she meant. Then it came back to him. But the trick with the crossbow seemed now a hundred years in the past. Everything seemed to have fallen into the past, the memory of darkness barring the way between him and everything that had ever happened prior to his little visit to Lord Death. He shuddered.

"The boy took no harm of it, and he favors you still," said Tenai, a trace of impatience in her tone. "Do not repine over it."

Daniel supposed he was lucky everyone could ascribe anything strange they saw in him to the crossbow incident. He didn't feel lucky at all. He cleared his throat. "Should I go find him?"

"He has not called for you. He assuredly will. This evening, I am certain, if not before." Tenai took a tray with goblets of spiced wine from the attendant who brought it, and carried one of the goblets across the room to Daniel.

Daniel took it, grateful to find that his hands were no longer trembling. The fragrant spices smelled wonderful, but he hesitated. "I didn't have anything to eat this morning. If a roll or something might be possible, I'd be grateful."

The request came out more tentatively than he'd intended, but Tenai still did not seem to hear anything amiss in his tone. She only glanced at the attendant, who whisked off to fetch food. Something bland, Daniel hoped. He looked at Tenai, trying to decide whether she looked as though she'd been receiving messages from ... well, from beyond the grave, so to speak. She only looked mildly impatient. Probably it wasn't realistic to expect Lord Death to have passed Daniel's warning along to her so quickly. Daniel found his hands inclined again to tremble, and quickly sipped wine. Its warmth was welcome, but didn't seem to touch the essential chill that beset him.

Food arrived: bread with soft, salty cheese and some sort of fruit compote. Daniel ate a bite of the bread plain and drank more wine. He sighed and closed his eyes, leaning back in his chair and turning his face to the warmth of the afternoon sun.

Tenai went back to her papers, taking up a sheet of vellum and dipping a feather pen in a clay bottle of ink.

In the moment of odd privacy this gave him, Daniel experimented with his strangely-afflicted eyesight. He studied the way the shadows in the room changed when he looked at them straight on versus sidelong; looked out the window over the palace, where the afternoon light poured over the walls and roofs; lifted his own hands to watch the shadow they cast. All the shadows, indoors or out, still seemed unsettlingly dark. Nor did the sunlight that fell between the shadows seem as bright as it should. The shadows of his hands seemed in some strange way to have gained a disturbing kind of solidity. Daniel opened and closed his fingers, watching the darkness shift and cling.

"You have been closeted here since morning, I am told," Tenai said, glancing up from her writing.

Daniel started and dropped his hands again to his lap, trying to pretend he hadn't ever seen anything odd about light or shadows in his life, and certainly not recently. Certainly not in this room or this moment. He prevented himself, by an effort of will, from glancing toward her sword.

Tenai said, again with that impatience in her tone, "You wished to see me, then?"

"Uh—" said Daniel, and opted for a small part of the truth: "I think I was just looking for a place to hide."

Tenai gave him a close look. That air of impatience eased. "My friend. I am sorry you should have so difficult a sojourn here: assassins and subtle courtiers and demanding kings. I would send you back to your own country at once if I could."

But it would take a human sacrifice to do it—if she could find somebody willing to be sacrificed. Which Daniel would certainly not have permitted, even if she could. Not even for Jenna's sake. But to make the shadows behave ... fortunately the temptation was nullified, because Tenai wouldn't do it anyway. He said, almost at random, "I didn't ... complicate things for you, did I?"

Another dismissive gesture. "I tell you, do not concern yourself, Daniel. Yes, you are correct: some of the less discerning believe I might have arranged for you to strike at the king. As Mitereh does not believe it, the suspicion is of little moment."

"He wouldn't think that," Daniel agreed. "I don't think he would." He cast around for some way to change the subject. "What's that you're working on?" The moment the words were out, he remembered that Keitah was listening to everything he said, everything anyone said to him. He added at once, "Never mind, I'm sure I wouldn't understand it anyway, since I don't know anything about Talasayan politics." He edged his chair a little forward, following the sun. Puffy summer clouds had formed, soft and full. One of them looked like it was going to block the sunlight in another few minutes. He set his teeth and tried not to watch it.

Tenai smiled. "You do not know many people here, of course, but you will understand enough when I tell you I am writing a letter a man who is a great nuisance. His name is Cardinal Imainan Tangan-sa-e." She finished a last line and blew gently on the ink to dry it. Then she rolled up the paper, slipped a ribbon around it, and summoned an attendant, to whom she gave the letter with an exaggerated gesture of relief. "This should calm him for a day and another day. May the Martyr grant me patience if I must deal with him again before at least that much time has passed."

The attendant had taken the letter with a small bow. "Shall I put this at once into the hands of a messenger, Nolas-e?"

Tenai waved a hand. "Yes. Go. I assure you, I shall not desire a reply. Tell the messenger he need not wait for one." She turned back to study Daniel.

He braced himself for dangerous curiosity, for some sort of probing question he would have to mislead or avoid. She said instead, with an odd note to her voice, "He trusts easily, this son of Encormio. I do take note of it."

Daniel eyed Tenai, drawn for the moment out of his own problems. She did not mean the way Mitereh trusted Daniel, he thought. She meant the way the king trusted her. He offered, "Not ... easily, I don't think."

"No? Perhaps not, then. But it is a decisive trust. An admirable quality, I am sure."

There might have been an edge of scorn in that. Or dislike. Or resentment. Or something else. Daniel wasn't certain. He said, keeping his own tone mild, "I think it is, actually. It wouldn't be helpful if the king refused to trust you, Tenai."

Tenai gave him a sharp, sidelong look. "Indeed. Certainly he makes use of me in many ways. Most lately, I have been engaged in alarming the current emissary from Imbaneh-se. It is not a difficult task, and it may yet yield something of worth."

He ventured, "You're still of the opinion that Imbaneh-se is most likely behind ... everything?" Once more he thought of charades and obscure references and hints Tenai might catch and

Keitah miss—but he'd already tried something that ought to work better than any subtle hint. Surely Lord Death would explain everything to Tenai tonight, if he hadn't done it yet.

Tenai was answering him, her tone absent. "I think it likely Imbaneh-se is involved, though I also strongly suspect a closer enemy. Perhaps this provoking cardinal, who may yet prove to be less a fool than he seems." She gazed at the remaining rolls of vellum on the table, perhaps considering what other letters she might write. Then, instead, she rolled out a different scroll and indicated a section of close angular writing. "Here we have the condensed reports of Mitereh's agents in the south. There have been interesting movements of men and resources there, not only near the border, but in the deeper south. These are coordinated movements: someone has formed broad plans. I hope to gain an understanding of the shape of those plans from these reports. Knowledge of what is intended to happen may lead us to a clearer understanding of who intends it."

Daniel nodded. This sounded reasonable.

"And I have ground of my own to prepare and sow, here in Talasayan," Tenai went on. Her tone was abstracted. Even uninvolved. She added, with no change in that tone, "If Mitereh were out of the way, I believe we would find the resulting situation exceedingly fluid."

Daniel looked at her sharply. He couldn't tell whether she was deliberately speaking to Keitah through him. He wanted to think so. He just couldn't tell. He asked, trying to keep his own tone ordinary, "Fluid in a bad way?"

"Events would likely become unpredictable and alliances ambiguous. Our enemy has likely laid long plans for such a time." Tenai's manner had become brisk. She rolled up the scroll of reports and slipped its ribbon back on. "There are people with whom I must meet this afternoon. Do you wish to remain here? Or return to your own room? If your thoughts and dreams trouble you, Daniel, I will prescribe a change of prospect and activity. You could be of service to me: I would value your opinion of the men I will see. Will you accompany me?"

"Gladly." Daniel stood up. Shadows swung around him with the movement and he swallowed and stood still for a moment to catch his balance. Then he had trouble walking because of a feeling that he might accidentally put a foot right down through the floor into the strange kingdom lying right beneath. It was a very odd feeling. Even sort of ... schizophrenic, in a way. *Out of touch with reality, Doctor?* he asked himself wryly, and it was even stranger to know that, instead, reality had in fact slipped out of true.

Fortunately Tenai had gone ahead of him out of her apartment and noticed nothing.

8

Morning brought sunlight through the trees, the chirps and trills of unseen birds, the low sounds of the waking camp, and a seriously stiff neck. Jenna sat up, groaning. Emel sat near her, his back against a tree, his hands linked around a drawn-up knee. He looked watchful, but not particularly tense.

The woman with the scarred mouth was stirring something in a pot ... leftover stew, Jenna thought. She hoped the pot had been kept hot all night or they'd probably all die of food poisoning. Men were mostly just sitting around. Nobody was helping the woman.

Kuomat came over and squatted down to talk to Emel, not even glancing at Jenna. "We have a number of possible activities open to us," Kuomat said. "We could try the Kinabana-Nerinesir road. There is a town with a good inn a little to the north where sometimes wealthy men stay; we could go look for opportunities there. Or we could slip south, work our way around the bay towns to the Gai-e road. Do you have, perhaps, a suggestion?"

"South might be as well," Emel said, in a tone that implied it didn't really matter.

"South it is," Kuomat agreed. He stood up. "We will wait for the rest of my people, however. You might want to sleep while we wait." Emel didn't say anything. Kuomat walked away.

"Is he mad because you watched all night?" Jenna asked.

"No. He wants me to know that he thinks I am a fool." Emel sounded amused. "He means that there are enough of his people here to kill me whether we keep watch or whether we do not."

"Oh."

"I want him to know that he will lose men if he tries me," said Emel. "I should bring you food. Forgive me that I must ask you instead to serve me."

He wasn't looking at her. More uncomfortable asking her to bring him breakfast than getting ready for a knife fight. Men were weird. Jenna went off and got a bowl of stew for him and one for her.

"You should get some sleep," she said, coming back and handing him his breakfast. "Since you didn't wake me up like you said you were going to."

"You were tired," he muttered. He ate the stew and lay down where he was. Jenna sat beside him. He didn't put his head on her leg, though.

She leaned back against the tree and watched the outlaw camp. Nobody was doing much. The woman put the rest of the stew into bowls to wait, she assumed, for other members of the camp to eat when they came in. She didn't cover the bowls. Flies were landing on the food. Jenna tried not to watch them. The woman had taken the pot over to a pool of standing water and was cleaning it ... not very thoroughly. Jenna sighed, got up, went over, took the pot away from her, and did the job herself, with a twist of coarse grass. It was heavy, and the remains of what appeared to be decades of meals made the job harder than it should have been. Jenna wished she had steel wool. She got a bigger handful of grass.

The woman had given Jenna a look when she took the pot ... not a grateful look. A look of anger and resentment. "What's your name?" Jenna asked her. She wasn't supposed to talk much, but surely that was safe.

But the woman spat at Jenna's feet. "Pretty girl," she said in a tone like a curse, and stalked away.

Jenna stared after her. She could see, on reflection, that the woman might resent a younger, prettier woman. But ... she sighed and finished cleaning the pot. What did she care if the woman liked her or not? These people were nothing to her. She hoped passionately that they would not have to stay with them long.

After scrubbing the pot again, she rinsed it out with water that probably wasn't anything like clean and heaved it up on the bank.

It was a wonder anybody had to hunt outlaws down and kill them. They all ought to die of dysentery.

Imbutaiyon came over and picked up the pot with one hand. "I'll carry this back for you," he offered. He smiled at her. "You're a pretty girl."

Jenna gave him a scornful look, took several steps back to make absolutely sure he couldn't grab her from behind, not that there weren't ways to deal with a man who grabbed you from behind, and went back to sit with Emel.

Behind her, Imbutaiyon said plaintively, "How did I offend?" and another man, watching, grinned and answered, loud enough for her to hear, "That's a flower that only wants one bee, man. Just as well, or Katawarin would cut off your parts and then how would you piss?"

Jenna ignored them both, though she wondered who, and where, Katawarin was. She glanced at Emel. He still looked deeply asleep. Good. He needed the rest. She leaned back against the tree and tried to relax.

After some time, Kuomat gave a low whistle and she looked up, but it seemed only to be a signal to break camp and pack everything up. Canvas got rolled up and the wooden frames for the lean-tos taken apart. The branches were discarded, the lashings carefully rolled up and tucked away. Men picked up weapons and other things. Everyone had a pack or a bag or at least a pouch.

Kuomat went over to the sick man, who was sitting near the fire, and talked to him in a low voice.

Somebody else whistled and everybody turned to look. Jenna put a hand on the heavy crossbow, seeing people approach, but it was apparently the rest of Kuomat's gang. Pack. Whatever. It seemed like a crowd. Jenna tried to remember how many people Kuomat had said he had. Should she wake Emel? He needed sleep. She glanced at him doubtfully. Despite all the activity, he was still asleep. Not that anyone was making a lot of noise, but still, he must be really tired. She was angry as well as worried: he should have let her take a watch last night.

The other people had come into the camp. There were two men, Jenna saw, and two women, and though they all seemed more interested in breakfast than in her or Emel, plenty of glances came their way. She could tell they were asking about the new recruits, and she could tell from his tone and attitude that Imbutaiyon was being flamboyant with his description. Imbutaiyon seemed to be a popular guy. Nobody was talking to Tantang. One of the men had gone to talk to Kuomat. The two women withdrew toward the edge of camp, with bowls of stew and no male company. The woman with the scarred mouth didn't join them.

Kuomat stepped up on a fallen tree, obviously calling for attention. Jenna reluctantly patted Emel's hand.

He woke up at once, this time without any scary jerks toward weapons. He sat up, took in the new arrivals, glanced at the outlaw leader, nodded.

"File order," Kuomat said, not loudly, with a tone that said he just assumed everybody would shut up and listen to him. Everybody did. "Medai, you and Bau will go first, and I want you ready to pass a signal back if you see anything out of the usual. Then Imbutaiyon. Imbutaiyon, you are in command if the front of the file discovers anything amiss in our way."

Imbutaiyon grinned and nodded.

"Then Saimadan, Katawarin and Panaih. Panaih, no talking. Tantang after that. Inasad will follow Tantang. Petat," he glanced at the sick man and received a resigned nod, "will stay here. Katawarin, put food aside for him. Petat, we will come back this way in not so many days and hope to find you recovered. If you can follow on, we are going to the camp down near Nemesen."

The sick man nodded again.

"The new man is Bukitraya," said Kuomat. "The woman is his." He didn't bother to give her name. "They will come last in the file, with me. Bukitraya, I will have my bow back."

Emel bent, picked up the crossbow, walked over to the outlaw, and handed it to him. Kuomat took the bow without comment, slung it by its strap over his shoulder, and walked away again, gesturing to his people to move out.

For a while, Jenna almost enjoyed the hike. There was no trail, but they were out of the marsh in about an hour and after that the walking was pretty easy. And the weather was nice. Not too hot yet. In some ways it was easier to walk than ride because at least she wasn't going to whap her leg into a tree or anything, and she wasn't tired yet. Emel and she came right at the tail end of the line—behind even Kuomat, which probably meant something or other. She hoped it wasn't supposed to be an insult, but she liked having all the brigands in front where she could see them.

Birds called. Squirrels whisked around tree trunks. Emel shot one, cleaned it beside the trail, wrapped it in leaves, and tucked it into a pouch. Katawarin shot another one. One of the other women paused at a patch of some kind of plant and pulled up some, collecting the white tubers that grew on the roots. Jenna began to feel like they were hunters and gatherers, some prehistoric tribe that should be carrying flint-tipped spears and clubs with stone heads. She wished she could joke about that with Emel, but he probably wouldn't get the joke, and besides, she wasn't supposed to talk.

The ground got rougher after that. Kuomat was taking them by ways horses couldn't manage, she assumed. Jenna only wished she could manage them better herself. The sun mounted higher in the sky and the temperature climbed. Biting insects came out, not as bad as in the marshy places but bad enough, and the hike stopped being nice and started being unpleasant. By the time they stopped for a break, Jenna was tired, hot, hungry, and in a thoroughly bad mood. Katawarin, an older and taller woman than Jenna, with strong arms and hands and a cold don't-touch-me aura, made a fire with a drop of blood. The woman with the scarred mouth—by now Jenna knew her name was Angana—cooked the squirrels and the tubers and everybody had a few bites, plus the rest of the bread.

Then they went on. At midafternoon they came to a small road. After a brief pause for Kuomat to consult with Imbutaiyon and one of the other men, they spread out along both sides of this road and settled down to rest. Emel and Jenna sat down near Kuomat, up on a slight rise on the east side of the road where brush screened them from view. Jenna could just barely see Katawarin, who was the only woman armed: she carried a heavy crossbow and sat now behind a screen of brush that hid her nearly completely, from the road and from Jenna too.

"If there should be a fight, you will stay here and quiet," Emel told her. "Yes?"

Jenna nodded, her mouth dry.

"Probably there will not be a fight," he said, and leaned back against a tree. "Wake me if there is need." He shut his eyes.

Jenna stared at him. Kuomat glanced at her and smiled, not a very kindly smile. She looked away, flushing, glad for the dye that made a blush less obvious.

After what seemed like a long time—Jenna wanted to go to sleep herself and was tensing and relaxing all her muscles in turn to try to stay awake—two men came down the road, walking beside an ox pulling a wagon. Jenna looked at Kuomat. The brigand leader looked perfectly unconcerned. His heavy crossbow still lay on the ground at his side. The men went by, slowly, talking companionably about weather and, Jenna thought, sheep.

More time crept past. Jenna began to think she might put roots down into the ground and turn into a tree herself. They ought to be pressing on toward Nerinesir and they were sitting here? Waiting, for God's sake, to ambush and rob some harmless person? How stupid. How surreal. Why were they putting themselves through all this again? Right, to hide from Keitah. Had they really been in such danger traveling alone that this waste of time was actually worth it?

No way to ask that question now. No way to pick up and leave just at this moment, regardless. She leaned her head back against the trunk of the tree and tried to count the leaves on the lowest branch. Just past two thousand she lost count. She started over.

A pair of women rode past, with an escort of soldiers. The outlaws didn't move. Emel opened his eyes, measured the party on the road, and shut his eyes again.

Shadows lengthened slowly. A whole afternoon gone. Lost. They could never get those hours back. Would her father be back in Nerinesir yet? Probably not. But close. So much closer than she'd managed to get. Would he have figured out a way to beat Keitah yet? Would he guess she'd escaped? Jenna could not persuade herself either was at all likely. Maybe Tenai would take one look at him and know something was wrong. She wondered again what Keitah had done to make sure he didn't just tell Tenai everything.

A pair of approaching men, escorting a single older woman, interrupted this increasingly disturbing train of thought. Their horses all moved at an gentle trot. Emel lifted his head again and this time stayed alert, though Jenna had no idea what made these particular travelers more interesting than any of the others. Kuomat got to his feet, quietly. So did Emel. Jenna stayed where she was, tucked up like a little mouse.

Kuomat raised his crossbow with a smooth motion and fired, without seeming particularly to aim. The black bolt thumped into the ground in front of one of the horses; two other bolts followed immediately. The horses startled and shied. The male riders cursed—the woman let out a small scream. One of the men reached for a bow slung at his saddle, the other for a sword. Katawarin lifted her bow and fired very carefully. Her bolt struck the man's crossbow, jolting it hard. The man swore, jerking his hand back. Jenna blinked. Wow. Katawarin could really shoot.

Kuomat walked forward so that he could be seen. "Enough!" he said coldly to the young men. "Be sensible or go to the dark kingdom; I've no patience with fools who think Lord Death will not hear the whisper of their names."

The rider with the bow dropped it. The one with the sword shoved it back in its sheath. The woman gripped her reins so hard Jenna thought her horse might try to rear, but it didn't.

Emel went past Kuomat, jumping lightly down to the road. He picked up the heavy bow and tossed it up to land at Kuomat's feet. He didn't even have his sword drawn, but tapped the young man's leg with his closed fist. "Down," he said.

"God curse you—" the man began, and Emel reached up unhurriedly, caught his arm, and jerked him off his horse. He hit the ground hard enough to cut off the rest of what he'd been going to say.

"Taya—" said the other rider, and the woman screamed again, though half-heartedly.

"Be quiet. Get down," said Emel. Three of the other outlaws had come out on the road; to Jenna's surprise one of them was Tantang. She could see the others: Saimadan was a heavy-jawed sullen-eyed thug who looked just the type to cow victims into submission, and the other one, Bau, was at least as big. But none of the three had a weapon out. Bows in the woods, that was the threat, Jenna understood. It was a good threat. The other young man, tight-lipped, swung down from his horse. The first one started to scramble to his feet and Emel casually knocked him down again and put a foot on his neck, pinning him in the dirt. He had his sword drawn suddenly, and touched the point firmly to his prisoner's back. The man stopped resisting and lay still. The woman hadn't yet dismounted. She was so scared Jenna could hardly stand it. An outlaw had the reins of her horse. Another one had disarmed the other young man while someone else took his horse.

"Down," Emel said to the woman. "Or I'll help you down." She stared at him, wide-eyed.

The young man still on his feet produced a knife from somewhere, a little black thing with a pale, gleaming hilt, and Kuomat cursed, sounding surprised and alarmed out of proportion to anything Jenna could see. Saimadan lunged forward, a knife of his own out, but Emel was faster—he moved with speed Jenna hadn't seen since they'd got away from Keitah's house, certainly with more urgency than he had in his knife-fight with Imbutaiyon.

He hit Saimadan to knock him out of the way, and the young man to make him drop the knife. The knife itself, he caught before it hit the ground and tossed away into the underbrush.

"Kill that fool," Kuomat said, his tone arctic.

Shocked, Jenna stared at him—then turned quickly back toward the road. Saimadan, his mouth twisted in a sneer, was moving to obey Kuomat's order. The young man made a hopeless attempt to get away, but Emel held him firmly. "No!" Jenna said.

"No," Emel agreed, and stopped Saimadan in his tracks with a look.

Saimadan looked at Kuomat. The big outlaw was grinning, but tightly, and Jenna thought he was afraid of Emel and wanted Kuomat to take over because of that, not just because Kuomat was in charge.

"Is this yours to decide?" Kuomat demanded, staring at Emel. "The young man knew very well what he did when he chose to draw that tasaya blade."

"He did not. He was a fool. Young men are fools," Emel answered. He looked perfectly relaxed. "Would you kill a man for stupidity? Few enough would remain. Likely this young man is important to someone. Why else would he have such a charm? You know it would be unwise to spill his blood. And there is no need. He is no danger to us now."

Kuomat shook his head, looking disgusted. Jenna was terrified he might simply shoot Emel where he stood. But he only lifted a hand and let it fall again in a gesture that Jenna translated as *whatever*. "I will speak to you later." He turned his shoulder toward the road, his attitude now disdainful. "Proceed."

Emel forced the young man he held to his knees with a foot behind his knee and said shortly, "Be still." The man looked like he took this order very seriously—really, he looked terrified, poor guy. Emel handed him over to Bau. Then he went patiently to the woman's side and held up a hand to her. "If you please," he said, more gently. "No one will harm you, Nola. But you must dismount."

Kuomat's expression took on an ironic cast, but he didn't say anything. The woman tentatively gave her hand to Emel, who helped her down from her horse. "Tantang," Kuomat said.

The Creep went quickly through everybody's saddlebags and then searched the young men. He seemed to have a knack for guessing where to look to find valuables they had wanted to keep hidden; it was Tantang who found a ring tucked into a hidden seam of the woman's saddle. When he went to search the woman herself, both men started to object. Emel shut them both up with a single hard stare, but the stare he turned on Tantang was a lot more threatening than the one he directed toward the prisoners.

Tantang sneered, took another look at the bigger man's face, and threw a glance over his shoulder to Kuomat. Kuomat only said, "Be quick, man." Tantang looked resentful, but searched the woman a lot more politely than he'd searched the men. He brought everything he'd found to the outlaw leader. Jenna couldn't see what any of it was from where she sat. Kuomat glanced through it and nodded as though it was pretty much what he'd expected. "Tie their hands and tether the horses," he ordered.

There were rustles as the brigands began to depart. Emel came up the slope, picked up the bow, slung its strap over his shoulder, and held out a hand to Jenna.

Not much later, there was a campsite, brigands scattering along the banks of a stream by ones and twos. Nobody made lean-tos, but people spread canvas and blankets out on the ground. Imbutaiyon and Katawarin put theirs together as a matter of course—if anybody had told Katawarin that Imbutaiyon had tried to get Jenna away from Emel, she didn't seem to mind. Her attitude made it clear she didn't regard any other woman as real competition. No wonder, as striking as she was, and as good with a bow.

The big man, Bau, caught Panaih by the wrist and she looked annoyed, but let him put her blanket with his. Angana made a fire, got the pot out, and started making supper without help and without looking at anybody.

Kuomat, standing near the fire, glanced around. "Bukitraya."

Emel, who had tossed canvas down well away from the other outlaws for Jenna and himself, looked over his shoulder, put his new bow down on the canvas, gave Jenna a stay-here gesture, and walked over to face the leader of the brigands. Jenna stayed by the bow and tried not to look nervous.

"You contradicted my order on the road," Kuomat said, his tone mild. "Do you then seek to challenge me?"

"No," said Emel. He didn't look scared or upset. If anything, Jenna thought he seemed resigned.

The other outlaws had drifted up to watch. Imbutaiyon, smiling, nudged Katawarin. Katawarin rolled her eyes.

Kuomat hit Emel, a hard backhanded blow across the face. Emel, who had obviously expected it, barely moved. Then Kuomat picked up a piece of the firewood Angana had gathered and hit him several more times in quick succession—a quick jabbing blow forward into the stomach and then twice down across the back as he dropped to one knee. Those last blows left Emel on his hands and knees. Tantang laughed, a high unpleasant giggle. Some of the other brigands laughed, too.

"Well?" said Kuomat. *He* wasn't laughing.

Emel slowly rocked back to his knees. Lifting his head, he looked into Kuomat's face. He seemed neither afraid or offended. "Forgive my defiance."

"Will it happen twice?"

"No," said Emel.

Kuomat tossed his club into the fire and walked away. The circle of outlaws broke up. Imbutaiyon, to Jenna's surprise, offered Emel a hand up, which after a slight hesitation he took. He nodded to Imbutaiyon then, and came back to Jenna's side, moving like it hurt.

"You're all right?" she asked anxiously. "You're sure? Oh, I could *kill* Kuomat!"

He gave her a brief nod, though she knew he must be badly

bruised. "Kuomat is not at fault." He touched his stomach, gingerly. "Next time I will find a more subtle way to object. Of course he was offended. His punishment was light enough. He might have been far more rough."

"If you're sure," Jenna said doubtfully. "Sit down. Let me get you some water." But he did seem basically all right. She brought water, and then some of the soup Angana made. The soup was even pretty good. They sipped it out of bowls and watched shadows lengthen and spread between the trees.

"Emel? What's a tasaya knife?" Jenna asked, after a careful look around to make sure no one but Emel was close enough to hear.

"Do not call me by my name," he warned her. "It is a knife enspelled to captivate rather than fight. Had the young man brought that blade to life, anyone who looked at it might have been bound to stand in that place, seeing nothing, aware of nothing, until the man or another sorcerer released the spell."

Jenna thought about that. "Well ... that seems really handy for a man surrounded by enemies. Why was he a fool to draw it?"

"He did not have time to bring it to life. He would have had to prime the blade with his own blood and then invoke the spellwork. He should have seen he could not manage that. He should have understood that Kuomat meant only a little robbery and not murder. His act only frightened the outlaws. This was foolish, the more so because by that attempt, the young man showed himself sufficiently schooled to be a threat. It was not at all remarkable that Kuomat should demand his death. Only that he should relent. Only a man secure in his authority would have permitted my protest to stand."

"Oh." Jenna turned that over in her head. "I thought for a minute he would shoot you right there."

Emel did not answer, by which she understood that he'd thought that, too. He said after a long moment, "I must ask your forgiveness. I was a greater fool than that young man, to risk leaving you alone among these rough folk."

"Oh, well." Jenna hesitated. "We couldn't let Kuomat kill that guy. It was a risk worth taking. I'm glad you did it."

Full dark had slid down around them. Jenna tucked herself behind some bushes and bathed as well as she could in the cold stream, with no soap and no clean clothing to change into afterward. Then she crept back through the night the short distance to where Emel was waiting.

"You could get a bath, too," she whispered. "I'd watch."

"Curs don't," he muttered back. "You may. You are young and female and clearly new to this life. But I should not."

"Oh. Too bad." For a moment, Jenna sat by him in silence. It was too dark to see him well. He was just a big, breathing presence near her. She imagined she could feel him there more than see him; she thought she would know he was near her even if she were actually blind. Even if she had no sense of smell. "Did you—were you nice to those people because of me?"

"Yes," he answered bluntly.

Jenna was quiet for a moment. Then she asked, "What if I'd fallen down a cliff this morning and broken my neck? Would you still have been nice to them?"

There was a slight pause. Then Emel's deep voice answered again, "Yes. Because I would know you would have been pleased."

"Oh." Jenna, oddly, did not feel tired. Emel certainly couldn't be, after sleeping all afternoon.

It was somehow easier to talk to him in the dark, when she couldn't actually see him. She asked, diffident and yet somehow feeling like she had the right to ask, "You couldn't ... you weren't ... you didn't really go around and hurt and kill people. Did you? Before Tenai?"

This time the silence was longer. But Emel might, like her, have found the darkness somehow allowed a greater intimacy than had been possible before. He said, "In that pack ... the leader of that pack was a man like Tantang. Stronger, but ... like. And that company was not like this one. It was far less subtle, far less inclined to pass quietly through the countryside. One could not ride in that pack and be kind."

Jenna turned that over in her mind. It seemed impossible. "I don't understand how you could have been in that company. I just ... I really don't."

"I think," said Emel, and paused. "I think because I felt I did not deserve better. I had been a long time on the road, you understand. I think I felt I was no better than they, and so I made that true. I think I felt no one deserved better, and so I was willing ... to do the things we did. I wanted everyone to be brought low, as I had been."

He paused again, then said, "And then, a pack of that sort ... it does not last. Lords hunt that kind of outlaw down with considerable will, far more swiftly than a pack such as this, led by a man more restrained. I ... I think I may have looked forward to that also. To the sword or the rope, or whatever death waited. Until I saw Nolas-Kuomon and knew that it would come in that very hour, and found that, indeed, I did not want to die."

There was a silence. Jenna did not know what to say.

Emel added, "You deserve a better man as your guard. Forgive me."

He did not get up, did not even shift his weight. Yet Jenna felt him pull back from her as though he had physically walked away.

"Nobody," she said fiercely, "nobody could be braver or—or more loyal. You aren't that man. Not anymore. Anyway," she added more calmly, "Anyway, the very first time I saw you, you know, you were being kind to that poor man who was dying."

"Ah." Emel was silent for a long time, and Jenna thought he would not say anything else, but his deep voice went on at last. "That boy made me think of the boy I had been. I was sorry he would become ... like me. I thought ... when he died, I thought, at least he would be spared that."

"Oh." After a moment, Jenna asked, unable to help herself, "Exactly what kinds of things did you do?"

Emel asked harshly, "Would you wish to know?"

"Uh ... I guess not."

"And yet, I did those things. It is not ... it is not possible for me to be other than I am."

Jenna thought about that. She said finally, "Maybe not. But it's possible for you to be other than what you were."

He didn't answer. But the sense of withdrawal eased, and Jenna, as she stretched out, felt ... not happy, exactly. But maybe a little happier.

9

The 'people' Tenai had mentioned proved to be half a dozen court officials, none of whom Daniel knew. And none of whom knew him, perhaps more to the point: he would surely be so strange and foreign to them that they wouldn't see anything odd in his manner while he was waiting for the shadows to settle back down into their ordinary nature. He could only hope the shadows *would* start behaving like ordinary shadows, eventually. He rubbed his fingertips across his eyes, blinking hard.

He could make out, barely, that it was a small, finely-appointed room filled with clusters of chairs and low tables: a conference room was evidently a conference room in any world. The officials were seated around a table near the west wall of the room, a wall that consisted largely of a single very large window flanked by smaller windows, all with their shutters drawn back to let in the afternoon sun. Two of the men in this room sat in strong light in front of windows, and Daniel could hardly see their faces at all because of the sharp-edged shadows that streamed past them.

Tenai was seated in an ornate chair. Once the initial round of bows and courtesies was over, Daniel had, at Tenai's nod, sat down a little to one side. She had said she wanted his opinion of these men, but Daniel suspected, once faced with their cautious curiosity, that she'd primarily wanted him with her so he could distract them. This was, at least, a role that demanded neither skill nor concentration. He did not really understand what the talk was about. It seemed to skirt around some sort of complicated relationship between Talasayan and a smaller neighboring country, not Imbaneh-se, but a country called Keneseh, which Daniel recalled Tenai mentioning, but not in any detail.

Daniel had not been looking forward to meeting Mitereh again today. Even so, he was almost grateful when one of the king's young men, Badayan, tracked him down and indicated that the king was expecting Daniel to join him in the morning room. Whatever a morning room might be. Not, evidently, a room used only in the morning. It was well on toward evening by the time Badayan found him.

Daniel stood up, bracing one hand on the arm and then the back of his chair in a hopefully unobtrusive attempt to maintain his balance. "Excuse me," he said to Tenai, and glanced around the room to generalize this to the room as a whole. All the men rose and murmured polite responses, and Tenai said, with a regal inclination of her head, "Convey my respects to the king, Daniel, if you would, and assure him I shall not fail of our meeting this evening."

Obviously this was meant for the court officials, who by their common reaction—a subtle but general flinching—heard more in the simple request than Daniel recognized. Feeling entirely out of his depth, Daniel nodded and muttered some response and retreated from the room, following Badayan. He almost put a hand on the wall for balance, but didn't dare do anything that would so obviously reveal his problem. Instead, he made himself navigate in a straight line right across the chasms that the shadows of the chairs drew across the floor. The chasms did not open up and swallow him ... he had not been sure they wouldn't, and found it hard to relax until he was safely past the long shadows. The interior halls of the palace were better. Lantern light seemed to behave more normally than natural light from windows.

The morning room, a room connected to the king's personal apartment, unfortunately turned out to have two entire walls that were essentially open-air balconies, one to the east that looked out over a long, winding avenue of flowering trees and a small lake, and one to the south that gave a view over an interior courtyard with a fountain and smaller trees bearing small round fruit of red-blushed gold. The clouds that had threatened earlier had cleared and late afternoon light poured, thick as honey, over both scenes. Yet, warm as it was, the light seemed a fragile thing to Daniel. He could imagine the darkness that underlay it. He felt that the sunlight might part like curtains to reveal the night beneath. He closed his eyes for a moment, setting a hand on the doorframe for balance in a gesture he hoped looked natural. Then, opening his eyes again, he tried hard to keep his attention solely for the room itself.

The balconies and interior of the morning room were finished with smooth pink stone and polished pale wood. Delicate vases set on every small table held sprays of pink and cream flowers. The king was seated at one of these tables, along with Taranah and another, older, woman.

Inkaimon and Torohoh stood to one side, quietly alert. And, rising and coming forward from a corner of the room where Daniel had not at first seen him, was Keitah Terusai-e.

Daniel stood frozen, afraid of what his face might show.

Mitereh stood up and came forward a step, with a little gesture of welcome. "Ah, Nola Danyel, here is Keitah, returned from Kinabana!"

Daniel managed to force himself from stiffness to a smile. He nodded to Keitah. "Nolas-ai Keitah. This is a surprise. I hadn't expected you for some time yet. Jenna—and the queen?—aren't with you?"

"I followed you closely the entire distance," Keitah said, smiling. "But, no, your daughter remains under careful guard in Kinabana, with the queen, until such time as we are perfectly certain they may be safe to return to court."

There was nothing in the words or the tone to suggest that this simple statement was a threat, but obviously it was. Nearly overwhelmed by loathing, Daniel could not for a moment manage any response.

Keitah said smoothly into the pause, before it could grow awkward, "Once you were departed, I found I wished I had gone with you, Nola Danyel. So I left Nola Jenna and Nolas-ai Niah in the capable hands of my staff and came after you."

"My queen and your daughter will follow on in a few days," Mitereh said, perfectly cheerful, gesturing both Daniel and Keitah toward the table. "Come, sit with us. Keitah, my friend, you have been corresponding with Mikanan, I believe, so you will know what has occurred in your absence."

Keitah laughed and spread his hands. "Elaborate the details, do, Mitereh. You know Mikanan Chauke-sa: I have had only the broadest strokes painted in for me."

Mitereh grinned, spun a chair around, and settled on it sideways with his arm draped casually across its back. "I confess, I should not expect detailed brushwork from Mikanan."

"To be sure." Keitah accepted a tall silver cup of chilled wine from Taranah with a nod and took a chair near Mitereh. Like the young king, he looked amused. *Blandly* amused. If Daniel had not known of the man's duplicity, he would never have guessed it now. He wanted to signal Mitereh somehow. At the same time, he was terrified that Keitah might interpret something he did or said—*anything* he did or said—as some kind of a signal, and take any resulting annoyance with Daniel out on Jenna. This conflict left him hardly able to move or speak at all.

"I am given to understand you swept the assassin into your hand," Keitah went on, glancing sideways at the king. "The man knew nothing, of course."

"One would hardly expect it," the king agreed.

"He gave us one or two useful tidbits," Taranah put in unexpectedly, her tone a shade cooler than usual. "Assuredly, his master told him nothing. But this did not prevent the man from sketching out a handful of conjectures."

"My aunt suspects Imbaneh-se's envoy," the king explained to Keitah.

Taranah gave Mitereh a look of broad patience. "My nephew finds this suspicion unfounded."

"I find it altogether too obvious," the king said, with an air of having repeated this same argument several times. "Our enemy is a man who works with subtlety, around the edges of our awareness.

The envoy—any emissary, but most decidedly this one—being centered in our eye, would be a fool to engage in such open treachery. Besides, he is not a subtle man. Or not in this manner."

Taranah waved one hand in a gesture that expressed a feeling like *Yes, yes*. "Even so, you do well to send Nolas-Kuomon prowling along that trail. A worried man—"

"Misses the snare in his path while looking over his shoulder," said Keitah, nodding. "Indeed, Nolas-ai Taranah, and if I am not mistaken, it was your hand that directed Chaisa-e along that trail? Yes. And you have indeed set a snare on that path?"

"Only if the man is guilty," Mitereh said, inclining his head when his aunt glanced his way. "Did I not say that Chaisa-e would be a knife I would throw into my court?"

"And have any of the startled birds surprised the eye?"

"Keitah, my friend, all birds surprise me—" the king broke off as Tenai herself tapped at the door and came in, her stride long and aggressive.

Tenai looked—well, there was nothing about her that Daniel could put his finger on, but a prickling chill went down his spine anyway. There was a dangerous satisfaction in her dark eyes; dangerous, he thought, because of the edge of fulfilled cruelty implicit in that satisfaction. He hadn't seen anything like that from her in years.

She spoke with no preliminary greeting. "Emtaitah Benainanon fears me. And he believes that you do not."

Mitereh had risen when Tenai came in. Now he gave her a regal little nod and indicated a chair at his left hand. "Sit," he said, and to Daniel, "Sit, Nola Danyel. Join me, if you please. We shall discuss strategy only a very little, I promise you. I have a gift for you. Inkaimon, if you would be pleased to bring this gift?"

The only chair remaining was to Keitah's right. Daniel took it, trying not to look like he'd rather sit down beside a coiled snake. Keitah smiled, a blandly warm expression.

Inkaimon went into another room of the apartment, but came back at once carrying a slim white falcon on his wrist. A tracery of pearl gray accented the bird's fierce yellow eyes and outlined each feather of its wings and back. Inkaimon held it up so they could all see it, then dropped his arm so that the falcon half spread its wings and shifted its grip on his arm. Daniel stood up, both admiring the bird and appalled by the idea of carrying this wild thing himself. Its talons looked half an inch long and sharp enough to go straight through to the bone.

Torohoh came forward a step, offering Daniel a long leather glove and a hood decorated with strands of white beads. He said, with a diffident bow, "If you will permit me, Nola Danyel, I would be pleased to take her for you now, and show you how to handle her at your leisure."

Torohoh taking responsibility for the actual handling of the bird sounded like a fine idea. Daniel said, "Thank you—yes, please. Thank you, Mitereh. Um, my king. She's beautiful."

Torohoh hooded the falcon and showed Daniel how to arrange her on his wrist and how to hold her jesses.

"A sai falcon, from the heights," said Tenai, trailing the back of one finger down the bird's breast once it was hooded. "They are said to fly so high their feathers brush the face of God. You should weave a feather into a chain of silver or iron, Daniel and wear it near your skin—that chain you are wearing now would do well to hold the feather. A fine bird, and," she added to the king, a slight edge to her tone, "a generous gift, Mitereh. You cannot have many of this kind in your mews."

"One other," the king answered, with obvious satisfaction at her comments. "My falconer prizes my sai above pearls."

"I'm overwhelmed by your generosity," Daniel said, regarding the falcon with even more respect. "You're certain you wish to give her to me?"

Mitereh looked almost smug. "Indeed, Nola Danyel, she is a perfect gift. Let all men see how I value you, and thus surmise the accord between Tenai Chaisa-e and myself."

The corner of Tenai's mouth crooked up slightly, in an expression that Daniel could not interpret. It was not simple humor. It was not, he thought, anything friendly. She said, "Indeed."

Mitereh's smile was far easier to read: it was the smile of a man pleased with the way his plans were unfolding. He leaned forward, resting his elbows on the table. "Now, Chaisa—tell me of Benainanon. Does the man regard me as a fool?"

Tenai gave a little jerk of her head back, meaning *No*. "Benainanon believes I am a weapon in your hand, Mitereh—and fears you will use me against your enemies." Again, there was a note to her tone that was hard to read.

"And counts himself among that number. You might be wise to bring him up hard, Mitereh," suggested Keitah.

"Emtaitah Benainamon is the best of enemies," Taranah disagreed. "Where he opposes us, he does so honestly. He need not be checked, nor should he be, I believe. If encouraged to oppose us, the man may set other enemies, as yet unseen, in motion." She turned to her nephew. "Well thought, to start a falcon at that hidden game, my dear."

The king gave his aunt a pleased little nod.

To Daniel, Tenai seemed pleased too—but, again, in a dangerous way. As though she might be satisfied to think that Mitereh's enemies had been set in motion, but not for the same reasons Taranah Berangilan-sa was pleased. Or else he was imagining things. Her dark eyes, when she turned her gaze toward the king, gave nothing away. He couldn't tell what had created the impression.

Tenai asked, "And for the morrow? What would you have me do, Mitereh?"

Daniel blinked. Though her tone had been unexceptional, the phrasing was decidedly antagonistic. Behind her unreadable expression he suddenly thought that he might see a trace of hidden rage after all. He was not shocked. The lack of shock suggested that he'd been subliminally aware of that hint of anger for some time. *Could* this be part of an act for his benefit—for Keitah's benefit? He found he could not believe the edge of rage he saw in her was anything but real.

He looked at Mitereh, at Taranah, at Keitah and the king's young men. No one else seemed to perceive anything exceptional in Tenai's tone or manner, though maybe that was because they were not attending closely. Taranah was murmuring to her woman companion, who was nodding with earnest concentration. Inkaimon and Torohoh were also speaking in low tones, their heads close together. And Keitah Terusai-e, of course, was probably thinking more about his own deception than about Tenai.

The king, to all appearances, simply accepted Tenai's question at face value and answered, "I wish to press the envoy from Keneseh hard. I would value clarity between myself and this man. I wish him to understand that, regardless of what may happen between Talasayan and Imbaneh-se, Keneseh would do well to remain quiet."

Tenai inclined her head. "I believe I may be able to convey this impression."

"I believe you may," Mitereh agreed.

Daniel could see that now, at this moment, the king didn't fear Tenai at all. Mitereh's lack of fear ought by rights to have pulled her in the right direction, toward trustworthiness. But the hint of hidden rage—mostly hidden—he wasn't certain. He wasn't certain of anything, except all his professional instincts told him that there might be, there was, a new, or newly intense, antagonism there. All on Tenai's side.

Mitereh turned to Keitah. "My friend, I have a task for you as well, if you will. I believe the envoy from Imbaneh-se has been successfully caught in a net of fears and possibilities. We will now see whether we have trapped his wits. You may draw the net tight and then offer a line out. Yes?"

Keitah smiled, with a ruthless edge to the expression—the first suggestion Daniel had seen of his true nature, and applied deliberately, where the young king could learn to trust that ruthlessness. No doubt this was a tactic Keitah had applied all along, visible to anyone who had eyes to see. Daniel closed his own eyes for a moment, bracing himself against showing anything that might give him away. Or give Keitah away, even worse from Jenna's point of view.

"This service will be my pleasure," Keitah was assuring the king. "I believe I will be able to spin a line that appears safe, but holds a sting at the end."

Daniel had absolutely no doubt he could.

A little later, after both Keitah and Tenai had gone, Daniel found himself out on the east balcony, looking blindly out over the unrolling landscape of trees and lake. Taranah Berangilan-sa said something to him that he didn't catch, and he turned toward her and said, "Excuse me?" and only then noticed that nothing about the gardens or the way the light lay over the them struck him as odd. He understood at once that the shadows had straightened themselves out as soon as he'd seen Keitah—that the shock of strong emotion at that moment had pulled him at last, even if rudely, wholly back into the real world from his Orpheus-like trip to the underworld. How ironic that it had been Keitah himself who had done him this favor! He just hoped it might be a permanent change back toward the ordinary. He suspected that Keitah himself, if he knew about this, would also appreciate the irony of proving to be an asset to Daniel. His mouth twisted.

"Shall I offer a crust of bread for your thoughts?" Taranah asked him, her silver eyes alive with humor and interest.

Daniel thought that she, also, would appreciate the dark humor implicit in his situation. He said, not quite able to keep the bitterness out of his tone, "You wouldn't get a bargain." And, remembering his manners, "Nolas-ai."

"I might be willing to deal at a loss," the king's aunt said lightly. She followed his gaze out over the winding avenue and the lake at its end and added, not quite so lightly, "You are troubled, I believe."

The sun, now riding low in the sky, sent long shadows skimming over iron-dark water. Daniel was infinitely grateful that the shadows just lay quietly where they were cast, like any ordinary shadows, and that the light between them seemed unwavering and steady, like any light. He pulled his gaze from the scene to look into Taranah's pleasant, strong-boned face. She was really a very attractive woman. Not striking, like Tenai; nor prettily fragile, like Niah. Hers was a warmer, more welcoming attractiveness.

At the moment, however, she looked concerned. So, Daniel surmised, he'd not done as thorough a job of hiding everything as he'd hoped. What was it they said here, about silver eyes seeing into the truth of men's hearts? How unfortunate that the king's aunt did not seem able to see the cold pit of Keitah's heart!

Wary of saying too little, Daniel offered, "I suppose I'm a little worried about Tenai."

Accepting this, Taranah sighed. She sketched a little gesture of acknowledgment. "She is like a lioness lying by one's hearth. One understands at every moment it is not merely a cat. I speak freely, Nola Danyel, though she is a friend to you."

"She meant it when she swore that oath to the king," Daniel said quickly. "That was a deliberate choice." But then he added, without quite meaning to, "But now I think I understand more about what that choice meant for her, and I wonder if I did the right thing when I advised her to make that choice."

Taranah did not protest, but only nodded with grave attention.

"I don't think there was another possible choice. Was there?"

"I do not believe there was. But sometimes none of the choices laid out before one offers what one would wish."

"No," Daniel said. "Yes. Tenai's been in that situation far too often in her life."

"As have we all."

Daniel sighed and tilted his head back, looking at the thin streamers of cloud that reached across the sky. "True."

After a little while, as the edges of the sky deepened from lavender to midnight blue and the clouds vanished into the reaching darkness, Taranah added, "Mitereh understands it is a lioness he holds on a silken leash, not a cat."

Daniel understood that she meant this as reassurance: that he did not need to go against the bonds of friendship to warn the king, for Mitereh already knew what he had brought into his court. Or more than that, that he did not need to worry for Tenai's sake, because Mitereh knew what Tenai was and already respected her as he ought to. Or both those things.

"If you wish, we might go in," Taranah said after another moment. "I believe Mitereh wishes an early supper. He must meet with several men yet tonight."

"No rest for ..." the rest of that probably wouldn't translate well, Daniel realized, and finished, "the head that wears the crown, I suppose. Where shall I—does it matter where I stay tonight?"

"You are courteous to ask. Either within Chaisa's household, or Mitereh's, as you prefer, Nola Danyel. So long as you are clearly welcomed within each household, Mitereh will be satisfied."

If he stayed in the king's apartment tonight, Keitah would probably expect an assassination attempt this very night. Daniel should have thought of that before he asked. Now he needed to get Taranah, or Mitereh himself, to send him back to Tenai's household tonight. And he needed to do it while seeming to suggest to Keitah, if the son of a bitch were listening, that he was angling for the exact opposite. This role was going to be impossible to maintain for long. Despair washed over Daniel, as though flung out of the night to overwhelm him. He set his teeth against it and strolled back toward the doorway, pretending a relaxation he certainly did not feel.

"Nola Danyel." Mitereh gave him a little nod as he and Taranah came back into the room. The king then tilted his head toward a newcomer, a man all in black, with a long white vest. "I make you known to Cardinal Uanan Erusa-go-e, a prelate of the Church in special service to the Martyr."

The cardinal was an older man, perhaps sixty or so, with a features that were strong, even harsh. His skin was about three shades darker than the king's; his hair, unusual for the people of Talasayan, was iron gray. Though he had a good deal more of it than Daniel. And, as with everyone here but Daniel, he looked to be in excellent physical shape.

The cardinal rose, acknowledging Daniel with a small bow and a forthright look. He said in a deep voice, "I am glad to meet the man who won Tenai Ponanon Chaisa-e from the service of Lord Sorrow."

Daniel returned the bow, more awkwardly. "Not Lord Death?"

"At the end, was Chaisa-e not seduced to the service of the forgotten past?" the cardinal responded. "Death is the darkest of the great lords, but never the grimmest. I have spoken to the lady twice since her return to Talasayan. I find her dark, but, by the grace of the Martyr, not so grim as in past years."

It was always a slight shock to Daniel to meet figures out of Tenai's past; he had spent so long assuming them all to be metaphorical. "I'd be curious to know what she was like when you knew her."

"And I, the same." The cardinal resumed his seat and opened a broad, strong-boned hand toward the chair beside him. "If you would oblige me, Nola Danyel. Though I am given to understand that the discussion this evening will turn and turn about Imbaneh-se and the unfortunate envoy from that country. You must assuredly join me in my home on some later evening, where we may perhaps discover more congenial topics upon which to converse."

"I'd like to," Daniel said honestly. He thought—he felt—that this man might be as close to a professional colleague as Talasayan offered. In fact, he rather thought the cardinal might remind him of Dr. Martin, director of Lindenwood hospital. He would, he realized, very much have liked to talk to Russell Martin. Especially if it meant he could do it in a world without Lord Death, Lord Sorrow, or magic of any kind.

"Not tomorrow evening," Mitereh said briskly. "I must claim that time myself for both of you, though I will not send you about identical tasks. Uanan, I would be pleased if you would bend your attention toward your brother cardinal, Imainan Tangan-sa-e. You might reinforce for me the work Chaisa has done there. And this evening I fear I must also ask your patience to exert yourself on my behalf with Cardinal Tairanai-e. The man has lately become intransigent."

Cardinal Uanan inclined his head with stately deference, and Daniel realized, without quite knowing how, that the two men, for all the differences of age and rank, were personal friends.

"Danyel—forgive me, but I must ask you to retire tonight to Chaisa's household," the king added. "My own will be all at odd angles, I fear, with such business as I must pursue."

Daniel tried not to show even a hint of relief. Was it possible Mitereh actually *did* know what was going on, that Daniel's crazy gambit had paid off, that the king was *deliberately* moving Daniel to a distance?

No way to know. Better not to count on it. Either way, he was very grateful for the reprieve. He tried not to let that show in his voice when he answered, "Of course. Whatever is convenient for you, um, my king." Then he took care to go on, in belated protest in case Keitah expected him to object. "If you're certain it won't send the wrong message to, well, whomever."

Mitereh gave a casual wave of his hand and answered with assurance. "By no means. The sai falcon is a gift that must illuminate my regard, Danyel. That gift should slant a light through the dimness of confusion for any who might doubt it."

Unable to think of any suitably flowery response, Daniel merely nodded. He supposed that, at his age, Mitereh could pull one all-nighter after another and be no worse for it. It certainly sounded as though the king had one planned for tonight. He wanted to ask him what he would be doing, but didn't, in case the answer might give some small detail away to Keitah that the man didn't already know. Or, worse thought, open up some obvious opportunity for murder that Keitah might expect him to take advantage of.

Food was brought in and served, small elaborate dishes that

Daniel noticed only intermittently. He tried to listen to the talk between Mitereh and the cardinal, but again found any focus difficult to maintain. Seated between Cardinal Uanan and the king's aunt, he found most of his attention had to be bent toward framing natural-sounding responses to Taranah's comments. But he thought that, though Taranah might be concerned about him, she was not actually suspicious. Nevertheless, it was not an enjoyable supper. Daniel was glad to retire—retreat—at the earliest possible moment.

And then he found, as he walked through the palace toward Tenai's apartment, that the shadows had once again become stretched: longer than they should be, and darker, and dangerously tangible. Daniel had to stop for several moments, breathing carefully and trying not to panic as he worked to disentangle the reaching darkness from the true solidity of mosaics and rugs and white stone tile. He could almost have wept. On top of everything else he'd already endured and would be forced to endure in the morning, having the shadows turn back into nightmares really seemed an unnecessary blow.

In his room, the same room he'd once found peaceful, Daniel found he now feared and disliked the dark, as had never been true even when he'd been a child. He could not sleep until he lit a candle and left it burning in the room. Actual flame in a bedroom: not a wonderful idea, but he could not stand the pressing darkness. Even the wavering shadows the candle created were better.

He truly did not know how he was going to handle pretending everything was normal in a world that seemed now as thin as the skim of reality over darkness. *You deal with the world you've got.* He'd always given that advice to patients. Well, fine. It would be a helpful piece of advice, if he could only figure out what that world *was*.

Lying sleeplessly in his bed, he almost began to think he heard Jenna screaming. This proved, when he listened closely to the pendant, to be his imagination. Or his memory. Either way, he was positive it wasn't real. Almost positive.

Uncertainty, Daniel decided, could be quite sufficient to drive one mad. Clearly he'd never given enough thought to this psychological factor in the past.

10

The dawn brought no deep conversations. In fact, if anything, Jenna felt a new constraint between Emel and herself. And yet it did not seem a harmful constraint. There was soup for breakfast. Nobody seemed in a hurry to get moving, except Jenna, who fretted. "This is so *slow*," she muttered to Emel. "Can't we go off on our own again? That was so much better."

"It would not be faster, if we were taken by Keitah's searchers," Emel pointed out.

This was hard to deny. Yet ... "We got pretty far without being caught."

It took a moment for Emel to answer. At last he murmured, "Once we had turned south ... I fear that we would quickly have met enemies. I would have delayed that turn as long as I dared, and avoided so much as a deer path ... but the urgency of our intention would have called out. I do fear so."

And he hadn't told her this because he hadn't seen anything to do about it, Jenna supposed. Except hope they fell in with outlaws and could turn south safely after all.

"I think we will be safe to slip this company in a few more days," Emel offered, giving her a tentative look, as though expecting Jenna to scream *A few days!* in frustration.

God knew, she wanted to. She made herself nod and tried to look patient.

Imbutaiyon and Katawarin went off after a while. Gerabak, the man who had taken away Emel's and Jenna's horses, turned up halfway through the morning with a sack of coarse dark loaves and some cheese and a small cask of—Jenna was surprised—pickled beets. They were very good pickled beets, which was not a consolation for the slow pace of the morning. Gerabak showed Kuomat the money he'd gotten for the horses, and Kuomat passed two-thirds of the price over to Emel without comment. Emel gave part of it to Jenna later. It seemed like a lot of money to her. Emel said Gerabak had probably skimmed a little off the top, but it was worth it to have the horses gone and untraceable. And a little money in their pockets couldn't hurt either.

Imbutaiyon and Katawarin came back with spare crossbow bolts, a dozen meat pies, and news that no one seemed to be trying to track the outlaws and in fact that no one yet seemed to have reported the robbery. Everyone loafed around some more. People talked, and some of the men played a game involving pebbles and twigs and a lot of good-natured cursing that only turned real once. It took a while for Jenna to realize that the prizes involved not only the rest of the pickled beets, but also who got to sleep with Panaih. Saimadan won her and took her off into the woods, to catcalls from the rest of the men. Panaih looked a little disgusted at the outcome, but didn't argue. Nobody tried to gamble for Katawarin's favors. Nobody seemed interested in Angana. Jenna couldn't believe the woman's scarred mouth stopped them.

"She's probably diseased," Emel told her later, when everybody had retired for the evening. "That won't stop a man who really wants a woman, but they have Panaih to trade back and forth."

Jenna made a face.

"Angana is fortunate they keep her. Men don't like having a diseased woman in their company."

"Yeah," Jenna muttered. "How lucky for her." Emel had found a chance to make her more dye, and she edged her way down the stream to rub it on her hands and then bathe as well as she could. Two baths in two days, wow. Still no soap, though.

The next day they moved on at last, thank God, heading almost due south. It rained. They walked most of the afternoon in an unpleasant drizzle that shortened tempers all around. They came to the big road from Kinabana to Nerinesir, and Katawarin did a spell to help them cross without being noticed by anybody who might be watching. Jenna thought they might stop there and wait for travelers to rob. She didn't know how she would stand the delay if they did, but they didn't. They just crossed the road and walked south for a while longer. Kuomat turned out to have a destination in mind: a tangle of old growth that hid the ruins of a big house and its outbuildings. There was nothing left of the house but the foundation and a bit of wall at one end, but the building that had once been the stables was still half-standing. The brigand pack greeted it as though they'd come home after a long journey, crowding up under the stable roof to get out of the rain and starting a fire in a fireplace made of broken stone. It was clear they'd stayed here before—there were pans and skillets on makeshift shelves to one side, and wood stored dry under the protection of what was left of the roof. Out in the courtyard there was a well, and it turned out there was even a bucket in the stable, its rope stored neatly coiled in it.

Most of the brigands stayed in the stable. Imbutaiyon and Katawarin claimed shelter in what was left of the big house, putting up canvas to keep off the continuing rain. Emel made a similar shelter for himself and Jenna at the edge of some scrubby brush, where the ground sloped enough that it wasn't too muddy.

Though there were still hours of light left, no one seemed inclined to do anything with it but sit around and complain about the rain, though that seemed at last to be tapering off. Saimadan and Gerabak gambled for Panaih. If Panaih had a preference, it wasn't obvious to Jenna, who sat in a bit of unclaimed space near the fire. Emel laid out his weapons and began to inspect and clean his sword.

The clouds broke up at last. Late sunlight turned the humid air to a sauna. The wet stones of the ruins steamed, but everybody's temper improved anyway. Katawarin drew up a bucket of water, took it behind a screen of young trees and brush, and came back much cleaner and in a different and cleaner shirt. She drew another bucket afterwards, came over to Jenna, and held out a little clay pot. Jenna looked at Emel, who didn't seem interested, and took the pot.

"You are very young, of course," said Katawarin, not unkindly. "It is soap."

"Oh!" said Jenna, taken aback. "Thank you!"

"I will go to a town tomorrow, so I must be clean," said the older woman, and added with a sly sideways look of amusement, "Imbutaiyon will have to bathe as well. It is a terrible trial for him. But not for me, yes?"

"Oh!" said Jenna again, and blushed.

"No one would know you. You could come also. The town is nothing, but it is somewhere you have not yet been, I think."

"No," said Emel, looking up for the first time. He sounded curt, but not angry. "Though she is grateful for your kindness. And I."

"Is she?" said Katawarin. "Are you?" She gave Emel a considering look and said to Jenna, "Well, then you might at least persuade your man to bathe. He might do it to please you." She walked away again, hips swaying.

"She's actually nice!" Jenna said to Emel, surprised.

"She is fortunate to have Imbutaiyon to protect her. But also she is probably curious about you, and more curious about me. If you had gone to town with them, I think they would have asked you many questions.

"Oh," Jenna said. She should have realized that. She went off to use the soap, ulterior motives or not.

The soap was wonderful. Jenna washed her shirt, too, and wore the spare one, which was much too big but considerably cleaner. Emel, without a word, used the rest of the soap himself and bought a clean shirt from Imbutaiyon.

Sure enough, in the morning Imbutaiyon and Katawarin strolled out of camp, in no obvious hurry. No one else seemed inclined to go anywhere.

Jenna watched them go and fretted. "How long are we going to stay here?" she whispered to Emel. "Couldn't we slip away?"

"Not yet," Emel counseled. "Abide in patience."

Jenna, scowling, tossed pebbles at an oak gall and considered whether she ought to insist. Presumably Emel knew what he was doing. But just how long were they going to be forced to 'abide in patience?' Days? Weeks? "We can't dawdle around here forever, no matter how many men are out combing the countryside for us," she whispered at last, fiercely. "My father must be in Nerinesir already!"

"Perhaps not yet." At her glare, Emel added, "Soon, yes."

"And how far behind will we be then?" Jenna demanded.

"We will see if we might slip this company in ... three days more, perhaps. If we travel even thirty or forty miles further in that time, I think we shall be far safer to go on independently. Can you abide so long?"

Clearly Jenna was supposed to say she could. She only shrugged. She wanted to shout *No* and insist that they break away from the outlaw pack and head south immediately. They were going to waste a whole *day* sitting here. Who knew what they might do tomorrow—more sitting? It was unbearable.

Getting caught by Keitah's men would be worse. Jenna made herself drop back to the ground. She tried to look relaxed. Probably her effort didn't fool anybody. She found Kuomat giving her a considering glance out of his silver eyes, and looked away, scowling again.

Imbutaiyon and Katawarin came back late in the day. Unlike Jenna, they looked genuinely relaxed and pleased with themselves. They had not just bread and cheese, but pies, a bag of apples, and a small barrel of beer. The beer was greeted with enthusiasm by everybody but Kuomat, who was exasperated. "We will not be able to go out at all tomorrow," he said to Imbutaiyon.

They *were* going to stay here another whole day? Jenna bit her tongue hard and refused to look at Emel. She knew he was looking at her, and she knew what his expression would be: neutral, but worried behind the neutrality.

Imbutaiyon only shrugged and laughed. "We have enough.

We don't have to work. Gerabak and Medai can go hunting. Or I can go buy a pig."

Kuomat gave him a disgusted look, but he didn't try to stop anybody from drinking the beer. Emel took a cup, and gave one to Jenna, who tasted it reluctantly and made a face; it was horribly bitter and seemed to be spiked with something she thought didn't belong in beer. "Everyone drinks it," said Emel, so Jenna sipped a little and tried to look like it was fine.

Saimadan got drunk and asked Emel if he couldn't buy an hour with her. When Emel wouldn't sell, he sat around and watched Jenna until she finally went back to the canvas lean-to she shared with Emel and got out of his sight. Saimadan had bad luck gambling all day and never got time with Panaih, so he tried again to get Emel to let him have Jenna. Kuomat hit Saimadan in the end, and Saimadan went away looking sullen. Emel gave Kuomat a little nod and didn't even get up.

They stayed at the ruined house until late the next day. Then they finally went south again, until they found themselves right on the bay. Jenna thought it was the ocean until Emel drew her another map. She really felt like they'd gotten pretty far from Kinabana—until Emel extended his map and she saw how much farther they still had to go.

Once they hit the shore, the outlaw pack turned more west as well as south, paralleling the bay. They didn't push themselves nearly as hard as Jenna would have liked, but they covered enough distance that she let Emel persuade her that they shouldn't break away on their own just yet. Even Emel probably regretted this after Kuomat insisted they set up a camp on a very disagreeable island. Though maybe not: Jenna had to agree that no one in his right mind would search thoroughly through this region. The whole place was swarming with biting insects and overgrown with knife-edged coarse grass that cut your hands and arms. They stayed there for a truly unpleasant night.

In the morning, they moved on at once, probably because there would have been a general rebellion if Kuomat had tried to make them stay in that horrible spot a minute longer. After a half-day's walk, they came to a much more pleasant camp up on a rocky slope hidden between two spring-fed creeks. From this camp, the outlaws went out to 'work' a road that Jenna gathered was only a short distance away.

In the afternoon, Saimadan came back to the camp early. Jenna was in camp with Panaih and Angana, waiting for everyone else to return. Jenna could just imagine what kind of excuse Saimadan had made to go off on his own, not that it mattered. She saw him first, realized he was alone, and got to her feet. Panaih turned her head, glanced at Jenna, and smiled spitefully. Angana muttered and went off by herself.

Saimadan was a big, coarse looking man with an unpleasant twist to his mouth and cold eyes. He was muscle, Jenna had learned; one of the 'outer' men who went into the road and let himself be seen by the victims. Some of the outlaws always stayed out of sight, like Imbutaiyon and Katawarin—that way they could go into towns and villages and spend the money the pack stole. It was a clever tactic, Emel had told her, and one not every pack had the sense to employ. Besides, bowmen were most useful if they stayed out of sight. And Katawarin was very good with a crossbow.

But Saimadan never went into towns. It was, Jenna realized, probably one of the reasons he was frustrated: Katawarin was taken, Angana diseased, and Panaih had to be shared with all the other men. "The women don't cause trouble," Kuomat had told Emel. Maybe they hadn't, but she, Jenna thought, was apparently one too many off-limits women for Saimadan to stand. She moved out into the open, away from anything she might trip over. Adrenaline went through her, seemingly from her belly up through her spine, in a rush. Her hands were trembling. Her back and neck went tight: she consciously relaxed them.

"I will not hurt you," Saimadan said. He'd stopped a few yards away. "You are a woman. It will not hurt you to act like a woman. If you tell Kuomat, he will punish me. But he won't kill me. And next chance I get, I *will* hurt you. Yes? You understand?"

The memory of striking those guards made Jenna sick. She had killed them. She'd used techniques she'd learned for fun and *killed* those men, and she'd thought she was over it, but it came back to her now and she wanted to throw up. And yet she could not, she *could not* let Saimadan touch her. But she didn't know if she could kill him, either. She didn't know if she could override all her training and actually go all the way with *any* technique, not with the memory of that other fight so horribly vivid—she started to speak, finding a tremor in her voice and wondering if that was good or bad, did she want him to think she was scared or did she want to sound confident? But it didn't matter, she couldn't get her voice steady anyway. "I won't have to tell Em—Bukitraya. He'll know. And he'll kill you."

Saimadan's lip curled. "I know you women. You can hide it if you want. Maybe I'll kill *him,* yes? Maybe I'll slide up on him in the dark, in the woods, hah, maybe? Kuomat would be angry, yes? But he would not kill me, and then you would have no man. Maybe he would give you to me. I would have the right if I killed your man. Yes?"

He might be able to do that, Jenna realized. The understanding was a coldness in her stomach. He might murder Emel if he thought he could. If he were willing to try. If she talked him out of trying to rape her, he might very well try that instead. She didn't hear the rest of what he said: she was too focused on the risk to Emel. Improbably, that threat steadied her where the danger to herself had just made her feel distracted and wobbly. She noticed without thinking about it that her hands had stopped shaking. She said submissively, "I'll do what you want. Don't hurt me," and took a step toward him.

Saimadan grinned, crossed the few remaining feet between them, took the hand she offered him, and pulled her to him.

Jenna stepped into the pull, broke his grip on her hand—that was easy, he wasn't expecting it at all—rolled her wrist around his, and caught his hand in an inside wrist lock. He yelled in pain. She didn't pay attention to that—she was too busy. She stepped and turned, popping his elbow up with the palm of her other hand, getting behind him: *Your attacker's feet are the base of a triangle,* Tenai's calm voice said in memory. *Pull toward the point of the triangle.* She pulled, not the gentle move from classes, but hard and sharp, and Saimadan screamed in earnest as his shoulder was dislocated. Or maybe broken, Jenna didn't know. He hit the ground and she was stepping out, in fighting stance. She realized at once that she was waiting for her opponent to bounce to his feet and offer her another opening. But *this* opponent wasn't going to get up and smile. He was going to get up mad, and maybe he was going to try to kill her, maybe try to ambush Emel in the woods.

He had rolled and gotten up to one knee. He was *looking* at her, his face twisted in rage and pain—he was going to get up, he was getting up now, but he was so clumsy—she stepped and stepped again, setting up the right angle, and did a jump side kick, rolling her hip over just like she'd been taught to get her whole body behind the kick. She'd meant to go right through whatever defense he could manage and hit him in the chest, but he moved faster than she'd thought and she kicked him in the solar plexus. He fell back, stunned, his mouth opening and closing as he tried to breathe. In contrast to the fight with Keitah's men, she felt only satisfaction. She landed from the side kick and instantly spun back the other way into an exchange jump roundhouse kick because she could really get her hip and body behind that kick from the angle she'd landed in, and she knew the kick was going to hit him exactly right on the side of the head, and it did, and he didn't get up after that.

Jenna stood back warily. Saimadan's head seemed to be set at an unpleasant angle, away from her so she couldn't see his face. She thought his neck might be broken, but she wasn't sure. She wanted to go touch his throat, feel for a pulse, see if he was dead, but what if he wasn't? Visions of him grabbing her hand horrified her, even though she knew her horror was stupid, that she could certainly take care of it if he did—too many horror movies, she knew that, but she still stayed back. What was she going to do if he wasn't dead? First aid? No, he could just lie there.

Panaih's horrified cry seemed to come very late, long after the whole fight was over. Jenna jumped and whirled, recalling for the first time that the other woman was even there: Panaih was standing stiffly on the other side of the camp, her hands fisted in front of her mouth, her eyes wide and stunned. Angana, drawn by that cry, came back from wherever she'd been and stood still, staring at the dead man. Then she looked at Jenna and smiled. It was not a nice smile at all. The scar twisted it strangely awry. But it was a smile; the first one Jenna had seen from Angana since they'd met.

Her foot didn't even hurt this time. It came from wearing boots to fight. Clumsy, but safer. She walked away, not quite turning her back on Saimadan—zombie movies again—and sat down in the shade.

Panaih stared at Jenna, stared at Saimadan, stared at Jenna ... finally edged up to Saimadan and put her hand on his chest. Jenna watched. She didn't understand why she wasn't more bothered by the dead man—by this time she was pretty sure he was dead—why didn't that bother her? Was it good or bad that it didn't bother her? She longed, with a sudden painful intensity, to talk to her father. She knew what *he* would think about Saimadan. He would be very, very happy that Saimadan was dead and that she was okay. But what would he think about the way she felt about it? Or didn't feel about it?

There was a rustling in the leaves, and Gerabak strode into camp, head turned, saying something cheerful over his shoulder to one of the other men. He didn't see Saimadan at once; when he did, he stopped so suddenly the man behind him—it was Medai— ran into him. Medai gave a muffled curse, shouldered his way past Gerabak, and also stopped. They stared at Saimadan, then at Angana. Angana shrugged and pointed at Jenna. Both men's heads swiveled around like they were puppets on the same string, staring now at Jenna. She flushed.

The rustling was louder: everyone coming back. Jenna stood

up, looking anxiously for Emel. He was about in the middle of the file, and came into camp with quick strides, warned perhaps by the quality of the silence ahead of him. Kuomat came in last, took in the scene thoughtfully, and turned to look at Jenna. His wintry eyes gave his gaze an intense quality. Jenna wanted to look away, but she wouldn't.

Emel came to her side and put an arm around her shoulders, turning to face Kuomat.

The leader of the brigands walked slowly to Saimadan's body and touched it with his foot. He nudged the man's head, observed the way it turned, loosely, like it wasn't connected to his body. Saimadan's head turned so his face was up; for the first time Jenna saw that his eyes were open. The open eyes made him look ... really dead. She looked away, feeling sick for the first time since the fight had ended.

"Well?" said Kuomat. Quietly. Looking at her, not at Emel. But ... Katawarin had her crossbow pointed almost at Emel, and so did Medai.

"She killed him!" Panaih said shrilly.

Jenna swallowed. "He tried ... he tried to ... he said if I didn't, that he would sneak up on—on Bukitraya in the woods and kill him, and then you would give me to him, he said."

"Is that what he said?" said Kuomat softly. But Katawarin was looking at Jenna with an odd expression, and her bow was pointed at the ground.

"We shall go," Emel offered. He had a sword, but he didn't draw it. His eyes were on the outlaw leader's face. "I shall take her and go. There is no need for trouble."

"You are a useful man. Why should I want to lose you? Everyone understands now that the woman is only yours."

"We'll go," Emel said, with finality.

Kuomat glanced at Imbutaiyon. Imbutaiyon shrugged. Kuomat turned a thoughtful stare on Emel, silver eyes cold. "You are far less useful, man, if you will not stay." It was clearly a threat. Medai brought his crossbow up to aim directly at Emel, and so did

Gerabak. But Katawarin left hers pointed down.

Emel reached into his shirt, took out the pouch of money he carried, and tossed it at Kuomat's feet.

Kuomat didn't look impressed. "That would be mine either way."

Jenna, on impulse, took a step toward Katawarin. "Please," she said. "He said he would kill Bukitraya. *You* would have shot him, if it was you. Wouldn't you?"

Katawarin tipped her head to one side, regarding Jenna curiously. "I would never have thought it, to look at you," she said at last. She looked at Imbutaiyon, eyebrows lifted. Imbutaiyon sighed, shrugged, and looked at Kuomat.

"Take the money," said Emel. Quietly.

Kuomat glanced down at the pouch. He gave Emel another long look. Then he opened a hand. "Then go."

Emel turned unhurriedly, drawing Jenna around with him, and they walked away into the woods. Jenna wanted to run, but Emel only walked, not too fast. Her back prickled. What would it feel like, to get shot in the back? But there were no bolts.

"I'm sorry," she whispered to Emel, once they were well away from the camp. "I did get us away. But this wasn't the way I would have picked to do it."

He shrugged, his eyes on the woods ahead of them. "As you say, it was time to leave them. We may well be far enough from Kinabana now to be safe from Keitah. Killing Saimadan ... carried more risk than the way I had intended. But all is well." He did glance at her then, briefly. "I had some hope that Kuomat would choose as he did. But what made you think to appeal to Katawarin?"

"Oh," said Jenna, surprised. "Anybody could see she really ... she loves Imbutaiyon, so, you know, she would understand why I ... couldn't let Saimadan threaten you. And anybody could see Imbutaiyon would want to do it her way if he could."

Emel gave her an odd, intense look. "Ah."

Jenna looked away, blushing, she wasn't sure why because she hadn't said anything that wasn't obvious. Her sheer physical awareness of Emel had faded over the days with the outlaws; it came back now, vividly. She said, almost at random, "It'll be dark soon."

"We will have to stop for a little. Just until the moon is well up. We should be farther away from Kuomat's pack, if we can go on for some time yet."

"I'm not tired. I didn't do anything all day but sit around." Except kill Saimadan. The memory was getting more disturbing. It wasn't ... it still wasn't as bad as when she'd killed Keitah's guards. She didn't feel sorry for Saimadan, exactly. Only it made her feel sick to think about him lying there, with his eyes open, sightlessly looking at the sky. She thought of how his head had moved, bonelessly, when Kuomat had shoved him with his toe, and turned abruptly aside to throw up.

Emel came after her uncertainly. "I'm all right," Jenna said indistinctly. She waved a hand, *go away*. "I'm all right." Emel hesitated for a moment, clearly wanting to hover, just as clearly not having a clue what to do. Then he backed away and left her alone, to her considerable relief. She didn't exactly feel better afterwards, but it was sort of a relief not to be able to kill somebody and just walk away, so she sort of felt better because of that. Emel didn't say anything about it when she rejoined him.

They found the road just before full dark, unrolling like a smooth white ribbon through the night, and actually walked along it for a while because they didn't need the moon to walk on the road. "Isn't this dangerous?" Jenna asked.

Emel shrugged and answered, "Curs and soldiers alike sleep at night." Even so, they turned off the road again once the moon was well up.

Now that they were finally moving, Jenna would have been fine with walking all night. How far could a person walk in one night? Off the road, with visibility not so great? But clouds came up, so it became harder and harder to see and the question less and less relevant. At last they found a place hidden under the downswept branches of an old tree and sat on the moist ground, leaning against the trunk. Jenna regretted the canvas and blankets they'd left in the outlaw's camp. "I don't suppose we have anything to eat?" she asked after a while. They didn't. No blankets, no spare clothing, no food, very little money—only what Jenna had been carrying, which wasn't much. How did they keep winding up in this situation? This time they didn't even have horses.

"We will get food in the morning," Emel said at last. "Can you rest?"

With no outlaws around to worry about? With no Tantang looking at her when he thought nobody was looking, no Saimadan watching her with hot, frustrated eyes? Of course she could rest. But then, once she thought of Saimadan, Jenna couldn't help but think of him as she'd seen him last, with his head tilted oddly and his dead eyes staring at the sky. She shuddered. Tired as she was, she felt at the moment that she might never sleep again.

11

"I intend that Mitereh will die within the next four days," Keitah told Daniel. "You will see to it, Nola Danyel."

Somehow this statement was shocking, even though Daniel had expected something like it as soon as he'd realized Keitah Terusai-e had found him alone. He'd hidden himself in the king's private library, a room with generous windows and plenty of light. There, he could pretend to read and hope no one would track him down. But of course Keitah had found him anyway. Keitah was in fine form this morning: the very picture of a collected, suave, thoughtful ... bastard, Daniel filled in, mentally. But that last seemed to remain thoroughly hidden from everybody but him.

Of course, he hadn't guessed it either, until Keitah had chosen to reveal the truth hiding behind the smooth façade.

Daniel had worked hard to avoid Keitah for the past few days; and even harder to avoid Tenai, who might yet see too much; and hardest of all to avoid the king—while trying not to let any casual observer or Mitereh guess he was avoiding him deliberately, and simultaneously make it seem to Keitah that he was missing encounters with the king despite every effort to the contrary. This effort had begun to take its toll: Daniel could feel the early warning of a migraine behind his eyes. He'd never had migraines in his life, except for that terrible period right after Kathy's ... death.

"Whether you strike him down publicly or manage to do so secretly is not important. I care little for the method, but I do care for the result. I trust you understand me."

Daniel wanted to spit in Keitah's face. He could not remember ever before having that particular uncouth desire. Only thinking hard about Jenna let him keep his tone humble. "I understand you perfectly, Nolas-ai."

Keitah gave him a narrow look. "I care little for the method. Only for the timing. I will have your daughter whipped in two days if Mitereh yet lives, and I shall see to it that you hear her cries through the pendant you wear. The next day, the same. If Mitereh is still alive the following day, I will begin to have her fingers cut off. Two fingers a day until the king is dead. All this, too, I trust you understand perfectly."

Daniel understood it. How he was going to find a way past Scylla and Charybdis, he did not know, his earlier attempts having failed.

Keitah, watching him narrowly for a moment that lengthened out into exquisite torture, at last gave a little satisfied nod and left.

Daniel sighed, pressing a hand over his eyes. Not so much trying to think, as to gather the remnants of his nerve and strength. Though he had watched carefully for any sign—any sign at all—that either Tenai or the king had received his message from Lord Death, he had seen nothing. On the contrary. Keitah was still obviously free and pursuing his plans. Nothing at all seemed to have changed. Tenai, when she spoke to Keitah, showed the same slightly antagonistic civility she had from the beginning. Mitereh still treated him as a loyal and trusted friend and advisor.

Nor did the king appear to avoid Daniel's company, or seem concerned about standing in front of high windows or whatever when they were in the same room—which sometimes Daniel could not plausibly prevent. Fortunately, one or two of Mitereh's personal guards were almost always with their young king. That had *seemed* fortunate. Daniel had not realized Keitah would expect Daniel to make away with the king while his young men were with him. Now it seemed that Keitah expected just that. Maybe it was actually better for Keitah's ambition to have Daniel—Tenai's protégé—blatantly assassinate the king.

Daniel rubbed his forehead. A headache was definitely coming on fast. And not an aspirin to be had. Much less anything stronger. He felt at the moment that nothing could be strong enough.

Certainly not his own nerve.

Despite himself, Daniel found himself turning over different ways he might get to the king, rather than ways he might get around both horns of the dilemma. He rubbed his chest, where the visceral memory of Tenai's sword sliding past his ribs could still return at night to jar him out of dreams. As it had returned now, unpleasantly vivid. The shadows at the edges of things began to ripple and deepen—a stress reaction, perhaps. He shut his eyes, turning his face toward the warmth of the sun. Sometimes, especially in a bright room, if he kept his eyes closed for several minutes, the patterns of light and shadows would settle back where they belonged. Sometimes they wouldn't. His skull seemed to pulse in time to his heartbeat: the threatening migraine, not quite ready to break through into full flower. Yet.

Two days. He didn't even want to know what kind of whip Keitah would have his thugs use on Jenna. Some whips left terrible wounds, didn't they? Horrible images shifted through his mind. He couldn't let that happen.

Daniel rubbed his forehead once more, harder. If he picked up Tenai's sword a second time—or better, some ordinary uncursed sword—he slitted his eyes open. Patterns of darkness and light shifted around him and he closed his eyes again, breathing deeply. Definitely he would not touch Tenai's sword a second time. No. But an ordinary sword. Could he pretend an attempt upon the king and somehow cut himself instead? Make it look enough like an accident? An accident serious enough that Keitah would have to grant him a delay?

What would it take to force the man to back off? Real injury, probably. Could he possibly manage a subtle enough job to make the bastard think he'd sincerely tried to do as he was told? When he'd never picked up a sword before in his life, except, well, he didn't want to think about it. Darkness pressed in on him. Even through his shut eyelids, he could feel it out there, condensing in some strange fashion right out of the light around him. He put a hand over his eyes, pressing hard; sometimes, he had found, that could make his vision settle.

If not a sword, maybe some other kind of accident? If they had buses in Talasayan, he might step in front of one. He supposed a fast-driven horse might have something of the same effect. Was there some way he could set up an apparent attempt on Mitereh's life in a way that would let Daniel himself get trampled?

Obviously that was a stupid idea. Probably he'd just get himself killed. What did he know about horses? And there was no guarantee Keitah would let Jenna off the hook even if that actually happened. He was just the sort of sociopath who might torture her simply to convince some other pawn of his that he meant his threats. No, Daniel had to be alive to press for an extension. Surely he was more likely to be able to persuade Keitah of his sincerity if he was around in person.

Someone nearby cleared his throat. Daniel flinched and opened his eyes: shadows swung around his chair and settled uneasily back into place between brighter areas.

Apana Pelat stood a little inside the doorway. Daniel blinked, then frowned as his sight cleared. There was a tentative air about the man, as though he had come in already thinking about retreat. That indecisiveness brought all of Daniel's professional antennae to attention. A wave of quite personal frustration swept through him: didn't he already have enough on his plate? Why did everyone have to badger him for attention or advice right now?

Of course, this feeling was as unjustified as it was normal, and Daniel was already trying to put it aside almost before the annoyance hit him. He rubbed a hand across his eyes and tried to focus his attention on the moment at hand.

Pelat had always seemed serious, even solemn, an effect intensified by his strong features and by the gray in his neat beard. But not even after the assassination attempt that had cost him his place as captain of the king's personal guards had he ever seemed *uncertain*. Daniel said, keeping his tone neutral, "Yes? Did you want to speak to me?"

Pelat took a step forward, then paused. Again, Daniel had the sense that the man was on the edge of withdrawing. If Daniel spoke again, even to urge him to stay, probably he would be gone. So instead of speaking, Daniel opened his hands on the arms of his chair and relaxed his face.

Pelat responded as expected, coming further into the room. "Nola Danyel. I do not know that I should speak with you." He spoke with slow care; not just deliberately, but more as though he was experiencing difficulty framing the words. "But you are ... you are not quite Chaisa's man. Nor quite the king's. You are ... a 'physician of the mind.' So it is said. I am told you have taken an oath to hold private any ... any confidence a man may set before you."

"Yes, that's an important part of my oath." Then Daniel swore mentally. Keitah was listening—he could hardly let Pelat tell him anything important or anything private. But the man had already come forward to take a chair near Daniel's, close enough to permit lowered voices. He sat stiffly, obviously uncomfortable. Daniel couldn't see how to stop him now. Maybe he could fake a sudden dire headache. Maybe he wouldn't have to fake it.

Before Daniel could decide how to stop him, Pelat said, "I am Chaisa's man now, as you know, Nola Danyel."

That, at least, was harmless. Everyone knew that. Keitah had been there when it happened. Daniel nodded, half his attention on the man before him and half on the man who might be listening.

"This was a gracious gesture, for Chaisa-e to take me up when ... when Mitereh was forced to set me aside." Pelat hesitated for a moment and then added in a low voice, "Was it not gracious of her?"

Ah. This was private, or should be, but now Daniel could guess that nothing Pelat said was likely to be actually dangerous for Keitah to overhear. "Her decision surprised you?" he asked.

Pelat sketched a small, self-deprecating gesture. "Chaisa-e is not naturally generous. Or I would have said she was not. And I had been accustomed to trust ..." he paused.

Daniel waited.

"My own judgment of people," Pelat said finally.

And then his confidence in himself had been shaken when Iodad, one of the king's personal guards, one of the men under Pelat's command, had betrayed them both by trying to assassinate Daniel. Yes, Daniel understood that clearly. He didn't say, *Everyone makes mistakes.* That wouldn't be at all helpful, no matter how true it was. He didn't want to say anything that would show this man's vulnerability to Keitah Terusai-e. He said instead, "You knew Tenai at a ... particularly difficult time in her life, though. To me, she often seemed kind. Especially with my daughter. With all the girls she taught."

Pelat opened his long hands, dark fingers like bars across the light. He was, of course, unaware of the confusion of light and shadow his gesture created for Daniel. His mouth crooked in a wry smile. "I am glad to hear so. Indeed, I am relieved to hear it." He went on, glancing down at his hands, which he had folded neatly across his knee. "One meets reverses in life. I looked to duty to be my grace until such time as Lord Sorrow should lift his hand from my shoulder. I have always found duty to be a chain that would bear any weight."

His words came haltingly. Clearly he was beginning to circle around the matter that had brought him to Daniel. That was fast. Daniel had hoped to find a way to cut him off before he got to anything that mattered to him.

Pelat was going on, still speaking slowly, "Yet that chain seems less strong to me now. It seems weak as a mere stem of grass stretched across a dark chasm."

A dark chasm. Yes. How ... vivid. Shaken, Daniel turned his face to the sunlight pouring in through the window, trying not to let the little shadows in the room grow into chasms. The light helped. He took deep, slow breaths, trying to draw the light itself into his lungs. He continued the fancy: the light might thread from his lungs into his very blood, and spread through his body, fed along with oxygen to every cell. At once, he felt warmer. Safer. More grounded; more present in the world of light and the living.

The triumph of imagination over ... what, a different sort of imagination? Probably he would do better if he were a little less introspective.

"I feel I have lost my hold on the world," Pelat said in a low voice.

Daniel shoved his own personal problems aside. He had to bring this to a close. Later—later, if they were all extremely lucky, maybe he'd have an opportunity to apologize to Pelat and offer a sympathetic ear without anyone else listening over his shoulder Right now, he tilted his head to the side, conveying subtle sympathy and said, his tone just brisk enough to push the other man away, "This was a greater reversal than you ever expected to meet, I suppose. Did the king take your suggestions for whom to promote to captain of his personal guard? For how to go about establishing the loyalty of all his guards?"

"Indeed," answered the other man.

Daniel lifted his eyebrows just a hair, suggesting that Pelat stop and think about that. "Even if you're not sure you trust your own judgment, the king doesn't seem to feel the same way. I expect that here in Talasayan, divided loyalties are pretty hard to bear." He kept his tone neutral, just a foreigner commenting on the customs of the country he visited. "In my country, we believe a man must first be true to himself, or else he can't have anything but, um," he found a phrase that ought to translate, "base coin to offer anyone else. Once a man achieves, hmm, knowledge of his own heart, then loyalties he owes elsewhere are much more likely to fall into place."

After a moment, Pelat gave a small nod.

That hadn't been quite right. Or not quite enough. Of course it wasn't reasonable to expect someone to rearrange his personal loyalties at the drop of a hat, but maybe Pelat thought he should have. Or something. Or ... Daniel thought that what Pelat really wanted, or needed, was a reason, or maybe an opportunity, to be honest with himself, and with everyone else. Or not *everyone*, probably. But with everyone to whom he owed loyalty.

Daniel spoke in a musing-out-loud tone that implied he was

simply wondering—nothing strong enough to be construed as a suggestion. "I wonder what Tenai would say, or do, if you simply told her about the, um, division in your heart. I don't suppose it would surprise her."

Pelat laughed; a reluctant sort of laugh, but not without humor.

"That bad?" Daniel asked sympathetically, implying with the minimal lift of an eyebrow that he doubted it.

"I ..." Pelat paused. "As you say, Nola Danyel, she would not be surprised. But such a thing could hardly be tolerated."

"Are you sure? Well, maybe you're right. Though, I don't know. She's probably accustomed to accommodating divided loyalties. This is a new and difficult situation for you, but I doubt it would seem either new or difficult to Tenai."

Pelat frowned, a thoughtful expression.

"Her own loyalties are divided, aren't they? I mean, she said something like that, didn't she? When she told the king her first fealty is to Lord Death. That didn't stop her from swearing an oath to Mitereh, though."

That got a reaction—a slight recoil at first, but by the end, a thoughtful nod. "Indeed. That is so. I cannot say that is not so."

Daniel gave him a minimal nod of acknowledgment and let him alone, and after a minute the other man said, "Perhaps you are right, Nola Danyel. I think that could be so."

"I don't know exactly what would be proper for you to do. I'm still a stranger here. But I imagine you know what's proper."

Another slow and thoughtful nod. Whatever realization he had come to—and Daniel was sure Pelat had reached some realization, though Daniel himself didn't know what it was—the other man seemed more comfortable. More comfortable with his position, poised between the king who still held his first loyalty, and Tenai? Daniel wasn't sure. But sometimes it happened like that: a man came in needing, not therapy as such, but really advice, and the doctor thought he saw something resolvable within his patient's stuck position and tapped exactly the right lever, half by intuition. Then the advisee, especially the sort who really knew his own mind anyway, was suddenly able to do the heavy lifting.

And, hopefully, without revealing too much of himself to unseen listeners. Pelat's manner had changed; he seemed more like himself, or more in charge of himself. More ready to think and act decisively, whatever he chose to do.

Pelat rose to his feet, offering Daniel a small bow. "I thank you for your wise counsel, Nola Danyel."

Daniel rose, too. "You already knew your own mind. If I helped you see more clearly what you already knew, then I'm glad, but I did very little." And thank God he hadn't needed to. He was going to have to make absolutely sure no one approached him like this again. Not while he wore Keitah's pendant.

The man bowed a second time, a little more deeply. "Wise, I say. I thank you." He bowed a third time, this time barely more than a simple inclination of the head, and withdrew.

To do what, Daniel didn't know. Maybe to go talk to Tenai, and if so, Daniel hoped she would be kind to him. He thought she would be. Even more likely, Pelat wouldn't actually do anything overt; maybe he would just test out his new insight, whatever it comprised. Daniel shook his head and sank back down into his chair. No wonder Keitah could hide everything about his mind and heart: even when people tried for understanding, for engagement, how opaque they remained to one another!

Daniel shifted his chair further into the sunlight and pressed his hand over his eyes, trying to think. It seemed a failing effort.

Another 'attempt' to murder the king. Another attempt that had to fail while looking real enough to fool Keitah. Another attempt that would also look enough like an accident so that Daniel himself could avoid suspicion. He would have to be unreasonably lucky, Daniel suspected, to achieve two out of three ... no, four: whatever he did would also have to look accidental to Tenai. Or pass unnoticed by her? That would be perfect. Even better if whatever trick he came up with was also unnoticed by Mitereh. Something only Keitah would recognize.

This seemed less and less possible.

And he had only two days to find a way to pull off whatever trick he could devise. Blood pounded behind his eyes as the migraine he'd hoped he'd avoided returned, this time with more force.

12

Morning brought brighter spirits, for Jenna at least. She stretched and yawned and realized that sleeping on the ground no longer made her stiff. Or maybe it was being free of the outlaw pack, so she'd been able to really relax. But she was very thirsty, and she was starving. Her stomach growled. She gave Emel an apologetic look.

There was a stream, which took care of the thirst, but there was nothing for breakfast but a handful of shoots and young leaves off a vine that Emel showed her how to collect, and a few raw tubers from reeds growing by the stream. "We need money," Emel said. "And clothing, and food." He took them back to the road. They walked along it, not too fast, watching for anybody else who might be moving this morning. Jenna wasn't too clear on what they meant to do if they spotted anybody. Maybe there just wasn't an actual plan—maybe there wouldn't be until they saw some fellow travelers and knew what they had to work with.

Though Jenna felt she'd been alert, it was still Emel who spotted the wagon first. It was still kind of far away. She could see there were a couple of people sitting in the front of the wagon, which was drawn by a pair of big sorrel horses. The rear of the wagon looked ... lumpy, she thought, and wondered what was under the canvas. Nothing very big. Adrenalin ran through her. She looked nervously at Emel.

"Wait," he murmured. "Have the bow ready, but wait for my signal. We may do nothing."

Kuomat had had a whole pack to rob people. Emel was by himself, except for her. She hadn't said a word even when she'd realized he meant to rob people to get what they needed. Maybe she'd gotten all used to the idea over the past days. But—God, what if it went wrong? What if someone was hurt? Killed? Someone else would be bad enough, but what if one of *them* was hurt or killed? Then what? They could do something else to get money for clothes and stuff. Something not illegal. Something not *dangerous*. She didn't know what. But something. Why hadn't she made him think about that? Because she'd been too impatient to get on with their journey to even care. Then. She bit her lip anxiously, trying to decide whether she should say something now.

The wagon came on. The man held the reins. The woman had a light crossbow resting on her thigh, taking a firm grip on it as they met on the road. Both the man and the woman looked comfortable, respectable—the man had a sharp, intelligent-looking face and a humorous, wry set to his mouth. The woman with him, surely not all that much older than Jenna, had much softer features and very dark skin. When she laughed at something the man said, her laugh sounded unforced and free. Jenna wondered why they were traveling by themselves, why they thought they were safe from outlaws—surely there was no trick, no trap, because Emel would have known.

Emel nodded and lifted a hand in polite salute to the couple, who eyed him askance anyway—that would be the lack of soap and general grunginess, Jenna suspected—but the people didn't seem especially alarmed, either. That part was maybe because it was Jenna who had the crossbow. Maybe women generally carried the bows in order to make their parties look civilized. Or maybe it was generally recognized that women needed the protection more? Or maybe it was just that men were supposed to be the ones with swords, and that was why they left bows for the women? She should ask Emel sometime.

The man had guided his wagon to the left side of the road, leaving plenty of room for pedestrians. Emel, Jenna at his side, just walked on past, and for a moment Jenna thought he'd changed his mind and they weren't going to try to rob the couple after all. She was immensely relieved.

Then Emel turned, walked up alongside the wagon so smoothly and quietly that not even the horses flicked an ear, reached up, caught the woman by one arm, and pulled her down into his arms. The crossbow she'd held went flying. The woman gave a single muffled squeak. The man made an inarticulate sound, reached back into the wagon, came up with a heavy crossbow, and stopped dead. Emel was standing as massively still as a large rock, holding the woman firmly in front of him. He had not drawn his sword, but his knife rested across her throat. His expression was sardonic.

The man on the wagon lifted his crossbow to point at the sky.

"Throw it away," said Emel.

The man hesitated ... and then brought it down instead, to point at Emel's face. "Do harm to her, and you will die next," he said. He'd gone ashen, but his bow was quite steady.

"Will that comfort you, if she is also dead?" asked Emel, not noticeably taken aback. "I swear before God, I will harm neither you nor this woman if you do as I tell you. But if you do not throw away the bow very soon, my friend there will shoot you, and then who will protect your wife?"

The man looked skeptical. Jenna shot into the dirt in front of his feet. Then she quickly reloaded the crossbow, fingers feeling stiff. But she got the bolt in and the string cranked back.

The man glanced at her and then looked back at Emel. His face was very still. He said to Emel, "You swear before God. You will not harm my wife. Not in any way."

"Or him!" put in the woman, quickly, from where she stood rigid with the knife dimpling the skin of her throat. Jenna approved. Good for her.

Emel gave the man a slight, reassuring nod. "Before God and the Martyr," he repeated. "So long as you put me to no trouble, you are both perfectly safe."

The man threw the bow away into the woods, not very far, and Emel gave him a second small nod. "Get out of the wagon," Emel said. And, when the man had reluctantly complied,

"Approach me. Stop. Turn your back to me. Kneel. Put your hands behind your back. Asih. Aim at this woman. Shoot her if he moves. Or if she moves, shoot the man. Yes?"

"Yes," said Jenna, a little shakily. She knew that she was not going to shoot either of them ... except what if Emel was in danger? She didn't know what she would do then, and bit her lip hard, praying both the, the victims would just be good little victims and cooperate.

Emel let go of the woman, went to the man, and bound his hands firmly behind his back. Neither the man nor the woman moved, but the man's head bowed a little once his hands had been bound. "Sit," Emel told him, his tone not unkind. "And you, sit," he added to the woman. She sank down beside her husband and they both stared at Emel. The woman was frightened, but trying to be brave. The man looked stiffly proud.

"Your coin," Emel said to the man.

The man said, "In a pouch in my shirt." He held still while Emel searched him and found the pouch.

Emel weighed the pouch in the palm of his hand and looked speculatively at the woman.

"No," said the man.

"No?" said Emel. He considered the man for a moment, then studied the wagon. "Asih," he said. "Shoot them if they move." Then he went to the wagon, knelt in the dirt next to it, and felt around underneath it. He came out with a second pouch, considerably larger than the first. The man had gone gray. The woman made a small sound and hid her face against his shoulder. Emel shook his head, mildly exasperated. "Men do hide coin there. You are far from the first. You should take more thought when you hide coin. The cleverest place I have seen was a hollowed axle. One must make the hollow with some care, to be sure, lest the axle break."

"Is there a lot there?" Jenna asked. She backed up a few steps, trying to watch the road and Emel and their prisoners all at once. The light bow felt slippery in her hands.

"Yes," said Emel, with a considering look at the couple.

"Well, we can't need that much. Take what we have to have and leave them the rest."

Both prisoners turned their heads and stared at her.

"We could do so. But with this much, we might buy good horses."

"We can walk," said Jenna. "It's not much slower."

Emel poured some of the coins out in his hand and tossed the rest of the pouch up into the wagon. He tucked the money he'd kept away in his own shirt and said to the man, "Hide the rest away with more care this time." He hesitated, and added, "We need clothing." And to Jenna, forestalling her objection, "We cannot walk into any town and buy better. We would draw too much attention—and the wrong sort. We must first *have* better. Then towns and villages will be open to us. This woman is near enough your size."

"The man is smaller than you."

"His clothing will serve." Emel looked at the man. "I do not wish to take the time to search everything. Where shall I look?"

The man hesitated, but the woman immediately described the appropriate chest. Emel threw back the canvas covering the wagon and found the clothing. It seemed to take an alarmingly long time to Jenna, who was now spending as much time looking anxiously along the road in both directions as watching the prisoners. She half expected to see Kuomat and his men appear out of the woods. But Emel seemed satisfied at last with the parcel he'd made up, and nobody else appeared on the road. Emel tossed the bundle out of the wagon and leaped down.

"We're done, right?" Jenna asked him tensely.

"Food. You are hungry." Emel found a packet behind the seat and tossed it to Jenna. He hesitated, appearing irresolute. Then he came back and knelt down on the road, looking steadily at the man from the same level. The man met his eyes with wary curiosity.

"Swear before God," Emel said quietly, "that you will speak to no one of us for three days. After that it will not matter. But swear that, and we are done."

The man lifted an ironic brow. "If I will not, you will do murder?" His glance slid to Jenna and came back to Emel.

"Of course you see I will not. But I must have your silence, so if you will not make the oath as I told you, I will beat you so you will not be able to speak."

He sounded absolutely serious. Jenna believed him. So did the woman, who said immediately, "We swear! Before God and the Martyr."

"You can make the oath only for yourself," Emel said to her, not looking away from the man.

"You do not this time threaten my wife?"

"I do not want you to hate me. I want you to do as you are told. Make the oath, or I will see to it you will not be able to speak for at least three days."

"Give the oath!" said the woman. "Kahisan, give the oath!"

The man bowed his head slightly. "Before God," he said, "I will tell no one of you for three days. Then I will describe you at great length to all my friends over a bottle. They will not believe me."

Emel smiled and stood up. But his voice was serious. "As you have sworn, so we will do you one more kindness. There is a cur pack working this road. They will be that way, likely not so far distant. Men not so courteous as we. You would be wise to travel with a good deal more company."

The man shook his head. "How do they dare?—how do you? Do you not know there are soldiers on this road? That the lord of Nemesen sent soldiers through here only a handful of days past, and will send more to clear this road as soon as he knows men have been robbed here?"

Emel shrugged. "There is a risk to everything. One learns to perceive an ambush and let soldiers pass. These brigands of whom I speak, these are experienced, clever men. You would do well to go back to Nemesen and give them the warning as I gave it to you, minding your oath to me, but I do not care if you give warning of curs on the road so long as you do not speak of us in any specific manner. If you are wise, you will find men in the town to bear you company on your road."

The man nodded slowly.

Emel took out his spare knife. The man tensed, but then relaxed when Emel offered the knife to his wife. "One may easily cut the wrist as well as the bonds," he told her, "so take care."

The woman nodded, taking the weapon gingerly.

Emel gathered up the parcel of clothing and simply walked into the woods. Jenna ran to catch up with him. She opened the packet of food and examined its contents. "Rolls. Chicken! Great. It's finger-lickin' good. Here." She handed Emel a drumstick and took one for herself. "Are we going to Nemesen? That's a town, right? Is it a real town, or just a village? How far away is it from here, do you know? I want a bath before we change into clean clothes. I guess you didn't find any soap in that wagon."

He gave her a sidelong look. "I did. I might have told you of it, only I feared you would tell me to take only a little and leave the rest."

After a startled second, Jenna laughed.

The soap was wonderful. They used it all once they were close enough to Nemesen to walk the rest of the way without getting too dusty. Emel made her wait while he made more dye for her—for her hair as well as her skin, because he said the roots were starting to show blond. She scrubbed all over and washed her hair three times, applied the dyes and washed again, luxuriating in the feeling of being *clean* for the first time in days. It seemed like weeks.

The woman's clothing fit pretty well. The skirt was a dark golden brown color, very full cut, with a weighted hem that swirled around Jenna's ankles. The blouse was a soft gold. It wouldn't have gone that well with her natural coloring, but she thought it probably looked great with the mocha color she got from the dye. There was a long vest to wear over the blouse, the same color as the skirt. She abandoned her filthy clothes in a pile and came out to show Emel her new finery, feeling shy and vain and smug and thoroughly female for the first time in days.

He looked at her without speaking for a moment. She thought a faint flush might have darkened his face, but his coloring made it hard to tell. He nodded at last. "You should have a net to put over your hair," he said, and looked faintly chagrined. "I did not think to look for such a thing. But ... I think no one would take you for a brigand's woman."

"You couldn't think of everything." Jenna felt quite cheerful. He looked much better, too. The shirt was too small. Obviously it would be. But he looked ... really good. The trousers were dark chocolate brown, the shirt almost the same color as her skirt, the vest a lighter golden cream. "No one would take you for a brigand."

Emel looked pleased, in his restrained way. "We will walk on the road and come into the town as respectable travelers. I think we will be safe to do so. I think even your own father would need to look four times to know you. There are precautions we shall take, but I think we should indeed be safe to go into Nemesen. We will have supper in an inn, like respectable folk, and sleep—" he faltered slightly—"sleep in real beds." He had been smiling, but now he looked away.

It occurred to Jenna that she could think of worse things than a private room with just one bed and supper for two ordered in ... but what would her father think? This wasn't like a simple fling with a college boy. Emel wasn't a simple boy, for one thing. Anyway, if she made any move that way, he'd probably think she was a slut. Talasayan was pretty straight-laced. Jenna felt her face heat. She cast around quickly for something to say. "And buy horses? Did you keep enough money for that"

Emel took this offered new topic with obvious relief. "I did not. We will buy seats on a public conveyance, I think. Even a fast carriage will not cost so much, and there will be less risk of ambush from curs or Keitah's soldiers. We will be back in Nerinesir in not so much longer. Three days, four days."

Nerinesir. Jenna looked down. How many days had it been

since her father had arrived back in Nerinesir? Several, she was sure. What would he be feeling, thinking she was still trapped in Kinabana? He would be so worried, so scared for her. What had he been doing, since he'd been back in Nerinesir? Had Emel even been right in his guess about Keitah's intentions? Surely ... surely her father hadn't done anything ... too irrevocable.

"We will hire the fastest possible conveyance," Emel said, watching her face, and she tried to smile.

Nemesen was a town on the shore of the bay that was its backdrop and its livelihood. It was built of gray slate, its houses roofed with red tile; a hundred small fishing boats were drawn up on the pale sands below the town, and a hundred sails were visible far out in the bay. A thick low wall, not even shoulder height, divided the town from the countryside. The wall was meant, Emel explained, to direct traffic onto the main streets of the town, not to guard against armies. A briny, fishy smell wafted inland on the sea breeze. Jenna wrinkled her nose, trying to decide if she liked the smell or not. She thought she might. Or that she might learn to.

"How big a town is this?" she asked Emel. They had circled around to enter the town from a road that ran along the shore of the bay from the north, avoiding any possible encounter with the couple they had robbed, in case they had taken Emel's advice and returned to Nemesen themselves. And also, of course, further reducing what Emel estimated was now only a small risk of running into soldiers from Kinabana. Keitah probably had agents in Nemesen. But he would not be likely, Emel had decided, to have so many they could cover all possible approaches. Especially as Nemesen was not a town on any of the most direct routes from Kinabana to Nerinesir.

"Twelve thousand, fifteen thousand?" Emel said now. "They fish, as you see, and they have pigs, though it is said the pork of Nemesen tastes of fish. They use clay for tiles and for plates. And Nemesen serves as one of several waystations on the way from Kinabana south to Gai-e in Imbaneh-se. They are not wealthy here, but neither are they poor. The lord is Balaiyan Teiskana-e; this province is Teiskana, from here north twenty miles, perhaps, and then all the way south and east to the farthest inland extent of the bay, and some way south toward Gai-e."

Jenna nodded.

"We will stay here as short a time as may be," Emel added. "The inns are along the roads. They are accustomed to the needs of travelers. We will find an inn near the eastern edge of town and arrange for conveyance there."

The road that led down toward Nemesen was paved with slate set firmly into a base of packed sand. It was a pleasure to walk on it because, though there was a certain amount of traffic, horses kept to the left side of the street, with the right-hand side of the road reserved for pedestrians. The people entering the town were a thoroughly mixed bag: all the better for Jenna and Emel to avoid notice themselves.

"We will separate to go through the gate," Emel told her. "You see that family, there, walking, with all the children? They are southern, I think. You will match them closely enough to be taken for one of their daughters. Walk closely with that family. Speak to one of the children as you go through the gate into town. Make the child laugh, if you can."

Jenna eyed her chosen camouflage. "All right. And where will you be?"

"I will offer my assistance to that old man there. You see his barrow is heavy. He will welcome a strong back to help him over the rough cobbles near the gate."

"And you look a little like him."

"He is my uncle, perhaps."

Like Emel's 'uncle,' some of the people entering the town—and most of the ones leaving—were pushing wheelbarrows; some had small four-wheeled carts that were pulled by large dogs instead of horses. Most of the wheelbarrows and carts on the way out were empty. Some held packages wrapped up in canvas or paper.

"Farmers," Emel explained. "Probably today was a market day. They have sold all that they brought and bought in return a little fish or oil—the things they cannot make for themselves. The inns here will serve good food tonight."

Jenna looked forward to it. She looked forward to decent food, and a real bed, and best of all, an early start in the morning back to Nerinesir and her father. She found herself tensing again at the thought of him. He would be all right. She was certain he would be fine. He would never have tried to kill Mitereh. Even if he was really afraid for her. No matter what Keitah had told him. Would he?

"We can get the news here, I guess," Jenna said to Emel. "If there is any."

"Yes," the big man answered, so firmly that Jenna realized he must also have been lost in worried thoughts. "You might ask the children of your family for news, and I will ask my old man."

Jenna nodded and let her stride lengthen as much as her new skirt would allow. Which was pretty far; it was generously cut. She put on a smile like it was part of her disguise, which she supposed it was. Drawing a breath, she prepared to produce lighthearted chatter for the benefit of the young woman shepherding the family's younger children at the rear of the group.

Separating was a good plan. It should have worked. It was a horrible shock when a crossbow bolt hit the road in front of Jenna's foot and skittered off sideways. The children scattered, yelling. Jenna stopped dead, staring after the bolt, too shocked to even scream. Behind her there were more shouts, and she knew without having to turn her head that men had targeted Emel as well.

Other travelers shied off quickly, scattering before way too many hurrying soldiers. The soldiers ignored everyone else. The men weren't wearing Keitah Terusai's badge, but they were his: whose else would they be? Jenna could see that running away would be hopeless. There was no cover anywhere, and all of Keitah's men had heavy crossbows.

"I am very sorry," Emel said to her in a low voice, coming forward to join her now that there was no reason to maintain the distance they'd barely had time to establish in the first place.

Jenna shook her head. "How did they spot us?"

Emel only shrugged, as baffled as she was. "Some magic I did not guard against—something I did not know to guard against. Or cleverness. Or many spies spread out everywhere, more than I imagined." He took a breath. Then he cautioned her. "We must not fight. There are too many bows. Probably these men will not be careless, although—" Emel looked like he was trying to reason out what Keitah's men might reasonably know and what they probably didn't—"they will not know you were a student of Nolas-Kuomon's. I think."

Because all of Keitah's men who had seen her fight were dead. Jenna felt like throwing up, maybe because of plain adrenalin, but she thought more because of the memory of fighting those men. Killing those men. She swallowed. She had killed Saimadan on purpose. She hated, *hated* the idea that she might have to do it again. She didn't know if she even could.

"A chance may therefore come," Emel finished quickly and quietly, while the men were still too far away to overhear. "For you, if not for me. If it comes—" he stopped, because the men were too close to say anything else without being overheard. But Jenna knew he'd been going to say, *take the chance and go, if you must, without me.*

And, Jenna thought, she might even make it alone, now. She was the one with a few coins in her pouch. And she'd just renewed the hair and skin dyes. She gave Emel a sidelong look. She didn't make any move to fight the man who took her arm, because a chance might indeed come, but she didn't need to be told that this wasn't it.

13

By dinnertime, Daniel still had not come up with any ideas that seemed better than insane. He spent some time morbidly figuring out exactly how many hours Keitah might mean when he said 'two days' and how many were left. Would that be two days from the time the warning had been given, or, say, two days from this evening? Probably to be safe he had better assume the former ...

"You are very quiet this evening," Taranah Berangilan-sa observed. Daniel had become her supper guest almost by default, Tenai being engaged in some job or other for Mitereh, and the king himself entertaining various powerful lords of the court whom Daniel did not know. Before all this had happened, Daniel would have been quite happy to spend his evening with the king's aunt. Now ... now he would have been glad of a quiet evening in which to think. But Taranah was far too courteous to leave Daniel at loose ends for the evening, especially when such engagements obviously were socially very important.

Daniel excused his inattention with an apologetic, "I'm afraid I have a headache," which was, God knew, perfectly true. The headache hadn't quite grown into a true migraine, but it was bad enough. And persistent.

"Oh, poor Danyel." Taranah patted his hand, instantly sympathetic. "Allow me to send for medicinal tea." She glanced at one of her women, Inaseh, who departed at once on this errand.

"Thank you," Daniel said, and tried to work out whether he could use indisposition to excuse an early departure. Paper, that's what he needed. And a pencil. Or quill pen, if that was all he could get. Anything that would help him *think*.

"You should not allow yourself to suffer for no purpose," Taranah scolded, in much the tone Daniel imagined she would use if she wanted to take Mitereh to task. "Here we are," she added, as Inaseh returned and proffered a tray. The tray held a small, round-bodied, red enamel pot and a matching cup; a short fat white candle; and a long silver skewer with a painted red design winding around its base. Inaseh poured steaming tea from the pot into the cup. Taranah herself lit the candle and pricked the tip of one finger with the skewer. A single drop of blood welled up.

"Oh ... look, it's not necessary ..." Daniel began, belatedly. He had not realized any sort of sorcery was involved; he forgotten until now that the king's aunt was a sorcerer. It certainly hadn't worked out well when he'd allowed Keitah to involve him in magic ...

Taranah barely even glanced up. "It's little enough trouble," she assured Daniel with brisk matter-of-factness. "I make tea a double handful of times every year for my nephew. Mitereh *will* work himself into headaches, disregarding all advice."

"*You* make tea for everyone who suffers a passing indisposition," murmured Inaseh Suaneni, apparently in mild disapproval.

"Well, and if I do? Does the world not contain enough unavoidable suffering? Thus it behooves us all to prevent what suffering we may."

That caught Daniel's attention. He found himself smiling. She was a wonderful woman, really. So matter-of-fact in her kindness. Impossible to distrust her, no matter how wrong he had been about Keitah.

Inaseh had lit a taper from one of the lanterns that hung above the table and handed the taper to Taranah, who now in turn lit the white candle. Then Taranah let the drop of blood fall from her finger into the flame. Crimson washed down the candle from top to bottom. Melting wax ran down its sides like blood. Taranah blotted her finger absently on a cloth and picked up the candle, letting a drop of the reddened wax fall into the cup Inaseh held waiting. Turning, she offered the cup to Daniel.

Daniel took it. The king's aunt gazed at him: practical, sympathetic, worldly, expectant. Absolutely as kind as she seemed. She hadn't suggested tea until he'd said he had a headache. Her attendants obviously thought this was something ordinary. They probably watched Taranah prepare this kind of sorcery-influenced tea all the time.

Besides, if she were actually a terrible, dangerous person, she obviously wasn't working with Keitah, so if Daniel found that out, maybe could set them against each other.

The whole idea was ludicrous. Everything about this situation was ludicrous. He couldn't think of any possible way to refuse the tea. And he just couldn't distrust Taranah. He hadn't contributed a drop of blood this time. Maybe that was the key. Taranah hadn't asked him to. Maybe that was an important indication that her intentions were exactly what they seemed.

He sipped the tea. Not much seemed to happen, not right away. The headache didn't ease, or not much. Perhaps the sorcery hadn't touched him.

"Thank you," he said.

Taranah gave a little dismissive wave of her hand. "It is a trivial thing. Do not trouble yourself, Danyel. If the headache returns, as it should not, but if it does, be sure to send word to me. At least, if Chaisa-e is not available, for I confess Chaisa-e is far more skilled than I. Now. What pursuits have you found, or has Mitereh found for you, to fill your hours? I do not believe I have glimpsed you more than twice in the past several days. I shall speak to my nephew if he forgets himself and tasks you as though you were one of his young men."

"Um ..." Daniel was unsure how to answer this. He'd been spending his time trying to avoid everyone, mostly.

But he was spared the necessity to answer, for there was a low apologetic cough from the doorway. Ranakai had appeared there, escorted by another of Taranah's attendants. He gave a little bow. "Forgive me, Nolas-ai Taranah, Nola Danyel. I must urgently request Nola Danyel to the king's presence."

Daniel sat up straight. "Why? What's—has something happened?" Something had, he realized. The young man was clearly upset. The moment strongly recalled an equally urgent summons to Lindenwood, that one in the middle of the night, to deal with a Tenai out of control and dangerous to herself and everyone around her. Daniel's heart sank.

Taranah sat back in her chair, frowning. "What has my nephew done, or discovered, or suffered?" she demanded.

"Is it Tenai?" Daniel asked, following his own fears.

The young man bowed to Daniel wordlessly, clearly an affirmative. Daniel stood up. "I'll come," he said unnecessarily.

Taranah was also on her feet, looking no happier than Daniel felt.

Mitereh was in a private audience chamber, one made of white marble and decorated with tapestries and rugs in jewel tones. He was pacing, a quick worried stride. Apana Pelat was present, standing stiffly with his hands clasped before him, tracking the king's movements with a serious, concerned expression.

Mitereh spun as Daniel and Taranah came in, dismissed Ranakai with a jerk of his head, and motioned the other two to approach. He said with no preliminaries, "I am deeply troubled regarding the mind and heart of Chaisa-e. So I sent for you, Nola Danyel; and I am glad of your presence also, my aunt. Nola Danyel, I am aware your own heart is divided. Nevertheless, I must ask you."

Daniel glanced in alarm from the king to Pelat to Taranah and back again to the king. "What's happened?"

Mitereh held out his hands palm-up, in a gesture Daniel read as uncertainty and distress. "I may have made an error," the king admitted. "You understand, Nola Danyel, Tenai Ponanon Chaisa-e married into that name? That she holds Chaisa because her husband's family is gone?"

"Yes ... "

"You see," said Mitereh rapidly, "it seemed to me expedient

to offer Chaisa to a man named Tantanad Kaingaran-se. Which I could not do, of course, save Chaisa-e herself is here to give up that right and that name." He stopped.

"Ah," said Daniel. He tried not to wince visibly.

"Worse," said the king, "My request that she renounce the name was made publicly, and cannot now easily withdraw the request. I did not ... the fault is mine. I confess I did not understand the depth of her attachment to Chaisa. She has spent less than one year in a hundred there! How could I know? I believed she would take another grant as easily. Worse than that—" he paused, lowered his voice, "Worse still, though she was angry, it seemed to me she would accept what I asked." He glanced at Pelat. "I understand now that this is not so."

Daniel shook his head, momentarily without words. Hadn't he had enough to deal with? Had the situation really needed this complication? Though—wait—might there be a way to somehow turn this problem to his own personal advantage?

"You thought the lady would give up Chaisa?" said Taranah, less distracted than Daniel. She sounded exasperated as well as worried. "Mitereh, did you not understand that all Tenai Ponanon's memories of peace, all her *dreams* of peace, are tied up in that estate and that land? Whatever small number of her hours she ever spent under its roof?"

"I understand it now," Mitereh said ruefully. "I confess, my aunt, I should have asked you for your opinion. But the moment arose unexpectedly and I thought to take it firmly and turn it to fit my purpose."

Daniel thought his headache might be getting worse, Taranah's tea notwithstanding. He pinched the bridge of his nose, then looked at Pelat, trying to focus on the moment. "So what did she tell you? I gather something else?"

Apana Pelat was as stiff as though he'd been carved out of marble. "The lady bade me make ready to ride south," he said tonelessly. He would not quite look at Daniel.

South, Daniel recalled after a moment, was Imbaneh-se.

"Instead, as you see, he came to me," said the king. "A thankless loyalty; necessarily so. For which I am nevertheless extremely grateful."

Pelat bowed his head, still refusing to meet Daniel's eye. Daniel, too preoccupied with his own concerns, could not spare much thought for parsing this avoidant behavior.

"Advise me," Mitereh said to Daniel and Taranah alike. "Shall I send to her, tell her I regret my rash haste? Promise her that Chaisa is hers? It would harm my pride, yet I might do it. Or command her obedience and let her word bind her? Will it? Advise me, Nola Danyel."

Taranah deferred to Daniel with a slight bow. Daniel said, "Uh ... maybe I'd better talk to her." Could he get Tenai to leave, *and* to compel him to go with her? That would get him away from Mitereh. Or would Keitah construe any such outcome as *de facto* defiance and have Jenna tortured? Regretfully, Daniel decided that Keitah would of course do exactly that, and reluctantly discarded this idea.

Oblivious of Daniel's distraction, Mitereh spread his hands in a little *Yes, please* gesture. "If she will speak with you, I should be profoundly grateful." The king hesitated, slid a sidelong glance at Apana Pelat. "Where the captain's best loyalty lies ... is a private matter, best left between himself and God. Do you understand me, Nola Danyel?"

"What? Oh ..." the king's meaning dawned on Daniel. "It's certainly not my business to question where Apana Pelat goes, or to whom he speaks, or about what."

"Exactly," agreed Mitereh. He gave Pelat a direct look. "I have no right to ask, and yet I must: will you go with Tenai Ponanon Chaisa-e, wheresoever she may go, and yet tell me where that may be and ... and apprise me of what counsel she takes, and of whom, as you see fit? I know it is a hard and bitter thing I ask."

Pelat glanced uncomfortably toward Daniel and then answered Mitereh in a low voice, "All else aside, I serve the king still."

"And you, Nola Danyel." The king came back to Daniel and laid a hand on his arm, a rare gesture, among the people of Talasayan and especially among the nobility. "I think you do not desire to see Nolas-Kuomon go to war. No? So I ask you to act as you may to ease her temper. Will you speak to Chaisa-e as you may? I understand that your loyalties also are divided. Yet will you bear word to me as seems good to that end?"

"Yes," Daniel promised.

"Then go," said Mitereh, and opened his hand, meaning, *Now, please*. "My aunt, if you will remain."

Daniel located Tenai in a courtyard behind one wing of the king's palace. It was easy to find her: he followed distraught looks and dismayed murmurs through hallways and down corridors and at last out into the blazing sunlight, which Tenai rendered weak and dim by contrast with her own scorching fury. The force of her anger swirled out from her to fill the courtyard; the other people there seemed small and cowed before it. Every shadow here seemed darker and deeper and sharper-edged than any natural shadow should. If the quarrel between Mitereh and Tenai was a ruse, it was a convincing one. Not that he had much hope that any such ruse was underway.

Tenai had her black sword slung at her hip. Daniel tried not to look at it. She was overseeing the loading of a single packhorse with as much concentrated ferocity as though directing supplies for an army. The packhorse fidgeted anxiously as men tried to balance its load with trembling hands. Tenai's own black mare, saddled and held off to the side along with a couple of other animals, tried to rear. A groom brought it down and whispered soothingly in its ear, to very little effect. It tried to rear again.

Daniel drew a quick breath and stepped out into the courtyard.

"Daniel," Tenai greeted him. He might have found it promising that she recognized him and was willing to speak to him, but there was nothing reassuring in her tone. Her flat stare had no give in it. She nodded toward one of the nervous animals the grooms held. "There is a horse for you, if you would take it."

"Ah ..." Daniel glanced that way and then back again. The force of Tenai's fury made it almost impossible to meet her eyes, even for him. If this was merely a show, then she deserved an Oscar. Or an Emmy, whatever award it was actors got. "Tenai, I suspect Mitereh is having second thoughts about, um, asking you to give up Chaisa."

"I care nothing for the opinion of a son of Encormio."

Daniel knew her anger was not directed at him personally. But the ferocity of her rage and the deep, reaching shadows reaching through the courtyard made it hard to think. If there was a way he could bend this situation toward his own and Jenna's safety, he couldn't see it.

Tenai stalked over to the cowering groom and took the reins of her horse. The animal rolled its eye at her and sidled sideways. She made an impatient sound, followed its nervous movements, got a hand on the front of the saddle, and smoothly gained its back.

Sandakan Gutai-e came into the courtyard. He had been running: his breathing was quick and urgent. But he came to an abrupt halt when he saw Tenai. She halted too, and the air between them seemed to go stiff and brittle.

"Well?" Tenai said sharply. "And has Encormio-na sent you to me, Gutai? Will you lift your sword against me? Have you a hundred men with bows beyond that gate?"

Those contemptuous words struck Sandakan a bit like the bolts from a hundred bows. Daniel had hardly seen the two of them together since their initial reunion. But if there had not been a strong bond between them still, she would surely not have been able to hurt him so badly. It was the flat contempt in her tone as much as what she said. Sandakan was too dark-skinned to exactly pale, but his silence was a speaking one. He unclipped his sword from his belt and flung it, still sheathed, at her feet; her horse reared.

Tenai spun the horse in a circle, bringing it again to a halt hardly a hand's breadth from Sandakan, where she held the animal still. The horse shivered, ears rotating nervously forward and back. Her expression had not exactly eased, but there was something in her face that had not been there previously. She said very softly, almost too softly for Daniel to hear, "Then will you come with me? Because I cannot bear to leave you a second time as an enemy at my back."

Daniel closed his eyes briefly, moved despite everything by this effortful move toward conciliation. Or reconciliation.

Sandakan took a step forward, laid a hand on the neck of her horse. He said nothing.

Tenai's expression hardened.

Sandakan said, "Will you stay? Because I cannot bear to watch you ride away from me as an enemy a second time."

Tenai backed her horse a single step, not taking her eyes off his.

Sandakan's hand fell slowly to his side. He said, "Mitereh erred, but he is young yet. He would not do ill of a purpose. Go back to him, Tenai. Do not ride alone away from life and the living into that dark country."

Tenai met his eyes. Her fury had been banked, but she showed no sign of softening. "I was a fool to think for even a moment I might serve a son of Encormio."

"Tenai. The war is over. That is a son of Sekuse Berangilan-sa. He owns no father. Can you not let it lie?"

"I cannot endure it," Tenai said quietly. She looked at Daniel. "Will you come?" But then she turned at once back to Sandakan, her tone sharpening. "Or have you indeed set men to shoot from the walls?"

Sandakan shook his head. "I have given no such order. I know bolts would avail nothing against you, and I will not strike down any who choose to go with you—though I ask Nola Danyel to remain."

Daniel looked helplessly from one of them to the other, trying to frame an answer, hopelessly off balance.

"Stay," Sandakan said again, without emphasis.

Not a command, Daniel thought, but a request. Even a plea. But he did not dare go. He took a step toward the general, wordlessly.

"So," said Tenai, and reined her mare about, reaching for the pack horse's lead rein.

Apana Pelat came into the courtyard at a dead run, jerked to a halt so sharply he staggered, and stared at Tenai. Then he went, abruptly and not quite steadily, to one knee on the flagstones.

Tenai drew her horse up and gazed back at him, face still. She jerked her head at the waiting horses.

Pelat got to his feet. He did not look at Daniel, nor at Sandakan Gutai-e, but went quickly to take one of the saddled horses. Mounting, he reined around and took the pack horse himself. When Tenai rode out of the courtyard, the hooves of her horse echoing like the drumbeat of time itself in the silence, he followed.

Daniel and Sandakan both watched them go. Only when he could no longer hear the hooves of the horses did Daniel turn back to look at the general.

"It's as well she has one man with her," Sandakan said at last, not returning the look. His eyes were on the gate. It was clear he wished he were that man. It wasn't nearly as obvious to Daniel whether he knew that Apana Pelat was really still a king's man and not Tenai's. Nor was it obvious how to inquire with any discretion. Daniel said nothing.

"I must report to Mitereh," Sandakan added, and sighed. His shoulders had bowed; he looked like he'd aged ten years.

Was it possible he was acting a part for Daniel's—or Keitah's—benefit? Daniel shook his head slightly, wanting to believe the whole thing had been staged. Yet he could hardly doubt the intensity of Tenai's rage, or of Sandakan's distress. When the general turned back toward the palace and the waiting king, he found nothing to do but trail after and wait for some kind of hint; if not of the truth, whatever that was, at least of what he might do to retrieve as much as possible from the evolving debacle.

Mitereh, listening to the report of Tenai's departure, remained expressionless. But it was a grim impassivity. Taranah had gone, no doubt about some urgent political duty.

"And now?" the king asked Sandakan. "What will she do?" Then he asked Daniel, "In your estimation, Nola Danyel, what may she choose now to do? Will she consider again and return? Have you *any* expectation she may choose so?"

Daniel doubted this. The dark fury in Tenai had been scorching.

"She will go to Imbaneh-se," Sandakan said quietly. "I have very little doubt of it."

"Yes, my general, I think you are surely correct." Mitereh sighed. Then he went on, speaking slowly. "Yet I think Imbaneh-se may find her a difficult asset. The Geraimani or others there will assuredly seek to turn her to their use; but I think perhaps she will turn *them* to *her* use instead. That may well dismay those who sought so hard to bring her to their side and their standard. Perhaps, should quarrels erupt in the south, I may yet persuade Nolas-Kuomon to return to my hand." The king turned back to Daniel. "Nola Danyel, may I ask your opinion?"

"I ... don't think so," Daniel said honestly. "Maybe. Probably not easily."

Mitereh tapped his fingers thoughtfully against the ornate arm of his chair. Daniel and Sandakan had both been invited to sit. Daniel sat uneasily upright in a stiff wooden chair, but Sandakan had elected to stand. The king said to him, "My general, we have won two small wars with Imbaneh-se in the past sixteen years. Are we so positioned as to defeat them again?"

"With Nolas-Kuomon to lead them? My king, I do not know."

"Having Tenai with them would truly make so much difference?" Daniel asked.

"So much difference? Yes. Would her banner set before theirs be enough to turn the age? That is a more difficult question. When Tenai warred against my father, half of Talasayan fought at her side and the other half at least sympathized with her aim to bring him low. That is not the case now." The king tapped his fingers some more. He added, "Men remember her final defeat. This, too, is to our benefit, if there should be war. We might defeat Imbaneh-se, isolate Nolas-Kuomon, and then hold her until the turning of the year. I do not disregard that possibility. But the outcome would be uncertain, and the cost great." Mitereh paused.

Then he added to Sandakan, "Send to Terusan, to Kaya-sa, to Kandun, to Patananir. Have Keitah send to Kinabana. Call up the levies from all those provinces. Leave Antiatan aside. How long to gather this army and set it in order?"

"With the foundation already laid so little time past, not long, my king. Seven days. Five for Kaya-sa. You would not choose to send the levy from Kaya-sa to Antiatan? That would not be too great a force to protect the young prince."

He meant Mitereh's younger brother, Daniel recalled after a moment. The boy was in Antiatan. Right. A good place for him, probably. Anyplace but here was probably a good place for the youngest son of Encormio, now.

"We may well need Kaya-sa here. Call them up," Mitereh said decisively. "See to it, my general. Also send men to the border and into Imbaneh-se to see what progresses there."

Sandakan bowed.

"And may God look with mercy on us all," the king added, and dismissed them both.

That was one prayer Daniel could get behind.

14

The man, though he held Jenna's arm, had focused most of his attention on Emel. He said crisply, "Your sword, man."

Emel handed it over without a word. One of the men searched him and took his knife. No one searched Jenna, but she hadn't had anything but the light bow and they took that.

The leader was the one who held Jenna. He was a handsome dark-skinned man, maybe thirty or thirty-five, with high cheekbones and fine elegant eyebrows and black eyes. But he handled Jenna like she was a dog or a horse, like to him she wasn't a person at all. Jenna thought that if Keitah cut off her feet, this man wouldn't even be interested. To him, she was something Keitah wanted, and as a plus she was also something he could use to control Emel.

The man glanced at some of the others, who hurried away into the town and came quickly back leading horses. The men took badges and marks of rank out of their saddlebags with unmistakable satisfaction and put them on. They were, of course, Keitah's men.

"You didn't get far," the captain of the small troop said to Emel, with even clearer satisfaction. "We will be back in Kinabana in three days. Less."

Emel bowed his head. Jenna wondered if the men surrounding them saw the fury masked in his eyes. If they did, she supposed they wouldn't care. She wondered whether anybody but her saw the sick fear behind the anger. If they did, probably they would care even less about that.

"How did you recognize us?" Emel asked.

The captain smiled and tapped a stone pendent he wore on a

leather thong about his neck. "You might hide from the eye, man, but from the spell? Nolas-ai Keitah said this would recognize the girl, and so it did. Nola," the leader of the soldiers added to Jenna, and held the bridle of a horse for her to mount. He didn't exactly sound sarcastic. It was more like her title didn't interest him at all, like he said it out of habit and it didn't matter to him one way or the other. Jenna, who had not thought she liked to have people call her 'Nola' and bow to her, found it a lot more uncomfortable to be addressed that way by someone who obviously didn't have a clue who she was and didn't care a bit.

Her horse, she found, didn't have reins on its bridle. It had only a lead-rope, held by one of the men. Nobody bothered to tie her hands, although they did tie Emel's, and then bound them to his saddle. Obviously no one thought she would do anything except meekly ride along with their captors. Jenna stroked the neck of her horse as they started forward at a trot, and wondered just how good a chance would have to be before she could reasonably try to escape.

Maybe if she jumped off her horse she could get away and lose herself in Nemesen before they could catch her? She glanced around speculatively. Nobody was paying her any attention. Maybe she could in fact take them totally by surprise. Yes, and what then? She couldn't outrun a crossbow bolt. Would they just shoot her? That captain of theirs might. Jenna studied him. He rode a little to the side of the rest of his company. He looked depressingly professional. All the soldiers did. The country around Nemesen was open; she supposed they could ride her down with no trouble even if she did totally surprise them. Then they would probably tie her hands to her saddle like Emel's. That wouldn't be much of an improvement.

Everybody else on the road pressed to the side to give Keitah's men room—plenty of them jumped right off the road onto the sandy soil rather than crowd the soldiers. They stared curiously at Jenna and Emel—not like they were concerned. More just curious, like people slowing down to stare at an accident on the highway. Somebody else having a really bad day, glad it's not us, now back to our own business.

If she could get away by herself, would she go? Jenna thought of her father again, alone in Nerinesir and worrying about her, and knew she would. If she could. Which did not, at the moment, look likely, hands free or not. There were seven men. With those numbers, she wasn't sure it mattered much whether they were careless with her or not. Maybe at night. Unless they tied her hands at night. Tied her to a tree, maybe. She thought maybe they would. That captain didn't seem stupid.

The horses moved at a brisk trot. The staccato beat of hooves sounded on the road, sharp on slate and muffled on sand, and then a more constant sound on hard-packed dirt as they moved farther away from Nemesen. The captain meant to get back to Kinabana as fast as possible, obviously. How far had they come? Jenna looked over her shoulder. The road must have gone around a long slow curve, because already the town was no longer in sight. To the left the bay stretched out, endlessly blue, dotted with the sails of Nemesen's small boats. To the right there was scrub that turned gradually to thin woodlands, and beyond that, where the hills began, thicker forest. Not enough cover to hide in close to the road. Maybe the forest would come closer to the road later. Like, by nightfall.

Or maybe not. Maybe the forest had been cleared back from the road on purpose, to reduce the risk of banditry on this road. Jenna tried to remember whether Kuomat or anybody had ever said anything about working this particular road. She could not remember. Could she manage to slip away if she had nothing but the dark for cover? Was the moon going to be full tonight, or just a sliver? She couldn't remember that, either.

It had been early afternoon when Jenna and Emel had tried to enter Nemesen. The sun crept downward in the sky, slowly descending toward the road in front of them. Jenna tried to estimate how many hours it might be till dusk. She had never been good at estimating time from the sun: too many years with a perfectly good watch, she supposed.

Emel, riding in front of her with a soldier on either side, rode without looking around. His head was bowed. He looked, in fact, like he had given up. Jenna was sure that was just an act. Probably he was waiting for a chance to create a distraction for her. So his quiet attitude now probably meant he knew there wasn't a chance right now and he was hoping she would just wait and not try to rush ahead with some stupid plan that couldn't work.

But every beat of the horses' hooves carried them farther from Nerinesir. Farther from the king, and Tenai, and her father. They might have traveled slowly with the outlaws, but at least they had traveled in the right direction. At this rate, it wasn't going to take long to undo all the progress they had made. Could they escape from Kinabana twice? Keitah would probably chain them in the kennel with his hounds. Jenna set her teeth and tried not to think about the passing of time, or about how desperately she wanted to jerk her horse around and ride as fast as she could go in the opposite direction.

Shadows lengthened, stretching down the road behind them. Traffic thinned, and thinned again: hardly anybody besides them was still on the road now. All the farmers who sold their produce in Nemesen probably lived closer to the town than this, Jenna supposed, or had at least left Nemesen early enough they were already home. She longed, suddenly and intensely, for her own home: for a normal house and a normal life, and her father talking to her about the best grad schools and *no worries* about war and death and the possibility of Keitah cutting off her feet. For some time, Jenna was almost blinded by the force of memory, and by her longing for home.

Her horse, stumbling over a rut in the road and lurching, recalled her to the present. Jenna looked up, blinking, and then around, trying to get her bearings. The road had shifted farther from the bay: the water was no longer visible to their left. To their right, the woods had thickened. That was good. But, she saw, the soldiers were alert. They watched carefully in all directions. That wasn't so good. Emel was, unfortunately, right: these men were not careless.

But the light was bad now, and getting worse. Surely they were not going to travel right through the night?

Just as Jenna began to wonder this, the captain of the small troop reined around to come up beside a man near her. "We will camp in that glade where the woods are thin," he said to the other man. "We should come to it before full dark."

The other man nodded, and the word passed through the troop. The horses had been kept mostly at a trot all afternoon. They were tired. But the men pressed them now to move a little more quickly, eager, no doubt, for a fire and hot food and a chance to sit on something that wasn't moving.

That eagerness was probably why they missed the ambush.

There were seven of Keitah's men in this company. Three, including the captain, fell immediately, bolts in their throats or chests. Another took a bolt in the thigh and cried out, fumbling for his own crossbow. Before he could get it ready, another bolt struck him in the throat and he fell limply back across his horse and slid to the ground.

Horses were squealing and plunging everywhere. If there were more bolts flying, Jenna missed them in the poor light and the confusion. She saw Emel trying to make his horse lunge against the horse of the only soldier still near him without falling off himself; that man, probably thinking that a dead prisoner was better than a live escapee, or maybe just because Emel was the only clear target available to shoot at, was trying to shoot him. But he was having trouble at such close quarters. Jenna saw him realize this and drop his bow, going for his knife instead.

Another soldier had leaped from his horse, probably to make himself less of a target: he grabbed at Jenna, evidently meaning to pull her out of the saddle as well—to kill her or use her as a hostage, Jenna didn't know which he had in mind and didn't care. A bolt went over his shoulder, but he only flinched and cursed and kept coming. She swung her leg over her horse's back and slid to the ground on the side nearest the approaching soldier. She stepped, and stepped again, blocking the man's first grab: her whole world narrowed for that moment to the man trying to take hold of her.

The man cursed again, furious and frightened. He was a big man, as big as Emel, really big for a person her size. Jenna wouldn't have wanted to spar him in competition. But this wasn't competition, and he didn't know what he was doing anyway. He reached toward her again, impatiently, like she was some helpless little thing, and Jenna grabbed the hand and wrist he offered her, hyperextended his elbow, and turned her body to force him past her and down. The man didn't believe she really had him and tried to fight her hold; Jenna broke his elbow, but flinched from the elbow strike that would have finished it. She let go and backed away from him instead, jumped aside from a frightened horse that rushed past, and turned quickly in a circle, trying to spot Emel—yes, there, not good: his opponent was down, but his horse was terrified and trying to spin in circles. She ran that way, meaning to grab the horse before it could throw Emel and drag him.

But somebody else got there first, catching the horse's lead-rope and talking to it soothingly until it calmed and stood trembling. It took Jenna a startled, disbelieving second to recognize this person as Medai. After that she saw that it was Gerabak checking the soldiers to see they were all dead. Tantang and Inasad were searching them for coin, and for whatever else they might have carried. And then Imbutaiyon came by her, leading two nervous horses, and Katawarin, examining one of the soldier's bows with a critical eye.

Kuomat came out of the woods and leaned against a tree beside the road, folding his arms over his chest and tilting his head. Early moonlight turned the gray in his hair to silver and made his pale eyes as colorless water. Jenna could see no expression in his face at all. But she sort of got the impression the outlaw leader regarded all this activity with a sort of bleak amusement. At the weirdness of the fate or luck that had thrown Emel and her back at his feet, Jenna supposed. She didn't find it all that funny herself.

Though anything was better than continuing to Kinabana to be thrown at Keitah's feet, and having their own cut off, oh yes.

Medai sliced through the cords binding Emel to his saddle, and without a word Emel swung down from the horse. He rubbed his wrists, turning his head to look for Jenna. She walked over to join him. He put a hand on her shoulder, looking her over quickly. She shook her head, meaning she wasn't hurt, and tried to smile. They both turned toward Kuomat, who lifted a hand at them, *Come here.*

"How is it," Jenna muttered to Emel, "that we keep winding up disarmed and surrounded? I think we must be doing something wrong. Next time I want to be the one with the weapons and the superior attitude."

Emel's mouth crooked a little. He nodded toward Kuomat, and they both went that way, stopping a few feet away from the outlaw leader.

"I thought you too wise to attack soldiers," Emel said.

Kuomat did not smile, but Jenna again got the impression he was amused. He waved a casual hand at the carnage in the road. "Man, that is not outlaw work. Outlaw curs might wait near a campsite for travelers, but why would they be interested in shooting down soldiers? So much risk for so little gain. Clearly that bloody work must be the act of your allies or partisans. So the Terusai will believe. Will he not?"

"Yes," said Emel, in a tone that suggested he was just realizing this was true. It *was* true, Jenna understood. In fact, impossible though it would have been, she'd half-expected to see *Tenai* come out of the woods, rescuing them at last. It made sense that allies would strike hard to rescue them. And, yes, a lot less sense that outlaws would. She wondered what allies Keitah would imagine they had found here, once he knew about his men's deaths.

"And what allies, I wonder, would those be?" Kuomat asked Emel, echoing that thought. "Who are you, man? Or should I ask, whose?"

Emel did not answer.

"An enemy of the Terusai's, clearly," said Imbutaiyon, stating the obvious with evident enjoyment. "I wouldn't have thought he'd have many living." He lifted his eyebrows at Emel, who looked back without expression.

Kuomat said to Jenna, "I thought Saimadan had turned his back to you. I thought he had been foolish enough to allow you to strike him down with a club. I did not find it easy to believe Panaih when she described to me how you killed him. But she was telling the truth. You might have killed that man out there, just now, if you had wished. Yes? Who are you?"

Any of them, Jenna realized, might have seen her take down Keitah's soldier. Probably Kuomat had been watching her particularly. Maybe he had even given orders to the rest of them to let a soldier threaten her, so he could see what she would do. He was the sort of man who might have thought of that. She said nothing.

"You would be useful to my pack," Kuomat said to Emel. "And you—" he eyed Jenna with considerable respect—"even more valuable, if you could teach my people some of your skill. But you have business of your own, I imagine. In the south? The east? Who are you?"

"No one whom you would do well to hinder," Emel answered.

There was a long silence. The breeze through the trees made a peaceful sound. It was too dark now to see the dead men in the road, though the hard metallic smell of their blood was way too strong even from the edge of the woods. One of the horses Imbutaiyon was holding made an uneasy sound and shifted its weight.

"What would Keitah Terusai-e give the man who brought you to him?" Kuomat wondered aloud.

"A knife across the throat and a quiet burial," said Emel shortly. "You would do well to avoid the paths of the great. Outlaw cur."

Jenna blinked and tried not to stare at Emel.

But, though Kuomat's mouth twisted, he did not seem angry. Jenna thought his expression was more one of wry agreement. He straightened abruptly and gave a jerk of his head, and his people began to make their quiet way into the woods. They brought the horses with them, which wasn't easy in the dark. They brought Emel and Jenna with them as well. No one, this time, seemed likely to let either of them near a bow or a sword.

There was a campsite, tucked in and among a wild tangle of thorny brush. Angana and Panaih were there, by a small fire that was all Kuomat seemed willing to risk at this site. The women seemed taken very much by surprise by the catch the rest of their pack had taken on the road. Bau, also waiting in the camp, his arm in a sling and his mood foul, seemed barely to notice.

The rest moved slowly to settle around the fire, taking cups of tea from Panaih. Angana began to dip bowls into the pot and pass those around as well. No one spoke. No one brought Emel or Jenna tea or soup. Eyes turned to Kuomat, and away. To Emel, and away again. Katawarin was leaning comfortably against a fallen tree. Jenna caught her eye for a second, but the tall woman lifted her chin and looked deliberately away.

Kuomat accepted a bowl of soup from Angana and sipped it slowly. Then he put the bowl down on the ground beside him. As he had by the road, he made a little beckoning gesture for his prisoners to approach. Emel stood at once and offered Jenna a hand up. They walked forward and knelt down on the ground in front of the outlaw leader. The ground was rocky and cold, but at least it was dry.

"Who are you?" Kuomat asked them both. His voice was low, calm, without obvious threat. He did not, of course, need to make his threats obvious.

Emel met the outlaw's pale eyes and said nothing at all.

Jenna thought that wasn't going to work out well as a long-term strategy. She cleared her throat. "Nolas-Kuomon," she said. She wished she'd had a chance to talk about this with Emel. But it was clear the outlaws did not intend to give them any opportunity to speak privately.

They all stared at her; all except Emel, who bowed his head and slowly let out his breath.

"We're hers," Jenna said, into the silence, which scrolled out into the endless night around them. "Keitah Terusai-e is her enemy. And the king's enemy, too. She doesn't know that, yet. Neither of them knows that. But he is. We need to get back to her, to tell her so."

"It is true," added Emel. "I swear to that, before God and the watchful Martyr."

Kuomat gazed at Jenna without expression. "The paths of the great, indeed." He tilted his head a little, considering. Imbutaiyon took a breath as though he meant to speak, but then didn't. He put an arm around Katawarin's shoulders. She shifted her weight to lean against him.

Gerabak said, "We should either kill them or let them go. We want no part of this, Kuomat." Inasad, sitting next to him, nodded emphatically.

"It can't be true," protested Medai. "Can it?"

Kuomat turned his gaze, silver as water, wordlessly to Medai, and the younger man flushed and looked down. The outlaw leader turned back to Jenna, thoughtfully.

Jenna wondered if it was true that silver eyes could see the truth in men's hearts. She wouldn't have been surprised to find Kuomat could. She met his eyes, wondering what he saw in her heart. She could see nothing of his; the hearts of men were hidden from her ordinary gaze, unfortunately.

"Give us two of the horses," Emel said. "We will go quickly, at dawn. As soon as there is enough light to see."

Kuomat considered this. He said slowly, "Whatever game is being played across Talasayan, you are surely more valuable to it than I had suspected."

"Not to you," Emel said at once.

"Then to whom? And whom should I prefer win this game?"

"Have you reason to cherish the Terusai? In despite of Mitereh Sekuse-go-e? No? Then leave the great to scatter the ruins of their wealth on the field of battle for the scavengers. You need do nothing to bring that moment, only wait for it to arrive."

A wintry, humorless smile glinted in Kuomat's pale eyes. "Is that what you advise? That I take no action? Would you have advised such inaction when the Terusai's men had you in their hard grip?"

This interrogation was not exactly a contest, Jenna thought. Or, kind of, sure. But what this really was, was Kuomat trying, blindly, to find a way for himself and his people through an unexpected and dangerous maze. She even sympathized, sort of. She said firmly, "You should support Tenai. Nolas-Kuomon. That's what you should do. Because she's the king's ally, so by supporting Tenai, you'd also be supporting Mitereh. Together they can bring peace to Talasayan, and Keitah Terusai-e can't and won't. He sure doesn't want to. He'll do anything and sacrifice anyone to get what he wants, and he's—he is terrible, he would be a terrible king, even if people accepted his rule, and I don't know why they should, but I bet he has a plan. It would be wrong to let him have things his way. So you should give us horses and let us go."

Kuomat's silver eyes met hers once more. His expression was unreadable. This time his stare wasn't a contest, Jenna thought, but maybe a kind of test. She held Kuomat's eyes with hers. She could feel herself beginning to shiver, although she was not cold. Nor did she exactly feel frightened. Not exactly.

"The Terusai is an enemy both to Nolas-Kuomon and to the young king," the outlaw leader said to her at last, in an absolutely level voice. "Both. They have made common cause, Nolas-Kuomon and Mitereh Sekuse-go-e. You assert that this is the truth."

"Yes!" said Jenna, wondering if an outlaw would care about that, and why. But she thought somehow that Kuomat did care.

"Yet they do not know that Terusai is their common enemy. Thus you go to bear word to Nolas-Kuomon, that she may act with the king her ally to bring him down." Kuomat's tone was so dry that Jenna winced. Maybe it had after all been a mistake to be so up-front and honest. Maybe if she'd just waited for a minute, Emel would have come up with something better than the truth, something more plausible—

"I swear before God and the Martyr that is the exact truth," said Emel, quietly, but with force.

"Do you, man? And shall I believe you have honor to set behind your oath?"

Emel flushed. He opened his mouth, but shut it again without speaking.

"Hey! He does. You do," Jenna said sharply, when she realized Emel might deny it. "Tenai gave you your honor back. You said so yourself. Anyway, I've never broken *my* oath to, to anybody! And," she swung back to face Kuomat, "it *is* true, every word!"

Kuomat's mouth twisted. He said, "You call Nolas-Kuomon by her name."

Jenna blinked. She'd forgotten that mattered so much, or she would have done it on purpose. She wasn't sure what to say now.

"She does," Emel said quietly. "I would never presume, but the young nola is a friend of Nolas-Kuomon. I swear this is true, but you need not take my word. As you see, she does call Nolas-Kuomon by her name. Who else do you think taught the young nola how to fight?"

Kuomat considered Emel. Then he said to Jenna, "Tell me again that Nolas-Kuomon is an ally of the king."

Jenna looked at him uncertainly. They'd already said so. She didn't understand why Kuomat wanted to hear it again. But finally she said, "It's absolutely true. Tenai is on Mitereh's side. She really is. He asked her to take oath to him, and she did. Keitah Terusai-e wanted to use Tenai against the king, but she knows someone wants that and she isn't going to permit it. But she doesn't know it's him. She has to know. She and Mitereh both have to know. You have to let us go, or who else is going to tell them?"

For another moment, Kuomat merely regarded her, expressionless. Then he got to his feet. He seemed to Jenna to have in that moment as much authority, even in his worn clothing and surrounded by his handful of ragged outlaws, as any lord standing in a great hall crowded with courtiers. Glancing around at everyone, he said, "I will take the first watch. Bau, you and Gerabak will have the second. Imbutaiyon and Katawarin will take the third." He looked down again at Jenna and Emel, still kneeling in the dirt. "At dawn," he told them, "you may take two of the horses and go. It would be foolish of you to struggle through the woods in the dark. You will rest here tonight. Must I set a guard on you?"

"No," said Emel, bowing his head a little.

The outlaw leader glanced at Panaih. "They may eat. Bring them something." He walked away.

15

They took the plainest of Keitah's horses in the morning, and arms to replace those Keitah's men had taken, and some of the money the soldiers had carried, which was really generous of Kuomat. Then they were back on the road to Nemesen maybe half an hour after dawn.

It had occurred to Jenna that Kuomat might have lied to them. To keep them calm, maybe, while he sent someone to Kinabana. That didn't make sense, and she knew that, but she had worried about it anyway. Sleep had come hard with that thought creeping around the edges of her mind, and she had not been able to dismiss it entirely until Kuomat, in the first gray light of the dawn, brought them the horses and weapons and a pouch of coins along with their breakfast bread.

Jenna hadn't been able to tell whether Emel had entertained similar thoughts. He'd held her horse without a word to her, and then got up on his. Then he'd just sat there for a moment, looking down at Kuomat.

The outlaw leader's eyes, truly silver in the pale dawn light, had seemed perfectly expressionless to Jenna. Emel might have seen something there. She did not know what. Neither man spoke. Emel only turned his horse and rode down the hill, leaving Jenna to follow him.

It felt, well, very strange, to turn their backs on the outlaws and ride away. Like an echo of the first time they had left Kuomat and his people standing behind them, not knowing if they might be shot in the back. Only, Jenna thought, it was not the same. She didn't trust Kuomat, only apparently she did really, because it *did* feel different this time. Although she listened to hear the swish of bolts behind them, she was not at all surprised when she didn't.

"Why do you suppose he let us go? Does he really care about the king?" Jenna asked, as they picked their way back toward the road. "I thought maybe he seemed to, but why should he? Or does he just hate Keitah for some reason?"

Emel took long enough to answer that Jenna thought maybe he wasn't going to, but eventually he said, "Few curs of the road were ever of good family. But once Kuomat had another name, I think; a name he left behind when his honor was broken. But though he cast it away, it informs him yet. I think ... I think last night he found he still cares for Talasayan. Perhaps he remembers old loyalties. Perhaps to Mitereh. Perhaps to Nolas-Kuomon."

"Oh." Jenna thought about this.

"And then," Emel added, "if Terusai-e is broken, and his house brought down, and even Kinabana, perhaps, ruined ... well, then, there will indeed be rich scavenging. I should expect Kuomat to take his pack toward Kinabana now, to watch there in the case such battle might be joined. He may yet feel the urgings of old loyalties, but he would never have survived so long on the road were he other than practical."

"Oh," Jenna said again. "Well ... as long as he let us go, I guess it doesn't matter." But it did, really. What people did mattered most, maybe, but the reasons they did things mattered, too. "I think ..." she began, but then the road came into sight, and she stopped.

The road was ugly even in the pale opalescent light of the early morning. Flies rose, buzzing, as Jenna and Emel rode past the bodies. The horses rolled their eyes and shied, ears back nervously, and Jenna put hers into a fast trot, passing Emel to take the lead. She found tears on her face and did not understand why. Those men had been enemies. She hadn't even known them. She was glad Kuomat's people had shot them; if they hadn't, she and Emel would still be on their way back to Kinabana, which didn't bear thinking about. She didn't *care* that the bodies lay tumbled on the road. She told herself that as fiercely as she could. But seeing them there hurt her anyway. She pushed her horse to a canter and let the wind dry her face, so that when Emel caught up to her he wouldn't know she had been crying. Maybe he was upset too, because even after he came up even with her, he didn't seem to want to talk any more than Jenna did. They rode in silence; canter and walk and trot and brief, swift canter.

Jenna had thought they had ridden away from Nemesen for hours and hours. But it must not really have been such a long time, because it was only mid-morning when they came back into sight of the bay, and still well before noon when the town itself appeared again in front of them.

This time, not to be idiots twice, they turned off the road before it turned to slate under their horses' hooves and rode well around Nemesen rather than entering the town through the gate. Houses and boats sprawled out along the shore, where there were no big streets. Women mending nets looked up in mild curiosity as they passed; an old man standing by a boat turned upside-down on the sand glanced around at the sound of the hooves and then went indifferently back to painstakingly spreading black pitch over the hull of his boat.

"We will leave the horses here, where they can be quietly stolen," Emel said, drawing rein in the shade of a ramshackle shack. No one was in evidence. In fact, Jenna thought the shack looked like it had been abandoned years ago and had been quietly going to pieces ever since.

"You think we have to do that, even though we're not coming in on the road?"

"I think we will be safer so." Emel glanced around carefully. "Even if these were not Keitah's horses, I think we will be safer to come into town on foot. We can come in by small ways, anonymous ways. Keitah cannot have all the little warrens of the town watched. We can purchase, not horses, but seats in a conveyance, as we initially planned. I think that will be safe, if we are careful in our choice. Many conveyances stop at the important inns. No one can watch them all.

Jenna hoped he was right. She doubted they could depend on Kuomat's people to rescue them a second time. Even if Kuomat actually did go to the trouble, wow, would that be embarrassing.

Buildings in Nemesen weren't clearly divided into houses and shops. As they came at last—on foot—into the town proper, Jenna got the idea that a lot of structures might be both. Buildings were small and kind of crammed together, but not in an ugly way. They might be made mostly of gray slate, but brightly painted signs hung in front of a lot of them. Advertisements, Jenna assumed, but the pictures were so stylized she couldn't make out what anybody was selling. Some of the shops were crowded; others nearly empty.

The streets were busy, men and women walking quickly on foot or riding past at a brisk pace. That was surely good: they could get lost in crowds like this, and yet Jenna found the bustle uncomfortable. Somehow the people seemed to Jenna not only busy, but tense.

Small tight knots of men sat at tables in front of what was obviously a bar of some kind, but they didn't seem cheerful. They sat in their little groups with their heads close together, muttering. A pair of women passed Jenna and Emel going the other direction, with worried looks on their faces. A man on horseback passed them without a glance at them or at anything else: he was completely absorbed in his own thoughts. From his tight expression, those thoughts must be grim. When a horde of little boys poured down a narrow ally, and ran, yelling, across the street in front of them, Jenna twitched in startled alarm. She glanced at Emel, who tipped his head slightly back in baffled unease. He said, "This town seems to have been well overset, but I do not know why. I do not think this can be Keitah's doing. He has no reason to stir this town to such anxiety."

Jenna shook her head. Well, we don't have to stay here long. How much farther do you think we have to go?"

Emel shrugged. "I have not been to this town. There should be inns along this road, closer to the edge of the town." He nodded the way they'd been going.

Eventually—really, not much later—they did find an inn, but though several public conveyances were indeed in the inn's yard, all the seats were taken. One of those was a big, decent-looking carriage drawn by four horses, which was about what Jenna had assumed when she'd heard the term *public conveyance*. Three others looked a lot more like farmer's wagons, with benches hastily nailed into place and horses that looked like they might be more used to pulling plows.

Jenna looked at Emel.

"I confess I am surprised," Emel told her, and moved a few steps aside to speak to a woman who obviously worked for the inn, judging by mugs she was handing out to the people waiting to board the conveyances. Emel dropped a couple of coins on the woman's tray and murmured to her.

"Had you not heard?" the woman asked, her voice louder and clearly audible. "Nolas-Kuomon broke with the king not two days past and rode for Imbaneh-se. We have only just gotten word this very morning. An army rose up to meet her and swear to her service before she even set foot across the border—so it is said. She is at the confluence, so we have heard, gathering men about her banner, and men say Kuanonai Geraimani-sa has carved a new throne out of a great oak and set his banner beside hers. Men are fleeing all this country, going north to Kinabana or Patananir, or south to Sotatan or even Kari-e. If my mother weren't ailing, I'd go as well."

Jenna felt stricken. Her throat had closed; she couldn't have spoken, even if she'd thought of something to say.

Emel had taken on his most closed, inexpressive look. "Do men say how they came to quarrel?"

"A thousand men, a thousand tales," said the woman, shrugging, then added with more relish than sympathy, "If you wish a conveyance, I fear you must be disappointed, for there are no seats to be had for any price, and no horses either."

Someone behind them cleared his throat. "I and my wife might have room in our wagon—for the right price."

Jenna turned quickly, Emel not as smoothly but even faster, his hand on the hilt of his sword. The narrow-faced man who stood there looked ... alarmingly familiar.

"I would ask a very reasonable fee," continued the man, in an even drier tone. His expression was amused and wary and sharply interested, all at once. "Perhaps you might have enough coins over to buy a shirt that better suits you. You need not be mistrustful. I am a man of my word, I assure you. We might even exchange oaths."

Emel let his breath out slowly. Jenna realized she was holding hers and resumed breathing with a whoosh. She would have liked something to lean on, but the only thing handy was Emel, and she doubted he wanted her tying up his sword arm.

"When we last met, my wife and I meant to go to Nerinesir," said the man. He was holding his hands well out from his sides, clearly—even ostentatiously—unarmed. "You sent us back to Nemesen, and now we see this was as well. We have decided Gai-e might be better. We could use a competent, experienced man in our company. The roads will become more perilous every moment. By tomorrow, I foresee there will be a thousand men on the road, and many will make dangerous company for honest folk"

"One might reasonably wish to press a grievance," suggested Emel. He had removed his hand from the hilt of his sword, but he sure didn't look very trusting.

The other man turned his hands palm outward. "I should say ... not reasonably. I might even suggest the opposite." He hesitated, then went on more slowly, "I should be more confident with a proven man to ward peril away from my wife. A man of honor, though perhaps recently hard-pressed by some mischance, might prove a useful companion. I would not ask what mischance might have led to our previous encounter. I am not trying to mislead you, man. I swear that is true. But I think you owe me something. In trade for frightening my wife, you might now prevent any worse brigands from coming near her."

Emel opened a hand, conceding the argument, though Jenna

supposed it wasn't an argument, exactly. He drew Jenna aside, leaving the man to wait. "I think this offer is in earnest," he said. "It is a good offer: Keitah's men, if there are more here, will have no reason to look for us in company with these ordinary folk. But would you choose Gai-e? From there we could go up the river to the confluence and Nolas-Kuomon. But you might rather take the road to Nerinesir and the king."

"Where do you think my father will be?"

"Nola, I cannot begin to guess."

How could he? How could she? Jenna rubbed her face with the tips of her fingers, trying to think. Wouldn't her father have gone with Tenai? If he could have? ... He couldn't possibly have killed the king, because they would surely have known all about that here if he had. But if he'd tried—surely he *wouldn't* have tried, but if he had—that might have made Tenai break with Mitereh, maybe? Could he have? Or what else was Tenai *doing?* Or—she didn't know, she couldn't guess, she felt her brain had turned to mud. "What do you want to do?"

"I confess I feel my duty to Nolas-Kuomon. Whatever has happened to drive her apart from the king, I am still her man. But she set me to guard you. If you desired to return to Nerinesir, I would feel myself drawn in both directions. But I would go to Nerinesir if you chose that."

"But you'd rather go meet Tenai?"

"I do confess so."

He was so formal suddenly. Jenna rubbed her face again, feeling desperately tired. "I guess ... I guess we should go to Gai-e. I guess that's what we should do. I think my father probably went with Tenai. I think he would have."

"And this man? We might go alone. We might slip out of Nemesen, steal horses later if none here are for sale."

"What do you think? You like him, don't you? I like them both."

"That is not altogether to the point," Emel said in a severe tone. "However, I think we should be more secure in company.

This person is correct: with what has happened, the roads will swiftly become crowded and perilous. Four people, all armed with bows ... that is not an enticing target, and four may watch the road more closely than you and I might if we traveled alone. And these folk ... they have coin. That is an advantage in many circumstances."

Jenna managed a smile. "I guess it's an advantage in almost any circumstance. All right. Tell him he's on."

Emel glanced at the man, who had been waiting quietly near the door, where they'd left him. Jenna didn't see Emel make any sign, but the man came over at once to join them. His expression was calm, but his eyes met theirs with a certain anxiety.

Emel said, "I swear before God and the Martyr, I will do good and not harm to you and your wife for so long as our roads may run together. But certainly so far as Gai-e."

The careful stillness of the man's expression eased. He said at once, "And I, the same, for you and your wife."

Emel gave him a measured nod. "I consider you are wise to be concerned about the safety of the road. If I may suggest, we should not wait for morning. I suggest we go at once."

The man hesitated. Then he said decisively, "As you say. I will inform my wife."

It took only two days to reach Gai-e from Nemesen. Well, two days and a night. They pushed hard because Emel said the road behind them would be a lot more crowded and dangerous than the road in front of them. So everybody walked except whoever was driving the wagon, which was Patanah at first and sometimes Jenna after she learned how. It seemed like a lot of reins at first, but really it wasn't too different from riding. Kahisan walked to one side of the horses or the other, his crossbow slung at his side where he could get to it in a hurry, and Emel usually walked on the other side of the horses or sometimes a little way ahead. Everyone had changed into rough traveling gear, but nobody had tried to make Emel or Jenna give back the clothing they'd stolen. Kahisan treated those clothes like they'd been a gift, except he took his shirt back after Emel got a different one that fit better. Keeping the clothes embarrassed Jenna, only it sure was nice to have decent clothing, even if it was packed away at the moment.

Kahisan and Patanah had, it turned out, been planning to move lock, stock, and barrel to Nerinesir and had had all their worldly goods loaded in their wagon. They'd sold a lot of it real quick to people in the inn and even given some things away, so the wagon was light and the horses could sometimes trot. Keeping up with trotting horses was hard for the people on foot, so they couldn't keep up that pace all the time. But it was such a pleasure to be able to keep to the road that the fast pace was almost a pleasure. Although not as much after the first hour or so.

Patanah was strained and nervous at first and flinched whenever Emel looked at her, even though he was carefully polite. It was pretty clear she would have been happier if she and her husband had stayed on their own. That lasted until a dozen riders from Nemesen came up with their wagon, late the first afternoon. They weren't polite at all, and it was Emel who made them go away. It was his attitude that did the job. So confident. He looked just bored by the whole idea of fighting. Like a dozen men were nothing to him, like he killed that many people every day and twice on Sundays and made a hobby of biting the heads off hamsters besides. After that Patanah was still scared of Emel, but she was glad he was there, too.

"You don't have to be afraid of him, you know," Jenna told her.

Patanah gave her a doubtful look.

"He really isn't at all mean," Jenna said earnestly. "He's just kind of shy."

"Shy!" said Patanah, and laughed a little.

"He is," said Jenna. "So he acts tough because he knows how to—to project that tough-guy attitude, you know, and it makes him not have to explain himself, you know?"

Patanah gave her a sidelong look. "You were not in truth ... brigands of the road, you and he?"

Jenna hesitated. "Only *very* temporarily," she explained at last.

"You ... would not have shot Kahisan?"

"*I* wouldn't," Jenna said, and hoped it was true. "Em—Bukitraya might, if he thought he had to, but he wouldn't *want* to."

"He would protect you," Patanah said, and seemed more comfortable after that. "You are his wife."

"Um—" Jenna didn't quite know how to correct this impression, or if she should.

"Clearly he treasures you," said Patanah very seriously. "You are very pretty—you have a very unusual face—many men must have desired you. And yet you esteem this one?"

"Um ... "

"Then if you say he is kind and ... and good to you, I will believe you," said Patanah, and after that was less afraid of Emel. So that was one problem solved, and a much pleasanter trip, so Jenna stopped wondering whether she should try to explain that they weren't married and just let it go.

Gai-e was a bigger town than Nemesen, and a prettier one. Like Nemesen, it had only a low wall. The stones were gray slate. A lot of Gai-e's buildings were made of the same gray slate, but there were also a lot of pretty little wooden houses with steeply-angled roofs, whitewashed and trimmed with bright paint. The boats drawn up on the shore had sails of plain canvas, but the boats themselves were painted pink or yellow or lavender: they looked, in the brilliant light of late afternoon, like somebody had cast a bushel of flowers out over the beach and into the ocean.

But there was the same sense of tension and unease in the streets, and the same edge of hostility from the people.

"They do not want a thousand strangers here," Emel said briefly, when Jenna commented on this. "But they will have them, whether they will or no. Folk who would evade difficulty would do well to go further south, to Sotatan, perhaps." He glanced at

Kahisan, who nodded sober agreement.

They had halted at an inn in the middle of Gai-e to buy grain for the horses and a meal for themselves. It was driving Jenna nuts to know how close they were now to Tenai and her father. She wished they could just press ahead at once. But she also knew they would part company with their companions here, and she was even sorrier about that because traveling with people you liked was really different from traveling with a bunch of outlaws.

Kahisan pulled a loaf of dark bread apart, slowly. He asked, just a little tentatively, "And do you go to Sotatan?"

Emel hesitated, and shook his head. "Along the Khadur." To where Tenai gathered her army, he meant, where the great upper Khadur River divided into the lower Khadur and the smaller Tese.

"Oh, *no!*" exclaimed Patanah, clearly dismayed. "Would you fight for Imbaneh-se against the king?" It seemed weird to Jenna that everybody was willing to duck for cover in Imbaneh-se cities while still talking about Imbaneh-se as an enemy, but everybody else seemed to take this for granted.

"Not willingly," Emel answered, rather dour at the thought. He glanced at Jenna.

"Maybe it won't come to that," Jenna said doubtfully. They had heard some of the news along the way, and none of it sounded good. Some of it sounded downright terrifying. But she had a hard time believing those parts. Whatever had happened between Tenai and Mitereh—and Jenna couldn't believe that her father could possibly had done something to set things off—but *whatever* had happened, Tenai surely could not have put the heads of captured loyalists up on pikes outside her camp? She surely could not have promised Imbaneh-se soldiers a chance to loot Nerinesir and fling everyone in Mitereh's court off the walls of his palace? All the stories like that must be false. Jenna was sure they were false. She looked at Emel and shrugged.

"We have no choice," he said to their companions. "We must go by the river road. However, if you will forgive my presumption to offer advice—"

"By all means," Kahisan promised earnestly.

"If you go through Imbaneh-se, I think you will lose your horses at the least. Sell them here, then—sell everything you can, and hire passage on a boat to take you south. I think Sotatan would be safer if there is trouble, but if war truly comes, I would leave Imbaneh-se altogether and go into Keneseh, and look for a place in Pitatan."

The other man nodded, very soberly. "I cannot furnish you with saddles, but I will ask you to take the horses."

Emel, taken thoroughly aback, opened his mouth but then closed it again without speaking. His expression made him look suddenly younger and ... Jenna tried to frame for herself just what his surprise did for him ... not so hard-used, she decided.

"And money for a saddler." Kahisan clearly enjoying the effect, produced a small pouch and pressed it on Emel—then gave it to Jenna when the bigger man hesitated. "Truly, my friend, we owe you at least so much. We would have encountered far worse difficulty had we taken the road alone; I have no doubt of that." He glanced at the sun coming in through the windows of the inn, and went on, "You will wish to go without delay, I think. I will wish you fair fortune, and for Lord Death to turn his gaze from you. And ... ah ... if you tell me your name, man, I will not die of curiosity. We will swear before God to repeat it to no one," he added hastily.

"We do swear," Patanah promised, her glance including Jenna in that vow as well as Emel. "Before God and the Martyr."

Emel started to speak, stopped, and said at last, "We would be glad to take your word. Forgive us, then, that duty forbids." His glance invited Jenna to agree, and she nodded seriously.

Kahisan's eyes widened slightly, and he offered a small bow. Jenna wondered what he had inferred from this refusal. But he said, "Be certain we will say nothing of you that any man might remark."

Emel nodded, turned it into a bow for Patanah, and rose. He held out a hand to Jenna, who took it and let him pull her up.

"Fair fortune," she said breathlessly to them both. "Thank you—" and hurried after Emel, who was striding away without looking back. They would, she thought, probably not ever meet again, or even know how anything came out for each other. She knew Emel was right, but that seemed ... so unfair.

It was nearly dusk before they had saddles and riding bridles, and whatever other equipment Emel thought they had to have—Jenna stayed with the horses and let him handle the details. The horses were big, bigger than Jenna was used to for riding, but good-tempered enough not to object with more than a pinned ear and a roll of the eye to being asked to go out on the road again so late.

There was a startling amount of traffic on the road that ran along the Khadur: barges, pulled slowly upstream by horses even larger than the ones they rode or riding the current back down; families coming west toward Gai-e; soldiers going the other way, toward the confluence. Twice a company of soldiers tried to steal their horses. Jenna listened anxiously as Emel argued them out of it, and still wasn't sure how he did it.

"They believe I am a soldier, too," he told her when she asked. "They think I am following my company. Fortunately the moment is sufficiently confused they have no clear idea which commanders are already in place and which are yet to arrive."

Jenna could believe that, but, "What do they think I am?" she asked doubtfully.

Emel gave her a slight shrug.

"Oh—your woman. Right." Her voice scaled upward with incredulity. "Do soldiers—soldiers don't take their women to battle?"

"Some do."

It seemed weird. But come to think of it, she *had* seen a handful of women with the last company of soldiers they'd met. Really weird. Did they like the traveling? Did anybody ask them? Jenna thought she would like nothing better than to settle down in one spot—one luxurious spot, with hot baths and soft cushions—for the next several years. Reminded of a more urgent question, she asked, "How far is it to the confluence, then?"

"Not far. Perhaps ... forty miles."

"Forty miles! We aren't going all the way tonight!" Though she was also ready to be persuaded that they should try.

Emel also obviously would have liked to press onward, but he said reluctantly, "The horses have been too hard-used of late to go so far. No. We will stop later and rest."

It seemed a lot later to Jenna, when Emel finally turned off the road. She groaned as she worked her way stiffly out of the saddle. The horse bent its head around and blew in her face, as tired as she was. She patted its nose, hobbled over to a convenient low tree, slipped its bit, and tethered it. It was like their first night out of Kinabana. Sort of. Well, not really, since nobody could be hunting them here. And they had blankets, and a change of clothes each, and food ... all the comforts, relatively speaking. And it was a pretty night. All soft breezes and stars stretching across the sky, and for once nobody else anywhere nearby ... Jenna tried not to look at Emel When her gaze did slide toward him, she found his eyes meeting hers, and they both instantly looked away. They needed a fire to give them something to stare into. Only Emel hadn't wanted to give any other traveler on this road that kind of sign that they were here, so there wasn't a fire.

She opened her mouth, and closed it again, finding herself with no idea what she might say. In the morning they would get back on their horses and ride to the confluence and find Tenai, and whatever else happened this ... interminable, uncomfortable, exhausting, dangerous, tedious, occasionally terrifying journey would be over. She and Emel would be pulled into the rush of events, whatever those events might include, and this ... opportunity, whatever it had included, would be gone. Lost. No wonder they said that opportunity only knocked once. She could feel it receding right this moment.

Turning her head, Jenna again found Emel looking at her. This time, even though she felt the blood rush back into her face, she didn't look away.

"Nola ..." Emel said. "Your father would kill me. He would be right to do so. I am nothing. You ..."

"You're not nothing," Jenna said, not hotly because he'd just think she was a girl with a crush, and it wasn't like that at *all*. But she put intensity into her voice. "You're strong, and brave, and quick-thinking, and kind, and the most, most *steadfast* person I've ever met. Without you, I ... it's not that I'm grateful. I mean, I *am* grateful, you've been ... but that's not what I care about, not now. And I don't care about what you used to be, or do, or—or anything. What I care about is the person you are *now*. You are what you do, not what you used to do in—in another life. What's in your past doesn't matter to me."

There was a long pause. He said quietly, "I beg you will believe that I cherish your regard above anyone's. But ... my past matters to me. Even if your father approved, even if Chaisa-e approved, I am not fit for you. *I am not fit.*"

Jenna drew breath. But the sheer endurance in the set of his shoulders stopped her. She could have argued. But she knew she wasn't going to change his mind, and worse, she would only make herself into something he had to endure. And she couldn't face that. So in the end she said nothing.

"We will ride out at dawn," he said, after it became clear she wasn't going to try again to change his mind. "I will watch."

Because he wasn't going to be able to sleep, she translated that mentally, and wondered when she had acquired the ability to translate what he said into what he would not say. So she didn't argue. She just pulled her blanket straight and lay down, and stared into the infinite depths of the sky.

16

City and court seemed, as soon as Tenai departed Nerinesir, to become simultaneously calmer and more anxious. Tension seemed to rise like steam from the very stones of the city, yet Tenai's departure, no matter how hasty and threatening, also meant that Nerinesir was no longer being continually stirred up by her presence. It was as though everyone had been waiting for Tenai to declare herself an enemy and now that she finally had, well, at least the waiting had ended. By this note of relief underlying the general apprehension, Daniel finally understood just how afraid everyone must have been, right from the beginning, about Tenai's return to Talasayan, whether she seemed Mitereh's ally and vassal or not.

Of course, for Daniel, there was no liberation in Tenai's defection or relief in her absence. His own position was worse than before she had left—and he had felt as though he was going down for the third time even then. How had he let the relationship between Tenai and Mitereh worsen to the point of actual desertion? Even if he couldn't have stopped the final explosion ... no. He should have been able to stop it. If he had been paying attention. If he had only found a way to show Tenai what was going on, she would never have flown into such a rage at the king: instead, she would have directed her formidable rage toward the *right* target, and no doubt found a way to rescue Jenna, and everything would be *over*. Daniel, sitting in the sun on one of the wide windowsills of the map room, leaned his cheek against the warm stone and let his eyes rest on the mosaic that eddied across the wall. It was a soothing thing, abstract gray and white tiles that led the eye in easy swirls around the room.

Mitereh was saying something, but not to Daniel, who—as

often happened these days—found it all but impossible to keep his mind focused on the discussion.

Had Keitah maneuvered Mitereh into that stupid decision to interfere between Tenai and Chaisa? Probably he had, Daniel decided. From things people said, Daniel had gathered that Keitah had not actually been present when the king had asked Tenai to let go of her grant. But that meant almost nothing. Even if he hadn't been in the room, Keitah could have been working behind the scenes to get Mitereh to make that request. More than one string on his bow, wasn't that the saying? One plan involving Daniel and assassination, and another involving Tenai and a final break away from the king and toward war. And other plans beyond those, each set up to reinforce the chance that Keitah Terusai-e would come out where he intended, on top and in control.

As best Daniel could guess, he had one day remaining before Keitah would order Jenna whipped. Certainly when he had come into the map room a moment ago and found Keitah there before him, Daniel had found the other man's eyes meeting his with a ruthless impatience that promised terrible things. That was when he'd lost all the threads of the current discussion. He tried to pay attention.

"The Geraimani will have an army ready for her hand," Mitereh was saying. "Probably she has already taken it up."

The king was standing beside the map room's enormous table, a long elaborate map rolled out before him. Pyramidal stones held down two corners, sheathed knives the other two corners. Daniel hadn't looked at the map. He assumed it showed the border between Imbaneh-se and Talasayan, but this didn't matter to him. He was a good deal more interested in those knives.

Mitereh, Keitah Terusai-e, Sandakan Gutai-e and three of Mitereh's young men had been moving counters about on the map for the past hour. Now Sandakan had gone, no doubt to put some sort of plan into action. Daniel hadn't been following the talk well enough to know what that plan might include.

"We should have set the Geraimani down hard ten years

past," Keitah declared. "Yes, Mitereh, I know I advised you otherwise at the time. I was wrong. Now we are in a difficult position." He tapped the map, scowling the forthright scowl of the honest man. The expression looked perfectly sincere.

"I confess I do not perceive so. Ten years past, your advice was wise," Mitereh disagreed. The king also tapped the map, then ran his thumb along a ragged blue line. "We could not have punished the Geraimani without clear and just cause, lest all Imbaneh-se rebel against our hand. Even now, our position would be well enough, save only the presence of Nolas-Kuomon."

"A chance we were wrong not to anticipate."

"Were men as wise as God, we would never err," Inkaimon murmured, with a deferential nod toward Keitah. "Being men, we must in the end contend with events as they occur. And now we have all that we have: the arrogant Geraimani daring to carve the oak throne anew, Imbaneh-se rising," he tapped the map, "and Nolas-Kuomon our enemy. Thus we act as wisely as we are able. I believe we do as well as men may. Have you advice that would redirect our attention, Nolas-ai Keitah?"

However deferential his manner, there was no question but that the new young captain of the king's guards was not pleased with Keitah's attitude. Daniel watched Keitah. The older man smiled and clapped Inkaimon on the shoulder, his manner easy and sincere. "Forgive an old man's regret for the lost peace in which he had hoped to spend his remaining years. Indeed, your words are wise, Inkaimon Umaira-na. We do as well and wisely as any men might, I do believe so. And with the favor of God and the Martyr, perhaps that shall suffice." He glanced toward Mitereh. "I shall go attend to your commands, then, if I may have leave, my king."

Mitereh inclined his head. "Indeed, my friend; and I will wish you all possible fortune and success. May the Martyr hold his hand above you."

"And God hold us all in his hand," Keitah returned. He bowed and withdrew.

Daniel wished he understood what the plan actually was and

what Keitah's part in it was, but he had not understood enough of what little of the discussion he had actually heard, and he could hardly ask now. He shivered involuntarily as Keitah departed, however: an actual physical reaction of relief. A stupid one. As long as he wore the pendant Keitah had forced him to take, it didn't matter whether the other man was physically present or not. But he could not help the relief.

"Go to Mikanan Chauke-sa," the king said to one of his young men, Bidau. "See that his part of this play is set properly in motion."

Bidau gave a sober little nod and went out, leaving only Daniel and two more of the king's guards in the map room.

And if he was ever going to find a better opportunity, Daniel could not imagine what it might be. He didn't think: there was no time to think, and if he had hesitated for thought he knew he would not have the nerve to proceed. He was out of time and out of options. So he simply took the few necessary steps, picked a knife up off the table, withdrew it from its sheath, and ripped Mitereh's shirt down to expose his chest. The king jerked back with an exclamation of surprise, but Daniel hardly noticed. All his attention was concentrated on his target: Mitereh's chest, at the level of the fourth and fifth ribs and on the left so that this stabbing would look like a real attempt to find the heart, but over far enough to miss everything important, and slanted to cut against the ribs rather than slip between them.

Mitereh did not fight back at once, undoubtedly too surprised. He'd put his free hand on the table, bracing himself against the pressure of Daniel's grip, but despite the weight recent worry and involuntary exercise had recently taken off, Daniel still outweighed the younger man by at least seventy pounds. He used his weight to pin Mitereh for the brief moment he needed—he had to do it fast, before Mitereh could tear himself free—if the king moved exactly the wrong way, Daniel might even injure him seriously—he should have been a surgeon rather than a psychiatrist—Mitereh finally seemed to understand that this was a real attack, and began at last to struggle in earnest, shouting. But Daniel stabbed him, at exactly the right angle. He knew it was right; he felt the knife grate against bone almost at once and turn in his hand—

The end of Mitereh's shout choked off in a gasp of shock and pain.

Daniel let go of the knife, not jerking it out because he didn't want the wound to bleed too much. He stepped back, forcing himself to watch with clinical detachment as Mitereh caught at the table, staggering. Behind him, Inkaimon's shout of horror was much louder than the low sound Mitereh managed.

Inkaimon sprang to his king's side, helping Mitereh to a chair and bending close to inspect the wound. Badayan, the other of the king's young men still present, had drawn his sword. Daniel thought for a moment the young man would simply strike him down where he stood; he had known that was a possibility. Mitereh must have thought so to; the king said huskily, "Do no harm to him!" and Badayan hesitated. Then the young guardsman instead put a hand on Daniel's shoulder and a foot behind his knee, forcing him to his knees in a move that was rough but not brutal. Both young men were ashen; they looked profoundly shocked. Inkaimon said in a hushed tone, "Mitereh, you should not try to speak. I shall call for your physician, I shall send for your aunt, for your sorcerers—"

The king managed a slight nod. His own hand had gone to the wound in his chest; his fingers flinched away when they encountered the knife. His color wasn't good; he'd gone almost gray. It took no skill to diagnose shock, and how long would it take that physician to get here?

Daniel stared at Mitereh's face. Even though he knew he hadn't dealt a serious injury—he *knew* that—but even so, he couldn't help but watch for the frothy exhalations that would mean the king had suffered a lung injury, for the deathly look that would suggest too much internal bleeding. But the young man looked all right, allowing for the shock. Blood was seeping from around the edges of the knife, but not very fast. Inkaimon fortunately had too much sense to pull the knife out; he left it where it was, only pressing Mitereh to lean back and murmuring to him to be still.

Daniel was not allowed to linger in the king's presence long enough to be absolutely certain the surgeons had adequate skill to cope with the wound. Badayan took him to an apartment high in one of the palace towers and left him there. Neither the apartment nor the situation was nearly as bad as Daniel had expected: the apartment was small and plain, with no rugs on the stone floors and only minimal furnishings, but, though the windows were narrow and placed high up on the walls and the door was barred, it was far from a stereotypical dungeon. And Mitereh's injunction to do no harm seemed—at least for the moment—to effectively restrain the king's young men from any, well, excesses.

Though their frozen disdain was not very pleasant, either, over the next few days, which passed very slowly. None of them would speak to him, nor did Daniel have the nerve to try to break into their deadly silence. Two of the young men would bring him a tray of food in the morning, one standing on guard while the other laid it on the room's only table and took away the previous day's dishes. Save for this uncomfortable interlude, there was nothing to break the steady monotony of the days.

The windows were set too high for Daniel to look out of them, unless he stood on his toes and craned his neck. He spent a good deal of time lying on the narrow bed, his hands laced behind his head, staring at the blank ceiling and trying to imagine Jenna—where she was, what she might be doing. Or suffering. Though his mind flinched away from that possibility, he could not keep it from recurring to him over and over. He listened carefully to the pendant he still wore, but he heard nothing. So surely Keitah must have been satisfied that his 'assassination attempt' had been in earnest. He believed that, with a firm effort. The belief felt increasingly fragile as each day followed the last.

Worse even than thoughts of Jenna was the time each day when the gathering shadows stretched out to engulf the city and—at last—the tower where Daniel was held. This tower was almost the last one left in sunlight, which somehow seemed to make the approaching darkness harder to bear. Perhaps this was because Daniel had so long to anticipate the coming of each night. To him, it felt as though the very stones of his tower would dissolve as the light left the sky. As though he would fall through them into the darkness, an endless tumbling fall. He could no longer sleep at night at all. After the third such night he finally ventured to ask for a lantern, or even for some candles; the first request he had made of his jailors. It was Torohoh whom he asked, hoping he of them all might choose to be generous. But Torohoh gave him a scornful look, as though he understood the childish terror that lay behind the plea, and left without answering.

No candles were brought. Not very surprising. Mitereh's young men were no doubt eager to make whatever small gestures of vengeance against him the king's injunction permitted. He did not blame them. But he was sorry not to have the candles.

But Mitereh himself came up to Daniel's high prison, late that same afternoon. Torohoh and Pitagainin were with him. Far more disturbingly ... so was Keitah Terusai-e. The older man's expression was reserved and chilly, exactly the expression of a loyal man forced to meet a treacherous one. He met Daniel's eyes without a trace of secret knowledge.

Daniel stood up slowly, tearing his gaze with an effort away from Keitah's face. His heart rate had quickened. His palms prickled. He felt ill. All simple physiology, of course. He'd dealt with stress before. There was no reason to take any of the physiological reactions personally. Knowing this helped a little.

Torohoh and Pitagainin took up posts on either side of the room's single door. Keitah drew the room's single chair around for Mitereh, who sat down in it. The king moved stiffly and his manner was restrained, but somehow the plain chair became very much like a throne at that moment.

Daniel wondered whether he should kneel, but chose to remain standing. Kneeling to the king would, after all, be a gesture of fealty, and in all Nerinesir he doubted there was any other man who'd more blatantly renounced fealty to Mitereh than he had.

Mitereh drew one leg up, wincing a little, and settled with his heel resting on a rung of his chair. Folding his hands across his knee, he looked steadily at Daniel.

Daniel, drawn by the quiet expectation in that look, cleared his throat. "I'm sorry," he said. He tried not to look at Keitah. "I never wanted to harm you."

The king lifted a hand to touch his chest where the knife had gone in. His mouth crooked in a wry expression.

"Yes," Daniel acknowledged. "But once it became clear how much you were harming Tenai—I know that wasn't your intention, but you—your demands, your presence, your very existence—were destroying her ... her balance. Her stability. What else could I do? I've known her sixteen years; she's been my patient; she's the one to whom I owe ..." he hesitated.

"Loyalty?" said Mitereh. There was an edge to the king's tone, but not the angry condemnation Daniel had expected. He sounded ... quiet, thoughtful. Like he was sincerely trying to understand what Daniel had done, and why.

That was dangerous. With Keitah Terusai-e in the room ... potentially very dangerous. Daniel would have rather faced rage than this cool assessment. He'd spent a good deal of time thinking how to justify the unjustifiable. If necessary, he meant to make up a reason based on Scientology or something, so utterly foreign to Talasayan that everyone here would decide there was just no understanding him. For now, he only said carefully, "Not as you mean the term, I think. But the kind of relationship we had ... it forms a bond. I have a responsibility for Tenai, for her well-being. I couldn't ... I couldn't let her fall back into, well, into madness."

The king inclined his head, evidently finding this sufficiently plausible to pass. "And it seemed to you that my death would end all the ill attending Nolas-Kuomon. Yes. And your people make no sacred oaths. I do recall you told me this. But I did not realize how lightly you would hold the one you made to me."

"I'm sorry," Daniel repeated. He did not permit himself to

glance at Keitah, though he felt the other man's gaze as almost a physical pressure against his skin.

"I do not forgive the blow," said the king, reclaiming Daniel's attention. "Indeed, I find no possible way to forgive it. But I believe I understand something of your reasons." He was silent for a moment. Eventually he went on, "Nolas-Kuomon we feared, and Nolas-Kuomon we have now among us, when we had all but set aside this fear. She has gone to our enemies, leaving you here, Nola Danyel. Though you remember her, I believe she has forgotten you."

This, though it hadn't been Daniel's immediate concern, seemed all too possible. He had no idea what to say. If Keitah had not been present—if Mitereh had still trusted him—if everything were different, Daniel would have asked for permission to go after Tenai. God knew what he could do if he found her. Not that there was much chance Keitah would permit any such thing. Daniel found himself wanting to look again at Keitah, try to judge by the other man's face what he thought, what he would do ... he shut his eyes, consciously trying to steady his breathing.

"This man is a danger to you, my king," Keitah said. His tone was neutral, but with just the faintest edge to it. "And he requires attention from your guard that they can ill spare."

"On the contrary, my friend, I perceive he may yet provide a useful check upon Chaisa." The king studied Daniel, an unreadable gaze. "The army out of Imbaneh-se has begun its advance, Nola Danyel. Nolas-Kuomon leads it. Thus you may have value to us, though she should set her foot on one road or yet another."

Meaning, if Daniel understood him correctly, that Mitereh might use him to try to get Tenai's attention ... or perhaps as a hostage. That at least explained why the king had kept Daniel guarded and safe. He waited.

"And Nola Jenna as well," the king concluded, and turned to Keitah, wincing a little as the movement pulled at his injury. "I shall ask you to send for her. I believe Niah and Inana had best remain in Kinabana for this present, however."

But Jenna would be brought into danger ... if Keitah allowed her to reach Nerinesir, rather than having a man of his drop her off some cliff on the way. Which in fact he would surely do. He could not afford to let her get back to Nerinesir. Daniel clenched his teeth, managed at last in a calm tone, "Surely it would be better to leave Jenna out of the way."

The king gave him a thoughtful stare. "Is it possible you consider I owe you regard, Danyel?"

Daniel tried not to flinch, probably not quite successfully.

"Send for Nola Jenna," the king said to Keitah. And to Torohoh, "Keep Nola Danyel safe. Keep him close."

Keitah inclined his head. Torohoh took a breath as though he would protest, but then bowed wordlessly.

"I will do justice upon him," Mitereh assured his man, "but in my own time and in a way that will be useful to me."

The young man bowed a second time, looking somewhat more content.

Daniel supposed he couldn't blame Torohoh for his vengeful attitude, but it still hurt; of all of the king's young men, Torohoh had become something like a friend. And so the younger man's heightened sense of betrayal, he realized. No wonder Torohoh had refused the candles; Daniel should have asked someone who felt less personally betrayed. He should have understood that more quickly, but then he had a surprisingly hard time believing that everyone truly thought he'd really tried to kill Mitereh, even though he'd gone to so much trouble to make them believe it.

Daniel took a small step forward, stopping when Torohoh stepped between him and the king. He eased back again at once, lifting his hands in token of peaceful intentions. "I'll try to stop Tenai for you, if I have a chance to do that," he said. "Whatever comes later. But if I can't ... Jenna might. Tenai is my friend. Even now, I think she is. But she and Jenna have always had a special relationship. Even if she's forgotten me, I don't think she will have forgotten my daughter." There: that was as close as he could come to reminding Keitah that if by any chance he thought he might need a hostage against Tenai, he had better not dispose of Jenna. Daniel could not quite stop himself from glancing at the older man: do you understand me? Was that clear? Kill my daughter and you won't have anything left to stop Tenai gunning for you, whatever else she does ...

From the tight set of Keitah's mouth, the message might have gotten through, and it wasn't one the man relished. Or else Daniel was reading far too much into a change of expression that was barely perceptible.

Even so, this tiny unspoken victory, if victory it was, afforded Daniel all the comfort he had once his visitors had withdrawn. He still had no candles. And the sun was already slipping down below the mountains. He went to the window and set his hands on the high sill, standing on his toes to look out: the lengthening shadows had already fallen across the furthest reaches of the city. Daniel could very easily imagine Lord Death walking through the streets there, his strange kingdom trailing like smoke at his heel, so that with a careless step anyone walking behind him might fall out of life and into the dark. Shuddering helplessly, he turned his back to the window.

17

Tenai's camp was a big one, and very orderly. No heads on pikes, Jenna noted with relief. Ranks and ranks of tents spread out into the flat floodplains where the great Khadur divided and gave rise to both the westward-flowing lower Khadur and the quick, bright Tese. This had all been farmlands a little while ago, that was obvious, but everything was thoroughly trampled now and Jenna couldn't even guess what sorts of crops had been growing. The road, following the northern bank of the Khadur, ran straight into the camp and vanished entirely under the shifting mass of men and horses waiting there. Banners were ranked along the river, where the greatest tents stood: a blaze of formless color to Jenna, who didn't know any of the devices.

Emel did, and read them off to her: "Pasaguan, of Ninivar. Bedukayan Simpanar-e, of Mihaninan. I think ... I think that blue-and-black is Kuanonai Geraimani-e, of Kuduvar. He is a great lord, of a family that styles itself a line of princes. Few of that family are left, for they are proud and stiff-necked and hate to own other men as their kings. Geraimani might well think to claim the oak throne."

"But is *Tenai* there?" Jenna asked impatiently.

"There." Emel pointed with his chin. "That black tent is hers, with its black banner. So she raises her standard as Nolas-Kuomon, and not as Chaisa-e." His tone was neutral, but she could tell he was worried. So he thought the stark black banner was a bad sign. Jenna bit her lip. But there was nothing to do but urge their tired horses to one last brief effort.

Watchful soldiers stopped them outside the camp. Jenna expected Emel to say he was a soldier and get through that way, but he said instead that they were spies. Nolas-Kuomon's own spies, back from a mission to the north with news for Nolas-Kuomon only. The sentries didn't question this, probably because it didn't occur to them that anybody would have the nerve to lie about any such thing. Nor did the officer the sentries summoned try to question them himself. He escorted them instead straight to Tenai's black tent.

They had gone down to the river that morning for a quick bath and change, so Jenna didn't feel quite as grubby and small as she might otherwise have felt, escorted through an encampment of several thousand men, between impeccable sentries, and into the great tent.

The tent was ribbed on the inside with smooth supports made of what appeared to be ivory, and a dozen porcelain lamps cast their warm light over jewel-toned rugs in blue and green. There was an ivory-colored couch against the far wall of the tent, and in front of the couch an ornate long-legged table with a dozen equally ornate chairs, spread with papers and lit by short white candles. And at this table, in the single chair at its head, sat Tenai, one hand lying lightly on a map that rolled out across the table before her.

She looked like a wild falcon, barely content to descend for a moment to some tame perch. She looked like a dark flame, summoned by sorcery to burn in a barely-contained blaze. She looked like a woman who might walk beside Lord Death and keep him company in his dark kingdom.

Then she glanced up to see what the officer had brought her. Her fierce eyes seemed to scorch what they looked on, so that Jenna felt momentarily bereft of any ability to speak or even think. She had never seen that look, never imagined Tenai might look like that—like a bad guy, like a movie villain, like the evil queen in some made-for-tv miniseries. That ferocious gaze touched on Emel, slid to Jenna, lingered for an instant. Then Tenai's eyes widened, and surprise came into them so that once again she seemed suddenly human and familiar. She rose.

A man with her said sharply, "What are these? Spies of yours, are they?"

So thoroughly did Tenai dominate the tent that this was the first moment in which Jenna noticed that she was not the only person present. Actually three men were with her: Apana Pelat, an intense young man Jenna didn't recognize, and a powerful-looking older man, also a stranger, standing close by her side at the table. This last man was the one who had spoken. That man was a presence in himself, or would have been if he hadn't been so eclipsed by Tenai. He was big and broad, with a hard, intelligent face and eyes as sharp as the edge of a sword.

"They are mine," Tenai said. "Yes." Her voice dominated the tent as much as her sheer silent presence had. "I will see them at once." Her gaze lingered on the man. And lingered, until he seemed to realize all at once that she meant for him to leave. He flushed, and snapped, "This is my army you have about you; any intelligence that affects it falls within my purview."

Tenai stood quite still. When she spoke, it was without emphasis, and yet with a flat brutality worse for that very lack of weight. "When you raised this army from the land, Geraimani-e, it was yours. When you brought it here in hope of me, it was yours, and you stood in authority before it. But now it is mine. And the authority, mine. Do you wait for me to command you?"

The man stared at her in a kind of blank outrage. But not a blind or sputtering kind of outrage. He looked more dangerous for his quiet. But when he drew breath to speak, Tenai cut him off with a frightening, chill precision: "Shall I set my standard crosswise to yours? Shall I cut yours down entire and cast it into the fire? What men here would challenge me if I chose to do so? Or if you set yourself against me, what of this army then? Well?"

The man didn't answer. His expression had gone tight and hard.

"Your aims and mine run together," said Tenai, "but you do not command me. You raised this army, but I could destroy it. Thus the authority here is mine. I advise you retire from this field, Geraimani-e."

The man started to speak, stopped, drew another breath and

said harshly, "I have a reasonable need to—"

"I bid you retire."

For a moment Jenna thought the man was going to break the stiff silence that followed this command by drawing his sword. His grip on its hilt was so hard his knuckles had gone pale. But the younger man set a hand on his arm, just a touch, but enough to make the older man pause. He glared at the young man, but he did not draw. He bowed instead, a short savage gesture like a shout of rage, turned on his heel, and stalked out.

Tenai looked at the young man, who had an ironic, wary expression. He gave her a very small bow and backed toward the tent's door.

Tenai said to Apana Pelat, "Remain," and Pelat, expressionless through all of this, inclined his head and turned a quiet, intense look on Jenna and Emel.

Jenna started to speak, to be cut off by a brisk gesture. Tenai's attitude had eased now that the tent had been cleared, the burning force within her banked now and merely warm. Though she was not quite smiling, her eyes held a familiar glint. She said, "We shall make sure no one may listen by any means," and shifted one of the candles toward her end of the table.

Drawing a knife, she touched it to the tip of one finger, allowing a single drop of blood to fall into the flame. Then she beckoned to Jenna, who came forward obediently and let Tenai prick one of her fingers as well. She poured some of the hot wax from the candle into the palm of her own hand, and though the candle was white, Jenna saw that the liquid wax had gone crimson. Tenai let the wax cool in her hand, rolled it while it was still malleable into a ball, set the ball on the table, and turned to take Jenna's hands and draw her forward into an embrace. "Now," she said warmly, directing Jenna toward a chair near hers, "tell me everything." She shifted her glance toward Emel, including him as well in that request.

Jenna tried, found her words tripping over themselves as she tried to give voice to what seemed an impossible clamor of memory. She fell silent in confusion. It was Emel who stepped in, with a deferential glance her way, and turned all the wild, confusing mess of the past days into a crisp, coherent, military-style briefing. Somehow ... the way he told it, all the awful bits got left out, or transmuted to brief matter-of-fact simplicity utterly different from the way she remembered them.

"Yes," Tenai said at length when he had finished. "Very good, Emelan." Then she spoke to Jenna. "You have done very well, my child, given Terusai-e set his spell upon you."

"That was really stupid of us, Tenai, I know that—"

"Assuredly unwise. But the error was mine, to send you into the hand of my enemy. Our enemy. A subtle man, Keitah Terusai-e, yet I would not have said so subtle as this."

"I should have known," Emel said quietly. "I did know, but then it was too late. I beg your pardon that I did not give warning of a truth I should have known, Nolas-e."

Tenai looked at him, her expression thoughtful. She said, "I grant pardon, as you ask, Emelan Terusai. But the fault was not yours. It was mine, and the king's. Mitereh mistook Keitah's heart entirely, while I … I have long been accustomed to judge men with some fair skill. This time, I saw what I expected to see and looked in every direction but the correct one. Keitah Terusai-e conceals his designs well, but this is more than that. We think he must be a far more skilled sorcerer than anyone had realized."

Emel made a muffled sound, instantly smothered. When Tenai glanced at him, he said, speaking far more clumsily than he'd delivered their report, "Then ... then you are not ... you have not ... forgive my presumption to ask, Nolas-e—"

"Mitereh and I ride the same road, with the same destination in mind," Tenai said. She was frowning again. Her face had gone still; her steady gaze was opaque, giving nothing away. "Few men know this. You must take care not to reveal it."

Emel bowed. Jenna said, in heartfelt relief, "Well, I'm glad *I* know it now! We were really worried!"

"As are all others, assuredly, save our common enemy, who

believes all his plans proceed in proper order. Save that he has lost you from his hand, and almost certainly does not know you have come to mine. You have managed excellently well." She included Emel in that assessment with a small nod. "Terusai-e has lost a hostage, and not the least of his hostages. Thus your father is relieved of constraint, my child."

Jenna leaned forward, hands clenching. "Is Daddy ... all right?"

That got her a direct look. "He remains with Mitereh in Nerinesir. He has been afraid for you. Nor, I fear, will we be able to inform him of your safe return. Terusai-e knows all that he says, all that is said to him. Mitereh will decide whether to inform him of anything, or by what means."

Jenna sat back in her chair and pressed a hand over her mouth. Keitah had bugged him somehow? And listened to everything he said. That explained some things. It also made her really furious. "Keitah tried to make him kill Mitereh, didn't he?"

"He did. Your father found his courage sufficient to take a different course. I regret that you cannot be reunited at once." Tenai set a hand lightly on Jenna's arm. "But it is as well you came here to me. Terusai is in Nerinesir himself. Better he does not learn you have made your way to my hand; *far* better he does not yet discover that he is known. We have all put ourselves to some difficulty to make certain he does not know. You need not fear for your father, child. He has been *exceedingly* brave and clever. It was he who found a way to make clear to us the perfidy of Keitah Terusai-e." She made a little gesture that took in the whole tent and by implication the camp that surrounded it. "Thus this ... show. But we must inform Mitereh that you have come safely to my hand."

"I would bear word to Nerinesir," Pelat offered. His manner was quiet, a little hesitant, as though he half expected rebuff.

"Of course you would," Tenai answered, with a slight nod. "Yet though I would send such word, I think I may have another task in mind for you, my captain. Have you another man you might trust with the task?"

Pelat ran a thoughtful hand across his chin, briefly ruffling his short neat beard. "I could find such a man," he said at last. "Yes, I know one who would do well."

Tenai drew a piece of paper to her place at the table, picked up a feather pen, dipped it in a jar of ink, and wrote briefly. Then she folded the paper and gave it to Apana. "This will get your man out of this camp. I do not think he will be able to return, however. I shall take Mitereh's part to remain as we discussed. Have your man tell Mitereh that *I* shall see to Niah. I shall take her from Keitah and take her into my hand. I swear before God I shall bend my attention to that task. Let him leave that to me. He should do nothing in that direction, lest he cross my path and so ruin the chance to recover his queen. Be sure your man is quite clear on that point, my captain."

Pelat bowed, took the paper and went out.

"Kuanonai Geraimani-e will not suspect collusion between you and the king?" Emel asked, a little tentatively.

Tenai tipped her head back absently, *No*. "Indeed, Geraimani-e cannot suspect me, or not of that, for without me he has nothing." She tapped the pen she held gently against the table, her eyes dark with thought. "What Keitah Terusai-e suspects ... that is more in question. Whatever comes later, Terusai-e must come foremost, and we must be quick to force his hand while he remains uncertain."

"Whatever comes later?" Jenna asked, confused.

Tenai shifted her attention, powerful as a searchlight, back to Jenna. "You have understood what Terusai-e intended for your father? That he was to do murder upon Mitereh?"

"Yes," Jenna agreed. "I mean, we thought so. We thought that was probably it."

"Indeed. He might have proven apt to the task, as sorcery does not easily constrain him. In the same way, no magic constraint touches you, my bright child. You crossed all of Kinabana's powerful wards as you left that house. For you, they were not even there. Nor would they be if you meant to go in rather than come out. That was useful once. Likely enough it might prove so again." She laid down the pen she held with a decisive little click.

Emel started to speak and clearly thought better of it.

Jenna leaned forward eagerly. "You think we could go get Niah? I didn't want to leave her or Inana, but we *had* to, we *couldn't* take her. Emel thought she might not even be willing to try to get away because she's really scared of Keitah. But we could go get her out now, right? You could do it, you could get her out, couldn't you, and we'd have him then—"

"Perhaps," Tenai murmured.

"Terusai-e is not so powerful a sorcerer as was Encormio," Emel said quietly. "But the wards set about Kinabana are ancient and formidable."

"Yes," Tenai agreed, but distantly, as though she were thinking about something else. "How long Terusai-e has intended something of this sort we do not know, but I suspect he has been long in the planning. Certainly he has schooled himself well for this moment. Let us all recall that it was his decision to recall me to Talasayan, and thus we may assume he is prepared to guard himself against me. Still ... still, I greatly desire to have Niah and the child safely in my hands and not in his. They are a weapon Mitereh's enemy may hold in reserve and use at the last. To rob Terusai-e of this weapon would be most desirable. Also, I have sworn now that I will take the little queen from Terusai, so I must assuredly do so."

Those dark eyes came back to Jenna. "He will have spies here in this camp, I have no doubt. But I believe we may yet conceal your return. The dye was well thought. I shall ask you to keep to that disguise. Let Terusai-e hope you perished on the road and feel safe to pursue his own aims. He means to crush Mitereh between this army and his own, so much is certain. I little doubt Kuanonai Geraimani-go-e had this army prepared from the moment Terusai-e brought me back through the veil, though I suspect both were dismayed when I did not come at once to take it into my hand. Also, I think the Geraimani has yet other intentions of his own he has not shared with his ... ally. And the other way about as well."

"Oh," said Jenna, trying to figure all this out.

"Indeed, I believe we are all of us vigorously maneuvering to betray one another," Tenai said, a touch drily. She rose. "I will keep you close. Both of you," she added to Emel. "And we shall press events a little, so that Terusai-e has no time to think. While armies move through the land, I think we shall have a chance to take Niah and her child from Kinabana, despite all possible wardings set about them."

Apana Pelat came back into the tent with a quiet nod: *It's done.*

"Your man is gone on his way? Good." Tcnai was looking at the captain with a strange intensity. "Find a close-kept place where Jenna and Emel may go to rest. Find them a man to serve them. And a woman, for Jenna." She lifted a hand when Jenna started to protest that she wasn't tired and they certainly didn't need servants. "You should be discreet," she said to them. "Particularly before the servants. What names would you use?"

Jenna told her their aliases, a little reluctantly. She'd thought they would be done with hiding when they found Tenai. She understood why that wasn't the case, but it was disappointing anyway.

"Then return," Tenai told Pelat, and added again to Jenna, "Take rest when it is offered. Emel will tell you: one is never certain of what will come, in war."

The tent Pelat found for them was near Tenai's, and furnished far better than Jenna had expected for its size. Which was as well, because Pelat gave brief clear instructions that they weren't to leave it without specific word from Tenai. Nor did Tenai send for them again that night as Jenna had more than half expected. Or the next morning. Jenna, hating the confinement and trying not to wish they were still on the road, paced and fretted. The servants they'd been sent were always about underfoot, so she couldn't even complain properly. Emel was no help. He simply absorbed this forced inaction with a bland placidity that promised to drive her nuts simply by its contrast with her own feelings.

Then the army flowed slowly into motion, and though that was a relief in a way, in another way it was actually worse. They had to ride surrounded by men who all seemed to know what they were doing and where they were supposed to be going and what their place was in the world, and Jenna felt like she'd never been less clear about her own place in the world in her whole life.

The Khadur rolled out on their right, a great gray river that spread out between wide banks at first, and then got narrower and faster as the land began to slope upward into hillier country. The army seemed to Jenna to stretch out like the river, endlessly before and behind. Mounted companies rode seven abreast, carrying long lances with steel points that flashed in the sunlight. Long files of foot soldiers carried swords and crossbows. Each company had its own standard, gold and blue, or scarlet and silver, or a somber brown and black. Jenna and Emel rode at the rear of Tenai's own company. Watching her stark black banner precede them gave Jenna an odd feeling in the pit of her stomach.

The first mountains appeared before them, looking amazingly far away, and the road got steeper and harsher. The army moved a little faster despite this, maybe just because it had gotten a little cooler as they climbed. They were truly in among the mountains by the day after that, and Jenna knew, because she asked Emel, that it would take only another day or two to reach Nerinesir even at the slow pace of the army.

Very late that night Tenai finally sent for them. Jenna, desperately relieved at not being forgotten, felt like hugging her until they actually got to her huge black tent and found Tenai looking severe and elegant and cold and not at all huggable. No one was with her except Apana Pelat. He was sitting at the table, very quiet and upright, his hands folded in front of him. His gaze had been on his hands until Jenna and Emel came into the tent. Then he raised his eyes, looked at Jenna for a heartbeat, and then dropped his gaze to his hands again. Jenna stared at him, transferred her stare to Tenai, and asked, "What's wrong? Is—is something wrong in Nerinesir?"

"Not so I am aware," Tenai said, her tone frighteningly distant. She indicated chairs at her long table, and Jenna came hesitantly forward to take one. Lanterns hanging over the table cast a warm light through the tent. Three tiny crimson knives lay beside a tall candle, not yet lit. A thin disk of some pale wood, golden in the yellow lantern light, lay next to the knives. Yet another knife, this one long and black, with a bone hilt, lay unsheathed on the other side of the wooden disk.

Emel did not sit, but stood at Jenna's back, his broad hands gripping the headboard of her chair. Jenna had never found his presence more comforting.

"We will break our camp in mere hours," Tenai stated without preamble. "By midmorning tomorrow we will be maneuvering on the field, or so I expect." She indicated a map that lay before her. Leaning forward, Jenna saw that it was a map of Nerinesir and the surrounding countryside.

"We will come in here," said Tenai, "where the land is not quite so rugged. We have moved quickly, but Mitereh will have known of our approach the moment we began our advance. He will have his forces here, and here. Keitah will have his men here, I think, or else here. We will cooperate with his intentions, or so we will seem to do. Once the battle is begun, he will have no time to consider larger schemes. This will render him vulnerable." She looked up, straight at Jenna. "As the battle commences, you will strike into his house and take from him the hostages he holds. There is some risk to this and I am sorry for it, but you are the weapon I hold most apt for the task and I dare not reserve you. If, of course, you will do this for me."

"Uh—" Jenna said. "I mean, I'd be glad to, but I don't see how I can do that by myself. Or even," she glanced over her shoulder at Emel, "even if I'm not by myself."

Tenai folded her hands together on the table and looked steadily at Jenna. "You will have several advantages possible for no other. I shall give you a knife—" she indicated the little ones on the table— "a charm, that, if you trust me, should turn a bolt or a glancing blow. And this charm shall also enable me to find you, so long as you are without Terusai's wards. Alas, not within."

Jenna nodded. So it ought to work for her, because scary as Tenai might seem right now, she knew she still trusted her. Another of these knives must be for Emel, but would it work for him? She hesitated a second, glancing over her shoulder at him, but took the little red knife that Tenai held out to her.

"You may pass freely where wards would prevent any other. Keitah's men will not expect a young woman to offer them threat, especially if they do not recognize you. And if they do recognize you, I believe they will hesitate to harm their lord's prisoner. Also, Niah will trust you … we must expect that you may persuade her to it, should she hesitate."

"How shall we go to Kinabana? And how shall we come away from that house after the queen is found, Nolas-e?" Emel asked Tenai, in a tone Jenna thought held a strange note. She glanced at him, puzzled.

"I shall send you there across the miles." She turned to Jenna. "When you have found the little queen, I shall pour power into the air between that place and the place I stand, and so bring you and everyone near you back again to safety."

"Nolas-e—" Emel began, looking thoroughly disturbed. Jenna glanced from one of them to the other, trying to figure out what the problem was.

Tenai ignored him. "There are few alternatives from which I may choose. I shall send you, Jenna my child, as the best among them, if you will do this for me and for Niah and for Mitereh. You must pass the wards and go into the house. Once within, you must find Niah and Inana. Once you have found them, first give Niah one of my charms and then bring her and her child out of the house. Then call to me." Tenai moved a hand, indicating the thin wooden disk. "I will set an enchantment on this and fill it with power. Break it in two and the power will be released, destroying any wards that attempt to contain it. To use this, it would be best if you were out of the house, near the outermost wards—that is, near the wall. Break this disk there, and I will feel the surge of power as the wards are destroyed. Then I will use that power to bring you back to me. You would do best to be very near the queen and the child at that moment, lest one or another be left behind in Kinabana. Better still if you have hold of them. That will make it easier for me to recall you all across the miles that will lie between us. Is this clear?"

"Oh, it's clear," Jenna said. "But, sorry, it's kind of nuts! How am I supposed to get to Niah? You think all Keitah's men will just let me stroll right up the stairs to her rooms, huh?"

"She will be—Nolas-e, you will lose her to Keitah, and he will once more have three hostages rather than only two," Emel put in, vehemently.

"If you cannot find the queen or find yourself too much at hazard, abandon all else, break the disk, and call to me," Tenai said to Jenna, glacially calm. "But consider also that this chance will not come again. Grasp it or let it slip, I believe this will be the sole opportunity to reclaim what has been lost."

Jenna thought about that.

"Assuredly you must send me also, then, that I may set the house aslant with confusion," Emel argued. "At least let us make the best use of the chance we shall have, Nolas-e."

"Hey," said Jenna, suddenly realizing how dangerous this would be for him. "No, listen, no way! Didn't you hear the plan? You'd get separated from me, you can't cross Keitah's wards! What if you get stuck there, what then? No!"

Tenai tilted her head slightly to one side, lantern light sliding across the elegant lines of her face and glinting in her dangerous, secretive eyes. "Emel is correct. Though he cannot enter the house, he may act from without to aid you as he may. Yet you may well be unable to find one another at the end. Should I fail to recall you," she said to Emel, "you must make your own way back. If you are captured, warn your captors that I value you and that their own lives are yoked to yours. Warn them most sternly that Keitah Terusai-e has failed of his ambition and that no clemency will be extended to those who make themselves my enemies."

Emel bowed his head in acknowledgment.

Jenna opened her mouth, looked at Emel's tight expression, and shut it again. When Tenai handed her the third little red knife charm, she took it and set it beside the first one, on the table in front of her. Then she frowned at Tenai. "What is it you're going to do that Emel hates so much?"

Tenai inclined her head in a gesture that held regret, but no lack of decision. "Power requires sacrifice. To do as I must in this, to send you across the miles and bring you back again with the queen and the child, I must have great power." She looked down the table toward Apana Pelat. "A man unshakably loyal to the king has agreed to be made the vessel of this sacrifice." Her voice, soft and dark, seemed somehow to come from a great distance away. "A man who loves and serves the king; a man who treasures the peace Mitereh has built these sixteen years past."

"No!" said Jenna violently, understanding suddenly what Tenai meant to do.

"It is not your choice," Tenai said, almost gently. "Nor mine."

"No!" Jenna exclaimed again, jumping to her feet. "It *is* my choice, because if I let you do this and then I screw it up, that means it'll all go for nothing! *No,* Tenai! There's no way!"

Apana Pelat cleared his throat. He said, "Nola Jenna ... will you agree that this choice is most nearly mine? I thank you for your care. But I am willing to make this sacrifice for the chance to strike through Terusai-e's defenses and snatch the queen from his grasp. If you fail, Nola, I will forgive that failure. Success is not certain in any mortal act. I ask you to accept the chance of failure so that you may strive for success."

Jenna stared at him, unable to speak.

"In war, men die."

"Not like that!" Jenna glared at him, then spun back to Tenai. "Not like this! No!"

Tenai tilted her head, candlelight sliding, opaque, across her eyes. She said softly, "Yet you also have decided what you would kill for, as well, perhaps, as what you would die for, have you not? Few indeed are so cowardly that they would not lay down their lives for *some* high purpose. Unfaltering courage turned to cool purpose is not so common, true, and that is the need here. That is a gift that cannot be compelled, but must be given."

Jenna shook her head.

"I intend to take the queen and her child from Terusai-e, that he may not use them in any cruel way. More than that, I wish to set you through the wards that surround Kinabana, and so make an opening through which I may bring down all those wards and render the estate and house useless to our enemy. *That* will balk Terusai-e in *all* his plans." Tenai added, relentlessly calm, "The wise general does not seek to spare the lives of her men, but to use them as well and wisely as may be. At uncountable moments in every battle, a soldier must choose whether to live or to spend his life."

"That's different!" Or maybe it was all exactly the same, but Jenna couldn't stand it, couldn't stand any of this. She said, "You can't—can't—" she couldn't put her protest into words, and looked in appeal at Emel. But he was silent. She could tell he agreed with Tenai—or maybe with Pelat, who was looking at Jenna with the same strict calm.

Pelat said quietly, "Terusai-e has laid careful plans, Nola Jenna. I believe now—I consider it certain—that he has held this ambition even since the age of Encormio. To fulfil this ambition, he would tear down my king and sacrifice all of Talasayan. Certainly he would sacrifice the queen and her child." His tone hardened. *"This I will not permit."*

Jenna stared at him.

Pelat went on, speaking with quiet intensity. "Nola Jenna, I would gladly take upon myself the effort and risk required to bring the queen and her daughter out of their peril, and if the chance fell so, I would willingly die in the attempt. I cannot serve in that way. But to confound Keitah Terusai-e and serve my king, I choose to serve in this way. It *is* my choice, freely made in the sight of God and of the Martyr, who himself chose death and sacrifice that others might be spared worse evil. I ask you to accept this sacrifice now and turn the power thus granted to the necessary purpose. I ask you to turn your thoughts from me and toward Niah—and toward Inana. Would you leave that child to the care of Mitereh's enemy? I would call that choice wrong. I ask, I most fervently ask that you permit me to make the choice for you as well as for myself, Nola Jenna, however difficult that may be for you." Then, still holding Jenna's eyes, he picked up the black-bladed knife by the blade and offered it to Tenai.

Jenna couldn't think of anything to say, although she knew—she absolutely knew—she had to say something. It had never occurred to her that the example of the legendary Martyr might be held up as justification for something like this. Now she saw she should have realized that long ago. It was awful—it was unendurable. But Apana Pelat's gaze was utterly steady. He wasn't going to change his mind. When she thought of Keitah threatening to cut off Inana's feet, she couldn't even say he *should* change his mind.

She said instead, "There has to be a different way to get them out!"

"Not quickly," Tenai answered with implacable calm. "Perhaps not at all. There is no estate in Talasayan better guarded than Kinabana. Encormio himself laid down those wards. Terusai-e planned well when he caused Mitereh to give him that grant. Now that house, which should be a place of refuge, serves not only as a prison for those Terusai-e holds; it is a stronghold to which he likely intends to retreat, should his plans go awry." She held her hand out to Pelat, who set the knife in her palm without changing expression.

Tenai continued in the same soft, deliberate tone, "But however one may strive to plan for every exigency, still exigency retains the capacity to surprise. Terusai-e will not expect anyone to lay his life in my hand—and if he did, he would surely never expect *you* to provide me the means to drive through every ward that surrounds Kinabana. I will open the veil and so make nothing of the miles between Kinabana and this camp. Then you will step into the guarded precincts of Kinabana, and so give me the opening I need to bring down the wards, so that Terusai-e loses both hostages and every possible retreat. Then I will bring you back to me, with the queen and her child. Your act in passing through the wards and giving me a way to bring them down will very likely be the pivot upon which this contest will turn." She picked up the wooden disk in her other hand and rose.

Pelat silently got to his feet as well. For the first time, Jenna saw that, beyond him, a low bench of black stone took up the far end of the tent. Tall white candles stood at each corner of the bench, and a wide black wooden bowl sat on the floor by its foot.

Pelat looked ... he wore the stiff, blank non-expression people here put on when they were concealing strong emotion. But he walked across to the stone bench without hesitation and turned to face Tenai.

"True sorcery is dark and bitter," Tenai said, still softly. She was speaking to Jenna, though she was not looking at her. Though she seemed at first simply composed, there was in fact a harsh stillness to her expression that suggested she found this more difficult than she wanted to let anybody see. "Death magic is the most terrible of sorceries: hail the Martyr, whose willing sacrifice forever broke the power of death sorcery over suffering men. Yet the power remains, so long as the death comes willing and aware to the knife. In unwilling death," she added, this time straight to Pelat, "there is no power. In the death of a fool or a dupe, there is no power. A man must know his own mind very clearly, assess the use of his own death with a fine judgment, and hold to his purpose with unwavering courage, or the sacrifice will spill its power uselessly and all will be for nothing."

"But it's wrong!" cried Jenna. Or she tried to cry it out loud, but her voice came out only a cracked whisper. Stumbling around the table, she caught Tenai's arm.

Tenai permitted it, pausing to gaze down at her with an expression that was sympathetic, but not giving.

"Yes," she said. "But it is necessary."

Jenna opened her mouth and shut it again. Tenai's tone was so cool and flat, and everything seemed so weird and horrible, that she couldn't speak.

Before Jenna could gather her wits or will for any further protest, Tenai turned to face Pelat. "Know you your own mind?" she asked him.

He answered in a low voice that was amazingly steady, "I know it."

"Are you resolute of purpose?"

"I am resolute," he said. He sat down on the bench and looked at Tenai, just at Tenai, like the two of them were alone in the tent.

It was obvious Pelat wouldn't welcome any interference from Jenna, and yet she couldn't bear just to stand by. But there didn't seem to be anything she could do. She drew a breath, not knowing what she was going to say, but Emel put a hand on her shoulder. She let her breath back out in a hiss of frustration and horror.

Tenai said to Pelat, "If your heart fails, you must tell me, for then the sorcery too will fail."

"I will tell you," he answered. "But it will not fail." He held out his hand, palm up, over the wide wooden bowl. His other hand he placed flat on the stone.

Tenai did not touch the candles, but they burst suddenly into flame—long white flames that reached much higher into the air than normal candle flames would have. She dropped the white disk into the bowl and took Pelat's hand in hers. She had the black knife in her other hand, but she did not cut right away: to Jenna she even seemed to hesitate a heartbeat. But then she drew a breath and made a swift confident cut the long way along his wrist. The blood was so dark a red it was almost black in the candlelight. It did not spurt or spray, but it ran out more quickly than Jenna would have believed possible; blood spiraled around Pelat's hand and ran in long rivulets down his fingers. The wooden basin caught it. Somehow, although the basin should have overflowed, it did not.

The disk floated in the blood, horribly like a child's toy in a tub. Tenai did not look at it, but at Pelat's face. Her own face was very still, her mouth drawn hard and thin. Jenna could not help but be glad if Tenai was not as untouched as she seemed, but even if she grieved for what she was doing, she wasn't going to stop. Pelat leaned back, then lay down on the stone and closed his eyes. Jenna saw his chest rise and fall as he sighed.

The candle flames took on a red tinge, and the wax that ran down the sides of the white candles was as crimson as blood.

Tenai laid the knife aside and rose, so that she stood over Apana Pelat like some kind of pagan priestess over a sacrificial altar. Yet, for all her lack of expression, Jenna felt her shudder once, sharply. Jenna herself felt cold, and sick to her stomach. She wanted to run from the tent, even knowing it wouldn't change anything if she did. She wanted to scream, to protest, to cry. None of that, either, would change anything that was happening. She knew that she would see this in her dreams for the rest of her life, however long she lived: the dying man on the stone and Tenai standing dark and tall above him. She wanted to look away, and yet it felt like it would be a kind of sacrilege not to bear witness to this death. She felt like the blood that flowed out of this man she hardly knew was a loss that chilled her own heart. She was conscious of Emel standing solidly at her back; it seemed to her that though he didn't touch her, still it was somehow his support that let her keep her feet.

Jenna knew when Pelat died, for the candle flames suddenly flared high and then went out. A strange, heady feeling ran through Jenna, from the soles of her feet rapidly up through her spine; she felt suddenly like she was twice as tall as she should be and weighed half as much. Power rose and surged like the tide of some vast unseen ocean, and it seemed to Jenna that she rose with it, was carried by it to some height which she had never before dreamed even existed. She thought she might have cried out, but she heard nothing but the rushing of power through the still air.

Lantern light from the other end of the tent filtered slowly back through the darkness. Or maybe, Jenna thought, it was her own ability to see that had been destroyed. It felt like that, like she might have lost sight and hearing and every sense that tied her to her body, and was only now regaining them.

Beside her, Tenai was holding the wooden disk in her hand. It was no longer pale, but crimson. The bowl on the floor was empty of blood. And Apana Pelat was lying on the stone bench, eyes open and glazed with shadows. Dead. Jenna's knees wanted to give; only Emel's hand beneath her elbow kept her on her feet.

Tenai held the disk out to Jenna, who stared back at her and wondered if she had ever known her. Tenai did not look in the least uncertain or regretful. She was dark and dangerous and no one Jenna knew. When Jenna did not move, it was Emel who reached out and took the disk. Tenai only said, harsh and expressionless, "It is power. Keitah will not be able to constrain it when it is loosed. Break it when you are close to his wards, but remember that it may be broken only once. Do you understand?"

"Yes," said Emel, when Jenna couldn't speak.

"Do not move until one hour past noon," said Tenai. "After that time, move as quickly as you may." And the world twisted around them while Jenna was still trying to figure out whether she could handle any of this or what she ought to say, or do, or decide. And then it was too late for all kinds of second thoughts.

18

Daniel couldn't see out his high, narrow windows well enough to know when Tenai came up the Khadur road and into view of the walls of Nerinesir. But shortly after she arrived, Mitereh had him brought to the high walk that led along the top of Nerinesir's outermost wall. From there, Daniel could see how the army spread out along the great, silver Khadur river, an alarmingly large and businesslike force.

Daniel stood between Torohoh and Inkaimon, looking down at the ground where companies of Mitereh's mounted soldiers with lances and bright banners maneuvered into position before and between companies of men on foot. It was a beautiful morning: sunlight ran across the bright banners and struck the tips of spears turning them to jewels. From the height and distance granted by a perch high on the walls, Mitereh's army bore a startling and disquieting resemblance to a vast collection of toy soldiers. High-pitched shouts and a lower mutter much like that of the sea reached him, dimly. More clearly, the bright mellow notes of horns rang out in mysterious commands.

The young king stood with his hands clasped lightly before him gazing out at the distant armies. He did not look at Daniel, but said quietly, "So we see the yield of all our efforts, and the cost of all our errors."

It wasn't our *errors*, Daniel wanted to shout at him. *Can't you guess, can't you* see*, who did this to you?* He set his teeth against the powerful urge to say any such thing. He found his hands were trembling, so strong was the impulse to take this final chance to warn Mitereh. The pendant at his throat weighed on him like an anchor. Or an albatross. Some symbol of duplicity and betrayal. He knew he should give up trying to protect Jenna and shout out the truth. He knew, seeing those armies maneuvering below, that everything had gotten too huge and important. He opened his mouth, he took a breath, but he couldn't make himself speak.

Mitereh went on. "I have sent to Nolas-Kuomon; I have sent four messages in all, in my own name and in that of Gutai-e, and then in yours and finally in that of your daughter. By my own personal guards I have sent them, and then by a man recommended by Gutai-e, and at last by a woman of my aunt's household. And I have received nothing in return save a blank hostility that recalls my father and does not answer me in any other terms."

Daniel nodded to show he was listening. He knew what he had to say. He had to tell the king about Keitah. He *had* to tell him he was betrayed. Nothing else could possibly be any use now. He had no choice. No matter what it might mean for Jenna.

Bracing himself, he began, "Mitereh, listen to me. I have to—" But that was all he had time for. Torohoh seized his arm and set a hard hand over his mouth, stopping him. Daniel tried to jerk away, but realized at once that there was no point in struggling. The young man was much stronger than he was. Daniel had left it too late, and now, if they wouldn't let him speak, there was nothing, absolutely nothing, he could do.

"There is no use in pleading now," murmured Mitereh. "When Chaisa comes beneath these walls, she will indeed find you, Danyel. Perhaps the shock of that will bring her to pause. Inkaimon, Torohoh. Bind this man to the rope we have prepared and cast him from this wall, that his hanging body may carry my defiance to my enemy."

Daniel stood frozen. He had wondered how he would meet death if he had to; now he found that he was too shocked to move. Nothing, in this moment, seemed real to him: not the arching blue sky overhead nor the city that spread out behind him nor the soldiers turning in their formations below. He could not think. He could not even breathe. He shaped Jenna's name, but only in his mind. She would be left in this terrible country all alone, a prisoner of Keitah's, without even Tenai to protect her because Tenai had fallen into bloodlust and forgotten her ... forgotten them both ... *oh, Jenna.*

Torohoh still gripped him by the left arm, and now Inkaimon took his right. Perhaps not willing to tolerate a potential scene, Torohoh kept his hand over Daniel's mouth. Even now, Daniel didn't fight them. He waited, numbly, for the two young men to carry out the king's command.

Then Mitereh stepped forward, gripped the pendant Daniel wore, and jerked it free. The chain popped against the back of Daniel's neck with astonishing ease. Mitereh turned on his heel and cast the pendant out over the wall's low balustrade. It fell through the air, glittering, and disappeared from sight.

Torohoh took his hand from Daniel's mouth. Both young men released him, a fact which seemed as unreal as the initial command. He found he still could not speak, and only looked at one young man and then the other, and then at the king, who gazed back with intense compassion. Daniel touched his chest where the pendant had lain against his skin. It seemed it should have left a mark, a burn ... there was no sign it had ever been there.

"Nola Danyel," said the king. He spoke gently now, his manner entirely different from the coldness of the past moments. "Through your efforts, you have wrought this moment. Lord Death gave to Tenai Ponanon Chaisa-e the name of our enemy, and Chaisa-e gave it to me. Thus this dangerous ruse of ours, for we must catch Terusai-e in a chain he cannot see, and he must be coaxed to forge many of the links himself."

Daniel opened his mouth, but closed it again without speaking.

Coming forward, the king took Daniel's arm and turned with him back toward the balustrade. "That is an army raised up by Imbaneh-se," he said. He faced Daniel again, his manner grave. "But Chaisa has it in her hand, and thus I will turn it to my own purpose. This is what you have done for me. I recognize that all the good possibilities of this day attend us because of your cleverness and bravery."

Daniel still could not speak. Mitereh waited, unshakably patient. Below them, armies shifted their ground in maneuvers that probably made sense if you understood military things. Daniel watched them without really seeing anything they did, trying to make sense, not of the movements of the armies, but of all that had happened near him and around him in the past days. He said at last, "The fight between you and Tenai, that sent her out of the city—"

"A play," the king said, still gently. "Only a play."

Daniel looked at Inkaimon, and then at Torohoh. He could see that both men had known everything all along. Inkaimon looked grim and satisfied, but Torohoh looked ashamed. "For my part, Nola Danyel ..." the young man began.

"I understand," Daniel said. He thought he did. Of course the king had told all the young men of his personal guard: not only for practical reasons, but, and this was the more important part, as a gesture of trust. After Iodad's betrayal, they would have needed a dramatic gesture of that kind in order to regain their self-respect. And probably Mitereh had also needed to offer such a gesture, in order to re-establish that relationship of trust and loyalty in his own mind as well. None of which could be addressed out loud; maybe only the pragmatic reasons had ever been consciously recognized by anyone involved. He said, still trying to believe this reprieve was truly real. "I thought—but it was all for Keitah's sake, then. You're all good actors. I was—I believed you."

Torohoh made a little gesture of agreement. "So did Nolas-ai Keitah, or we hope this is so."

Mitereh said, "Your daughter is safe. She escaped from Kinabana with the swift daring of a lioness and came into Chaisa's hand several days past. Chaisa sent me word. Nola Danyel, I wished very much to inform you. But I could not take that risk."

If Torohoh hadn't caught his arm again, Daniel might have staggered. He closed his eyes, trying to adjust to this new version of reality. Struggling to fit everything that had happened in the past days into this new understanding. Safe. Jenna was safe. He could not believe it. But he could feel belief struggling to be born, rising out of the terror and despair that had haunted him. Jenna was safe. She would return to him, unharmed. Everything would be just fine. Just ... He opened his eyes again. "I did stab you." He tried to gauge the king's reaction to this.

Mitereh inclined his head. "Did you mean to murder me? I ask and command you will speak truth to me. I swear before God that if you intended such an act, I shall pardon it."

But not precisely forgive it, whatever he himself might believe. Or so Daniel judged. And if the king would not in fact believe the truth, that was where they would be. He met Mitereh's eyes. "I was working very hard to deceive Keitah, but even for Jenna, I wouldn't have done it for real. I swear ... I swear before God, I was trying to make it *look* real, but I meant to turn the knife against your ribs. Mitereh, I'm a physician, not only of the mind. I do know where to put a knife." He hesitated. "It ... something could have gone wrong so easily. It was an enormous risk. I chose to take that risk. I would never have forgiven myself if you'd died, but it was a deliberate choice."

"We have all been pressed to make difficult choices, in this. I confess this is what I wished to believe." Mitereh gave him a grave little nod. "I do believe your words. It was well done, Danyel, for it gave me reason to guard you closely and then to destroy you, and now Terusai-e will have no time to realize I have not done so. Remain, if you wish, Nola Danyel, and witness the final steps of this dance for which you have drawn so strong a melody."

Daniel obediently looked down, though he could not yet muster much interest in anything beyond the simple truth that he was safe, that Jenna was safe, that Mitereh and Tenai were working together. He leaned on the balustrade, taking deep breaths, ignoring the movements of the men below. Nothing he could see made the slightest sense, and he couldn't focus on anything anyway. He was starting to shiver—shock, he understood distantly.

Torohoh moved close again, ready to catch him, he realized, if he fainted. He felt he might.

Mitereh set a hand on his arm, both reassurance and support. The king nodded down toward the battlefield, pretending not to notice Daniel's unsteadiness. "The Geraimani must have been pleased to find a chance to put their army to use after the hope had seemed to fail. That house has always fancied itself ... potentially royal, as perhaps you have gathered, Nola Danyel. Still, I would not think any Geraimani challenges Chaisa's command of that army now. Nolas-Kuomon was never known for sharing power. Especially at the last."

Daniel took a deep breath. Let it out. Finally he said, "So you're sure she has control down there?"

"Oh, yes." The king was not smiling. His gaze, directed outward and down toward the field of battle, had become abstracted. "When Nolas-Kuomon raises her banner, Lord Death himself walks upon the battlefield. Those who swear to follow that banner will not lightly turn aside from their oaths. Every general of Imbaneh-sa will have sworn to her service. She would not have accepted less. Indeed, I know she would not. We discussed exactly that before we began our pageant. No doubt Kuanonai Geraimani-e intends to use her for his own purpose, but he will not find Nolas-Kuomon apt for his use, I do assure you."

This whole conversation still seemed unreal. Daniel tried to focus on it. It *was* important, though that fact had a slightly distant, unreal feel to it. Keitah was down on that field with a large chunk of the Talasayan army under his command. "Can she ... what is she going to do, attack Keitah's, um, position when he doesn't expect it?"

The king gave a little tip of his head back, *No*. "Nothing so obvious. Or not at once. Terusai-e remains dangerous. A direct advance against him would permit him to show his strength. More, should Chaisa move to engage merely Terusai, this would create great doubt within our own forces and increased peril to us from the Imbaneh-se army. No. We wish to draw Terusai's poison without allowing him even to realize he is discovered."

"That sounds ... it has to be ... "

"It presents a challenge," the king admitted. He laid his hands flat on the balustrade, studying the situation below. No doubt he saw a great deal more down there than Daniel could. He added in a low voice, "What we must do, we shall do, and ask God's grace and the Martyr's favor that we may do as we must."

This had the flavor of a quote or an aphorism, and for a moment all of them stood in silence on the wall, letting the king's words reverberate.

"So ..." Daniel said at last, "when do you suppose Tenai's army will actually, um, engage, then? And how will she ... what will she do, if not attack Keitah?"

Mitereh opened a hand in a gesture of uncertainty. "I confess I should be surprised if her horns did not call for the advance before noon. But for all we strive, events on the field are not well subject to the will of any general or king. We intend to jointly craft Terusai's destruction. How we shall do this is subject to the vagaries of the moment."

"Um ... and Keitah thinks he's in overall command? Isn't that how you set it up?" Daniel tried to keep the dubious note out of his voice. What exactly *would* Keitah Terusai-e be planning to do? If Keitah thought he was going to be able to use Tenai herself like a knife, then presumably Tenai thought she could counter him. That army down there was in fact Tenai's own ... bludgeon, Daniel thought. Certainly nothing quick and small and sharp. As a tool, a whole army seemed a little, well, short of subtle.

"Terusai-e commands the south wing. Sandakan Gutai-e has overall command," corrected the king, his tone now abstracted. He was leaning out over the balustrade, watching the movements below. "He is far the best general I possess, as Terusai-e himself must acknowledge; thus Terusai did not expect the highest command. You see, the banners there declare Gutai's command. Terusai believes he is Gutai's second. But that place will be held by Belagaiyan Tenom-e once Terusai is brought down."

"Ah." Daniel rocked back and forth gently, trying not to grit his teeth.

No fighter planes. No tanks. Just an agonizingly slow maneuvering of men and horses along the banks of the silver Khadur.

"They're getting closer. That black banner is Tenai?" Daniel asked, lifting a hand to point. The banner in question was distant, but even so its grim blankness drew the eye.

"Yes," answered Mitereh "You see, there, we are preparing to engage."

Daniel could see nothing of the sort. To him, it was all just a chaotic jumble. He produced a kind of wordless murmur.

"She is herself riding far toward her northern flank," Torohoh offered in a low voice. "You see, Nola Danyel?" The young man indicated the shifting companies of men below the city. "She will allow her force to engage Nolas-ai Keitah in the southern part of the field while holding back elsewhere. To hold men is difficult, and thus she sets herself in place there to enforce her commands."

"That makes sense," Daniel said, almost at random. He supposed it made sense; at the moment it seemed just another part of the incomprehensible day. Then it did come clear, with the suddenness of receding shock, and he took a step forward, craning to see. "She won't face Keitah herself?" He was surprised by the urgency of his disappointment; he had not even known how much he wanted to see that particular confrontation.

"Not at once," said Torohoh. Perhaps divining something of Daniel's disappointment, he added, "Likely at the last."

"At the last," the king said, each word clipped and distinct, "and saving the wild chance of battle, that will be mine to do."

Everyone was silent for a moment, in respect of that declaration. "I'm sorry," Daniel said at last. "I know he was ... you thought he was your friend."

"My father once said," Mitereh began, and cut that off. He seldom referred to Encormio. But this time, after a short pause he went on, "My father once told me, Nola Danyel, that kings have no friends, but only men who have not yet forgotten their proper loyalty. It is not a unique observation, I am aware, but my father meant more than that. He thought little of ordinary men, you understand. He might as well have said, *Any dog may bite*."

"Nice little father-son chats." Daniel allowed his tone to become dry, by implication rejecting the advice as well as the giver of that advice.

"I do not accept this advice," Mitereh agreed. He kept nearly all the pain out of his voice.

Daniel heard it anyway, as clearly as though the king had shouted it aloud. But he also gathered that Mitereh's rejection of his father's advice served really as a statement of faith. Or perhaps of will. I *will* not accept this advice ... and Inkaimon and Torohoh were listening. That had been meant for Daniel, but the king had been speaking to them as well.

Then Mitereh leaned forward again, studying the scene below with renewed intensity, and the moment passed. A low murmur passed among the observers on the wall, their numbers increasing as a dozen or so more men joined them in their high vantage.

Daniel craned uneasily to see. "What? What?"

"They have engaged."

"Tangentially," commented Inkaimon.

"Decisively, if Gutai-e turns," said Torohoh. "Yes, there, you see, he is turning now."

"She risks herself," objected another man who, with his own retinue, had come up just now to join them on the wall. Cardinal Uanan Erusa-go-e. The man set one broad hand on the balustrade and regarded the beginnings of the battle with concentrated intensity, his strong features set in harsh lines with strain. He looked years older than when Daniel had first met him, mere weeks ago. "What will she do if Terusai-e turns as well and comes against that one wing of her army?"

"That is Nolas-Kuomon," Mitereh reminded the cardinal. "And that is Gutai-e opposite her. I think we may all be confident she perceives the possibility. And I think we may all expect that she and Sandakan Gutai-e will dance together on the field as smoothly as the most accomplished courtiers may dance on a polished floor."

There were grim nods all around: a lot of them, then, had known the truth. How many men could keep a secret? Mitereh seemed to have been optimistic on that one—though Daniel could see that some of the other men had been taken aback and were now looking down at the battle with new speculation as they understood what their king had just said. In an odd way, their surprise made him feel better—that others here had struggled under a burden of doubt and fear as he had.

Time passed, with gradually intensifying sounds of clashing metal and a wordless, roaring sea-sound that was different from any ordinary crowd noise Daniel had ever heard. The occasional high scream pierced through the clamor with disturbing clarity.

Daniel could follow, with Torohoh's occasional commentary, a little of what was happening. Keitah's forces had pulled back, so that the southern wing of Tenai's army struck forward between a wing of his men and a wing of Sandakan's.

"Wait—wait," said the man suddenly. "Observe Terusai—"

It took Daniel a moment to work out what everyone else probably saw at once: Keitah's men were shifting again, sideways and back, closing up against Sandakan's from both the rear and one side.

"So," Inkaimon said grimly, "see how he leaves his position, for all Gutai-e signals him back. So the serpent strikes, without warning and from below."

"And you see," added Torohoh, for Daniel's benefit, "Chaisa-e holds the greater part of her men, for all they would take the opening Terusai-e provides them. She holds them—they do not close."

Mitereh said nothing. He didn't move. He stood with his hands folded neatly before him, looking quite calm. After a moment, he said in a low voice, "Nolas-Kuomon is moving."

"I confess I do not perceive so," Inkaimon admitted.

"Not the men. No. They hold that position. It is Nolas-Kuomon herself who is moving."

She was. Daniel could see now that grim black banner plunging across the field, trailed by a sweeping arc of her Imbaneh-se force—though, as the king had observed, the main part of the Imbaneh-se army was holding its place.

Below, half of Sandakan's part of the army turned smoothly and engaged Keitah's men. And the single company that Tenai led swept out and tucked itself around, and suddenly it was Keitah's force, not Sandakan's that was pinned between two enemies, with the Imbaneh-se army blocking his way south and the city walls blocking any retreat north.

Cardinal Uanan said in a quiet voice, "So the trap has closed as we would have it and not as Terusai-e would have had it. He will be given no opportunity to slip destruction now."

"Just so." The king moved his hand slowly along the stone of the balustrade. He said in a remote tone, "So it ends. This part of the play is over, or nearly so. Now … now we shall see what we may salvage from the blood and the shame of this day." There was a brief pause. Then the king said curtly to Torohoh, "My friend, if you will stay with Nola Danyel. Come down when you consider the risk permits." The king himself turned toward the stair that led down from the wall. Torohoh had drawn a breath to protest, but then he let it out without speaking.

"I'm sorry," Daniel said. "I know you'd rather be with the king."

"As you have no personal guards of your own, Nola Danyel, of course Mitereh must set a man of his at your back. I would not have you believe I would have protested in that regard. Indeed, I am honored to serve you, Nola Danyel."

"I'm sure of it. Thank you." Daniel looked down and out. "Can you tell me what's going on out there?"

That battle might be half staged, more than half, but it was real enough that people were getting hurt. Getting killed. It occurred to him to wonder, exactly how *did* one stop an army, two armies, when one changed one's mind about having the war?

The answer to that seemed to be: with difficulty. As Torohoh explained, it was very useful to have an enemy with whom everybody actually could do battle, but neither he nor anyone else could guess how long it would take for the Imbaneh-se army to realize that they'd been pulled off Sandakan's forces and pointed exclusively against Keitah's. Or how long after that the Imbaneh-se officers would understand that the maneuvers in which they were engaged were being done in actual *cooperation* with Sandakan. Or how long after *that* they would start trying to get control of their own men back from Tenai. Daniel suspected that it couldn't be much longer.

"There," Torohoh said tersely, laying a hand momentarily on Daniel's arm and nodding toward the battle.

Daniel followed the gesture, finding Tenai, at that moment clearly in view, all in black and riding a black horse. The sword she carried was also black, which should not have been perceptible at this distance, but Gomantang drank in the afternoon light like a black hole. Light and souls. Daniel winced and looked away as Tenai took the head right off one young officer who was, he supposed, trying to countermand her orders. That blow only required a single slash of her unearthly sword. The body of the officer folded in on itself and vanished. Daniel tried not to see that or think about it; all around him shadows trembled and expanded.

"Even those in the dark kingdom of Lord Death remain in the hand of God," Cardinal Uanan murmured.

Something in his deep voice made the shadows slip once more back toward their ordinary places. Daniel shuddered in relief and gave the other man a long look: what he saw in the cardinal's deep-set eyes suggested that Cardinal Uanan might know—probably did know—that Daniel had visited that dark kingdom and what aftereffects he'd suffered from that visit.

Uanan answered the unspoken question implicit in that look. "From time to time in the long ages of the world, a man has gone where you have gone and returned. Yet no mortal man returns unscathed. The touch of Lord Death is not for mortal men to endure; the very air of his kingdom scars our lungs and his darkness invades our sight."

"You did something to help, didn't you? Did you?"

The cardinal bent his head, the afternoon light casting his harsh features into strong relief and shining in his iron-gray hair. He looked, in that moment, every bit a sorcerer. "But little. I only set my hand for a moment between the daylit kingdom and the reaching shadows. Would that I had been able to do as much for you at once, Nola Danyel. But Mitereh forbade it, I think wisely, that our enemy should not guess what long journey you had undertaken."

Even if the effect didn't last, Daniel was grateful for the moment's respite. Now that he could see again, he found that the men Tenai was commanding had, unsurprisingly, followed the sweeping gesture she made with Gomantang and turned to support Sandakan. Tenai left them to it, evidently trusting them to keep going without her—nothing like sincere terror—and rode ferociously across the front of another section of the Imbaneh-se army, pulling it after her by, as far as Daniel could tell, the sheer force of her dark charisma. After that she was lost to view.

In deliberate counterpoint to Tenai, Mitereh moved now to control his own forces and pull them back from the battle: Sandakan Gutai-e might be in operational command, but it was Mitereh who rode across the field to draw the eyes and the attention of the Talasayan soldiers. Shouts and cheers rang out where the young king rode, in blazing white and on a white horse. Men turned with alacrity to obey his commands. The young men of his personal guard rode around him, defending their king against occasional resistance from the Imbaneh-se forces.

While Daniel had been watching Mitereh, Torohoh had been keeping an eye on the whole field. Now he leaned forward, suddenly intent. Daniel turned to see what had caught the young man's attention, but he could see nothing—nothing that made any sense: only the same pounding, clamoring chaos out on the field of battle. Tenai wasn't in sight any longer, and even Mitereh in his white had been half-lost in the confusion. "What do you see?" Daniel asked.

"A difficulty rising there. Look, do you see? I am aware that Terusai-e is pinned in place and subject to the greatest possible pressure, yet is that not a wing of the Imbaneh-se army moving to trap Mitereh against Terusai's remaining force?"

"Trapped or no, those are good soldiers Terusai-e commands," the cardinal said grimly. "I should say the serpent, though caught, still has fangs."

"But they're going to win, right?" Daniel demanded. "Tenai and the king?"

"Nolas-Kuomon will assuredly take the day," Cardinal Uanan answered. "Terusai will assuredly lose all that he holds, including his life. None of that is at question, Nola Danyel."

Given which assurances were missing from that statement, Daniel surmised that the king might indeed be in danger down there—and that neither the cardinal nor Torohoh trusted Tenai to get him out of it.

19

After the darkness folded around them and then folded back again, Jenna found herself, with Emel, in the humid prickly woods outside Kinabana. Tenai had set them almost within sight of the estate walls, so that less than ten minutes brought them to the edge of the woodlands. From here, they could look across maybe a mile of cleared land toward the sprawling walled mansion. The lake, surrounded with willows and great spreading oaks, sparkled silvery and inviting in the early light. Innocent. That was how the scene looked: innocent. The sight of the house and lake made Jenna feel strange, like the past days had been a dream: like they'd never walked through the woods with outlaws or stolen money and clothes from passersby or found Tenai in a black tent in the midst of an army. Like they'd never stood in the light of tall candles and watched Apana Pelat bleed out his life.

But the sick feeling in the pit of her stomach, that was real.

The worry in Emel's face when he looked at her, that was real too. Jenna said, striving for a matter-of-fact tone, "Over the wall and in, find Niah, get Inana, fight off the bad guys, get out. It's perfectly simple. What could possibly go wrong?"

A reluctant smile crooked the big man's mouth. "I will go that way." He nodded to the left, where the road led up to the main gates. "I will find a way to make a disturbance."

"But not too soon. An hour after noon. That's a long time." How long were the days here? Well, it was about midsummer. Six hours, say. It seemed an eternity.

"Thus we shall have time to discover many methods by which we may create distractions."

"Yes ..." Jenna paused. "I wonder," she said, thinking it over, "if anybody else might be hanging about, ready to make—or use—a disturbance. You know?"

There was a pause. Then Emel said, not with any great enthusiasm, "You are thinking of Kuomat?"

"Well ... yes, kind of. I mean, you did say he was probably going to bring his pack to hang out near Kinabana, in case there was a battle here, remember? And you have to agree, everything about this will be dangerous. I'm sure you can create a fine disturbance, but no matter how good you are at stirring up trouble, it'll be even more dangerous if it's not *enough* trouble. I bet Kuomat's people would be really good at disturbing the peace in, you know, a big way."

Emel tipped his head back, *No*. Or, in this context probably it was, *Really stupid idea, Nola Jenna*. "Or he would kill us both for interfering in his affairs, or turn us over to Terusai's men because he decides that after all he might try for a reward. Outlaw curs are not reliable men, Nola Jenna."

"Well ... but he might be really interested in hearing that Keitah's wards are going to go down. Don't you think?"

This time, the pause was longer and more thoughtful.

"Of course, maybe we wouldn't be able to find him anyway, even if he's here with hundreds of his best buddies. I bet he's got a great hiding place fixed up for his people. But we could try. I mean, we do have quite a while to wait, don't we? You probably know just how to look for them. And if you can't find them, we can always arrange our own distraction after all, can't we?"

Emel sighed. But he said, "I shall first consider how best to arrange a distraction. But yes, after that, perhaps I might look in one or two likely places, if you think it wise to do so, Nola Jenna."

"I don't know about wise, but I do think he'll want to help us. I really do think so."

Emel sighed again. But he didn't disagree.

In the end, Emel went alone to see if he could find Kuomat's pack. He argued, and Jenna had to agree, that if anything went wrong with Jenna's brilliant idea, it would be a lot better if the outlaws didn't have her in their hands. Or even know where she was, shame though it would be to miss old-home week. If Kuomat got any ideas about turning Emel over to Keitah, well, Emel wouldn't be there to make a distraction, but in that case *she* might constitute a distraction for *him*. He'd pointed out a couple of ways Jenna could get everybody looking in all kinds of different directions. In over the wall and through the wards and let the horses out of their paddock, that was one idea. Let the hounds out of the kennel, lead them to the house, and let them into the kitchens and the rest of the house—that was another. Either way, in the uproar, she'd surely have a good chance of getting Niah and Inana out.

"I really don't want to try it by myself, though," Jenna had told Emel. "So be persuasive!"

"Nola, I shall assiduously obey your command," he assured her, in so serious a tone that at first she wasn't sure it was a joke. Then she had to grin, but it was harder to keep smiling as he disappeared.

Smiling got harder as the morning wore on. Jenna didn't dare move around: what if some kind of patrol spotted her? Or even some innocent person who happened by and pointed and said to a companion, *Now who could that be?* Waiting was exhausting; a lot worse than clambering around looking for an outlaw hideaway, she was sure. It was both boring and nerve-wracking, with a generous serving of discomfort thrown in and nothing to distract her from any of her worries. Of which she had more than seemed her fair share.

She watched the sun crawl across the sky and made plans about how she would get the dogs into the house—she ought to have brought sausages or something, but a quick stop by the kitchen midden might provide something that would appeal to dogs. Anyway, start some trouble and then slip up to Niah's apartment. She tried to plan out what she would do if the queen wasn't there, what she would do if Niah was there but Inana wasn't, what she would do if somebody pointed and shouted "You!" while she was sneaking up the stairs … oh, making plans was easy. Probably nothing she thought of would help a bit when push came to shove. No, it wouldn't be anything she thought of that went wrong; it would be something that had never crossed her mind.

Like, maybe being shot by Katawarin. When the woman's shadow fell across her, Jenna rolled over, looked into her humorless face, studied the sharp end of the crossbow bolt pointed her way, and wondered seriously just how bad an idea she'd had. Katawarin didn't look amused at all.

Imbutaiyon did, though, when he appeared. He had kind of an air of taking their reappearance outside Kinabana for a joke, one directed at Kuomat, and one that he was prepared to enjoy.

Kuomat himself, third in line behind Imbutaiyon, didn't seem to think the joke was very funny. He surveyed Jenna in silence for a long moment. She was really glad to see Emel behind Kuomat. He didn't look exactly happy as he brushed past the outlaws to come to her, but at least he didn't look like he thought they were in deep trouble, either.

Accepting the hand up he offered, she murmured, "I thought you weren't going to bring them back here?"

"Kuomat declared he might assist us, Nola Jenna, but only if he spoke with you again," Emel muttered back, his deep voice even more gravelly than usual. "It seems he considers you more persuasive than he finds me. He did swear by the Martyr that he would do no harm to you. A cur will foreswear himself easily enough, but not this time, I think."

Jenna made a face at him and turned back toward Kuomat, trying to feel persuasive. Unfortunately, he really didn't look all that persuadable. She gave him a cautious nod.

Kuomat flicked a hand and the rest of his people slipped up and made places for themselves among the prickly undergrowth. Kuomat said, "Nola, is it?"

Jenna said briskly, "Mitereh said so, yes." She didn't have the title pegged down exactly, but she knew it meant some kind of minor noble. She doubted Kuomat cared about the title, but she hoped using the king's name might help here—she thought it would. "You wanted to talk to me?"

"Your companion explained your intentions to me. I wish you to explain this as well. If you will," Kuomat added, the courtesy plainly an afterthought.

Jenna found she had relaxed a little. She might have found Kuomat's demand, his very presence, a threat. But somehow she didn't. It might have been the steadiness of his gaze: he looked like he was thinking, like he was weighing everything, but he didn't look like he meant to make threats. His eyes were as pale as water. If he could see the truth of men's hearts ... that seemed a reassurance, now.

The whole thing seemed crazy, but not actually difficult to explain. "I'm going to go in there and get Niah and her daughter so that Keitah can't hold them hostage against Mitereh. Then I'm going to take down the wards Keitah's got around the house and signal Tenai, and she'll pull Niah and Inana and me out of here." She glanced at Emel. "Emel's going to make a distraction so I have a better chance to get to Niah. We thought you might like to help with that part. I mean, if the wards are broken and everybody's rushing around in a panic, wouldn't you find that helpful? I mean, if you wanted to break in and steal things? And then Emel would have a better chance of getting away, too."

"Useful. Indeed." Kuomat looked her up and down, a searching glance, but too impersonal to be insulting. "You are a powerful sorcerer, do I understand so? Thus you may slip the wards around this house."

Jenna hesitated. She didn't want to lie to Kuomat. She didn't think that would go well—and it shouldn't be necessary to lie anyway. "Not exactly. I mean, it's nothing I do on purpose. I can walk through those wards, I guarantee that, and Tenai gave me something I can use to break the wards from inside so Niah and Inana can get out."

"The girl has the right of it," Imbutaiyon offered. "That is indeed a wealthy house. I'd regret missing prey that fat, if the wards come down and we're not in position to slip in."

"I say no," Katawarin argued, her tone flat and unfriendly. "This proposal carries too much risk, I say. Bukitraya, or Emel as may be—whatever his name, the words he spoke that other time were truth enough for me: it's unwise for ordinary men to trouble the affairs of the great. How much worse for us? I say we should head south. The hunting will be good along the border, whatever happens here." She glanced at Jenna. "We needn't take any path here, neither to help nor to hinder."

"Katawarin's right," Inasad agreed. "We should just leave well alone and get right out of it. Merchants on the road, that's prey wealthy enough for us. I wouldn't even know what to take out of a house like that. And there'll be guards thick as bees in a hive all through that house."

"But they'll be distracted," Imbutaiyon pointed out. "And they'll be out on the grounds, not inside with their eyes pointed at the Terusai's wealth. Kuomat would know what to take, and Medai might make a guess—so might I. Gerabak? How about you?"

Gerabak shrugged, meaning, *Yes.* "We wouldn't all need to go in—some would have to stay out here to keep our retreat clear. Bau and Tantang and Inasad could stay out here, with Katawarin in charge. That would leave four of us to get in and out. I think we could. Especially if we found proper clothing, with the proper badges. A house as big as that, men come and go every day. Nobody's likely to know everybody else."

"We could get clothing," Imbutaiyon said, in a bright tone that suggested he'd enjoy knocking guards on the head in order to steal their uniforms.

"If we chose to," Katawarin said darkly, and glared at Kuomat.

The outlaw leader sent a lingering glance around at his people, with a little nod for Katawarin, as though to say, *Yes, I hear you.* Then he turned back toward Jenna. "You act with good will toward the queen and her child, and toward Mitereh Sekuse-go-e. You swear this. Do you so?"

Jenna had already believed that Kuomat might support the king if he were given the chance. Even so, she was startled by such a non-pragmatic focus just at the moment. "Well, yes!" she said. "I mean, I wanted to get her out before, but we couldn't, there just wasn't a way—but now there is, and I told Tenai I'd help because—you know what Keitah does to people who defy him, don't you? I mean, I *like* Niah! And Inana's just a baby."

"And you are determined to aid the king against his enemies, though you are Nolas-Kuomon's partisan." Kuomat sounded just a little skeptical. Sunlight shifted across his pale eyes, rendering them opaque and impossible to read.

By the sun, Jenna guessed it was maybe about an hour till noon, maybe a bit less. Plenty of time to play twenty questions. It didn't feel like plenty of time. She tried not to look impatient. "Sure. He's a good guy, isn't he? Anybody can see he's a good king—my father says so and he wouldn't if it weren't true. Tenai thinks so too, even if Mitereh is Encormio's son. Besides, nobody ought to have his wife used as a hostage against him like Keitah wants to do. I'd want to get Niah and Inana clear even if I didn't care two bits for Mitereh."

"We shall assist you," Kuomat stated. He gave Emel a look Jenna couldn't interpret. "Indeed, I shall wish you every success in your endeavor. But I will not endanger my own people more than I must."

Katawarin made a small, scornful noise.

"Consider how we will proceed," Kuomat said to her. "You will command outside the house. Inasad, Tantang, go scout out possible means of distraction and bring your conclusions to Katawarin. You have one hour from this moment. Imbutaiyon, take Gerabak and Bau and set up a path of retreat. Several paths. We do not, I think, wish to discover what the Terusai does to men who strike a blow against him." He turned to Emel, "Well, man, are you able to produce a plan of the house? Draw this for me, if you please. Medai, attend."

Everyone scattered. Jenna settled near Emel to watch him draw the floor plan of the house. Far from objecting to Kuomat taking over, she was glad to let him. Honestly, if they couldn't have Tenai herself in tactical command, it was probably hard to beat Kuomat. Especially since—and she didn't think she was wrong about this—he seemed to want them to succeed in getting Niah and Inana out at least as much as he wanted to succeed in robbing the house. In fact, she had to wonder if Mitereh would have a name in mind, if she asked him about tall men her father's age who had silver eyes and had disappeared years ago under a cloud. Or, no, the one to ask was *Taranah*. Jenna just bet the king's aunt would be able to make a shrewd guess about what the outlaw leader's name might have been before he'd become Kuomat. She was dying to know, now.

Another reason to survive all this nonsense. How else would she ever be able to satisfy her curiosity?

Waiting was really not much fun at all. Waiting by herself had been worse, and waiting in company with Kuomat's outlaw pack hadn't been great either. But waiting after Kuomat and his people had disappeared to set up their part of the caper was worst of all, because what if he decided to betray them after all? In fact, what if he'd hated Encormio—everybody had—and far from being on their side was really taking this opportunity for vengeance against Encormio's son?

While Kuomat had been actually present, this hadn't even crossed Jenna's mind. Was that a sign that she'd been picking up his real feelings, or a sign that he was a con artist? Surely the former. But what if, what if, what if ... possibilities spun themselves out in her head, and she couldn't even pace. What if *Katawarin* turned on them? She was not real happy about this little job. On the other hand, if she weren't trustworthy, Kuomat wouldn't trust her. Especially if he could see into a person's heart. Which she sort of thought he could. Maybe.

"Do you think," Jenna began, looking up, but Emel interrupted her thought with an abrupt little gesture. Ordinarily he wouldn't interrupt her, so she thought probably he was having just as hard a time as she was with all the waiting. At least, he didn't seem to have spotted any kind of danger. He was just looking at the sun. "Time to go?" she asked.

"Yes." Emel swept a long, careful look across the open land between them and the house. No one moving anywhere out there as far as Jenna could see. He said, "Once you are within the house, in a very few moments you may depend upon a great show of trouble, especially by the main gate. Remember that Keitah's men will believe the gate is their great vulnerability. They will rush to guard it. But you will take the queen out the other way."

He must be nervous all right, or he wouldn't be repeating everything. Jenna said, "Everybody can set off fireworks by the main gate, sure, but whatever Kuomat's people pull off, you get close to the wall near the kitchens as quick as you can, you hear?" Because once the wards went down, they'd be able to get out anywhere. Or *he'd* be able to get *in*, anywhere. And they'd settled on the kitchen to try for as a meeting place. "I want us all to leave together. Right? Well?"

Emel was quiet for a moment. All along he'd maintained that she should forget him as soon as she got over the wall. Which, fine, he had a point, but Jenna didn't like planning for failure—not even a partial failure. But he said at last, "The queen's safety is paramount. And her daughter's safety. Understand this: if they are harmed, or if you fail to free them, or if you are yourself taken, then all that we do here is nothing, and Keitah retains a great weapon for his extremity."

"Well, yes, I *know* that—"

"You must break the disk as soon as you may. If I am there, good; but if I am not, then you must not hesitate. Do you understand?"

"Yes, I know, all right? I understand."

"Swear before God you will take the first chance that offers and depart. You will not wait. You will not think of me, nor hesitate for any reason."

"I'll think of you if I want to," Jenna said shortly, but she knew he was right, really. The whole *point* was to rescue Niah and Inana. She said reluctantly, "I promise I'll put Niah and her daughter first, and get them away. Now you swear *you'll* get clear, too. If you can't meet up with us, okay, but you won't throw yourself away. You won't let yourself be caught or, or killed."

"I swear before God I will try to meet you, or if I cannot, I will strive to escape and live."

Jenna nodded, satisfied that he meant it. She looked out across the cleared land toward the mansion. "Okay, then. How do I get over the wall?"

Emel stood up and held a broad hand down to her. "We will go openly."

Jenna looked out again over the fields that lay between them and their target. "We will?"

Emel looked like he was trying not to smile. "Men do. With their young women. We will walk down to the lake, where it is cool and pleasant. No one will be surprised to see us walk that way."

"Right," Jenna said dubiously, but she took Emel's hand and let him lift her to her feet. They walked out into the field hand-in-hand.

The ground was rough: not a lawn. A pasture, maybe. Not the easiest walking in the world, until they came to a path. That was better. Jenna felt horribly exposed, especially when they got close enough to see the occasional man walking along the top of the wall. But, just as Emel had said, though they must have been seen, no one seemed at all upset about them walking out to the lake.

They got to the trees eventually. It felt like it'd been a lot longer than a mile. Jenna let her breath out with relief when they stepped into the shade, though she knew it was silly to feel safer. And there was the lake at last. And, as they turned to walk along the shore, there was the wall. Stone, heavy construction, maybe eight feet high. Plenty of hand- and toeholds if you wanted to climb it. Not much of a barrier. But it wasn't the wall, it was the wards, and whatever magic was on the wall didn't matter to Jenna, because she was special. Right.

Jenna let her breath out and looked at the sun.

"You will go over the wall. Be quick to get over, and then go on as though you are meant to be within," Emel said, voice low but not whispering. "The distractions will begin soon after. But you may move even while all is calm. No one will be watching for you here. Do nothing to draw the eye."

"Yes," whispered Jenna. She cleared her throat and said in a stronger tone, "Right."

Emel looked at her, not moving.

"Right," Jenna said again, more firmly still. "Be *careful*. You've got your charm?" Jenna thought hers would work. She wasn't sure about his. But she wanted to be sure he had it.

Emel nodded and offered her his cupped hands. Jenna put her foot in his palm and he tossed her upward like she weighed nothing, which given his size and hers was about right. Jenna lay on top of the wall and peeked over cautiously, then waved back an okay, pulled herself up and dropped down again on the other side.

No one shouted. No one came running. No guard was set on the wall, since nobody was supposed to be able to come over it. Well, since it was insane for her to have come back, Jenna supposed Keitah could be forgiven for not thinking she might.

The house was just visible through a screen of rounded big-leaved shrubs and delicate ethereal-looking trees. Jenna crept in that direction, trying not to think of everything that might go wrong. Once she saw the house clearly, she realized that she had sort of forgotten how big it was. To the right, the paved courtyard ran back around the house to the stables and kennels. In front of her, four generous stories of slate and stone and wood and glass reared up—five, where the mansion flowed back into its long wings. Big windows, at least. The better to climb through.

Nobody was looking for her, she reminded herself. So, a bold walk straight across the lawn and right in through the big bay window—the room was one of the dining halls, with an intricate wooden floor and a long, long wooden table, and a fabulous chandelier with real candles. No one was in the room, which made sense at this time of day. Jenna threw a quick look around and hurried to the door.

There were servants: almost as soon as she was out in the hallway, she passed somebody carrying a stack of linen, and somebody else with a wooden ladder, and it occurred to Jenna that if she'd wanted to go unnoticed she ought to have come in with a bucket of soapy water. In fact, there were several women sweeping a long flagstone hallway right in front of her. The women looked up curiously, but she walked right past them and they didn't even stop chatting with one another. An urge to laugh welled up in her, so that she had to hold her breath for a minute.

Stairs, a long sweeping curve of stairs with an ornate banister that looked just right for sliding down, and there was her first armed guard, a man who didn't even glance at her. Jenna let her breath out. She was trying not to think about having to fight somebody—having to kill somebody. She couldn't really stand to think about it. Up another flight of stairs, and a third, and it was down a hall and through a long gallery and up yet another flight of stairs. And there was Niah's apartment, right in front of her, with a man on the door.

The guard straightened when Jenna approached him, looking at her in some confusion but with no recognition. When she'd been here as a guest, probably all he'd noticed was her light coloring. There was no wariness in his stance when he started to speak.

"Is Inana with the queen?" Jenna interrupted the guard, in a shy little voice and with a downward glance.

"Her nurse has only just taken her away," said the man, in some confusion. "And have you been—just when were you assigned to the child, woman?"

"Only this morning," Jenna answered, cursing mentally because, *damn*, couldn't the nurse have waited a few minutes longer to take Inana away? She made a tentative little movement like she would go right past the guardsmen.

The man put a hand in her way, not aggressively, but with a strange mix of indecision and firmness. He didn't look suspicious, though—sometimes it was good to be a woman. Jenna bet he'd have suspected a man.

"The lord himself sent me to serve the king's daughter," she said, trying to look shy, edged forward into kicking range—*don't think about it, just do it*—she didn't *want* to hurt him—somewhere in the distance there were shouts. She had to move now, no choice, no way to back out—if they were caught, would Keitah *really* cut off their hands and feet?

The guard, startled or maybe even beginning to be alarmed, seized Jenna by the shoulder with his right hand. And then thought wasn't even necessary, because that set him right up for self-defense seven, which was Jenna's favorite. The move came automatically: grab the man's hand, set her forearm over his wrist, step forward and twist the hand over and up, in a direction it was not meant to bend. The hard part was to do it for real and not hold back. Jenna thought she could do it, she tried to do it, but even so she flinched and lightened her grip when the guard made a startled sound of pain.

He had gone involuntarily to his knees, but he wasn't going to stay there if she didn't do something else. Jenna snapped her elbow into his temple. It hurt her arm, but it didn't seem real—nothing about this little scuffle seemed real, it was like somebody else was doing these things and she was just watching. Everything seemed suddenly slow and kind of far away, and she thought that was good except that actually she wanted to throw up, so maybe she wasn't as distant from it all as she'd thought.

The guard collapsed. That made a noise, so that Jenna jumped, shuddering. But though she stood still for a few seconds after that, there were no indications that anybody had heard the clatter and thumping. She could feel her heartbeat in her throat, in her wrists. And she still felt like she was going to throw up.

The shouting from outside was louder, though. She had to move. Right now. No time to feel sick, no time for second thoughts. She stepped past the downed guard gingerly, trying not to look at him, and slipped through the unlocked door into Niah's antechamber.

There was a woman in the little room, but Jenna went past her with such assurance the woman didn't try to stop her. Niah, as small and slender and exquisite as ever but with wide frightened eyes, turned swiftly as Jenna shoved open the door to her inner chamber. A dozen or so other women were with the queen, which was not great. None of them recognized her, except Niah did, Jenna realized, maybe because the queen's fear made her extra sensitive to people around her. The queen didn't look very trusting. Certainly she didn't leap forward to meet her rescue with a glad cry.

"Niah—" said Jenna, breathlessly, wondering what she was supposed to do with all these women. She touched Tenai's disk, safe in her pouch. If only they were out of here already, ready to break the disk and let Tenai bring them home—

Niah's female guard, Merai, studied the queen's face and then looked suspiciously at Jenna. There was no recognition in Merai's eyes, but the woman knew something was wrong—she wasn't a total idiot—she was going to shout, Jenna realized. She took two quick steps forward and kicked Merai in the solar plexus, a simple front snap kick, trying not to do it too hard. The woman folded up around her abdomen with a *whoosh* of lost breath. Her mouth opened and closed, voiceless, the air thoroughly knocked out of her. All the other women scattered back and away, some with stifled little cries.

"Come on—" Jenna said quickly to the queen, almost as breathless as Merai. "We need to find Inana—"

The queen actually took a step backward. "He will—I will—he will be so angry—" her voice, a little kitten's voice, shook badly.

"It's all planned," Jenna told her desperately. "This is your one chance to get Inana out, and *Mitereh* is depending on you, Niah, come *on.*"

The queen quit dithering and came forward at last, even taking the red knife-charm Jenna pressed on her. A couple of her women looked like they might try to stop her, so Jenna kicked the nearest in the thigh, a simple roundhouse kick, trying just to knock her down and not hurt her. The woman fell over with a cry, more of surprise than pain, Jenna thought, and Jenna caught up one of the omnipresent candles and tossed it against a wall. Then, on that thought, she threw a hanging up over a burning sconce. It blazed up at once. Jenna followed Niah out with the crackle of flames behind her, and if all those women burned to death, Jenna supposed she would be living with the guilt of it for a good many years, if she was lucky, but the fire surely wouldn't catch that fast. Probably it would just go out.

Right over the guard Jenna had hit, with Jenna trying to pretend that she thought he was really okay and knowing he probably wasn't; down the hall, down the stairs—behind them there was plenty of screaming now.

"Where's Inana?" Jenna gasped.

Niah caught her hand and drew her quickly down the gallery toward the stairs. "Her woman took her back to the gardens!"

The gardens: good. Outside was good. Jenna touched the wooden disk for luck and ran with Niah, down the stairs, two at a time. Off in the distance the shouting was much louder. Armed men passed them, walking quickly down the hall. At first they did not seem to notice the two women, but then one of them, a dark-skinned older man with a gray beard, slowed and turned his head to stare at them, frowning.

"Back stairs!" Jenna suggested, and she and Niah ducked sideways away from the men, past a surprised servant, and into a steep, dark stairwell. Bad, bad place to be caught, and Jenna suspected at once that it had been a mistake to come this way. This impression was confirmed by a sudden shout above them—the suspicious man with the beard. Worse, there was an answering shout from the landing below them: two more guardsmen, where did Keitah *get* them all? Didn't they have something better to do?

Like attend to whatever Emel and Kuomat had cooked up for a distraction, maybe?

Niah, in front, hesitated. Jenna ducked around the other woman and kicked the man in front in the knee, feeling the jar of the blow all the way up her own leg. He went down, and she flowed right into a really nice aggressive jump side kick to take out the other man, but at the last instant she couldn't make herself do it right, no follow-through at all—but it got the second man out of the way and she and Niah ran past. They raced down the stairs and burst out into a narrow hallway. Jenna hesitated.

"The gardens, that way," Niah said quickly.

"Right," said Jenna, and they both ran. There were people everywhere, men and women, servants mostly rather than guardsmen. But there were men behind them and a guardsman at the door. Without pausing, she and Niah swerved into a parlor or something and went right out an open window there and then they were out in the gardens. The shouting was much louder once they were outside, but whatever was going on wasn't visible from where they were. No one behind them was shouting for them to stop or anything, and at last Jenna realized that this was because they weren't supposed to be able to get out except through the gates, so the men didn't think there was anywhere for them to go.

And there wasn't, if they couldn't find Inana. So, quick along a path, away from the main gates. "This way," said Niah, and ran toward the fish pool. Jenna followed her, hoping the young queen knew what she was doing. And she must have, because *there* was Inana's nurse, hurrying toward them from the direction of the pool with the little girl in her arms. The woman's face lit with relief when she saw them.

"What is happening?" she asked Niah when they met. "Are we safe? Is all well?"

Niah reached for her daughter, ignoring everything else.

"Everything's fine," Jenna assured the woman. Just how close to the wall did they need to be? It was only about forty feet away, surely that was close enough? She stepped up close to Niah, offered an inarticulate prayer for Emel's safety to Whoever might be listening, took the wooden disk out of her pouch, and broke it in two. The *snap* it made when it broke was like a dry twig breaking, crisp but not loud. A breeze seemed to come out of it, whisking their hair back and swishing past their faces. The breeze strengthened to a wind, so that Niah exclaimed in surprise. Then it died.

Nothing else happened.

Jenna had stupidly forgotten to ask Tenai what *ought* to happen when she broke that disk. Yes, the wards should go down, but she should have asked what that might look like, feel like, how she could tell it had worked. It seemed an awful lot like it hadn't.

Not ten yards away the bearded man came around a curve in the path, three other men with him, walking fast. Seeing the women, the bearded man gave a shout. He didn't sound excited. More commanding, like he couldn't imagine they'd try to resist him.

Niah said hopelessly, "We are discovered." She sounded resigned, as though she'd never expected to get away. Inana, held tight in her arms, had realized that something was wrong; her eyes were wide and frightened.

"Damn," said Jenna, with a good deal of emphasis. "Tenai was—is supposed to pull us *out* of here. I don't know—" She didn't know what had gone wrong, she didn't know for sure if something *had* gone wrong; she hadn't thought to ask how long it might take Tenai to reach out from Nerinesir to pull them out of Kinabana. But either it hadn't worked or it was going to take a while.

She grabbed Niah's arm and dragged the young queen into a run for the kitchen gate, quite a distance away around the house, because that was where Emel *ought* to be, and maybe some of Kuomat's people, and if Tenai couldn't get them out of here, then they were going to need as much help as possible.

Crossbow bolts went past. One hit Jenna, but skidded away— the charm obviously worked. But then the bolts suddenly stopped coming their way—that would be the bearded man stopping his men from shooting near the queen, Jenna thought. Then somebody was shooting back at the guards. It took her a second to realize it was Katawarin, standing on something outside the garden wall, aiming and shooting a heavy crossbow with cool concentration. The queen wasn't anywhere near Katawarin; the guardsmen were suddenly turning their own bows that way, and just as it looked like Katawarin was certain to have her liver skewered for sure, there was a heavy crashing roar and everybody turned and stared in amazement as half the nearest wing of Keitah's mansion went up in a violent blaze.

"Wow," said Jenna, staring with the rest. Whatever Kuomat's people had done for a distraction, she bet she'd just topped it. Setting the whole house on fire, damn. What had those stupid women done, stood around wringing their hands and weeping while the blaze caught? It was hard to look away from the flames, pale as they were in the bright sunlight. Niah caught Jenna's hand this time, and drew them both into a run for the gate. Jenna spared a glance for the wall, but Katawarin was no longer shooting over it.

Around a turn in the path, then, and right through a gap in a flowering hedge, with bees thrumming around them and the scent of crushed flowers hanging in the air. Jenna ducked and twisted, losing bits of her clothing and skin on unexpected thorns. Niah pressed through grimly ahead of her. Inana wiggled to get down until her mother said, "Cease!" in the sharpest tone Jenna had ever heard from her.

Then they were through the hedge and faced the kitchen gardens, on the other side of a large lawn lined with flowers and scattered with small trees and one huge smooth-barked giant with branches that reached nearly to the wall, and there was the gate at last. Guarded, of course. Jenna couldn't see how many men were there. Plenty, she bet. Definitely more than a couple.

Not that it actually mattered. How far were they going to get, even if they made it through that gate? She wouldn't have bet a dime they'd make it a hundred yards—

"There is a plan?" Niah asked, looking ahead to the guards waiting at the gate. She'd stopped under the huge tree, so that Jenna had to stop too. Which was all right, since she couldn't imagine what they'd do if they kept going. Niah was shaking, a fine trembling that was not reflected in her voice.

"Well, *I* sure thought so." And *damn* Tenai, *where* was that rescue? Jenna had now spotted at least five men at the gate, two of them on horses and all of them with crossbows. And the guardsmen they'd got away from at the house had found horses, too, and were around the hedge now, too. As they got closer, it became obvious that the one in charge of that group was the bearded man. He really looked mad. Maybe he was the sort of guy Keitah kept around to cut people's feet off. He looked like he might enjoy it.

Caught between the men at the gate and the men coming up behind them, there just didn't seem to be a lot of options. Men with bows, Jenna thought, were a lot like men with guns: once they got in range, there was only so far martial arts would take you, and after that if the bad guys could shoot you and you couldn't shoot back, you were just going to *die*.

The bearded man, face set and hard, stopped his horse a few yards from them and looked them over, a slow up-and-down examination. He didn't look impressed. Jenna knew she'd flushed, and was glad of the dye that kept it from showing so plainly.

There was some noise from the gate, and three men began to cross the lawn toward them from that direction too. Jenna saw after a moment that Emel was one of them, and that he was apparently hurt—at least, he was lame. She couldn't tell how badly he was hurt. She was sorry to see him, really sorry, and yet she couldn't help but feel her heart lift just because he was with them, with her, again. Which was stupid, but it was the way she felt.

The bearded man looked Emel over with the same disdain he'd shown for the women. Dismissing the man, he turned his attention back to Niah and made a short angry gesture to her, like, *Come here.*

The queen, her arms tightly closed around Inana, shuddered. She was ashen, so scared it hurt to look at her. She didn't glance at Jenna, not even really at the man who beckoned her; she walked forward with small hesitant steps. The child squirmed, and she put her down, holding her hand firmly when the little girl tried to pull away. It occurred to Jenna that once she was separated from the rest of them, there was nothing to stop the guardsmen standing back and shooting at her and Emel until, charms or no charms, they were both feathered like fowl. But she didn't know what they could do about that, and what were Kuomat's people doing, breaking in on the other side of the house and ignoring this little drama? And most of all, *where where where* was *Tenai?*

The man, looking angry and satisfied, reached down from his horse and grabbed Niah's wrist. He turned his horse, clearing a stirrup for her so she could mount: obviously he wanted to take Niah and her child back into the house and then the quote rescue party unquote would no doubt be cut to pieces.

Jenna started to say something, but then she stopped. Up ahead of them, Niah had let go of her daughter's hand, put a foot in the offered stirrup, lifted herself up to face the guardsman, and stabbed him with the little crimson knife Jenna had given her: she set the knife straight into his stomach and ripped it viciously upward. It might be tiny, it might have been made as a protective charm against edged weapons, but it still worked just fine as a knife. Niah's delicate face was twisted with fury and terror, but she moved with a dancer's decisive grace, grabbing the horse's mane with one hand and the man's big bow with the other and twisting her hips to throw him down off the horse into the road. The horse shied sideways, but Jenna already had Inana in her arms and safe. Safer. Emel shoved both of them behind his own body and turned to face the men—brave but stupid, if anything Jenna should hold *Inana* up as a shield, but she couldn't make herself do that even though it'd probably work, because what if it didn't? She crowded up to Emel and said through her teeth, "Get up close to Niah, they don't want to shoot at *her.*"

Emel must have heard her; he moved—grunted sharply, and she knew he'd probably been shot, but he didn't stop, and then the queen got herself set in the saddle and the horse under control, and started pulling bolts out of the quiver behind the saddle, shooting at the other guardsmen. Men ducked and shouted because they couldn't shoot back. Niah shot one man in the chest, then missed her next shot, and missed again, but suddenly she wasn't the only one shooting—that was Katawarin, back up on the wall, and Imbutaiyon and Kuomat himself with her, so the outlaws hadn't deserted them after all and who would have expected that? Crossbow bolts were going every which way, but not toward Niah, and now Emel, still on his feet, thank God, had a grip on her horse's bridle.

Niah ran out of bolts and threw her bow down, reaching down for Inana: she would take the little girl and—well, what?—run for it on her own? Well, but Kuomat might look out for her, Jenna really thought he might—

And then, *finally*, as Jenna reached up to hand Inana to her mother, the world skidded suddenly out from under them, and they fell at last into the black and were gone.

20

The battle had not become easier to follow, exactly, but Daniel had at least learned to recognize a handful of the most important banners. He could see the king's spiky blue spiral in two places, on a brown background over on the left and, further away on the right, on a white background. He didn't know what the different background colors meant. The king himself certainly stood out, all that shining white, surrounded by a frighteningly small detachment of soldiers. To one side of the king, a lot of Keitah's men; that was one banner Daniel knew: a jagged black triangle on a gray background. To the other side, different banners he didn't recognize, but knew belonged to Imbaneh-se.

He could not, at the moment, see Tenai's black Nolas-Kuomon banner anywhere. She had gone out of sight around the curve of the city wall, apparently—or back too far to see—or her banner had been cut down, maybe. Banners did fall sometimes, and then there might be a pause until some other soldier got to the fallen banner and raised it up again.

There was, at the moment, relatively little fighting close to the city walls. Lots of men, but relatively little action, so far as Daniel could tell. The noise had swelled, but now ebbed. Not many individual voices stood out from this height, but now and then a shout or scream or the ringing blow of metal against metal came clearly despite the background clamor. Daniel had given up any hope of understanding exactly what was going on down there, but it almost seemed to him that the Imbaneh-se army seemed reluctant to press hard against the king—maybe they thought Keitah's men would support Mitereh, maybe they didn't realize the reverse was probably true. Or maybe something else was stopping them. Or maybe he was just wrong entirely and this apparent lull meant someone was preparing to drive forward any second.

Swords were terrible weapons, dealing horrific wounds. He didn't need to be down there on the field of battle to know that. Arrows, too. Crossbow bolts, whatever. At least the people here hadn't developed cannons yet, but by this time he'd realized that a handful of catapults guarded the city walls. A twenty-pound stone thrown by a catapult might not be a cannonball, but it was no joke either.

Horns called, their clear notes rising in a counterpoint above the cries of men. Maybe this experience would have been easier to bear if he'd understood the signals of the horns, understood more of what was happening. But Daniel doubted that. Probably this would be unbearable no matter what he understood.

Torohoh, beside him, let out a breath. Cardinal Uanan said quietly, "So, that should do," in a relieved tone.

"What?" Daniel asked them both. *"Is* the king out of danger? Or has something else happened?"

Torohoh pointed. "I would not venture to say the day is won or the risk ended, Nola Danyel, but look there. Do you see? Gutai-e must have recognized the king's peril before we saw it. He sent a detachment to guard the king; plainly he set that detachment in motion as soon as the king came out through the gates. That is why the Imbaneh-se troops have held back; some commander there knew that before we did. Perhaps Chaisa-e has also maintained command; that I cannot tell, but the danger is much less."

"Not ended," murmured the cardinal.

"No, not ended," agreed Torohoh. "But his position is as well as may be contrived when the battle has not yet ended, as it has not. But see, those Imbaneh-se troops have turned aside. They will press Terusai and leave be Gutai-e and the king. They are pressing forward now."

Daniel could see this, after a minute, now that Torohoh had explained what he should look for. Yes, all right, the blazing white figure of the king had moved off to one side, surrounded by his own people, and he could see that someone with a banner showing three ovals against a red ground was driving forward against Keitah's force. And Sandakan Gutai-e pressing from another side, yes. The city walls blocked any possible retreat. All at once he could see that Keitah's position was actually pretty terrible.

"Someone is pressing Terusai hard from the other side as well," Torohoh told him. "That will be Chaisa-e, or so we may hope. I think it must be, or Terusai would attempt to break away to the south. The enemy he faces in that direction must be even stronger than those he faces here, where we can see better. I think it must be Chaisa."

"I think it is," Cardinal Uanan agreed. "I do think so, Nola Danyel." He was standing differently, still gripping the balustrade, his back still straight, but much of the tension easing. He said to Torohoh, "You say the battle is not yet ended. I would not disagree, but I think the day may be said to have turned decisively. Let us go down. By the time we come there, I think we will see the matter very nearly at an end."

Torohoh nodded, but he said stiffly, "The king bade me stay with Nola Danyel."

"That's fine, because I'm going down," Daniel said firmly. "I want to—I need to—" he stopped, not sure what he'd meant to say. Face Keitah and *see* the man killed? He shied away from that ugly thought almost before he recognized it. No, he wanted to find *Jenna*. He held to that sudden urgency. Find his daughter; yes. That was what he wanted, above everything. He said, "I'm going down, Torohoh."

The young man hesitated for one more moment. But he wanted to agree; anyone could see that. After that moment, he nodded with decision. "Yes," he said. "Yes, Nola, I agree. You should attend upon the king. I will take you to him."

Mitereh wasn't Daniel's primary concern, not anymore. But he didn't argue. He could draw a simple line with no trouble, from the king to Tenai and then to his daughter. He just nodded, and headed for the stairs that led down from the wall.

They found the king and his retinue hard against the walls of Nerinesir, the center of a stillness that had, by the time they had collected horses and come out through the gates, folded outward across the battlefield. The king's personal banner was pretty easy to spot, and then the shining white of the king's clothing. He was on a chestnut horse now, not the white one, so peril must have come very near Mitereh after all. But the king himself seemed unharmed. When Cardinal Uanan and Torohoh and Daniel rode up, Inkaimon recognized them with a nod and waved for them to be allowed through the tight lines of soldiers that surrounded the king.

Once they'd come that far, Daniel could see Keitah as well, surrounded by a knot of his own men, but held tightly at bay against the wall. Sandakan had drawn up a force of soldiers to one side. To the other, a harshly-controlled detachment of Tenai's Imbaneh-se troops waited. Small bits of the remaining Imbaneh-se army, isolated and confused, had pulled into defensive formations. The Talasayan divisions were mostly edging slowly over toward ... Daniel wasn't certain, but he thought that huge and relatively orderly mass of men might be the main mass of the Imbaneh-se army. He couldn't see Tenai, or, when he remembered to look for it, her black banner.

Keitah had apparently surrendered just at this moment. Daniel stared across the open ground toward him, feeling ... oddly blank. The men over there, plainly exhausted and disheartened, were grounding the tips of their swords against the torn earth. Sandakan's men were shifting to one side and another to leave the king an open path toward his enemy. As those soldiers moved aside, Daniel finally spotted Tenai. She was visible beyond Keitah's small defensive formation, sitting like a dark statue on a black horse at the head of a pretty large company of soldiers.

Sandakan Gutai-e appeared, riding forward to meet Mitereh, greeting the king with a bow and a level look. He seemed tired, satisfied, and grim in about equal proportions. He said in a clear, loud voice, "Behold, my king, your enemy is brought low."

"Well done, my general," Mitereh answered, also in a carrying voice. He rode forward slowly to face Keitah.

Keitah Terusai-e similarly edged forward past his own men. He was on foot, but he did not seem badly injured. Daniel was taken aback by the depth of his own sudden disappointment that Keitah had not been wounded; was not, right at this moment, lying gasping in the mud and blood among all the men who had been brought to this field, suffering because of his ambition. Daniel had not known it was possible to really *want* the death of another man; now he found he could easily desire worse than that.

Keitah wore a hard, closed expression. He did not seem inclined to pretend that he didn't understand why Mitereh had turned on him, which Daniel, at least, found something of a relief.

For a moment the two men faced one another in silence. Then Keitah said, not pitched to carry but only for the king, "Niah is still in my house and my hands. What will you offer me for her and for your child of her?"

Mitereh didn't answer. He looked past the older man, to Tenai.

Tenai reined her horse to the side and rode at a measured pace through all the gathered soldiers until she was near enough to speak and be heard easily. Then she said calmly and clearly, but with a cruel edge to her voice, "Your house is in disarray this day, Keitah Terusai-e. The queen and her child are in my hands and not in yours."

Mitereh nodded. He said to Keitah, "Have you anything now to say to me, Terusai?"

Keitah said nothing at all.

Mitereh lifted a hand, and dropped it. At his side, Sandakan Gutai-e repeated that gesture. A dozen men lifted bows and began shooting. It became immediately obvious that Keitah had some sort of magical protection against bolts. A little after that, it became clear that this sort of protection had its limitations. Daniel found, somewhat to his relief, that he did not actually enjoy watching this ... process. Execution.

After Keitah was dead, soldiers shot the men who had stayed by him. None of them asked for quarter, and no quarter was given. They had no such protection, at least, so it didn't take as long. Even so ... that was ugly to watch.

Tenai's men—the Imbaneh-se troops—took no part in the execution. They stood like stone, watching. At their head, Tenai was also like stone, or something colder and harder. Iron, maybe. After it was finished, she spoke to the man at her side, who, face blank, lifted a horn and blew a flurry of incongruously sweet, mellow notes. Behind her and all around, the army of Imbaneh-se began to withdraw in surprisingly good order.

Neither Mitereh nor Sandakan made any attempt to stop this measured retreat. The general had lines of frustration and weariness engraved at the corners of his eyes and beside his mouth. The king had no expression at all.

Tenai waited until it was perfectly clear that they would not try. Then she said, the cruelty in her tone clearer and more dangerous than before, "When you would reclaim your wife and child, Mitereh Encormio-na, come to me and ask. Perhaps I may consider your request, if your manner is sufficiently humble." Then she turned her horse and rode away without a glance back. She had not looked at Daniel at all.

He almost went after her. He thought about it. He thought of Jenna and almost nudged his horse in that direction. Torohoh stopped him, reaching across to catch his rein. He shook his head, wordlessly forbidding that movement. Mitereh glanced over, noticing this, and made a curt gesture, signaling everyone, or everyone near them, to ride back toward the city gates.

This was not something Daniel had anticipated at all: that everything would have been a pageant put on for Keitah's benefit ... and that it would also turn out, in the end, to be real.

Not long afterward, Mitereh, composed but pale, occupied his chair at the head of the table in a small chamber high up in his palace; Sandakan Gutai-e sat at his right and down a little from him, Mikanan Chauke-sa to his left, and the heavyset Belagaiyan Tenom-e, whom Daniel did not really know, past him. Cardinal Uanan Erusa-go-e was also present, beyond Sandakan. Daniel didn't know whether the cardinal was there as a formal representative of the church, or as a personal advisor of the king. Perhaps both. Mitereh's young men filled up the rest of the places. And Daniel, seated uneasily in a place of honor at the foot of the table.

Mitereh had been sitting quietly, his hands folded on the table in front of him and his eyes fixed on his hands. Everybody else waited for him: even still like that he drew all eyes. Lost in thought, Daniel wondered, or in some dark morass of fear and despair? Daniel was afraid the king would have a right to the latter.

Finally, Mitereh sighed and lifted his head. He said to the room at large, "I call you all to witness." The quiet in the room intensified. Mitereh stood up, came around the table, and held out his hands to Daniel. Daniel, startled, let the king take his hands and draw him to his feet. The king went smoothly to one knee and pressed Daniel's hands to his forehead. Daniel, taken completely aback, stared down at the top of the younger man's bowed head.

Mitereh lifted his eyes to meet Daniel's and rose as neatly as he'd knelt. He did not release Daniel's hands. "Before God, I hold myself to be deeply in your debt, Nola Danyel. But for your courage and integrity placed between Keitah Terusai-e and myself, this day would have been ... I do not know what would have occurred, but I think it would have been very different."

Daniel knew he must have flushed. "It was the only thing I could think of. And ... I'm not sure it's turned out as well as I ... as I thought it would."

"Even so," said Mitereh. "I do not have honor enough to give you." He lifted Daniel's hands once more to his forehead, then released him and turned back to the rest of the room.

From the various expressions of the men assembled, Daniel surmised that everyone here had been in on, well, everything, except himself. He was no longer surprised by this, except apparently he still was, on some level. On some deep level of his mind he apparently still really believed it had all been real, and not just a play for an audience of one. Or, counting both Keitah and himself, two. He was impressed, in retrospect, at their acting ability. Though everyone seemed to be trained in low affect, in this culture. And then, real necessity was inspiring, he supposed. In fact, he'd found that out himself. He sat down again, slowly.

"Now," said Mitereh, "What is the situation as you see it?" His glance took in everyone present and settled on Sandakan. He did not go back to his chair, but leaned his hip on the edge of the long table, folding his arms over his chest.

Sandakan Gutai-e looked up, his expression bleak. "She did not say Niah and Inana were in your hands, but in hers. It is impossible that she misspoke. If she did not mean to use them as weapons against you, she would have sent for them on the field and returned them to your care there."

Daniel agreed that this was almost certainly the case. And Jenna, he supposed, was with the queen. He couldn't believe his daughter wasn't safe in Tenai's hands. He couldn't believe she *was* safe, in the hands of the woman he'd seen out on that field. In the hands of Nolas-Kuomon.

"And if she meant to turn against the Geraimani," said Mikanan Chauke-sa, in a hard tone, "then why not do so at once? Imbaneh-se is in better order out there than I am happy to see."

Sandakan bent his head in agreement. "I fear … I much fear that Nolas-Kuomon has found an army at her back and the walls of Nerinesir before her eyes, with a son of Encormio behind those walls, and she has forgotten that the sixteen years past … are past."

Mitereh gave a grim little nod. "I fear you are right."

Daniel cleared his throat. He said, in the sudden sharpening of attention that resulted, "I don't exactly disagree. I think that's very likely correct. But … Mitereh, you said once that all the choices were hers, that nobody else had any choices. Is that still true? *Could* she make the Imbaneh-se army withdraw or surrender if she wanted to, or would she lose control if she tried?"

"She could turn that army," Mitereh said. "Those men are hers to fling forward or cast down; no one else's." He sounded very sure. He must have seen Daniel's doubt, because he added, "There are the walls of Nerinesir, and there is Sandakan Gutai-e, and there is what remains of Keitah's army, which must now reclaim what honor it may, if the chance is offered it. Beyond all this, that is Lord Death's Lady, and Lord Death himself stalked that battlefield today. No. If Nolas-Kuomon turned on her own force, we would surely break it. The men of Imbaneh-se will know that well, Geraimani pride or no."

"In that case ..." Daniel paused. He shook his head, trying to get his thoughts in order. "I think Sandakan is right—I think the habit of war just swept her up like a tsunami and she's caught in the flood. The question is how to help her get out of it. So ... how can we, what can you do, to make this less like a war and more like ... a triumph?"

There was a thoughtful silence.

"Last time, winning wasn't enough. This time, I think it might be. Especially if ... what if you pulled back your men and opened the gates and had the cardinals ring the bells, like you were celebrating. And people lined the walls and cheered and threw confetti."

"Confetti?"

"Bits of colored paper—it doesn't matter, whatever your people do when they're celebrating. Flowers, maybe. What if Tenai came into Nerinesir, perhaps even at the head of an army, and you met her as a friend? A savior, even. Didn't she nail Keitah for you? Didn't she save the queen? She's a hero. Why not treat her like one? Don't you think that would take her by surprise? Wake her up out of the memory she's caught in?"

"A novel suggestion," murmured Sandakan. He looked like he was trying to decide whether he thought it was a stroke of genius or the stupidest damn idea he'd ever heard.

"Plus, you say Tenai has control of the Imbaneh-se army, so that should be all right—as long as Tenai comes to—" *herself, her senses*—"comes to realize we're all on the same side. Anyway, wouldn't the Imbaneh-se soldiers hesitate to slaughter a bunch of ordinary folk who are cheering their arrival as though they were allies? Or," Daniel went on, "If you don't think that would work, you could go out to her, Mitereh, just as she invited you to, remember? Only you could go like you believed everything was fine. Not with an army—not even with a guard. Sandakan, maybe. And me, of course." He probably should have insisted on going after her right there on the field of battle. Although ... maybe not, maybe it might be better to go with Mitereh. He thought that could be useful, now that he had framed the idea. He went on, more certain now. "I'm nothing to do with war. I'm all wrapped up for her with not-war, with building a life that didn't have anything to do with any of you. If I'm with you, I think that will help her see past her ... her memories of Encormio."

Mitereh came back around the table and took his seat, looking thoughtful. Picking up a quill pen, he turned it over in his hand, stroking the feather gently through his fingers.

"If you go into that camp, there is no likelihood you will come out," Mikanan Chauke-sa objected, leaning forward. "It is not only Nolas-Kuomon you will find there, but Kuanonai Geraimani-e and his allies. The Geraimani want nothing if they do not want you dead, my king. Do you truly believe that Chaisa-e controls all that passes within that camp? Will you set your life and Talasayan's good on that belief?"

"Mm." The king turned the quill over again in his fingers. "I believe ... that this is perhaps a loaf of bread we may break and yet have whole."

"My king?" Chauke-sa sounded wary, clearly suspecting he wasn't going to like whatever Mitereh decided.

Mitereh set the quill down on the table in a decisive little gesture. "Sandakan."

"My king," answered the general, in a tone that suggested he was willing to be persuaded to almost any idea. A grasping-at-straws kind of tone.

"If you brought your men back into Nerinesir ... you might then take them out again, yes? Through the Gate of Pearl, perhaps."

Sandakan lifted his eyebrows, interested. But he said, "The Geraimani is not a fool. He will have all gates watched."

"In an ordinary campaign, certainly. In this one? He is distracted. And he is not in command, do we agree? Nolas-Kuomon commands, yes? And she is not only distracted, but, we may hope, also divided in her mind and her heart. As that army, indeed, must be. Divisions all through it, cracks everywhere ... someone may be watching the gates, or not, but to whom go the reports? Do those who take reports even speak plainly to one another, in that camp? I will take your leave to doubt it."

"Perhaps," the general allowed. "That is likely true."

"So you might slip your men out through the Gate of Pearl, and set them behind the Imbaneh-se force, well down along the river, where they will not be seen and yet may come up rapidly."

"Yes," Sandakan acknowledged. "And the city? How will you defend Nerinesir?"

"I will not. The River Gate will be opened, and the people told to rejoice." The king looked at Cardinal Uanan.

The cardinal inclined his head. "As you desire, so it will be done, my king."

Mitereh nodded. "I will go out to her." He held up a hand to forestall the immediate objections and went on, "As Nola Danyel suggests, I will go out to meet Chaisa-e as though I go to meet a friend, and the gates will stand open behind me. Not the gates of the Serpentine Wall, however. The bells will be set ringing. The people will rejoice to know there is no war ... we shall hope to redeem our word to them. Sandakan Gutai-e will take ... half, I think ... of our armies around the rear of the Imbaneh-se force and stand ready to come in and pin them against the Serpentine Wall, if the need arises. We will make barricades ready down each side-street so that at need we can prevent the Imbaneh-se army from spreading out into the city. And we must be quite certain the River

Gate cannot be closed behind the Imbaneh-se force, so that if Gutai-e must come at their backs and drive them against the barricades, he may do so." He gave a look to Belagaiyan Tenom-e, who nodded, accepting this responsibility.

"My king, you will surely not go alone," Inkaimon put in.

"I will go as though to the house of a friend." The king's gaze turned to Daniel. "Yes, Nola Danyel? You and I will go alone, do you judge this would be best?"

Daniel thought about it. He wanted, badly to go with the king himself. He wanted, more than nearly anything, to see Jenna with his own eyes, *see* that she was all right, that she hadn't been hurt in any of this; he wanted to see Tenai, see if he could talk her down. But was that a good idea? *Should* he go?

Should the king's young men? What statement would it make if Mitereh came with them? Without them? What difference would the men of his personal guard make, if they came along? He said slowly, "In practice, your guard can't make any difference to your safety. Can they?"

"Likely they cannot," agreed the king. He made a little soothing gesture toward Inkaimon, who clearly wanted to protest.

"I'd say ... yes. You and I should go. I honestly do think that would be best," he added placatingly to Inkaimon and Torohoh and the rest.

"I concur," said Mitereh. "Inkaimon, Badayan, Pitagainin, Torohoh, Bedau, Ranakai—forgive me that I must ask you to assist elsewhere. Before God, I swear I regret the necessity."

The young men looked, if not precisely satisfied, at least resigned.

The king looked around the room at all of them. Then he focused on Sandakan. "If all goes well with me, Sandakan, you must yet be ready to come against the Imbaneh-se army and force their true surrender, if they are reluctant to yield the field and the day and accept Talasayan authority. If what I will do goes ill, then all the choices are yours. I give my authority into your hands to hold in trust for Tegaitan, with all my hope that you will eventually set a peaceful and prosperous country into my brother's hands. Cardinal Uanan, should this become necessary, I ask you to assist Gutai-e in this endeavor."

Both men bowed their heads.

"I will not desire vengeance," added the king. "But I would not consider a Geraimani on the ivory throne a satisfactory outcome. Please bend your efforts to prevent that."

Sandakan inclined his head. "I understand. I will ask Mikanan to take the force that will wait down the river. I will ask Belagaiyan to command the force within the city. If the need arises, I will myself meet Tenai Chaisa-e at the River Gate. I will then take what action seems good to me. I swear before God and the Martyr, I will do my utmost to persuade Nolas-Kuomon to retire her banner and take up her place in Chaisa. I will not yield Talasayan to any Geraimani, nor any other lord of Imbaneh-se."

The king signed acceptance of this statement. Then he rose.

"Now?" said Mikanan Chauke-sa, startled and not happy.

"When would be better?" asked the king. "There are hours yet to pass before the coming of the dark. I will go out at dusk ... that will give Gutai-e time to bring in his armies and arrange what his men will do, and the cover of the night in which to do it." His gaze passed once more across all the assembled men, and settled last on Cardinal Uanan. "Prayers," he ended gently, "would surely not be amiss."

Daniel certainly agreed with that.

21

The darkness folded back almost before it had closed around Jenna, opening out into shattering light and sound, a sensory confusion that made her stagger. She tightened her hold on Inana, who, brave through everything else, cried out now in a high, piercing wail. Niah's horse tried to rear, but Emel brought it down again with his grip on its bridle. He was staggering too, and the horse plunged dangerously. Emel reached up instead, grabbing the queen's arm and dragging her down, swinging her around, away from the hooves. The horse bolted, swerved one way and another, and vanished from sight. A lot of people were shouting—Jenna was almost sure a lot of people were shouting—there was a huge, roaring tumult, men shouting and screaming and the clash of metal, and nothing made *sense*—

"Jenna!" Emel shouted to her, and grabbed her arm the way he'd grabbed the queen, hauling them both sideways, hard, dragging them with him.

Even stunned as she was, Jenna had a flashing thought that this was the first time he'd called her just by name with no title or anything. Then, under the pressing urgency of everything else, the thought disappeared. She let Niah take Inana—the queen was determined—and tried to cooperate with Emel, since he seemed to have some idea what was going on, or at least was *really clear* about what direction he wanted them to go.

Horn notes lifted above the clamor, and men on horses thundered past, not very close but not *so* far away, and suddenly, as though the world snapped itself into focus, the situation sorted itself out so that Jenna understood where they were and what was happening. This was a battle, they were in a battle—or not really *in* a battle, actually, kind of *adjacent* to a battle. *Way* too close, but not actually surrounded by fighting soldiers or in immediate danger of being trampled or stabbed or whatever. But, yeah, a whole lot too close, and Emel was dragging them toward a … an overturned wagon, that was probably what it was, and oh, right, here was a road underfoot, she hadn't noticed because everything was so insane.

"That is Nolas-Kuomon," Emel said curtly, nodding to one side and another.

Not literally. Tenai was nowhere in sight. Black banners. That was what he meant. Long black banners streaming out in a sharp breeze. Not close, but closer than any other company of soldiers. That was probably good, though … yeah, when one of those companies suddenly peeled off and thundered right toward them, it didn't feel exactly good.

Niah pulled away from Emel, handed her daughter back to Jenna, raised her chin, and stepped out in front of them all, clear of the dubious shelter of the upturned wagon. Wow. Jenna was impressed, even though she'd already realized that Niah was no pushover once she got going. She held Inana tightly, though she wasn't sure what she could do if those men didn't turn out to be friendly. Something. If she had to. They were Tenai's men—or working with Tenai, or—Jenna wasn't sure, that was the truth. Inana clung to her just as tightly, not fussing, her eyes huge as she twisted around, staring at everything. Not crying or screaming, which was pretty amazing for a kid as little as Inana. Jenna murmured to her, wordlessly, hoping those *weren't* enemies.

But, no, it looked like those soldiers were drawing up after all, some of them swinging out to each side, surrounding the wagon—but wheeling their horses, too, facing outward, taking a defensive stance, not a threatening one.

One of the men, not the banner-carrier, a different man, plainly the officer in command, rode out from the rest and swung down from his horse, nodding respectfully to Niah. "Queen of Talasayan," he said to her—so he knew who she was, probably who they all were. He went on. "I am Nuan Geraimani-na. Nolas-Kuomon has directed me to take you into my care. Have no fear. I will deal with you courteously."

Niah's manner had already been stiff. Jenna didn't think hearing the young man's name helped at all, despite the officer's civilized manner. If anything, the queen's manner became more glacial still. Emel had also gone still in a different way. Frightened, both of them—or at least not sure what this officer might do, even if he did seem polite so far. Jenna sort of remembered hearing the name Geraimani. Ambitious Imbaneh-se family, she was pretty sure that was it. She studied the young officer. He did seem faintly familiar. After a second, she decided she might recognize him. She thought possibly this was the young man who had been present with Tenai when she and Emel had first found her in the midst of the Imbaneh-se encampment. She wasn't sure. But she thought so.

Whoever he was, Nuan Geraimani-na nodded to Jenna too. "Nola," he said in the same respectful tone. "Nolas-Kuomon directs that you be taken back beyond the lines and made safe; your hurts tended and all your needs supplied." He added to Emel, "Can you ride?"

Turning, Jenna stared at Emel. She had not had even a second to realize this before, but *now* she could see he had the broken-off stub of a crossbow bolt sticking out of his abdomen, low down, just above the hip. She set her teeth against an exclamation. She remembered now that she'd thought he'd been struck, just before Tenai pulled them out. Then in all the confusion she'd forgotten, and he hadn't seemed hurt, not when he was dragging her and Niah around. But that didn't look good. That was definitely not a good place to get shot.

"I can ride, Nolas-e," Emel said stiffly.

Jenna had her doubts about that, but the officer studied him and said, "I think you will do. This will be only a short distance. A sorcerer will attend you as swiftly as may be." He raised his hand for horses to be brought up, and issued rapid commands that Jenna couldn't follow. She wasn't really trying to follow them. She was trying to figure out how badly Emel was hurt—from the solid way he stood, either the wound wasn't that bad or else he wanted people to think it wasn't that bad.

And besides that, she was trying to see if she could spot Tenai anywhere. And besides *that,* though she knew it was stupid, she was trying to spot her father, even though she knew he wouldn't be anywhere *near* this battlefield. She knew that. But she couldn't help but look.

Someone had brought her a horse. Niah was already mounted, so Jenna handed Inana up to her mother, then turned and lifted herself into the saddle. Then watched narrowly to be sure someone helped Emel, who was definitely not going to be leaping on and off horses with a crossbow bolt stuck in his abdomen like that. She didn't plan to let him try, even if he were stubborn enough to want to make the attempt … no, good, the officer, Nuan Geraimani, was gesturing to a couple of sturdy-looking soldiers to help. Emel let them help, too, which said a lot about that injury.

The day seemed to have gone on forever, though when she looked at the sun, she estimated it probably wasn't much past two in the afternoon, something like that. She really, really hoped it was getting pretty close to over.

Nuan Geraimani took them to a tent back some distance from the battle. Just a handful of tents had been set up here. At the moment, no one seemed to be anywhere nearby. A command post, maybe, but if so abandoned now because everyone had gone forward. The battle itself wasn't so far distant the clamor was completely inaudible, but just about far enough that Jenna wouldn't have known what she was hearing, if she hadn't known what she was hearing. The banner outside the tent was black, which was probably good. Jenna flinched from the candles and bowls and things on the table, but at least there were chairs and cushions and other ordinary things, and no obvious threats of any kind.

Jenna helped Emel sit down—by this time, he either wasn't trying to hide how badly he was hurt, or else he couldn't. He'd gone as pale as a guy with his coloring could, a sort of greenish shade, and his jaw was visibly clenched. She sat on the edge of the table so that she could hold his hand, not caring if he felt it hurt his pride or something. He didn't seem to be too worried about that, actually, and gripped her hand back so hard it hurt. Jenna didn't protest or pull away, only held on harder herself. She was positive he was hurt a lot worse than he pretended.

"The sorcerer will be here at once," Nuan told Emel, told them all. Then he addressed Niah. "We have no women to attend you, Niah Madalan Kuyad-sa, for which I ask your forgiveness. I give you my personal assurance that my soldiers will conduct themselves respectfully. Forgive me if I do not remain. My duties call me away."

"Yes," Niah said. She had not settled into a chair, but she had finally lowered Inana to stand rather than keeping her daughter in her arms. She held Inana's hand about as tightly as Jenna held Emel's, but Inana clung to her mother and didn't make a sound. Her eyes were still huge. What a thing to put a kid through. Jenna hoped she'd get over it. What a *risk* they'd all taken, hauling a baby like Inana through all this craziness.

Then Jenna had to stop and remember why they'd all taken that kind of risk, because Niah asked, her voice soft but steady, "How's goes the battle, if I may ask, Nolas-e? May I ask regarding Keitah Terusai-e and regarding my husband?"

The young man hesitated. "Peculiarly," he said at last. "Nolas-Kuomon's strategy is …" he opened a hand and shrugged. "Perhaps not entirely as expected. What the day will bring, neither I nor any man can say. But, as you ask, I will say this much: my belief is that Terusai-e may not have anything as he would wish, regardless of the rest. I believe—I may be mistaken. But I believe perhaps Nolas-Kuomon means that he should not leave this field."

Niah gave a small, regal nod.

Nuan added kindly, "The king of Talasayan had not taken the field when last I saw. If I have word of him, I will send to you."

"Yes," Niah whispered. "Thank you, Nolas-e."

The officer inclined his head and went out, brushing the tent flap back. Jenna heard him speak to someone there—guards, maybe—but maybe just the sorcerer, who came in hardly a heartbeat later. She ought to look out and see if soldiers did stand outside the tent, just to know, but she would have had to let go of Emel's hand. She stayed where she was.

The sorcerer, when he arrived, proved to be an older man, carrying a tray cluttered with candles and knives and bowls and all sorts of things. His blood-spattered clothing and his harassed look made it clear he'd been working for some time to heal wounded men, which was reassuring in a way, but brought home the reality of that battle out there in a way that, honestly, nothing really had until that moment.

The sorcerer nodded to Niah and Jenna without really seeming to notice them. Most of his attention was on Emel. He gave him a long, assessing look and a curt nod. "Good sense, leaving the head in, but you'll be cut to pieces in there. Next time, make them bring a litter."

"This is assuredly good advice," Emel answered. No doubt that meant he didn't plan to take it. Jenna made a mental note to talk to him about stupid male posturing, sometime when they had the leisure for it.

The sorcerer probably heard that answer the same way Jenna had, because he snorted. But he also drew a knife and began cutting away Emel's shirt. "Not so very deep," he observed. "You were lucky in the angle. The head is right up against the bone."

"I know."

"If you know such things from the feel of the wound, you have taken too many wounds in your life." The sorcerer's tone was dry. "I advise you set your foot on a different road, soldier, before you find this one shorter than you might prefer. Now, let us see what we have here." He touched the end of the crossbow bolt lightly, which made Emel draw in a breath and then set his jaw. The sorcerer nodded. He turned to the side, lit a candle with a gesture, and picked up a knife with a thin handle and narrow, angular blade—more like a scalpel than a regular knife.

Jenna had to look away after that. She heard Emel's breath hiss between his teeth, but by the time she could bring herself to look again, the previously white candle had turned red, the broken bolt was lying discarded on the table, and the wound itself was closed, looking a lot like an injury taken a week or ten days ago.

"Well done. Good. Wound fever should not trouble you," the sorcerer said, pressing lightly around the wound in a way that made Emel hiss between his teeth. The sorcerer didn't seem displeased by that, though. He nodded, straightening. "This will do, I think. In four days, five, if the wound troubles you, find a sorcerer whom you trust enough that the healing may proceed more efficaciously. But I think you did well enough."

"I think few of your patients need trouble themselves to seek a second sorcerer," Emel said, his tone hard to read. "Thank you for your care."

The sorcerer clapped Emel on the shoulder, smiling for the first time. "The ones that live, generally not. You'll do, soldier." He took the time to look Jenna and Niah and Inana each over with a swift abstraction that suggested that if none of them was injured, he was not remotely interested in any of them. Then he picked up his tray and walked out.

"A very good battlefield sorcerer," Emel murmured, gazing after the man. "The kind who cares far more for the sorcery he works than for his patients."

"That's a good thing?"

Emel smiled. "Anyone may trust him; enemy soldiers as well as those belonging to his own lord. He cares nothing for the battle and everything for the art."

"Oh." Jenna filed that away. That was definitely a new take on bedside manner, but it sort of made sense. Emel certainly looked better. Especially, well, never mind. Maybe someone would bring him a new shirt eventually. She looked away, at Niah and Inana. Then she hopped off the table and crossed the tent. "Hey," she said, as reassuringly as she could. "It's all right. I'm sure it will be, anyway. You're here, you're safe, and you heard what that officer said—whatever happens, probably Keitah's finished."

And if Keitah Terusai-e died out there on that battlefield, Jenna herself might be partly responsible for that. What a strange idea. She wasn't sure she liked it. Despite everything, she was pretty sure she didn't. She shook that thought away and said instead, "You're fine, Inana's fine, we're safe. Here, sit down." She coaxed Niah into a chair so that Inana could crawl into her mother's lap. There. That would be better for both of them.

Niah permitted herself to be coaxed and folded her daughter in her arms, but she also murmured, "The Geraimani are here. I have no doubt Kuanonai Geraimani-e is here himself. He is my husband's enemy—all the Geraimani are my husband's enemies—"

"Nuan seemed nice enough."

"He is a *Geraimani!*"

The queen's voice had risen, not to hysteria or anything, but she was obviously upset. Jenna answered in the firmest tone she could manage. "Don't *worry,* Niah—Tenai's working *with* Mitereh. She really is. Everything's *fine.* Tenai can handle whoever else is here." She looked at Emel. "She can, right?"

Emel had gathered up the pieces of his shirt. It was really too torn up to be worth messing with. He must have decided that too, because he sighed and sat down again, still shirtless. He said, "Nola Jenna, I have no doubt she can do so." Then he added to Niah, "She bade Kuanonai Geraimani-e to come and go, not many days gone. I witnessed this myself. This is *Nolas-Kuomon,* Lord Death's *own lady.* Kuanonai will not lightly gainsay her—and if he does, his own men must hesitate to take his orders over hers. I do not doubt that half the men on that field were at Antiatan. They know well that the black banner she raises up is not hers alone. It belongs to Lord Death. Those who oppose her ride under that doom. Kuanonai is not Encormio, to drive men against Lord Death's lady."

Niah looked at him. Then she raised her chin slightly. "You were there yourself."

"I was. Very few men who rode with *or* against Nolas-Kuomon in those dark days would wish to do so again. I am very certain. If any man would dare, it would be Sandakan Gutai-e—and today, he will be dancing *with* the dark lady on that battlefield. Ambitious the Geraimani may be, and all Imbaneh-se may be ambitious, but when they see the black banner set itself beside Talasayan's banner, that will end the day. You heard that Geraimani officer own Nolas-Kuomon and not his own lord when he gathered us up."

Niah thought about this for a little while. After some time, she said, not a question, *"You* are Terusai. If Keitah does not live through the day, you are Terusai-e. He has no heir that would stand before a brother."

"That is not my name," Emel answered firmly. "Not for many years. I belong to Nolas-Kuomon now, and to Nola Jenna, and take my honor from them and not from Terusai."

Niah did not look away from him, but he didn't lower his gaze either. Jenna cleared her throat so they would both look at her. "Okay!" she said in her brightest tone. "I'm going to peek out and see what's going on."

Both Niah and Emel straightened in alarm. "Soldiers will have been set to guard this tent," Emel warned her.

"Then maybe they'll *know what's going on*," Jenna said. "I'll ask them!" She jumped to her feet, but she didn't head for the tent flap after all, because all of a sudden there was a lot of noise out there—horses, mainly, and a few voices, indistinguishable, but mostly in the short, choppy tones of people giving orders.

And Tenai's voice too, sharp and decisive.

Hardly a heartbeat later, she swept the entry back and strode in. At once, the spacious tent seemed far smaller, and, oddly, darker—as though every shadow darkened and stretched out. Men were with her, Jenna was aware of that, but they seemed small and insignificant, as though Tenai were a towering black flame and everyone else dim by comparison.

Her gaze flicked across the tent, taking them all in, Emel,

Niah, Inana, Jenna, flick flick flick, without registering much of a reaction. She said curtly, to someone or everyone, "Enough. Obey my orders now or later, but now would be simpler for us all, Geraimani-e. I will come shortly, and expect to find all arranged according to my command."

Jenna realized that the other Geraimani, the lord of that name, must be here. Kuanonai. Oh, yes, there he was, with a look of balked fury that was actually just the same as last time. Oh, and Nuan had come in with Tenai too—Jenna hadn't realized that either. Even after she'd spotted them, Tenai still drew the eye so strongly that Jenna could barely focus on either of the Geraimani even when she made a deliberate effort to do it. If she hadn't been making that kind of effort, she wouldn't have seen Nuan lay his hand on the older man's arm and draw him back and away.

Even the other time, in the other camp, when Tenai had ordered Kuanonai Geraimani-e out of her presence, she hadn't looked like this, *felt* like this, radiated this cold ferocity. Jenna realized she was holding her breath only because her chest began to ache. She exhaled as quietly as she could, afraid to draw attention.

No matter how unobtrusive she had tried to be, Tenai's attention came to her instantly.

Tenai did not speak or smile. She said to Jenna, her tone hardly warmer than when she had spoken to Kuanonai, "Well done. Very well done. By means of your courage, you set Terusai-e into my hands—and now Mitereh is in my hands as well. Excellently done."

"Um. Um …" Jenna was having trouble responding to that. "Right, Tenai, so, I bet Niah would really like to go home."

"I have no doubt of it," Tenai responded, smiling. "Perhaps she may. Who can say what chances may lie before us?"

That smile was not friendly, or kind, or even amused. Tenai was not exactly a demonstrative person, but this … this was different. "Tenai …" Jenna said. "Are you all right?"

That drew a long look. "Of course," Tenai said, her tone dismissive. "Have no concern. My lord is ascendant. Today, his shadow falls across all the world. None shall gainsay his will, or mine. No man anywhere would dare raise his hand against you or to your father now, nor against any other life I claim for my own. You have nothing to fear."

Jenna hesitated. "Okay. Ah ..."

From outside, someone shouted, and someone else answered. Jenna couldn't make out any words, maybe because it was so hard to pay attention to anyone but Tenai, but Tenai turned her head. She ordered impatiently, "Stay here." Then, turning, she walked out.

Jenna let out her breath with a whoosh, only then realizing she had started holding her breath again. That had been ... a very strange ninety seconds. And very uncomfortable. Tenai had looked at her without exactly *seeing* her, not really, or that's what it had seemed like. Plus she'd looked at Niah the way she might have looked at ... a prize she had won. All that had been bad enough. But Tenai hadn't glanced at Emel at all. Somehow that had been worse. As though she expected that naturally men would be hurt and maybe die in her service and she didn't care. As though she wouldn't even *notice*.

She said to Emel, her voice a little shaky, "So ... I thought ... I didn't think ... I thought that was Tenai, at first. But I guess maybe that was actually *Nolas-Kuomon*."

"Yes," he said, not quite meeting her eyes. "Yes, Nola Jenna. I fear that was indeed Nolas-Kuomon."

"Wow." Jenna was silent for a moment. She'd never exactly understood the story of Antiatan before. She thought maybe she understood something about that now.

The woman she'd known all her life had been her father's friend and Mitereh's ally. Even right before opening the veil to send Jenna and Emel across the miles to Kinabana, Tenai had been herself. Or mostly. She had been *recognizable*. Now ...

Oh. *Oh*. Jenna had thought Apana Pelat's sacrifice was the worst thing she'd ever seen, would ever have to see. *Now* she thought it had been *even worse than that*. The shadow of that sacrifice seemed to her now to lie, long and endlessly dark, between the woman she had known all her life and the woman who had just stepped into this tent, frozen Jenna's heart with that cold ferocity, and walked out again. Between Tenai, who was almost an ordinary woman, and Nolas-Kuomon, Lord Death's lady.

22

Daniel rode beside Mitereh through the last of the afternoon sun, down the sloping city streets, through the white court and outer city and across the torn earth where armies had so recently marched and fought, toward the ranked presence of the Imbanehse army.

The army was quite a distance from the city's walls; he didn't know what tactical or political considerations were responsible for that. There was a great black tent foremost, with an austere black standard before it; he did not need to ask whether that was their destination. Off to the side, the Talasayan army was furling its banners and filing in order back into the city. Daniel wondered what the men thought about their orders—how many knew what the plan actually was? Any of them? What was the emotional cost, to shutting up and soldiering on while your commanding officers acted like lunatics?

Probably he should be planning what to say to Tenai, what to ask her, how to figure out what was going on in her head, how to help her straighten things out if he had to. He didn't find himself up to the effort. Which might be just as well: too many expectations and you'd start to miss the signals you actually got in real-time. He sighed.

"I think," Mitereh said to him, in a slightly hesitant tone as though not quite certain his comment would be welcome, "I think you, at least, have little need to fear. I think Chaisa-e will not find in her heart a need for *your* death, Danyel."

Daniel couldn't believe she would, either, but—"That's not actually the point," he said slowly, finding the words as he sorted out his thoughts. "The point is ... if she needs *your* death, then she's not ... well. And I thought she was. Environmental cues, I suppose. Put people back in a screwed-up situation they'd got out of and you can just watch them get screwed up all over again ... I thought, when I saw Tenai in Chaisa, and then later with you, even in Nerinesir ... I thought she was past that risk. Guess I was wrong."

"You are seldom wrong?"

"Oh ... about as often as anybody, I guess. It doesn't usually come with quite so large a price tag."

Mitereh's mouth crooked upward in a wry smile.

Yes, Daniel thought: the king, young as he was, would know all about price tags. "So ... you know for sure that my daughter is safe?"

"A day past ... two days, now ... I knew so." The king gave him a sidelong glance. "I was sorry I could not tell you."

Daniel was sorry about that, too. "I'm grateful to know it now." They were coming up on that black tent rather more quickly now; Daniel estimated they would arrive at it just about with the last of the light. And what would they find there? He both longed for and dreaded their arrival, both emotions so strong that he barely had time to notice the growing shadows, which was a small mercy, as he did not look forward to being out in the open countryside in the dark.

The ranked tents of the Imbaneh-se army looked a lot more extensive and worlds more intimidating from this close distance. Fires burned in the dark: neat small fires arranged in precise rows. Did that precision comfort the men whose lives were wrapped up in the military? Or was it just meant to daunt their enemies?

There were sentries: Daniel jumped at the hail, though he supposed he should have expected it. Of course an army would set men to watch what their enemies might do. And it wasn't like their approach had been at all secretive. Should they have had a white flag or something? Because they didn't. Daniel wondered what the chances were that they were about to get shot full of crossbow bolts.

Mitereh did not even twitch. He rode forward a few more

measured strides and drew his horse to a halt where the red light of the sunset could most clearly reveal his face. He said in a level voice, "Inform Nolas-Kuomon I would trouble her for a moment of her time, should she have the leisure."

There was a pause while the sentries looked at each other. One of them withdrew. The other came forward and laid a deferential hand on the bridle of Mitereh's horse. No one offered to shoot anybody. Mitereh asked the sentry, his tone merely conversational, "Whom do you own, man, if I may ask?"

It took Daniel a moment to remember how these people used that word, that phrase. Then he was as interested in the answer as Mitereh. The sentry met the king's eyes, startled, then glanced down. Then he lifted his gaze again and admitted, "One hardly knows, o king. Bedukayan Simpanar-e holds my oath, yet I confess I believe my orders now come from Nolas-Kuomon, who commanded that the king of Talasayan should be passed through to her unharmed if he should come to speak with her."

"This is a difficult time," Mitereh commented.

The sentry turned his free hand palm up and bowed his head in agreement. The other man came back then and nodded, and the first man released the king's horse and turned to walk before them to the black tent. Men turned and watched, but there was no show about it, nothing like the pageants everyone had arranged for important events in previous days. Daniel couldn't tell what Mitereh thought of their reception.

The tent was a big one—imposing, with heavy black spars like whale ribs, or so Daniel imagined, supporting great sheets of canvas pegged down with what appeared to be wrought iron stakes the size of swords. The tent had a high awning over the door, supported by black wooden pillars more than a foot in diameter and carved with deep spiral grooves. The black standard was on a lance set into the ground on one side of this awning. It snapped in the sharp breeze off the mountains with a sound like the crack of a whip.

Within the black tent, porcelain lamps cast a soft glow over rugs and hangings that were, thank God, not black—cream-colored, and blue and green. On the inside, the spars that supported the tent were white, and not only lanterns but also glittering crystal candelabra hung from them. There was plenty of room in the tent's single room for your average performance of *Henry IV,* but in fact the room was empty save for a single heavy, ornate chair and, hard against the far side of the tent, what appeared to be a small black stone table or altar.

In the chair, of course, sat Tenai.

She filled the eye like a flame in the dark, like a falcon cutting in swift flight through an empty sky, like a stroke of lighting striking through a storm. For the first time, Daniel saw, looking at her, an echo in her dark eyes of a greater darkness: of the limitless darkness of Death's kingdom. No wonder, then ... no wonder her eyes, her face, had always held such power. Even that slight echo was enough to lend her gaze a compelling strength that was simply and truly other than human.

Her gaze, now, was fixed steadily on Mitereh. So fierce was that opaque stare that it was virtually impossible to look away from her. Mitereh met her eyes and held them, a tactic that might not be wise. But he could scarcely do otherwise, Daniel supposed; he was, after all, a king. Tenai did not seem even to notice Daniel. She looked only at the king: a dangerous and disturbing fixation that did not offer a promising way to help her remember that sixteen years had passed since her war had ended. He made himself look around, to see what, if anything, might be surmised from what, or who, might be present.

In fact, hardly anyone else was in the tent: only behind Tenai and to one side stood Niah, with Inana in her arms—was their presence meant as a reassurance or a threat? Daniel wanted to believe the former, but suspected the latter. Inana wiggled impatiently, and the queen shifted her to her other hip. There was another young woman by the queen's side, whom at first Daniel barely noticed. Emel stood behind the women, and it was his presence that first brought Daniel's eye back to that young woman.

He stared. Then, dismissing any possible considerations of protocol and tactics, he crossed the room in a dozen strides and folded his daughter into a hard embrace.

Jenna put her arms around him, too, and tucked her head down against his chest like a child. He thought—he was afraid—she might be crying, and when he pushed her back to arm's length and looked anxiously into her face, she *was* crying, but she was also laughing. "You're all right," he said, with such an profound depth of relief he could hardly speak. "Thank God. Oh, thank God." And, involuntarily, "What did you do to your *hair?*"

Jenna laughed out loud and hugged him again; he found, with a slight shock, that she was very nearly as tall as he was. He had known that, and yet in this moment it still came as a shock. She said, "Don't you think it suits me? I was in disguise. The dye doesn't come off no matter what you do—and there's nothing for the length but to let it grow out again." She spoke quickly and cheerfully, but with a tiny tremor in her voice that suggested something other than cheer. Daniel thought he caught the slightest flick of his daughter's eyes toward Tenai.

She went on rapidly, with that same deliberate cheerfulness, "Are you okay? I was so worried about you—because I knew you'd be so worried about me. But I knew you had to be all right really, because you were with Mitereh and I knew, I *knew* you wouldn't do anything stupid no matter what Keitah threatened—you didn't, did you? No, of course you didn't, or Mitereh'd be dead, wouldn't he?" And she sent a swift blazing smile across the tent at the king, whose mouth crooked up just a little.

"Stupid is arguable," said Daniel, aware that his insouciant young daughter was in fact deliberately trying to lighten the atmosphere—to draw Tenai out of that dangerous mood, to get her off her current fix on Mitereh. He was immensely proud of her, even in the midst of his terror. He said, keeping half an eye on Tenai himself, "But I tried not to do anything ..." *immoral* sounded so priggish—"... permanent."

"Oh." Jenna looked suddenly solemn. "Permanent."

Daniel turned to Tenai. She was indeed watching them. Her attention had been pulled off Mitereh, very good; he would have gone to Jenna anyway, but the impulse had evidently been good tactics as well as irresistible. Tenai now looked serious, but not angry: the fire banked, or just hidden? He said, "Thank you for taking care of her for me."

Tenai made a little gesture with one hand, like throwing something away. "I ... hardly did that, Daniel. Rather the opposite. She quite ably took care of herself, I believe."

Jenna said quickly, "Emel took care of me."

The big man looked like he was prepared to object, and Jenna gave him a stern look and said, "Oh, all right—we took care of each other, then." She turned back to Daniel. "He was wonderful. Don't let him tell you otherwise."

When Daniel caught Emelan's eye, the man looked away at once, flushing. Daniel felt his eyebrows lift.

"And will you also disclaim responsibility for my wife?" Mitereh asked Tenai softly. It was the first time he'd spoken to her: was it Daniel's imagination, or was that a dark glitter of anger that entered her eyes at the mere sound of his voice?

"She saved herself, too," Jenna told him, with a quick sidelong look at the queen. "At the end. She was really brave."

Niah flushed and lowered her gaze. Inana wiggled in her arms, but the queen murmured to her daughter and the child quieted. Niah had not tried to go to her husband: why not? She did not set the child down to run to him: again, why not? Daniel tried to study Tenai without being caught looking worried.

"But it was Tenai's idea, how to get her out," added Jenna. "It was ... it was clever, I guess." She sounded doubtful about this, and her eyes flicked to Daniel's with unspoken emphasis.

Daniel wondered just what Tenai had done, and just how awful it had been, and just how far it might go toward explaining the change he saw in her. But Jenna was going on quickly, "Keitah was just horrible to Niah, you know." Was there a faint emphasis on Keitah's name? As though she wanted Mitereh to know that

Tenai hadn't been? Or to be sure Tenai knew Jenna expected better things from her?

Mitereh gave Jenna a bare nod. He didn't even glance at his wife, but only came a step closer to Tenai. "Then I am indebted to you for your care of her."

"Are you?" said Tenai, consideringly. There was nothing easy or friendly in her manner now. She looked at the king with ... not obvious rage, but with the same cold edge of hostility she'd shown in the field during the denouement with Keitah.

"Am I not? Is she not safe in your care, Chaisa?"

Tenai settled back in her chair, gazing without expression at the king. "She is quite safe. And the child."

"I am glad to take your word," said Mitereh. "Should I not then be grateful?" He paused. "And I? For I see I have offended you, Chaisa. Tell me, then, what is my offense? Have I not played my role as necessary? Have you not done the same?" Or had she stopped playing a role and made it real; Daniel got that question, not quite asked, with no trouble.

Though there was no obvious shift of muscle, no clear change in position, nevertheless Tenai's whole manner seemed to darken, to become colder. "Encormio-na. Dare you ask me?"

Mitereh glanced down, seeming to gather himself. He looked up again. "Do you—" he stopped. Daniel wondered what he'd been about to say, what question he'd restrained himself from asking. His expression was calm, but ... that hesitancy in his manner was very unlike him.

A sudden minor commotion from outside, and whatever the king might have said was interrupted. Daniel didn't know the man who erupted into the tent. He was a big, heavyset man: forceful and harsh-featured. The kind of man who might well tend to try to overawe his opponents rather than persuade them: surely a man used to being in charge. And men behind him, Imbaneh-se soldiers—officers, Daniel revised his initial impression. Few of them young. Senior officers. His estimation of the newcomer rose. He guessed this must be one of the infamous Geraimani.

"Encormio-na," the man said harshly to Mitereh.

Mitereh was standing very still. He answered this hail with a frigid inclination of his head. "Kuanonai Geraimani-e. I see, to my astonishment, that you have learned to take lightly the oaths you once swore."

Kuanonai's head lifted proudly, angrily; his lip curled. "A forced oath is no oath at all."

"Was your oath to me forced? I confess I do not remember so." Though Mitereh spoke to Kuanonai, his attention was almost entirely on Tenai. She said nothing. She remained tightly focused on the king; she might not have even noticed the arrival of the Imbaneh-se people.

Mitereh turned his shoulder to Kuanonai Geraimani-e, took a step closer to Tenai, and said in a low voice, "And *your* oath, Chaisa-e? I believed you swore freely. I pressed you to swear to me, I acknowledge that, but I had no possible way to force that oath. All the choices then were yours; did I not say so? And so it is again tonight: you hold every choice in your hands."

Tenai rose. The sense of danger in the tent increased. Mitereh did not move, but everyone else drew back. Daniel found himself tucking his daughter closer to his side. Niah edged a step closer to him on his other side: taking him for a source of protection or merely seeking human contact.

Tenai's sword was in her hand, though Daniel hadn't seen her draw it. It did not glint in the lantern light. Its dull blackness was an emptiness into which light was simply absorbed. Daniel swallowed, aware of Jenna's stillness beside him.

Tenai's eyes met Mitereh's. Hers were cold, opaque, secretive. Daniel could not see the king's face, but his shoulders had stiffened.

Her hand moved. The sword drifted down, lightly, until it rested at the base of Mitereh's throat. He did not step away, but his head tipped back, and Daniel saw the movement of his throat as he swallowed.

"Encormio-na," Tenai said. Expressionlessly. "I would have

you humbled. I would have you kneeling at my feet."

There was a pause. It lengthened. Finally the king said, "You are aware, Nolas-Kuomon, I cannot."

At Daniel's side, Niah flinched and made a small sound, barely audible, and Daniel put an arm around her shoulders as though she were also his daughter. She was shivering, fine tremors that did not show; she clung to her little girl as though to an anchor. One point of surety in a world of storm: Daniel understood that, oh, yes. He wanted to speak, he wanted to say something useful, something that would *work*, something that would defuse the moment. He couldn't think of anything at all, and his mouth was too dry to speak anyway.

But Tenai did not thrust her sword forward. She did not move at all for a long moment. Then, though she did not sheathe her sword, she shifted it to rest point-down on the floor of the tent. Her expression was odd, combining hostility with a kind of arctic amusement that owed very little to humor. She demanded, "What would you have of me, Mitereh Encormio-na?"

The king opened a hand, palm up. "Your good will, Nolas-Kuomon."

She laughed briefly.

"Peace, then."

Tenai shook her head—which was not, Daniel thought, a refusal or denial. That gesture was something else: wonder or mockery. Or self-mockery. She said, "Is that what you ask?"

Mitereh answered with some intensity, "I have had your oath before now, Nolas-Kuomon. You gave me that. Will you not keep it?"

"Hah." Tenai studied the young man, so like her ... in stillness, in presence, in features, but there was nothing in him of her cold anger. Against his steady calm, the edge of that anger seemed blunted.

And the Imbaneh-se general must have sensed that too: the slipping away of the moment, the loss of opportunity. He moved, a long smooth stride, snatched Tenai's black sword from her, and pivoted to aim a powerful blow against Mitereh's side and chest.

Tenai shouted with outrage and fury; but too late. There was no blood. But the sword had cut deep into Mitereh's chest, and the king's body was folding up around that dark blade in a way that was horribly familiar. Around the edges of Daniel's vision, shadows began to creep and expand.

Without even thinking, because there was no time for thought, Daniel threw himself forward and caught Mitereh's wrist in a hard grip.

The world twisted around the two of them, and they stood on a wide, dark plain of ice: a darkling plain, Daniel thought, and wondered for an instant from what sources poets drew their inspiration. Above was an infinite starless desolation; around them, nothing; before them, an unornamented gate of cold black iron, set between pillars of black stone. Beyond that gate, nothing visible. Before it, patient and terrible, Lord Death.

Mitereh, beside Daniel, shuddered violently. Daniel glanced at him quickly, but the young man's expression, as befitted a king, was calm. He gave Daniel a wry sidelong look, opened a hand in a gesture of resignation, drew breath to speak, and then evidently could think of nothing to say.

Daniel understood the feeling. What *was* there to say? And where was there to go, but forward?

Lord Death, standing before his gate, bent his gaze on them as they approached. His face was almost like the face of a man, but his hollow eyes seemed to open into infinite depths.

Mitereh bowed low. Then, straightening, he spoke clearly. "So your hand has touched my heart, o Death, and I am come into your kingdom."

Indeed. And is it now *my* good will you desire? asked Lord Death. His voice struck heavily through the perfect silence of his dark kingdom like the tolling of a great bell.

Mitereh didn't try to answer that. He dropped to one knee and bowed his head.

Daniel said, "He was never Tenai's enemy, you know." Those

terrible eyes turned to him, and he went on quickly, "And you said ... you did say I might ask you for one more favor."

You ask for his life? said Lord Death. **Not for your own?**

That might indeed, Daniel realized, count as two favors. His heart sank. He said slowly, "You said you owed me another favor. But if it's owed ... if it's earned, is it a favor at all?"

Do you debate me? asked Lord Death.

He might have been amused, or offended, or utterly unmoved; Daniel could not tell. "No, Lord," Daniel said at once. "I would not ... I don't think I would dare. I only ask. Knowing you will bestow what favors you will, for whatever reasons you will. Or ... or not."

"Be generous, o Death, and spare the innocent," said Mitereh in a low voice.

I am often suspected of a capacity for generosity, answered Lord Death. There was nothing generous in that ice-hard face. He moved a hand to rest on the back of the young king's bowed head.

Mitereh shuddered under that touch. He did not look up. But he said in a voice that was only a little unsteady at the end, "Because sometimes you are indeed generous, Lord. I was fairly struck by the dark sword, but this man is here in your kingdom only because, trusting your word, he cast himself forward into your hand for my sake. Will you not be gracious now and open your hand for him?"

Perhaps I may. And do you ask that I open my hand for *you*, Encormio-na?

Mitereh answered, "Before God all things are small, and the sufferings of men are transient. But I am only a man, and to me small things are great, and the years seem long."

Ah, the length of years! said Lord Death, with dark irony. He shifted restlessly, lifting his hand.

"Without Mitereh in her life, I don't know that Tenai will ever move past her long hatred of Encormio," said Daniel, slowly. "Because how will she ever decide to choose a path that doesn't include that hatred, that rage? It's the choice that matters. She ... I thought she had made it, but I think now she will have to choose again. And again, until her mind and soul have beaten a broad path through the dark so that she no longer has to fight ..." he tangled in his metaphor and stopped.

Lord Death turned his head, settling his attention on Daniel. It was like having the weight of a mountain come down on you. Daniel almost thought he could feel his bones creak under that strain. He said with an effort, "She's my friend, and ... and my patient, I guess, in a way, even now. She's strong, but I want her to be well as well as strong. I want her to be happy. I don't know what she is to you. Or what you want for her. Or what moves you to be generous."

There was a long silence. Lord Death considered him. Bent his head to study Mitereh, kneeling in proud supplication at his feet. He said at length, **As you ask me, Daniel, I shall spare Mitereh Encormio-na. To please my lady, I shall spare you. If you choose. There is the Gate: you may pass through it and find there the greater kingdom. Or turn, and I shall permit you to return once again to the country of the ephemeral day.** Stepping aside, he lifted a hand to indicate the wide gate.

Once attention had been drawn to it, that gate was compelling. Daniel set his teeth and thought of Jenna; he didn't know what Mitereh thought of. He again held the young king's wrist, and Mitereh gripped his; he did not know whether he helped Mitereh get to his feet and turn away from the gate which waited ajar, or whether the king rose and helped him. But they both turned. And were bracing each other, suddenly, amid the dazzling uncertainty of lantern-light and the disorienting shouts of men.

Jenna was screaming, Daniel heard that above all other sounds, and turned blindly toward her. His hands found her before his eyes had relearned how to focus in the light, and he clung to her, steadied by her very solidity.

Then, driven by a sense of urgency—though, for the first moment, he did not remember why he should feel that tense urgency—he looked for the king.

Mitereh was standing in the center of the tent, much as he had been standing before ... right, before the Imbaneh-se general had grabbed Tenai's sword and struck him. Right. Yes. Daniel shuddered helplessly, all that memory rising again, like a dark tide through his mind..

Tenai had the sword back in her own hand now, thank God, and she looked murderously ready to use it. The Imbaneh-se general, Kuanonai Geraimani-e, and his officers were standing very still, staring incredulously at Mitereh and at Daniel. Mitereh himself ... the king was gazing at his hands, turning them over and opening the fingers, as though taken aback by the miracle of living flesh. The light of the lamps gave his dark skin a warm cast.

Niah moved a step toward him, and stopped.

Mitereh looked up at his wife and smiled, a grave, tender smile. He walked forward and touched her cheek. Inana, who had been shocked still, tucked herself against his chest, and he bent his head low over hers and murmured something to her.

So it was the same for both of them, Daniel thought: family and child, and what's the gate of God's kingdom to that? Then Mitereh looked back toward Tenai, and Daniel was no longer sure of his conclusion, because that look held the same grave intensity the king had bent on his wife, though ... not the tenderness. Though no hostility, either. Nor even fear.

Mitereh gave his daughter back to Niah and turned to approach Tenai; he did not even glance at Geraimani-e, who had murdered him. Geraimani-e and the other Imbaneh-se officers regarded the king with disquiet. Mitereh did not speak.

Tenai gave a slight, impatient jerk of her hand. "I was at fault. I do acknowledge it."

"An unforeseen contingency," Mitereh answered. "For which I do not hold you to blame." He was silent again for a moment, then added, with a direct simplicity, "I had no choice but to ask for your oath. I still consider so. As the oath was given, I ask: will you not hold to it even now?"

There was another small silence. The king bowed his head, lifted his gaze again, and asked her, "Or shall I release you from it? I shall do so if you ask, only so you set the army raised up by Imbaneh-se into my hand."

Kuanonai Geraimani-e exclaimed wordlessly. Neither Tenai nor Mitereh seemed to notice. Both of them ignored everyone else. Tenai asked after a moment, "Was that a promise you gave my Lord Death? Was that the bargain you struck?"

"There was no bargain. Lord Death merely chose to open his hand. A grace freely offered. Shall I do less?"

"I confess I am astounded," Tenai said. She sheathed her dark sword, absently, and the tent seemed suddenly to grow a little brighter. It had been something to do for the slight delay it occasioned, Daniel surmised, because when the sword was sheathed she seemed, uncharacteristically, at something of a loss.

"The falcon is beautiful in flight," said Mitereh. "Jessed and hooded, it is less than a falcon. It must be set free if it is to fly." He asked again, "Shall I do less?"

"Can you do so much?" Tenai asked him.

"Do you ask it? Set the army you led against me into my hand, Chaisa-e, and I will have far less need to hold you. Do as I ask and I shall release you from your oath. I confess, I would prefer to let the oath stand. I ask that, Tenai Chaisa-e."

There was a pause.

Tenai said at last, "I will set Imbaneh-se into your hands, Mitereh. As for my oath ... I do not ask for you to release me from it. I hardly need to lay out every manner in which that might cause difficulty. No. Very well. Let it stand."

The Imbaneh-se general, Kuanonai Geraimani-e, made a low inarticulate sound and strode forward. He caught Tenai by the shoulder, spun her around to face him; a dangerous move, but Geraimani-e was too angry, Daniel thought, to be thinking of his own danger. There was nothing cold about *his* anger.

Tenai knocked the man's hand away, but she didn't hit him, a restraint which surprised Daniel immensely. Nor did she speak, but met his rage impassively.

"This is our moment!" the man said harshly. "This is our time! If Imbaneh-se fails now to break the grip of the Encormio line, it will never be broken, and we shall be subject forever!"

"Our?" said Tenai. "We?"

It took Kuanonai aback only for a second. Then he made a furious gesture and said violently, "You have taken my folk into your hand, you have spent their blood and made them yours; will you now cast them at the feet of this Encormio scion? The wave that bore you on has foundered, so you will leave all those carried by that wave stranded in your wake? Is this how Nolas-Kuomon acts toward those who have entered into peril in her service?"

"My service?" said Tenai. "You speak harshly to me, Kuanonai Geraimani-e, but is it not true that you meant me to serve as your tool, to use me to set Imbaneh-se free from a broken Talasayan? It is you who lifted your own banners and set mine before them. And after, what? A place of honor in your household? Was that your intention? I think not."

The big man opened his mouth, and shut it again. The force had not gone out of him, but it had damped down; he looked now more bleak than angry.

"But you took the banners," he said at last. "You led the men. You brought them here and made this battle serve your own purposes, whatever I meant to do; and now you will turn on them? And for what? For a place of honor in the household of this son of Encormio? Now, here, at this moment all the pieces are in your hands: look, he has put himself into your hands! And you will turn on *us?*" His voice rose in passionate disbelief, and Daniel winced.

"What was your own purpose?" Tenai demanded coldly.

"Freedom!" he shouted at her.

"An Encormio hegemony traded for a Terusai one?" said Tenai. "When you chose to align yourself with Keitah Terusai-e, did you believe he intended less? Did you tell yourself you believed that? An honest young man cast down in favor of one who spins his plans of treachery and betrayal across the wide span of years?

Well played, o Geraimani!"

"I could have handled Terusai-e. Do you think I did not know what he was?"

"And you would have handed Talasayan to him, even so," murmured Mitereh. His tone was one of wonder, and of condemnation.

The bigger man turned to face Mitereh directly. "My obligation is to Imbaneh-se."

"How simple that must make your life, Kuanonai Geraimani-e. Mine is to both Talasayan and Imbaneh-se."

There was a silence. "You don't mean that," Geraimani-e said at last. "You have always claimed so, but that has never been the truth. And if it was, you would still have no *right*."

"All kings become so because of conquest. Geraimani kings no less than any; you know the histories as well as I. How then is your right greater than mine? Because you are so wise you know men's hearts and God's intentions?" Mitereh's voice gained intensity, though he spoke no more loudly. "You would have swept both Imbaneh-se and Talasayan to war, Geraimani-e, and *for what?*"

"We would be free of *you,* Encormio-na!"

"*You* would raise up your banner. *You* would take and hold power, at the cost of raising up a treacherous king to rule Talasayan. I see that would have benefitted the *Geraimani*. I ask again, how would that benefit *your people?* Do you think *Imbaneh-se* would have done better with Keitah Terusai-e on the throne of Talasayan? I confess I do not see how that could be so." Mitereh waited, but this time Kuanonai Geraimani-e was not so quick to answer.

After a long moment, Mitereh turned to Tenai. He said quietly, "All the pieces are in your hands. Will you set this army gently into my hands, Nolas-Kuomon? Can you do so? Or must it be broken on the field? I confess I am sick to death of blood."

"I will set the men of Imbaneh-se into your hands, Mitereh Sekuse-go-e." Tenai lifted her hand as Geraimani-e made a wordless exclamation and moved sharply toward the door of the tent, pushing through the men he had brought with him. Though she had not called after him, the gesture alone stopped him, stopped all their confused movement.

Kuanonai turned, though with seeming reluctance, to face her. She had not drawn her sword, but she had her hand again on its hilt. She said, "You will not leave this tent before I give you leave to go, Geraimani-e. You will yield to me, or to Mitereh Sekuse-go-e, and you will not raise half this army to fight the other half. Can you not see that this struggle is ended?"

He looked at her, and now there was no mistaking the bleakness. He had lost, and knew it. Now it was only a question of whether he would try to pull as many of the rest of them down with him as he could.

One of the other Imbaneh-se officers said quietly, "We will yield." He was a dark young man, with sharply-cut features and a bitter, wry set to his mouth. It was the first time any of the other Imbaneh-se officers had said anything, which might have been why his words seemed to stand out as though he had shouted them.

Kuanonai Geraimani-e made a sharp, dismissive gesture, but he did not contradict the younger man. Nor did he turn again to stride out of the tent, though for a moment Daniel thought he would.

"Shall we face both Gutai-e and Nolas-Kuomon on this field?" asked the young man, speaking straight to Geraimani-e. There was a similarity to them, Daniel saw; not so much in any individual feature but in the impression given by the whole. Maybe a similarity of attitude, more than one of face or body. A son, a nephew, a cousin? It became plainer why the Imbaneh-se general had let this young man stop him.

The officer said, speaking now both to Kuanonai Geraimani-e and to Mitereh, "We have lost. It is an experience," he added with bitter irony, "to which Imbaneh-se has surely become accustomed. There is nothing now but to make the defeat cost as little as may be." He took his sheathed sword from his belt, walked past the other Imbaneh-se officers, and knelt to lay it down at Mitereh's feet. Then he looked up into the king's face and said quietly and with no irony at all, "But we were all game-pieces in your hand. Though the men of Imbaneh-se did your will blindly, still it was your purpose for which they fought, in the end. May I ask pardon for them, now that they have served the purpose you intended?"

"What is your name?" Mitereh asked him.

"Nuan Geraimani-na," answered the young man.

Mitereh inclined his head. "Whatever decision I make regarding the Geraimani, I will grant the broadest possible pardon to the men you led, provided they yield now to my hand."

The young man bowed his head briefly, rose, and stood aside, with a meaningful glance toward the other officers; they looked at him, at Kuanonai Geraimani-e, at Tenai, and last at Mitereh, who waited patiently. Then one after another, they came forward to lay their swords at his feet. Kuanonai Geraimani-e stood rigidly silent while they did this, but he did not try to prevent them. And at the end, Kuanonai, too, unbuckled his sword from his belt and cast it violently to the floor. Then he glared in furious challenge at Mitereh.

Ignoring him, the king said, "Draw up your companies in good order and bring them into Nerinesir at dawn. There will be no need to disarm your men; I have confidence there will be no fighting. I will have men ready to show them which barracks are theirs. Their officers may stay with them, but when I am ready I shall send for all officers of rank higher than captain, and these must come before me unarmed. Is this clear?"

"Clear, and, I confess, gracious beyond any possible expectation," answered Nuan Geraimani-na. "Before God, I swear, all shall be done as you require."

"I am glad," said Mitereh, "to take your word." He looked deliberately at one man after another, and each in turn nodded soberly. Finally he looked at Kuanonai, a stare that lengthened until the older man at last said savagely, "Before God, then, and curse your bones, Encormio-na; all shall be done as you demand." He turned on his heel and went out, taking the rest of the Imbaneh-se officers with him.

Mitereh, looking tired beyond exhaustion now that it was safe to do so, went at last to his wife. She clung to him silently and bowed her head against his chest. He picked up Inana and put her on his shoulder, where she held solemnly to his hair, evidently not at all sure whether the danger had passed.

Neither was Daniel. He said to the king, "They could be waiting out there to kill you, I suppose."

"They will not," Tenai said, sounding almost as tired as Mitereh looked. "But I will escort you to the gates of Nerinesir."

"Not within?" the king asked her.

"I will stay here tonight, that we may be certain all occurs as you require. Kuanonai Geraimani-e will be bitter."

Mitereh did not question this. He would trust her now, Daniel understood, as he had before, trying by his very faith to ensure her trustworthiness. "He gave me his oath."

"He did so before. And beyond that, I will have very many tasks to do before the sun touches the eastern sky."

Mitereh nodded wearily. "I shall be glad of your escort."

So it was a larger party that rode back to the city than had left it: the king and his wife and daughter; Daniel and Jenna side by side, and Emel protectively on Jenna's other side. An inspired choice as a guard, apparently, and Daniel wanted very much to hear the whole story, but it was enough at this moment that his daughter was with him, and safe. Safe. Though not *entirely* safe, he supposed, until she was within walls and this Imbaneh-se army had been disbanded and sent home.

On the other hand, Tenai rode with them as escort, and that was a safety better than walls, probably. He should stir himself, go talk to her, make sure she was all right ... well, she *was*. After all, she had let her oath to Mitereh stand. That was huge. Daniel thought he understood, at last, just how huge that was. But she might want to talk about it, and what other sounding board did she have, here? Lord Death? That was literally almost unimaginable.

Later maybe he might suggest Sandakan find her. He probably

wouldn't have to suggest it. But … that would have to wait. The moment he had now was one to cling to. Daniel let his eyes rest on Jenna's slim form beside him, and that was enough.

23

Jenna had expected a huge celebration, bells ringing, people dancing in the streets. And there was all of that. The Imbaneh-se soldiers marched with set faces into Nerinesir at dawn and found, no doubt to their astonishment, that the rejoicing had no edge to it; that the people of Nerinesir cheered them as victorious allies rather than scorning them as defeated enemies. That was why Mitereh had left them their swords; her father had explained that. Because the king wanted everybody to think of them as allies who had helped win a victory. He even wanted them to think of *themselves* that way, if he could get that to happen. The king had let even the highest-ranking officers carry their arms into Nerinesir. He wanted Imbaneh-se to accept being ruled by Talasayan, really accept it, so that this strange, brief war would be the last one. Maybe Mitereh could pull it off.

Jenna leaned her elbows on the windowsill of her high chamber, and gazed out at the late morning sun that turned the city below blindingly gold and white, or further away struck light out of the black marble of the nobles' city. The slate of the outer city looked blue as the sea in this light. It truly looked like a day for rejoicing. And it was. Everything had turned out just fine. Why did she feel so … so let down?

Niah was safe in her own apartment in the palace, next to the king's. She had her own women about her, and Inana stayed with her all the time, seeming completely untouched by the violence of the past days or the dark weirdness of the previous night. Jenna had had breakfast with the queen. Well, brunch, really, because everybody had stayed up late assuring each other they were fine and so she, at least, had slept in. Niah spoke less when she was happy, but smiled a great deal more. Whatever one word might describe the queen now, Jenna wouldn't have picked *resigned*. Maybe ... grateful.

If Jenna had to pick one word for herself, now, it might have been *waiting*. But she was not sure why she felt that nothing was finished, when everything was over.

Her father was fine. He'd had an awful time. Well, so had she, but in a totally different way, and she was grateful she hadn't had his part to play: everybody acting a role and her father trying to guess what was really going on underneath and thinking he'd failed and knowing all the time that Keitah was listening to every word that came out of his mouth. That was an idea that made Jenna feel sick when she thought about it too much. She'd heard about her father pretending to try to assassinate the king, about his using Tenai's sword to, well, kill himself, so he could tell Lord Death what was going on. And he'd never known, all through that, what Keitah might be doing to her in Kinabana.

Better, much better, to be riding, or even walking, through the woods with a clear destination and one person beside you whom you could truly depend on.

That was it, Jenna realized. She hadn't had time to think about it before because she'd been worried about Niah, and about Tenai, and most of all about her father. But, just as on the road the night before they entered Tenai's camp, she was sorry it was over, that part, the journey. Not sorry to leave behind the bugs, the drizzle, the tense company of outlaws, the constant fear of discovery or attack. But sorry to lose Emel's steady presence at her back. Because he was still with her, even in the palace, but he wasn't *with* her any more. He said "Nola" and wouldn't meet her eyes. Opportunity had gone, and she didn't know whether she would ever be able to coax it back. Until she figured that out, how could things feel finished?

She sighed.

He came into the room behind her; she recognized his step and didn't turn. He was shy of interrupting her even though she wasn't doing anything, and for a moment said nothing. But at last he told her, "Nola Jenna, the king asks you to attend him."

Mitereh would be dealing with all kinds of private business this afternoon, Jenna knew. Tomorrow was for all the public declarations: rewards, mostly, because the king wanted it to be another day of rejoicing. Though Kuanonai Geraimani-e would probably be publicly condemned and executed. Not for raising or leading the Imbaneh-se army, exactly, because Mitereh was going to forgive that, but for conspiring with Keitah. Jenna didn't like to think about it. She was glad Keitah was dead, and she hadn't really ever met Kuanonai Geraimani-e, much less liked him, but she still didn't like to think about it.

Today, Mitereh was going over everything that had happened and making a lot of decisions about what ought to happen next. The king had been closeted with Tenai and Mikanan Chauke-sa and Belagaiyan Tenom-e and Cardinal Uanan Erusa-go-e and some other people all morning. Her father had been there part of the time, too. Now it was her turn. She'd be glad to get it over with, but she was still reluctant to turn and nod and go with Emel, because there was also a lot she honestly didn't want to talk about.

No choice, though. So she turned and nodded, and turned toward the door. Emel wanted to fall back and walk behind her. She gestured impatiently, stopping that. He knew exactly what she meant when she waved her hand, and fell into step beside her instead. He didn't smile. Neither did Jenna. But he didn't argue either. That made her feel just a little better, though she wasn't exactly sure why.

Mitereh wasn't surrounded by advisors and counselors now. And he wasn't on a throne or anything like that, either. He sat, looking like an ordinary man, in a perfectly ordinary chair, in a small airy room with sunlight coming in through large windows. There were other chairs, but only one was occupied: Cardinal Uanan was with the king, sitting in a second chair drawn up close to Mitereh's. They had clearly been discussing something important. Mitereh was frowning, and the cardinal looked grim. Of course, on the few occasions Jenna had seen him, Cardinal Uanan had usually looked a bit grim. A plain wooden table near at hand held neatly-bound scrolls and blank paper and pens and things. A second table, smaller and more ornate, held a pot of tea and a set of tall, narrow cups.

Mitereh looked up as Emel escorted Jenna into the room. The force of the king's gaze made her hesitate in the doorway. Then he smiled, rose to his feet and held out his hands.

Feeling unaccountably shy, Jenna crossed the room and let the king take her hands in his. Emel started to go out, but the king released Jenna's hands and held up one of his and Emel stopped.

"Emelan Terusai," the king said, but gently.

"No," said Emel at once.

"Is it *No* you will tell me?" The king leaned his hip on the larger table and folded his arms, regarding Emel. He was frowning again, but thoughtfully, not like he was angry. "I understand why you do not wish to bear that name. But whatever your name, you have put yourself in my way. Or the hard hand of the Martyr has set you here before me. Do you think it possible to step now off the road onto which you have set your foot? I confess, I see no possible way to permit any such retreat."

Emel didn't answer. He met the king's eyes, but with a helpless sort of defiance, as though he both wanted to yield to the king's demand, whatever that was, and at the same time wanted to run screaming from the room and never come back.

"While you were merely Chaisa's nameless dog, I was willing to stand clear," the king went on. His tone was still gentle, but it was an inexorable gentleness. "But whatever you intended to do, whatever road you expected to walk, you have become something other than that now. I understand you would not own your brother. Nevertheless, he was your brother. You are his heir, Emelan Terusai-na. He has no other. Now I must see your heart." The king glanced at Cardinal Uanan.

The cardinal stood up. "I will do more than see your heart,

young man. I will weigh your soul in my hand." He strode across the room, opened a door that led into a smaller room, and stood aside, looking expectantly at Emel.

Emel didn't move. Jenna wanted to help him, but had no idea what she should say or do that would help. She sort of had an idea that anything she said might turn out to be wrong. So she didn't say anything. Emel didn't glance at her, either. His gaze was on the cardinal. Wasn't there something about birds being hypnotized by snakes? He looked a little like that.

"Young man, I understand you do not lack pride," Cardinal Uanan said. His tone was stern, but somehow not unsympathetic. "I am asking you to set it aside."

There was a pause as everyone waited. Emel drew a deep breath, finally. He started to look around, maybe to look at the king, maybe to turn back toward Jenna, she couldn't tell. But he stopped, let out his breath, and bowed his head. Then he walked across the room and through the door the cardinal held for him without looking back.

Cardinal Uanan gave the king a little nod, followed Emel into the other room, and shut the door firmly behind them.

Jenna looked at that door, which was nothing special, just a door, and thought it really ought to say *Abandon Hope, All Ye Who Enter Here* above it. Or no. Maybe it should be more like, *Endure Hope* ... she swallowed and looked away, her eyes prickling.

"He will be well. You may trust Uanan," the king told her. He poured her a cup of tea and nodded toward a chair near his. He'd changed again, once more seeming an ordinary man. Almost, anyway.

"Yes," said Jenna, through the lump in her throat.

The king was kind enough not to notice the waver in her tone. He held out the tea he'd poured and said, "Nola Jenna, I do not need to see your heart. I trust your soul is bright before God. But I would like to see through your eyes, if you will permit me. When I meant to send you into safety, I sent you into danger. Through your courage, you redeemed this error. I believe I understand the broad sketch of what took place. Would you now draw in the details?"

Jenna took the tea and held the cup in her hands. The warmth was comforting. She sat down, since he so clearly expected her to. She wouldn't have thought she could stand to talk about it, about the bad parts, anyway, and yet something about Mitereh's grave attention made her want to. Like he would hear her in a way even her father couldn't—her father couldn't just listen to her, he also had to bear all his retroactive fears for her. She didn't have to worry about protecting Mitereh. She somehow felt that Mitereh would understand just what she meant, even if she couldn't find the exact right words.

It took a surprisingly long time to tell the whole story. Jenna found herself putting in a lot that she hadn't told her father. She had told her father how it felt to creep along a ledge thirty feet up and how much it had hurt to leave Niah behind in Keitah's house. But she hadn't told him what it was like to kick a man for real and know you'd killed him: that had been too hard. She could tell Mitereh about that. It occurred to her that the king was after all getting a pretty good look at her heart or her soul or whatever. Whatever he'd said, she doubted this was accidental.

She had told her father about Emel's courage and resourcefulness, but she hadn't wanted to emphasize just how dangerous everything had been. It scared even her to think about it in retrospect; her father would have been horrified. She had only said vaguely, *Oh, we traveled with an outlaw gang for a while and then left them and joined up with a couple going south and went with them to Gai-e.*

Now she found herself telling Mitereh a lot more than that. She told him about Kuomat and his cold silver eyes and how she had thought he would kill them both when they left. She told him why they had had to leave, and even how it had made her sick when Saimadan's head rolled loosely under a nudge from Kuomat's foot. The king listened gravely, not horrified, offering neither condemnation nor approval. Just careful attention. This neutral attentiveness was exactly what she had needed. How had he known that? Was that part of being a king? She told him how she and Emel had robbed Kahisan and Patanah for money and clothes, and how that had led to a really good team later, after they'd been captured by Keitah's people and rescued by Kuomat's pack.

Mitereh stirred at that, surprised.

"I know," Jenna agreed. "And later, Kuomat helped us rescue Niah—I'll tell you about that in a minute. I don't know his real name, but I actually thought you might. Or Taranah, maybe. I think he's close to her age. He helped us when we were caught because he was curious, I guess, but what kind of outlaw would be curious enough about us to shoot soldiers?"

"Or maybe, curious enough about Keitah," Mitereh murmured.

"Right, maybe. But I'd swear it was your name that made him decide to let us go then and help us later, when we went in to get Niah and Inana."

"You must assuredly describe this man carefully for my aunt, that she may see him through your eyes. Will you describe this rescue for me?"

"Oh, well—that was awful. Not the rescue," Jenna added hastily. "I mean, parts of that were pretty bad, too. But I meant the way Tenai set it up." She described the way Tenai had killed poor Apana Pelat, though she suspected he must know about that already, and how terribly grim Tenai had been that night. She even told the king about how, on that raid, she had lost her nerve and failed to really kick a man when she'd needed to, and how she'd accidentally set the whole house on fire, or a lot of it anyway.

"You went alone into the house of our enemy and led my wife out of her imprisonment," Mitereh observed. "You did not falter when Niah was afraid to go with you at once. The mission you took on yourself was successful. Do not reproach yourself because you have discovered that war is not your calling."

This was actually comforting. Maybe knowing the right things to say was also part of being a king. Jenna drank the rest of her tea to hide her confusion—it had gone cold—and tried to relax. She said, "Then when we came back, when Tenai brought us back, she was so different. I think ... okay, look, I guess Captain Pelat knew what he was doing and what he chose, and I'm not saying Tenai was wrong to ask him to do it. I mean, she was wrong, obviously, but ..." she set her cup down and waved a hand in frustration. "It's complicated, and I know that, and I get that awful things happen in war, or when you're trying to head off war, or whatever. I *get* that. But doing that to him ..." She hunted for words. "It hurt her," Jenna said finally. "That was when she went so dark. I'm sure that's what did it. That was the kind of choice Nolas-Kuomon would have made, probably did make, lots of times. When Tenai made that choice, it was like ... like she picked that name and all that, I don't know, all that history, all that rage, back up. And then she got stuck, and couldn't put any of it away again."

Mitereh had listened with quiet attention to all this. "You tried to make her remember herself, and remember me. This you did, as well as anyone might."

"Yes, I tried, but ..." Jenna opened her hands in remembered helplessness. "She was terrifying. What happened to her was terrifying. But I think she tried. I think she was trying, even at the worst part, to ... I don't know. To remember not to be like that, or—or something."

"I think this was clearly so, yes. She was trying to make a decision other than war, even before Geraimani-e seized her sword." The king paused, thinking. After a little while, he went on. "I am glad to know all that you have told me. I am grateful for all you have done. If you had not reminded Nolas-Kuomon of recent choices, if your father had not done so, I believe that even at the end, events might have fallen out far otherwise. I will recognize your bravery publicly when it comes time to do so."

"Oh, no! I didn't do so much, and anyway," Jenna said hastily, hoping to get out of what would probably be a way-too-public occasion. "It was poor Captain Pelat who deserves everything."

"Do not protest; I will recognize all whose courage served to turn the age. How should I not? I will indeed recognize my brave captain." The king opened a hand, palm upward, in a gesture of resignation. "Alas that such recognition must come after he has gone into the hand of God!"

"I know it was wrong."

"In war, sometimes sacrifices must be made. Wrong? Yes, but the good that came from the sacrifice shines through the darkness. No other man who died in all this difficulty died to such clear purpose. Surely this knowledge comforts you."

Put that way, it even did, in a weird way.

Rising, Mitereh took her hands. When Jenna stood up, a little uncertainly, he bowed and brought her hands to his forehead. "For your service to me and to my house," he said formally, "for your bright courage and your rescue of my wife and child, I am in your debt, Nola Jenna."

Jenna stared at him, aware she must be blushing with confusion.

Bowing once more, Mitereh gestured her back toward her chair and turned his head to glance impatiently at the door through which Cardinal Uanan had taken Emel—how long ago had it been? It felt like hours. Days.

As though this glance had been a signal, that door opened. Emel hesitated on the threshold. He looked utterly wrung out; Jenna jumped up to go to him and then didn't know if she should and stood still, irresolute. He glanced her way, but dropped his gaze at once. He didn't want to see her—he probably wanted to see her less than anybody else—Jenna actually understood this. She looked away, trying to keep her own expression completely neutral, which was the closest she could come to actually being absent.

Cardinal Uanan came through the door after Emel. He gave Jenna a long summing look and Mitereh a short nod. "I'll lay out the parts of the tale you must know, later. You need not ask further, if you will trust my judgment."

Mitereh inclined his head. "Implicitly, I promise you. You are then satisfied? You approve my intention in this regard?"

"I am, and I do. I've imposed suitable penance, which has

been accepted. You need not inquire."

"A man's penance lies between him and God. I assuredly will not ask." Mitereh turned back to Jenna. "Nola Jenna, permit me once more to express my gratitude and permit me to ask you to withdraw. I will speak with you once more in a little time, if you would be generous to wait."

"Of course," Jenna said, glancing uncertainly at Emel. He still wouldn't look at her. Surely Mitereh would be grateful for his part in Niah's rescue—in her own escape, for that matter—but Emel would know that. Knowing that wouldn't help him. No, he would fear the king's praise almost more, maybe really more, than he would have feared his censure. She didn't know how she knew this. It didn't even make sense to her. But she knew it was true. There was nothing she could say that would make anything easier for him. She retreated.

Her father was out in Mitereh's antechamber, Jenna found, and a couple of men who looked slightly familiar, and a woman she knew was one of the queen's attendants. The woman slipped in quickly to speak to Mitereh and then went away, back to Niah presumably. Jenna sat down at first near her father, but couldn't bear to stay still and jumped up, pacing instead from one window to another and back again. Then she caught him looking worried and sat down again, carefully too far away for him to easily speak to her. She folded her hands in her lap and tried to pretend everything was fine.

Emel seemed to be closeted with Mitereh for a long time. Probably Mitereh wanted to hear all about the escape from Kinabana and about Niah's rescue and everything from him, as he'd heard about it from her. Damn, that might take forever, if Mitereh wanted the story in as much detail from Emel as he'd had it from her.

Attendants brought food on platters and offered it around. Jenna wasn't hungry and only shook her head impatiently at the man who offered her a tray. She couldn't sit still, but got up and paced some more, then perched uneasily on a window ledge and tried to look out at a city she didn't even see.

At last the door opened, and Emel came out. He looked even more exhausted and pale than he had before, if that were possible. Again, Jenna wanted to go to him, and again she hesitated. He didn't look her in the face, but said only, "He will see you again. And Nola Danyel."

Jenna couldn't keep herself from asking him, "Are you all right?"

He didn't answer, but gave a very slight, even involuntary, backwards jerk of his head, *No*. She bit her lip and went past him, back into the cheerful little room. Mitereh was standing by the table and Emel didn't take a chair, so neither did Jenna. Nor did her father.

The king said without preamble, "As the Terusai family ends with Keitah save his brother take back the name, Emelan has agreed to own it. Chaisa-e will release him from her service, that he may claim his rightful estate."

Jenna looked at Emel quickly. He didn't return her gaze. He wasn't looking at any of them. Her father had on his blandest, most neutral expression.

"To be sure," said Mitereh, with a steady look her way, "it would be preferable for the Terusai name to be secured. I have therefore commanded Emelan to marry. Indeed, if you will have him, Nola Jenna, and if Nola Danyel will permit, I have commanded him to take you for his wife."

Her father, taken by surprise, exclaimed. Jenna, her eyes on Emel, felt like she'd never been less surprised by anything in her life. He hadn't met her gaze, even yet. He had folded his hands tightly before him, she knew to hide their shaking, and studied the far wall with great intensity.

Jenna walked across to him and took his hands in hers. They were indeed trembling. She was sorry about that, and yet it made her happy, too. He wouldn't look at her at first, but she waited, and at last, bracing as though to take a blow, he turned his honey-colored eyes reluctantly to meet hers. She liked the color of his eyes, she decided. She liked the strong bones of his face. She liked the broad strength in his hands. She said, "I won't marry you," and watched the color wash suddenly back into his face and as suddenly run out again. His expression didn't change, but he closed his eyes.

She said quickly, "Unless you *want* to marry me."

His eyes opened. He looked at her, really at her, and she knew, with an amazing sense of protectiveness she'd never felt before, that she had tremendous power, that he was utterly vulnerable; that she could wound him beyond bearing with a word. The awareness both frightened and steadied her, and she said fiercely, "I'm not a bauble for somebody to give away. I won't be a prize. Or a—a command performance. Or, damn it, a penance. I won't stand up on a pedestal and be treated like I'm made of porcelain and let you treat yourself like you're dirt. If you've got feet of clay, well, so do I, and I haven't noticed a lot of perfection going around, and I won't play Miranda to anybody's Caliban."

It was quite a speech, and it produced a space of total silence. But the color had come back into Emel's face, this time to stay. And his hands had stopped trembling.

"I did not intend to be overly forward with your affections, Nola Jenna. Forgive the offense," the king said softly.

Jenna had almost forgotten anybody else besides Emel was even there. She said, "None taken," and let go of Emel's hands abruptly—it was harder than she'd expected—so she could turn to her father.

He said, "Jenna—" and stopped.

She said to Mitereh with, she knew, a slight curl of her lip that she just couldn't help, "I don't need anybody's *permission* to marry, thank you very much. But," and she turned back to her father, "I wouldn't want to marry without your approval." She didn't say she *wouldn't* do it, though, and she knew he noticed that, too.

"Jenna," he began, and stopped, and held out a hand to her, looking oddly vulnerable now himself. "Are you sure this what you want?"

"Why?" she said, and heard a note of warning in her tone that she'd never heard there before. "Don't you think he's fit?"

"I—trust your judgment," he said helplessly. And then, more soberly, "I do, you know. But ... you want to stay in Talasayan? Are you sure?"

"Oh!" Somehow, she hadn't thought of that. Or she had, but not about what that actually meant. "You want to go home," she said. "I mean, obviously. Of course you do." That was—she didn't know what to say. She couldn't look at Emel.

Mitereh said softly, "The veil cannot be laid open until midwinter. As the season turns, perhaps if you decide you are pleased to remain, Nola Jenna, then Nola Danyel may find himself content as well."

"Not exactly subtle," her father said drily.

The king opened a hand, a gesture of concession. "Subtlety is not my intent. I declare openly that I should indeed prefer that you remain, Nola Danyel. I should prefer that you both remain. For several reasons."

"For Tenai's sake."

"Indeed, Nola Danyel. That is foremost among my reasons. You understand, I will offer every inducement I can contrive. I will pour honor into your hands and cover your feet with gold and pearls. But the choice will, of course, be yours. And, to be sure, Nola Jenna's. If she would choose to marry a man of Talasayan, I would be very pleased."

"Well ..." Her father looked at Jenna. He sighed. "I don't know. But if you decide you want to stay ... we can talk about it. Midwinter's a long time from now, Jen. You don't need to decide right away, but eventually you're going to have to decide what *you* want, not arrange your whole life according to what you imagine *I* want, so ..." he opened his own hands, exactly the same gesture Mitereh had made.

Jenna studied him narrowly. But she was pretty sure he meant it. She was almost totally sure. She said to Emel, "I won't marry you if you don't want to marry me. I won't marry anybody just because he's been *ordered* to marry me. But you can court me. Until midwinter." She added, "And I'll court *you*. That's only fair. And then we'll see who's fit and who wants to marry whom."

"Nola—" said Emel, and stopped.

"I'll get Mitereh to order you to court me," she warned him. "And *don't* call me 'Nola.'"

"An order ... will not be necessary," he said. This time, he was the one who captured her hands.

Jenna gave Mitereh a smug look. The king was clearly trying not to laugh. His eyes laughed. But he said in a perfectly sober tone, "If the bargain you have proposed is more acceptable to all those concerned, I must assuredly declare myself perfectly content." He added more seriously, "You understand, Nola Jenna, he cannot offer you Kinabana. Terusai's customary grant is Kandun. That is a smaller province, in harsher country."

Jenna shrugged. "Like I care? What, you think I had such a great time in Kinabana I want to go back?" She had a warm feeling in the center of her body, that seemed to be spreading outward. It made it hard to stop smiling. It made it hard to think, except for warm fuzzy thoughts.

Her father, not quite so distracted, asked, "Who are you going to give Kinabana to?"

The king moved his shoulders in a minimal shrug. "I confess I do not know. Perhaps my brother, when he is of age."

"Declare Inana your heir and give it to her, when she's old enough," Jenna suggested, and the king's shocked look cut right through the warm fuzzies. "What? Isn't your heir one of the people who's supposed to be able to hold Kinabana? Inana's bright and energetic and brave; do you think there's something *wrong* with her just because she's a girl?" She gave the king a narrow-eyed stare, daring him to endorse such complete stupidity.

Mitereh gazed at her wordlessly. Emel had a blank look over his face, but this time he was the one hiding laughter.

Her father said mildly, "If you had a declared heir, wouldn't your advisors have to stop pressing you to take another wife?"

By his expression, the king found this, at least, a cogent

argument. He said firmly, "I will consider what you say," meaning, obviously, *But not right now.* He cleared his throat, shook his head, and added, "Nola Danyel, Nolas-e Emelan, I would like you to stay, to witness this next interview. Nola Jenna, you may stay or go."

Jenna imagined an agenda with little check marks next to all their names, and wondered what, or who, came next on it. No one that Mitereh seemed all that happy about. The warm feeling was still there, but the rest of the world was already coming back into sharper focus, and she was curious. Emel looked grim; did he know, then? She thought her father also seemed to know what was going on. Had she been so distracted earlier she'd missed something obvious? She said, "I'd like to stay, please."

Mitereh nodded gravely. Emel began rearranging the chairs in the room into a smooth semi-circle. He nodded to the one on the end for her, so Jenna sat down and folded her hands in her lap. She wondered who the other chairs were for. Except the one in the middle. That one was clearly for the king himself. One for him, one for her, one for her father, that left four chairs. Hmm.

One of them turned out to be, unsurprisingly, for Tenai. She was dressed very formally, embroidery black-on-black on her vest and the cuffs of her blouse. Jenna had hardly seen her since ... that night when she hadn't killed Mitereh. She looked better, less coldly distant, more like herself. She exchanged one long glance with Daddy, gave Jenna a small nod, and took her seat as a matter of course at the king's left hand.

Another chair was for Mikanan Chauke-se, on the king's right. The one between Chauke-se and her father was for Cardinal Uanan Erusa-go-e, who had changed into what Jenna supposed must be formal vestments. And the last on her side, between Jenna and Tenai, was for Sandakan Gutai-e. He did not take his seat, but stood behind Tenai's chair with a hand resting on its back. Emel eyed him sidelong and would have taken a similar post behind Jenna's chair, except Mitereh waved him impatiently to the unoccupied chair, so he sat down beside her himself. Someone had brought the king a much more formal vest than the one he'd been wearing, and a plain gold circlet that, against all odds, didn't look the least bit silly.

Most of the king's personal guards were also present, standing to either side of the chairs. They didn't have their swords drawn, but the threat was palpable. Jenna drew a slow breath, understanding at last for whom all this show was intended. So she was not, after all, surprised when Kuanonai Geraimani-e was brought in.

His hands had been bound before his body, but he walked with his shoulders back and his head proudly erect. His face was expressionless, except for the bitter set of his strong jaw. He walked between his guards like he didn't know they were there, and deliberately failed to notice any of them but the king.

Jenna thought he might shout at Mitereh with defiant rage, or else maybe curse him in a savage whisper. But he didn't. He walked straight through the double line of the king's guards until he was directly before Mitereh's chair, went heavily to both knees, and contented himself with glaring in silence.

"Geraimani-e," the king said formally. He was so much younger, so much slighter, and yet unquestionably in command of the situation; he gave the impression that he'd still have been the stronger of the two even if he had been the one bound. Jenna wondered how he did it.

The other man started to answer, stopped, and said after a moment, "Sekuse-go-e."

Mitereh gave him a little nod. "I will freely pardon all your men, and all your officers ranked as captains or below: I will make all my dispositions tomorrow and declare it then."

"You are gracious, o king," Geraimani-e conceded, like it was a painful admission for him to make.

"And of the rest ... I have been considering this. How many Geraimani are here among your officers?"

Kuanonai Geraimani-e jerked his chin up in what seemed an involuntary movement; it made him seem somehow more human and much more sympathetic. He hesitated for just a heartbeat, then said, "Four. My uncle, my son, my brother, and his son."

"So many? Are there any left in Imbaneh-se?"

"Hardly," Kuanonai muttered. His chin jerked up again and he said reluctantly, "My brother's daughter. And my uncle's wife, with her two daughters."

"No male heir of the line direct? Will you swear that before God, and you so near His kingdom?"

A longer hesitation this time. Then the older man's shoulders slumped a little. He said, "My niece's child. That was a boy-infant, born this spring."

Mitereh made a small gesture of acknowledgment. "I had heard of the birth," he said in a neutral tone.

Kuanonai nodded as though he wasn't surprised. "Will you spare him, o king? He is only an infant."

Jenna had not believed the man could bring himself to plead, and saw now she had been wrong. She closed her eyes in sympathy, but that was worse than watching and she opened them again. Would Mitereh really order a baby killed? She looked at his still, calm face and did not know.

"You knew you risked him when you cut a great oak to carve a throne," the king said. "And all your line. Even the women, who may yet bear more sons if they are left free."

Kuanonai Geraimani-e nodded again. He said grimly, "I thought we would win. It did not occur to me that Tenai Nolas-Kuomon would set her banner below that of a son of Encormio." He gave Tenai an accusatory stare. She said nothing, and he turned his gaze back to the king. "As you are gracious, o king, will you not spare him?"

Mitereh opened a hand. "Though your own life is certainly forfeit, Geraimani-e, I shall spare all the rest of your house, or none. I do not know yet which path I shall take." He set his hand back on the arm of his chair. "You claim you fight for the freedom of Imbaneh-se. Freedom to do what? To set your armies across the Khadur? To press for lands that have not been yours for a thousand years and more?"

"To raise up our own throne!" snapped the older man. "To set our own law within our borders and never apply to a king of Talasayan for leave to come and go in our own country!"

"Well," Mitereh said mildly, "that is little enough."

"You say so!"

"I say so. And whose opinion is more important than mine?" Mitereh tapped the arm of his chair thoughtfully. "Yours is a warlike people, Geraimani-e. That is why Tenai Nolas-Kuomon raised one army after another from your land: you were accustomed to fight my father's tight-drawn rein. I will not give Imbaneh-se freedom to press Talasayan. A throne in Sotatan is something I will not suffer to exist. On the other side ... an oak throne here, below the ivory throne, so that all might see Imbaneh-se still yields to Talasayan ... that, I might allow. A king of your own, to set your own law ... if that law did not conflict too greatly with mine, I might allow that. A king of Imbaneh-se, to grant and take back fealty within the borders of Imbaneh-se ... if this king were himself held in fealty to me, I might allow even that."

Kuanonai Geraimani-e stared at him, speechless.

"And who better to hold the oak throne than a Geraimani?" asked Mitereh softly. "Would this not please Imbaneh-se? If any Geraimani would bend his stiff neck. Not you. Your uncle, your son, your brother, your nephew. Which, if you would choose?"

For the first time, Jenna actually admired Kuanonai, as she watched him ruthlessly subordinate all his pride and anger to this question. He did not waste time or breath cursing Mitereh or railing that the king meant to deceive him; he only shut his eyes for a moment, opened them, and said harshly, "Not my uncle. He lacks ambition. Imbaneh-se would destroy him. Not my son. He is too ambitious. No matter how light your rein, he would fight it, and you would destroy him."

"I think your brother will hate me too much after your death. I am aware you are close. So. Your nephew, then, if you think he is fit, Geraimani-e."

Kuanonai glared at the king. But he said after a moment. "He would do well. You have met him. He pleased you, when he yielded to you and forced me to yield. Well ... I confess he was right. He is wise beyond his years." The man seemed to have forgotten that he spoke to a man even younger than his nephew. "And strong, and clever."

"Ambitious enough for Imbaneh-se," suggested Mitereh, "but not too ambitious for me."

"Before God, I swear that is my honest opinion."

"I think it is." Mitereh leaned his chin on his hand, regarding the older man. "Shall I do this? Shall I give Nuan Geraimani-na leave to raise the oak throne in my hall? Shall I ask him to be king of Imbaneh-se, yielding only to me? Shall I make him the gateway through which my authority flows to Imbaneh-se? And shall I then leave long the rein and see what gait he chooses?"

"Will your people permit it?"

Mitereh glanced both ways along the row of chairs and raised an inquiring eyebrow. No one said anything. "No one objects," he said to the older man. "Indeed, we and others of mine spent much of the morning discussing only this. All are willing to be ruled by my opinion. With Nolas-Kuomon at my side to enforce a certain caution among any ... potential enemies. And so what say you?"

"I say ... that it is not enough, but I confess that if your father had offered so much, then Nolas-Kuomon would have had more difficulty raising armies in Imbaneh-se."

"My father never gave up power willingly."

"And you do?" Kuanonai Geraimani-e sounded skeptical.

Mitereh made a gesture as though he tossed something into the air. "A falcon jessed to its perch will not be lost, but neither will it bring down game for its master. I prefer to loose the falcon to fly, expecting always it will come of its own will back to my fist. If your nephew is an honorable man, I may safely let him fly. Honor alone will hold him where he would fight the jess. Shall I believe that he is an honorable man?"

"Make him your offer. He will take it, I have no doubt, and

when he takes wing, you will find out."

Mitereh inclined his head and gave a little get-up wave of his hand. The other man hesitated and then climbed to his feet, shaking off a guard's helpful hand with disdain. "You have surprised me," Kuanonai admitted. "I do confess it. May I ask one favor for myself alone, imposing on your generosity?"

"Ask."

"I do not ask for my life. But to live long enough to see my brother's son take your offer ... that, I do ask. Will you permit me this?"

"I am not perfectly certain I will offer this ... opportunity ... to your nephew. If not to him, to no one; and if I do not spare him, I will spare no one of your line, not though they be women or infants at the breast. I will test him tomorrow, when I make all my dispositions among my people and yours, and neither you nor I knows whether he will stand the test. You may find it bitter, to live so long you must bear witness. Will you choose that risk?"

Kuanonai answered confidently, "My nephew will stand any test you set, Sekuse-go-e. I hold to my request."

"Then I grant it," said the king, and gave another little dismissive wave. Kuanonai turned on his heel and walked out, holding himself proudly. None of the guards touched him.

Mitereh leaned back in his chair, his expression distant. Everyone else was stirring, getting to their feet. None of them had said even a word. Silent witnesses. So this had been what they all discussed this morning, while Jenna slept late and then had a leisurely breakfast with the queen. No wonder the king looked tired. She shook her head and let Emel offer her a hand to help her to her feet. A faint physical shock went through her at the touch of his fingers against hers, and Jenna smiled: so that was still there, and still real. She saw he'd felt it too, and knew her smile took on a satisfied edge.

24

Daniel thought his daughter would join him after that intense little scene Mitereh had engineered with Kuanonai Geraimani-e. But she didn't. She vanished—with Emel, he presumed—and left her poor old father to fend for himself. Well, no doubt she would be in later, but her absence underlined an uncomfortable truth: Jenna would almost certainly want to stay in Talasayan. But Daniel didn't know whether he could bear to stay here.

He would have to give up so much. Every part of his life, except one. That one part was so important. Nothing else was more important. But … Jenna wasn't the *only* important thing in his life. Lindenwood … his patients … true, Martin would find someone else, someone good, someone who wanted, or needed, Lindenwood's unusual focus on and flexibility regarding individualized patient care. Lindenwood's director had a remarkable combination of professional expertise and administrative ability … he'd find someone solid.

In a few years, not so long, Russell Martin would be retiring. He'd find someone good there too; someone who could handle Lindenwood's board of trustees on the one hand and the staff on the other. But the hospital would change, once Martin stepped down. That was inevitable.

Come to think of it, in not so very many years, Daniel would have been thinking about retirement himself. And then what? He had no idea. He'd never really thought that far ahead.

Midwinter. The longest night of the year, when the veil that separated the dark kingdom of Lord Death from—what was the phrase?—the ephemeral kingdom of men?—was thinnest and least secure. The one night when he might step out of this sorcery-ridden world and back to his own. If Jenna would come. If, by then, he even thought he had a right to ask her to come. If not ... he didn't know.

Not wanting anybody else's company, Daniel tucked himself away in his own apartment. He and Jenna were no longer part of anybody else's household, but had an apartment in their own right, complete with a handful of attendants Daniel barely recognized but hadn't been able to refuse. It was a good apartment, with big south-facing windows that admitted plenty of light. Whatever complicated political signal the separate household was supposed to send, Daniel was glad of the new privacy. Among other advantages, it allowed him the luxury of a nice little indulgent bout of self-pity. Though he had better get over it by evening; there would certainly be an invitation from someone later.

Daniel closed his eyes and leaned his face against the smooth stone of the window frame, letting the late-afternoon sun fall on his face ... maybe he ought to get out, go for a walk ... maybe he'd run into Jenna, she might well have gone out for a walk of her own, she liked to walk when she needed to think things over ... it was strange, and strangely discomfiting, to be able to let his thoughts turn toward his daughter without instantly flinching. Wherever she was, she was safe. With, no doubt, Emel.

Daniel opened his eyes again, gazing out over the terraced orchards that spilled away down below the southern wing of the palace. Fruit was visible among the leaves, glowing gold and red like jewels in the rich light. But he lost sight of the orchards as his thoughts turned inward again.

Well, though Emel might not be exactly the man a father would pick out for his daughter, still, his redemption was something good that had come out of the whole grim tangled mess of the last few weeks. A chance for life and—Daniel winced slightly—possibly even love. What was that worth? Memories of Kathy as she had been when she was young and happy presented themselves forcefully to his attention, not for the first time in the past day. What would he have given to keep her that way? Nearly anything, he concluded. Certainly his own life. His mouth crooked. Was it possible to believe that anyone in all the world really loved the way you'd once loved yourself? He didn't believe Jenna loved that way. But he might be wrong. Or she might grow into that kind of love, in time. With, maybe, Emel.

If Jenna actually loved Emel, if he would make her happy, then wasn't that alone worth everything either of them had gone through, all the fear and pain? Even if the man was ten years too old and far too experienced in all the wrong ways and not at all the sort of young man Daniel would have voluntarily chosen as a son-in-law. Although *brave* and *devoted to Jenna* counted for a lot.

Jenna seemed sure of her choice. That had been quite a speech about pedestals and feet of clay. Daniel grinned despite himself. That had been so *Jenna*.

Well, and what father ever got anywhere by standing in his daughter's way when she decided whom she wanted? No—as far as that went, he supposed he would have to chalk it up as one for the good guys and give Jenna's future over to luck and life and, he supposed, God's good grace.

Behind him, there was a tap on the door. Daniel straightened, sighing. Somebody coming with an invitation, of course; the sort that was really a polite order. From Cardinal Uanan, he hoped, or else Taranah; if he had to go out, he would like to join someone he could talk to without watching every word. He might even like to talk to Taranah, now that neither of them was forced to play a role … But his guess was wrong. It was Emel at the door.

There could surely be no one Emel less wanted to approach than Jenna's father. And yet here he was, presenting himself with such decent, plain courage that Daniel could only admire it, however little the man matched his idea of Prince Charming.

"Nola Danyel," Emel said, offering a small bow.

A deferential bow, and was that appropriate? Daniel took a step back and half turned, tacitly inviting the other man to come further into the apartment. "Let me send for wine. Nolas-e, is it now? Not Nolas-ai, as for your brother?" Either way, Emel now outranked Daniel—here in this country where hierarchy mattered so much. It hardly seemed right.

He might have allowed a faint edge to creep into his tone. Emel winced just perceptibly, but he didn't deny the title. "Nolas-e is correct. Kandun is the traditional Terusai grant, Nola Danyel. It is not as high a grant as Kinabana. Likely the king will now give Kinabana to his brother and hope for better from that."

Well, Daniel had never met the young prince, but Tegaitan was virtually certain to prove a big step up in terms of trustworthiness. As Emel himself would, no doubt. Jenna thought so. Daniel supposed it would only be fair to start with that presumption.

"I would never have asked for her. I know I am not such a man as should have her."

Such direct, painful honesty. Daniel could see with perfect clarity just how he could take this man apart. Every word Emel spoke, every deferential glance and gesture, delineated the fracture lines Daniel might use to shatter Emel's vulnerable new sense of self-worth. If he didn't want him to marry Jenna, well, here was a fine chance to prevent it.

And if Daniel could have done anything more contemptible, more unworthy of his profession, or more likely to make his daughter hate him forever, he had no idea what it could be. He said instead, "It's a mistake, I think, to fixate on the past. Nothing there can be changed. Only what you do in the present is under your control. My daughter has always had good judgment in choosing her friends."

"I respect her greatly," Emel assured him with touching earnestness.

"I believe mutual respect is considered quite a solid foundation for a relationship."

The wine arrived. Daniel took the carafe and glasses the attendant provided and gestured Emel toward a chair. "Perhaps you would tell me a bit more about what happened in Kinabana after I ... left. About your escape. I've heard about it from my daughter, but, you know, I *can* spot holes in a story if they're big enough. She doesn't want to worry me, of course."

Emel accepted both the wine and the chair. Not the best chair. That was the one nearest the windows, and Daniel wanted the sunlight for himself. He didn't know what he'd do in the winter … he'd probably have a horrible case of seasonal affective disorder for the rest of his life. "If you don't mind. What about these outlaws?"

The tale as Emel told it was hair-raising. And even he must surely be toning it down a notch or two. Several times Daniel's professional antennae quivered at something softened or glossed over or left out entirely. He let the moments go, as he would have let such a moment go for a patient on his first appointment. He found he was automatically keeping an eye out for the word or phrase or lifted eyebrow that would support Emel, that would strengthen one of those lines of vulnerability he perceived.

"Yes," he murmured, "Jenna told me about that. Just what kinds of distractions did you and the outlaws get up to while she was inside Keitah's house? I wondered. She told me she burned the house down …"

Emel didn't exactly laugh; he didn't even really smile. But his sober look lightened. "Only one wing of the house, I think. She throws herself forward with such enthusiasm into all that she does—it is a wonder she left any stone of that house standing atop another!" He remembered he was speaking to Jenna's father and closed down again, but not quite as far.

Daniel caught himself smiling. He liked the younger man's enthusiasm, given its direction. He liked the man himself for expressing it. It made him look less a thug, more like a man who simply happened to be big and tough. A man who had made some bad choices and lived through a rough ten years, and who had now come out the other side to a different sense of who he was, who he could be.

"We did nothing outside the house to equal the fire," Emel said, grave again, but with the memory of that enthusiasm glinting in his eyes. "We found a party out with falcons. There were not many men, but every one removed made one fewer. But we also loosed the best of the birds near the wall. It was a fine bird, good enough we knew it must belong to a lord and so they would not care to mislay it. Thus we lured more men away from the house as they tried to recover it. Katawarin ran up the gate with a tale of outlaws and mayhem on the very borders of the estate, an insult to … Keitah. So his men must answer it, and more were drawn away. When we knew Nola Jenna was within, we began to shoot through windows on the other side of the house. Katawarin returned in time to join that effort, and she shot a jar out of the hands of one of Keitah's servants. This created some confusion."

"The, ah, the wards around the house didn't stop bolts coming over the wall?"

"We took the metal heads off the bolts, so for all the wards could tell we were merely throwing sticks. Even blunted, a crossbow bolt will bruise, and of course being struck by one will frighten a man. So there was some commotion from that. Then the wards went down, so we knew Nola Jenna had brought the queen and her child out of the house. After that, of course, we could use entire bolts, and that was far more distracting. Even so …"

Even so, it had been a touch-and-go exercise. Yes. Daniel didn't want to dwell on the details. "And then Niah made her surprise move, and finally Tenai pulled you all out. Very good." And then Emel and Jenna had found themselves facing Nolas-Kuomon, dark and deadly, with blood on her hands and blood, so to speak, in her eye. He didn't care to dwell on that thought, either. "It sounds to me like you all did very well."

Emel at once made a little self-deprecating gesture. "Nola Jenna did very well. I, whom she trusted to protect her, was taken by Keitah's men and redeemed from failure only by the capricious hand of fortune."

"We seldom judge ourselves as accurately as others judge us," Daniel observed. "Especially not once we have become accustomed to our own harshness. You might consider that if the king and Cardinal Uanan and Jenna all agree, then your own opinion might be too unforgiving. You may be sure I've considered that."

Emel, startled, looked up. Looked for hidden condescension, probably. Of course, he could see nothing of the sort behind Daniel's deliberate neutrality—even if Daniel had been insincere, he trusted he could have kept that insincerity off his face and out of his manner. But in fact he meant exactly what he said. And he'd found that generally honesty could be felt through even quite profound confusion, if it was spoken plainly.

Emel said at last, "You are generous, Nola Danyel."

Daniel shrugged dismissively, sitting back in his chair. "Generosity isn't my intention."

"Your nature, perhaps."

It was Daniel's turn to be startled. "Well ... it's good to think so."

Emel drew a breath and stood, decisively. And went to one knee, a dramatic gesture to which Daniel doubted he'd ever become accustomed. He said formally, "Nola Danyel, as you are generous, I ask your permission to court your daughter. Or forbid me and I will withdraw. Many women would be pleased to marry any man called Terusai-e of Kandun. His humor aside, the king will hardly refuse me if I should declare for another. Nola Jenna is young: her heart will settle elsewhere."

Daniel studied the other man. This unexpected offer made him think better of the other man. The humility wasn't assumed, he thought. It might signify an uncomfortable tendency toward self-abnegation, but it didn't seem to him to arise from, say, the defective sense of self-worth that plagued some depressives. In fact, it seemed more an aspect of a robust sense of the ... what, fitness of things? A more outward-directed feeling than one would expect of an emotionally disturbed person. Yes. That was why he suddenly felt more comfortable with this man as a prospective partner for Jenna: because he read this gesture as an expression of fundamental health.

The pause was threatening to become too fraught. Daniel said, "I don't quite think Jenna would approve either you or me taking over her decision. If you want her, court her." And he might encourage a few other young men to do the same; who knew what might happen between now and midwinter? But saying so would be ... too much honesty, surely.

Emel looked thrown a little off balance, as though this wasn't what he'd expected Daniel to say. But he gathered himself then, and rose to his feet. "Well ..." he began. "Well, Nola Danyel, then I thank you."

Daniel held up a hand, stopping that right there. "You're not beholden to me," he said, putting deliberate surprise into his voice. "Why should you think so? She makes her own choices. If you win her, it'll be because of who you are." And if he didn't, well, Daniel could stand that, too, but this he didn't put into words.

When Emel had gone—looking much happier—Daniel retreated into the interior of his apartment and paced. Jenna still wasn't back—just as well, Emel wouldn't have wanted to run into her here, but then where was she? With Tenai? Taranah? He wouldn't have thought either woman would have time for Jenna on this particular night. And wherever she'd gone, he wanted her back. With him. He needed to see her, look at her, know again that she was safe and well.

When an invitation to supper came from Cardinal Uanan, he took a bold step, pleaded indisposition, and turned it down.

What he didn't expect, having done so, was for Uanan to then show up in person at his own apartment.

"Cardinal," he said, trying to mask the surprise he felt when an attendant bowed his visitor into his study, where he was sitting in the last of the late sun. He hadn't thought it was done, for a higher-ranking person to come in person to visit a lesser. Instead, an invitation that was really a summons would arrive; that was the rule. He'd known he was committing a *faux pas*, turning down an invitation from the cardinal. But he hadn't suspected he would get a personal—what? Rebuke? He stepped back, knowing he'd flushed, angry because he simply wasn't in any mood to adjust to anyone else's customs and expectations, not tonight.

"If you will forgive the imposition," murmured Uanan. The cardinal was dressed a good deal less formally than he had been earlier, in clothing much like that normally worn by the laity, but this did little to reduce his air of authority.

"Of course." Daniel, though still annoyed, made himself add politely. "Forgive me. It's been a long day. I'd thought to, well, stay in tonight and catch my breath—and I'm waiting for my daughter—"

"Thus I must beg your indulgence for my intrusion." The cardinal gave Daniel a long look, then glanced across to the windows and the lingering sun. "May I sit?" He brushed aside a second apology, accepted an offer of wine with a brisk nod, and settled into a chair. "Now," he said, tenting his fingers before his chest and fixing Daniel with his severe gaze, "Tell me of this second journey of yours to the dark kingdom."

"Oh," said Daniel. A *professional* visit. He felt suddenly as though he'd come out of shifting sand onto firm ground. Good. This was fine. He dropped back into his own chair—then immediately rose again and went around the room lighting lanterns and candles, because the sun was fairly well down by this time and he didn't want the darkness pressing too hard into this room.

Cardinal Uanan watched him, frowning. He said, "Lord Death is not evil, Danyel; nor is his darkness evil. Foreign to mortal people, yes, and hard to bear, but not essentially antithetical to the ephemeral world or to Godly folk."

"Well, that's comforting," Daniel said drily. He moved his chair away from the window and closed the shutters, then moved a lantern to the table nearest the chair and sat down. And then stood up again and moved a second lantern to the floor on the other side of the chair. Then he seated himself once more and tried to relax.

"Meaning you do not feel the truth of these words." The cardinal was still frowning. "This second journey of yours, for which I indeed commend you—but permit me to ask, was it as hard for you to return as from the first?"

"No," Daniel admitted. "Not really. It was, well, a *reminder* of the dark. But the darkness really could not get any more ... aggressive. You—if there's anything you could do, I would certainly be grateful. Last time, you said you set your hand between the sunlit kingdom and the shadows, or something like that, didn't you?"

"Which I may do again, for a passing moment. And tomorrow, for another." But Uanan didn't look pleased about this. "Danyel, if you will permit me, I would prefer to help you become more comfortable with the darkness."

"Comfortable!" Daniel found himself on his feet, stopped, and sat back down. "The days are all right. But the nights ... I haven't been sleeping well." He glanced around the room, at the shadows gathering at the edges of things where the lanterns' light did not reach. He wanted to get up again, but made himself sit still with an effort. "Though last night was better ... I wish Jenna were here." Her presence would help, he knew: just having her near him was like lighting a dozen extra lanterns.

"She is with Taranah Berangilan-sa, I believe," Uanan said absently.

"Is she?" That was all right, then. Or better, at least. Daniel tried to relax.

Cardinal Uanan brought his hand down hard on the arm of his chair with a sound like a gunshot, making Daniel jump. "Danyel!" he said sharply. "Attend me, if you will! You are nervous as a man set to be executed rather than fêted on the morrow. Well, you may trust me that I understand this, but I think you will find this mood an uncomfortable one to carry throughout life!"

Daniel flushed. "You understand, do you?"

"I assure you that I do. Do you think a servant of God and the Martyr unacquainted with darkness? I have watched through many midwinter nights, I promise you, and witnessed the darkness enfold the world. And seen the dawn arrive all the same, timely as ever. Now, *will* you attend me, man?"

It took a moment to gather his wits. Then Daniel said more humbly, "All right."

The cardinal rose. He took one of the lit candles and moved it to the table nearest Daniel's chair, setting the lantern on the floor instead. Then he produced a small white-hilted knife from some hidden pocket and laid it down on the table next to the candle. "Your immunity to sorcery renders you a difficult man to assist," he remarked, his tone absent. He stepped back and gazed at his arrangement, head tilted to one side, his air much as Daniel imagined a painter's would be while arranging a still life.

"The last time I allowed a man to work sorcery on me, it didn't turn out very well," Daniel pointed out.

"Indeed. You must decide whether you may trust me," answered the cardinal. He went to the door and called for a bowl—"Bone or bleached wood," he told the young attendant who came to answer his request. "Nothing metal, mind. And a jug of water. Not a metal jug!"

The young man produced a ceramic jug of water and a shallow bowl carved of bone, exactly as though both were normal household implements. Daniel supposed they were. He leaned back in his chair and watched the cardinal's continuing preparations.

"Tenai Chaisa-e might do this for you," Uanan said, pouring water into the bowl and bringing a second, shorter, candle to set beside the first. "But I suspect she no longer understands fear of the dark. The kind of sorcery I intend, if you will permit me, is truly priest's work. Your specific immunity to sorcery aside, it is not customary for priests to work any sort of spell on any person without his consent. If you will stand here by this table, Danyel, and give me your hand."

Daniel sighed, rose to his feet, and moved to stand as directed.

Cardinal Uanan took Daniel's left hand in a firm grip and turned it palm up. "Blood is life," he commented. "It is not merely a representation, as so much of what we do in sorcery depends on representation. Bone, as one would expect, is an adjunct of blood.

And fire, of course, is an ally of life and blood." He laid the blade of the bone-hilted knife in Daniel's palm and let him go. "Gently— the blade is quite sharp."

Daniel looked into the cardinal's face for a moment. Uanan's harsh, strong features could hardly appear gentle. But his deep-set eyes were calm. Assured. Intent, but as a surgeon's eyes might be intent as he began some complicated work. A surgeon would also be using a knife.

Daniel drew the barest tip of the blade across his palm, tracing a vivid thread of blood against his skin.

"Good." Uanan took his wrist firmly again. "This will hurt, I fear. So many of the important acts we choose must involve pain. And more: pain willingly borne." He lifted the first candle, its flame leaping high and white as he touched it, and traced the line of blood across Daniel's palm with the flame. Not too quickly. The flame turned crimson as blood as he completed the exercise.

It did hurt, of course. Daniel endured the pain, trying to keep his hand still.

Moving swiftly, the cardinal set the first candle back on the table, picked up the knife, and passed the blade through its crimson flame. The flame turned white again. The cardinal made a pleased sound. "I see we shall not require the second candle," he said. "Well done, Danyel. Pour the water from the bowl across your hand."

Daniel was glad to. The water didn't help the pain as he'd initially hoped and expected, but evaporated as it ran across his burned hand.

No. It didn't evaporate. It turned to light, a light that filled the room with a soft radiance a good deal more subtle than candlelight, and that lingered rather than fading.

"Good! The Martyr favors us." Uanan sent a glance around the room and then turned his intense gaze on Daniel. "Now. Blow out the candles."

"But—" said Daniel.

"Blow them out," repeated the cardinal, inexorably. "Let in

the dark. Dark and light are each the same, to God."

"But—" But he'd already gone along with the cardinal this far. Bending, he blew out the candles, one good hard puff of air, like blowing out the candles on a cake.

The candles weren't the only lights to go out. All the lanterns and candles all over the room flared up and went out. The soft radiance that had been created from the water lingered, but that was not enough to hold back the dark, which crashed like silent thunder through the room.

Daniel might have shouted; afterward, he could not remember. If he did, the darkness swallowed the sound, for all sound, like all light, seemed to have been erased. He staggered, losing his balance along with all frame of reference; Uanan's hand clamped hard on his arm and Daniel grabbed the cardinal's arm in turn, gaining another point of stability in the featureless dark. He stared into the darkness, eyes wide, unable to see—

Or, no. He became aware at last that not quite all light had been stripped from the room. That pale luminosity from the bowl of water was still present, even in this suffocating dark. Yet this light didn't illuminate anything, exactly, but seemed instead a strangely bodiless kind of luminance. No. It wasn't actually light at all, was it?

"You see it?" Cardinal Uanan's deep voice came out of the dark, as though the darkness itself formed that voice.

"Yes. I think so." Daniel's own voice was shaky.

"One may see by darkness as well as by light. Do you understand this, Daniel?"

This didn't make any physical sense. And yet, it almost seemed to be true. "I think so," Daniel said again.

"To God, light and dark are the same. You may walk surrounded by light or by darkness, and this matters not, to God. You need not love the darkness, Danyel. But you must learn to accept it. Light may vanish, and the darkness may engulf you. But you will not drown in it. Lord Death's kingdom may lie before your next step; you may fall through a stray shadow into that dark kingdom. But you will remain within the greater Kingdom of God. You are not bereft. Do you understand?"

"Yes," Daniel said. His voice came out husky and too hesitant; he cleared his throat and said again, more strongly, "I understand you."

"Do you see me, here where there is no light?"

No. But if the dark luminance didn't allow Daniel to actually see the cardinal, somehow it did seem to make him *aware* of him, in a way that wasn't sight and yet restored a sense of balance to the room. Daniel let go of the cardinal's arm and straightened, slowly, testing this new sense of stability.

"Good," said Cardinal Uanan. Light bloomed around the room as he called fire once more to all the lanterns and candles.

Daniel looked around at them all, at the room thus illuminated with their ordinary, straightforward light. At the shadows each little flame cast. The shadows were dark, and they still shifted and trembled and showed a tendency to creep out from behind objects. But he saw now that each shadow held its share of that strange dark luminance.

The shadows still made him uneasy. But he was no longer so desperately afraid of them.

"Thank you," he said, turning toward the cardinal. "I don't think—I don't think I understand even half of what you did. And this—" he waved a vague hand around the room—"this isn't exactly what I expected."

Cardinal Uanan smiled, an expression that couldn't soften his features, but lent them a comforting quality nevertheless. "But it will do?"

Daniel glanced around the room again. "Yes," he said. "I think this—I—will do. Now."

The cardinal inclined his head. "Very good. This time, Danyel, the change is in you, and should last. So that should be well enough. I'll leave you to your rest, so bravely earned. You will need rest, I believe. It will be a long day, the coming morrow, and though I hope God will smile to look down upon it, still, we are not all either young or immortal. I shall expect your company for breakfast—if I may? Good. I shall send a man for you." He went out.

Daniel looked once more around the room—exactly the same as it had been an hour ago, and yet so different. Then he blew out all the candles and all the lanterns except one. This one he hung on its chain near the door. He opened the shutters to let in the air from the gardens, and stood for a moment looking out into the night. It wasn't actually very dark outside: the moon, nearly full, rode behind thin wisps of cloud that didn't block much of its light, and there were great round white lanterns on tall posts all through the gardens, and light from higher palace windows. Where the darkness gathered around the edges of all those lights, well, it wasn't so forbidding and grim a darkness as it had been.

And tomorrow there would be a dawn, and a long day. Daniel went to bed.

25

After being dismissed from the king's company, Jenna wandered aimlessly around the palace for a little while. She didn't want to see her father. It took her a little while to figure out that this was because of an obscure feeling that, after telling everything to Mitereh, she didn't have much of an excuse not to tell all that stuff to her father. Only she didn't want to.

She wanted to be with Emel, but knew he needed time to recover his self-possession. She felt like that herself. Well, not really, but she knew somehow that that was how *he* felt. Maybe it was a guy thing. And, oh, God, he was going to be all stiff and shy with her father, she knew he was, and her father was going to see him at his worst and wonder about bad-boy romance, or else he was going to think she'd fallen for Emel just because they'd been in danger together, or something stupid like that.

She really wanted maybe a week or so to walk through the woods with Emel, in nice weather, with no one after them and nowhere special they needed to be, with no danger or outlaws or whatever, *before* she had to deal with him and her father together in the same room.

Everybody in the palace, in the city, was so happy, and she felt like she ought to be, and kind of like she was letting down the team because she wasn't. Couldn't be. She ought to be happy about Emel, too. And she was. But that sense of letdown had returned as well and she still couldn't figure out exactly why.

And on top of everything else, it seemed like every single person knew who she was, even though her skin and hair were still dyed dark. Their recognition gave her a weird feeling, like she was impersonating the person they all thought she was.

So Jenna wandered down hallways and galleries until she found an unoccupied balcony that looked out over the palace gardens and the surrounding city, and settled finally onto a white stone bench by the railing. Sounds rose from the city: bells, and a high thin ripple of flute-like notes, and some kind of buzzing, humming instrument not like anything she knew. And people shouting way far away, but a cheerful kind of shouting; and all of them going places and doing things in a considerable hurry. None of that bustle seemed to apply to her. Did she feel left out, or just relieved?

"Nola Jenna," a woman said from the doorway, and Jenna turned quickly, to find Mitereh's aunt Taranah Berangilan-sa. Taranah was wearing a wonderful embroidered skirt and an even more wonderful net of silver and amethysts over her hair; the silver brought out the paleness of her eyes. Silver eyes, right. Jenna had all but forgotten that Taranah had eyes like that.

Jenna started to stand up, but Taranah waved a casual hand and said with brisk good cheer, "Oh, no, Nola, certainly you must not disturb yourself. You have had a most adventurous time, I understand. So energetic, adventures. Though I suppose you are young enough to be splendidly energetic yourself."

"Actually, I think I've decided I don't much like adventures," Jenna admitted.

"Yes," said Taranah, with a shrewdness that surprised Jenna. "Such difficult events, and hard to reconcile with ordinary life afterwards. I understand from Mitereh that you have reclaimed the younger Terusai for us. That was well done. It is a hard thing to lose a great house."

Jenna felt herself relaxing a little. The king's aunt somehow seemed a comfortable woman to talk to. Taranah sounded like she both understood and approved of the way Mitereh had arranged to get Emel and Jenna together. And sympathetic, and, well, just nice.

"He seems a fine young man," added Taranah. "though damaged by his past. He greatly desires to reclaim honor and earn respect, I believe."

"He has," said Jenna, trying not to sound offended.

"He has certainly begun to." Taranah smiled warmly at Jenna. "So that is well done, my dear, and if not the greatest of your recent accomplishments, perhaps the one that most pleases the heart."

Jenna hesitated and then said, "He thinks I'm too good for him. He thinks he's not fit to touch the hem of my skirt." She was in fact wearing the very same dark-gold skirt he'd stolen for her outside of Nemesen.

"He will recover his senses," Taranah predicted confidently. She added a touch wryly, "And you shall come to believe you are worthy of him, too, I am certain. But not too quickly. Early courtship is so exciting on both sides. I advise you enjoy it, as it will pass soon enough."

Jenna stared at her. Taranah raised an eyebrow, not quite smiling. But her eyes were smiling. Jenna wanted suddenly to laugh, but didn't know if it was at herself or at Emel or at the whole crazy situation.

"And your father?" Taranah inquired comfortably.

Strangely, this didn't feel intrusive. Maybe because of the woman's obviously sincere concern. "I haven't really talked to him about anything," Jenna admitted. "There wasn't time ... and then it didn't seem like the *right* time, exactly ... and I didn't understand as fast as I should have that, you know, if *I* stay in Talasayan with Emel, well, obviously my father's going to feel like he ought to stay *too*, and how can I ask him to do that? How can I possibly? He's got the hospital back home, patients, things to do. He's hated every minute of the past few weeks, he's had it much harder than I have, you know, all that waiting and worrying and nothing to take his mind off, well, anything. I'm sure he wants to go home. And here I am," she finished penitently, "saying Emel can court me and never mind what that means for my father."

Taranah listened attentively to all this. She said after a thoughtful moment, "I cannot, to be sure, speak for Nola Danyel. Yet I should expect you may trust him to know his own mind. My dear, I advise you ask him whether his heart truly belongs so irrevocably to your own world; whether he cannot be content in Talasayan. Of course we understand he is a man of high regard in his own country, but then, should he remain here, Mitereh will cover his feet with pearls and gold, you are aware? Wealth and honor have reconciled many men to foreign lands; perhaps he will not be so unhappy to remain as you believe. And as for Emelan Terusai-e, I believe you may trust your father to act there with discernment and kindness."

That might be so, but—"Yes, but ... he could really hurt Emel," Jenna said, and knew suddenly and with relief that this, this exact worry, was the one that she'd really been circling around. Since way before Mitereh had brought the whole thing out in the open. Way before that. All the way along on that endless journey back from Kinabana. Except it hadn't been endless and here they all were and life was still moving forward, even though she wanted to step out in its path and yell for it to stop, to just hold still for a while.

Taranah nodded as though she understood. Jenna even thought she really might. She was suddenly intensely glad the other woman had happened by.

Taranah said seriously, like she knew, "Never apologize for your lover to your father. That cannot succeed. Begin by assuming your father will approve and then retreat, if you must, to assuming he will at least maintain a civil manner. Nola Danyel will, I believe, trust you to know your own mind. Yes?"

"He said he trusted my judgment," Jenna admitted.

"Then you need not assume otherwise. If I may presume—"

"Oh, yes. Please."

"You are gracious to permit an older woman's interference," Taranah said, smiling. "Nola Jenna, I think you will do well to assume that your father indeed has faith in your judgment, as he asserts so, and to trust his as well. Tell him what is in your heart, if you are so inclined. This pleases fathers, to know they are trusted by their daughters. Thus you may explain to him what you feel, if he will hear you; and what you see in the young Terusai, if he will hear that. Otherwise how will he know?"

Jenna nodded slowly. This advice seemed really right. The warm feeling inside was joined by a completely new bubbling affection for the whole world, but particularly for Taranah. "I bet you have daughters, don't you?"

The older woman gave her a little nod before turning to look out over the city. "Three, my dear, and all well settled and I think happy with it. And two sons. My lord was a fine man, may he rest gently in the Kingdom of God, but he was not a man to release his daughters easily. Nola Danyel is, I think, a man who may more clearly judge the hearts of men."

Taranah sounded warmly approving. Jenna gave her a careful look, and after a moment, smiled. Obviously it wasn't happenstance at all; obviously the king's aunt had deliberately looked for her. This had to be because of Daddy. That was fine. Taranah was really nice. And clever. Jenna felt much happier.

Somewhere not too far away, the notes of a single harp rose above all the varied sounds of the court and the city and scattered music like a handful of sparks across the court. Behind the harp, the bells were still sounding in slow, mellow reverberations. The sun, sinking, cast long shadows out across the white court of Nerinesir, but there was no terror waiting in the dark or the coming day, and that seemed gift enough for now.

Jenna didn't go back to her own apartment at all that night. Taranah seeming to find nothing at all odd about Jenna's continuing reluctance to face the men in her life.

"You wish to rest," Taranah said briskly. "You wish to recover your own sense of yourself. Who would not? You may send Nola Danyel a note and then you may help me find appropriate clothing for you for tomorrow." She sounded like she enjoyed the idea. "We must remove that dye. I shall do it with magic if I must. We must search out fabrics and jewels that will set off that unusual coloring of yours. I think nothing of mine will suit you, my dear, but if we must we shall summon women from every shop in the court until we find the perfect materials."

Jenna laughed. "That's resting?"

"Of course," Taranah assured her, her pale eyes glinting with laughter of her own.

And, of course, it turned out that it was. It was fun, exactly the kind of totally unimportant fun that Jenna found she'd been missing without even knowing it; a perfect antidote to way too much serious stuff. She spent hours with Taranah, trying on the most wonderful clothing and watching with fascination as the king's aunt and her women used magic and amazingly quick hands with needles to alter things to fit. There was a late supper in Taranah's private rooms, jewels pushed casually aside to make room for bowls of soup, and finally a comfortable guest room.

Taranah was gone in the morning when Jenna woke up. There was bread and fruit and a carafe of sweet wine that Jenna sipped cautiously. One of Taranah's women helped her dress in the clothing they'd laid out the previous night, all pale blue and pale violet, with a net of silver and pale blue crystals for her hair, and long dangling earrings of pearls and more crystals to go with it. She looked at herself in the tall mirror in Taranah's dressing room, finding her own fair coloring unfamiliar after so long dyed dark. Usually she didn't mind being the center of attention. Today she wouldn't have minded blending in a little.

Taranah had left on the table a note from Niah, an invitation to attend the queen during the procession and all the ... ceremonies, or whatever, that would fill the day and, well, settle everything, Jenna supposed. At least, she supposed everything was going to be settled, one way or the other. For Kuanonai, and for his nephew, and everybody else.

She wondered where Emel would be; where Daddy would be. Where Kuanonai Geraimani-e would be. In chains, prominently displayed? Or removed to a private prison somewhere in the city? Or no, the king had promised Kuanonai that he could watch his nephew accept Mitereh's offer. *If* the king actually made it. She wondered uneasily how Mitereh would decide. What had he meant when he'd said he would 'test' the nephew? If Kuanonai's nephew failed the test; would the king have all the Geraimani executed right there? How about the others, the women left in Imbaneh-se, the baby? Jenna wondered unhappily whether Mitereh would send Tenai after them, and if he did, whether she would go.

She found she was sorry she hadn't gone to find her father last night after all. Worse, the lack of Emel's solid presence at her back was as uncomfortable as a newly missing tooth, surprising her every time she thought of it. She would have liked Taranah with her. Probably she was with the king, though.

But she hurried down the hall and joined Niah. The queen did not seem to be suffering any moments of doubt or worry. She was so quietly happy that Jenna couldn't help but find her own mood lightening in response.

The ceremonies and everything, Jenna gathered, were actually to be held at the Badan Kulirang, the House of the Oak. There wasn't room there for more than a few hundred people, but everybody else would spread out on rooftops to get a view, and lots of them would watch by scrying in bowls of water or in clear glass. Like television, only weirder, Jenna supposed.

The queen left Inana with a nurse for the first time since she'd been rescued from Keitah's house and went down to the Badan Kulirang by litter, with some of her attendants riding alongside. Jenna was one of those. Lots of noble women were riding in litters, which was the first time Jenna had seen any since the day Mitereh had brought Tenai into Nerinesir and showed her to everybody and told them to rejoice. Ceremonial things, she supposed, and for everyday use, more trouble than they were worth She was glad she was riding.

The black bridge was wider close up than it had looked when they'd passed it at a distance before, which was just as well, because it was handling a lot of traffic today. There was a steady stream of jeweled people in carriages or litters or on horses going one way, and a stream in reverse of servants taking horses and carriages and litters away empty—it took a little while for Jenna to figure this out, but then it made sense: there was no room for so many animals and carriages and things right by the pavilion, so they were sent out of the way. She wondered how long it would take everybody to get sorted out again afterwards. Probably not a problem for the queen, though.

The pavilion itself was much bigger than Jenna had imagined, more the size of a small amphitheater, which was good because there was a huge crowd already present. She couldn't imagine how it had been made. It looked like it had been carved in one piece from a chunk of marble the size of a small mountain. Maybe it had been; who knew what magic could do with stone? Plants that had looked like shrubs around its base turned out to be small trees, some of them bearing little bell-shaped white flowers. The oak inside was huge, big enough it would have taken four or five men to reach all the way around it. It was isolated in a great swath of fine white gravel that was in turn surrounded by a circle of banners. A single banner hung from the oak itself: Mitereh's, of course. Several more were set beneath its shade in what was probably a very calculated order, not that Jenna could read the nuances. One of them, the third from the front, was Tenai's stark Nolas-Kuomon black, with Chaisa's silver half-oval on brown set below it on the same staff.

Nobody had chairs, though, except there were two ornate ones right up by the oak. A throne for the king, Jenna assumed, and the other one would be for the queen, which Niah at once confirmed by moving toward it. Mitereh wasn't present yet. Jenna looked in vain for her father or for Emel, or for Taranah, but they weren't here yet, either.

But—her heart sank a little—there was Kuanonai Geraimani-e, his wrists chained together, standing between guards. A little distance away was a small group of, she surmised, the other Geraimani, also bound and surrounded by guards, except for one man who had his arm in a sling. Beyond the guards, ranks and ranks of soldiers, and then lots and lots of nobles from the court.

Niah didn't seem at all self-conscious about being the first to make her way through the crowds—though her attendants made a path for her, so it wasn't much trouble—to take her place beneath the shade of the oak. She beckoned Jenna to stand by her chair. Jenna moved dutifully to stand at the queen's left hand and tried to look like she stood in front of huge crowds every day. She felt self-conscious enough for both of them. She tried not to fidget, or fuss with her hair, or scratch her nose.

It seemed to be a long time, but probably wasn't, before there was a stir through the jewel-toned crowd and everybody else was arriving all at once: Mitereh and his close advisers, Taranah, a couple of younger women Jenna didn't recognize. And the young men of the king's personal guard, and there was her father at last. Somebody had found clothing for him that made him look dignified and formal. Jenna had not noticed before, but he had really lost a lot of weight. All that riding, and of course a lot of worrying ... had he been eating all right? She would have to make sure he did, but he did look good now. Distinguished, even.

Oh, and there was Emel at last with some of the lords of the court—well, of course, Emel *was* a lord of this country now. So he was with the king on his own account, and not because he attended Tenai. Though of course Tenai was also there, like a shadow in her formal black, walking at the king's left hand.

Mitereh took his throne, with a smile for his wife and a grave nod for Jenna. Her father came and stood near her, and Emel right after him among the other lords, though his was a slightly more anxious look than anybody else's, she thought. She smiled at them both and wished again she'd found them last night after all, because there was no way now to do more than smile.

After that things began to move more quickly. No long speeches, which was fine. But Mitereh singled out men from his army; one or two out of a company. For each man he had a word, too quiet for anyone to hear but the man to whom he spoke, and then a gift, brought forward by one or another of his attendants: a hollow coin with a pearl suspended in its center; a scroll bound with a white ribbon, or a red ribbon, or a lavender ribbon; a wooden disk with intricate carving on its face; another scroll. Medals and awards, Jenna assumed. A man with a clear, trained voice called out the name of each man and a brief phrase that probably indicated what kind of medal he'd been awarded.

Each man so honored, from the youngest soldier to Sandakan Gutai-e, who was called out last, knelt and kissed the king's hand. And each time, the king finished the ceremony by taking the man's hand in both of his and lifting it briefly to touch his forehead. Fealty in the kiss, Jenna thought: not a word she had thought much about before, but she knew *fealty* went beyond loyalty or obedience. *My life and my honor in your hands* ... they meant it here, and sometimes the king called for both, which she understood much better now. And, in return, equally formally, the king acknowledged the debt he owed for such service. Fealty and service; honor and gratitude. No wonder Mitereh projected such quiet power: surely the pressure of all those gathered hopes and expectations must weigh like stone and produce a kind of forced concentration of character.

Then it was Emel's turn, which Jenna had expected and dreaded on his behalf. He had gone so pale and quiet Jenna was afraid he was going to faint right there in front of God and everybody. She watched with intense if covert worry.

The herald announced him as Emelan Terusai-e, which produced a stark silence all through the crowd, although surely rumors had been flying. Emel knelt at the king's feet and kissed his hands, and the king pardoned all the acts he had ever committed against the laws of God or man without specifying what those had been—the silence, if anything, deepened at that—and confirmed him as Terusai-e and confirmed Kandun as his to hold, and gave him all his brother's honors. Then he formally commended him for his part in recovering the queen, without mentioning that it was his brother's treachery that had made the rescue necessary. Standing, Mitereh drew Emel to his feet. Then he bowed low himself, lifting the other man's hands to his forehead. Emel tried to draw away—maybe only Jenna saw that—but Mitereh refused to let him go, and

Emel set his teeth and endured the burden of the king's gratitude.

Straightening at last, Mitereh spoke to him, just a few words. The herald did not call these out, and as they were just too far away to overhear, Jenna had no idea what he said. Emel tried to go back to his knees, but the king seized his arms and wouldn't let him. He spoke again, quietly and intensely, and this time Emel stood still, listening. Then he bent his head and answered, briefly. The king grinned, clapped him on the shoulder, and went back to his throne, and Emel, face set in a formal mask, went back to his place near Jenna. She wanted to look at him, touch his hand, anything, but she couldn't because then it was her turn.

Nobody, Jenna realized, had ever asked *her* for any kind of fealty or anything, before. Not Mitereh, not Niah, certainly not Tenai. It felt harder and stronger and more dangerous than she had expected to kneel in front of Mitereh and kiss his hand. Not like just a promise, but like an almost physical exchange, as though something really was going out from her to him. She was giving him ... her life and her honor, she supposed. How strange. How ... fraught.

When he stood, and drew her up, too, she expected that he would lift her hands to his forehead, and he did. But, where before she had only felt uncomfortable at this gesture, now she felt like something was coming back from him to her: a binding that was metaphorical and yet real and true. She had never understood before that something metaphorical could also be absolutely real.

Then he straightened and released her.

"What did you say to Emel?" she asked him directly, which she hadn't planned to.

He grinned at her and said, "Ask him." Then he went back to his throne and gave her an estate in her own name, near Kandun, and a house in the white court of Nerinesir, and formally declared her to be a member of the queen's household, which didn't actually mean she was adopted or anything, but was more than just saying she was under royal protection. Everybody cheered, which sounded just weird when it was for her, and she blushed fiercely and retreated to her place behind Niah.

After that it was her father's turn, and he very soberly renewed his oath of fealty and received in return that dangerous, profound gesture of gratitude and trust. Then the king had small, ornate caskets brought out, each carried by one of the young men of his personal guard. Each young man opened his casket and poured the contents out over her father's feet. Small gold coins and fat white pearls: the king was *literally* covering her father's feet with gold and pearls. Jenna had thought that was a *figure of speech*, but no. Half a dozen little caskets made for a lot of pearls and gold. Her father stood still, pretending not to be embarrassed, but actually blushing. Finally the young men gathered up the coins and the pearls again and set the caskets to one side, while Mitereh, smiling, also gave her father formal and permanent title to an apartment in the palace itself. Every possible inducement, the king had said. He had sure meant it.

And after that, though Jenna had kind of expected the king to call Tenai out, it turned out he wanted the Geraimani instead. Jenna had expected them to be called forward, and she had been dreading it. What if the king had Kuanonai Geraimani-e put to death right before his throne? She thought he might, and she wasn't sure she could stand to watch. And she was afraid that Nuan Geraimani-na would fail whatever test Mitereh meant for him, and then maybe the king would then have all the Geraimani killed, and she knew for sure she wouldn't be able to stand *that*.

Kuanonai Geraimani-e was brought forward first, and made to kneel in front of Mitereh; behind him, the other four Geraimani knelt in a row. They all had proud, blank expressions. The defeat still showed through. It wasn't just the chains that bound their wrists, Jenna thought; it was something that went deeper and set its mark on the soul.

The older man behind Kuanonai, with a resigned expression, must be his uncle. He didn't look much like a soldier; more like a humanities professor. Somebody absent-minded and kind, but death on grammatical errors in student papers.

Kuanonai's brother, then, would be the man who, of them all, seemed to be having difficulty hiding fear behind his set expression. And, of course, Jenna recognized the brother's son, Kuanonai's nephew, Nuan Geraimani-na. And Kuanonai's son was then the other young man, the one who looked almost openly angry.

"Kuanonai Geraimani-e," said the king. The herald picked up his words and called them out for everyone else, but Jenna found the king's quiet voice infinitely more compelling. "For your part in conspiring with Keitah Terusai-e to murder me, and for your attempt to break the peace of the land and set country against country, your life is forfeit. You will die tonight, by the knife of the assassin sent against me. Because I have no wish to be cruel, I will permit your death to be private, and your body to be returned to your own country for burial."

Kuanonai only gave a curt nod to this, but behind him his brother had closed his eyes. The man had a hopeless expression on his face; when he opened his eyes, his gaze went helplessly to his own son. Jenna understood all at once that he, of all of them, had held a desperate hope of mercy, but that now he expected they would all die, and he could not bear it because he thought his son would die too. It was far too easy to imagine how he must feel.

"Nuan Geraimani-na," said Mitereh, and the young man looked up in surprise. Nuan's father jerked a little as the king spoke his son's name, then sank back. His face was now very still.

At the king's gesture, the young man got to his feet and walked forward. Evidently seeing that Kuanonai alone had not been surprised by this summons, he gave his uncle a curious look as he passed him. He stopped a few steps from Mitereh's chair and started to kneel, but stopped at a slight gesture from the king and stood instead in an attitude of respectful attention.

"I am weary of Imbaneh-se's aggression," stated the king. "I am wearied beyond description at the thought of fighting this war yet again in another generation. Of my brother Tegaitan, or a son of mine, eventually fighting it again. Perhaps against your sister's son." He stopped.

Nuan Geraimani-na listened with an utterly neutral manner. Then, as it apparently occurred to him to wonder again why Mitereh had chosen him to speak to, rather than his uncle, his look became suddenly more speculative.

"My father tried the direct elimination of your country's capacity for aggression," Mitereh went on, speaking to the other man with a direct simplicity that Jenna, at least, found powerful. "His ruthlessness indeed achieved his will ... for a time. Do not mistake me. I am willing to eliminate your house entirely. I am willing to do more than that, if I am sufficiently hard-pressed. But another way has occurred to me." He paused.

"I do not expect I would object to it, given the alternative you suggest," said Nuan, with some irony.

Mitereh fixed him with a long stare, so that Nuan clearly regretted he'd said anything. Again the Geraimani tried to kneel. Again Mitereh moved a hand in a gesture that prevented him. The king said, "Imbaneh-se chafes at a tight rein. I discussed this with your uncle. We agreed that your country might do better bridled more lightly. A throne of its own, perhaps, with a king of its own blood."

Nuan drew a breath. He said after a moment, "A throne beneath yours? Not in Sotatan. Here? A Geraimani king. Held, I should expect, in fealty to you?"

Mitereh, watching the other man with close attention, opened his hand slightly.

Nuan started to look back over his shoulder at the men kneeling behind him, but stopped himself. He asked, "Why me?"

"You are my choice," said Mitereh, without explanation.

Nuan stood still for a moment, thinking. Then he said, carefully, "I ask merely to know. What if I will not?"

"Then all your house will die," Mitereh said flatly. "To the last and least; and as many others of your country as will ensure peace for the coming generation."

"Then I will do whatever you require," Nuan Geraimani-na

said at once, smoothly. Behind him, his uncle twitched, as though he suspected that that had been Mitereh's test, and that his nephew had failed it. At least, that was what Jenna herself suspected.

Mitereh leaned back in his chair and studied the young man. Well, not so young: older than Mitereh himself, Jenna supposed. But not by a lot. There was something alike about them. It wasn't anything about their features. More something about the directness, maybe. Or something in the way they held themselves.

"You must swear fealty to me," Mitereh said softly.

Nuan answered, "I understood that. I have said I will do whatever you require of me, and so I will. I will swear any oath you demand, in the sight of men and God."

"Will you so?" said Mitereh. He put out a hand. Tenai, behind him, drew her sword and set the hilt into his hand. Light slid into the black blade. All around them, shadows seemed suddenly to creep out a little longer and a little wider, and grow a little darker. The king said, "You will make your vow to me before Lord Death, upon Gomantang."

Nuan drew a breath. Behind him, his uncle muttered a soft curse, and his father closed his eyes, face rigid. Nuan did not glance back at them. He came a step closer to Mitereh and this time did drop to one knee. He rested his bound wrists across his other knee and lowered his voice so no one further away than Niah or Jenna could have heard him. "Will you permit me to beg you? I understand no false oath can be laid before Lord Death. I intended to swear fealty falsely; so you suspected, and I confess it. But, Mitereh Sekuse-go-e, I will do anything you ask. I will play any part you demand. I swear before God, no one will guess from any word or act of mine that I cannot do so with a whole heart. O Martyr, hear me!" he said in a low, intense tone. "If I cannot swear honestly, I promise at least the unfailing pretense. O king, do not loose your anger against my family or against Imbaneh-se!"

Mitereh's face showed nothing. At his shoulder, Tenai was equally impassive. Niah looked frightened and sick; Jenna felt the same way and rested a hand on the queen's shoulder. Beyond her,

her father might have been just far enough away that he had not made out the words; he was looking at Jenna with concern, but his attention was mostly on Tenai's sword.

A beat passed. Another. Nuan's intense expression eased toward despair, and he bowed his head.

Mitereh said softly, "A pretense will not content me. It is a real king I would raise up for Imbaneh-se. Not a mockery. It is a true road to peace I seek for both countries; how should I gain that with a lie? Yes, your throne would rest below mine. Yes, you would swear fealty to me in the sight of men and God. Yes, you must do so with a sincere heart. If that is truly impossible, then you must tell me so, for I cannot and will not accept falsity from you, Nuan Geraimani-na. You must speak truth to me and never falsehood. Any oath you make to me must be made honestly."

Nuan listened to him carefully, his head still bowed. When the king stopped, for a long time, Nuan did not move. Mitereh waited patiently. At last, Nuan lifted his head and spoke, in a far more tentative way than before. "You truly mean to make a king for Imbaneh-se?"

"I should like to make the attempt," Mitereh answered, gently. Their eyes met, and held. "Will you make that attempt as well, Nuan Geraimani-na? I ask that you do so. I ask you again whether you will swear fealty to me, upon Gomantang, before Lord Death."

A long pause. Finally Nuan said, "I will try. If Lord Death strikes me down for laying a false oath at his feet, I ask you to believe I tried to swear honestly, and I ask you to be merciful to my family and my people."

Mitereh considered him. Eventually, he answered, "Let us say ... let us say that today you will swear obedience and honesty, not fealty. In a year's time, when we have come to know one another better, you will swear fealty. At that time, if you cannot swear honestly, I warn you, Nuan Geraimani-na, I will put you to death. Then I will either elevate someone less stiff-necked or destroy the oak throne entirely."

Nuan bent his head, thinking. Finally he lifted his gaze to

meet the king's eyes. "I agree to that. I will swear to that, upon Gomantang and before Lord Death."

"Good," Mitereh said softly. Rising, he set the tip of Tenai's black sword against the earth, his hands resting one over the other on the pommel, and waited.

Nuan hesitated for one moment longer. Then he reached across the small distance required and gripped the black sword with both hands. He said clearly, his eyes holding the king's, "Mitereh Sekuse-go-e, son of Encormio, before God and the Martyr, I vow to you my obedience. I shall answer to your voice and obey your commands. I shall speak truth to you, and not falsehood; I shall do good to you and not evil. A year from this day, I shall swear fealty; or if not, then I will submit to your judgment and accept whatever fate you decree." Still holding the king's gaze, he slid his palm gently against the edges of the black sword, so that one crimson drop of blood and then another ran down the length of the blade and dripped onto the white gravel.

Every shadow seemed suddenly much darker and much deeper. There was a long pause. Neither Mitereh nor Nuan moved. They each stayed very still, their eyes locked together, waiting.

Jenna held her breath. She felt like anything might happen: Nuan might fold into himself and vanish into the dark kingdom; Lord Death might step into the living world; anything. She looked at Tenai, who showed no sign that she expected anything too appalling to happen. One corner of her mouth was crooked up in an ironic expression.

Finally, Mitereh inclined his head. "I think we can be certain you swore honestly. Very well. All that you swore, I accept. Nuan Geraimani-na, before God and the Martyr, I swear I have spoken truth to you and not falsehood. Do you keep faith with me, and I swear I will with you, and do good to you and Imbaneh-se, and not evil. I declare you are this day king of Imbaneh-se. As you will take your kingship from my hands, so I grant it to you, for the coming year and I hope for many years that will come after this." Reaching down the blade with one hand, he drew his hand along the edge, so that a few drops of his blood, too, ran down to mingle with the other man's.

Again Jenna held her breath; but this time she didn't really expect anything too dramatic to happen. Nothing did. Lord Death might be listening; he must be listening. But he did not pull Mitereh into his kingdom, nor step into the bright world of the living.

Nuan released the sword. Mitereh, turning, gave Gomantang back to Tenai, who took it, her expression unrevealing, and sheathed the dark blade. Then the king turned back to Nuan, reached out and just touched the chain that bound the other man. The chain fell away—magic, Jenna supposed. The king held his cut hand down to Nuan, drawing him to his feet in a silence that seemed deep enough to ring like a bell.

Then he let go.

Nuan Geraimani-na turned and walked a few steps away, toward the great oak. He touched its trunk with his hand and leaned there a moment, head bowed. Then he turned again. He glanced at his uncle, and past him, at his father and cousin and great-uncle. Whatever he felt, his face was quite still. Turning, he came back to Mitereh, knelt again, opened his blood-streaked hand in a gesture of relinquishment, and asked the king, "What shall I do with these Geraimani of Imbaneh-se, who were your enemies?"

"As you choose," Mitereh answered, holding his eyes.

Wry humor crooked Nuan's mouth. He said, "I set these men into your hands, my king, to suffer your judgment."

Mitereh made a little gesture that also suggested amusement. "I spare them, only so they offer you fealty. I trust they will be able to swear honestly with far less inducement. Save Kuanonai Geraimani-e, whose life I have already declared forfeit." Neither of them seemed to find that last part cause for amusement, at least.

Nuan rose again and went to the other Geraimani. One by one they swore fealty to him, his father first and gladly, his cousin last and, it seemed to Jenna, less so. But they all swore. Except Kuanonai Geraimani-e, who waited to see this through, then got to his feet on his own and strode directly to Mitereh. Nuan cast a look after him, but saw Mitereh's lifted hand and let his uncle past.

"Well," growled Kuanonai, "I confess, Encormio-na, you showed more graciousness than I expected." He lifted his head with a sharp arrogance. "That nephew of mine will make a fine king for Imbaneh-se."

"I do expect so," Mitereh said politely.

"Well," repeated the older man, but seemed then at a loss for words.

"All that I said I would do, I will do."

Kuanonai nodded curtly and glanced beyond the king, to where Tenai stood silently as his shadow. "Not that sword," he said sharply, almost defiantly.

"It will be the assassin's knife, as I said," said Mitereh.

"It makes no difference to my Lord," Tenai said in her darkest, most velvety voice, "in the end."

And Jenna realized that the shadows that lay on the ground didn't need Tenai's black sword to darken them: the sun had all but set, and she had hardly noticed the changing light. It was night, or nearly, and the day, which seemed to have gone on forever, was finally over.

26

So the long day was over at last, and, Daniel supposed, everyone was ready to live happily ever after. Except Kuanonai Geraimani-e, of course. One last death, to tie off the whole conspiracy of blood and murder, of treason from within and rebellion from without. And was that a fair price to pay for the new beginning Mitereh was trying to forge for Imbaneh-se and Talasayan? Would Kuanonai himself think so, as he faced the knife?

Daniel, leaning on the wide windowsill of Tenai's private study and looking out at the night, imagined that he might. The man had been willing to risk everything he had, everyone he presumably loved, on that chance. And he had in fact lost it all. And then received a whole lot back, through Mitereh's rather incredible act of generosity.

Kuanonai might already be dead. It was full dark, now. It would be darker still, in the kingdom of Lord Death. On that thought, Daniel stepped back from the window and closed the shutters. He moved quietly about the room, using the single candle burning on the table to light the lamp that stood over her desk. He might find the darkness more acceptable now, but light was still welcome. The flames cast a soft warmth over the study, which Daniel recognized as the merest illusion of light stretched thin across a vast reality of darkness. So are we changed by our own unique experiences, Daniel thought wryly. Psychiatrists categorize everything and expect certain characteristic reactions to particular stimuli. But in the end we all respond uniquely to what we meet in life.

Daniel was very tired, but not at all inclined toward sleep. He could not even bring himself to sit down. He would have liked to pace, but the room was not very large. He paced anyway, three steps one way and three steps back.

Behind him, the door opened, letting in a bar of light from the hall. He turned.

Tenai stood silhouetted against the brighter light of the hall. He did not have to see her face to recognize her. He would have known her just by the force of her presence, even if he had been altogether blind. But she came in and shut the door again behind her, and the light from the lamp on the desk revealed her expression, which was distinctly weary.

Her sword, sheathed, was in her hand; his eyes went to it involuntarily. But she put it aside, on a long low table by the door, and said, "Daniel. My attendants said you were here."

He nodded a greeting. "Is it ... done, then?"

"It is all finished," she answered, and crossed the room to sink into a chair.

"How did it ... go?"

"He died bravely. As one would expect. Nuan Geraimani-na wanted to be there, but Mitereh would not permit him, which was likely a kindness to them both. So besides the king there was only I to witness. As was fitting," she added, "as, of course, it was I who betrayed Kuanonai Geraimani-e to his death."

Daniel opened his mouth, and shut it again.

"Yes," said Tenai, watching his face, "far from the worst betrayal I might have made, when I must choose one or the other."

"You were true to every oath, in the end," Daniel said.

Tenai moved a hand, miming a rather horrible gesture, as though she was running somebody through with a sword, and lifted one eyebrow.

"Well, yes, but that wasn't you; that was Kuanonai. *You* weren't going to do it. You'd already changed your mind, even before he grabbed your sword."

"Perhaps. Or perhaps I might have struck Mitereh down myself, had Kuanonai restrained himself a moment longer." Her gaze had become distant. "I meant to destroy him. I believe I intended that."

"I didn't say you never intended to do it. I said you'd changed your mind. Sort of like stepping off a cliff, but then grabbing a ledge."

"Or a rope a friend flings after you. I thought I was done with such choices, before we left Chaisa. Or I would not have left it."

"You could never have stayed closed off in Chaisa. And I told Lord Death," Daniel said gently, "that I thought you might be making that particular choice for the rest of your life."

"Do you mean to comfort me?" Tenai was half-smiling. "Did you come here to say that to me?"

"Not really. I'm sure you already knew it." Daniel moved restlessly, glancing across the room toward the table that held her sword, and then quickly away.

Tenai caught that glance. "Shall I put him out of sight?"

"No, no." Daniel dropped into a chair and rubbing his face. He felt both incredibly tense and logy with exhaustion. He asked, on some impulse, "Was Sandakan there?"

There was a brief pause. "No," said Tenai.

Right. She'd said perfectly plainly only she and Mitereh had attended the execution. He sighed. "Right. Of course. You said that. So … will you go back to Chaisa, now?"

"I think I may."

"I think you ought to. Mitereh wouldn't mind now, surely. I think you could use some time … offstage, so to speak. Jenna and I could stay here in Nerinesir. You might consider inviting Sandakan along for the ride."

This time the pause was a little longer. Then Tenai sat back in her chair and smiled with real amusement. "Daniel. Do you seek to manage me?"

"What else are friends for?"

"Ah, indeed. And do you regard Emelan with favor?"

Daniel smiled despite himself. "I gather you think I ought to."

"He was an honorable man once, Daniel. I would be

astonished if he were not so again."

"I don't doubt it. He did come see me. He's not—well, I think every father has an image of Prince Charming in his mind, and Emel isn't much like mine. But ... I think he may do. And after all, it's not like they're going to elope next week. A lot can happen in half a year."

"A measureless amount."

"Right." But not everything. Not, sometimes, anything that mattered. And so now he found himself here to no purpose. It wasn't like he didn't know it was to no purpose. He got up to leave, but then stood, irresolute.

"Daniel?" said Tenai. Her dark voice came out of the pool of lamplight like the voice of the night.

Daniel turned without a word, walked to the table by the door, and laid a hand on the hilt of her sword. Even the hilt was more than he wanted to touch: it was colder than metal should be, and it seemed to cling to his fingers. He resisted the urge to pull his hand away.

"Ah," murmured Tenai, watching him. She asked nothing.

"I keep thinking about Kathy. My wife. She died so long ago. She committed suicide, you know." Daniel's mouth twisted. "The great psychiatrist. I couldn't even make sure my own wife stayed on her meds. The usual story: in the highs she didn't think she needed them, and in the lows she couldn't imagine they would help. And one day she dropped into a low so deep she couldn't handle it, and never came out the other side. I wondered ... I only wondered whether ... and I never thought to ask." That was the worst part: that he had been in a position to ask, twice, and had not thought of it.

"Daniel," she said gently, understanding. "The long dead are gone from us. They do not linger. Those who inhabit Lord Death's dark kingdom are no less departed than those who are gone through the Gate. Do you think I have not desired over and again to call back into life those who have died?"

"I came back," Daniel said, helplessly unable to let go of the idea. "Lord Death permitted that. Twice. And Mitereh came back. If I begged him—if *you* asked him—"

"You went to Lord Death by Gomantang's gateway. That is not the same. Daniel. Forgive me that I must take this hope from your hand. She is gone from you. Let the dead past die. Look for life from the living."

Daniel stared at her for a long moment, trying to decide if he blamed her—it would be a stupid, irrational response, but he was surely as capable of stupid irrationality as anybody. No, he thought. He just felt tired. He took his hand off the hilt of her sword. "I'm sorry."

"Can you believe she is gone? It is easier," Tenai said, still very gently, "if one can permit the dead to depart."

He tried to smile. "And you would know?"

"It took me a long time to learn it."

Four hundred years? He thought it might take him about that long. "I thought I'd accepted it," he admitted painfully. "We all fool ourselves. It's a protective mechanism, you know. I thought I'd moved on. Only then I found out I hadn't. The hardest part ... this is actually funny ... the hardest part is that I find myself wanting *Emel* to be more like Kathy. Vicarious living through Jenna, obviously. How stupid is that? Lord, what fools these mortals be!" He came back to his chair, threw himself into it, and put a hand over his eyes.

Tenai said nothing.

After a moment, Daniel asked her, "She's really gone?"

"Beyond any mortal ken."

"Right." The soft, regretful certainty in her voice might have done it: somewhere behind his breastbone, he thought he felt the first true belief begin to take hold. It was not exactly like a scarring over of the heart's injury, he thought. He was intimately familiar with that. This was something different. Less fragile. "Thank you."

She opened a hand in acknowledgment and apology. "Forgive me."

He understood what she meant. He said, proper return, "Go

to Chaisa. And when you go ... Tenai, I think, I truly do think, that you should ask Sandakan Gutai-e to go with you."

Their eyes met. After a moment, he said, "Look for life from the living. Or is Lord Death that jealous of his lady?"

"He will die," she said, after a long pause.

"Everybody dies. As you just pointed out to me. Love them and, if you have to, let them go. Just ... don't hold yourself bound to love only death and the darkness."

She bent her head slightly. "No," she said. And, eventually, "Thank you."

"We'll both be in each other's debt so far we'll never climb out. And isn't that what life is for, if you're lucky?" Daniel got to his feet and looked at her for a moment. She was, it occurred to him, the most striking woman he had ever known. And all he could think of was to get her together with Sandakan Gutai-e. Life was full of irony. But strangely satisfying irony, sometimes.

He was still desperately tired. But for the first time since Kinabana, he actually felt that he might be able to rest. He said, "After everything that's happened, this is going to sound stupid ... but, all in all ... I'm not altogether sorry I came along for the ride."

Tenai smiled, stood up, and took his hands in hers. "God makes us gifts in life, that if we are wise enough we sometimes recognize. Ask Mitereh to build you a hospital here in this city. Or in Kandun, if that pleases you."

A hospital. Here in Talasayan. Daniel stood still, so startled by this idea he could not at first even really process it. He said at last, "With no medications?" and then felt ridiculous: was one not a psychiatrist if one had no pharmacy? Was that the measure of a doctor?

But Tenai answered seriously, "Perhaps you can make what you desire. You should have a sorcerer to work with you, Daniel. You are aware ... Taranah Berangilan-sa is a sorcerer."

Daniel blinked. He thought about this. At last, he began to smile.

ENDNOTES

I hope you enjoyed reading the Death's Lady Trilogy! It's a little different from anything else I've ever written; challenging in several ways. I enjoyed writing it, though for a while there I was calling it The Tenai Trilogy: An Exploration of Eternal Revision.

I'm sure Daniel and Jenna will go on to have interesting and perhaps exciting lives in Talasayan, and, as I have a novella written that's set after this trilogy, perhaps readers will have a chance to see them again.

If you enjoyed this story, I hope you'll take a moment to leave a brief review at Amazon or Goodreads.

ALSO BY

Urban Fantasy: The Black Dog Series

    BLACK DOG

    BLACK DOG SHORT STORIES I

    PURE MAGIC

    BLACK DOG SHORT STORIES II

    BLACK DOG SHORT STORIES I & II (collection)

    SHADOW TWIN

    BLACK DOG SHORT STORIES III

    COPPER MOUNTAIN

    BLACK DOG SHORT STORIES IV, forthcoming

    SILVER CIRCLE, forthcoming

Young Adult Fantasy

    THE CITY IN THE LAKE

The Floating Islands duology:

THE FLOATING ISLANDS

THE SPHERE OF THE WINDS

THE KEEPER OF THE MIST

THE WHITE ROAD OF THE MOON

Adult Fantasy

The Griffin Mage trilogy:

LORD OF THE CHANGING WINDS

LAND OF THE BURNING SANDS

LAW OF THE BROKEN EARTH

The House of Shadows duology

HOUSE OF SHADOWS

DOOR INTO LIGHT

THE MOUNTAIN OF KEPT MEMORY

WINTER OF ICE AND IRON

The Tuyo series

TUYO

NIKOLES

TARASHANA

KERAUNANI, forthcoming

TASMAKAT, forthcoming

Collections

    BEYOND THE DREAMS WE KNOW